WET WORK

MARK A. HEWITT

Black Rose Writing | Texas

ISBN: 978-1-68433-360-8
PUBLISHED BY BLACK ROSE WRITING
www.blackrosewriting.com

Printed in the United States of America
Suggested Retail Price (SRP) $25.95

Wet Work is printed in Book Antiqua

Wet Work is a euphemism for murder or assassination, alluding to "spilling blood." During the days of the Soviet Union, these operations were reputed to have been handled by *Spetsbureau 13*, at the KGB, colorfully known as the Thirteenth Directorate or the "Directorate of Wet Affairs."

It is generally against the policy of the Communist Party to resort to assassination. However, it requires two criteria and a high level policy decision. The criteria for the individual in question are that he must be highly effective and it must serve some sort of example — some sort of highly effective example.

—Che Guevara

WET WORK

PROLOGUE

April 1938
Baltimore, Maryland

Three loud raps on the mansion's old oak door broke the silence within. A cloud of cigar smoke roiled between door and jamb as Colonel Boris Bykov stepped inside. He was dripping wet from the nor'easter swirling over Maryland as it moved up the coast. As he stomped his feet to shed the water from his shoes, he presented a challenge coin, the Order of the KGB was proof of his bona fides and authority to enter the secret gathering of intelligence officers. The presentation of the coin was just as natural as a policeman flashing his badge to gain entry to a crime scene. The coin was the size of an American silver dollar; a brass shield and sword were set against a sea of black enamel; a polished red star with a hammer and sickle were centered atop the sword. On the front of the coin was the three-dimensional likeness of Joseph Stalin surrounded by the red flag of the Soviet Union, all encased in scarlet glass. At the bottom of the coin, in Cyrillic: *C.C.C.P.*

Bykov ignored the man incautiously pointing a TT-30 pistol at him. The two men knew each other well; Bykov didn't have time for the bluffing. Soviet officers don't generally shoot other Soviet officers, at least not in America.

The man who opened the old oak door barked at the intruder, "I can't believe you interrupted our game! I was winning!" Then he sneered, *"This better be very good."* Bykov returned the special coin to his pocket, removed his soaked fedora, and pushed aside the man with the Tokarev semi-automatic. Rainwater cascaded onto the carpet as he withdrew a shoebox-sized package cross-tied with hemp rope. He handed the package to the man with the gun who growled, "This better be cigars!"

Bykov shook more water from his short red hair and snapped, "No Comrade. More diaries. But that's not what I'm here for. He's gone!" *I knew he couldn't be trusted!* Bykov thought. He blamed himself. Comrade Stalin would blame him too.

The group of intelligence officers in the middle of the classical European mansion's library listened intently and stopped playing the old Russian card game *vint*, which meant "a screw" in the vernacular. Some used the interruption to tap cigar ashes into trays and raise their eyes to see if there would be a murder at the front door. Anyone interrupting their game of *vint* should have been screwed to a piece of wood and left to die in a thunderstorm.

Colonel Filipp Ivanovich Golikov looked at Bykov's gift dangling from his hand and rolled his eyes. He closed the door against the rain and wind and slipped the 7.62 mm self-loading pistol into his suitcoat pocket. He sighed in frustration and squinted his smoke-saturated, bloodshot eyes behind dirty round spectacles. He tossed the package onto a table. Exasperated, he asked, "Who is gone, Comrade Bykov?" Golikov's long thick cigar bounced up and down between his lips as he spoke.

Bykov was never invited to the card games at the mansion. He was distrustful and vituperative, and was considered a cheat with a personality disorder. Any minor thing could set him off. Golikov regretted not shooting the spy handler before he stepped inside. He anticipated another of Bykov's outbursts. At the very least, it would have saved the carpet from being drenched.

Bykov spat, "*Chambers!*" The name rolled off his tongue with contempt, like a man reporting a colossal failure while trying to shift the blame and the focus from himself. A classic paranoid.

Golikov squeezed his eyes shut. He removed the panatela with one hand and rubbed his face with the other. The other men were stunned and stopped puffing their Cubans. If true, this news was bad. Very bad. *Could another American communist have defected? Americans are so unreliable....* Golikov didn't want to believe the news and stuttered, "Are...are you...sure, Comrade Bykov?"

"Yes, Comrade Golikov. I've been his case officer for some time. We have an established schedule. We were to meet at the safe house to photograph a new shipment of documents. Chambers had been very reliable and punctual when he brings documents. But this time, he didn't arrive. After waiting the required fifteen-minutes, I left to determine if he had car trouble. His house...in Baltimore...is unoccupied. Chambers' family is also gone...as if they left for holiday."

Colonel Golikov, the Intelligence Directorate Chief at the Soviet Union's embassy in Washington D.C., dropped his head in disgust. A dozen intricate silver medals and enameled badges bedecked the tunic of his uniform. He led intelligence-gathering and surveillance missions in the coastal cities of New York City, Los Angeles, Baltimore, Washington D.C., and Philadelphia. His men terrorized White Russian émigrés and other opponents of the regime who fled the Bolshevik Revolution of 1917. This development with Chambers wouldn't please his superiors.

Golikov glared at the men at the poker table for moral support as Colonel Proskurov, the Air Attaché, murmured, "Maybe he heard the screams," a clear reference to the ongoing purge where countless souls were marched to the basement of the Lubyanka Prison to be butchered. He laughed to himself. Safe from Stalin's purges with an assignment in the United States, the problem wasn't his for the foreseeable future, and without fear of reprisal he could be as nasty as he wanted to be to the case officer.

No one in the room wanted to believe another Communist had defected. *You can be shot by them or be shot by us.* There had been several defections over the previous few years. Stalin's purges were in full Soviet efficiency, and blood ran freely into the drains of the Lubyanka. Being recalled to Moscow during the purges could mean only one thing, you would be killed. If you were a soldier, your honorifics, your badges and medals would be stripped from your uniform for failing the Communist Party. Men wailed in their cells in the basement of the Lubyanka before being dragged to a dungeon wall and shot. For women, a bullet to the head only meant their sufferings were no longer required by predatory prison guards who raped all women brought to them, alive or dead.

One of the well-dressed, officious men sitting at the heavily ornate card table, a table where the Russian Tsar Nicholas had once played cards with his children, cleared his throat in preparation to speak. Colonel Andriy Ivan Panfilov was the Soviet embassy's security chief. He wore a dark suit and bow tie to offset his bushy brows and mustache. He gestured with a corona in hand, "Maybe he had a family emergency. He has children. One of them may have required hospitalization...." Another man at the circular table gestured indifferently with his cigar, an inch-long ash held on miraculously through the gesticulations. With a malicious smile he said, "Children can be so clumsy."

With a look, Bykov asked for Golikov's permission to shed his dripping Macintosh. Golikov frowned a tacit approval. Bykov gave Golikov a nod and then nodded vigorously at the Security Chief, "Yes, Comrade Panfilov. I thought of that. I stopped at the local hospitals. I know his license number. I know his vehicle. I looked for him everywhere. No Chambers."

"Maybe he used an alias?" Filipp Golikov suggested. He couldn't believe Chambers, his best man and most productive resource, a loyal member of the Communist Party had vanished. It was improbable. No, it was impossible. He felt his blood pressure rise, presaging the migraine that would surely come. He turned his eyes to one of the mansion's library walls and contemplated the news, as if the cumulative knowledge in the rows of books could explain a loyal Communist's sudden disappearance.

Colonel Ivan Proskurov and Colonel Andriy Orlov, a lawyer who usually remained silent during the card games, found their cigars no longer tasted of wintergreen or spice but now tasted of bitters, as if a concoction of reground black pepper had been blown up their noses. Panfilov, Orlov, and Proskurov snuffed out their cigars in sequence as if the activity was choreographed. Once the old butts had been crushed into overfull ashtrays, the five men looked at each other with the dawning realization that Chambers had committed the ultimate sin in the Communist Party. He had defected and may have gotten away unscathed. This could not stand.

As the men looked around the table at each other, they realized they could be in great danger. Police. The FBI. The American Army. Stalin. The NKVD, the People's Commissariat of Internal Affairs. They had their own special group to take care of those who ran or defected. They may have diplomatic immunity but it was time to return to the safety of the Soviet Embassy, to file reports, develop a plan. They must report the news in such a way to ensure that they'd stay alive. The old Romanov mansion on the Chesapeake, once pictured on the cover of Club House cigar boxes, was no longer a safe haven.

One question ricocheted in their craniums: *Why did you do it, Chambers?* One answer was acknowledged and implied: *You have likely killed us all.*

Whittaker Chambers had held a position of significant importance and trust within the Communist Party of America—he alone ran the highest-placed Soviet spy in the American government, the urbane Alger Hiss. Chambers was a quiet genius, *blasé*, a thinner, frumpier version of the matinee heavyweight Sidney Greenstreet. He was the perfect handler for the perfectly placed Soviet spy. In a crowd no one noticed him; people looked through him or looked away. He didn't elicit any second glances, and in his typical dull suit he could remain anonymous in a receiving line. That is until he spoke. Chambers worked furiously to hide a mouthful of discolored teeth skewed in acute and oblique angles. People remembered bad teeth. His best disguise was being himself.

For several years Chambers had photographed every classified piece of paper given to him by Alger Hiss, documents that had crossed the desks of the Assistant Secretaries of State, the Deputy Secretary of State, and the Secretary of State. Chambers routinely delivered countless rolls of microfilm to Comrade Bykov, his Soviet handler and case officer in Baltimore. For his expert handling of the effete yet productive Hiss, Chambers was considered a hero in the Kremlin. Somewhere in a Moscow safe lay an Order of Lenin medal for Whittaker Chambers.

Looking more like he belonged on Broadway or in Hollywood than in the pale green halls of the U.S. State Department, the polished and cultured Alger Hiss was the quintessential diplomat. He was poised, suave, and debonair. He was a strong, determined man with a firm and resolute character. He was a devout and committed Communist holding a position of great trust and confidence in the U.S. government. He was a politically active intellectual who believed capitalism was collapsing at a time when the Soviet Union's revolution and industrialization had demonstrated the vigor and promise of socialism. He didn't commit espionage for remuneration but for the ideal of socialism. Spying was what good Communists did in the employ of the U.S. government.

He spied for the Soviet Union, not for money. Joseph Stalin had awarded *ALES*, Hiss' KGB codename, several medals with corresponding cash awards *in absentia*. Order of the Red Star, the silver Order of Lenin.

ALES hinted to Chambers that a true patriot would find it unpatriotic to accept money for his work, for making revolution against such a powerful and vicious enemy as the United States of America should have been reward enough. Only Colonel Filipp Golikov of the Soviet embassy was responsible for distributing the funds set aside for *ALES*. Reward money would be accrued until such time as the source requested it.

Hiss had worked his way up the civil service ladder to one of the most senior executive positions in the U.S. State Department. He was "one of the essentials," a position which routinely placed him in the company of the top leaders of government. Hiss was above reproach as Special Assistant to the Director of the Office of Far Eastern Affairs. Yet he had copied and smuggled thousands of top secret documents out of Foggy Bottom, using his personal Woodstock typewriter. Alger Hiss retyped the classified documents and handed the copies to Chambers for his discretion. Hiss always returned the originals to their file folder before they were moved to a safe as required by security procedures.

Colonel Golikov pinched the bridge of his nose and hung his head. Their greatest and most successful spying operation was unraveling faster than his cigar. His stomach began roiling like the nor'easter churning outside. They were all shattered by the news and collectively sighed as their careers dissipated with the smoke.

Filipp Golikov transported the bundle of diaries to another table. He knew this bad news must be moved as quickly as possible to the next level on the chain of command. Someone would likely die for this unforeseen security failure. Golikov wasn't ready to give up his own life. A Stalinist, he feared that, like several other American Communists and Soviet intelligence officers before him, he'd be called to Moscow to deliver his report in person.

If he did stay in the U.S., the Kremlin would likely send someone to America to kill him, his family, and anyone else associated with the sleeper cell handling Alger Hiss. The savagery of the assassination squad would send a signal to others in the American Communist intelligence network: *Comply and don't ever contemplate leaving The Party. Defections will not be tolerated!*

Colonel Bykov continued, as if relating more details of Chambers' treachery would begin to ameliorate the situation, "I've done everything possible to find him. I'm convinced he has left his home and the city."

The attorney Orlov stood and announced, "He has likely defected. We need to get ahead of the GRU. We need to get ahead of the assassin's bullet. There's no telling how much Yezhov is spending to accomplish this…this *wet business*. Filipp, you must tell the leadership. I don't envy you, sir."

The other colonels pushed their chairs away from the table. The game was ruined. The atmosphere had been compromised. It was time to leave and reassess their futures.

"This is very bad, Comrades. Comrade Stalin…yes, even our infamous Chief of the Soviet Secret Police Yezhov will be furious."

Bykov said, "Yezhov's days are numbered, I assure you. The only reason Stalin hasn't killed him is that he knows where the bodies are buried."

Golikov thought, *But not the unclaimed award monies. For all he knows ALES has been paid in full. Returning to Moscow will invite a trip to the Lubyanka for all of us. We have to be smart about this.* Golikov couldn't help but consider defecting from the Communist Party and going into hiding. Such a traitorous action could be the only way to save his own life and the lives of his family. He was a distinguished intelligence officer, due a promotion after his tour of duty at the embassy. He swallowed hard. "This Chambers had to have planned this, his getaway. We'll all be *recalled* for not seeing the obvious. It took years to get someone of *ALES'* stature into position. His production has been simply fantastic. Now all is lost."

Golikov used the code name of the Soviet spy in the U.S. State Department, as if everyone in the room knew who Alger Hiss was. As senior intelligence officials in the Soviet Government, they had been briefed on *ALES* and signed non-disclosure agreements. The agreements were like death warrants kept on file by Comrade Stalin.

They knew there was a well-placed spy deep within the U.S. government, but only the Chief, Golikov, knew the man's name. With Chambers on the loose, the secret cell, Alger Hiss, and his code name could be splashed across the front pages of America's largest newspapers. The complete operation with the names of the Soviet contacts and Chambers' handlers could be unmasked. Chambers could spell out the program's particulars for the Federal Bureau of Investigation, or worse, have an interview with a reporter who could plaster Alger Hiss' name and the Soviet Union's spying on the front page of the *Washington Post* or the *New York Times*.

The still dripping Bykov offered, "I'm not confident they'll recall us to Moscow. We have many *resources* embedded in the government. *ALES* was simply the highest placed resource. Chamber's position is meritorious only because he runs *ALES*."

"*Ran*," spat Golikov.

Bykov ignored the correction and said, "These things happen in this business." He hoped his assessment of the damage would somehow spare him.

The Air Attaché, Colonel Proskurov, harrumphed. "If we aren't recalled, then they'll *send someone*. Someone who has experience in finding those who failed the Communist Party, those who run, those who defect, those who don't wish to be found."

The lawyer, Colonel Orlov, feigned flamboyancy and waved an effeminate hand. "Hopefully the NKVD can find him. They can leave us alone. They'll leave us alone, won't they, Filipp?"

Boris Bykov raked the last vestiges of water from his hair and announced, "I'm concerned Chambers *has evidence*. I've always suspected that man! If he has defected and has documents he could trade microfilm for security and safety. Comrades, please accept, I always ensured he destroyed the papers he brought after photography. I witnessed their burning."

The lawyer said, "He could have copied them before delivering them to you, Comrade. And he could have kept a diary." It was a feeble attempt by Bykov to clear his name of failure, but it didn't work.

Golikov regripped the pistol in his coat pocket at the mention of Chambers' possible "diary." He offered, "I've known of this Chambers for a year. He's not as dumb as he looks. I wasn't able to detect any unrest or uneasiness with him. Even so, I agree, it's possible he has bargaining chips. We should expect it." Golikov thought, *He could have kept a diary….* The man gritted his teeth and made a decision.

The sound of poker chips being returned to their racks reverberated from the card table.

Bykov shook his head and said, "I always believed Chambers was a good Communist, but I didn't trust him. I tested him repeatedly, but he always demonstrated that he was a loyal and faithful resource. That success should take some pressure off of us; do you not agree, Comrades?"

Golikov shook his head like a man condemned. He didn't agree. Bykov lost Alger Hiss, the number-three man at the State Department.

Colonel Ivan Proskurov, the air attaché, ignored Golikov and Bykov and replied to his playing partners across the table. "Apparently, he wasn't all that good. If you were going to run, what would you do? Where would you go?"

Colonel Panfilov, the embassy's security chief, raised bushy eyebrows and said, "*Da.* One would protect himself if he could. He'd take or have immediate access to whatever he had of value. And as you said, he could have kept a diary. No one is so stupid to throw in their hand when you hold trump cards. We are talking about several thousand documents. Golikov, you say *ALES* has been uncommonly productive?"

"*Da!*"

Panfilov asked, "Then the real question is, does Chambers have information on us or other incriminating evidence? He only knows you and Bykov by your aliases."

Colonel Bykov admitted, "I'm his supervisor and case officer. He knows my name and all other names of the many *apparatuses* in Washington, New York, Los Angeles and Chicago. The people he could identify in the Communist Party…could be in the hundreds."

That wasn't the answer they wanted to hear. Now they knew they were living on borrowed time. The grumpy old colonels left the card table, donned their fedoras and coats, and shuffled out of the library, leaving Bykov and Golikov to deal with the problem of Chambers.

The two communists stood quietly, trying to find the right solution. Finding none, they uncomfortably and awkwardly gazed upon the walls of leather-bound books, a wall with a huge fireplace full of ashes, and a wall of windows which overlooked the coastline of the Chesapeake Bay. Comrade Joseph Stalin registered his disgust from his portrait perched over the thick railroad tie-sized mantel. Bykov said, "Fifteen diaries from politicians and military men in New York City."

Golikov ignored Bykov. He listened for and heard the other colonels' vehicles start and drive away. He announced, "I'll walk you to the shoreline. I doubt the FBI is out in this miserable weather. Where will you go Comrade Bykov?"

"Comrade Golikov, I'm still operating out of the consulate in New York City. I only come to Maryland when I have acquired sufficient diaries to deliver to you or when there's a shipment from *ALES*."

"My thoughts are that Chambers may still show his face, leave you a mark. There could be another reason for his absence. I suggest you give Chambers a few days before returning. You shouldn't contact the members of your cells. Think about a plan to get away if Chambers fails to emerge from whatever hellhole he's climbed into." Golikov's expression changed from pensive to thoughtful. He asked, "Do you need some money?" Bykov nodded in appreciation.

Golikov removed a cigar box from a table and carried it to the door. He joined Bykov on the stoop; they donned their rain gear. Before stepping outside, Colonel Bykov took one last look at the inside of the library as if he'd remember where every piece of furniture was situated, where every book resided on a shelf, where every diary he had delivered to the intelligence chief was ensconced behind glass cabinet doors. The old Romanov mansion, the Soviet Union's embassy getaway and sometimes Communist Party of USA's Washington D.C. area secret meeting location, would likely have to be abandoned. Bykov had made his grand entrance and ruined everyone's evening. The Communist Party of USA's most successful infiltration operation of the American government had been compromised. The worsening weather, lightning, and driving rain punctuated their failure.

Bykov responded to Golikov's gentle pressure and went out the door. Never before had his superior officer volunteered to walk him outside, in the moonlight or in the middle of a thunderstorm.

Colonel Golikov handed the cigar box to Bykov. They didn't speak as they walked to the edge of the river. During an extended period of lightning, Bykov stuck his hand out to shake Golikov's hand one last time only to touch the barrel of a gun. Bykov recoiled and glared at the old colonel in disbelief. The first shot went through Bykov's hand and stomach. The next shot went through Bykov's heart, and he collapsed forward in a pool of water and blood. The next shot went through the back of his head.

Golikov rolled Bykov over and stuck the barrel of the gun in the dead man's mouth and pulled the trigger. The back of Bykov's head exploded. The extended thunder drowned out the pistol's reports. Golikov thought, *You failed me for the last time, Comrade Bykov.*

He pulled the cigar box from Bykov's arm then fished the car key, the Red Banner badge, and Bykov's Soviet identification book from the dead man's pocket. Like a starving gulag prison guard, Golikov quickly liberated the man of his possessions. He removed the man's pocketbook and stripped off most of Bykov's clothes. Golikov rolled the semi-naked fleshy corpse into the turbulent muddy water. After a few crashing waves, the intelligence officer's body disappeared in the undertow to feed a cast of Maryland's famous blue crabs. Golikov clutched the cigar box closely. He was breathing hard from the exertion as he slowly made his way back to the mansion through puddles that flooded his shoes.

Once inside, Golikov headed straight for the portrait of Stalin. He unfastened a hidden latch under the mantel, and the portrait swung open. A hidden safe was exposed. It wasn't locked. One at a time, he withdrew six cigar boxes, each with an image of King Edward VII on the lid. He looked into each box to ensure stacks of crisp uncirculated 1934 $500, $1,000, $5,000, $10,000, and $100,000 United States Federal Reserve Notes were nestled inside. The $5,000,000 was the accumulated reward for the extraordinary services, the theft of some 5,000 top secret documents by the Soviet spy Alger Hiss.

The cigars in the box that Golikov had given to the dead Bykov were ruined. He tossed the soaked box of cigars into the fireplace. Golikov placed all of the other cigar boxes from the safe in a black physician's bag. Bykov's belongings followed. Golikov walked through the library one last time to ensure all evidence of their presence had been cleared from the room.

The neatly bundled package of diaries beckoned, the remains of Bykov's thundering entrance. Golikov still hadn't recovered from all the exertion rendered in turning the handler into fish food; he sighed and thought, *Stupid diaries.*

Golikov rolled around in his head what he should do with the package. Comrade Stalin had ordered all intelligence officers in every Soviet Union embassy to acquire the personal journals and diaries of their British, American, French, and German enemies through whatever means was necessary. The Chesapeake Bay mansion held over two thousand of the small notebooks behind locked doors, waiting for intelligence officers to analyze their contents for any intelligence-related information. It may have been a well-thought out program in Moscow but no one in America could be trusted to read the diaries of the evil *haute bourgeoisie* and not be influenced. *I will return and deal with these later.*

The colonels knew how to clean up after themselves; there should have been nothing but cigar ashes and those had been dumped into the fireplace. Golikov extinguished the lights as he left the mansion. He and the others wouldn't be coming back anytime soon. *ALES* wouldn't be collecting any fees for services rendered in support of spying for the Union of Soviet Socialist Republics.

Colonel Filipp Golikov walked out into the pouring rain. He slipped into the rear seat of the black Lincoln Town Car, placed the black bag close to him, and kicked off his wet shoes. He told the driver, "Embassy."

1

July 4
Indianola, Iowa

Tommy Larrabee's mother laughed hysterically when he told her what his job entailed; she thought he wasn't being serious. He always had an impish quality about him and he could get a little onery when she least expected it. When he was a child, he sometimes made up stories, usually after watching a James Bond movie with all the action and fascinating gadgets. He had boobytrapped an old cigar box his father had given him with a rubber band, a paper clip, and a button; safeguarding the juvenile contraption against an unauthorized peekaboo. Tommy called it his "007 safe."

When Mother Larrabee discovered he was serious about his job description and duties, she began to worry about him. She knew enough of the Democratic Party's behind-the-scenes operations and machinations to know her only son could be walking on a one-way tightrope without a net.

He wrote letters to her because he refused to communicate with her through her unencrypted computer or smart phone. He told her, "It's too unsafe. If you want to use a computer, then we need encryption. Lots of encryption." She wrote letters to her son's post office box, and he sent cards to her Iowa post office box, a box that her husband didn't know she had.

Tommy was much closer to his mother than his father. Although she claimed to vote a straight Democratic ticket at every election, he suspected his mother was a closet Republican and quietly voted for Republican candidates. When he asked which way she voted, she demurred. Her non-answer coupled with a sly "who-me" smile was an answer. She knew how to keep a secret, and her real political feelings would always be their little secret. Tommy wanted his mother to be proud of him, and she undoubedly was, but now she was worried about his career path, him, and his safety.

Tommy had surprised his mother when he extracted his lanky frame from an Uber pickup that stopped at the mailbox at the end of the driveway. With a backpack and a bag, he ran up the drive, opened the screen door, and rushed into the kitchen, completely unannounced, completely unscheduled. She was completely floored and chided all six-foot-one of him for not telling her he was coming to visit. He loved surprising her and making her smile. Had she had known Tommy was coming for a spell, she would have made his favorite meal of chicken and dumplings, key lime pie, and homemade ice cream. With frozen strawberries. As far as Tommy was concerned, his mother was the best cook in Iowa. In Washington, he missed her cooking.

Tommy was agitated as he confided to his mother, "I can't do this anymore. I'm in a criminal organization. You can't possibly conceive what these people have done. What they are doing." He shook his head as if shaking hairy worms from his ears. "I came across some files…there were names of people I was unfamiliar with. Researched a couple only to find…that they'd either been killed mysteriously or had a suspicious heart attack or committed suicide. At first, I wasn't sure if the DNC had anything to do with their deaths."

"But now?" She was worried and increduous.

"Now? Now, I'm sure of it. But I don't have a good grip on how they do it. I dig up dirt, I don't dig up killers. At least I didn't."

"Tommy, that's not a good situation to be in. You sound like a modern-day James Walter McCord, Jr."

Tommy smiled as if he was an eight-year-old caught cheating at Uno. The former CIA intelligence officer was instrumental in leading the Watergate break-in. McCord and four Cuban nationals made up the burglary team, known as the "plumbers," and broke into the DNC headquarters in the Watergate building.

Maude said, "I read about him recently. The last of the 'plumbers.' He's still alive but not in good health."

"McCord and the others were the exact reason the DNC established an official opposition research department and why we live and work in the shadows."

She asked, "Kind of like the CIA?"

"Yes, we modeled our capability after theirs and the Navy's fighter weapons school. What do you know about him?" Tommy was suddenly curious. He allowed a passing thought, *Would he end up like McCord?*

Mother Larrabee smiled at the Top Gun reference. She was a huge Tom Cruise fan. She had visions of her son becoming *Maverick*, a Navy fighter pilot but her husband insisted "no son of his would ever be a Republican, that his son would attend Harvard law school, like his father." She was still a very proud mother. Maude Larrabee sighed, "He was the most puzzling of all the Watergate characters. Retired from the CIA. Like all those guys who would like to talk about their secret life but can't, he somehow ended up on Nixon's re-election campaign security team."

Tommy smiled at his mother. He knew the story of Watergate, a story of a president desperately trying to hold onto power, but it sounded better when his mother told it. His mother had the gift of Goldilocks; whatever Tommy did was either too little or too much but whatever mother touched or said was always "just right." He said, "Watergate was Nixon's way to get dirt on his political opponents, whether it was their sex lives, tax records, drinking habits, or marital problems. The Republicans were bumbling fools and remain so in this area. We're the Top Gun of opposition research."

Maude Larrabee smiled and nodded at his confidence. *Maybe my Tommy's the Maverick of the DNC.*

Tommy nodded and continued his train of thought, "I also did something I probably shouldn't have. I tried to look into the history of Dr. Z. Every month he authorizes the transfer of tens of millions of donation dollars to offshore entities. The DNC pays consulting companies overseas to create—not report, but create out of whole cloth—detrimental dirt, doctored documents, damaging dossiers, and deleterious information on adversaries. Depending on the candidate, the leadership, meaning Dr. Z, pays a third party to manufacture false information from which studies and personal files are generated. There are a dozen federal election laws and conspiracy laws being broken when they use false information against Republican opponents or some Democrats who have fallen out of favor. Their attacks on President Hernandez are wholly manufactured. And the cigar-smoking DNC Chairman, Dr. Zhavrazhinov, is the orchestra leader."

"What do you mean, manufactured?"

He laughed at the walls and returned to his mother. "Democrats control the Senate and all of the leadership positions in several departments, such as State, the DOJ and FBI. I understand we used to have several high-level contacts within the CIA, but they seem to have vaporized. There's a new guy in charge, a new director. Although he's on record for voting for President Mazibuike, he was handpicked by President Hernandez. He was a retired spook. His appointment was totally unexpected. *Unapproved.*"

"He's viewed, *officially*, as a former Democrat, now a closet Republican, and as such he's reforming the CIA. The DNC leadership has tried to approach him but the Agency man has no time for Dr. Z and steers clear of him at political functions. All of this was after Dr. Rothwell vanished. Then after President Mazibuike resigned and disappeared, I saw the documents and approvals that allowed the DNC to send millions to third parties and the media to fund programs to undermine President Hernandez, and kill him with paper. Money to newspapers. Money to Congressmen. Money to fund protests.... I'm sure Dr. Zhavrazhinov planted the seed for the FBI to begin an investigation that President Hernandez was being blackmailed by the Russians.... Dr. Z has amazing pull. Completely ridiculous, manufactured things like that. I've seen Hernandez's file. He's as clean as a boy scout. With one exception."

"What's that?" Tommy's mother was curious.

"Seems he had a sister who was a flight attendant on a jet that exploded shortly after takeoff. The rumor was it was shot down by a terrorist."

Maude Larrabee shrugged her shoulders to articulate, *So what?*

"Well, he has been very aggressive in rooting out the worst terrorists on the planet. Something like the top 100 or so international terrorists on the terrorism watch list have dropped off the grid. They've been *eliminated*. Rumors on the dark web suggests they'd been shot 'by a ghost. That fact alone smells of CIA involvement. The DNC Chairman thinks we can use that information to hurt Hernandez come election time. Expose his Agency's black operations or two. Maybe an October surprise. I wish we had proof."

Mother was indignant for a moment. All at once she didn't like or trust the DNC Chairman. She had always thought of him as a Communist plant. A spy. Zhavrazhinov reminded her of another communist spy, Alger Hiss. She obliquely smiled at the impure thoughts that Dr. Z was Alger Hiss' doppelganger with white hair and a white Fu Manchu. She said, "President Hernandez may be tough on Islamist terrorists and jihadis, but it shouldn't make any difference if a terrorist is linked to the murder of his sister, it seems to me the president is just doing his job. A job he didn't ask for. He was appointed; he wasn't elected. And, he isn't a cigar smoker or a drinker."

"Doesn't matter. He's a Republican. He's the enemy. He holds the office, and he has decided to run for the office, and most of the Republicans support him. The DNC's job is to stop him and elect our candidate."

"How do you plan to do that?" Now she was curious.

"We sell info. I dig up dirt."

"You dig up dirt and sell information?" Her face turned into a scowl.

Tommy nodded and said, "I don't see any money. There are other offices. Front companies disguised as law firms. The DNC Chairman assigns those issues personally to the Opposition Operations

Department. Sometimes they build a criminal record for the opposition. My office, Opposition Research, I find and expose their sordid little histories which they must refute. But because of political purposes, or their families, or they just can't afford an attorney to fight the charges, they quit. Much of my work is fed to Opposition Operations. The dark web is full of sordid stories just waiting to be used against an adversary."

Oh, Tommy….

"Once a candidate has been broken, they either lack the will or the resources to fight back. Through their credit card purchases, I find out what they do, what they purchase, who they call, where they go, where they are, who they lunch with, who paid, what they ate, where they travel, what they're working on, etc. Everything is available. If I have time I use those data to create a history. Real or false. If I'm any good, and I am, I selectively edit the opposing candidate's record, turn him into a felon or an adulterer or a homosexual, at the very least—whatever is necessary to annihilate the candidate's chances. If I don't have the time or bandwidth, I send the information over to the DNC Chair who sends it to the Opposition Operations Department. They have dozens of people who can counterfeit credit card statements and create other documents. They can show the Pope met with a hooker in a massage parlor in New York City or Moscow, with photographs."

Mother Larrabee frowned.

She has to hear it all. "These people aren't independently wealthy; if they were they could fight back. Millionaires might fight back but billionaires…they have more money than God and aren't intimidated by bogus opposition research. It's as if they know what we can do to them and they just don't care. We can't hurt them. So, overall, it's better for the others to withdraw from the race than for their *history* to be given to the media, to be subjected to the level of scrutiny that they can't hope to overcome. In virtually every case it's too expensive to fight back, monetarily or personally. These guys built an impeccable reputation and must maintain it for future income. So when you can kill their reputation and candidacy using the threat of bogus documents, that's exceptional opposition research."

His mother challenged him, "But when he was a Congressman, Hernandez had nothing to do with the release of the CIA file on Mazibuike or the vice president's suicide. He was the Speaker of the House. He couldn't have been responsible. He was completely out of the loop." His mother was suddenly afraid for her son.

He waved a finger at her. "Mother, first, he's a Republican—that makes him enemy number one at the DNC. The RNC is clueless, they aren't at war with the DNC, but we are at war with them. Hernandez could have cured cancer, and we'd have a stinging rebuttal of some sort. Another office handles retorts. Strategic planning, I think. Anyway, Washington Democrats ignore the obvious truths and work with the media to develop other narratives that are in line with or beneficial to the DNC. Then the narrative is leaked to the media that he's somehow responsible, that the Russians helped the CIA build that file on President Mazibuike, and that it was someone in the CIA who released that file to the media and Congress."

"Who at the CIA had a file on Mazibuike?"

"Apparently there were several files on our former president. We had an extensive file on 3M. We wouldn't have released that info, but there was someone who wanted that information into the bloodstream of public knowledge. Dr. Z was livid as he thought parts of 3M's file was part of an official DNC release, but it wasn't Opposition Operations. Or me. There was other close-hold information from the other intelligence services — Brits, Germans, Israeli — that we didn't have in our file."

Maude Larrabee looked at her son strangely. "I didn't think you'd do something like that."

Tommy shook his head. "To hurt Mazibuike? I would not. That would have been political suicide. But I started a file on Hernandez because I had nothing on him. President Hernandez is one of a very select few on Capitol Hill who are squeaky clean. Others have a history they don't want exposed. I tried to generate a false history — documents and photos.... You have to be creative but extremely careful if you try to create a false history on someone who's clean. It requires amazing amounts of research, like dates-times, locations, people. I manufacture credibility, when I'm not drilling for dirt. Those are the reasons for getting access to their bank records, credit cards, and recurring bills. They never know where the information comes from. So if you can't get them to quit, at the very least you can create doubt in the minds of a spouse or the voters. And if voters think he held a personal vendetta and had a terrorist killed....*assassinated*, they might think he was less than honest or worse, vindictive."

Mother Larrabee was vocal. "But Tussy is the most dishonest politician this country has ever seen!" She watched her son shake his head as if he was defeated. "The people you work with are disgusting. That's criminal activity. They're losing it. I suppose facts and timelines don't matter."

"You have no idea, Mother. If there's one topic which would have the greatest political impact, it would be the unmasking of the Republican who released President Mazibuike's CIA file."

She raised a hand to interject a comment, but Tommy continued. "Every week another congressman threatens to impeach the president, accusing him of imaginary crimes. Every month another member of the Senate threatens to hold the CIA Director in contempt of Congress. He just yawns at them. He wasn't even in the CIA when 3M's file was being built or when it was released. The truth doesn't matter. Only the narrative as dictated by the DNC. Zhavrazhinov."

Maude Larrabee quietly asked, "Tommy, what's the real story on Mazibuike?"

"What we know is that the Chief of the Near East Division in the Central Intelligence Agency started a file on the young Maxim Mohammad Mazibuike in the 1990s. Culled from embassy dispatches from Islamabad, the Mazibuike file began with photographs and witness statements about how the tall skinny man and his traveling partners tried to be inconspicuous as they moved through hotels and markets, before dashing into a mosque known for its fiery imam who railed against the Great Satan and Israel."

"The file grew as additional Agency dispatches and case officer notes came across the daily wire on the curious young man from England. British Intelligence and other intelligence agencies were helpful. Xeroxed copies of British passports and visas under an alias came to the Near East Division Chief's office via double-wrapped packages. One of the last of the bogus documents was the man's U.S. passport."

"When the man appeared on national television as the keynote speaker for the Democratic National Convention, warning bells went off inside the Near East Division. The Mazibuike file was the hottest document on the planet, for it proved he wasn't the man he claimed to be, that he was aided and abetted by the DNC with fraudulent and bogus documents to create a history. The liberal media picked up its cues from the DNC, while the RNC screamed, 'the media never vetted the man.'"

"When this thing—when Mazibuike's file had been released—when it first broke as news, Dr. Zhavrazhinov gave me some time to find the culprit who released it. I'm sure he didn't think my office was behind the release, although we had a copy of virtually every document contained within that unauthorized release, we just lacked the foreign intel. So, for weeks, I tried my best to find a lead. I developed a list of potential players; I scanned all of the files in the GOP and the DNC's archives and active databases…but to no avail. The most important info was that there was absolutely no connective tissue, no intersection between Mazibuike's file and President Hernandez."

"Now that we know that President Hernandez will be the Republican nominee, the Chairman is furious that we haven't been able to crack that nut. If President Hernandez isn't part of the Mazibuike's file then who is? Zhavrazhinov is convinced someone, some *Republican*, knows that that information 'is out there.' It's an utter shock and embarrassment within the DNC, at least in my office, that we still don't have a hint who released it. *We know or are supposed to know everything!* Even our partners overseas don't have a clue. They're protecting whoever released that information like pros. I swear it smells of high-level CIA, but the FBI has crawled up their ass and has found every hidden dime in every pile of pony shit and still don't have an inkling of who did it. Anyone who even touched any remnant of the original file has had multiple polygraphs. And still nothing."

Maude Larrabee smiled for the person who released Mazibuike's file. Whoever it was, was a hero in her eyes.

Tommy slyly smiled back at his mother and continued, "At least that's what I'm led to believe. I know…I have *access* to everything that's in the RNC archives and their servers. No related info is there. They didn't have it and they didn't generate it. I'm convinced it wasn't one of their guys. I saw their email traffic—they were just as surprised as everyone else when that file was released."

He shook his head as if trying to shake off a bad dream. "And how that file was released was a work of art. A credit card issued for a California DNC front company was used to pay for copying the file, binding the documents into a book, and delivered to Congress and the media. But it just has to be the CIA. Eliminate the distractors, and there's only one agency left who had the means and the wherewithal to collect, file, and analyze the data. CIA. We know a little…that some—but not all—of that information was in the possession of a CIA analyst. In fact, we know who developed it. Collated it. A woman replaced him. What we don't have is a good handle on is who touched it last."

Maude Larrabee closed her eyes and asked, "Why doesn't someone ask him, the person who developed it?"

"He was killed. No one knows who or how or why. Some classified message traffic indicated some weird special bullet hit him in the middle of the chest."

His mother turned her head away. A rising wave of fear for her son washed over her like a riptide that dragged her from the beach. She thought, *A weird special bullet hit him in the middle of the chest….* She said,

"I see on television where they continually pull the CIA Director in front of a congressional committee hearing, it seems like every month. The Republicans say the same thing. That there's no direct or indirect evidence to even hint that President Hernandez had anything to do with that file. He's clean and they know it. Tommy, you can't continue to do this."

He ignored her entreaty and said, "The new CIA Director was retired in '95 and had no access to the CIA. The day he hit 'mandatory retirement' age he was gone. As a political appointee, President Hernandez didn't have to grant him an age waiver in order to serve as the CIA Director. All I have on him is that he's supercilious to a fault; he owns several adult toys but nothing egregious like a jet. A large sailboat and an airplane and a little sports car. A *Porsche*. He married into old money and is set for life. Big boy retirement toys for the rich and clandestine. We believe the Republican president gave the retired Democrat spook an offer he couldn't refuse."

"I'd think something like Mazibuike's file would have been worth millions to someone."

"You are right, of course. Something that explosive should have—no, would have been shopped to some partisan Republican billionaire, not the media—even if it was overseas. And if it had been, we'd have known about it—open web and the dark web. If it was ever available, that's information you just can't hide for long. But because it wasn't, I'm convinced it came from a lower-level partisan Republican. Dumped in his lap."

"Not a *her*?"

"Women don't do those things. He didn't release it for money, he just wanted to expose Mazibuike as a fraud. Like a Republican Julius Rosenberg—whoever did it stole the file and dropped a thermonuclear device on the Washington Democrats and their friends in the media. And it's nearly killed…at least heavily damaged, the Democrats. That and more. And when Mazibuike quit and ran, well that just proved that the contents of that file were the unvarnished truth. Zhavrazhinov was in shock. We didn't have time to generate a backstory."

"Mazibuike was a fraud." She didn't like saying his name in her house.

Tommy changed direction. "The only saving grace is that the polls show the Democrats' strategy to paint Hernandez in a bad conspiratorial light is…working. May be working. He's down double digits."

She sighed. "All I know is that Eleanor Tussy's entire campaign has been predicated on the notion that we must make history and elect the first woman president. That it's her time. That we must rally behind her. Just her. Eleanor. I cannot. I'm sorry…that woman's voice is enough for me to vote against her. You do know she sounds like a billy goat?" Maude Larrabee mocked the Democrat nominee and made impolite goat braying sounds. Her husband wouldn't approve, but mother and son laughed in a moment of fun.

"Mother, I can't do this any longer. But, I have to find the right time to leave." Tommy was quiet for a short period. A thought had taken hold of him. He couldn't articulate, *I'm positive that Dr. Z doesn't know I tried to investigate him. If he suspected….*

Maude Larrabee interrupted his reverie. She was very surprised and said so. "I think I'm going to make a Republican out of you yet. I knew one day you'd see the light.…"

"We can't tell father." He grinned at his mother. "We generate lies, manufacture false stories, and basically direct disinformation studies. The media believe they're an integral part of political opposition, they're no longer journalists. The DNC has a strategic plan to crush the GOP, eliminate Republican leaders, to disarm America, and infiltrate the government with Democrats loyal to 3M, Tussy, and you shouldn't be too surprised, Moscow."

She shook her head. "Moscow?"

He nodded and said, "We had an election strategy, and it was good. Her whole BS slogan, by design, makes this election about Eleanor Tussy, not the country. The DNC Chair is livid—he had a theme and a narrative and a plan, but she apparently knows more than Dr. Zhavrazhinov."

Maude Larrabee said, "The Democrats booed God at their convention and she attacks Americans in flyover country. Like Iowa. I'd never vote for that…that… *bitch.*"

He grinned and said, "I didn't think it was a good strategy to attack the American people, that farmers and ranchers and flyover country are somehow irredeemable and isn't real America. She wasn't my first choice. She's a piece of work. Not in a good way." He thought of making another goat sound but thought better of it.

It was time to go.

2

July 4
Indianola, Iowa

Tommy and Maude jumped into her car, racing against the clock to get him to the airport so he could catch a jet to Washington D.C. Once on the way, Tommy told her, "The DNC has been melting down ever since 3M left. They want Hernandez gone. Whatever it takes. I'm getting out of there. But I have a few more things I need to do before I leave."

"Son, what does that mean—whatever it takes?"

"The Democrats are under so much pressure to win back the presidency—they raised and spent over two billion dollars to ensure she wins; they don't want to see her fold. There's a belief that with a couple of billion big-ones, she should be a shoe-in."

Mother Larrabee asked, "What if *he* wins?"

He looked straight ahead. "He just might. Actually, I think she'll lose. There's a difference. But more importantly, the DNC now thinks *she can lose.* Some pollster indicated the Democrats were drinking their own bathwater. Democrats are a lying bunch. They believed everything that was being sold to them without questioning its veracity. So Chairman Zhavrazhinov and the leadership are getting some insurance to protect themselves."

She asked, "Insurance?"

Off handed he said, "Pay for another set of files; created overseas; Russia, China, I found someone to do it. On the dark web all things are possible. Impossible to verify, and the final product will probably have a Russian flavor to it. The Chinese are horrible. One of the most senior members of the DNC had their honeymoon in Moscow. These guys know all the Russians and they know all the right Russian spies in all the right places. Islam worked as a secret wedge for 3M, but it won't work for a Latino. Latinos are Christian; and generally, they don't generally convert to Islam."

Those Russians.... He sighed, his chest heaved. He didn't want to tell her what he only surmised, but he found it therapeutic telling the only person he could trust. "Mother...if something goes wrong, if the election goes awry and he's elected, I don't know for a fact, but I get the sense there are other plans to try and forcibly remove him. There's been some email traffic from the campaign to Dr. Z. It was coded; I wasn't supposed to see it."

She found this unbelievable. "How's it possible to remove a sitting president? The Democrats don't have the numbers in the House to impeach him....unless they think they're going to win the Congress this term, and I don't see that. Your father knows it doesn't look good for the Democrat Party House members. Is it true the DNC is worried several dozen Muslims will win their seats but won't be good Democrats?"

He nodded. Tommy looked under his brow at his mother. If looks could kill.... *When all else fails....*

Then it hit her, and she realized what her son was thinking. Why he was in such turmoil. *They may try to kill the president if he's elected. It wasn't about killing him or destroying him with paper but with a bullet or a bomb. My Tommy really is defecting from the Democrat Party! He may have to run. Hide. He's not going to want to hide here. This may be the last time I see him! This is why he came to see me and tell me what he has been doing. Oh my!* Now she was terrified for her son.

He continued, "There's nothing they wouldn't do to achieve more power or the presidency. With Mazibuike, they were *so close* to transforming the U.S. into a Russian-style dictatorship, an intelligence dictatorship. If you control the intelligence community, you can also control the Justice Department, the government. I believe they'll find a way to take down President Hernandez if he's elected. They couldn't embarrass him sufficiently to get him to quit before. Trying to accuse him of avenging a personal vendetta will probably be a bust. He's proven to be very resilient and won't go easily if he's elected. My opinion, the DNC and Eleanor Tussy will freak out if that happens. There's no telling what they'll do."

Maude Larrabee put fingers to her mouth to keep her from screaming.

"They're...the Democrats.... I've seen the document which suggest they're also likely trafficking in sex slaves, at the very least they're involved in human trafficking. They're...they have a place in the Carribean. Sometimes I drop in on a special file from the Chairman's office, I see receipts for first class one-way airline tickets—but no returns. Sometimes singles, sometimes duos. I've seen the email traffic to know they're even laundering money—those things are too large to hide. I can't get too close, but from what I've seen it appears that they're turning terrorist assets into legitimate currencies—and in the hundreds of millions of dollars.... The DNC is a criminal organization."

Maude Larrabee was past being shocked. She begged pitifully, "*How...?*"

"Most recently, they're turning stolen Lybian oil into cash. The Islamic State of Iraq and Syria, ISIS, steals the oil, someone high up in the Democrat Party foodchain negotiates a deal to buy the oil, DNC funds are paid out, and hours later we get these huge donations. Another one of my jobs is to hide these from the IRS."

"Oh my God."

Tommy shrugged and kept his mother's vehicle on the road. "And they're so cozy with Russia; I swear, Mother, they're helping Russia bring down America. And if it isn't the Russians, then it's the Islamists. Not the blustering al-Qaeda, but the quiet Islamic Underground. If it's not the Islamists, then it's the mobsters. New York mobs. The trafficking of documents, the raw espionage is so blatant that if we weren't paying the Washington D.C. Metro Police and the FBI heavyweights on the seventh floor to look the other way, I swear we'd all be in jail. It's good to be a Democrat."

Maude Larrabee said, "Eleanor Tussy should be in jail for the things she did when she worked for President Mazibuike."

"There have been a number of right-wing legal defense funds that have sued the FBI for information because she violated the Espionage Act. *Repeatedly!* Like a third rail, the FBI won't touch it. They don't dare touch her — she's the nominee, so all of this crap goes away.... The FBI exonerated her before they even talked to her. When she wins...."

Maude Larrabee whispered, "...when she wins."

"And when she wins, do you think that info will ever see the light of day? That's another incentive for her winning. If Hernandez wins, there will be bloody massacres; the blood will run freely into the Potomac. DOJ. The FBI. State Department. The Left has become so crazy — murderous. If he wins, they'll eat their own to survive."

His mother could hear fear in his raspy voice. "I suppose there never has been a case in the United States where the holdovers from the previous administration openly attacks a sitting president. Like a turd world...*third world* country. But the DOJ? The FBI? Seriously?"

"A few in top leadership positions, I'm speculating. I don't know who exactly. I'm not authorized to know that information. You have to remember, when Mazibuike was the president, he was able to nominate, lobby, and control who got the top jobs at the DOJ and the FBI and the CIA. The DNC has been able to weaponize the FBI and the DOJ against their political adversaries. The Agency has a new director who immediately polygraphed everyone that came in under the Mazibuike administration *multiple times*. The layoffs have been in the hundreds. Islamic Underground, Islamic National Party members — gone. He's not with the in-crowd, so I'm assuming he's somehow a friend or close acquiantence of President Hernandez. That makes him off limits."

"Do you know these people…at the FBI?"

"No. I'm not supposed to know who they are at the FBI, but I've narrowed it down to the executive suite on the seventh floor. If they took money there's a trail and I, for the most part, have access to it. But most of these guys do it for *the Party*. For free. There's this thing in the military, I'm told — commander's intent. The head guy or commander, or in this case President Mazibuike…all he has to say is, 'She didn't intend to harm the United States.' So right there, the FBI Director looks at that as commander's intent, and responds in kind. There's no intent. He finds a way to exonerate her.…"

Maude Larrabee said, "He becomes a Democrat Party hero."

He continued, "…so he can get invited to the special parties in Washington D.C., New York City, and other places." Tommy thought of the DNC's *other places*.

Maude Larrabee said, "The FBI Director is another person hired not for his character but for his loyalty to Mazibuike, and likely identity politics attributes. You do know he voted for the Presidential candidate for the Communist Party? This shows a lot about how leftists view law enforcement — as something to tolerate corruption in, and something to use on one's enemies. It's like the rule of law isn't even part of the equation and the result is that the law enforcement agencies themselves start to resemble gangsters in an organized crime family."

Tommy nodded. "And, while this new CIA Director isn't a political player, there's evidence to lead me to believe that there may be a couple of CIA dudes on the payroll. The FBI is too *exposed*. I know who at the FBI gets DNC money. I can only think Zhavrazhinov must be able to contact someone other than the FBI when he needs… certain… *services*. You won't believe it. Especially out here in the midwest you can't believe it, but the truth is the CIA has been very involved with Democrat politics since before FDR. I've been in the archives. The old DNC chairmen wrote detailed internal memoranda. The Kennedy stories.…"

He thought wistfully for a moment of how he had learned that the CIA's counterintelligence chief had a habit of turning up in the houses of dead people, people with CIA connections or certain leaders of the DNC, or someone the president or his chief of staff might be concerned about. He returned to his line of thought. "At least I think that's the case. I get the chairman's calendar electronically and every once in a while, there's this special annotation."

"You think he's meeting an Agency....contact?"

"CIA or FBI. I don't know. For that level of detail you have to go to his paper calendar in a small Moleskine notebook. He has a dozen of them, different cover colors. He must have a system. Those, I don't have access to, and he keeps them close. Nor do I know the extent of the possible services. I think they're real partisans and are paid very well. I don't know where he goes, and I think it would be suicide to follow him." *But I can do other things....*

She rolled her eyes as she came to grips with the obvious. *He may be a man, but my dear boy is in great danger! What was it that Tom Senior said to me when he attained his senior post, "Say nothing and no harm will come to you or your family?" That's it.* Maude Larrabee wanted to scream *Turn this car around!*

As Tommy Larrabee steered the car onto the airport access road, he asked his mother to contact a well-respected journalist on his behalf. The man he had in mind was a regular contributor on television, with several specials on some very explosive subjects. Young Larrabee respected the man's work. He had done an intelligent and honest job of covering sensitive topics like *Escape From The Devil's Hole* where he interviewed a young woman who had been kidnapped in Texas and held as a sex slave in the United Arab Emirates. And in *Is your Neighborhood Mosque a Sleeper Cell?* a piece on the curious activities which could be traced back to some mosques inside the USA. But Demetrius Eastwood's article on Eleanor Tussy, *Was it Espionage*, sold him as the right person to entrust his secrets.

A commercial jet flew over their heads as they approached the airport. Tommy was talking faster now and Maude Larrabee began to wonder if her son might have been exaggerating or embellishing the high and low points of his job. At a stop light, he reached into the backseat for his backpack. She watched him with interest. He reached inside the black bag and handed her a dark brown cigar box; he said it was "filled with USB flash drives." He called them memory or "USB sticks" and "insurance" in case anything happened to him.

Colonel Demetrius Eastwood could also access the special email account Tommy had set up for his mother and review the information in the "draft" folder. Larrabee had learned a few things about how to send and receive messages without sending them over the internet. The shared email account thwarted the National Security Agency codebreakers and the DNC's own sureveillance software because the email message was never transmitted over the internet, so the NSA and the DNC couldn't capture the message and the metadata.

Without alarming his mother, Larrabee bet his life that he wasn't under any surveillance, and the encrypted mail service would be a safe way to communicate with his mother.

Tommy and his mother developed a system of simple codes that would be sufficiently innocuous to a trained investigator while transmitting hard information. He said, "Dad is extremely proud of the Cubans in the humidor at the National Democratic Club. Any reference to 'taking a cigar' means that you have made contact with the target correspondent and any reference to a 'cigar box' means you have been able to give him the contents."

"You mean like, 'Tommy, if you take another cigar out of that humidor, your father will positively kill you. Something like that?"

"Exactly." Tommy nodded, grinned, and hugged his mother.

Maude Larrabee wasn't eager to agree. There was a part of her that thought her son's discussion bordered on the unbelievable yet there was an element of truth to it. And she didn't want to hear anything that endangered her son.

He stopped under the American Airlines sign at the Des Moines Airport. They got out. He kissed her goodbye. She held on to him much longer than she should. He disappeared into the terminal. She cried all the way home.

3

July 11
Washington, D.C.

The National Counter Terrorism Center (NCTC) Director exchanged concerned looks with her boss. She had delivered the President's Daily Brief (PDB) in her usual thorough and professional manner and now they'd returned to the Director of the Central Intelligence Agency's inner sanctum, his sprawling corner office on the seventh floor of CIA Headquarters. The President had asked dozens of questions on the intelligence community's most recent security breach where an NSA contractor had effectively downloaded what the media called "the crown jewels" of the American intelligence archives. President Hernandez had articulated several approvals to include approving the Agency's request to infiltrate the Islamic Republic of Iran to extract a high value defector. He also approved the Agency's request to immediately evacuate the ambassador and a small group from the U.S. Embassy in South Africa.

There was also presidential direction, a "tasker." The CIA Director knew what he wanted to do to fulfill the president's directive but pride was interfering.

Specifically, the president wanted to eliminate the remaining terrorist targets from his spreadsheet. The *Disposition Matrix* had been the CIA's and the president's private terrorist targeting list. At one point there had been over 150 men on the *Disposition Matrix*, now there were only four. President Hernandez had looked up at the CIA executives with a sense of purpose and concern. It was discussed tangentially and understood that the President might not win the upcoming election and his possible successor was a closet socialist and Marxist, like his predecessor, and she'd never target the enemies of America, so this was likely the Agency's last chance to find and eradicate the final group of high value, "most wanted" terrorists who had killed many Americans. The CIA Director believed he had detected the sense of urgency in the president's voice. The CIA Director said, "Mr. President, we'll do whatever's in the art of the possible."

When the CIA executives stood to leave the Oval Office, President

Javier Hernandez asked, "Is Duncan available?" The NCTC Director was ready to say, "Yes" but one look from Director Lynche forced her to keep her thoughts and her words to herself.

After leaving the White House, Lynche had asked Nazy if her husband would be interested in the work. "If not Duncan, would this be something Kelly Horne could do?" Lynche had been grooming the young pilot and looked for a special mission for her to demonstrate her flying expertise and expand her growing portfolio of successes.

The CIA Director and the NCTC Director sat and stared at one another. When looking at each other without saying anything proved fruitless, they allowed their eyes to wander around the office. It was more a museum than an office. Photographs of former CIA Directors and the current president adorned one wall. There were officious chairs and a conference table made of mahogany, zebrawood, and ebony. The rare woods had been smuggled out of Africa in orange diplomatic bags, and the men from the Science & Technology Directorate had crafted the one of a kind conference table. The walls were filled with photographs from previous Directors and famous operations. Bookcases were filled with autographed books from the icons of foreign policy and the intelligence community as well as mementos from classified operations and historic events. There was missile debris from A-12 OXCART encased in Lucite, a piece of concrete from the collapsed Berlin Wall, and a twisted piece of metal from the World Trade Center. Three walls full of Agency history surrounded the two career intelligence officers. The focus of the day was before them. One had things to do; she was a busy woman. She broke the impasse.

Nazy knew the National Clandestine Service pilot well and rejected the idea of using her. "She's too young and inexperienced. Kelly isn't the right pilot for a job like this. This mission is a radical departure from the aerial eradication of opium poppies. I believe our only realistic option is to use Duncan. He has the right airplane to do the job."

Lynche knew the assessment of his NCTC Director was correct. Nazy indicated that the ground intel on the four men and the defector was still developing; an intercept could be possible. Lynche didn't like dealing with defectors, in part, paradoxically, because their motives were always suspect. And if defectors brought hard information in the form of documents, it required a great deal of time and effort to determine if their information was any good or relevant; or if any of it had value. The Agency had been burned many times when defectors promised to tell the CIA or the FBI things the spy agencies wanted to hear but once they were brought to the U.S., oftentimes those defectors just simply vanished. Many times the defectors didn't have any real secrets that would help the spy agencies. They just wanted to get out of Russia. When a defector brought substantial archives then the IC had to thoroughly process the information to ensure it was valid and verifiable. And when a defector showed up on your doorstep, *a bluebird*, these people have an expectation that they'll be treated like kings or queens, even when they have nothing of value. Those that have just wanted to escape their former life complained bitterly about the treatment they perceived as "hostile" from CIA and FBI handlers. *Bluebirds* were rarely worth the effort.

Rare was the defector who stole U.S. secrets and ran to the former Soviet Union. Now Greg Lynche had one of those to worry about and all of the murder that would likely come when the traitor shared his information with the Russians. Assassination teams would be dispatched to eliminate the Agency's spies whose cover had just been blown. There was nothing more to do with that issue. Lynche was focused on the president's directions. And he had questions.

Nazy's mind raced to anticipate Lynche's questions. Arranging for a defector to be picked up and spirited away by aircraft was a topic that needed to be discussed with her husband. There was a very narrow window which was ephemeral, even mercurial. Intel, especially coming from Iran, was like *Bluebirds*. Dispatches took forever and the intel wasn't firming up adequately for the secret event, 48-hours away. If there was a bright spot on the possible mission it was that the defector might be part of the wedding party. Everything had to go perfectly but with these missions, usually chaos reigned supreme.

Then there was the issue of the Republic of South Africa. Their congress had passed a number of laws essentially outlawing their Caucasian population's existence. The President's Daily Brief included photographs of billboard-sized signs that had been erected throughout South Africa: MURDER MURDER

YOU CAN KILL WHITES BLACKS CAN DO ANYTHING! CONTACT YOUR NEAREST ANC OFFICE NOW! YOU WILL NOT BE PUNISHED VOTE ANC! YOU WILL GET A WHITE FARM.

As if the local population took their cue from the colorful signs, white South Africans were being indiscriminately murdered from Johannesburg to Cape Town. It was time for the United States to demonstrate their displeasure and the President ordered U.S. Embassy personnel and other Americans to be evacuated immediately. Nazy indicated that as the situation developed in Iran, her husband would be interested in the lift to and from South Africa evacuating the ambassador and his staff. The operation had been approved by the

President but the request, the movement order, needed to come from the CIA Director.

That wasn't the response Lynche wanted. He tugged on his cufflinks as a way to delay. They were 1908 five dollar gold Indian head cufflinks; a gift from his best friend. *Why did I pick these today? That crazy ass Hunter has a thing for gold coins. Porsches, and old watches.* He checked his watch, it wasn't gold but an antique *Longines* 13ZN chronograph that was identical to the wristwatch Amelia Earhart wore. Another birthday gift from Hunter, the *Longines* was made especially for pilots before the Great War. Lynche sighed and looked at Nazy obliquely.

Duncan Hunter was assigned to a unique CIA special access program, an Eyes Only program. Besides Nazy, no one else in the CIA knew of the existence of the SAP or what the program's scope of work entailed. Duncan was Nazy's husband.

Fifteen years ago Nazy Cunningham had been striking, just another pretty face and curvaceous body in a sea of pulchritudinous women in government. Now she was impossibly beautiful, when she turned to look at someone straight-on, they knew they had seen that face before. It was as if a young Elizabeth Taylor had been hired as an analyst; in the early days people saw Sophia Loren, now it was the face of Marilù Tolo with five feet of hair. She could have been a movie star or a model working in front of a camera, but Nazy was a lawyer and analyst by training, and hunted down the most vicious terrorists hiding in Africa and the Middle East. She saw herself as average, with a nose that was too big and boobs that matched. She thought other women, especially the blondes and redheads with their tiny noses, puffy lips, and athletic breasts were much more beautiful than she.

Older professional men would look at the young striking women and know they'd never have a chance sexual encounter with any of them. They found that the mature women with exotic looks who took exquisite care of themselves were infinitely more desirable. And the older men found it difficult to look away from something so unique as Nazy Cunningham.

Part of Nazy's cover was that she was a widow, the wife of a U.S. Navy carrier pilot on assignment with the British Royal Navy. Admirers always noticed her ladies gold Rolex President with a diamond bezel and a wedding band from one of the boutique jewelers in Tel Aviv. The three diamonds reeked of DeBeers with the finest, flawless and most dramatic facets a professional diamond cutter could produce. American jewelers knew at a glance those weren't mass produced diamonds for the *hoi polloi*.

Her green eyes flashed behind round tortoise shell glasses in anticipation of a decision. There was an element of trepidation in the way she hid behind a layer of hair that fell over one eye. Her chin rested on her chest in angst and hid a stylized gold cross suspended on a delicate gold chain.

Greg Lynche rubbed his temples and made faces as if to head off an expected migraine. He was uncharacteristically introspective; something heavy was weighing on his mind.

He wasn't distracted by a planned, organized, and routine extraction of embassy personnel from an increasingly hostile foreign capital. Those were State Department problems. Nor was he concerned about extracting a nuclear scientist from Iran or killing a quartet of terrorists on the FBI's Most Wanted List. He was over seventy and afraid of speaking with Duncan Hunter, his best friend, and he felt foolish.

He finally noticed that Nazy looked as if she had been sewn into her navy Burberry business suit. The buttons from her striped silk blouse weren't under strain, but she was wound up tight in a pique of aggravation. Her arms were crossed under her beasts, her bare legs were crossed, and the free leg bounced in nervous syncopation. Her Christian Louboutin pumps were keeping time as she waited for him to make a decision.

He didn't move, other than to unconsciously tap a Vertex pen on a pad. Much like Spencer Tracy's *Santiago* character from *The Old Man and the Sea*, Lynche was thin and heavily-tanned from many years of racing J/105 sailboats or being underway on his fifty-foot yacht. Fishing wasn't his forte but drinking coffee and racing were, and several J/105 racing trophies, including a national championship, were sprinkled among the shelves of the Agency's historical artifacts in his office.

His white hair was quickly thinning, his grey Brooks Brothers suits were getting shiny in the seat and showing the telltale signs that he was losing weight. He was the oldest CIA Director ever to hold the office and was too busy to take time and replace his old clothes. After two thoroughly corrupt CIA Directors, he had been pulled from retirement to return trust, discipline, and operational sanity to the Agency. He was also tasked to extirpate the political partisans and Islamists who were allowed to infiltrate the Agency under the previous president and his rogue CIA Directors.

Lynche had been working like a madman since he had assumed his position. He had no time for his passion of sailing. There was so much to do in an organization the size of the CIA. Hundred hour work-weeks were the norm for the top executives, leaving time only to commute, eat, and sleep.

The undeclared Mexican standoff lasted for a minute until Nazy suddenly stood from the chair next to his desk, flipped her hair behind her shoulders, and leaned over the CIA Director's bank of telephones. *Time we don't have is wasting. What's he afraid of?* If he wasn't going to call, she'd take the initiative. She braced herself against the desk and engaged one of the phones. She selected the speaker phone feature, which clearly annoyed her boss as he generated even more displeasure with her with a facial tic. Nazy depressed the sequence of numbers she knew by heart. She waited for several seconds as the encryption technology raced through its protocols to ensure the conversation would be secure. The speakerphone emitted swooshing noises as a way of indicating the secret communication system was working.

As she leaned over the phone, Lynche took advantage of a window of opportunity that, like most men, he couldn't resist; his eyes drifted across her bosom like ball bearings' attracted to a magnet. He was embarrassed for being so weak and spun around in his chair to put space between him and the NCTC Director's breasts.

Lynche ground his teeth. He wouldn't talk with Hunter. It was time for him to get out of his own office, leaving his subordinate to make the telephone call he was too ashamed to make.

Nazy wanted the two men in her life to reconcile and resolve their differences. She thought the director's offer of work was a way of signaling that he was going to be the adult in the room and ask forgiveness from his best friend. But Lynche walked out of the office.

The telephone connection finally completed. She knew it would be a surprise for Duncan to see that the coded number in his Blackberry was from the CIA Director's office. She lifted the receiver, killing the speakerphone. He said, "Hello, good looking."

She smiled. "How did you know it was me?" Nazy's British accent was evident, she beamed like a school girl at hearing his voice. She unconsciously curled her toes in her shoes.

"Greg always uses another line to call me. I'm probably on speed dial. Number ten or 100 or something. What's up?" He asked very suggestively, "What can I do for *you*? You know I have some ideas."

She smiled at him before she became serious. "We need you for some work. Three parts. Possible *Wraith* operation, if it materializes in Iran; intel still developing. May not go. For the other, have you seen what's going on in South Africa?"

"I've seen the signs. They changed the law. Now they're murdering people. So, you need to evacuate the embassy? My jet isn't that big."

"Yes on the evacuation, but it's a skeleton crew. Maybe ten; maybe a dozen men. I thought it would be something you'd like to do, and if the situation we are watching develops, you'll be in the area to respond immediately." Nazy wouldn't use the aircraft's old military designation over the telephone, instead she used its code name. "We'll have the *Whiskey* and crew in place, just in case the intel firms up for a unique opportunity." *Whiskey* was code for *Wraith*.

He asked what it was; she told him in vague coded terms.

Two thousand miles away he nodded. "I can be heading that way inside of an hour. Will I have to fight my way into the airport? If this is anything like Zimbabwe's extermination efforts, none of the locals can be considered trustworthy."

"President Hernandez offered to dispatch some Marines to secure the airport and extract our embassy personnel, but their president said it wasn't necessary for the U.S. military to flex its muscles. He has ensured safe passage to the airport. Not the international airport. He assured the president that no harm will come to Americans wanting to leave."

Hunter frowned. "That's good. Are we evacuating your guys or State's"

"Our guys, the ambassador and a couple of guests."

"By 'guests' you mean locals."

"Yes, the former head of their intelligence service and their minister of defense."

"What about State's people? The Embassy Marines?"

"Marines and most of the State Department contingent are gone, evacuated by Marine Corps helicopters. Our guys are the last, they know how to close shop in an event like this."

Hunter had visions of CIA operations officers feeding documents into shredders. Computers and electronic storage devices would be dumped into disintegrators that could turn a Chevy Impala into deer dropping-sized pieces. Then he asked, "NCS?" The three letters hung on the line like mildewed laundry.

Nazy knew this could be a problem. Her husband had developed some serious issues with unknown members of the National Clandestine Service. Several *Wraith* missions had been strikingly and surgically interrupted as if the terrorist leaders knew not only who was coming for them but *how*. Hunter had been shot at, shot down, and even captured. Operations officers from the NCS had always provided the base actionable intelligence for the counterterrorism missions, they just didn't know who would be executing a possible operation. Hunter was convinced that someone from the NCS leadership had discovered his mission, likely from previous CIA Directors or that an NCS executive had achieved some unofficial backdoor entry into the special access program, and that they were trying to discover who was treading into their territory. Many of the missions involved significant treasure, usually gold.

The intelligence communities and military special operations were extremely territorial, and fights over jurisdiction were common, loud, and sometimes violent. Technically, the Agency and Special Operations Command worked hand-in-glove with each other but when they were on an operation in the field, violent clashes of personalities between the two organizations were expected. No one had been killed, but there had been plenty of damaged equipment and egos. Hunter believed the circumstances and evidence during and after his flight missions suggested that the NCS had somehow been following him and possibly even targeting him. He wondered, *Why and how and who?*

Hunter had become nearly paranoid about meeting anyone from the NCS. Their instructors taught the course on how to kill a person with a bug or some lethal chemical cocktail and you wouldn't even know it until you were on your death bed. The CIA had long touted the operations officers of the NCS were some of the finest patriots in the intelligence community and as such, they were always on the side of America and her war on terrorists. Even Director Lynche had been NCS in his early days; teaching among other things, bomb making and the defensive driving course. He even rose to the top of the clandestine food chain to become the NCS Director before his retirement.

Nazy knew things had happened to Hunter that were simply inexplicable, except for the lone possibility that NCS was likely conducting probing activities, running interference on some missions in Africa and the Middle East. The special access program Hunter was commissioned to perform was designed so that there were no divisions within the NCS that could be completely and operationally "in the loop." No one from the NCS had ever been read-in onto any part of any of his missions, even so, they had a strange and disconcerting way of being in the same location at the same time as Hunter and his airplane.

Nazy tried to assuage his concerns. "There are two low-level junior guys who are part of the ambassador's personal security detail. Not even a SAP. Your cover is simple—you are just a contracted business aircraft. Pick them up and fly them to Djibouti. You can go in disguise. You probably should do that."

He said, "I think it's fourteen, fifteen hours to Johannesburg. That still ok?"

"Duncan, darling, it'll take us two days to contract for immediate airlift. The Marines and their helicopters have been gone for about a week. You're the quickest solution. I can bill the lift from my office."

"And I work really cheap. Got it; I'm already on contract. Ok, I'll do it. Anything for you." Both of them smiled across a few thousand miles. "I have to add some things to my go-bag. I have to stop at FedEx, drop off a box. Let Greg know I'll take Bill, if he can get away. Regardless, I'll find someone to act as co-pilot."

She said, "Kelly is in Mexico. She's out." She breathed deeply. Her chest heaved. "Greg wanted to know if she could do phase two and three into Iran...."

And not use me? What's Greg thinking?

Before Hunter could veto the crazy idea, Nazy said, "I nixed that thought. She's the wrong person for that work — you really are the only show in town. Back to South Africa. We'll provide contact information...."

"That will be helpful."

"Okay, darling Duncan, someone will call you when we receive it. Things are..., uh, *fluid* in South Africa right now. The ANC (African National Congress) has erected hundreds of signs saying it's ok to murder white South Africans. That you can take the farm and all of the white farmer's possessions. The State Department doesn't want to lose another ambassador." *Like Libya*, she thought.

Hunter wasn't impressed with the ambassador or his actions. "He should have returned to the U.S. long ago. In case Greg has forgotten, the jet's satphone has an RJ-11 jack for a STU or whatever they call encrypted comm this week. I have one so not to worry. Can do easy."

She smiled as she turned to the door to ensure no one was listening. Nazy's words came out sultry when she was aroused. Thoughts of him always aroused her. She asked, "I know you've been busy...will you be able...*to see me* when you're done?"

"Baby, that's the only reason I'm doing this. I can't wait to do this for you...come see you and put my arms around you. But, ah, I have to tell you, you'll have to be gentle with me."

Her smile became a frown. "Okay, Mr. Hunter. What have you done now?"

He looked at his naked torso in the mirror, side view. A wide hideous blue and purple bruise ran from his hip to his knee; it was as wide and as dark as a rack of beef ribs. He said, "I remember the days being able to get up without making sound effects. I dove for a racquetball and landed a little funny. If something isn't creaking or grinding, then I'm groaning. I have a, let's call it a 'bruise.' But I've been taking it easy. I know they'll come a time when I'll just have to get this hip replaced."

And your knee…. Nazy nodded and smiled at his acknowledgment that he was human and mortal, and a bit juvenile.

"And just to let you know, while I've been nursing this thing, I've actually read the *Washington Post*. I was so hot I wrote a couple of articles for my Marine Corps buddy to review."

"Colonel Eastwood?" She was confused for a moment. *Since when did Duncan start writing articles? He never reads the Post! Is he confined to bed?* Always looking to protect him, she asked, "Are you going to have to clear that with Greg? Publication Review Board?"

"I don't think so. It's nothing to do with *your place*, but everything about the corrupt head of one of the political parties running for office. Besides, I don't exist in your database any longer. Greg had me killed and buried in Arlington."

"He had to do it. We thought they were getting close to discovering you."

"I know, Baby. Anyway, Colonel Eastwood has already published one article under his name and it got such good reviews that Eastwood said his network is making it into a television special. I'm sending him another proposal."

Her concerns about him writing were assuaged for the moment. "But you are ok?"

"I'm ok. I cannot wait to see you. I love and miss you, Miss Cunningham. I'll call when I get close."

She smiled and shook her head. *You're over sixty and you're still diving for racquetballs?* She said, "*You better!* I'll say 'thank you' for Greg. He'll appreciate it even if he can't articulate it. See you soon, Baby. Be safe." She hung up and returned to her chair. She waited for her boss to reappear.

As if he had heard her terminate the secure comm link, Director Greg Lynche walked back into his office, took a seat, and looked at his protégé. He waited for her to respond to the question he had asked minutes ago. She crossed her bare legs politely and waited for him to speak. Her kneecap stared back at him.

This time it was easy to keep his eyes above her nose. Exasperated, he finally asked the question with a Polish salute.

Nazy decided she wouldn't tell her boss her husband was writing articles. She nodded, smiled, and said, "Of course, he'll do it. He'll do anything for you, and you know that. You could have talked to him. He probably would have told you he's been reading the *Washington Post*."

He made a face. At first, he didn't believe her. "Duncan never reads the *Washington Post* or the *New York Times*." Since Nazy wasn't the type to kid around, he took her news as nothing more than a data point. He returned to the mission. "So, he'll do all three?" She nodded and then he nodded. She smiled and then he smiled. *She's right. She's always right.* "Thank you, Nazy."

It was an innocuous statement. A follow-on to her news that Duncan was somehow reading liberal newspapers when he wouldn't touch them to line a birdcage. Lynche pinched his lips. The look on his face telegraphed that the discussion was over. She stood, stepped behind her chair and gripped the back of it as if for protection. "You know, one of you is going to have to say they're sorry."

Lynche frowned and said, "Let me know when he lands in Djibouti."

She turned and walked away. With anguish in her deep, sultry Londonshire voice, she said, "Wilco," a word she learned from her pilot of a husband. It made her smile to use his lingo.

He lifted his eyes from the desk and followed her intently. Her wildly long hair swayed from side to side across her derriere as her heels left crush marks in the carpet. Lynche picked up a top secret file, one of about twenty in an IN box as his last vision of Nazy was her tight skirt disappearing through the door.

It was hard to get that woman and her husband out of his mind. He turned to the thick file in his hands. The Agency's Inspector General's report and executive summary on Eric Snowden, a former CIA and NSA employee, would occupy his thoughts for hours. As a contracted employee, Snowden had downloaded millions of files and been able to steal, what senior intelligence executives were saying privately, the American intelligence community's "crown jewels." Millions of the highest classified documents from the National Security Agency had been copied onto USB memory sticks and turned over to the Russians.

Lynche threw the package on his desk, turned in his chair and stared outside. After a few minutes of thinking and contemplating this *Great Game*, he thought of the business of defecting and defectors. *We do it to them, they do it to us. But we don't kill their defectors.*

He turned, looked up toward his door, and imagined Nazy walking out on him. When the image of her dissolved into his best friend, he excoriated himself. *I'll call Duncan when he gets back.*

4

July 11
The Farm

Two white and green-trimmed Cessna 310s touched down, one after the other, on the 5,000-foot Runway 23 near the remains of Bigler's Mill. At the end of the runway, the pilots steered right to the parking ramp, stopped and shut down the aircraft's engines. There wasn't a sign to announce to the pilots and their passengers that they'd landed in the heart of Camp Peary, known colloquially as "The Farm," the Central Intelligence Agency's primary training facility to train National Clandestine Service officers. The first passenger to step from the Agency's airplane needed no introductions. He was Steven Castaño, the Director of the National Clandestine Service.

The other men stepping from the aircraft worked for Castaño. Galvan Fässler was Chief Counterterrorism. Jarvis Bomarito was Chief Special Activities Division and Bennett Troxel was Chief Special Operations Group. They shared the flying duties to the Farm's landing strip. The four men wore the same style of sunglasses as they walked to the aircraft hangar. They went inside and met a small group of Agency scientists who were introduced as the masterminds behind the latest achievement in sniper weapons technology.

The NCS executives were as impressed as the S&T scientists were as secretive. A new sniper rifle would be a tremendous advantage to NCS officers in the field. Castaño and his men were convinced the S&T scientists were holding something back. Something that probably made the new sniper weapon unique among the ultra-long range sniper rifles. They'd have to wait for the great "reveal."

Bearded and bedecked in white lab coats, the subordinate scientists stayed mum as their boss ran through a slide presentation. The NCS men sat stoically, legs and arms crossed, silently demanding the S&T Director to get to the point. When the next slide, with top secret headers and footers, announced the sniper rifle had a ten mile range with a probability of kill greater than 97 percent, the NCS execs had to be convinced. The group broke up and reorganized on the roof of the hangar under an awning. When the S&T Director removed the cover from the sniper rifle, the NCS men stood in awe at what they were seeing. The scientists encouraged the men to come closer and touch it.

Castaño said, "It's definitely a new concept. I've never seen anything like it."

The Terminator Sniper System, nicknamed the *Terminator* or TS2, was a fully programmable weapon that used a very powerful, gyroscopically-stabilized spotting telescope which was electronically coupled with an internal infrared laser designator.

Sample ammunition the size and shape of an A-10 Warthog 30mm projectile and resembled *Orion's Bullets* in color, were handed to the four NCS leaders. The men were surprised at the weight; bullets from spent uranium slugs were expected to be heavy. They were more surprised to find the bullet tips were made of blue glass, like an eyeball from a tiny primate.

The S&T scientist commented that the state of technology had progressed to the point where the TS2's experimental ammunition could be manufactured with a tiny glass seeker head similar to the laser-guided seeker heads of anti-aircraft missiles. "And it has tiny 'wings,' and the microelectronics imprinted on a hearing aid battery can withstand a thousand Gs when fired." He demonstrated the firing sequence of the weapon; he explained the special bullets fired from the *Terminator* would essentially "ride the laser beam" and strike the laser-illuminated spot one hundred percent of the time for targets within five miles. He said, "At ten miles, the P-sub K; uh, the probability of kill, is reduced slightly to 97-98%. At ten miles, some targets move just enough for the laser designator to break lock." He motioned for the Agency's top clandestine service executives to gather around the weapon for a little show-and-tell. The weapon's container was the size, color, and shape of a Husqvarna chain saw. Heavy yet portable.

He demonstrated, "You just have to pull it out of its carrying case, unfold the tripod, and set the weapon on its electrically-driven plinth. You can do this in ten seconds. The barrel is synchronized with the movement of the telescope by a joystick, for coarse adjustments and there are knobs for fine adjustments. The image in the telescope can be carried remotely, via a wireless signal, to a touch-screen laptop or tablet device. As you know, the number one killer of snipers is another sniper aiming on a sniper weapon. With the TS2, the operator never unduly exposes himself to lines of fire."

One of the NCS men asked a question about how the system worked. The scientist said, "This uses artificial intelligence, the *AI* and electronics within the TS2, are constantly computing an aiming spot and sending adjustment signals to slave the barrel in the same direction where the laser designator is pointed and where the laser spot is focused. The main point is that you can set up the TS2 in seconds, load it, fire it up, move away from it, check that the weapon's computer is synchronized with your laptop, aim and 'tag' your target, and touch the fire button or the AI will pull the trigger for you, if you want it too."

"At ten miles?" The NCS executive asked incredulously. He was still not convinced. He'd need a demonstration.

Every one of the four NCS men wanted to try out the TS2. They fussed over the dull black and gunmetal weapon like children competing for turns at a merry-go-round.

Designed to kill competing snipers on the battlefield, the full range of capabilities of the TS2 hadn't gone unnoticed. While the effective range of an enemy sniper's weapon was at best, one or two miles, the *Terminator* round had five times the maximum effective range of any other known sniper weapon. The S&T scientist claimed, "We are about twenty years ahead of any competing weapon. A TS2 round is heavy enough to smash through the thickest sniper hide. A bullet can blow through brick walls, heavy armor, steel safes. Enemy snipers are no longer safe outside of two miles. You won't believe what the TS2 can do. Let me show you how easy the *Terminator* is to use."

The men from the National Clandestine Service took turns firing the top secret weapon. Each man was able to hit a ten-mile target the size of a man's wallet, the first time they attempted to use the *Terminator*. It didn't require any special skills to deploy, aim, or fire. Anyone laser designated and "tagged" in the telescope was a dead man.

It was the perfect sniper weapon. And no sniper team would ever conceive of its existence.

The National Clandestine Service Director crossed his arms and smiled at his subordinates. *This is something The Judge would want to know about.* They seemed to know what he was thinking.

The S&T scientist was extremely pleased with himself as he transferred custody of the weapon to Bennett Troxel. There wasn't a custody card; no one asked for a signature. *They're the National Clandestine Service. This is what we do for them. Help them do their job better.* He said, "This is disruptive technology. Nothing like it on any company's internal research and development programs."

The NCS Director reached to shake the S&T scientist's hand and said, "We can't wait for our operations officers to use the TS2 on an actual target." He left an NCS challenge coin in the S&T scientist's hand as a token of his appreciation. The scientist was shocked at the gift. The S&T rarely received appreciation and accolades for the great work done in the CIA's laboratories. He clutched the rare NSC coin in a death grip and said, "Thank you, Director Castaño."

The NCS Director paused, lowered his head, and stood in deep thought; his breathing came out in chuffs. His subordinates thought he was on the precipice of having one of legendary Tourette's-induced outbursts but relaxed when the man raised his head and looked at the S&T scientist from under his eyebrows. It was something of a villainous look that Vincent Price would make. The NCS executives held their collective breath. The S&T scientist wondered what the man was experiencing. It was as if an evilness of thought and manner had come over Director Castaño when he hissed, "Can this weapon be mounted on an airplane?"

5

July 11
Johannesburg, South Africa

Duncan Hunter expected the worst as he set up for the approach at Lanseria International Airport. It was an unknown airport and it was raining, and he had no contact with the group to be evacuated. They could be waiting for him or they could be held as hostages, used as bait. Or they could be dead. He thought, *And we are rushing into this mess to save the day? Crap!*

Published flight information indicated the airport was open 24-hours a day and once Hunter flew under the overcast, he was surprised to find the airport was actually open and operating in the early morning hours. There was virtually no traffic but his jet, on final. Straight-in approach. He couldn't tell if the situation on the ground was good or bad. The rain put him in a foul mood.

South Africa was under a moderate and steady rain with a low ceiling. Penetrating the cloud deck provided the typical bumpy ride as the Gulfstream IVSP gyrated up and down with the gusting winds. Hunter was quietly thankful there were no thunderstorms or high crosswinds to contend with as the prevailing winds were running right down the runway. As they approached the runway threshold, the jet's powerful landing lights illuminated the three-kilometer long runway. The copilot smiled at touchdown, at the smoothest landing he had ever experienced.

Hunter always assumed the worst possible conditions when flying into and out of Africa, and was surprised the runway was in excellent shape, as was the taxiway. There was no ponding or running water anywhere to interfere with steering the business jet on the taxiway. Hunter commented to his copilot that the airport seemed to be running with an unexpected sense of normalcy. "The locals are reportedly killing white people. We may have landed in the middle of a civil war or just an airport. We'll find out."

In some remote British dialect, the aircraft ground controller provided directions to the executive terminal. Former U.S. Navy SEAL Bill McGee expressed his confusion, and said, "I thought we'd find the country melting down. I'm still afraid we're going to get funneled into a place where we won't be able to get out. I hate being trapped like a rat in a sewer." The huge African American man with the grey flattop and round glasses continually hawked outside the jet looking for any sign of trouble.

Hunter reached behind his seat for his helmet bag and withdrew his helmet with the latest color night vision goggles. He donned the helmet, fired up the device, and scanned the areas in front and to the side of the jet.

Hunter said, "Nothing out there. I expected chaos and we have ops normal. Nazy said their president indicated Americans could leave without issue. Maybe someone called a truce while we were airborne."

McGee said, "Maybe they put up some new signs that said killing white men is now a no-no."

"Like that's going to happen."

Bill McGee then broke out in a poor rendition of Eddie Murphy's classic Saturday Night Live sketch, "*I'm gonna get me a shotgun and kill all the whitey's I see…. I'm gonna get me a shotgun and kill all the whitey's I see…. When I kill all the whiteys I see, then whitey he won't bother me… I'm gonna get me a shotgun and kill all the whiteys I see…*" As McGee laughed, Hunter grinned and flipped the NVGs away from his eyes and continued to taxi to the front of the terminal. He brought the jet to a stop when the marshaler in front of the jet crossed his lighted wands over his head. Hunter took one final look through the NVGs and didn't see anything out of the ordinary.

As he removed his helmet, the air traffic controller asked Hunter if he needed a fuel truck. Hunter shook his head and McGee transmitted, "Not tonight, sir. Thank you." Hunter wasn't about to risk having possibly contaminated fuel introduced into his jet. *When they're in the middle of a civil war, you can't trust anyone!* The Gulfstream had additional fuel tanks in the belly, so they had plenty of fuel to get them to their next stop and the passengers' final destination in Djibouti. Hunter shutdown the port engine and moved the starboard engine throttle to idle.

McGee remained in the cockpit and watched as Hunter donned his spider-silk body armor and pulled a sports coat over his shoulder holster. A six-inch Colt Python .357 magnum revolver with five hollow-point rounds fit snuggly in the custom holster under his left arm. Hunter buttoned his jacket and cautiously opened the aircraft door and lowered the airstairs. Adrenaline flooded his veins. He fully expected to be shot or at least chased back inside by a hail of gunfire. They were in an aluminum tube and the outside visibility was atrocious. The lighting on the ramp was nonexistent. Anyone could sneak up on them. He bounded down the airstairs and found the illumination was marginally better, at least enough to see details in the distance. His hip was extremely stiff from the lengthy flight. As he limped from the jet he surveyed the parking ramp for anything suspicious. He hobbled into the executive terminal as if he were an injured football player trying to leave the field of play.

A black man and eleven mature white men in the waiting area looked at him with relief and hope. Behind a counter three young black women with cobalt polo shirts and braided hair styles smiled pleasantly.

He read the passengers' faces, looking for a sign that he had been tricked, that it was all a trap, and that he was just seconds away from being ambushed and captured. But those expressions weren't on the faces of the men; he saw only the anticipation of escape, deliverance from something heinous, vulgar, and vile that had been left outside on the other side of a security gate, like the ANC sign promoting the murder of white men in exchange for receiving the deeds to the white men's farms. For the moment, evil was outside the confines of the airport, unable to penetrate the executive terminal.

Hunter nodded to the assembly and proceeded to act normally, like he was just another transient corporate pilot picking up business executives. He ensured his sports coat was buttoned as he presented an American Express card to a pretty black girl with a bright uniform and a customer service smile. If she tried to pull a gun on him, he wouldn't hesitate to shoot her. But she greeted him warmly as if he was one of their best repeat customers. She asked and he confirmed that he didn't need a fuel truck. He said he'd like to pay for all the landing and ground handling fees; he expected an expedited departure.

Her eyes rocked toward the group of mostly white people, and she asked if he had come for the group.

He didn't answer her directly; he just nodded gently as if he were listening to an announcement on a public address system. He continued to scan the inside of the terminal for soldiers with weapons, but there was nothing. This wasn't what he expected, but he was going to take advantage of the situation before it got worse.

Since takeoff, the State Department had provided him with hourly updates on the crisis in Johannesburg. Now that he and McGee were on site, the crisis situation wasn't as dire as reported, but it was surreal. He had raced across half of the globe to rescue and evacuate Americans and a couple of locals, and there was fatigue in their faces but little sense of urgency.

The executive terminal was a morbidly interesting place. Hunter half-expected to find relatively fresh bullet holes and anti-white messages of the rebels on the walls and windows. During their descent into Johannesburg fresh intelligence from the State Department cited there had been a major bloodbath in a secure compound a few miles from the airport. Over 100 whites were killed, some found shot in the back of the head. Tensions were very high.

After signing and receiving a receipt, Hunter thanked the woman behind the counter, turned and walked to the group of men. As he walked into the middle of them, they stood. He mentally separated the Americans from the locals. Even in Africa most Americans buy and wear American clothing and footwear; the South Africans had their own style of dress and shoes. Hunter asked for a private word with the man who matched the emailed photos of the U.S. Ambassador; he leaned close and challenged the African American Ambassador for "the password." Hunter breathed a sigh of relief that it was authenticated; he responded with his own, and the man shook his hand. "You ok, sir?" Hunter asked.

"Just waiting for you to get us out of here."

"What's the threat? Are we going to have problems leaving?"

"I don't think so. White members of the South African Army have protected us from the very beginning. If you meant, have you just walked into a trap, no, I don't think so. We have been perfectly safe. Frightened, but safe."

Hunter nodded. As if he were giving directions to a lost tourist, he said to the group in a forceful command voice, "I assume everyone is able to travel. You need to go to the washroom here; you won't be able to use the lavatory when we are aboard. And we can't take everything you have brought with you. Essentials only. Medicines, passports, important documents. Keys, computers, currency. Small bags only. Leave everything else here. I plan to be airborne in two minutes."

The men weren't shocked. Few availed themselves of the restroom facilities, and those that did hurried as if their bladders were about to burst.

Hunter stood impatiently for sixty seconds until the last person emerged from the restroom. He silently turned, nodded for the ambassador to follow him and escorted the group to the jet. His cowboy boots' thick stacked leather heels thudded out of the terminal. To the surprise of everyone, he quickly frisked them before they climbed the airstairs. Once he was satisfied no one was armed, he allowed them to board. He kicked the chocks away from the nosewheel, then climbed the airstairs and closed the aircraft door. He ripped off his sports jacket, slipped into the cockpit, and started the number one engine. He handed McGee his flight helmet.

As the jet's engine spooled up, he radioed ground control for permission to taxi to the runway for takeoff. When the air traffic controller said to "standby," Hunter said to McGee, "Like hell!" and jammed the throttles to the firewall to get the business jet rolling. He mashed the nose wheel steering button and touched the brake; he spun the jet's nose radically to the right and powered toward the runway. McGee had the NVGs over his eyes and he scanned the side window for any sign of trouble. He reported he didn't see any military vehicles rolling toward them or a platoon of soldiers with weapons. While he scanned the parking apron and taxiway, he asked, "So, 'standby' wasn't an option?"

The jet approached a turnoff. Hunter said, "What did you do during SERE training when you approached an unexpected checkpoint? A roadblock?"

"I yelled, back up! Back up! Back up!" McGee turned from the window to nod his understanding and smiled conspiratorially before returning his NVG scan of the airport.

"We can't backup; we're getting out of here before they try to stop us. I paid my bill; I'm never coming back here. Only an idiot would be flying in this crap."

"That us!"

Hunter shut off the taxi lights and all of the jet's external lights as he negotiated the jet toward the nearest entry point to the runway. The taxiway and runway lights remained illuminated as Hunter steered the darkened jet to the main runway. He mashed a brake pedal and turned onto the runway so quickly that one of the main landing gear nearly slid off the wet surface. His passengers were getting bounced around in the cabin by the aggressive movements. Hunter set the controls for takeoff. The nose hadn't fully come around to point directly down the centerline of the runway when Hunter slammed the throttles to the firewall. The engines responded nearly instantaneously.

He said, "You have to have the nose pointed down the runway, otherwise when the engines spool up, you will shoot off in the direction the nose is pointed. This isn't a commercial jet where it takes a few seconds for the engines to spool up and you can get away with the nose coming around."

"Sounds like the wisdom of someone who had to find out the hard way."

Hunter grinned and nodded. *Guilty as charged.*

The Gulfstream picked up speed quickly, and when there was sufficient airspeed for the nose wheel to lift off from the ground, Hunter raised the landing gear handle. Then the flaps. He kept the nose low, and the aircraft quickly accelerated. He flew low over the city until he pulled hard on the yoke and shot through the overcast. Once he was "clear on top" he flew the darkened jet just inside the clouds, as if he were trying to hide after stealing a jet. No other aircraft appeared to be in the vicinity, they weren't being chased. The Gulfstream raced across the border on a northeasterly heading toward the Indian Ocean. McGee returned the helmet to Hunter's flight bag.

Once the aircraft cleared the South African airspace and attained cruising altitude, Hunter set the autopilot, left the cockpit, and entered the cabin. Each of the evacuees was wide awake and looked at the pilot with the menacing black revolver slung under his arm. He ignored the pain in his hip and began asking questions of his passengers. Their stories were the same. Ten of the men were the last Americans to man the U.S. Embassy.

Safe in the jet, the Ambassador was now in a state of shock. Evacuating your embassy without a fight was as bad as not going down with your ship. When the indigenous population became suddenly hostile and murderous, it was hard not to remember what had happened to the U.S. Ambassador to Libya in Benghazi. Regardless of his skin color, the Ambassador had fully expected to be captured, tortured, and killed by the South African rebels who had succeeded in getting the laws changed and putting a bullseye on the backs of white people. Many in the ANC had been calling for the death of all white men in South Africa. Then they put up the signs and all hell broke loose.

The *chargé d'affaires* claimed they were given safe passage by the South African military because the new rulers didn't want to have poor relations with the United States. It was only a matter of time before the South African military yielded to the rebels and attacked the remains of the American delegation.

The two older men were obviously South African with their white hair, heavy black glasses, square-pointed shoes, and deeply lined faces. Duncan knelt in front of them and said, "I've been instructed to ask you if you need a satphone. If not, we're going to Djibouti and there will be people there to take care of you." No one asked to use the phone or the lavatory.

Hunter never offered his name and neither did any of the twelve men.

Upon arrival at Camp Lemonnier, the former French Foreign Legion garrison and current United States Naval Expeditionary Base in Djibouti, there was no fanfare, no ceremony, or official greeting. The U.S. Navy was all business. Hunter lowered the airstairs and shook the hands of the men as they departed the jet. The U.S. Ambassador debarked first, shook Duncan's hand and pressed a coin into his hand. The passengers were met by helmeted men in camouflage battle dress uniforms who escorted the refugees to black Suburbans with blacked-out windows.

Hunter didn't have a moment to look at the ambassador's coin or watch the passengers depart as a fuel truck pulled along the side of the jet and began refueling. Hunter walked around the jet inspecting the outside and underside for damage. Bill McGee offloaded his and Hunter's bags, a matte black Halliburton Zero briefcase, and a white Yeti cooler. A contingent of soldiers drove up in a tug and a tow bar, and once the refueling operation was complete, the Gulfstream IVSP was pushed into a nearby hangar.

An Air Force pilot emerged from an office within the hangar and introduced himself to Hunter and McGee. Passwords, challenges, and authentications were made quietly yet formally. He helped them lug their belongings to a U.S. Air Force Special Operations C-130 with its auxiliary powerplant running. Waiting near the C-130, an Agency operations officer handed Hunter a double wrapped package the size of an oversized document folder. After the C-130 settled into its cruising altitude, Hunter cut away the tape using an oversized Bowie knife from his helmet bag; he and McGee read the operations order.

The first phase of the mission was to land at a remote airfield in southern Iraq and debark the *Wraith* and make it ready for flight. For phase two, Hunter would fly the YO-3A across the Iranian border and locate a substantial compound situated in the Zagros Mountains in Khorramabad, near Keeyow Lake. Coordinates of the compound and the lake and satellite and ground-level photographs were provided. A single sheet assessment of the observable security inside and outside the compound was marked at the header and footer in red ink: TOP SECRET. The intelligence indicated there would be a wedding and at least four of the invited guests were on the FBI's Most Wanted Terrorists list. Photographs and information data cards were provided on those who were expected to attend. A "flash drive" containing photographs of the major terrorists was also included in the package.

Hunter disregarded the minor players and those of the wedding party. Phase three was as incredible as it was impossible: Find four men. Hunter knew what to do if and when he found them; assassination orders are never written down. He shared the data sheet and photographs with McGee. Bill McGee recognized the terrorists from his counterterrorism days as a U.S. Navy SEAL.

Mohammed Ali Hammadi had been convicted in a West German court of law for air piracy and murder for his part in the 1985 hijacking of TWA Flight 847. Hammadi had murdered U.S. Navy diver, Robert Stethem and dumped his body onto the tarmac in Beirut, Lebanon. Ibrahim Salih Mohammed Al-Yacoub had been indicted and tried *in absentia* for his part in the 1996 bombing of the Khobar Towers military housing complex in Dhahran, Kingdom of Saudi Arabia. Nineteen U.S. Air Force personnel and a Saudi local were killed. Abdullah Ahmed Abdullah had been indicted for his involvement in the 1998 bombings of the U.S. Embassies in Dar es Salaam, Tanzania and Nairobi, Kenya. Two truck bombs killed 224 people. Ahmed Jibril had led the 1988 plot to down PamAm Flight 103. He was paid millions of pounds by Tehran to mastermind the attack.

Then there was the man who provided the wedding information to a member of the Iranian resistance, a CIA insider. He traded the information for extraction from Iran.

McGee and Hunter shared a quiet moment. The men profiled were the four remaining terrorists on the U.S. President's Disposition Matrix, the list of terrorists to be eliminated. Once the targets were all crossed off, the special access program *Wraith* would end. Mission completion meant mission termination.

Hunter explained to McGee that before landing and unloading the little black spyplane, he'd use a "flash drive" to upload the defector and the four terrorists' photographs into the aircraft's mission computer. The basic plan was simple. After locating the compound identified by the intelligence sources on the ground, the aircraft's forward-looking infrared sensor would scan the faces of the wedding party and activate facial recognition software to positively identify the men in the sensor display. If Hunter could "take the shot," he was cleared to do so. After flying to the rendezvous point for extracting the defector, Hunter would verify his identity by the photo loaded in the database.

Bill McGee asked, "How's that possible? I've seen FLIR images and they're not the best. I'd think there's a lot of room for error. Mistakes."

"All of that it true, G.I. Dog, but today's facial recognition systems are based on geometry and distance, not clarity. The software analyzes over fifty data points, the ears and eyes, the nose and mouth—the distances between all of them can all be measured and cataloged, and a face is given a certain value. FLIR images faithfully replicate facial geometry and can be compared against a photograph. Instead of analyzing fingerprints, it analyzes 'faceprints.' I understand it's years ahead of anything in corporate labs today, and it works. At least, that's what I've been promised."

McGee and Hunter shared grins and nods as Hunter got up and entered the shipping container in the belly of the cargo airplane. McGee followed. A switch illuminated the inside of the forty-foot long home of the *Wraith*, one of Lockheed's three matte-black spyplanes, and the only one with a propeller. Hunter loaded the photographs into the aircraft mission computer and briefed McGee on the conduct of the flight. Bill McGee dragged a finger across the black fuselage; he shook his head in amazement at the special coating. Hunter knew McGee had loaded the aircraft's gun several times on previous flights, but Hunter indicated the gun had been replaced by a newer model. He showed McGee the new features. The only thing that didn't change was the location of the gun's magazine receiver.

As he had done over a hundred times, Hunter would deploy the aircraft's unique gun. From under the rear seat, the weapon and its targeting system would unfold into the airstream. To achieve high probability of killing distances out to a theoretical distance of ten miles, the system used the same revolutionary ammunition employing laser-seeking optics within the bullet head. If the mission required more than ten rounds, Hunter couldn't remove and replace an empty magazine for a loaded one.

For over one-hundred seek and destroy missions, the aircraft's gun had been the primary weapon to eliminate the masters of terrorism. Conditions had to be just perfect, sometimes requiring Hunter to wait for hours before the target appeared or conditions on the ground improved so he was able to "take the shot." Hunter and McGee scrutinized satellite photos and didn't like what they saw. The extraction of Osama bin Laden from his Pakistani hideout had galvanized terrorists across the world to make additional security improvements to their compounds and headquarters buildings. High-angle targeting was now impossible. Hunter wouldn't have hours to spend in the area hoping that a target would step into an open space of the compound or stand in front of a window. The defector had to be in the agreed location at the specified time, otherwise he wouldn't be extracted by the CIA aircraft.

To Hunter, the intelligence may have been outstanding and good, but it looked like detecting the terrorists Hammadi, al-Yacoub, Abdullah, and Jibril would likely be an abject failure. Duncan Hunter had seen it coming, the day when the YO-3A and all of its quiet and stealth technologies would be defeated by terrorists who had been studying how a hundred of their compatriots had been killed in the middle of the night with a single very large caliber bullet in some of the most inaccessible or protected locations on earth.

The anticipated location of the wedding was a closely guarded secret in Iran. If the location was top secret, so was the guest list. The Iranian government had long provided safe haven for terrorists on the run from U.S. and European intelligence agencies. No unmanned aerial vehicles armed with Hellfire missiles would be sent into the Islamic Republic of Iran to seek and destroy the old terrorists. Missiles would leave residue and collateral damage that could only be explained by American clandestine firepower. No U.S. manned missions had been flown into Iran, officially, in decades. Now, Duncan Hunter was planning to execute two in the same night.

After buttoning up the *Wraith's* conex, Hunter and McGee sat impassively and discussed the mission ahead. They agreed the incursion into Iran could be for naught. McGee got up and retrieved the black Halliburton case that he had brought from Texas. He grinned as he held the briefcase high. "At some point someone will use these to kill someone; might as well be us."

McGee said as he opened the case, "We only have eight operational drones. They're first generation, but they're packed with capability."

"So, technically, all we have to do is download their photographs and drop them over the target?"

"That's what you asked of our lab boys. This is what they came up with. They've been tested. There's only one problem."

"I understand I can't watch what they're doing or where they go."

McGee said, "Yeah, it's a bandwidth thing. It's easy to have tiny cellphone cameras but to add a transmitter….maybe the next generation drone. But the AI is the best we can get our hands on."

Hunter nodded. "Yeah, that's probably too much too soon. I asked for whatever we had and these will have to do. I appreciate the effort, don't misunderstand me. If I can't use the aircraft's gun, these give us other…opportunities."

"We may never know what they do. They could go stupid and kill kids." McGee raised eyebrows under the crewcut. He pulled his tiny round glasses from his face and dug sleepy sand from the corners of his eyes with a thick finger. It'd been a long flight.

Hunter thought about McGee's scenario and rejected it. He peppered his friend with questions. How far can they fall before they come alive and start flying? Can they be swatted away? How much battery life do they have?

McGee answered as only the CEO of the company could. Satisfied, Hunter plugged in USB cables from his laptop computer to each of the tiny rotorcraft drones and programmed a pair of drones for each terrorist. After the download, McGee handed the eight drones to Hunter who gingerly placed them in the pockets of his flight helmet bag.

As with all new products undergoing real-world field trials, the drones were on an order of magnitude more complicated and kinetic than the small helicopter drones found buzzing around America's largest shopping malls. The drones were outfitted with artificial intelligence algorithms and facial recognition systems to seek out specific targets. They were tiny, innocuous, the size and shape of an ancient first-generation BlackBerry, and combined the computing power of a smartphone, multiple cameras, four arms with four rotors, and a very small contact-explosive charge.

McGee said, "During testing, when a drone hunted down and made contact with the head of a goat, the one-ounce shaped-charge warhead detonated and penetrated its skull using the Munroe Effect. The explosive charge collapsed a metal foil liner inside the warhead to form a high-velocity superplastic jet of liquid metal. The brain was destroyed, cooked in its cranium by hot expanding gasses. The goat's eyeballs shot out of their sockets. Death was instantaneous."

Hunter asked impishly, "Do these work on Democrats?"

McGee frowned. "I guess we should have used them on donkeys."

"And I thought I was bad." The men laughed irreverently.

6

July 11
Iraq

After the C-130 landed at Prince Ali Base in Iraq, the *Wraith* was quietly unloaded. As the little spyplane rolled to a stop about fifty feet from the C-130's ramp, the U.S. Air Force aircrew watched the two old men and the pilot attach long, black glider-like wings to a black fuselage. The paint on the aircraft and wings played tricks with their eyes. They could make out the aircraft's basic outline but looking directly at the paint yielded no definition. It was as if the aircraft wasn't a three-dimensional solid structure but just a shadow. No one dared ask what it was that they were seeing.

Bill McGee crossed his arms and sidled over to the pilot and copilot and said, "What you are seeing, or not seeing, is the latest in nanotube coatings. I call it "black hole" because it sucks nearly 100% of any light that hits it. In a few years your *Hercules* will be painted with the stuff. Let's just say, it has some amazing anti-missile properties as well as a very low thermal signature. Keep this under your hat for now; our little secret. Ok?"

The aircrew agreed vigorously.

The aircraft was fueled, the battery was connected, it was ready for flight. As Hunter nestled into the cockpit of the airplane, McGee mimicked Oliver Hardy and said to Hunter, "This is another fine mess you've gotten us into." McGee's was a bass, and when he tried to raise his voice to sound like Andrea Bocelli, it came out as a rumble. Hunter laughed out loud and asked, "What's this us shit, *kemosabe*?" He transferred a pair of handcuffs from his helmet bag to his lower flight suit pocket, which elicited a look from McGee, massive body-builder arms akimbo. Hunter responded, "You can never be too careful with these guys."

Hunter was airborne just as darkness fell on the airfield. The YO-3A crossed star-filled skies above and the inkiness of desert Iraq below with the Iranian border on the nose.

Talil, the former U.S. Air Force Base in southern Iraq, had once been the temporary home for hundreds of airmen and Marines and their jets.

Now it was largely abandoned and had been renamed Prince Ali Base. It was the perfect location from which to conduct an incursion into the Islamic Republic of Iran. The last time Hunter had tried such a flight, an Iranian anti-aircraft battery had detected him and tried to shoot him down. Hunter's fighter pilot training saved him and the aircraft that night; it took months for the aircraft to be repaired after all of the stresses he put on it. He had nearly pulled the wings off the YO-3A during missile evasion maneuvers and nearly collided with the ground. The wild evasive maneuvers confused the surface-to-air missile's tracking computer, it's internal radar broke lock on the little spyplane, and impacted the ground. While Hunter's original YO-3A, serial number 007, was being repaired, he flew another identically-equipped Yo-Yo for continuous aerial eradication missions.

Tonight would be different. The *Wraith* had a new suite of stealth technologies, which not only made the aircraft invisible to visual detection but also made it invisible to radar, at least the engineers promised it should be. There was nothing like a live demonstration of the new coating's effectiveness. Hunter used the forward-looking infrared (FLIR) to quickly locate the thermal imagery of a Russian-made S-400 *Triumf* anti-aircraft battery near the Iraq-Iranian border. With what felt like gallons of adrenaline being injected into his body, Hunter focused on the FLIR as he flew the black glider-like aircraft, low and slow, a couple hundred feet above ground level, right over the radar dish on the Iranian's radar control van. Duncan Hunter was in awe. *American scientists are so damn smart!* There was someone outside the radar control van smoking a cigar, and he didn't flinch when Duncan flew over his head. Hunter started breathing again as he passed over the missile battery. He shook his helmeted head, *Like I wasn't even there!*

Finding the compound was quick and routine. Finding and identifying the targets in the FLIR wasn't a complete failure, but targeting them was. The FLIR and the facial recognition system returned confirmations that the four old terrorists were in the compound, but the compound's passive countermeasures gave the aircraft's systems fits. Within the first thirty minutes of surveilling the compound and wedding participants, Hunter assessed that the conditions and possible firing lanes to intercept the targets would never be in his favor. He couldn't see any way to kill all of the old terrorists with the gun. If he took a shot at one, then the bullet's acoustical report would alert the wedding party, and they'd take appropriate countermeasures and hide. One of four wasn't immediate mission success.

He could hear his wife's British-accented voice, "It might be years before we ever have another chance like this. If ever."

Hunter hadn't come to Iran to fail; he came to Iran to kill four murderers of Americans. He wouldn't be able to use the aircraft's gun. If he wanted to eliminate the four men, he had no other choice but to execute a contingency plan. He set up an orbit and engaged the autopilot to hold his attitude and altitude. He reached into the pockets of his helmet bag, and one-by-one, switched on the eight drones, a green flashing light from each confirmed they were ready to go. When Hunter guided the YO-3A silently over the compound, he pushed the octet of drones through an access door immediately above the aircraft's throttle. They vanished in the night, in the slipstream. Hunter turned the YO-3A for the next phase and the most dangerous part of the mission.

The wedding party effort was anticlimactic. Hunter said to himself, "That's as much as I can do. I could have got one but never would have gotten a shot at the others." He lamented, "How many times have I gone home, mission incomplete?"

Hunter knew there had been a handful of missed opportunities, but he had always been able to return the following night to complete the task. With the way the house and the compound had been set up, he could see that the Iranians knew exactly what they were doing to protect themselves from missile strikes from an unmanned platform. The compound was a fortress—with concrete overhangs so that satellites couldn't see anything or anyone. He said to himself, "Yes, they learned from bin Laden's compound."

Hunter was minutes away from the rendezvous point with the defector. He remained positive. *With the artificial intelligence, those drones are essentially 'fire and forget' weapons. The cameras will acquire, track, and guide the drone to its attack point, but there's no capability to watch the mischief and mayhem. The best I can hope for is that sometime in the future the intelligence gets out and confirms the drones did what they were programmed to do, that those men died from a pack of killer drones that chased them down and rammed their tiny warheads into carbuncled foreheads. Somehow I doubt I'll ever know. You know how some of those guys in the clandestine service can be. No need to know.*

Hunter checked the time and confirmed he was in the intercept window. The FLIR scanned the remote road and its surroundings out to five miles. There was one vehicle with a cooling motor in the distance and the thermal image of a single human with his arms over his head, hands touching. "That's the signal." Hunter engaged the laser designator and in a tight orbit over the man, typed commands into the multifunction panel. Hunter depressed the LD switch and the words

Lay flat on your belly, face down were spelled out in red letters. The thermal image of the man quickly complied. *That's a good sign.*

He cross-controlled the flight controls to get the aircraft to fall from the sky. Right before touchdown, Hunter centered the rudder pedals and control stick, and flared the little airplane as it touched down on the road 25 feet from the man on his belly. A judicious application of brakes ensured the tail wouldn't lift off of the ground and the propeller wouldn't strike the pavement.

Hunter rushed out of the cockpit as best he could with his balky hip, pulled his revolver, and stepped onto Iranian soil. He'd shoot the man if it was necessary. He frisked the man and when he was sure he didn't have a weapon, Hunter rolled him over and patted the man's chest only to find himself patting a pair of women's boobs. He was surprised. The mission was to extract an Iranian male and now, under the moonlight, he was looking into the face of a beautiful, older, smiling woman. He couldn't make himself handcuff her.

Hunter had a decision to make. Does he take this unknown woman or leave her. A man was the evacuation target, not a woman.

She could tell he was conflicted. She said in the most perfect English, "The Revolutionary Guard commander killed my son, Nassar. My life is worth nothing now. I've the information your government seeks." She tapped a square cloth bag across her shoulder. "We must go, quickly."

He mashed his lips, helped the woman to her feet, and prodded her to an airplane she couldn't see or hear. Hunter nearly threw her into the rear cockpit. He stepped onto the wing, buckled her into the seat, hobbled to the front cockpit, and lowered and locked the canopy as he powered up and sped down the road. He had so many questions that he was afraid he'd fail to adequately scan the area with the FLIR, and was surprised that there were still no vehicles in the area. Hunter cleared the area; it looked as if they'd get away undetected. He pointed the nose toward Iraq and retracted the gun.

Hunter flew a reverse-course over the Soviet-made anti-aircraft battery on the Iran-Iraq border. Two hours later, the YO-3A landed at Prince Ali Base. A contingent of CIA operations officers were stunned when a woman stepped from the aircraft instead of the man they'd been sent to recover. Hunter helped the woman from the spyplane. There was a meeting on the tarmac of the CIA's Baghdad Chief of Station, the woman, Hunter and McGee. The woman's English continued to surprise him; she didn't display any emotion as she articulated how her son had come to be killed by the Iranian Revolutionary Guard. She lifted the intricately embroidered bag to emphasize that whatever her son had been killed for, she had brought with her. She didn't transfer ownership of her handbag to the CIA man; she just stood there and looked into the eyes of each of the men.

The Chief of Station explained that the original target, Karzan Peyghambarian, had been a top nuclear weapons scientist doing research for years under the rubric of the Atomic Energy Organization of Iran. His mother, Raha Peyghambarian, was even more valuable than her son. She was the highest placed American agent in the Iranian Intelligence service.

With a strong commanding voice she said, "I respectfully request asylum in the United States of America,"

The CIA's Chief of Station said, "We never thought we'd be able to get you out. I'm here to grant you asylum and safe passage to America."

Once the formalities were completed, Raha Peyghambarian said she had wanted her son to escape and she was going to drive him to his rendezvous point, but when he had been caught downloading files, the Iranian Revolutionary Guard commander killed him. She tugged her bag and said, "Karzan told me what he needed to do to leave Iran. The signals. He'd trade freedom for the archives of Iran's nuclear weapons programs."

Standing on the tarmac, under the shadow of the cargo airplane's wing, she explained what she thought had happened. The Chief of Station didn't want her debriefing anyone but she was excited and fearless. Raha said, "He wasn't a trained spy and I'm afraid Karzan had gotten careless. He had been in a hurry and had copied the latest files on the latest advances. I believe his cover had been blown when he unwittingly triggered computer safeguards. I believe he recognized the people around him were acting differently. When Karzan realized his actions were being monitored, that he had been exposed, he left his office. I don't know how he smuggled the USB memory sticks out of his office but they were in a small cigar box under the seat of my auto. Karzan called me and told me to run. I knew they'd come for me, that I'd be next to be executed. They have special *procedures* for traitors."

Hunter inhaled deeply and said, "So you took his place."

She nodded and smiled meekly. She began to tremble from her emotions. The Chief of Station said, "We need to leave."

The Peyghambarian woman hugged Duncan Hunter as her savior and cried in his arms. When she was through, Hunter unwrapped his arms as she wiped her cheeks with the edge of her handbag. The four said their goodbyes as the Chief of Station turned and led the woman onto a white business jet, chatting with her all the way to the aircraft's stairs. Hunter and McGee watched her go.

When the spook and defector reached the aircraft, she opened the bag from her shoulder, withdrew a small flat box, and handed it to the CIA officer. As soon as the aircraft's door was closed, the Learjet began to taxi.

Hunter hadn't spoken to the woman during the whole flight and didn't know exactly why. Then he remembered—he hadn't given her a helmet or a headset or a pair of earplugs. It was a form of punishment for changing the rules on him without consulting him. But she couldn't have consulted with him beforehand. She was at the appointed place and time, and provided the requisite secret hand-and-arm signals to indicate, "I'm the one to be picked up." It was unusual for Hunter to be so thoughtless, and when he realized he had basically molested her to ensure she wasn't carrying a weapon, he felt like shit.

He had been so concerned for his own safety that he hadn't taken time to discuss why the defector was a woman and not a man. *But she said her son had been killed.* There had been great potential for the person Hunter had commanded to lay on the ground to commit some level of treachery, like roll-over onto her back and blow up her rescuer with a suicide vest, but when Duncan determined the defector was a woman, he had ignored the safety protocols meant to protect him and had expedited their departure from Iran.

It was something he had never considered, that a treasonous son would confide in his mother of his treachery. He was embarrassed that he hadn't taken better care of the woman and vowed not to let something like that happen again.

Over the years, he had extracted several defectors from Islamic lands, but never a woman. Islamic terrorism was the sole purview of Muslim men. Muslim women were different, they were never brought into the leadership fold, and they weren't to be touched by a male not of their family. With a male defector, usually some nuclear or chemical scientist, Hunter had manhandled them to get them into and out of his airplane. He always handcuffed them. But with the woman, he sighed at his failure to treat her with respect and ignored the successful extraction. Then he thought *Maybe I did treat her with respect. I didn't handcuff her.* He knew the truth. He was so shocked that he was frisking a woman that he hadn't even considered handcuffing her.

He'd likely never see the Peyghambarian woman again. That was the nature of the business of managing and debriefing defectors.

By the time the CIA jet had taken the runway, the *Wraith* had been disassembled by Hunter's two mechanics, Bob Jones and Bob Smith. It had been rolled back into its container aboard the Air Force C-130. The

Hercules' aircrew closed the cargo ramp and door, started the four turboprops, and were soon barreling down the runway.

On a return heading to Djibouti, the two Bobs, Bill McGee and Duncan Hunter snored atop sleeping bags laid across the Herc's troop seats.

●　　●　　●　　●　　●

The sticky note on the office door indicated the building manager had "mail," a small shipping container. Demetrius Eastwood had only received mail at the office once before, when his benefactor told him to expect a box. At that time, Duncan Hunter's text message didn't provide any clues as to what might be in the "box." But when it arrived, there were multiple shipping, FRAGILE, and FedEx labels on a shipping crate designed to ship precision or delicate instruments. Eastwood had borrowed a hand truck to move the grey square box to his office. It barely fit through the office door. When he unlatched the fasteners, Eastwood was completely taken aback. He had never seen a 1927 Woodstock typewriter before. He had only heard of them tangentially, in conversation with collectors of antique and rare typewriters. The Woodstock was in pristine condition, professionally restored. It came in a black metal traveling case, also restored to like-new condition.

Now there was another box waiting to be retrieved from the building's management office. It had to be from Hunter. He was the only person who knew Eastwood was living in the building.

The box was identical to the previous grey shipping container and required a hand truck to handle the bulky fiberglass box, just like the last time. Like an excited child at Christmas, Eastwood unlatched the lid and unwrapped protective plastic that enveloped the inner box. Another typewriter, obviously. Opening the travel case provided a wonderful surprise. Like before.

A sheet of paper was perfectly aligned between the paper table and platen. It was a proposal for another article. Hunter had typed, "I cannot research this, but this story needs to be told. I'm not looking for credit. Is this something you'd be willing to research and put your name to? The topic and this professionally restored 1934 Royal Standard Desktop typewriter is another shameless incentive to engage your services, good sir. Semper Fi."

Dory Eastwood, retired Marine Corps officer and combat correspondent, smiled when he read the paragraphs. Admiring the ancient typewriter and the cleverness of his benefactor, he said, "This will also be my pleasure, good sir."

Eastwood reread the proposal: In an effort to discredit and attack the POTUS, the media and the DNC have recently reported that the POTUS may have had the CIA assassinate a terrorist who killed his sister. Someone, likely in the DNC's opposition research department, determined that President Hernandez's sister had been a flight attendant on the jet that inexplicably exploded over Long Island in the late 1990s. While the official cause of that aircraft accident was "bad wiring," Congress knew the truth and began having hearings on the proliferation of shoulder-launched, anti-aircraft missiles and strategies to protect American air carriers. They wanted to ensure that there would never be another American commercial airliner shot down by a missile. The DOD looked to install anti-aircraft missile countermeasures on commercial aircraft. FedEx offered some of their cargo jets to be used as test beds. Somehow, the DNC (probably from democrat congressional leaders who had been in the hearings and/or the media), learned of the top secret truth. This sensitive information went against public policy and had never before been acknowledged, released or leaked—the U.S. paid an annual tribute to an unknown terrorist as insurance to prevent other commercial airliners from being attacked with anti-aircraft missiles.

The nature of the tribute had never been disclosed, but now the media suggests it involved the transfer of hundreds of millions of dollars in untraceable gold coins every year. The DNC and the media complex are accusing POTUS that, immediately after being sworn in, Hernandez tasked the CIA with finding the terrorist who shot down the TWA jet that killed his sister and dispatch him with extreme prejudice.

The article I envision would ask, "So what if the president tasked the CIA to find the person who shot down American airliners and held America hostage—the Democrats have a presidential candidate who's an unindicted criminal guilty of hundreds of counts of espionage. She's the modern day Alger Hiss on steroids, spying for the Russians. The FBI Director reluctantly but meticulously laid out the case against Eleanor Tussy but he wouldn't refer her for indictment." Thanks for looking, Dory. DH

Eastwood rolled his eyes into the back of his head. He had heard the latest media charge against President Hernandez, but it had been drowned out by their latest attempt to throw a scurrilous charge against the wall to see if something would stick. The media hated the president, and they made up the most incredible stories to demean him and injure him in the eyes of the voting public. Eastwood pulled out his smartphone and texted Hunter, "Thank you for the typewriter" and that he was, "On the case."

He turned to his computer and opened his email account. At the head of hundreds of unopened emails was something from the *Associated Press*. He had submitted an article for consideration. Attached was a rejection letter. Eastwood frowned as he reread his proposed article.

Morton Sobell spied for Stalinist Russia. An American engineer, he worked on military and government contracts and was subsequently found guilty of spying for the Soviets as a part of a technology smuggling ring that included Ethel and Julius Rosenberg. The ring provided top-secret information about radar, sonar, and jet propulsion engines as well as transmitting valuable nuclear weapon designs to the Soviet Union. Sobell maintained his innocence throughout the trial and was convicted of espionage in 1951, sentenced to 30 years, and was released after spending almost eighteen years in prison. Years after his release, Sobell reflected of his belief in Communism. Referring to himself as a "bona fide convicted spy" in a letter to the editor of *The Nation*, he wrote, "Now I know it was an illusion. I was taken in."

Alger Hiss was a democrat lawyer and senior State Department official with access to some of America's most sensitive secrets and the most powerful leaders of World War II. There are photographs of Hiss standing behind the wartime leaders of Joseph Stalin, Winston Churchill, and Franklin D. Roosevelt. Hiss was accused of being a Soviet spy and convicted of perjury in connection with this charge in 1950. Whittaker Chambers, a former U.S. Communist Party member, testified that Hiss was secretly a Communist and passed top secret documents to him. Hiss denied ever meeting Chambers and maintained his innocence until his death. Whittaker Chambers produced evidence of Alger Hiss' treachery with copies of the top secret State Department documents that were recovered from a hollowed out pumpkin which have become known as the Pumpkin Papers. Every Halloween, a group of patriots gather in Washington, D.C., to celebrate Chamber's defection from the Communist Party and his victory over the communist Alger Hiss, in a ritual spanning over forty years called the Pumpkin Papers Irregulars Dinner.

Former Attorney General, Eleanor Tussy, is the latest closet communist to be caught using her executive position to engage in rampant espionage and collusion with the Russians in a "pay to play scheme." Leveraging her position as the nation's top law enforcement officer, she circumvented the government's secret communications systems with a "homebrew" server and allowed American technology to be transferred to the former Soviet Union. The FBI Director had laid out a clear-cut case against the Democrat candidate for president, but in an unprecedented action, he refused to refer Eleanor Tussy to the grand jury. She maintains that she's innocent and justice is being subverted to serve political goals.

These three treasonous actors sowed bitterness and division by promoting a dubious story that depicted the U.S. government as a paranoid institution that mistook progressives for traitors when in reality, the U.S. government made the opposite mistake, confusing red-diaper babies, closet Communist Party members, and others devoted to the cult of Lenin and Stalin for patriots.

While the useful idiots Sobell, Hiss, and Tussy betrayed their country, the U.S. government erred in not adequately detecting and preventing them from abusing their positions to access and steal America's secrets and give them to a foreign power.

Eastwood didn't want to waste any time with rejections. He turned away from his computer, got up and placed the ancient typewriter along a long worktable beside Hunter's earlier bribe, the 1927 Woodstock typewriter.

He placed a hand on the old Woodstock and was hit by the unexpected success of Hunter's base article, *Was it Espionage?* Eastwood felt a little guilty that several papers around the country reprinted the article under his name. It was the deal he and Hunter worked out; Duncan didn't want to leave any fingerprints, any indication that he had been the author, and Eastwood was a little naïve, never imagining that the hard-hitting article would turn him into a journalistic rock star.

The theme of Hunter's article was simple. He asked if the former attorney general had been using the protection of her office to effectively conduct espionage. Before submitting Hunter's article for publishing, Eastwood researched the genesis of the article and was blown away by what he had found. He patted the typewriter gently and thought, *Hunter's article mentioned this specific 1927 Woodstock typewriter in the context of a famous Soviet spy who was exposed conducting espionage in the 1930s and 40s. And now the Democrat candidate for president is also conducting a similar level of espionage for the Russians? Using her government-issued BlackBerry? This can't be happening in America.*

7

July 18
Washington, D.C.

With every passing fast-moving waiter, table candles flickered to near extinction in the dark and moody restaurant of the National Democratic Club. Light from barely illuminated chandeliers created the desired ambience but wasn't bright enough for scrutinizing the patrons or the food spread out across the thick elegant linen tablecloths. The steaks, seafood, and desserts were as good as anything the Capital Grille could produce without raising an expense account challenge by the corporate finance officer. Patrons didn't usually come to the National Democratic Club for the food but to be seen or discuss the calculus of power, either attaining power, using power, or keeping power. The National Democratic Club was the perfect place to get away after a grueling week at the Democratic National Committee (DNC) offices. The alcohol flowed liberally, the food was non-GMO and family farm raised, and the labor was union. The prices reflected all of these facts.

Tonight was a special evening; the President of the United States was, officially, "under investigation." The Federal Bureau of Investigation was investigating potential high crimes and misdemeanors of America's chief executive. The DNC Chairman was in a celebratory mood; a president under investigation in an election year was as good as a win for his candidate, and he was off in a banquent room meeting with the latest class of candidates for Congress.

The DNC Chairman's voice intermittently penetrated the ballroom doors. "The Hernandez administration is dangerous to the world! When he challenged the Democrat Party, he became the criminal we call him today! I give President Hernandez credit for motivating his supporters brilliantly but he has also created a greater number of core opponents. That is why I expect you to win, the Democrat Party will win by a landslide! I regard his time in office as an aberration, a temporary phenomenon that will disappear with the election of Eleanor Tussy!" Inside the Red Room, the crowd roared.

Any ambience the restaurant usually enjoyed had been destroyed by the riotous and bositrous laughter coming from the Red Room. The

Red Room had been painted in the color of revolution, of blood, and named as a tribute for the sacrifice of radicals and revolutionaries across the globe who marched under red banners and flags of the Communist Party.

The National Democratic Club wasn't a platinum five-star dinner resturant where century-old artwork adorned the walls but it was a nice little place where ornate frames with large portraits of famous Democrats covered every wall. Black and white photographs of historical events, Democrats shaking hands or posing with domestic and international politicians adorned every vertical surface, even on the walls in the toilet and over the urinals. In the Red Room, there were photographs of radicals and communists, Fidel Castro, Che Guevara, Mao, and Joseph Stalin shaking hands with prominent Democrats.

The dining room was always filled with congressmen and senators, lobbyists and billionaires, ambassadors and diplomats, music and movie stars, Hollywood moguls and leading ladies, Grammy and Oscar recipients, and other icons from the business and entertainment worlds, people who donated vast sums of money to support the cause. And nearly everyone who was someone in the Democratic Party had their favorite wine or champange locked away in one of the massive wine racks which dominated the entryway. You could walk past the wine rack and view the brass badges to see what special or rare *vino* had been set aside by sitting senators or congressmen or lobbyists. The wine rack was enormous; it could hold a dozen bottles for 150 democrats.

To exit the building you had to pass by the walk-in humidor where the finest embargoed cigars from Cuba were protected by lock and key. The humidor was the odd attraction in the building. Its glass walls with a hundred private and locked cubbies held countless rare and unique cigar boxes. The glass-lined humidor fascinated newcomers as did the dedicated smoking room off of the dining room.

Tommy Larrabee II pushed an empty plate to the center of the table and tackled the house special dessert. He nibbled the slab of key lime pie a bite at a time like he was a distracted or disinterested diner. As he checked his watch, a Tag Heuer Grand Carrera he couldn't afford but was a gift from his parents for graduating law school, he surreptitiously looked to see if any of the doors to the Red Room would burst open. Tommy gave the unruly crowd in the Red Room a few thoughts before deciding he wasn't interested in their celebrations. He no longer cared about such things. He was done with them.

He tossed his napkin near the smartphone on the table as a shield for what he was about to do. Tommy swiped the screen twice to bring it to life, tapped a couple of icons, and when he arrived at the special application screen, he breathed deeply. One tap of the app would have activated the security software on his office computer. Adrenaline took over his heart. His finger hovered over the icon for a few seconds and then he touched the capacitive touchscreen. Tommy looked up and smiled to himself.

He returned the smartphone to an inside suit pocket and celebrated, *It's done. No backing out now!* Tommy looked around at the dinner crowd, everyone seemed to be having a great time. He would too as soon as he calmed himself. Another check of his watch and he determined it was almost time to leave if he was to meet the old war correspondent at the appointed place and time. His heart pounded in his chest; his feet felt like they were in freshly poured concrete. He was anxious to leave, but moving was a struggle. Tommy forcibly calmed himself while thinking, *Let's get this show on the road!*

Larrabee had a few things to give Eastwood, politically explosive things that would most likely completely upset the upcoming presidential election. Larrabee scanned the dining room one last time. No one looked the least bit interested in him.

He had made up his mind that he'd be leaving and wouldn't be coming back. Leaving the Club forever was the least important thing on his mind. He ran his fingers through his thick brown hair and pushed a few wild strands back behind his ears. *Where I'm going I'm not getting a haircut.* He tugged his chin. *No shaving either! I'll hide in Montana or Wyoming or Alaska.*

With a few minutes remaining before his self-imposed deadline expired, Larrabee acknowledged that the high and mighty of the Democratic Party never looked his way. They weren't even curious. It wasn't that he was a nobody in the DNC. He just hadn't achieved sufficent status, that special notoriety one achieves through some meritorious action or effort or knowing a certain major power broker. That's what he needed to be invited to the special dinners and evening parties reserved for the truly famous, the truly rich, the truly gifted politicians. It had taken him years to move from a glorified extra at the rear of a bar scene to "the go-to guy" who found, created, and delivered the dirtiest information in the political world that would, figureatively speaking, kill or knock a competitor out of a race. He thought he had achieved sufficient success to be invited to the mythical place, "Palacio de la Paranza." The Hideaway Palace. But the invitations never came.

Lower-level funtionaries envisioned Palacio de la Paranza as a place only for Washington Democrat elites, a special place to get away and relax, a place where one's fantasies could come true somewhere on a private island in the Caribbean. As grist for the rumor mill, Palacio de la Paranza was envisioned as the merger of the old Studio 54 and the Happy Valley Nudist Colony, all on a sprawling 5,000-acre resort on a discrete Carribean island. Masks were required. Pajamas were optional. Invitations, mandatory.

Larrabee had never seen any Republicans in the National Democratic Club, although he had heard the senior senator from Arizona liked to dine with the head of the DNC when the Maryland Jumbo Lump Crab Cake Sandwich was the Special of the Day. Larrabee made several special trips from the DNC headquarters to the Club on those special lunch Thursdays to see if the rumor was true, but for weeks on end, neither man showed. He knew the head of the DNC personally from his days in law school. There was a time when Larrabee would have asked him if the rumor was true. Now it didn't matter. He'd never see his old professor or the inside of the National Democratic Club again. Or the inside of the DNC. He was going to do everything in his power to blow it up.

He sighed after checking his watch. 8:39 p.m. It still wasn't quite time to leave. Another sixty seconds. He was a little nervous, even though he didn't anticipate any problems getting to his meeting. He had timed the route beforehand. He reflected on where he was and where he was going. He reflected on who he was now; a defector, defecting.

At the DNC, he was just a minnow in an ocean of barracudas and sharks. Tommy Larrabee was no longer fresh out of law school, nor was he just getting started in the Democrat Party, not after six years. He had quickly and quietly become one of the most trusted of trusted agents. He could pick a computer lock, tiptoe through a corporate server, take a peek at the contents, maybe copy some incriminating information, and leave the scene of the crime without leaving any traces. Some of the sharks and barracudas in the National Democratic Club, in their thousand-dollar suits, used and appreciated his opposition research work, even if they didn't realize he was now sharing their air.

He had little choice of his political party affiliation. Tommy Larrabee's father was a rabid Democrat and his only son had grown up to be a good Democrat like his father, like his father's father. Larrabee's dad had managed Tommy's political career to perfection and he had guided his son through the traps and pitfalls of being labeled a Democrat "in name only" while being involved in political, cultural, and educational activities supported by the Communist Party of the USA. After Junior's graduation but before the Bar exam, the elder Larrabee politicked the new DNC Chairman for a position for his son in the Democratic National Committee in Washington D.C. *Junior had a special talent.*

Tommy's mother couldn't believe her son had moved up the organization so quickly, landing a plum job as the Deputy Director of Operations. Unofficially, he was *Director of Opposition Research.* He was responsible for mining the political universe for the most deleterious information which could be used to leverage Democrats' chances and cripple or disqualify Republicans from running for office.

He belonged to the oldest group of computer hackers in America, the Cult of the Dead Cow. The cult took their name from an abandoned Texas slaughterhouse; members worked as a team to develop tools which, over time, allowed them to hack into the government's Microsoft Windows-based computers.

At first, Tommy just wanted to be "part of a community" who took to internet bulletin boards to connect with people. But when he received his first computer, friends encouraged him to visit chat rooms and find interesting bulletin boards. As technology improved more computer hackers traded information into how to break in and enter a company's secret files, and an underground industry soon formed. The demand for secret files drove the beginnings of the dark web.

On his sixteenth birthday, he hacked AMTRAK and Microsoft and an oil giant; he stole a boxfull of secure files and accessed customer accounts, but like most young hackers who poked into places they shouldn't have, he didn't know what to do with the purloined files. The best part of hacking wasn't the breaking and entering of secured files but getting away without getting caught by the authorities.

Framed with his law degree were a Masters in Computer Science and a Masters in Cyber Security. As a hacktivist, he used the illicit tools of the trade to hack into the computers of adversaries, steal passwords and siphon files, infiltrate and kill the computer systems of Republican candidates. Not only did he know his way around the dark side of cyberspace, the dark net, he had become an expert.

He was exceptionally good at his job. Like the best hackers outside of the government, he hadn't been discovered or unmasked. With greater successes at the DNC, he soon had the permissions for unfettered access to the heart and soul of the Democrat Party and the DNC—all of its databases and all of its archives.

Working within the dark net, Tommy Larrabee could hide his identity and avoid the laws, regulations, and government surveillance systems. He employed the most advanced software to cover any trace of his activities. It was the perfect cover to hack, capture, and transfer thousands of files from Republican candidates or the RNC. Once in,

Larrabee could move information to other secure DNC off-site servers or to a thumb drive with a click of a mouse. He had enough dirt on Republicans to bury all of them a mile deep in a mud-filled Grand Canyon. But the nature of being a hacking beast was that he also had dirt on Democrats, the Party, and the DNC, even the DNC Chairman.

When Dr. Zhavrazhinov had asked him to install a powerful private computer and program it to send and receive the private email messages for the incoming Attorney General, Eleanor Tussy, Larrabee had a hundred questions banging around his head, but he eagerly agreed. Not just anyone would have been asked to do the work, which obviously had an ulterior motive. The federal government had several classified communication systems its executives were expected to use. Why would a professional politician want such a private system? The server would be used to bypass the federal systems and store purloined secret files.

Before the private email server was operational, the DNC Chairman instructed Larrabee to ensure that his office was given Administrative rights to the Attorney General's server. Larrabee complied and also established himself as a hidden system administrator. He also set up a program that would automatically send a blind carbon copy (bcc) to an electronic drop box at the DNC for any email received or sent by the Attorney General.

When DNC Chairman, Nikita Zhavrazhinov, had hired Larrabee, he had told him, "Everyone has a history. We need you to find that history—all of it. Dig it up. Good, bad, ugly. On all candidates. Especially the ugly. Then you can disassemble it, categorize it, and extract the political entrails. Then we will leverage that information."

"No one can research and assimilate information like a lawyer. Your additional degrees in computer science and cyber make you uniquely qualified to get inside the bowels of the RNC and Republican candidates' working databases, files, and archives. There's no one like you. The only question is, do you want to do that kind of work? The pay is good, but don't be flashy with it." Zhavrazhinov offered, "Have a big front door and a small back door. Take as much as you can and spend as little as you can."

The DNC Chairman was a tall, handsome, Harvard-trained lawyer with an impeccable pedigree. He wore his thick white hair pulled back and knotted in a short clipped ponytail. His suits were from the House of Lagerfeld; high collared starched shirts and ostentatiously large ties tied in bizarre knots. At night he wore dark sunglasses; during the day he did his best to stay out of the sun which explained his pasty skin. He was a dandy of the first order, he exuded his preference of men over women.

A professor emeritus at Harvard University, Zhavrazhinov specialized in constitutional law. His more liberal students were surprised to see him occassionally at socialist conventions and Communist Party meetings in the New England area. His transition into Marxism was in his blood.

Months before the Russian Empire collapsed, his paternal grandparents, a Russian nobleman of the minor opposition party, and his young beautiful wife had escaped the surprise attacks on the Menchevicks by the murderous and rapacious Bolsheviks. The Zhavrazhinovs fled to the United Kingdom, facilitated by three hundred 10-ruble gold coins. A few gold coins with Czar Nicholas II on the obverse secured immediate passage to the United States aboard an empty freighter returning to America for more war supplies. The couple settled in a Russian émigré community in New York City where Ivan found menial work in a tobacco shop while Nadya worked in one of the mills dominated by hard working Russian women. Information out of the newly formed Soviet Union was scarce. But when the Zhavrazhinovs became part of the émigré community, they weren't surprised to hear that the Bolsheviks, led by Vladimir Lenin, had eradicated the Romanovs and confiscated the wealth of the Russian aristocracy before banishing them to the gulags to work in the gold and silver mines. They had escaped with their lives.

•　　•　　•　　•　　•

Professor Zhavrazhinov hated conversations with intellectuals and female students. He viewed others as inferior and only cared about his own opinion. Most students viewed him as a tyrant while others appreciated the man's genius. Very infrequently, some of the male students would catch his eye, both sexually and intellectually. He had been very impressed with the young Larrabee and would challenge him in class. Tommy could compete with the Democrat Party icon like the tennis novice earning a draw from the tennis pro.

During one lecture, Zhavrazhinov had led Larrabee into one of his favorite arguments, problems with constitutions and how to overcome them. "In Article Two of the United States Constitution, the phrase 'natural born citizen' describes a category of citizenship distinct from that described by the phrase 'U.S. Citizen.' This unique distinction was discussed during the constitutional convention of 1787. While it's true that 'natural born citizen' isn't defined anywhere within the text of the

Constitution, and that the Constitution makes use of the phrase 'citizen' and 'natural born citizen,' Supreme Court decisions have long considered the distinction to be between natural-born and naturalized citizenship."

Without being prodded, Tommy Larrabee responded, "It's a well-known fact that 'native-born' citizens, those born in the United States, qualify as natural born. It's also clear that persons born abroad of alien parents, who later become citizens by naturalization, don't. But the question hasn't been tested or resolved at the U.S. Supreme Court whether a person born abroad of American parents or of one American and one alien parent qualifies as 'natural born.' This was the essential point in a previous election. Not birth certificates. Not birthplaces. Not anything else. How could a child of a foreign national become president? Only through a disinformation campaign led by the media."

Zhavrazhinov applauded Larrabee's analysis and insight, commented how the media managed and controlled the narrative, forcing Republicans to respond to a false narrative while silently demonstrating how the U.S. Constitution could be usurped with a bold candidate who dared to be taken to court and have his *bona fides* questioned. He demanded his law student submit an article for the Law Review. Larrabee eagerly complied. His article argued that the constitutional phrase "natural born citizen" included citizens born outside the United States to parents who are U.S. citizens and disqualified all children of one American and one alien parent under the "natural born" requirement, because they were de facto "dual nationals," citizens of two countries.

This always reminded Larrabee of the failed presidential candidacy of the senior Arizona senator; it always made him smile. *If he hadn't been such a coward, that lawsuit would have been one for the ages!*

8

July 18
Washington, D.C.

Tommy Larrabee took one last look around the club. No one looked back. He wasn't a natty dresser flashing a solid gold Rolex President so why would they? *It's better this way.* Larrabee stood, refreshed his suitcoat, and straightened his trouser creases. He checked his breathing as he glanced at the bartender. He couldn't imagine that there was a bar in Washington D.C. that could be more political.

On his way out of the building, he stopped at the club's private, locked humidor where his father kept a few outlawed Cuban *Havanas* but mostly non-Cubans from the Dominican Republic and Nicaragua. He pulled a handfull of finely aged *Punch Sabrosos* from a numbered box, slipped them into a shirt pocket, and then grabbed an unopened box of rare and expensive *My Father The Judge*. As an aficionado, Tommy knew how special *The Judge* was as it had won the prestigious Cigar of the Year award on two different occasions. He tucked the box under his arm and headed for Seward Square.

As he stepped outside, Tommy held the door open for a pair of women who may have been men or alternative rock stars—he couldn't tell. They scowled at him for his unappreciated display of archaic chivalry, pulled each other close, and hurried inside. Larrabee stopped, pulled a cigar out of his pocket, clipped the end, and lit the thick rough tobacco torpedo. He looked at the building in amusement. *This is what defection looks like.* It would be the last time he'd come to this place. Like he didn't have a care in the world, he turned and sauntered off in the direction of Pennsylvania Avenue.

His rendezvous point was the northbound bus stop on Pennsylvania Avenue, at the northeastern corner of Seward Square. He'd get on the bus and meet the journalist. Another check of his Tag Heuer, 8:45 p.m., indicated he'd likely be a little early with his rendezvous with destiny. Since the buses always ran a little late, he slowed his pace and shoved his hands into his pockets. He played with the six memory sticks in his pocket like they were marbles. They carried the most recent files from the DNC.

Before Larrabee crossed the well-illuminated 2nd Street, he looked up toward Folger Park and noticed naked people meandering around the small area under street lamps. Nude wasn't an appropriate term, "painted" was more apropos. About thirty naked women were painted from head to toe in outlandish colors, various sceneries, mythical creatures, and a Picasso Claymation figure. A few nude men were similarly painted. There were several clowns in face paint and painted-on costumes with the wildly bright and oversized red, white, and blue clown shoes. One man in white clownface was dressed in a red fluffy costume made famous by a television clown. He spewed flames from his mouth, frightening some of the painted ladies. The disturbing face paint and fire breathing would have given children nightmares.

Larrabee winced at the idea of painting one's genitals. *Maybe if I was a liberal....* There was music to which some danced, not the onlookers, just the ladies in their special paint. It was hard not to stop and stare. Most of the painted women, even those lacquered up with the Sistine Chapel intricately detailed across pendulous breasts, were fairly attractive. He knew better than to stop; he had an appointment, and he wanted to be early. He artfully negotiated the perimeter of the park without succumbing to staring like a voyeur. He could have looked at the women all day, but not the men. Some things you just don't want to see, because they couldn't be unseen. The sounds from the sybaritic party behind him and the road noise in front of him were very loud.

Larrabee had practiced what he wanted to say to the old war correspondent. Circumspection was the order of the day for the neophyte spy. He wanted to be able to whisper, to tell the war hero-turned-journalist just how he had lost the faith and could no longer stomach the Democrat Party. He also wanted to tell him that he hadn't only stumbled into the secret archives and operational files of the DNC, but that he had copied them. There was treachery and treason, and he wanted someone to know that the Washington Democrats and the DNC weren't the people Americans think they are.

He stopped and waited for the pedestrian crossing signal to indicate it was safe to cross the last street before Pennsylvania. He rocked on his heels as the numerals counted down the seconds. Larrabee sucked air like a rhino with a full head of steam; his heart pounded. He continued to fumble with the flash drives as if they were lucky rabbit's feet. *If these don't do the job, then I still have my back-up plan...in case something happens to me.* If he failed to sign onto in his computer every day, a subprogram he had built and installed functioned like a "dead man's switch." Once activated, his computer would automatically trigger the release of archival documents to an encrypted mailbox to the international non-profit organization, *Whistleblowers*, that published secret information, news leaks, and classified media from anonymous sources across the globe.

With ten seconds to go, he released his grip on the small storage devices and pulled the crushed wet cigar from his mouth to discard the first hints of ash. He liked the smoke and the leathery taste of the *Sabrosos* on his tongue, and he smiled. He had been waiting for this moment for some time, and it was nearly upon him. The red neon timer on the traffic light pole ticked away…5, 4, 3, 2, 1…. He leaned forward, anticipating the light change, when a lone motorcycle roared in the distance and raced to speed through the intersection. Larrabee spit and replaced the cigar in the corner of his mouth. His heart beat wildly. He wanted to break out into a run, but it wouldn't be prudent to step in front of a speeding motorcyclist. The old black Harley Davidson Panhead rocketed through the intersection; its exhaust deafening.

Tommy Larrabee didn't hear the clown in the fluffy red clown suit approach from behind. He never heard the .38 caliber round that entered the base of his skull. He never felt the impact from falling on his face and his teeth shattering. He didn't know he dropped his box of cigars. He never felt the man with the white clownface jam a hand into his pocket and remove the half-dozen electronic flash drives. He didn't know he had been stripped of his watch. And he never heard the clown scamper away toward the rendezvous point with a box of cigars in one hand and a fistful of memory sticks in the other.

A block away, a Metro bus painted in sweeping patriotic colors as expected in the nation's capital waited at the Seward Square bus stop for several seconds. A lone rider had pulled the cord to request a stop. No one got off and no one got on. The famous war correspondent and combat journalist, Demetrius Eastwood, stood and turned and cautiously scanned the left and right rearmost windows of the empty bus, looking for his contact. A half-a-block away the shadow of a man, possibly a mime or a clown with a white painted face and an odd red clown costume, emerged from under a streetlight. Eastwood squinted to see better in the distance. He confirmed the man was likely a clown. Eastwood bit his lower lip and said to himself, "I think that clown missed his bus…." His eyes didn't leave the man under the streetlamp. He wondered why the clown would just stand where he was, unmoving, staring at the bus without reacting to it. *If he's going to catch this bus, he better get moving! I'll enjoy hollering at the driver to tell him that "Stop! There's a clown trying to catch this bus!"*

Eastwood was confused and returned to his seat. Not making

contact wasn't the end of the world. He'd be able to reschedule. But if the clown had wanted the bus, why doesn't he try to run to catch it before it pulled away from the curb? Even with the poor street lighting, Eastwood shifted in his seat to be able to keep watching the clown. *Was he really carrying a box of cigars?* Eastwood shook his head gently as the clown stood there watching the bus. *What's he waiting for?*

With no potential passengers within eyeshot, the bus driver closed the door. The air brakes released with a hiss. Eastwood turned from the window and stared at the back of the head of the bus driver as the bus accelerated. In his periphery was the diminishing view of Seward Square. In his memory was a clown in his ridiculous uniform, red and rotund, like an apple with a marshmallow on top. He shook his head; whoever heard of or seen a clown carrying a box of cigars?

Since he had missed his contact, Demetrius Eastwood rode into the heart of the District of Columbia. He bid the bus driver a "good night" as he left. The driver thought he had seen the man before, but that's how it is in Washington, you couldn't swing a dead rat without hitting a politician or a Russian spy or someone who was considered momentarily famous. Eastwood reverted to journalist mode as he waited for a taxi to take him to the Washington Convention Center. The president was holding one of his many campaign rallies in the cavernous convention center, and it was packed to the rafters with supporters. Hundreds more lined up outside waiting to get in. He hoped he'd be able to capture the size and spirit of the rally "on the floor" for his network.

President Hernandez had just started his speech as Eastwood arrived at the PRESS ONLY line. Although he was recognized by the security crew, he flashed his press credentials and placed his backpack on the conveyor belt for the X-ray machine. He stepped through a magnetometer and was wanded by two black-uniformed Secret Service guards before being allowed to pass.

Eastwood could feel the crowd roar. They always roared when the president mocked the media or his challenger, and it shook the building to the ceiling. President Hernandez spoke to them as if they were acquaintances in an office, telling some outrageous story that made the men smile and the ladies blush. The crowd was immense. Every seat was taken. Standing room only. It was like that whenever he toured the country.

The man who had been thrust into the spotlight and the White House had greatly refined his speaking abilities. Eastwood stopped trying to improve his position and just listened. He heard the president say, "Two years ago Americans awoke to the news that their president wasn't the man he claimed to be. The political establishment and the media did everything within their power to persuade you that the documents stolen from the CIA and released to the American people were a vast right wing conspiracy, that they were counterfeit documents, and it was all lies. It was a case of Democrats saying: who are you going to believe—we Democrats and our media friends or your lying eyes?"

The crowd first roared their approval and then booed with delight. Eastwood crossed his arms and smiled like a youngster fingering the pages of a Playboy magazine. This was political porn at its finest. And he loved it.

"It took an unknown patriot to release those documents so Americans could see what so many people knew in their hearts and minds, that their president—a Democrat president mind you—was a charlatan, a fake American, and someone who worked on behalf of, at the very least, radical or terrorist organizations. The co-conspirator media never vetted him. There's a reason he ran away. No telling where he's now. And no one cares but the media." Loud continuous boos rained down on the former president's supporters in the network media boxes.

"And Americans knew positively, that in order for a bogus president to be sworn into to the highest office in the land, he had to have had extraordinary help…likely by a group of shady creatures, as Alexander Hamilton would have undoubtedly called them. We can call them Democrats; we can call them the media. I'll call them collectively 'the dark state,' a corrupt and intensely political shadow government dedicated to the overthrow of the government…."

More booing from the throng of Republicans. For some reason unknown to Eastwood, the booing just made him smile even more. When the president took another shot at the media by saying, "…and their corrupt political media," Eastwood howled with laughter and clapped his approval along with the other people. He acknowledged, *The media are corrupt. I work in this industry and it's absolutely corrupt on the other side.*

The president continued, "The unmasking of President Mazibuike proved many things, exposed many things. But know this, there's nothing the political establishment won't do, there's no lie they will not tell to hold on to their power. And it'll all be at your expense. It's us versus them. Since being sworn in as your president, I can tell you we have interrupted their plans. And they don't like it. It's clear to you and me that he and Democratic Party leaders wanted to transform the U.S.

into a Russian-style dictatorship. Single party rule. Implement socialism."

"My fellow Americans, I can say they nearly succeeded. I've begun the process of dismantling the charlatan president's agenda. And I can say without equivocation, that agenda has been stopped in critical key areas, beginning with the appointment of a new CIA Director, an American patriot. Our movement is gaining strength; the truth is getting out there, and Americans are listening. The dark state is a parasite; it's entrenched and is working hard to diminish or negate your vote. So I ask you today, I need your vote so we can stop what the former president set into motion. My opponent, Eleanor Tussy, was his right-hand person. She'll try to continue the legacy of President Mazibuike and resume what the dark state has been working toward. Socialism. Infiltration of the Islamic Underground. It's not my imagination or yours; their goals are real. The Democratic Party's open Marxism and embrace of the Islamic Underground is a national disgrace and a national emergency."

Eastwood and the teeming masses hollered and clapped like teenagers at their first high school football game. He looked around at the many network cameras and reporter's booths. He saw the ravishing lead anchor of Russia Television Network in front of the camera, illuminated by powerful lights, probably giving her analysis of the president's speech. Eastwood thought, *That woman is a goddess, unfortunately, she's also a Communist.* He shook his head in disappointment and returned to the president.

"Americans are waking up to the fact that this president is with *you.* I'm not one of 'them.' You know what the problem is—and you know what's needed to save our country. An outsider! Not another establishment politician. No closet socialist trying to establish a new Socialist Republic in North America. Together we'll reject the corruption of the other party and replace a failed and corrupt political establishment with a new government controlled by you, the American people. The American people...now...know that the Washington establishment, and the financial and media corporations that fund it, exist for only one reason: to protect and enrich themselves. They'll stop at nothing to bleed you dry and turn America into another socialist shithole like Venezuela, Cuba, and Russia!"

At the word "Russia," Eastwood turned and looked for the response of the brightly illuminated and animated RTN anchor—Viviana Vaslakova. With eyes on the Russian's network box, he mumbled to himself, "The only reason to watch RTN is you, Miss Vaslakova." There was a significant age difference between him and the Russian woman, but he didn't care. There were just so few women he knew in journalism circles who excited him enough to turn his head.

As if she had heard him, Viviana Vaslakova looked down and momentarily caught the eye of Demetrius Eastwood. Then, just as quickly, she returned to her teleprompter and her camera. Eastwood thought, *And working for RTN, I'm sure you probably had to register as an agent of a foreign government. That makes you in all probability an intelligence agent in journalist clothes. Another Russian spy. But what a beauty; what a supreme waste.* He spun around, sighed, and headed for an exit. For this evening, the president won the tug of war in Eastwood's head. Eastwood thought, *Wow! He knows how to fire them up. He might not be much of an orator, but his speechwriter knows what to say and which buttons to push.*

•　　•　　•　　•

At precisely 1:10 a.m., electrical power failed in the neighborhood adjacent to Seward Square, sending the rows of Brownstones into an uneasy darkness. The power outage wasn't widespread as adjacent streets remained on the electrical grid. Those streetlamps and houses remained illuminated. The utility company's grid monitors were alerted to the failure, a blown transformer appeared to be the culprit. A manager was tasked to troubleshoot the problem remotely before sending a repair crew to the scene with a replacement transformer. Transformers failed all the time. Replacing them took a few hours.

For those still awake at one o'clock, it was time to either break out the candles or just go to bed. Cloud cover extinguished any illumination from the moon, although the lights of the District of Columbia, blocks away did reflect off the overcast.

A lone man emerged from a dirty unwashed four door car. He had wrapped himself tightly in a dull Burberry trench coat; one hand ensured a dark homburg of the Indiana Jones variety wouldn't fly off of his head, while the other carried an ancient leather Gladstone. He looked up to check his bearings as he approached the row of modestly painted brownstones. If someone were to poke their face out of a window, they would have seen their street in total darkness. They couldn't have seen the worn out college professor trying to find the way to his house by the Braille method.

He stumbled and staggered to the painted white four-story on the end and struggled with the stairs leading to a dingy solid oak door. He stopped on the landing and leaned against the ancient hatch as if he were searching for keys. Latex-gloved hands picked the lock quickly with special tools he had for that purpose.

Once inside, night vision goggles replaced the hat. The search of Tommy Larrabee's studio was completed in minutes. A laptop, an address book, notebooks, and other personal items, seen in shades of green in the NGVs, were stuffed into the portmanteau. A suitcase was open on the bed, half-packed. A shaving kit remained unassembled in the bathroom; something to be added at the very last, perhaps. An open and inviting computer bag. A potential trip interrupted? The computer bag was closed and tossed over a shoulder. NGVs were slipped in the Burberry's pocket.

As easy as it was for the intruder to enter the dead man's home, it was easier exiting the building. He was in the last and most critical phase of the impersonation operation. From under the hat, he scanned the area for any activity or movement. Anyone with a light wasn't his friend. The only noise came from the elevated I-395 highway to the east. The best news was that no one was out walking a dog. No one to confront or stop and chat. With the streetlights out in this section of Washington D.C., it wasn't especially safe to be out and about, unless the dog needing relief was a Doberman.

He strolled purposely away from the building. As he reached the tired unwashed Crown Victoria, he masterfully scanned the area one final time. There was no one in the area, and no one had seen him. He entered the vehicle and drove away without lights until he positively needed them. He fiddled with a BlackBerry smart phone and transmitted an acknowledgement that he was safe and returning to base.

As he cleared the neighborhood, streetlights appeared to chase him out of the area as electrical power was restored.

With indications that electrical power suddenly returned from the spot outage near Seward Park, the utility company's grid monitors and power distribution technicians gathered in the company's operations center. A spontaneous "return to service" condition was unheard of, unique. A blown transformer doesn't magically heal itself and automatically reset manual circuit breakers. Technicians ran diagnostics. Computer monitoring and control systems were troubleshot. After ten tense minutes the duty manager pushed himself away from his workstation and announced in disgust, "I think we were hacked."

•   •   •   •   •

Eastwood took a taxi to Union Station. First class ticket on the Acela to New York City. Unlicensed taxi from Union Station to 7 World Trade Center. No Uber, no Lyft, no licensed taxi. The unlicensed taxis that weren't Indian or Muslim or Chinese spies were mobster-run. They were in the business of taking your money "on the side." They were good for keeping their mouths shut, since they were an illegal operation. There were several added benefits to the mob-run taxis; their cars didn't carry cameras or microphones, and they were driven by Russians, not Muslims or Chinese. Mob drivers received their money from the "fare" before they left the curb. Neither passenger nor driver engaged in small talk.

There were times when he thought all of the counter-surveillance measures he instituted for his personal safety were overkill, until he heard that liberal activists had learned how to identify and surreptitiously follow right-wing journalists and reporters from their office buildings to their homes. Within hours of determining the addresses of the correspondents, the activists would splash the information on several websites dedicated to activism, anarchy, and revolution. Telephone numbers, daily routines, and the schools where the reporters' children attended as well as the schedules of their children's extracurricular activities were available for the Democrat Party and their left-wing followers. Threatening and menacing phone calls followed. Private vehicles would be vandalized. Organized marches and protests seemed to magically appear on the lawns of the conservative network and politically right-leaning television reporters. Police were always slow to respond.

As an accomplished right-wing reporter, Eastwood knew he was a marked man and was forced to live off the normal grid in an office building instead of a hotel or a house in the Hamptons. He told his producer, *They're relentless and aggressive, they should be wearing grey uniforms and red armbands.*

He arrived at his office in 7 World Trade Center before daybreak. He had written his report on the train then transferred it to his office computer so he could fix the obvious problems his laptop's software didn't catch or auto-correct. Eastwood polished his report one final time before sending it to his editor via his encrypted email account.

He still had a few scattered thoughts among the linear ones, wondering if the president could win and if he could overcome the disparity in the polls that showed that the POTUS was being far outclassed by the professional Democrat politician, if the media and the polls were to be believed.

Eastwood also allowed the hard thoughts of what it might mean that his DNC contact hadn't met him at the scheduled rendezvous point. At the top of his list: he had been discovered. He shook the poisonous dreadful thought from his mind. *I missed my contact. We'll try again. I hope he's ok. I hope he's alive!* He sent a quick email to the contact's mother via the encrypted service. *Missed him — need to reschedule.*

He returned to work. An email stood apart from the rest. From his producer he read: "The executive planning board approved your proposal for a TV special. Must be complete before October 1. Can you meet the timetable and deadline?" *Yes*, he responded, pounding out the reply with two fingers. *We can start shooting immediately!*

He thought *Before the election! That's very brave. An October surprise but in this case it'll be the Republicans who'll surprise the Democrats.* Eastwood knew his producer would demand something in return. Quid pro quo. *Ok! I'm on for my special. My trip report is done and on its way — now all I've left is the article.* He pushed around scraps of paper with notes scribbled on them. His way of writing an article for the big newspapers.

He read one note that wasn't important. *She was a former lawyer, a former senator, a former cabinet member, current presidential candidate. Would President Hernandez add to her résumé: losing presidential candidate?*

After a couple of hours, Eastwood tidied up the email submission, ensured there was the obligatory boilerplate fawning submission sentence he used from his Marine Corps days: *I respectfully submit….*

Could he…could President Hernandez stop her? It was a good question, he ascertained. He said to no one in the room, "Not going to happen without a lot of help."

9

October 30
New York City

Halfway up the east face of the 52-story 7 World Trade Center, one corner office space hinted at being illuminated, like grey pixels on the edge of a black monitor. Several stories both above and below the corner office were completely dark, giving the impression that either some idiot had forgotten to turn off a desk lamp before leaving for the evening or contract cleaning crews making their rounds had left a light on. Roving building security checked to see if the solid oak door was locked and passed the stark and austere office space without knowing if anyone was inside. The unmarked space at 2613 was designed to be overlooked or ignored and appeared to be deserted.

The corner office was as spacious as a Texas ranch house and what furnishings there were looked as if a Marine Corps fighter pilot had purchased pieces with a mix of minimalist and bohemian flair. A nine-foot leather sofa, a venerable Leopold office desk from the 1960s, a black judge's chair, a parquet chair mat, and a teak double extendable dining table. An antique green eyeshade lamp from a turn-of-the century bank sat at the corner of the computer desk and a 1957 Herman Miller Eames lounge chair faced an oversized Sony high-definition television monitor. Freestanding partitions prevented anyone in adjacent buildings from seeing who was in the office or what journalistic magic Eastwood performed.

When the sole occupant was at home, what little light there was came from the ancient lamp, a laptop computer, and a desktop monitor that spilled over the partitions. The unremarkable and private office was the primary residence and hideout of the international journalist and war correspondent, Demetrius "Dory" Eastwood.

Eastwood's name was recognized in political circles; his face was recognized in the heartland of America and anywhere among American troops on Middle Eastern battlefields. Eastwood had a strong chiseled face so familiar that sometimes it made his life challenging and finding lodging problematic. He was a perpetual target of the unholy warriors of the radical Islamic jihad. This office space was kept dark purposely to thwart possible snipers from the Islamic Underground. The women in journalism found him interesting but too old for a serious relationship.

Dory Eastwood was tall, broad shouldered, and had a full head of very short, very gray hair. He had a voice that resonated in mess halls. He eschewed hats unless he was among his kind—short-haired helmet-wearing military guys in combat zones. Then he preferred an olive Tilley's *Wanderer* to protect his standard Marine Corps haircut and to keep the tops of his ears from getting sunburned. When he was with the troops, kids far from high school cheerleaders and mom's apple pie, he wore baggy cargo pants which were impervious to pickpockets and a white long sleeve denim shirt. Soft green Merrill boots with the hard Vibram lugs kept him from slipping or falling and becoming a causality of a broken hip. Supremely fit for a man of 75, there wasn't a lazy bone in his body. His doctor told him to slow down because if he broke something, especially out in the field, "there are no spare parts for you, and when we patch you up, you're not going to heal as fast as you used to."

The former infantry officer had unwittingly become a household name while working on behalf of a Republican president; he had been accused of being the point man in a scheme of trading weapons for hostages. A picture of him in his dress uniform—complete with medals and badges—had been splashed over every major newspaper and magazine cover of the leftist media hostile to the president.

After being forced to retire from his beloved Marine Corps, he found a new life as an embedded correspondent in war zones, reporting from the front lines of a battlefield. He ate, slept, and worked alongside Marines, soldiers, airmen, sailors, and Navy SEALs—young and old—in the crappiest of shitholes from Afghanistan to Zimbabwe. Places where names looked as if letters had been randomly picked from a Scrabble box. Where tropical parasites and diseases didn't have names and remedies relied on experimental drugs. Depending on altitude, the air was either clean or fecalized from burning dung for cooking meals or for providing heat. From the mountains, one could see the layer of dirty air below and the crystal clear skies above.

Energy and excitement oozed from his pores when he was among "his guys." Through it all, he reported the news factually, the good and the bad, without the liberal spin from most of the "embeds," and garnered the respect of men and women in uniform everywhere. Not surprisingly, liberal journalists and Democrat Party politicians hated him. He called men, men and women, women—not one of the fifty-eight dubious genders listed like a Chinese menu on some social media websites.

The retired Marine Corps lieutenant colonel had found it uncommonly difficult to find a conventional and safe location in which to sleep and work. There were lease agreements, building directories, and electrical and wireless bills to pay — all clues to his whereabouts for a private detective to discover. Having another company lease the office space and pay the bills helped Eastwood live safely in New York City, "in the city that never sweeps," as his benefactor would say, a debasement of the city's unofficial slogan, "The City that Never Sleeps." After interviewing Duncan Hunter he had accepted his Marine Corps buddy's offer to use his New York City office. The space was huge for a private office — 4,000 square feet. Hunter was responsible for all of the furnishings and had installed a fully functional kitchen, private bathrooms, and a shower that could hose down a Clydesdale.

While the suite gave Eastwood much needed journalistic cover, he had developed a routine to get into and out of the office unnoticed. On odd numbered days, he'd get off the elevator at the 24th or the 28th floor and walk up or down to the 26th. Even numbered days, three floors below or three floors above. For several years, the building with the famous name had been a very safe location for him when he needed a place to bed down in the center of the city.

The original 7 World Trade Center structure was completed in 1987 and destroyed in the September 11 attacks. When it was rebuilt five years later it was five stories taller and maintained its distinguished name and address. When the new building opened for business, new and established companies jockeyed for the best locations and filled the floors. They took great pleasure in posting expensive signage to announce their new spaces.

A few individual offices on the higher floors were built-out for smaller, discrete companies. These were intentionally bland, and it was rarely advertised who was on the other side of the door. If an inquisitive detective attempted to determine the identity of one of these tenants, they'd find the largely abandoned office at 2613 was leased to QAS, Quiet Aero Systems, an obscure aviation company in Texas. For a single $50 gold eagle, the building manager assured the man who leased the property that the main directory on the first floor never listed the occupants at 2613.

Osama bin Laden had been the first to slap a *fatwa* on Eastwood. He learned to avoid hotels and restaurants and other situations with natural choke points where a pissed off *jihadi* could wait to ambush and kill him, just as Sirhan Sirhan ambushed and killed Bobby Kennedy in a cramped and packed kitchen. No one saw the kitchen for what it was until it was too late. To stay ahead of the assassin's bullet you had to look at every situation from a different angle, in a different light—*if I go there, how will I succeed, how will I die? What are the lines of sight for weapons to be fired? Which avenue of approach is best?* When there are too many distractions and too many people, there are also too many different ways and opportunities to be killed.

Eastwood had learned his contact, Tommy Larrabee, had found a way to die that was all too pedestrian for Washington D.C. The day after the blown rendezvous, Larrabee's mother contacted him through her secure email system. Up until that day, her emails had been terse but friendly but nothing like the chilling *Tommy's dead* in the subject line. It was all that she could write that day. Dory Eastwood hung his head in sorrow. He and Mrs. Larrabee agreed to meet in Iowa. When they did, two months after Tommy's funeral, she handed Eastwood a cigar box full of USB memory sticks. They were the records and archives of the Democratic National Committee. Maude Larrabee knew why her son had been killed, but the Washington D.C. police didn't and didn't seem to be interested. It was as if the police knew who killed Tommy, but didn't dare investigate.

Because of the success of his interrogatively-titled article and television special, *Was it Espionage?*, an exposé on Eleanor Tussy's actions as attorney general under President Mazibuike, Eastwood had been invited to network parties in Washington D.C. and New York City to celebrate the TV special's stratospheric ratings. But since the Larrabee murder, Eastwood wasn't in the mood for large parties. He remembered how JFK's brother had died. Being caught out in the open or in a hotel lobby always scared the crap out of him, and he politely demurred for safety reasons. The network celebrated the success of Eastwood's work *in absentia*.

When he was ensconced in the office for days, focused and working on an article or storyboarding one of his television specials, Eastwood wouldn't shave or comb his hair. His clothes looked like those of a homeless man who had been forced to sleep in the back of a hotel between dumpsters. Eastwood ran his hand through the stubble on his head and pushed away from the marble-topped desk. He scratched a two-day old beard, stretched and ignoring the threats on his life, sauntered to one of the floor-to-ceiling windows. He looked down at the masses below who were standing, walking, and driving in the light drizzle, not going anywhere fast, but getting wetter by the second.

Eastwood didn't dally but returned to his desk and focused on the large monitor in front of him. He nodded absentmindedly, proud of his work on the topic that would surely not get approved. It would be *spiked*.

Knowing he had other things more pressing to do, he shouldn't have wasted the time on an article that would be killed by a senior editor who had issues with him or his apparent politics. But when a topic entered his consciousness, the only way Eastwood knew to kill those thoughts was to put them on paper. Some of his musings would be sent to newspapers for consideration, some to weblogs, usually conservative blogs. Some went straight to the trash. Computer lingo: Deleted.

Dory Eastwood returned to the window, jammed hands in his pockets, and yawned. It was late. He needed to get some sleep. He had an early train in the morning. Washington, D.C. He'd be running the gauntlet again. From the basement of 7 World Trade Center, he'd take the subway to Grand Central Station. First Class on the *Acela*. Eastwood would dare the *jihadis* to find him, box him in, and slip a shiv between his ribs. That's why he also wore body armor. Always. When he was in "the house" he'd drape his bulky body armor over the back of his office chair.

He slipped into the leather high-back armchair and reread his 500-word article. No new edits. Eastwood lifted his eyes to the square cigar box sitting on the desk. He shook his head as he reached for the box. *My Father The Judge* was spelled out in gold lettering on the top. He slid the lid toward him revealing twenty aluminum cigar tubes with computer flash drives inside. He knew the answer to his question in his article. He closed the box and the file and transmitted the article directly to the office of the editor of the most virulently anti-Republican newspaper, the *Washington Post*, daring them to publish it.

Submission for the Editorial Page
By: Demetrius Eastwood
Title: Was the DNC Responsible for Tommy Larrabee's Death?
The most insidious power of the media is their power to ignore. While the July 2016 murder of a Democratic National Committee staff member near Seward Square continues to capture the conservative media's interest, the mainstream liberal media refuses to make even the most rudimentary of inquiries. Last summer, Tommy Larrabee, a 33-year-old DNC staff member, was fatally shot in the back of the head. Local news outlets reported he was the victim of a botched robbery. Washington Metropolitan Police reported that there was no evidence of

a struggle between Larrabee and his killer. There were no witnesses. The cameras hidden in the traffic signal near where the body was found had strangely failed to record anything at the intersection. The police claimed that all of Larrabee's personal effects—his wallet, cellphone, keys, and a handful of cigars—were still on his person when his body was found. The police report was silent on the whereabouts of Tommy Larrabee's watch. A retired police chief suggested that in his forty years in law enforcement, the Larrabee case could be that rare and unique botched robbery. Maybe the murderer was only after Larrabee's expensive watch. Maybe the murderer was forced to leave when someone approached. We'll likely never know.

Tommy Larrabee's last living hours were well known. He had walked from his DNC office and dined at the National Democratic Club. He had crab cakes and fries with key lime pie for desert. He selected a box of cigars from the family's humidor. Minutes later, he walked past a group of artists and entertainers at Folger Park. He was found a few blocks away, on his face. The front of his face had been blown away from a heavy-caliber gunshot to the base of his brain. No one saw a thing. No one heard a thing. Metro Police said it was the first killing of the year in that particular neighborhood. They also indicated that there had been two armed robberies in the same neighborhood within weeks of Larrabee's killing. Watches, smartphones, and wallets were lifted. No violence, no murders. According to the Metro Police, Tommy was the exception. The Larrabee family inquired about the watch they gave their law school graduate. Even after a thorough search of his Brownstone apartment, Tommy's watch has never been found.

In a statement from the DNC chair, Dr. Nikita Zhavrazhinov, called Larrabee, "...one of the brightest and most dedicated public servants the Democrat Party had in their employ. He saw the great potential of our nation and believed that together we could make the world a better place. Tommy Larrabee was the DNC's deputy director of operations. He investigated advanced analytical methods to help DNC leaders and candidates make better decisions."

There has been a profound lack of interest in the murder of Tommy Larrabee. A gun crime had been committed "against one of their own" and the usually vociferous gun control lobby within the Democrat Party couldn't find a single politician to utter a single line of phony sanctimonious outrage. Washington Metro Police say they're working on the case, but it's not active. The media have gone "radio silent" on the topic of his death. The DNC has been unusually quiet; they didn't organize a memorial, nor did the DNC send flowers to the grieving family. No one at the DNC thought to offer a reward for information that would lead to the arrest of the killer of their staff member.

Whistleblowers, the international non-profit organization that publishes secret information, news leaks, and classified media provided by anonymous sources, received tens of thousands of emails it said came from the DNC immediately after Tommy's body was found. The juxtaposition of Larrabee's death with the release of sensitive Democrat Party information has led some right-wing media personalities and outlets to tout the theory that Larrabee had been in contact with *Whistleblowers* before he was killed and that he was murdered as part of a cover-up. If Larrabee was suspected of releasing information detrimental to the candidacy of Eleanor Tussy, then one could understand why the DNC wouldn't have offered a reward for information on his murder. The absence of an expected action may reveal much, in the same way that the media chooses to investigate and report on topics which are beneficial to them.

Whistleblowers' founder, editor-in-chief, and director, Henrik Milner offered a reward for information leading to the arrest of Larrabee's murderer. Milner suggested that the DNC is a significant, powerful, and malignant influence, and that they leveraged their influence on the Metropolitan Police Department to ultimately kill the investigation on Larrabee's death. The police department has strongly denied the allegation. The FBI has stated they wouldn't investigate, citing Larrabee's death as a local matter for the Washington Metropolitan Police.

There are several curious connections regarding Larrabee's murder, beginning with the camera-shy DNC Chairman, Dr. Nikita Zhavrazhinov. When the lanky, urbane Dr. Zhavrazhinov was a professor at Harvard Law School, Tommy Larrabee was one of his students. He was very impressed with the young Democrat and encouraged Larrabee into opposition research.

As a graduate research project, Larrabee was awarded an independent study course at the National Archives. With Dr. Zhavrazhinov as his mentor, Larrabee researched an obscure topic: Presidential Eligibility, and his research paper was entitled *The Natural-Born Citizen Clause: A Case for the U.S. Supreme Court to Resolve Two Hundred Years of Political Ambiguity*. Larrabee's paper was the very topic which should have been explored and debated when Democratic candidate Maxim Mohammad Mazibuike began to run for President of the United States. The media stifled and killed any discussion on President Mazibuike's dual nationality and obvious ineligibility to be America's president.

Since the death of Tommy Larrabee, Harvard Law School has removed any trace of his article from their archives.

Those who live in the Washington D.C. area learned today that an FBI informant was scheduled to testify before Congress. The informant had been under the protection of a round-the-clock personal security detail. Today, he was found dead in his hotel room.

Individually, the deaths of Tommy Larrabee and the FBI informant would garner little more than a yawn in the pages of the *Washington Post* or the *New York Times*. It's too early to speculate on the death of the FBI informant. Has enough time passed for journalists to investigate why a DNC staff member would be murdered? Normally the handgun murder of a Democrat would have created a howling cry from the Left, but they've been curiously quiet. The DNC didn't offer a dollar in reward for information leading to the arrest of Larrabee's murder. Did the DNC kill Tommy Larrabee, or was it a random murder? I'll never believe it was random.

●　　●　　●　　●　　●

With the editorial dispatched to Washington, D.C., Eastwood had one final task to perform before calling it a night. A larger article, one that was a continuation of another on the obvious espionage of one Eleanor Tussy, the former attorney general and the Democrat Party's nominee for President of the United States. A few clicks of the mouse, and the complete 1,200 word article was plastered on the dual monitors at 150% resolution. He leaned onto the desk top, arms crossed, and reread the article one final time. Aloud.

Eastwood was happy with it; he saved and closed the file. He then opened his encrypted email service and composed a message. It went to the editor of an on-line daily internet publication. With a few more clicks of the computer mouse, he attached the article he had just proofread, sent the message, and closed down the computer.

Then Eastwood closed himself down. He staggered over to and curled up on the couch. He had a long day ahead of him tomorrow in the nation's capital.

●　　●　　●　　●　　●

The alarm in his smartphone went off. He got up, turned the computer on, and selected the website from his list of favorites. The speakers blared out a recognizable riff of music from Carlos Santana's *Black Magic Woman* as the introduction to a Washington D.C. radio show. Eastwood pushed away from the computer table and padded barefoot to the shower.

Mornings on the Mall was the early morning show that featured a pair of men reporting on the weather, traffic, and the latest political tomfoolery from the political parties. The main topic was the latest talking points from the Democrat Party that had been trotted out the previous evening. They played the soundbite: *If by some miracle the president wins the election, he'll be impeached when the Democrats regain the House and Senate. They say it's beyond dispute that President Hernandez has committed a smorgasbord of high crimes and misdemeanors; their issue is that the Republicans in the House of Representatives have ignored his crimes and have not held him accountable. When Democrats regain the House, they'll immediately rectify the Congressional malfeasance of the House Republicans.*

One radio personality asked his partner, "What has the president allegedly done this time?"

"Well, there's this little issue of the Democrat Party nominee, Eleanor Tussy, violating the Espionage Act of 1917 while she was the Attorney General. After seeing Colonel Eastwood's television special, it's pretty obvious she was engaged in espionage, but because of who she is, the Democrats don't want to see her indicted. You know, it might look bad if your absolute best candidate for president is being investigated by the FBI and should be in jail, not on the campaign trail, and definitely not in office."

"Colonel Eastwood's special is going to leave a mark. And speaking of marks, we have breaking news from London. Karl Marx's grave has been vandalized twice in the past month. The words the 'doctrine of hate,' 'terror and oppression,' and 'architect of genocide' were painted in red on the Highgate Cemetery memorial. On the steps of the Capitol, a spokesman from the Communist Party of the USA stated, 'Daubing paint on the grave of someone who exposed how capitalists control and exploit the majority won't prevent his vision of a better leaderless cooperative moneyless world becoming reality.' You know, I think the snowflakes are quite mad."

"Is that another *double entendre*? I think you are quite right. These people aren't *Dolittle Raiders*; if they got a splinter in their foot, they'd be laid up for months."

"In other words, it's just another glorious day in our nation's capital. I can see by the clock that it's time for a traffic update with our own Abby Gore—take it away Abigail!"

10

October 31
Washington, D.C.

The website, *The American Thinker*, headlined Demetrius Eastwood's latest thought piece on the possible crimes committed by the former attorney general and current Democrat Party's nominee for president.

Title: The Espionage Act of 1917, a follow-up

Last month my television special, *Was it Espionage?* focused on the bizarre email practices of the Democrat Party's nominee for president, Eleanor Tussy. The former attorney general insisted that she "had broken no rules" in conducting government business through the use of a private email server in lieu of the U.S. government's unclassified and classified systems. The U.S. government uses a system of interconnected computer networks to transmit classified information. There are also other closed encrypted systems used to communicate within the intelligence community.

The U.S. government spent billions of dollars developing, deploying, and protecting its networks in order to enable authorized officials to conduct the business of government.

The Democratic presidential candidate, Eleanor Tussy, once under investigation by the FBI, had disclosed that her aides had deleted more than 25,000 documents and emails that she deemed personal. These 25,000 documents and emails, if printed out, represent a stack of 50 reams of paper, a stack over eight feet tall. When the FBI retrieved the spools of Whittaker Chambers' microfilm, the Alger Hiss "Pumpkin Papers" printed out to a mere stack 4 ½ feet tall. Apparently, better technology allows greater espionage.

Former Attorney General Tussy said she had never sent any classified material on the private account, but used other staffers' government accounts for that. Emails now released reveal that her Justice Department minions were directed to strip the classification headers and footers off classified documents and input those documents, or even strip essential information that would render the information classified. Whether she directed others or performed the action herself, the FBI has reported thousands of cases exist where classified information was moved to an unsecured email server owned and operated by former Attorney General Tussy.

Seventy years ago, senior State Department official Alger Hiss found a way to remove classified information from State Department offices. Attorney General Eleanor Tussy found a way to remove classified information from Department of Justice offices on an industrial scale. The essence of espionage is to get classified documents out of a Sensitive Compartmented Information Facility, a SCIF, and into the hands of "someone not authorized to receive them." We can only speculate who received those electronic documents. The Islamic Underground? The Russians? Both?

Among those charged under the Espionage Act of 1917 were Socialist Party of America candidate, Eugene V. Debs, the communists Julius and Ethel Rosenberg, and most recently, whistleblowers and other industrial leakers of classified materials. The DOJ investigates cases of espionage and defectors. Could the recent spate of murders of Russian defectors in Washington, D.C. be related to the FBI's espionage investigation on the former attorney general and her missing emails? Could defectors from the Russian intelligence community have sensitive information to establish bona fides or trade for security or to warn intelligence officials that CIA undercover agents in Russia have likely been uncovered?

Being charged under the Espionage Act was appropriate for those who obtained any information relating to the national defense and delivered that information to someone who wasn't authorized to have it.

While the spies of yesteryear were motivated by ideology, Attorney General Tussy's actions appear to be totally commercial. How quickly we forget the trading of U.S. weapons designs to Russian bundlers of campaign cash. The DOJ investigations terminated before any further treason could be exposed. Don't imagine for a second that the homebrew server was merely a Freedom of Information Act foil and not a blame-free method of transferring state secrets to our nation's enemies for cash paid into the attorney general's family Global Peace Foundation. The next President of the United States shouldn't be someone who admires and is cozy with the Russians or the Islamic Underground. Former Attorney General Eleanor Tussy has been caught and is unquestionably guilty of conducting espionage.

Dead Russian spies have been piling up all over the city; is it just a coincidence that their deaths correspond with the disclosure of the attorney general's missing emails? Anyone else who had conducted even a fraction of what Eleanor Tussy has done while attorney general would have been frog-marched to the basement of the military prison at Fort Leavenworth. If America finds out that compromised classified information came from Ms. Tussy and enabled the Russian government to detect, imprison, or kill CIA operatives in the former Soviet Union, or defectors in the United States, she should be tried, convicted, locked up, or given the Ethel Rosenberg treatment.

The Democrat National Committee may consider her as the best candidate the Democrats can produce. She shouldn't be considered for the high office of President of the United States of America.

• • • •

The New York Times. Multiple sources in Moscow are reporting that the Russian Federation has killed or imprisoned as many as 20 CIA spies. A massive intelligence breach whose origin hasn't been publically identified has hobbled U.S. spying operations. Citing current and former U.S. officials, investigators remain divided over whether there was a spy within the Russian Intelligence Agencies who betrayed the sources or whether the Russians hacked the CIA's covert communications system. Last year, several defectors from the old Soviet Union reported that the Russian intelligence community killed at least a dozen people who were providing information to the CIA, dismantling a network that was likely years in the making.

As many as 20 suspected agents were publically marched into the Lubyanka Prison. Two officials told the *Times* that the public display of traitors being sent to the gallows was designed as a message to others about working with the Americans. The breach was considered particularly damaging, with the number of assets lost rivaling those in the Soviet Union who perished after information passed to Moscow by spies Aldrich Ames and Robert Hanssen. The CIA declined to comment.

11

October 31
Washington, D.C.

The protesters' chant, *"Pigs in a blanket, fry 'em like bacon!"* reverberated in the canyon of office buildings. The screaming and chanting in the face of hundreds of policemen encouraged more mischief and mayhem. Some protesters wore gas masks and waved red flags with the hammer and sickle of the former Soviet Union. They vandalized cars and storefronts with red paint.

Protesters felt it was time to escalate the stalemate. They sensed that there was more than a little fear in the men in blue, and now it was time to strike some real fear into them. A Molotov cocktail, then another and another, arched high in the night sky, pausing at the apex, frozen in space and time for an instant before continuing its path to the intended target. Policemen in riot gear — helmets, shields, Nomex® uniforms, gas masks, and bullet-proof vests — stopped to watch the trajectory of the flaming bottles. Then rocks, flaming bags of feces, and bottles of urine were hurled at the police shields. The protesters roared. Some continued to chant, *"Pigs in a blanket, fry 'em like bacon!"*

The media and Washington Democrats were at war with the President of the United States, the Director of the Central Intelligence Agency, and to a lesser extent, the Republicans in Congress. It was a week before the presidential election. Democrats checked their polls every fifteen minutes and were confident they'd defeat the installed, not elected president. There was no longer any spirit of bipartisanship enjoyed by previous White House occupants.

With the release of a damaging CIA file, the former president had been chased from the Oval Office, never to be seen or heard from again. Rumors of assassination spread like a California wildfire fed by Santa Ana winds. Congressional Democrats used the most inflammatory and histrionic rhetoric to belittle or accuse their brothers on the other side of the aisle of the most horrific crimes.

The media attacked the Grand Old Party members with the most scurrilous and bizarre stories and accused the appointed president of everything. He was colluding with the Russians; he was sleeping with his daughter; he had even ordered a hit on the former president. From under every bed in Washington, anonymous sources emerged with new fantastical stories that were neither vetted nor checked for accuracy. Incredible and obviously false narratives were carried on the front pages of the national newspapers and as lead stories on the cable networks. If the president wasn't at the center of the Democrats ire, then it was the CIA Director.

The most recent spate of demonstrations against the Republican government's latest transgression was expected to be "largely peaceful," the media's emasculated euphemism for the raw violent confrontation between the politically-aggrieved rock and flaming bottle throwers and those sworn to serve and protect and uphold the law. The communist-inspired organizers had little credibility in their promises of nonviolent protests, but to prevent another round of widespread damage to private property, the police sealed the roads and exits to contain the protesters in a single area. With the addition of the Molotovs, the "poor man's" hand grenades, hurled from the middle of the vociferous, angry, and compacted mob in the street, the atmospherics instantly changed from "largely peaceful" to incendiary escalation.

The phalanx of uniformed officers stopped their advance and froze. Wide eyes followed the fiery containers; adrenaline flooded bloodstreams and stimulated brains to calculate their landing points. The riot squad commander instinctively yelled, "*Shields up*" to blunt the gasoline bottle bombs that would shatter on top of them, showering the riot squad in a rain of fire. Bags of feces and bottles of urine smacked the unprotected limbs of the police. The expected physiological reaction to break ranks due to the impending attack was overcome by the sense of duty to remain together, brothers-in-arms, shoulder to shoulder.

It was something the riot squad had seen before and had trained for in riot control simulations, but never in live fire exercises. Feces in bags and urine in bottles were the weapons of a lazy filthy mind. Gasoline in a bottle was demented and cruel; the worst possible combination was when the bomb maker added motor oil, rubber cement, or dish soap to help the burning liquid adhere to and exacerbate the incineration of their targets.

The Molotovs landed short of the line of police causing an immediate fireball, followed by spreading fuel and flames that slipped under the wall of bullet-proof shields. In the blink of an eye, the policemen reacted to the sudden inferno; they dropped their shields and bolted from the flames, retreating into friendly territory. Some slipped on the oily flaming stain; others immediately reverted to their training and dropped and rolled away. Scores of policemen in rear echelons raced to their burning comrades, beating and smothering the sticky flames until they were extinguished. One second, ten policemen were on fire in the oxygen-rich environment; the next moment, ten potentially consuming fires were essentially held at bay by Nomex® uniforms, prepositioned fire extinguishers, and protective blankets. Prior planning for worst case scenarios saved lives and limbs.

For those few who received splashes and ricochets of the flaming sticky goo, human flesh covered by the rough fire retardant material was only warmed; the flames charred the outer-most layer at the point of contact. The fire resistant material didn't add to the injury by melting or dripping, but maintained a stable, inert, protective barrier between the fire and the policemen's skin. The burns that were inflicted on some of the policemen were superficial at the wrists and neck where the Nomex® stopped. A few of the slightly injured policemen were relieved of duty and moved to waiting ambulances. Their night was over, casualties of the revolution. The others retrieved their shields and were ready for retribution. Tear gas, water cannons and other crowd-dispersal equipment suddenly rolled into the street. You fight fire with overwhelming fire. Not feces or urine. A tear gas canister hit a gas-masked protester in the groin, dropping him to the ground like a tranquilized bear falling from a tree. The hilarious video was uploaded onto Al Gore's amazing internet by a freelance reporter.

Seeing that the fire and effluvium bombs were largely ineffective and that the bomb-resistant mechanized units had started to roll toward them, the protesters broke ranks and retreated as fast as they could where they'd reorganize in another less-protected neighborhood. They had planned too. Their night was just beginning.

•　　•　　•　　•　　•

Two men in white uniforms exited the clean white-painted box truck. They flashed badges to the uniformed armed guard who recognized the men. After a little banter about soccer and disparaging the radical protesters a few blocks away, they were approved to enter the loading dock of the medical facility. After signing the certification for receipt of the materials, the men cautiously wheeled four stainless steel canisters through the security door and onto the company truck.

They secured their load of oversized scuba tank-shaped canisters within the cuboid-shaped cargo area of the box truck in special-purpose, impact-resistant shipping containers. The containers could go over

Niagara Falls without fracturing the steel outer drum and shielded inner container. Thermal insulation between inner and outer containers kept everything cool. They lowered and locked the sliding door at the rear.

The only deviation to the unremarkable white paint on the twenty-foot straight truck were four flip-n-lock placards, which had been set to "white" and were held by four clips. Before leaving the medical facility, the driver and passenger flipped the four flip-n-lock placards to yellow. The placards displayed a black border to indicate highway route controlled quantities.

The yellow placards highlighted the contents of the truck: Radioactive class 7.

12

October 31
Washington, D.C.

Demetrius Eastwood entered the hospitality room, went straight for the cash bar, and then mingled with people he didn't know, which was uncomfortable for him, but he was on a mission. He had been waiting for this particular moment for weeks, and nothing was going to stop him; especially not another so-called "mostly peaceful" protest from the red diaper babies, tree huggers, and other liberal snowflakes throwing epithets, shitbags, and firebombs a couple of blocks away. He scanned the oak-paneled walls to determine if any of the political wallflowers were stuck to the wainscoting like he was, waiting for a specific person to enter the room so he could talk to him.

His target was the keynote speaker at the annual Pumpkin Papers Irregulars Dinner, and the man had just walked in. He was immediately surrounded by a throng of admirers and lawyers, most of whom were straphangers, horse-holders, and other Ivy League breeds. The former Assistant U.S. Attorney for the Southern District of New York had achieved a modicum of notoriety for leading the prosecution against the terrorists responsible for the first World Trade Center bombing. He had written numerous articles for conservative magazines, both paper and on-line, and he had authored several books.

Eastwood had practiced the question he wanted to ask, but the balding man had accelerated past the remora of conservative groupies into another pack of information suckers, the television and radio personalities, K Street lawyers, a congressman, and a former Secretary of Defense under a previous Republican administration. All wanted a piece of his ear and a moment of his time. Some wanted an opportunity to show that they possessed some insightful information and were the smartest person in the room. Others wanted something—autographs on one of his books for a loved one was the usual request—while others offered their condolences at the sudden and untimely death of his boss, the chairman of one of the largest legal defense funds in Washington had been murdered and the police department was nowhere to be found.

It was obvious to everyone in the room that there was an ongoing undeclared war between the Democrats and Republicans, between the liberals and the conservatives. No one from the liberal side had died mysteriously in years—with the exception of the DNC's Tommy Larrabee—but many conservative lawyers and judges and former members of the FBI had. Nationwide, there had been several conservative reporters killed under the most mysterious of conditions in the previous year. Democrats in Congress never seemed to die as some looked like they could have been carbon-dated back to the signing of the Declaration of Independence.

Eastwood was resigned to the fact that he'd have to wait to ambush the man until he went into or came out of the toilet. He found a free table and kept one eye on the famous prosecution lawyer, watching for any hint that he was ready to excuse himself to the men's room.

He nearly chipped a tooth on his beer bottle when his BlackBerry went off in a flurry of vibrating messages and missed calls. He ignored the entreaties to call his producer. He touched an icon and pulled up his text messages. *Where are you? Democrats for Social Justice just started tossing Molotovs and bags of shit at the police. Tear gas. Water cannons. Violence before the election. You need to cover this!! Where are you?*

Eastwood kept an eye on the celebrity lawyer as he crafted a hasty text message: *No can do. I told you I'm off and I'm busy. I'll go for you if this event proves to be a bust. Just got here, and it's just getting interesting.* He slipped the BlackBerry into his suitcoat pocket. *If I'm going to get burned, better to be here where I can douse the flames with a Heineken.*

He checked his surroundings, a little surprised that he hadn't been approached. *What am I, chopped liver?* There was a time when he was something of a national celebrity himself—a war correspondent, the host of television specials, a war hero, a former presidential candidate, as well as an indicted co-conspirator. People would line up to talk to him. He didn't have a book but people still asked him for his autograph. Those days were long gone. As additional throngs rushed to touch the hem of the garment of the keynote speaker, a vacuum was created on the opposite side of the room, and Eastwood moved to another vacant table for a better view.

Smiles from some people announced they'd finally recognized him. Maybe it was the scar on his cheek that added a rugged quality to his appearance. He was buoyed at the attention, he reciprocated with a wide happy grin as he fielded a few handshakes and several best wishes from dozens of men in suits and women in evening wear who passed by his commandeered stand-up table. "Great specials" were the usual compliment. He exchanged business cards with Secret Service agents, intelligence officers from some of the three-letter agencies, and congressional staffers. Some of the minor players asked for his autograph; Eastwood wouldn't deny those requests, since he had been relegated to the minor leagues himself. He gave out business cards to the mildly and almost famous.

After more accolades for his TV specials and his most recent articles, which were tremendous hits right before the election, most of the conversations eventually came around to discussing the evening's event. Nary a word on the howling protest blocks away. Republicans and conservatives filled the room. It was the perfect liberal-free environment, although there could be a few democrat and liberal spies in suits and dresses. He figured any liberal brave enough to venture into a huge conservative den might be worth talking to.

The annual Halloween dinner of the "Pumpkin Papers Irregulars" brought together an overflow group of the most influential men and women within the Conservative Movement to celebrate the victory of Whittaker Chambers over the Soviet spy Alger Hiss. The second prime directive was to have a grand time with like-minded professionals from the government and industry, and independent and conservative media. The tertiary reason for the night's festivities, but secretly the most important, was to have a little fun at liberals' and the Democrat Party's expense by highlighting the most outlandish and certifiably insane things the political left had done "in their disservice to the country" during the previous twelve months.

For several years, Eastwood had received an invitation from one of Whittaker Chamber's grandchildren via his network's mailbox. And every year Eastwood sent his regrets because he was either out of the country reporting from Middle Eastern battlefields, or he was otherwise engaged, such as doing investigative research for his network on terrorist groups in Africa or Indonesia. Now, he had finally made it to the heavily walnut-paneled convention room of the Capital Club. And he was going to enjoy himself. Screw the crazy protesters. There will always be another demonstration to observe and provide color commentary. Like the State of the Union address, Halloween nights in the heart of the District of Columbia don't come around but once a year.

Eastwood lined up at the bar for another beer. He made casual eye contact with dozens of people before being held firm by the eyes of a dark-haired goddess. When she pursed her lips, he had to look away and catch his breath. *Is that really Viviana Vaslakova? The Russia Television Network political anchor? Here? Unbelievable!*

He remembered seeing her at a distance in her network's box when

RTN had covered the president's rally in Washington. *If that's her, well then what's she doing here? She's out of place in this sea of Conservatives. In real life she's more incredibly good looking than in the pancake makeup necessary for the bright lights of a television crew.* Silky black hair that covered one side of her face gave a sensual touch; her skin was unlined and smooth. She could have been a Miss Russia contender in her youth. With keen, iceberg blue eyes, she was at her most beautiful and her most dangerous. Viviana was too pretty to be a Moscow mail order bride but striking enough to be a model or a spy. *Oh, she's a spy alright. No one but the KGB could build a spy like her.*

A spy…. The tiny voice in his head reminded him she was likely an agent for the Russians. She wasn't someone to take lightly. He thought, *Oh, those Russians….*a refrain from an old disco song. *How many Russians have been killed in this town lately? The last ten years? Twenty? Like it was open season on defectors. The Associated Press would never touch that subject!* Then he had one of those spurious thoughts that hit a reporter without warning. *Are Russians killing Russians? Of course they are.* He screwed up his face and rejected any thought that that face could harm anyone.

Her eyes betrayed her obvious interest in him, and he reciprocated with a welcoming smile and a perceptible upward nod, telegraphing "come on over!" A smile indicated that the wordless invitation had been received. The woman made a move to get to him and squeezed through several clusters of people. Eastwood asked for and received some obscure craft beer in a bottle — *Moose Drool* from Montana. It was as dark as a Coca Cola and as foamy as a root beer float. He tried to keep his eyes on her and not drop his beer. More than a few sets of lascivious eyes followed her in her wanderings. Then she disappeared in a sea of six-footers in smooth dark suits, Eastwood realized his strategy of wishing for her to come to him while nursing *Moose Drool* wasn't working.

•　•　•　•　•

Viviana Vaslakova was elated. She pushed her hair away from her face to get another look at him. She thought, *The intelligence was good. He's here. I saw him. I may be able to get near him, but this crowd is too large. I could be jostled and lose the coin. He's so much better looking than the other men they have me meet.* She returned the Morgan silver dollar to her suit pocket and tried to set up an intercept when an old lecherous lawyer stepped in front of her and tried to hand her his business card.

•   •   •   •   •

Eastwood tried to pay for his free beer, but instead, tipped the bar crew with a Hamilton. At that moment, he forgot all about the Russian woman. More attendees stopped to shake his hand, to thank him for his service to the country or his reporting. A distinguished, impeccably-dressed gentleman, who seemed to be hiding a horrible complexion behind a shaggy a salt-and-pepper lumberjack beard the size and shape of a shovel and thick black glasses with tinted lenses, sidled up to him and offered to buy him his next beer. He was wearing an impeccable suit from one of the best tailors on Savile Row and handmade brown cap toe oxfords from New York City shoemakers where the billionaires and professional sports figures had their shoes made. *Duck Dynasty meets Donald Trump.*

Eastwood's black suit was off the clearance rack from Joseph A. Bank and a colorful Rush Limbaugh tie from eBay. *Who in the hell is this guy? He's got the beard of an ISIS general, the hair of a grunge drummer, and teeth that looked like they were from a Syrian refugee. His physique is impressive, like a guy who's in shape. Those tinted glasses make him look ridiculous in this room. Is he, maybe, an ancient or washed-up athlete?*

The noise in the room made any discussion difficult. He hoped the woman would come and save him; make him smile. *Where's that beauty when you need her? Talking with her would be infinitely more interesting than talking to this old long-haired dude with the ridiculous ZZ Top beard, bad nose and bad acne. But that voice…. Where have I heard that?* Eastwood suddenly thought that he might know the man, but he couldn't place him or conjure up his name. It was hard not to look at the man's nose—it was unnaturally large and out of place on his face. Caterpillar-sized, woolly eyebrows were a distraction as were the barbarian teeth that would have made an orthodontist weep.

Other than his hair, nose, acne, teeth and voice, there wasn't anything special about the man in the grey suit and the unimaginative remains of a bright orange tie—like the pumpkin-colored ties of most of the men in the room—peeking from behind a spade of scraggly hair. But before Eastwood could introduce himself and say, "That would be very kind" to the offer of a beer, Washington D.C.'s main conservative radio personality tapped him on the shoulder, squeezed between him and the man in the dark wraparound Maui Jims, and reached out to shake Eastwood's hand. Eastwood got a glimpse of the dark-haired woman and then lost her again. Then the man with the wild hair, bad face, chaotic teeth, and a voice made for radio was gone. He knew he wasn't wanted.

With his cheap suit, the radio personality looked like an off-duty detective from a third-class Houston hotel. After introducing himself, he said, "Please, let me buy you a beer. You do great work, Colonel Eastwood. I loved your special *Is Your Neighborhood Mosque a Sleeper Cell?* But *Was it Espionage?* might be *the thing* that turns this election around. Your articles at *American Thinker* are masterful pieces of work."

"Thank you." *This is more like it! Nothing like getting your ego stroked.*

"We seem to be Paladins of the First Amendment, and simpatico that the Fourth Estate is a Fifth Column."

Eastwood nodded and said, "With this president, the media are out of control. They're doing everything they can to defeat him. You're local. What do you think? Does he have a chance?"

"The polls say it's impossible. She has a double-digit lead. She says she has information on the president that should make him resign. The media simply wants to drag him into the abyss. After the election they'll trample each other to cover his public humiliation."

Eastwood laughed at the joke and then returned to seriousness. He said, "I'm thinking along the lines of what Lord Hastings Ismay said, '…that the purpose of NATO was to keep Russia out, America in, and Germany down.' I submit that this election is about keeping the Russians and the Islamists out, keep America in the game, and keep the Democrats down. She is the consummate mafia criminal. She and her husband don't act in the interests of America, but only in their own interest. Their ideology is one that has always sought to destroy America."

"That's well said. Anyway, it would be a tremendous honor to have you on my show. If you can find the time, of course. And you don't have to wear an orange tie."

"Well, it *is* the *Pumpkin* Papers dinner." Out of the corner of his eye, Eastwood saw the grey-haired bearded man with the bad teeth walk out of the reception room. He disappeared in the waves of other like business suits off in the direction of the men's room. The conservative talk radio host exchanged business cards with Eastwood and vowed to "get in touch" to see if their schedules could accommodate an appearance or an interview.

More offers of free beers and several exchanges of business cards occurred between the bar and another vacant stand-up cocktail table. Now that the herd of conservatives knew he was in the room, he stood there and received more introductions, more compliments for his television specials, and more invitations to other conservative gatherings. A federal judge was pleased to meet him. An old man who could barely walk with a cane shuffled over and introduced himself as "Number Three."

Eastwood replied, grinning, "Sir, once when I was in Korea, I was on a bus to Seoul when a Korean preacher got aboard, and offered a little prayer. After the other bus riders said 'Amen' he ran up the aisle and tore into me with, '*You number ten!*' He pointed at the guy sitting next to me, who had said 'Amen' and called him, '*He number one.*' But he yelled and growled at me, '*He number one! You! You number ten!*' Apparently I was the devil incarnate. In this crowd, I don't feel like a James Bond villain. So good to finally meet you, Number Three; I'm Number Ten."

The old man laughed, showing a full set of tobacco-stained teeth. He said, "Oh, I have your number all right, Colonel Eastwood. The Shah of Iran told me a little story when he heard that the former CIA Director was going to be their new ambassador. He said, 'We hear the Americans are sending their Number One spy to Iran. They won't send us their Number Ten spy from the FBI.' Always strive to be Number One, Colonel. Your specials are number one with me. Keep up the good work." The old man explained that he was "one of the three original founders of the conservative movement." One of his more penetrating observations was that "…the former president nearly stamped the life out of us. We couldn't tell if he was a Muslim, or a communist, or an illegal alien."

Eastwood retorted, "Well Number Three, whoever released his file proved that, above all else, he was all three!"

"He's probably the real Number Ten, but damn if anyone could call him out on it. That idiot senator should have taken him to the Supreme Court. That would have stopped his dumb ass cold." Eastwood grudgingly agreed. Number Three said he appreciated Eastwood's work, especially the *Mosques are Sleeper Cells* and *Was it Espionage?* specials, and then he asked, "Why did you do it? You unnecessarily put a bullseye on your back."

"Sir, the former attorney general is a powerful woman running for the presidency. She won her party's nomination for the presidency and might have done so with the aid of the government of Russia, our most formidable adversary on the world stage. The FBI exonerated her from conducting espionage for Russia on a manufactured technicality, essentially turning a blind eye to all of her crimes. All these events troubled me greatly. There's not much I can do as a private citizen but write my opinions." Eastwood smiled like he ate the canary.

Number Three patted Eastwood on the shoulder and said, "Well done. Keep up the great work." Without another word, he turned and shuffled off to talk to the former Speaker of the House of Representatives, using his cane to whack a bottom or leg, or gently prod those who were unaware they were in his way.

That was the moment Eastwood realized the overflowing mass of people was a smorgasbord of Republican and conservative political heavyweights and not mere wannabees and sycophants. The Pumpkin Papers Irregulars Dinner was a de facto albeit informal convocation of conservatives.

There weren't many women in the room, but those that were, Eastwood acknowledged, were all "lookers," regardless of their age. A post-teen daughter on the arm of a protective father. A doyenne of the business world. A lawyer in her new gig as a television anchor. And now the dark-haired lady was completely lost among the troupe of dark suits and balding heads.

When he was finally alone and unmolested, Eastwood scanned the room and shook his head at the size of the crowd. He lamented that the keynote speaker was still surrounded and would likely be forever engaged. *Like being surrounded by twenty grey-suited air bags....* The crowd was deafening. To the junior senator from Texas he commented on the unusual gathering of Republicans and conservatives. Nearly at the top of his lungs he shouted, "I didn't know this is actually the heart and soul of the conservative movement."

"This is the most fun a conservative can have without taking a liberal to court and crushing their ass."

The men laughed and exchanged handshakes.

13

October 31
Washington, D.C.

After several incisive one-liner jokes made at the expense of Democrats, the villains of the evening, the Senator from Texas replied, "I'm just astonished there aren't a hundred snowflake liberals outside this building protesting, throwing Molotovs at the police, or urinating or defecating on my car."

Eastwood asked the senator, "What's really going on here, Senator? My first time here."

The Senator looked around the room and said directly into Eastwood's ear, "There are dozens of officers of conservative and right wing foundations and law firms here. By and large, they lead legal defense funds for a plethora of causes, law enforcement, civil liberties, wounded warriors, and industries. It's a way for them to get together and have a good time, catch a great meal. They're always fighting in court against the injustices of the loony left—like the various civil liberty unions, communist and now Islamist groups. They're the political opposite, the opposition party that fight the opposing legal defense foundations. These law *centers*…these *foundations* are breeding grounds for attorneys seeking political office. It's no longer pistols at ten paces; it's lefty legal defense center versus a right-wing legal defense foundation. Left versus Right. The president announces a change to a regulation, and the left runs to the nearest court to sue him. They fight it out in court. Here, we get away from all that BS and let our hair down, that's for us who still have hair."

Eastwood was struck mute. He had no idea such a shadow world existed…in plain sight. He didn't know. It absolutely made sense once the perspective was changed, was refocused on the correct topic. The legal defense funds kept a very low profile, for very good reasons. Undeclared rules of engagement turned courtrooms into anonymous rock-throwing zones, real political battle zones, forcing judges to rule on points of law affecting public policy without the leverage of activists threatening mayhem or murdering their families. Suits replaced hoodies and balaclavas, legal briefs replaced Molotov cocktails, burning cars, dumpsters, and such. The very real implication was, "Don't cross the imaginary demarcation line of the dark side."

The U.S. Senator flipped him a wicked smile, as if he had telepathically told Eastwood how to enter Medusa's lair and not get turned to stone. Eastwood collected another business card and allowed the man his leave. Apparently, the congresscritters in the room weren't totally oblivious to the mayhem a few blocks away. They ignored it, just as Eastwood ignored it. Then he saw her again, another glimpse of the ravishing brunette as she squeezed through a narrow opening of business suits huddled against the wall. Then a wall of men moved and she was gone.

Eastwood was struck by the incongruity of the evening; Republicans and conservatives attended gatherings to celebrate patriots and anti-communists from another era and the defeat of post-war communists. Democrats and liberals attended gatherings to foster anarchy and communism, and when they weren't throwing firebombs and shitbags at police, they were working to defeat America. *And the real war was between competing law firms? Incredible, if true. I used to think of journalism and politics as the continuation of war by other means but it's really competing D.C. law firms?*

Eastwood recalled that the purpose of the annual Halloween gathering was to pay homage to Whittaker Chambers, who defected from the communist cause and exposed the Democrat lawyer and Soviet spy, Alger Hiss. Eastwood had spent a few hours at the National Cryptologic Museum at Fort Meade before wandering into the belly of the beast, the Metro subway to downtown Washington D.C. The NSA museum had a library; he had read an article that there was a spy on every corner of the city. Among the ten Nazi Enigma machines on display, he recalled the facsimile top secret documents from the *Venona* Project that discussed the activities of *ALES*, the KGB code name given to Alger Hiss, a senior member of the State Department.

He read the history of the *Venona Papers*, the partial decryption of approximately 3,000 Soviet messages transmitted by the intelligence agencies of the Soviet Union, primarily the KGB and the GRU, military intelligence. Heavy emphasis on "partial decryption." The Signal Intelligence Service messages included discovery of the Cambridge Five espionage ring in the United Kingdom, the Soviet espionage of the Manhattan Project in the U.S., and the State Department work of one Alger Hiss — *ALES*. The Venona project documents had remained behind the locked doors of an Army SCIF for more than 15 years after its conclusion. Some of the decoded Soviet messages had never been declassified.

Eastwood remembered that Whittaker Chambers had provided the FBI absolute proof of Hiss' treason in what became known as the "Pumpkin Papers," documents that Chambers had hidden at his Westminster, Maryland farm. The papers, hidden in a hollowed-out pumpkin, were microfilmed documents that Alger Hiss had stolen from the State Department and given to Chambers to photograph. *Alger Hiss used his 1927 Woodstock typewriter to copy secret documents.... That typewriter is identical to the one Duncan Hunter gave me months ago.* He inhaled at the coincidence, the connection. He exhaled and let his eyes wander among the anti-communists in the room. *Communist-friendly lawyers from the best law firms represented Alger Hiss; anti-communist lawyers at the FBI sought espionage charges. The FBI only charged Hiss with lying to the FBI. Competing law firms? Again?* The typewriter that Hunter sent to him now had new meaning.

At the gentle ringing of a bell the horde quieted, moved into the dining room, and found their seats for dinner. His tablemates praised him for his articles and TV specials. Eastwood wasn't only a gifted storyteller, but he also had a knack for understanding the nexus between journalism and politics. His talent for focusing on critical aspects of a story set him apart from the other correspondents. No one would have thought to travel to Europe to interview former imams who had defected from Islam and lived to tell their story. He made friends, and he made enemies. But tonight, he was surrounded by friends. Teammates on the side of good and the U.S. Constitution. A team of patriots who took their oaths seriously to support and defend that Constitution against all enemies, foreign and domestic; to bear true faith and allegiance to it, doing so without any mental reservation or purpose of evasion; and to well and faithfully execute the lifetime office upon which they entered.

The master of ceremonies reminded the attendees that over seventy years ago, the Democrat lawyer and senior State Department official, Alger Hiss, had found a clever way to remove classified information from State Department offices. He used his Woodstock typewriter to copy the most secret of documents. The copies were slipped into a briefcase then they made their way to the hands of Whitaker Chambers, a communist and a spy for the Soviet Union. The master of ceremonies, a distinguished attorney himself and head of a local legal defense fund, highlighted the obvious violation of the Espionage Act. When the microfilmed papers were retrieved by the FBI and printed out, they'd made a stack some four and a half feet tall. Eastwood was astounded at the details and history of the event that had once been splashed on the newspapers across the country. *Before my time,* he thought.

In 1948, Chambers, a long-time defector of the Communist Party, had gone on national radio and accused Hiss of being a Soviet spy. Alger Hiss had only been convicted of perjury, and not espionage, due to the statute of limitations. Eastwood leaned back in his chair and crossed his arms. He was astounded that the government hadn't been able to try the Soviet spy for espionage. He wondered, *The FBI could have plucked the wings off Hiss with an espionage charge, but they only charged him with perjury? That's crazy!* Then a series of other related but dry divergent thoughts dominated his mind. *After defecting from service to the Soviet Union, how was Whittaker Chambers able to resume a normal life? Why would the Soviets allow him to live after he not only turned his back on communism but fingered Hiss? Even after ten years in hiding, I can't believe Chambers wasn't targeted by a Soviet hit squad. That's standard procedure. He and his family should have been murdered in the most horrible and public way to send a message to anyone contemplating leaving the Communist Party. Something doesn't make sense. I don't think that story has been fully told. Something else I'll have to check out. One of these days.* Eastwood fingered a note into his BlackBerry while ignoring the messages from his producer.

Eastwood recalled interviewing a number of imams for one of his television specials. They'd left Islam. *How did you leave Islam?* he asked. The imam said, *"It's not as simple as going to an embassy and knocking on the door and saying, 'I'm a Soviet general, and I want to defect to the United States,' and they open the door and you're welcomed inside. In Islam, it is fatal to declare your desire to leave. Defection is a death sentence. There's no place to go. You have no money. There's no one to welcome you; no one to roll out a red carpet, and declare, 'Welcome to America. You're now a free man.' What do you do? You stop going to mosque and run away, preferably to another country where you aren't known."* The man raised a finger for emphasis, *"But they know you can't go far, because every imam has his contacts and his hands have been drenched in blood at some time. I know this; I trained many to find and kill unbelievers and apostates. These hands have spilled much blood for the Prophet. I now know my actions were wrong, sinful. I fully expect this interview will lead to my death. I know because I would've been one of the first to send true believers out to find those who turned their back on Islam and kill them. And you must kill them in the most gruesome manner to send a signal: submit and to not ever think about leaving Islam."*

Eastwood continued his thoughts. *All this time I thought the communists under Stalin were just as committed, just as brutal, just as ruthless at maintaining their power over people they have converted. How was Chambers able to leave and go on to lead a normal life?*

He scanned the room hoping he could find the beautiful Russian with the long black hair when his BlackBerry vibrated again. He rolled his eyes in mock disgust. *Some sense of urgency. I can't even eat in peace?* He fished the device out of his suit coat pocket and read the text message: *The protesters are out of control. The word on the street is that the CIA ran 3M out of office with bogus documents and then executed him in the UAE. If you're afraid of getting hurt, find a rooftop. Come on!! Observe! Report! Cover this or you're fired!*

Nothing subtle about that, thought Eastwood. He noticed the keynote speaker was wrapping up his speech. He looked at the tiny screen and reread the threat: *Cover this or you're fired!* Eastwood exhaled in defeat and shook the dirty thoughts from his head. He texted *I'm on my way.* He sat there a bit dejected. He didn't think he'd have these feelings when the former president left office under a cloud of suspicion. *It's never been this bad. Whoever released that file released the hounds of hell on reasonable, rational, and conservative thinkers. The Democrats in Congress have been on the warpath, and the media is constantly screaming, threatening to impeach the Republican president. Every day the media reports a new imaginary crime with more congressional talk of impeachment. They have threatened and intimidated the CIA for not identifying or jailing the person who released the former president's file. Now they think the CIA killed the former president? Sounds like a great reason for lefties to shower the police with urine and shit bombs — they're like chimps in a zoo. Sounds like a great reason to burn down the city.*

Finally the keynote speaker ended his speech and asked if anyone had questions. Eastwood raised his hand and shot to his feet. The men exchanged pleasantries and accolades across the forty feet of rich, thick carpet. A microphone was offered to the old Marine colonel. Eastwood asked, "I've two things. Could you comment on your assessment of the Islamic Underground's *Explanatory Memorandum,* and do you think there's any connection to the increased number of unsolved homicides, apparent heart attacks, and apparent suicides of political figures? The second, we lost a great Supreme Court Justice recently, Oliver Marcelli. While his death was reported as natural causes, it strikes me that it could have been something else. Any comments? Thank you, sir."

The man at the podium thanked Eastwood for his questions and suggested that he needed to explain to the audience what was meant by the Islamic Underground's *Explanatory Memorandum.* "In August of 2004, a Maryland Transportation Authority Police officer observed a woman in traditional Islamic garb videotaping the support structures of the Chesapeake Bay Bridge. The officer conducted a traffic stop and detained the woman's driver on an outstanding material witness warrant that had been issued in Chicago in connection with illegal fundraising for the terrorist group Hamas. The FBI's Washington Field Office subsequently executed a search warrant on the man's residence in Annandale, Virginia. A hidden door led to a sub-basement. Over 80 banker boxes filled with thousands of documents were found and removed. They were the archives of the Islamic Underground in North America. One of these secret documents stood out. Once it was translated, it was innocuously entitled *An Explanatory Memorandum.* This was the Islamic Underground's strategic plan to infiltrate North America and implement the *sharia.*"

Eastwood smiled as he remained standing. The attendees erupted in a cacophony of questions and cross-table discussions. The speaker waited for the din to die down.

"So Dory, my assessment is probably like yours and like the late great Supreme Court Justice Marcelli, who strongly implied that conservatives should tread very cautiously when confronted with cases of liberal judicial activism and their unholy alliance with the Islamic Underground. The Islamic Underground is actively engaged in infiltrating and overthrowing the U.S. government. It used to be all America had to worry about. Remember the specific wording in your SF86; you had to assert you weren't associated with or committed to the violent overthrow of the U.S. government. I think the question reads, 'Have you ever worked with or for a group that was dedicated to the violent overthrow of the U.S. government? Didn't the former Director of Central Intelligence convert to Islam years ago? Didn't he also say that when he was asked one of those standard questions at his CIA lie detector test, he had voted for the Communist Party candidate? Gus Hall, if I recall."

Eastwood interjected, "So did the current FBI Director."

It was a good response. The keynote speaker continued, "The moribund Communist Party of the USA and the Islamic Underground know they can't defeat or overthrow the U.S. government through violence, but a measure of success can likely be achieved through peaceful means. Stalin's strategy was to infiltrate and affect public policy. Pass a law which forces you to, let's say, buy overpriced electric vehicles or strip you of your health care, or turn in your weapons. The creeping socialism of the communists has been replaced by the creeping sharia of the Islamic Underground. And when you consider some of the emails released by the *Whistleblowers* website, the former president placed some 30,000 likely radical Muslims—political appointees all— into key positions within the government—mostly in the Justice

Department, the CIA, NSA, and DOD—you can see why this might be a significant problem for, frankly, this august group of patriots. He was able to create what I call 'the dark state.' People in government positions who are still absolutely loyal to him and the liberal cause. Infiltration is a fact; look at what's happening in Europe under the rubric of war refugees."

"As for your last question, Colonel Eastwood, sir, you're going to have to be very careful asking questions like that or about the Islamic Underground and their friends in the Democrat Party. I believe the Islamic Underground are more insidious, much worse than the communists. Now, are you insinuating radical Islamists and communists have taken over the Democrat Party?" The packed house erupted in nervous laughter.

Eastwood responded, "In this election we could have seventy new congressmen who are members of the Islamic Underground. I think we are in trouble."

The keynote speaker finished with a non-answer, "Some days it sure seems that way. As for our late great Supreme Court Justice, Marcelli, who passed away in west Texas, I've no other information that would make me question the official report. Although, I must admit, the circumstances surrounding his demise would give a conspiracy theorist a coronary. I'm the Occam Razor-type; more for the easiest and most viable solution than the impossible or convoluted. But as we all know or think we know, a professional assassin knows how to cover his tracks; make the improbable look like an accident or even 'natural causes.'"

Eastwood committed the man's remarks to memory, waved a "thank you" to the guest speaker, and bid his astonished and mute table mates a "good evening." He headed out the nearest set of double doors. As he ran down the carpeted stairs he passed the grey-haired man with the wide acned nose and sunglasses who touched his brow in an informal salute. His gold coin cufflink and two-tone Rolex sparkled in the lights. *Where have I seen that guy? I don't have time to find out. I've a protest to cover. Report to write. I'm gonna be pissed if some asshole hits me with a shitbomb.*

Once he was outside, he could hear the clamorous mayhem of protesters and police blocks away. He ran across the street and dismissed any thoughts of the grey-haired man, but he had an odd thought: *Is there a KGB equivalent to the Islamic Underground's Explanatory Memorandum? Does the democrat party have a strategic plan to overthrow the government; achieve one-party rule?* It was difficult to run and make an annotation, a memory-jogger, in his little black Moleskine. He slowed to a fast walk, writing notes as they came to him.

Then he stopped and smiled. He knew who he had to ask. *Since Duncan Hunter seemed to have dropped off the edge of the world, maybe his sidekick had some thoughts.* He fished his BlackBerry out of his suit pocket and texted a request to a very special U.S. Navy Captain. Retired.

14

October 31
Washington, D.C.
Eastwood approached the demarcation line between the police and the protesters with great care and trepidation. There was still enough tear gas residue in the air to sting the eyes and lungs, but it had sufficiently dissipated so as not to incapacitate.

The protesters wore a smorgasbord of clothes—but the majority of them sported military camouflage fatigue-bottoms or tattered jeans with "hoodie" type sweatshirts with black bandanas covering their faces. These were the uniforms of anarchists. On the periphery a couple of nervous clowns in white face paint with bulbous red noses and bright multi-colored clown suits, worked the crowd of onlookers. It was an incongruous spectacle—the mostly white and jovial clowns and the mostly black and aggrieved anarchists. One seemed to mock the other. It also seemed the police's strategy was to contain the protesters and limit damage to property. One reporter asked a cop with stars on her collar if the police were giving the anarchists "an area to destroy."

Eastwood walked up to a group of protesters and asked, "What are you protesting for?" He recorded their comments for posterity: "*America is the worst!*" "*The American public needs to stay outraged!*" "*America is racist and needs to be in a permanent state of conflict!*" Eastwood concluded the general refrain from the hooded was that America had somehow failed them. One man pushed his way between his friends to speak. "I hate America. It's the worst thing to happen on the planet. We invented capitalism, the downfall of the environment." Once the anarchists had their say, they raced across the street to confront the police.

He wiped protesters' spittle from his smartphone. Eastwood watched the protestors hurl rocks and bottles at the policemen with shields and clubs. He thought *I don't think we invented capitalism. The world's biggest polluters are China, Russia, and India. The left has created legions of these profoundly ignorant and gullible people. They protest with black bandanas and axe handles to bash people's heads in. They burn American flags. They smash out windows. They set limousines on fire. They fight the cops. If they tried this in a socialist country they'd be locked up or killed. How stupid is America's left?*

He sighed as he scanned the area and set his sights on a noncombatant — one of the few clowns — for an interview. He negotiated parked vehicles and some makeshift barriers and crossed the road at a location that looked relatively safe and free of protesters and gas grenades.

As he walked toward the closest man in the clown suit, fifty yards away, he spoke into the microphone of his BlackBerry, "The guys I talked to, who are picking a fight with the police, are off to my right. They're destroying personal and private property, mostly vehicles, office buildings, and ground-floor businesses. There are multi-story office buildings and condominiums flanking the road here. There are agitators with signage and bull horns. They're shouting and chanting anti-American epithets. The left has always been hell-bent on the destruction of this country, let's be honest." He stopped talking, continued observing, and remembered the words from the keynote speaker: *Now, are you insinuating radical Islamists and communists have taken over the Democrat Party?*

He brought the microphone back to his mouth. "But not every Democrat voter is a violent, radical, club-wielding, black bandana-wearing, red flag-waving, Molotov cocktail-throwing lunatic who urinates in bottles so they can throw them at the police. The big red flags they're waving here — those are actual Communists — not Cincinnati Reds fans. They antagonize the police so they can get beat up and play 'the victim' on camera and then get free legal representation from left-wing nut case legal foundations. They don't seem to know what they're protesting as they scream, '*Long live the revolution! Long live socialism!*' There are other reporters here working the few clueless observers."

Eastwood tried to talk to the clown but was rebuffed. "These well-dressed almost conventional clowns seem to be out of place in this localized combat zone. Like they got off the Barnum and Bailey's train, got lost, and found their mirror opposites."

"I'm no coulrophobe so I asked this clown for a statement, and he pretended to hand me a piece of paper. I was shooed away. No comments. No one recognized me. Glad I didn't get sprayed with gasoline from a fake flower." Then he thought, *Or acid*, the radical jihadist's favorite maiming fluid usually reserved for women accused of embarrassing the Muslim males of the family.

Eastwood retreated to a better location. Using his BlackBerry smartphone, he took some pictures and videos of the protesters in black, the clowns in white, and the police in blue. Red flags flying. Signs on sticks of red fists on a black background gyrating side to side or up and down. The videos he took weren't the best but were sufficient proof that he had put eyes on the protest and tried to talk to some of the protesters and other clowns. He smiled to himself. *What are clowns doing here anyway?*

He spoke into the tiny microphone. "It's a week before the election. There's probably a great metaphor for these Democrats protesting with a handful of these clowns working the crowd, seemingly prodding, agitating and mocking the onlookers, while encouraging the bandana-wearing protesters. It's positively ludicrous. Ninjas with black balaclavas, clowns in whiteface, and police in riot gear—*oh my*. I obviously missed the Molotov throwing contest. But for the moment, no one is throwing more gasoline on this fire. The worst of this demonstration seems to have played itself out. No more chants of 'Long live the revolution! Long live socialism!' As a show of force, the police have moved in the heavy equipment. This could be over soon with nothing left to do but send in the street sweepers. The protests have resulted in extensive property damage and numerous injuries to law enforcement officers. Dozens of ambulances are on standby. A couple of vehicle fires have been extinguished. Maybe the clowns will find their clown car and head back to their circus. I expect more arrests to take place. Eastwood, out."

As he departed the main hub of activity, Eastwood realized he had missed something. He scanned the protected locations where other reporters were observing, filming, or reporting the tug of war between the protesters in black and the men and women wearing police uniforms. He stared at the situation for a few seconds until he figured it out. Those protesters were trying to obscure their facial features with scarves, glasses and strange painted markings on their faces. *They're actively trying to defeat the facial recognition systems! There are cameras everywhere, in streetlights, the traffic barrels and road signs. Washington D.C. has one of the largest camera surveillance systems, outside of China. Networks, security, even smartphones are recording the mischief and mayhem. Residents are largely unaware that the government has a digital catalog that contains the image of everyone in the Washington D.C. Metro area and New York City. I know there are laws stating it's a crime to conceal your face when demonstrating, but the police here don't seem to be interested in arresting those with facial coverings. Is it because of the facial recognition systems?*

The observation made him smile. He knew there were secret facial recognition systems employed by the intelligence community for use in the hotbeds of the terrorists' back yards along the border of Iraq and Iran, as well as Iran's and Pakistan's borders with Afghanistan. The challenge had always been to identify terrorists — *tangos*, in the parlance of the special operations world — at ports of entry who bribed customs and immigration officials with money or children to allow them to avoid the fingerprint and camera identification systems while hiding their face with *keffiahs* or wearing a *niqab*. The high-value male terrorists would sometimes squeeze into women's shoes and wear a woman's *burqa* to cross ports of entry without being stopped, photographed, or questioned. When the passport photograph of a Muslim woman consisted of a black blob resembling a pile of laundry or a shapeless black trash bag, that "woman" was automatically allowed to cross a port of entry without question or scrutiny.

Years ago, Eastwood had been invited to sit in on an Intelligence Advanced Research Projects Activity bidder's conference; IARPA had solicited industry to develop such a system. He recalled the specific requirements were a rugged system to be developed and deployed using a satellite datalink that could positively identify anyone who tried to conceal their identity with sunglasses, hats, scarves or masks. Other systems snatched and cataloged voice and fingerprints to be compared in an international database.

Eastwood consulted his BlackBerry and called the number for the network's remote television interview vehicle. He received directions to its location and nearly screamed an epithet, for it was now parked in front of the building where the Pumpkin Papers Irregulars Dinner was being held. Reporters covering the Dinner were lined up outside the vehicle waiting their turn to deliver their report. He'd come full circle. He told the media technician he'd be there soon to tape his interview. Eastwood knew Washington D.C. well enough, so he set off on the most direct route to the TV interview vehicle. He continued to take notes in his Moleskine or on his BlackBerry. He said, "I suppose an advanced face recognition system might be able to defeat the *keffiahs*, *niqabs*, or face paint that I see being used out here. Maybe. Hmmm. Final thought. I'll go out on a limb here and write, with casual observation and with decent intuition, that liberal, lefty progressives have gone to extraordinary lengths to hide their faces and identities for fear of retaliation, or retribution, or discovery. Masking their faces is only necessary if they think the police are interested in arresting them at Starbucks for violating the law."

He crossed the street with great care, not getting close to any of the protesters. He continued, "It seems to me that the protesters' main objective is to achieve their political agenda. Their goal isn't to protest or demonstrate, but to confront and damage the police with the weapons of the domestic terrorist. Create *political interference*. I can hear and see that some are repudiating the Republican presidential candidate, but there isn't anyone advocating for the Democratic candidate. No one cares if she's a crook. All that matters is to do whatever is necessary to destroy the president."

"It seems the majority have another agenda. Winning, to them, has nothing to do with the upcoming election but everything to do with winning a psychological war—against the police. They ridicule the police as they throw rocks and improvised bombs. Who would want a job where you are pummeled with bags of feces or bottles of urine or acid or get firebombed? Night after night. These activists threaten the police. It must weigh heavily on the police officers; they know that these unknown adversaries will find them and target them and their families. They always have to worry about being a target of violence or assassination, or worse. Do they really think their actions could lead to a dilution, an exodus of officers from the police force?"

Eastwood pocketed the smartphone and uttered to himself, "Inquiring minds want to know who's really orchestrating these protests. Is the Democratic Party playing some role in the growing civil unrest in the cities of America? Is it some lefty billionaire? Or two or three. Or is it something else?" He thought he had an answer. But he wasn't sure. *Could the DNC be behind these protests? I've been to a number of these things, it's always been some Communist Party affiliate like the Revolutionary Communist Party or the American Socialists for Justice who made the signs and distributed them to protestors. Their little red fist—no hammer or sickle stamped in the corner of those posters.* Eastwood frowned. As he walked to the network van, he thought he saw *her.* He caught a glimpse of the dark-haired woman he had exchanged glances with at the Pumpkin Papers Irregulars Dinner leaving the network truck. As she disappeared around a corner, he had a wild thought, *If that was her, then I guess she really was doing journalist work too. I should have spent more time trying to find her and speak with her. But…you have to be very careful getting close to a Russian spy. Bad juju.*

Eastwood kept glancing over his shoulder for another sighting of the dark-haired beauty from Russia Television Network, but no joy. He found the interview vehicle, slipped behind the faux table and fixed himself in a mirror. The media tech lowered behind him a sharp nighttime photograph of National Harbor with its Ferris wheel and the National Gaylord Hotel. He had Eastwood connected to his network inside of sixty seconds. Grateful to be wearing one of his best suits, he remained calm in the hot seat for twenty minutes, which was more time than his producer had anticipated, but it gave him enough workable observations for the evening's news.

Eastwood's producer regretted that not a single protester repeated the rumor that the CIA ran the former president out of office or that someone had executed him in the UAE. He wasn't happy and he let Eastwood have it.

15

October 31
Washington, D.C.

Three men and three women impeccably dressed for the evening waited for one of the elevators to come to the lobby of the Army and Navy Club. As the lift settled to a stop and the doors opened, two of the men held the doors open and allowed the women to enter first. The men were well positioned to steal glances of the bosomy woman in the low-cut little black zipper dress stepping into the elevator car. With long, loose, wavy, raven hair that seemed to fall about nine inches short of her ankles, she was dressed to the nines, with five inches of cleavage held at bay by an oversized zipper pull. A heavy thick scar snaked between the cleft of her breasts, suggesting the woman might have had heart surgery or something worse. While the men and women stole glances at her chest, the woman moved to a place in the elevator car which would hide her face from the elevator's camera and artfully conceal her right leg which was extensively pocked with scars, deep thick marks from the shrapnel of a bomb blast.

The other women, blonde but not as buxom, entered the elevator and glanced at the woman's sparkling diamond earrings and choker necklace. Their blue eyes met her devastating green-platinum eyes with a touch of envy. All but one set of eyes had followed her inside as the men repeatedly strained not to stare at her improbably large bust. Was it unadulterated curiosity that led their eyes to the size of her bosom or the disfiguring scar between her breasts?

She looked straight ahead. If she was a little embarrassed by the unwanted scrutiny she didn't show it. The hairy man was unfazed by the beautiful women. He took a thumbnail and scratched his eyebrow a couple of times while waiting for the door to close. He wore dark Hawaiian sunglasses favored by aging movie stars; his grey hair and nearly two feet of greying beard gave him the look of a contestant from the National Beard and Mustache Contest. He was the most unattractive of the three men, and everyone on the elevator car completely ignored him in favor of the distraction in the little black dress in the corner. He could have had a bloody axe over his shoulder and the response would have been the same. While they overlooked him, they wouldn't look directly at the sculptress either.

Maybe he should get closer to her, but that would mean moving, and he liked where he was. Inconspicuous, with a great view. His head was down, turned away just enough to foil the camera in the elevator control panel but perfectly positioned to marvel upon the woman's curviness, smooth legs, and pretty feet in designer shoes. Maybe he'd try to look at her a little more directly, to see what it was that made people's eyes dart or turn their heads when she moved. Then again, maybe not. He already knew. She dragged her thumbnail across her eyebrow. Once, and then again. It could have been an itch. A little spot needing a tiny scratch. The innocuous gesture was ignored by the men and women on the lift; their eyes were finding purchase elsewhere.

Couple by couple, the men and women stepped off the elevator on succeeding floors until there was just the two of them. *The Beauty and the Beast*. They kept their eyes down, waiting for the doors to open at their floor. They knew where the surveillance cameras were in the hallway and moved gracefully and purposefully to block their faces from being recorded. When the doors finally opened, the woman held her tiny bag to her brow as they passed beneath the silver half-ball containing hallway cameras. He fidgeted with an imaginary zit on his forehead, his hand covering his face. He was limping slightly and struggled to keep up with the woman's purposeful pace. She was obviously in a hurry. She had a spot that needed far more scratching than her brow.

Side by side at the far end of the hallway, they reached the Presidential Suite. He inserted his electronic key into the lock, opened the door, and let her in. He followed and took a longing glance at the small tight derrière in the skin-tight cocktail dress. Her scars didn't register in his mind.

Once the door was closed she turned, pecked him on the lips, scraped his wizard-length beard with a loving finger, and immediately turned away, apologetically. Nazy Cunningham ran to the bathroom squealing, "*I have to pee!*" Her long black hair streamed behind her as if she were face-first in a wind tunnel. She tossed her purse in a chair as she left a trail of heel prints in the carpet. Duncan Hunter's eyes slid down her backside. *The best legs on the planet!*

After weeks of separation, seeing Nazy now in black stiletto heels and a long-sleeved, little black dress with a zipper up the front created a massive chemical reaction in Hunter, like mixing rocket fuel with oxygen for a wildly combustible concoction. All he needed was ignition and that would come when she emerged from the loo. Free of the distraction of surveillance cameras, he was instantly aroused. He locked the door and inspected the room. He pulled out his BlackBerry and took pictures from the four corners of each room. He could hear Nazy finishing up. He knew she wouldn't come out until he said it was safe to do so.

He ignored the Tumi roll aboard and removed a laptop computer and a green donut-looking device from a well-worn Saddleback leather computer bag. He removed his fake teeth and nasal bone prosthetic as he fired up one of the electronic devices and waited for the software to kick in. He connected a USB cable between BlackBerry and laptop, hit a few keys, and waited for the program to do its magic. Hunter pulled glue residue from the nasal bone prosthetic, a counter-facial recognition device designed to radically alter the geometry of the inner corners of the eye. Facial recognition software relied on the two data points as the standard for all additional measurements. Pushing the corners of the eye points outward, where "sleep" accumulated, defeated the software.

The green Growler was in standby, waiting for the opportunity to kill any electronic eavesdropping or surveillance equipment in the suite. Until Hunter returned the computer to its shielded compartment in the computer bag, any hidden cameras would be temporarily disabled; any microphones would be squelched with electronic noise. And any other electronic device in the room would be rendered useless as long as the little green light flashed every six seconds.

The computer program downloaded the pictures from his BlackBerry and compared them with the pictures he had taken immediately before he left the room. The software could detect the tiniest deviation between before and after pictures. Other than his computer bag, nothing had been disturbed.

That was just what he wanted to see. No variations in the photographs told him many things. First, in his disguise he likely hadn't been unmasked. Second, the Army and Navy Club hadn't been compromised since he deposited his luggage in the room prior to attending the Pumpkin Papers Irregulars Dinner. And third, it was probably safe to make love to his wife without worrying about a camera or two. Hunter smiled as he executed a hard shutdown of the computer and took the Growler out of standby. He removed a doorjammer from his bag and blocked the door. If someone wanted to breach the hotel door, they'd have to work at it. He removed his jacket, his shoulder holster, his Submariner, and gold coin cufflinks and set them on the table. Then he peeled off the straggly combination of beard, mustache and sideburns, leaving the nose.

He walked to the bathroom door and knocked. It opened a couple of inches—a broad smirk looked back at him. He whispered in a tantalizing deep Clark Gable, "The coast...is clear...my dear."

Nazy Cunningham stepped out of the bathroom, ignoring him as she walked to the middle of the bedroom. She wanted him to get a good long uninterrupted look. She was naturally bronzed; impossibly beautiful, intoxicating, and alluring. And she had the most amazing eyes he had ever seen. Duncan had always been mesmerized by Nazy's eyes. Green with platinum and silver streaks, they sparkled with a special glossiness. Anyone who looked into her eyes knew immediately she was lively and brilliant. Sometimes he saw fear in them, as if she were still haunted by her past, her enemies, her torturers. Hunter looked for the clues to determine what she was feeling for he'd go to extraordinary lengths to ensure she felt safe and secure for when she felt safe, she'd give herself totally to him.

Hunter shook his head in wonder. Her eyes indicated it would be a good night. The former Muslima who had been sent to spy on him, who had trembled and feared for her life, who had worked like a dog as a CIA analyst for the last fifteen years was now so comfortable in her American skin that she could walk into the middle of a room and wait to be undressed by him alone. Slowly, without worry, in anticipation of what would come.

He ensured his hands were warm as he ran his fingernails across her ass. He kissed her neck and slowly unzipped the LBD, from décolletage to her knees, and let it fall to the floor. She had that come hither look of a steamy starlet and asked warmly, "Were you gazing at my legs?"

Hunter hummed a little reply. He cooed in her ear, "In the interest of complete fairness, I afforded them equal time."

Nazy unbuckled his belt. Before he nibbled on her ear, he whispered in his best dark and husky voice, "What is it about little black dresses that turn men to mush? I so missed you!"

Her eyes telegraphed she wasn't ready. She was distracted by the fake nose and by pieces of adhesive still attached to his face from the fake beard. She picked at him until he was sufficiently clean, then she slowly unfastened his trousers. When they fell to the floor, Nazy turned her head to the side and asked, "Did you call Greg?"

Duncan moaned when she didn't remove the phony nose. Without missing a beat, he bypassed her lips and continued to deliver sweet tender kisses to her arched neck. Between kisses he fiddled with the clasp of the necklace until it was free. He placed the necklace onto his computer. He said, "He knows my number." A bit sarcastic and all too flippant.

Hunter was taken aback when Nazy finally reached up and removed the prosthetic nose, fuzzy eyebrows, and cheek pads as easily as a clown would remove his red rubber, bulbous nose and accoutrements. She flung the masses of latex and hairy brows toward the door. She picked more rubber detritus from his face until it was free of makeup and glue. "That's so much better. Those things are hideous!"

"That's three hours work, gone in an instant, just so I could see you. Worth every second." Hunter smiled mischievously, nodded and thought that he might be able to get her to stop talking about work if he just kissed her. He ran his fingers down her back to her tiny buttocks. She moved under his hands. "It ties the facial recognition systems up in knots. At least, I hope it does." He kissed her. Deeply, passionately, lovingly. Their tongues played sensually. Their fingers were in no rush. The room was heating up quickly.

She pulled away, braced her legs, and ripped off his shirt. Buttons flew across the room. She loved doing that. He looked surprised at the sudden display of power. She gently scolded him, "He'll find out you were in town and didn't call." Then Nazy remembered an embarrassing nugget of intelligence. "Oh, and did you enjoy playing with the breasts of that Iranian woman? *Duncan Hunter!* I thought I was the only woman for you!"

He tried to kiss her to shut her up, change the topic. "I didn't know she was a woman. I was just glad the things strapped to her chest were boobs and not bombs." Nazy's smile telegraphed she had forgiven him. Hunter began to wonder how his wife could have known about that episode when he realized Nazy probably personally debriefed the Iranian intelligence officer he rescued from Iran. *Of course!*

As Nazy removed her earrings, Hunter removed the remnants of his shirt. He kicked off his shoes, stripped off his socks, and kicked his pants that were around his ankles across the room. The bending motion sent a spike of pain through his hip; he tried his best to hide the discomfort but Nazy sensed something was wrong. Wives always know.

"Are you okay?"

Hunter sensed the romantic moment could be gone. "My hip is acting up when I twist or bend the wrong way. I'll be fine."

"So you've seen a doctor?"

"I have prescription meds. I'm okay. Now, how's he going to find out unless you tell him? Besides, if he wants to talk to me, he'll call. He knows my number." Then, sarcastically, "I know I'm number one on his speed dial."

Mindful of the previous pain in his hip, he gingerly dropped to the floor, kissing her torso and tickling the backs of her legs. Then he went for her shoes. Under normal circumstances, removing her shoes as she towered over him would be more than erotic. He was forever-smitten; he could hardly believe that this woman wasn't only his lover, but also his wife. He finished an abbreviated prayer—*Oh, thank you, oh Lord!* He finally got control of his fumbling, bumbling fingers but still could not figure out how to undo the wild crisscrossing straps of her platform sandals; her shoes were simply Gordian, confusing. Distracted by her legs, he ran his hands over them. Nazy had the legs of a tennis professional, firm, taught. They were simply spectacular, even with hundreds of faint scars from being caught in a bomb blast where shrapnel pocked the back of her arms, torso, and legs. He was enjoying the view and was too distracted to figure out how to extricate her feet from her shoes.

Nazy thought he was taking too long. "You do know they have little zippers in the back?" After a few seconds of regaining his bearings, he found the tiny zipper, then unzipped and slipped her shoes off. He stood and she placed her arms over his shoulders. He was fully aroused. She was naked but not aroused. Her mind was still someplace else.

"I think sometimes you and Greg act like children."

Attempting to change her focus, Hunter pressed into her, he nuzzled her ear and neck and buzzed into her ear, "Uh huh. How did you get away?"

"My security detail went home when I was safely in the lobby. I gave them the night off."

He kissed and nibbled her neck. Then he moved his lips to her ear. "That's how Greg will know I'm in town. You get all dolled up and looking like a million bucks. This isn't the uniform to go to the library. They'll have to report you. Obviously you're making contact with someone that won't get put on an official contact list."

"He's happy. Things are quiet in McLean. He hasn't been called before Congress in a while. No one is threatening him with impeachment or accusing him of lying to Congress. We're days away from the election. The only real news is that we received a dispatch...."

Hunter kissed her to stop her from talking. After a minute of tongue play, he pulled away and Nazy continued her thought. "...that the Iranians buried Hammadi, al-Yacoub, Abdullah Ahmed Abdullah, and Ahmed Jibril. Their cause of death wasn't provided."

The information made Hunter pull away, smile and raise an eyebrow. *Holy moly! Those little drones did their job.*

"Greg thought you'd failed. You said in your after action report you never had a clear shot. He growled at me as he has no idea how you did it."

"One of these days I'll tell him."

"The president is ecstatic. That's the last of them."

The last of them; the last of me. They resumed kissing with no more discussion of work.

This was how it had always been, before they were married and after. Hunter would fly into town and as soon as Nazy was able to leave her office or the CIA headquarters compound, they'd meet at The Army and Navy Club, the JW Marriott, or the National Gaylord instead of her house in Bethesda. After several hours of lovemaking, talking, and napping, Hunter would call for room service. Early in the relationship they tried to talk about things other than work, but that proved to be impossible. Sometimes they'd talk national politics but always end up talking about work, which necessitated the use of the Growler.

He had grown into his role as an unofficial intelligence officer without the formal training at Camp Perry. She had renounced her Muslim faith, converted to Christianity, and after an extensive battery of interviews and polygraphs, had become an intelligence officer for the Central Intelligence Agency. Nazy was like a seven-year-old, wide-eyed kid turned loose in a Gummi Bear factory. Counterterrorism was fascinating and exciting, yet mentally tough and challenging. She wanted to share every new experience with Duncan. Without the Growler they couldn't begin to think about sharing intelligence information on terrorists or their organizations.

In the beginning, Hunter knew only tangentially what Nazy was doing for the Agency. He was "just a contract pilot" and had no need to know anything but his next mission. They played the "need to know" game to the letter of the law. Nazy was completely enthralled with learning the art of tradecraft, espionage, running spies, and analyzing or writing top secret documents. She had no clue what Duncan did, other than he was a pilot, and it wasn't good for them to be seen together. So when he was in town, he practiced the tradecraft while she practiced being invisible in little black or white dresses. Since she refused to wear a disguise when Duncan was in town, it was impossible to ignore or miss Nazy Cunningham.

The two lovers had agreed long ago not to disclose their missions until that day Duncan was almost killed by a sniper. Their self-imposed rules changed when Duncan announced that he and Greg Lynche were going to retrieve a very special *tango*, a very special terrorist and do what the previous president, Maxim Mohammad Mazibuike, didn't want the CIA to do. They were going to interrogate the head of the al-

Qaeda terrorist network.

The former president had confirmed on national television that Osama bin Laden had been killed. A few weeks later, after taking custody of one very alive Osama bin Laden from the Navy SEALs who had spirited him out of his Pakistani compound, Hunter and Lynche flew the master terrorist to a remote airfield outside Monrovia, Liberia.

Greg Lynche, Hunter's co-pilot, best friend, and mentor didn't want to have anything to do with what the press called "enhanced interrogation techniques." Duncan Hunter acted as the "bad cop" and offered bin Laden a choice. Since Osama bin Laden was already officially declared "dead" by the American president, Hunter threatened to torture bin Laden with a car battery and jumper cables attached to his testicles. For a little information, bin Laden could avoid the pain and suffering. If he provided simple answers to simple questions, Hunter promised to let him go and put bin Laden "on a jet."

Nazy Cunningham wore an *abaya* and played the "good cop." She counteracted Hunter's systematic aggressiveness and threats of torture as she interrogated the compliant and largely unhurt bin Laden for 12 hours.

Hunter was a man of his word and put bin Laden "on a jet" when they were through. But only Hunter and a Navy SEAL knew the whole truth. The docile and cowardly master terrorist was chloroformed and duct taped to the pilot's seat of an abandoned Russian jet far off in the weeds of the Liberian airport. The Yak-40, still visible from satellite photographs, was the home of rats and itinerant black mambas. No one had been in the aircraft since the former owner and pilot, Viktor Bout, the Merchant of Death, had aborted the takeoff when a flock of white necked ravens flew into the engine intakes. Soviet jets were expendable and airframe carcasses were scattered all across African airports.

Now, the derelict Yak in tall grass contained a carcass.

16

November 1
Washington, D.C.

After room service delivered a cart full of food, they sat in bathrobes at a table for two, legs touching, gently stroking each other. The aroma of the hot breakfast overpowered the remnants of sex in the air. Hunter handed Nazy a full glass of water and lifted his own. Goblets tinkled and they began to eat. He said, "You're hiding one of the Seven Wonders of the World in that robe, Miss Cunningham." As he pointed with his left index finger, the sleeve of his robe slipped above his wrist to reveal the hideous scar where his hand had been reattached.

Nazy smiled and gripped her bathrobe's collar. "This thing swallows me!" Dark red enameled nails contrasted with the bright white bathrobe. She looked at him with her unique smile that was part bashful, part sensual, full of wonder.

Hunter thought, *The first time I saw that particular smile she was in my room at the Naval War College. The second time, she was freezing.*

"I want to go ice skating," she had said. "I may never get another chance." Now that she was unleashed and unburdened from Islam, she had offered that unique smile, a freedom smile. He had never seen anyone like her, and he had seen his share of gorgeous and breathtaking women. He had taken her hand as they stared out his picture window. Over a foot of snow covered the cars in the parking lot, and it was still falling, obscuring the lights of Newport Bridge in the distance. Whoever had answered the telephone at the outdoor rink said they were open.

With no clothes other than her little white dress, he bundled her up in layers of his extra-large, long sleeve T-shirts, sweatshirts, and sweat pants. An oversized yellow Corvette sweatshirt was big enough to contain her very large breasts. Miss Marwa Kamal looked like a long-time resident of a homeless shelter. He worried that she'd get too cold. That she could barely move wasn't the issue. She insisted that she'd be warm enough, even in the subfreezing weather. He used a remote starter switch to fire up his four-wheel drive truck to warm the interior. It took an hour to slog through fresh snow on the previously plowed roads to the skating rink.

She had never been ice skating and was afraid of falling. He comforted her and told her "not to worry." As the Zamboni took the ice, he got down on his knees and laced up her skates; always looking up into her amazing green eyes. When the ice had been resurfaced and free of snow, Hunter took her by the hand and carefully led her out onto the ice. He told her what to do, and she complied, smiling like she was having the kind of fun only a child with new ice skates could have. He bought hot chocolates from a machine, and they shared her triumphs and laughed at her near-spills. She never fell. He was always there to save her.

With her incredible smile that melted his heart she said, "You're an amazing man, Duncan Hunter. I think you really would do anything for me."

It was at that moment fourteen years ago that he became hers forever.

Now she wanted to know what he had been doing in Wyoming, or Texas, or wherever he had been hiding from the people who wanted to kill him. She slid a foot up to his still sticky crotch and grinned. Her robe opened in the front exposing her girls.

He demurred. "You're teasing me. You are an incredible distraction. How does anyone get any work done when you're around? Especially when you're in a dress. I'd have to move my desk to the janitor's closet just so I could concentrate and get some work done. And I know if you were to bend over, I'd fall out of my chair, break my neck. I'd be a permanent fixture on a hospital ward."

She laughed at him. "I wear skirts, Mr. Hunter. Suits. Rarely a dress. You're avoiding me."

Hunter's eyes fell on the wide raised scar that emerged from under Nazy's right breast and extended to her sternum. Bill McGee and Dory Eastwood had worked to reattach her breast after a murderous Muslim troglodyte tried to remove it as a trophy.

He reached for and rubbed her smooth leg. "How could I ever avoid you? I'm worse than Pavlov's dog. You ring and I start to pant."

"You are mine forever, do you know that?" Her kilowatt smile brightened the room.

He nodded and smiled back at her, as if she was being silly.

It was the typical banter whenever they got together after an extended period of separation. Same silly drivel, same old dialogue, like content old married couples. They couldn't get enough of each other, and like two parts of a binary weapon, they generated a lot of heat when they got close. They were soulmates.

Hunter stood and moved to Nazy. He took her hands and brought her to her feet, and she laid her head on his chest. Their movement unleashed new hints of their lovemaking into the air. He untied her robe, stroked her hair with one hand and wrapped his arm around her naked waist to bring her closer. She reached down and dislodged the knot of his belt. Their robes fell. They stood toe-to-toe, embracing tightly. Hunter could feel her heart pounding against his chest. Something was bothering her.

She whispered, "If something were to happen to you I would…just die."

"Oh, Baby…." Hunter buried his face in her hair.

"I don't know if I can do many more of these separations. Greg has me locked up at HQ or at his house. There hasn't been another credible attempt on me in months. I feel safe enough to drive the Mercedes to and from work, but he insists on the security detail. Now that I think they're no longer after me, I worry about you. I can't help but be worried sick about you. They have been unrelenting."

He was reluctant to admit that her analysis of the threat on his life was on target. The attacks from al-Qaeda and the Islamic Underground hadn't only increased year over year but they'd gotten closer to succeeding, learning something new with every failure. He pushed away a bit to look at her watering eyes. "What you're really saying is that it's time. We've done our part—it's time for someone else to take over. Like the guy on the assembly line—he does his part, and then when his shift is over, it's up to others to finish the car. I think I can give it up. We have finished what we started. No more bad guys on the Matrix. So we are done. We can disappear."

Nazy nodded. "That's part of it. Look at us. We're both in hiding. We have a partial life. We can't even live together. Can't trust anyone but ourselves. Are we always going to have a Growler in our room?"

"Greg?"

"You know what I mean. Greg, Bill, and not many others. I think I'm ready to call it quits too. And it may be a *fait accompli* if the president loses and that…*woman* becomes president. You know they'll fire Greg and order his replacement to find you."

"Have you talked to Greg? I'm sure he wouldn't be surprised. Probably supportive."

She held him closer, her breasts still crushed against his chest. There wasn't anything sexual or sensual in her movements. "You probably think I'm losing my mind. What I'm really thinking is they're getting closer to you. To me. To us. The calm before the storm. Don't ask me how or why. It's just dominates my thoughts. I know that if I were looking for someone like you on the dark side of the internet, I'd be able to find you. And quickly."

Sounds like women's intuition. Hunter said, "Like you found bin

Laden."

Nazy nodded. "Everyone leaves a trace. A trail. I know where to look. Know what resources to employ. I thought I'd be able to find you easy and know I've tried. I know Moscow and the DNC have also tried. That is what is so surprising. Why Moscow and why the DNC? We've gone after Islamist terrorists, not Russian spies. I'm convinced a new director would have the whole Agency looking for the man who unmasked Mazibuike."

"Seriously?" Hunter wasn't sure of her hyperbole.

"Baby, I don't think you realize just how massive of a trail you leave wherever you go."

Hunter wasn't being serious. "Greg seems to think I have the carbon footprint of Ouagadougou."

"Not everyone knows where Burkina Faso is and not everyone flies a jet like you do. Jet travel…. That's a huge… *billboard* that screams 'look at me.' It might help you to be safe to move around the country, avoid commercial airlines and airports, but it isn't smart to always travel like that unless you're Mick Jagger. You might be able to hide among the jets of the corporate executives for a time, but someone will figure it out that you are a little different. With pictures. Telephoto lens."

"I do a good job avoiding the communist *Tailwatchers*." He referred to the organization in Moscow dedicated to monitoring the worldwide departures and arrivals of corporate aircraft from jet-capable runways and executive terminals and airports. When leftist and anarchist groups spotted business-type aircraft at an airport and reported it to the *Tailwatchers* website, they instantly received funds electronically for their work. The CIA was horrified when *Tailwatchers* accurately tracked *rendition aircraft*, those aircraft used to move captured, high-value terrorists from the battlefield to an interrogation facility, sometimes in a foreign country, and reported the CIA aircrafts' movements to the media.

Nazy was saddened. "I know, Baby."

Hunter frowned. "I *have* been a bit lackadaisical. Gotten old and indifferent. Maybe thinking I'm bulletproof." He shook his head. Not the discussion he wanted to have, but he knew the day would come when he'd have to change his *modus operandi*. He offered, "I've a couple of new airplanes that aren't as ostentatious as the Gulfstreams…." He sighed, "…and not as fast. But they're nice and I'm sure *Tailwatchers* wouldn't be interested in them."

Nazy nodded, smiled, and said, "No one is bulletproof." It came out almost as a squeak.

The hallmark of an arrogant assassin is they literally or figuratively write the name of their target on a bullet. Airmen in World War II would use spray paint or chalk to write "Hitler" across bombs' noses in the hopes of sending it to the proper address. An assassin's bullet would have their target's name on it, figuratively. So far, Hunter had avoided the assassin's bullet with his name on it. It was always on his mind. *They have gotten close. Too close. Had to move. Sometimes I feel like a Russian defector with the KGB on my ass, always thinking, Will they be able to find me this time?*

Nazy continued, "I can be on the elliptical or the treadmill and I can't help it, my mind wanders and I'm afraid for you. I don't want to lose you."

"I'll be okay, Baby. I promise. I'll find something else to do. Open a gun range or breed big beautiful Friesians. Or Texas Longhorns. I'll name each one after the colors of your nail polish or something."

She couldn't see her husband working in a gun shop, and she didn't know what Friesians were, but she had seen Texas Longhorns. She smiled broadly at the nail polish comment. She continued, "Look at us. We literally have the scars of being caught and...." Nazy couldn't say *dismembered*. She didn't touch his scar, and he didn't touch hers except when they were soaping each other in the shower. She finished, "...they say you can never get away from it. Can we?"

"I know the special ops boys sometimes find it's impossible to get away from it. It's like a narcotic. Like when I flew a fighter. There's nothing like it, and you think you are the luckiest guy on the planet for experiencing something few ever experience. There's nothing like working for the secret government. I know it's like being in a secret society."

Hunter kissed her lightly. "They don't have anything else to go to, so they remain in the business. We, on the other hand, have plenty of things to keep us occupied. We can travel. We have the house in Wyoming. I think that's a good start. There's a mosque in Gillette but nothing in Jackson. They'll have to work at finding me. Then there's the house...it's in Carlos' name and can't be traced to me or the company."

Nazy smiled at the thought of Carlos and Theresa Yazzie, Duncan's dedicated housekeepers, living in Wyoming and taking care of Duncan. *Theresa spoils him with huevos rancheros every day. But they're getting up in age, too.*

Since their prime threat was from Islamists, the implication was that there would be few Islamists to worry about in a place like Jackson Hole, Wyoming, where Islamists didn't have a local base of operations. Generally, the al-Qaeda-types didn't ski in thobes and were more adept at riding camels in desert operations than riding a snowmobile or a T-bar and plowing through feet of snow powder.

She nodded against his chest. "You have two jets. Airports are wide open for someone with a telephoto lens."

Hunter almost ignored the comment. He wanted to discontinue the line of conversation but said, "Yeah, one of these days when we stop working for your place, I'll return the Gulfstreams. I haven't told you I have a couple of *old* executive airplanes I'm restoring. I'm sure you'll love them."

Nazy appeared to sense his discomfort and dropped the topic. She was glad he had been thinking about leaving the CIA.

"Well, Baby. It'll be *a fait accompli* if she wins the election. That's days away. The Democrats think she's a lock for the job, and the Republicans are scared shitless that President Hernandez will lose." Hunter disparagingly referenced Washington Democrats, "The *Dhimmis* have thrown everything they could at him to wound him, disqualify him, kill him politically. You can't tell me the FBI leadership hasn't helped her by refusing to charge her with a crime. There will be hell to pay if the president somehow wins."

Nazy said, "I don't know. Colonel Eastwood's articles have set the media on fire. Will that energy translate to votes?"

"The death threats against the president increase every day. I don't know how he does it; just like I don't know how we do it. I don't think we are the crazy ones."

They held each other tight. They rocked back and forth ever so slightly. Nazy dragged her brilliant red fingernails across Hunter's bare ass just enough to get his attention. She said, "I don't want to leave yet. I want to stay here. Until you have to go." She pulled away from him; she took his hand and never let their eyes break contact. She slowly dragged him to the edge of the bed. She pushed him onto the mattress and then climbed on top of him. They kissed until they fell asleep.

●　　●　　●　　●　　●

Viviana Vaslakova pulled the *shemagh* across her head, nose and mouth, allowing only her eyes to be visible. She admonished herself for losing sight of the journalist Eastwood. He was especially nimble and moved quickly for an older man. Being in the middle of a rock-throwing, bomb-throwing protest wasn't part of her duties. It would only be a matter of time before something bad happened, something that she couldn't control. She'd have to protect herself in the best way she could without a pistol. Some of the old survival training kicked in, primarily her expertise in *krav maga*, the military self-defense and fighting system developed for the Israeli security forces. Any one of the protestors could be wearing a suicide vest, and she didn't want to give crazy American liberals a chance to suck her into their silly movement to be killed or injured by a bomb-throwing or bomb-wearing freak from the Middle East.

Now wasn't the time to get involved. A five-minute hurried walk toward the White House placed her well outside the effective range of any bomb, tossed or worn.

She wedged herself close to the closed door of a Subway sandwich shop. She used her smartphone to summon an Uber cab. One arrived within minutes. From the moment she got in, she knew it was a mistake. She deflated the driver's frequent advances and questioned his circuitous wanderings. The man paid more attention to the rearview mirror than the road. When her smart phone indicated she was close to her hotel, she jumped out of the car when it was stopped at a traffic light.

Viviana Vaslakova, the daughter of former KGB Russian intelligence officers, managed to make it to her hotel suite at the Key Bridges Marriott across the Potomac River from Georgetown. She retired to her room, fired up her computer, and filed her report. She had made contact with Colonel Demetrius Eastwood, however the opportunity to deliver the package didn't present itself. She shutdown her computer. Viviana slipped out of her clothes and drew herself a very hot bath. *Tomorrow would be a better day.*

17

November 4
Mexico

Tired and drenched with sweat, Kelly Horne lined up for her final pass of the night, double checking the GPS to ensure she was properly aligned on the area to be treated. She rolled the aircraft to a tight 30-degree angle of bank turn and mashed the "Fire" button on the control stick to activate the system of lasers. The multi-head ultra-violet laser irradiated a patch of plants, sucking the life out of thousands of baby poppies before they could grow into adult opium-producing plants. Mexican opium poppies were the head of the snake as U.S. counternarcotics organizations worked night and day to stem the headwaters of the heroin trade in the northern hemisphere. Every night that Kelly successfully flew the aerial eradication missions, she eliminated a quarter billion dollars from drug cartels' coffers.

After the prescribed number of minutes irradiating poppy plants, she released the Fire button, relaxed the pressure on the control stick, and rolled wings level. She breathed a sigh of relief and flipped up her night vision goggles.

She was exhausted from the hours of precision flying and fighting the aircraft's controls during the many runs. Her long knotted hair cascading from under her flight helmet and down her back was soaked. The nighttime air should have contributed to smooth flying, but unseasonably high winds and residual thermals had bounced her all over the sky for five straight nights. A former U.S. Air Force jet pilot, Kelly was used to turbulence, but this final night of the mission almost had her reaching for a barf bag.

The YO-3A's seventy-five feet of thin wings provided plenty of lift but also made flying treacherous in high winds. It was like bouncing up and down and side-to-side in an ancient Willy's Jeep on one of Colorado's high-altitude and abandoned mining roads.

Thirty-year-old Kelly was one of the unlikeliest of CIA operations officers fighting the drug wars. Born to a strict evangelical family from Liberal, Kansas, her mother died in childbirth. Red-headed and freckled, Kelly was raised by her grandparents. Grandmother Katherine

Horne had promised her daughter, Kimberly, that she'd never reveal the identity of her baby's father and she nearly took that information to her grave.

Kelly had been a devout Catholic her entire life. She attended the U.S. Air Force Academy, like her mother, and attended Bible studies on campus while others drifted to the sports bars in Colorado Springs that catered to the cadet crowd. But Kelly had always wondered who her father was, and remarkably, found the answer upon her grandmother's passing. Her mother's diary was in her grandparents' estate. It opened the door to the 25-year-old mystery. She found a single name in the story of how her mother met a most fascinating man. Kelly tracked him down. It was more than a coincidence that her father was an adjunct professor teaching a college course at the Air Force base where she was assigned as a flight instructor. She was convinced God had a hand in it.

She thought her father was a very impressive man. Smart, articulate, good looking. He was well respected among his students. He had a good, but sometimes incisive sense of humor. She had been extremely nervous when she decided to tell him who she was. She had done it quickly before either of them could turn and run away. She had convinced herself, *I can tell him. I can tell him. I want him to know. It'll be ok!* Kelly had taken one deep breath and then another. Her adrenaline spiked and sent her heart racing as she blurted, "My mother was Kimberly Horne, and I'm your daughter."

Although Duncan Hunter had been shocked, he knew the charge must be true and embraced her with open arms. He broke the protocol and told his daughter who he worked for, that his businesses, and lecturing, and teaching graduate school were only his cover. Thinking there had to be more to life than training student pilots for the Air Force, Kelly badgered her father to help get her into the Agency.

A retired CIA executive facilitated Kelly's entry—just like Hunter had done one winter day for Nazy. The CIA had turned the Jordanian refugee and Islamic Underground defector, Marwa Kamal, into Nazy Cunningham, Intelligence Officer and Near East Analyst, and they turned the Air Force pilot, Kelly Horne, into an operations officer in the National Clandestine Service. Special Activities Division. Air Branch.

Her specialized flying skills were always in demand. There was often a call for the pretty, freckled girl with the ginger hair to fly some executive, some cargo, or some aircraft to places with landing strips that barely qualified as runways. She did it expertly, without comment or concern, and often in the dead of night. The quiet, Bible-carrying, cross-wearing Kelly Horne was also on the front lines of the war on drugs, killing drug crops beginning at midnight. Discovery of the operation would likely have fatal consequences.

Before executing a *Weedbusters* run, Kelly always checked the surrounding area with the FLIR to ensure that there were no thermal images of humans within miles of the poppy fields. The rationale for thoroughly checking the area for people came down to one hard fact: if someone on the ground had their eyes damaged from the operation, it would indicate a laser was being used in the area. Her cover would be blown, and the secret aerial eradication mission would be compromised.

The concept of using the YO-3A, a low-level and virtually silent airplane from the Vietnam era was fitted with a drug-crop-killing laser that couldn't be detected visually. The combination of aircraft and laser system was a unique and tremendous drug war fighting capability. The program was more successful than their creators ever imagined. But all that success came with several challenges. If poppy, cannabis, or coca farmers came up blind or with "welder's flash," a temporary partial-blindness condition, it would be sure to arouse the suspicion of the drug cartels. Nothing says, "special operations are being conducted here" like inadvertent blindness from a laser source. The cartels would spend whatever was necessary to find the source that created blindness—however temporary—and exterminate it. The cartels were known to go to extraordinary lengths to protect their operations.

The prime reason for the *Wraith's* success as the ultimate drug crop eradication tool was that it left no trace, no "fingerprints." No human could detect the aircraft aurally; no human could detect the UV laser beam visually, and the *Weedbusters* system didn't leave any residue. What it did leave in its wake were dead or dying plants, poppies that appeared to be sick, opium poppies that shriveled up and turned brown. It was as if all of the moisture had been sucked out of the little baby plants.

A quiet aircraft and its powerful laser system was the perfect combination to find and over-irradiate the alkaloid-producing plants before they reached maturity. Every night, Kelly irradiated puny poppy plants by the tens of thousands, effectively breaking off a major branch of the drug trafficking tree.

During a week-long counternarcotics air campaign, Kelly pulverized hundreds of acres of drug crops and determined the coordinates of the cartel labs used to process opium and deadly heroin derivatives. The CIA Chief of Station handed the specific coordinates of the drug labs to his Mexican counterpart, and the Mexican Air Force targeted and bombed the opium-processing labs. Their successes weren't normally found in the pages of the local newspapers. The Agency connection was never made.

At the controls of the YO-3A, Kelly Horne had a very narrow window of opportunity to be effective. She had to fly at the lowest possible speed, at the optimum altitude, using an exact laser wavelength with longest possible dwell time. If she flew too fast the plants wouldn't receive the required dwell time to kill them; too slow, the airplane would fall out of the sky. At low altitude, with no altitude to inflate a parachute, falling out of the sky would be fatal.

Kelly pitched off her final run, and stowed the *Weedbusters* laser system, but not the FLIR. She slowly combed the sides of the mountainous valley looking for the telltale heat signatures of narco-terrorists cooking narcotics at night. She located several labs in the jungle and an underground staging facility. Kelly marked them on the aircraft's on-board videorecorder, then turned and headed for the Mexican air base. She retracted the FLIR, engaged the autopilot, and flipped her ANVIS-9 night vision goggles over her eyes. She was back in the world of thirty shades of green. Kelly was sweating profusely even with the aircraft's air vents fully open.

She left poppy farmers to try and explain the amorphous patches and stench of thousands of dying poppies to their narco-terrorist masters. There were healthy plants next to patches of sick plants. There was no clue what had caused the widespread blight.

The drug cartels would be quick to believe Americans, beginning with the CIA and ending at the State Department, were using crop dusters at night; spraying fields with herbicides, just as the Russians had done some thirty years ago in Afghanistan. But no one ever saw or heard any aircraft, and poppy farmers never found the telltale herbicide residue on any of the affected immature poppies. The problem was widespread but not consistent with strip crop dusting, suggesting it had to be some disease. Some plants were sent off to laboratories. Biologists would say the leaves had all their moisture sucked away, maybe even boiled off. The findings were simply unbelievable. It was as if moonlight had scorched the plants to death.

The Mexican military and the DEA didn't go after the farmers who were growing opium poppy. Farmers were compelled to grow the drug crop. Farmers who balked at serving the drug cartels found their sons murdered or their wives and daughters pressed into the sex trade.

After landing, Kelly was grateful that the week-long mission was over. It had been one of the smoothest short-notice *Weedbusters* missions she had ever accomplished. The YO-3A and its suite of sensors had performed flawlessly. The mothership, a U.S. Air Force cargo aircraft, had been completely responsive and on time. The disassembly of the YO-3A's wings and disconnecting the flight controls were choreographed as well as any NASCAR pit crew at Talladega. In less than five minutes, the *Wraith* crew, the Bobs—Bob Jones and Bob Smith—had removed the wings and rolled the YO-3A back into its container in the rear of the C-130 *Hercules*. Kelly handed a video-recording tape of the flight to the eagerly awaiting Chief of Station. He thanked her profusely and promised the information on the laboratories would get into the proper hands.

After takeoff in the C-130, Kelly Horne left the cockpit of the Hercules, thanking the aircrew for their work and professionalism and found a seat near the Bobs, who were perusing a local newspaper. She chatted with them for a minute and thanked them for their help. She was exhausted. She put on noise-cancelling headphones and a sleep mask. Kelly was asleep seconds after climbing atop a sleeping bag spread across a row of troop seats.

Bob Jones showed Bob Smith a couple of articles. The first was indirect evidence of the success of Kelly Horne's first mission. The second was a topic being replicated across the planet.

•   •   •   •   •

MEXICO CITY (Reuters) - Mexican marines said they'd discovered an underground drug lab in the mountains outside the capital of Sinaloa state where they destroyed 50 tons of methamphetamine. "Marines found the lab after intelligence reports indicated that tons of drugs were being produced in the area of Alcoyonqui municipality, about 12 miles (19 km) outside the state capital of Culiacan," the ministry of the navy said in a statement. In photos provided by the ministry, two marines in hazmat suits can be seen examining dozens of plastic containers in a mountain forest.

The statement said the drugs were hidden underground in two areas, along with barrels of the chemicals used to produce meth. The drugs were incinerated on site due to the difficult access of the remote location, the ministry said. Mexico is a major supplier of methamphetamine to the United States and is the top source of heroin, which is fueling a surge in opioid addiction. The country is also the principal highway for cocaine trafficked north. Sinaloa is the seat of the powerful cartel formerly run by Joaquin "El Chapo" Guzman, who's facing trial in the United States.

KIEV (Reuters) - Ukraine's security service said it had captured a Russian military intelligence hit squad responsible for the attempted murder of a Ukrainian military spy in the run-up to the presidential election.

The issue of how to deal with Russia, which annexed Crimea in 2014 and backs pro-Russian separatists in eastern Ukraine, is prominent ahead of the vote, with the incumbent Petro Poroshenko casting himself as the commander-in-chief Ukraine needs to defend the country.

Vasyl Hrytsak, the head of the SBU, the main intelligence agency, told a news conference in Kiev that seven members of the Russian group had been detained and charged and that an eighth person had been detained.

A spokesman for Ukraine's security service has reported before that it has captured groups belonging to Russian special agencies. "Those detained were involved in the attempted murder of an employee of the Ukrainian defense ministry's intelligence service...in Kiev in April. The group had planted a bomb beneath the man's car which had gone off prematurely, badly injuring one of the accused." The Ukrainian security service released a video from a security camera of the same incident which showed a man placing the bomb under a car before a big explosion. The video showed a man lying in a hospital bed with part of his right arm missing saying he was Russian and born in Moscow.

18

November 6
Washington, D.C.

The two women looked at each other as they heard a vehicle come to a stop in the rain just outside the apartment. They jumped when they heard car doors slamming. The older woman, the mother-in-law, was a Navy veteran who supervised casualty notification visits. She had conducted many; the worst ones were during thunderstorms when a pilot or an aircrew tangled with the winds, lightning, and hailstones of an unexpected storm and lost. With more curiosity than trepidation, she quickly stood and moved to the French doors.

Times like these were always troublesome. Her son was "in the Middle East," that was nearly all the information that he'd be able to tell his mother and his wife. They'd become used to living with the knowledge that he had been a United States Navy SEAL; on call 24/7 to confront the enemies of America, but would never reveal where in the world he'd be. Now he worked for one of the intelligence agencies. They knew which one.

She pulled the curtain aside to see two men walking toward the front door of the house. Her last conscious thought was that her son had lost his life. She fainted and collapsed in a heap between tables and chairs, miraculously avoiding injury.

The younger mother, Amy May, wasn't new to the game of midnight casualty visits either. She ran to her mother-in-law, clutching her infant, and trembled with fear. All signs pointed to something horrible had happened to her husband. She wanted to scream, "No! No!" and reject the spurious sounds outside as innocuous. She hadn't received a call. There hadn't been a knock at the door. It could still be a false alarm. Or maybe the duty officer charged with notifying the next of kin was going next door to the apartment across the walkway.

When three raps on the door reverberated in the room, she broke down on her knees and wailed. The knocks could only mean one thing — her husband was dead, and two men were bringing her the news that would shatter her life forever. Amy couldn't bear to walk to the door and let them in. She wouldn't open the door. She could avoid them and did. She moved to the sofa and sobbed, staring at the door as her baby cried.

But the door opened and *he* entered the apartment. *He* didn't say anything. *He* looked right at her and she knew who *he* was: Frank's boss. The Director of the National Clandestine Service, Steve Castaño. She looked for answers in his dark eyes and found nothing but emptiness. She didn't like the man, Frank's big boss. Never did. Castaño always stared at her boobs full of milk, and he always gave her the creeps. Her husband didn't like him either, but he was the boss, and it was better to deploy to faraway shithole countries and make 115% of his base pay than deal with the man's reported erratic behavior and lunacy.

Castaño didn't apologize for picking the lock outside, for entering her house, or for interrupting her privacy. He said, "Amy, Frank is missing. So you know why I'm here." He pointed at her, warning her. "I don't want any hysterics from you." He looked over at the mother-in-law in a heap of nightgown and terry cloth robe. He didn't care. He had a job to do.

She couldn't move; she stared at him with loathsome eyes. He had no heart, he was unable to say comforting words to the grieving wife, the potential grieving widow. His scarred hands were the hands of a demon. He was raw evil invading her home when her husband was on a mission to "who knows where." She knew where, and that made the unannounced visit especially painful. The families of CIA operations officers didn't get a visit from the director unless it was to announce a loved one had died on some remote or secret battlefield. There would be no mention that the Agency might not ever be able to recover Frank's body. Such were the pitfalls of intelligence work overseas.

He waved his scarred hands around like he was framing a picture, developing a plan to start his search for anything of value which might prove useful to a foreign agent. Castaño knew where to look. Like previous DDOs and National Clandestine Service Directors had done before him, he found the hiding places and safes. He found the obvious things he needed to confiscate—a laptop computer which went into an old doctor's folding bag. Castaño found a two-drawer file cabinet and emptied the contents into an orange plastic bag he pulled from under his raincoat. He found a day-planner, and it too was tossed into the orange bag. Anything and everything that could be used to incriminate the CIA.

Castaño tore through the house while the mother-in-law still lay unconscious on the living room floor. He searched drawers, closets, and the like for weapons or notes or books. He worked around the older woman, bumping her with his foot to rouse her. Without saying goodbye or that Castaño would be in touch when he received more intelligence regarding the status of her husband, he left.

When the door closed behind Castaño, Amy broke down and cried. Her baby, little Frankie, wailed along with her.

19

November 6
Washington, D.C.

"The Islamic Underground is a terrorist organization and it has infiltrated the U.S. government," announced the Director of the Central Intelligence Agency. Greg Lynche's opening statement before the United States Senate Select Committee on Intelligence wasn't wholly unexpected. However, his tone carried a measure of concern and warning. "The Islamic Underground has become highly skilled in infiltrating our institutions and exploiting the civil liberties afforded to Americans. Their sole purpose is to destroy the United States. They understand they can't defeat America through violence, so they have adopted a long view. Infiltration. They have a strategic plan and they're following it to a 'T'."

"Well prior to the morning of September 11, 2001, members of the Islamic Underground had worked for many years spreading out across America, finding work in American airports and settling into senior airport security positions. While some learned to fly airplanes, others performed passenger and cargo screening services. They facilitated the tragedies in New York City, Washington, D.C., and near Shanksville, Pennsylvania. As a consequence of the Islamic Underground's infiltration of airport security across the country, the United States government federalized airport security. You have the secret volume of the 9/11 Commission Report. You know this to be true. There should be no question about their will to infiltrate other sectors of our many security agencies and programs. They are relentless."

"There should also be no question how and why our former president facilitated the hiring and placement of some 30,000 members of the Islamic Underground into key and top level jobs in government and the intelligence community. Through a cleverly articulated, government-mandated 'diversity hiring program,' human resources managers were forced to hire controversial employees with questionable backgrounds and suspicious histories."

"All across the heartland of America and from coast to coast, the Islamic Underground has achieved significant success in infiltration, bringing the *shariah*. The Islamic Underground's clandestine spy network has threatened and blackmailed corporate executives, journalists, and government employees mostly along east and west coast regions. They have kidnapped, detained, and threatened family members to facilitate entry into buildings, newsrooms, and government facilities. And like they did with the airport security firms prior to September 11, they have thoroughly infiltrated the United States government and its many departments. With the tacit approval of President Mazibuike, they have been especially successful in penetrating the intelligence community."

One Democrat senator after another attempted to cut off the DCI's statement. Lynche tuned out the group of senators who interrupted when one nearly jumped to his pigeon toed feet to claim control of the microphone. Lynche strained to keep a straight face. He recalled breaking out in laughter when Duncan Hunter called the senator, "Jerry Waddler; not the Burgess Meredith 'Penguin' *waddler* but more the Danny DeVito 'Penguin' *waddler*. That man's an imbecile."

The chairman of the Senate Select Committee on Intelligence admonished the members of the committee. He was forced to pound his gavel several times to restore order. Once calm was restored, he asked CIA Director Lynche to continue.

A striking red-headed woman of about thirty entered the hearing room. Dressed in a neat, dark, form-fitted business suit, she negotiated through the reporters and onlookers and directly approached the Director's table. She handed Lynche a note which he immediately read. As he pushed his chair back, he asked the chairman to be excused and for the hearing to be rescheduled. Before the gavel was struck adjourning the hearing, Greg Lynche and his aide rushed out of the door.

The CIA Director's sudden departure from the halls of Congress sparked curiosity from the audience and sent the committee, journalists, and visitors in the chambers into a frenzy.

• • • • •

The *Bad to the Bone* ringtone resonated loudly in the underground room, drowning out Boney M's *Rasputin* playing in the background from an ancient Bose Wave music system. Duncan Hunter immediately placed his hand out as a micro rotorcraft with four tiny rotor blades landed in the palm of his hand. The miniature rotor blades stopped, and the green light on the side of the device blinked off. He was momentarily annoyed at the interruption, for by the sound of the ringtone he knew who was calling and it made him smile. *It was about time.*

He quieted the music after its energetic finish.

Ra Ra Rasputin, Lover of the Russian queen
They didn't quit, they wanted his head.
Ra Ra Rasputin, Russia's greatest love machine,
And so they shot him till he was dead.

The numbers on the BlackBerry's tiny screen read 0000. Whatever code was transmitted on the cell carrier, he knew it to be the private office number of the Director of the Central Intelligence Agency. Duncan Hunter pushed a Bluetooth earpiece into his ear, and pressed the BlackBerry's connect key. He said, "Hello, good sir. I didn't expect you." He placed the little helicopter on the workbench.

His words echoed in the spacious basement. The genteel but annoyed raspy voice of Greg Lynche came through the tiny speaker in his ear, "I need you."

"I'm retired. You killed me off, remember? Technically, I can't even vote now." He unholstered a matte black Colt Python revolver from under his arm.

"I'm still buying your fuel. You owe me." Two-thousand miles away, the DCI grinned and breathed a sigh of relief. *He didn't yell at me.*

Hunter grinned at being reminded and reprimanded. "You have a point. This must be important. I didn't think you wanted to talk to me." He checked the laser sight by aiming the weapon at the nearest wall. Hunter opened the cylinder to ensure there were five rounds and no bullet lined up with the barrel. He lovingly admired both sides of the weapon before placing it on the workbench, cylinder open, and then listened for his best friend to speak. He knew Lynche would take some time to grovel so Hunter went to work on servicing his gun.

In the world of revolvers, the Colt Python was undisputedly the most beautiful revolver ever made. One of seven Colt handguns named after snakes, the six-shot Python was a beefy, all steel revolver chambered in .357 Magnum. A full length ventilated rib ran the length of the barrel, all the way to the muzzle, leading to the sloping front sight. Pythons were made the old fashioned way. Parts were fitted by hand by a skilled machinist with the eye and patience of a watchmaker who would take the time to perfectly match, adjust, and polish the fifty-seven parts that made up a Colt Python until everything fit perfectly. The pistol's black grips could have been mistaken for rubber but were rare Gabon ebony. Hunter was sure there was an environmentalist somewhere who would have squealed his displeasure at the cosmetic use of the beautiful jet-black unstriated wood. He treated the metal parts of the Python with gun oil and rubbed the grips with linseed.

Hunter could hear Lynche's breathing, but there were no hints of an apology. He returned the Python to the shoulder holster and then connected the four-rotor device with a USB port to charge its battery. He smiled at the little invention his scientists in Texas had built. Hunter waited for the conversation to resume.

"You think too much. Yes, it's important. Pack your trash, *Maverick*." Hunter pulled one side of his mouth into a vicious grin. *Trash* was Hunter's catch-all word for his flight gear and a "go-bag." It was some of the vernacular the old spook at the other end of the line had picked up from the old fighter pilot. Lynche wasn't off the hook.

"Yes, sir. Will we need Bullfrog?" Hunter used the call sign of the legendary U.S. Navy SEAL, Bill McGee.

"Not this time."

Hunter was surprised. *A solo mission. Hmmm.* "Okay…. Greg, a couple of things."

"Go!" Lynche was annoyed but didn't mince words.

"You need me, I need something. I have to know that there will be no NCS, no SAD, no SOG involved." Hunter spelled out the acronyms for emphasis.

The demands set the CIA Director back on his heels and torqued his jaws. *That shit about the NCS again? He's still paranoid that someone inside the Agency is out to get him?* Lynche shook his head and took inventory of the men involved on the impending mission. This was a "pop-up." There really wasn't anyone from the National Clandestine Service, Special Activities Division, or Special Operations Group involved with this operation…with two exceptions—the NCS Director, who was also the Deputy Director of Operations (DDO), and his personal aide, Hunter's daughter Kelly Horne. The NCS Director shouldn't be an issue. Although he was one of the most trusted men in the CIA and the national intelligence apparatus, the man was a few months away from scheduled retirement. The man was acting more like he was already retired than still on active duty. *On the road.* Lynche said, "You got it, *Mav*. I'll get a PPR for you for Andrews." Prior permission required was necessary to land at the sprawling Air Force Base.

"Thank you."

"Hurry. *Wraith* is inbound. I think it's a four-hour trip. What's your ETA?"

"I'll find a healthy tailwind. See you in three."

"See you on the ramp."

•　　•　　•　　•　　•

All of the men and some of the women in the gym of the National Counter Terrorism Center endeavored to remain focused on their own workouts and keep their eyes from wandering across to the woman on the elliptical. It wasn't odd for the NCTC Director to be in the exercise room during the lunch hour but maintaining ones composure when *she* was "in the house" wasn't easy. If she moved suddenly, everyone in the gym who was watching her would jerk, as if a minor electric shock had collectively zapped everyone in the room. Eyes would race to follow her movement, or to catch her eye, or get a glimpse of her bosom. Men who wouldn't normally be found in a fitness center were motivated to get to the gym by the curvaceous woman. As for the women in the room, they wondered *How could anyone be born with those looks?*

They'd been jealous of her, not only for her appearance but for her successes. Most career intelligence officers could chalk up one or two significant achievements in career, episodes worthy of a medal or citation. Her record was one of unimaginable monthly achievements where medals, citations, and promotions just became insufficient awards for incredible work. Nazy found Osama bin Laden hiding in Pakistan. She located the missing weapons of mass destruction from Iraq in Syria. She found the Iraqi general in charge of Saddam Hussein's procurements who kept meticulous records on all illegal and embargoed transactions. And she interrogated the worst of al-Qaeda and the Taliban. Nazy Cunningham became the go-to person for any problem deemed improbable or impossible or too difficult for a man to do.

Like every day she went to the fitness center, her voluptuous body was covered, this time by peach-colored yoga pants and a matching long-sleeved top. The woman with the ridiculously long black hair worked the elliptical hard, pulling on the counter-oscillating bars opposite of the deep steps. Every day she wore a new hairstyle— sometimes it was straight and pulled back over her ears, sometimes it was braided in a multitude of different ways, sometimes it was just tied in a huge knot, and sometimes she wore it curly. On rare occasions she wore it up on her head, skewered in place with crochet needles. Her hips rocked back and forth with every cycle of the exercise machine; her long hair tied in an elaborate string of knots created a perfect sinusoidal wave across her back.

She flaunted the length and volume of her hair, a simple but emphatic rejection of her Muslim heritage when she was forced to wear the veil and cover every strand of hair that tried to escape the headscarf.

Muslim women were proud of their hair and often grew it to extraordinary lengths. They found creative ways to bundle or knot their hair under billowy hijabs as an unsubtle protest to the Islamic dress codes of fundamentalist imams while mocking the local modesty police in their own way.

She had rejected the change in Islamic tradition, forced upon women after the 1976 Iranian revolution. After years of enjoying western attire—dresses, skirts, and slacks—it became a crime to expose bare legs and arms. Nazy went so far as to expose her breasts in public at an outdoor hookah bar, yelling at her cheating cruel husband that "he'd never see them again." She took the next jet out of Jordan for America to start a new life where there were no prohibitions against a woman's hair and she could let her hair down without fear of being chastised or beaten or have acid thrown into her face.

Nazy often seemed to be an otherworldly presence, a creature of such off-the-charts pulchritude that the humans around her were exposed for what they were: human, all too human. She was oblivious to the clandestine stares. She ignored her surroundings and just worked out reading something non-fiction from her office library as tiny ear buds piped in The Moody Blues, *The Other Side of Life*. She was a breathtaking woman who just wanted to work and to be invisible.

Nazy was startled by her pager flashing and vibrating on her book, she dismounted the exercise machine. She recognized the number. The boss. She fished her BlackBerry from her gym bag and called the DCI's office. Sweat dribbled down her back and between the cleft of her breasts as she waited for the encryption to work and connect the telephones. She toweled her face and neck as Lynche said without salutation, "I'm meeting Duncan at Andrews in about three hours. I think you can help, if you can get away."

Her heart jumped. "I will clear my schedule."

"I assume you have a go bag."

She said, "I do."

"Good. My office as soon as you can. I have to read you in."

Unconsciously she nodded her answer before articulating it.

Nazy was taken aback when Lynche asked for some personal information. "Nazy, I think you and Connie are about the same size. I'm sure you're a size four or six; five ten-ish, boot size seven and a half...eight." He tried to find the right wording for the next question.

With a frown Nazy asked, "Are you fitting me for a uniform or a coffin?"

Lynche said, "Flight suit. We're going to Amman. The Air Force wanted to know if we needed flight suits, and I said yes. So I need your height, your inseam, and I'm a little embarrassed to say, I also need your bust size. Flight suits for women are made different than men's."

She told him her Betty Brosmer-like measurements without thought or concern or embarrassment and confirmed her shoe size.

He thought, *Wowzers.* His eyes did loop-the-loops. *That woman is going to kill me one of these days…. So glad she's "family."* He said, "Thank you, Nazy. Bring your passports. See you shortly. Be careful, it's raining and the roads are slick."

20

November 6
Over the Appalachian Mountains

Demetrius Eastwood was enjoying the first class accommodations aboard the American Airlines 737. He could get some work done aboard the jet. With no seat partner, he used the additional space for his computer bag. As his laptop fired up, he pulled a couple of paper files from his bag for reference. He scribbled some notes in the margins as reminders to insert a line or consider deleting a phrase. Once his computer was connected to the internet via ViaSat, he checked his email. He expected junk mail, spam, trash, pleas for money from Nigerian princes, and tips from other writers and journalists.

His inbox announced new mail from his friend Mary Katherine Wentworth, an award-winning chief intelligence and Pentagon correspondent. Her connections within the Department of Defense and the intelligence community were tight, unimpeachable. She was the approved correspondent for the CIA, NSA, NGA and all of the three-letter guys in the IC whose business was to make secrets, keep secrets, or to steal secrets. He could barely believe what he was reading. *Another one? Two?*

Of the first article, Mary Katherine reported, "On the eve of a planned meeting with the U.S. Justice Department, the former media tsar of the Russian Federation was found dead in his Du Pont Circle hotel room in Washington, DC. The official cause of Mikhail Globloshnik's death was ruled as accidental suicide 'due to a series of drunken falls after days of excessive consumption of alcohol.'"

Her email continued, "Two FBI agents, new to the case, cast new doubts on the U.S. government's official explanation of his death. The investigation continues."

Eastwood read the rest of the email. "Washington DC police publicly declared that during a three-year investigation, none of the twelve suspicious deaths of foreign nationals on American soil involved foul play." *Twelve? There's only been twelve? Officially? I know of thirty! In D.C. alone. Another twenty in New York City.*

Mary Katherine provided, "U.S. intelligence officials privately suggested that many of those deaths had been linked to Russian mafia gangs or security services. The public has been kept in the dark about what national security officials have long suspected: Russian assassins may have murdered their turncoats in the U.S. with impunity."

He mouthed, *"No shit, Sherlock!"* he turned to the next article provided by Mary Katherine. "Law enforcement officials have finally ruled that the accidental death of the Russian defector and dissenter, Yuri Raschtipov, on Valentine's Day in Philadelphia, Pennsylvania, has been ruled a suicide. The coroner's office contend Raschtipov was depressed and despondent, likely from his failure to sell hundreds of top secret documents that he personally stole from Russia's Central Committee (RCC) archives. During a February press conference, Raschtipov claimed that the RCC documents demonstrated, irrefutably, that American politicians, networks, and the Democratic National Committee were willingly and repeatedly working on behalf of and colluding with Russian intelligence services during America's presidential elections. He said, 'The major publishing houses said they were interested in publishing the archives but demanded that I needed to fundamentally alter its content by downplaying the infiltration of America and her allies by Russia. This I couldn't do.' Raschtipov insisted the archives demonstrated the decades-long extensive infiltration of the U.S. government and the media by the Soviet Union and then the Russian Federation, and that stripping any reference to infiltration or media influence would render the documents useless. When no American publisher would touch the archives, Raschtipov was compelled to walk away and go into hiding."

"The stolen documents told the story of the men and women who engaged in collusion between America's major networks, the U.S. government and Russia's Central Committee. One secret RCC document from a presidential election detailed secret collaboration between the Democrat president, the networks, and the Soviet Union to boost the candidate's popularity, advance highly questionable political objectives, and trick Americans into liking communist Russia. Other documents of that era detailed how the Democrat president secretly collaborated with the Russian president to limit America's nuclear weapons."

When Eastwood reached the end of the email he screwed his face into a tornadic scowl. He said with a heavy dose of sarcasm, "I could be wrong, but I think it's very difficult for a death to be a suicide when there are multiple blunt-force injuries to the head, neck, and torso."

The official findings of the two cases of suicide left Eastwood thinking, and he replied to Mary Katherine Wentworth, "Those are complete BS. It's obvious they were bludgeoned to death. No one with two brain cells to rub together would believe those guys got drunk, fell down, and died. What are their history? I think they were whacked, and that either Vladimir or the SVR were behind it."

He said to himself, dejectedly, "Add these to the list. A pair of Russians assassinated." He filed them under, *Political Assassinations. Numbers 31 and 32.*

When Mary Katherine Wentworth didn't immediately respond, Eastwood moved to other emails and deleted the majority of them. He came to an article forwarded by an unknown sender, but he hesitated to kick it into the spam file. He questioned the validity of the Subject line: Must Read. He tentatively opened the email hoping his anti-virus and anti-spyware software would catch and kill any hidden bug. When the email opened Eastwood was both relieved and intrigued. Unsigned, the email appeared to have been a copy of a copy of a copy. The original came directly from the National Security Council. *Was this a leak?* Eastwood rarely received "leaked information." He read on.

"'Political warfare' doesn't concern activities associated with the American political process, but is one of the five components of a communist insurgency. In Communist insurgencies, the formation of a counter-state is essential to seizing state power. Functioning as a hostile state acting within an existing state, it's an alternate infrastructure. This approach envisions the direct use of non-violent operations, arts, and tactics as elements of combat power. Political warfare methods can be implemented at strategic, operational, or tactical levels of operation."

"Political warfare is combat by administrative means. They principally operate through documents and narratives. Because the left is aligned with Islamist organizations at local, national and international levels, recognition should be given to the fact that they seamlessly operate through coordinated synchronized narratives. They operate in social media, television, the 24-hour news cycle in all forms of media. This is the world of the 'dark state.'"

Eastwood said aloud, "This is the world of the 'dark state.'" *Is this…is this what's going on between the Republicans and Democrats, between the conservatives and the liberals? Not just politics as usual but political warfare? I think I could make a good case today's Democrats aren't 'Kennedy's Democrats;' they have been hijacked by the communists and socialists, while today's Republicans are Democrat-light.*

He hadn't ever heard the term "political warfare" used in such a context. Nor had he heard of the "dark state." But it made him think about the political reality of Washington D.C. and establishment politicians. *The communists, the Marxists, the left have become more aligned with Islamist organizations at local, national and international levels.* But that's common knowledge if you have a top secret security clearance and hang out with in-the-know Republicans.

Eastwood had always suspected Islamic Underground infiltration, but there had been no proof. Few people outside the intelligence community knew that Senator Maxim Mohammad Mazibuike, before he became President Maxim Mohammad Mazibuike, had been a clandestine member of the Islamic National Party and that all of his senatorial staff members were also Islamic National Party or members of the Islamic Underground. The media longed to brush up against the hem of his perfectly pressed garments; they have been complicit in hiding the truth, especially political truth. Political truth would give the papers and the networks the vapors. They ignored the truth.

The pretty flight attendant came by, picked up his glass, and reminded him that they were about to land. Eastwood closed his laptop and slipped a twenty dollar bill into her apron pocket. He received a ten-dollar smile in change.

21

November 6
Hondo, Texas

The petite dark-haired waitress in a bright flowery Mexican costume set down a large bowl of chips and salsa and two miniature pitchers of ice water. Letty Pineda smiled and caught herself before welcoming the white man in Spanish. "Welcome to the *Azteca*; may I take your order?" She had an old blue Bic poised above the pale yellow guest check pad.

The man smiled and made subtle gestures and murmurs that he was still perusing the menu, but that he was close to choosing something. Letty had no other tables at the moment so she waited.

The big burly African-American man with him was a regular. He said in the deepest baritone anyone in town had ever heard, "My usual, Letty." He'd usually come with other big burly men. Mostly in twos, rarely in threes, never in fours. Men of different races and skin tones. Even the black men were heavily tanned, as evidenced by two-toned oversized biceps poking out of their uniform white polo shirts. He would come two, sometimes three times a week to the *Azteca*. He didn't miss Fridays when the *carne asada* fajita salads were the special.

He and his friends always carried pistols. Big black pistols. Other men who came into the restaurant also carried pistols on their belts. Sometimes they wore a badge and a grey "cover" of the Texas State Troopers. The big black man always wore a silver-white cowboy hat and took the rear-most booth where he could look out of the window toward the street from Hondo's downtown hole-in-the-wall, the *El Restaurante Azteca*. His silver belly Resistol John Wayne War Wagon sat on the seat next to him. The best Texas cowboy hats had the best names.

This time, like all the other times, he brought a small but conspicuous thing which could have easily been mistaken for a toy. A light-neon green, rubberized device the size and shape of a donut also had a pulsating green light. It was placed in the middle of the table. The "Growler" generated a bubble of electronic noise and prevented anyone and anything from electronically eavesdropping on a conversation. If anyone tried, the only sound they'd hear was a growl reminiscent of a Rottweiler guarding his food dish. Adjacent cell phones were rendered useless. Television pictures became snowstorms. The men could speak without concern that their words were being recorded or monitored electronically.

Letty's boss had said he was the head of the big training center north of town, north of the airport. The man had been famous for something, but he couldn't recall exactly what it was or who had told him. Maybe he had been a famous weightlifter for he was as huge as two grown men. All she knew was that the black man and his friends loved the food at the *Azteca,* and especially the chips and salsa from the border town of Del Rio. Buckets of chips and gallons of salsa, the best in Texas.

If the men weren't able to come to town, then the *Azteca* would cater events at the training center. They ordered the dinner-sized portion for lunch and smothered salsa and cheese sauce on their food. They were a little protective of Letty, as if she were one of their daughters, and they always tipped heavily. Maybe *gringos* didn't know how to eat authentic Mexican food correctly, but they could put it away by the truckload.

Letty could see that his lunch companion today was a little different. He wasn't like the usual muscular or mustachioed men who came into town with the black man. He was taller, thinner, and was more relaxed than the others. He was also visibly older. He carried a paper sack and a notebook, which was open to a page with indecipherable scribblings. She looked at him for a little longer than she should — she had seen him before, but she couldn't place where or when. Maybe television.

She subconsciously turned her head to the television in the bar, but it was showing nothing, a product of a bad connection or something. Sometimes a rancher would cut the fiber optic cable running from San Antonio, along Highway 90, killing television and internet connections.

Her boss would know him. He could have fit in with the black man's friends, with his billowy khaki bush shirt, cargo pants, and boots. They all wore cowboy hats and Justin or Tecovas boots from the huge clearance malls in San Antonio. It was Texas after all. This man strolled in with dark green Merrill's on his feet and something green and crushable for a hat which looked to be an Indiana Jones movie prop. He carried no obvious weapon.

Before Letty Pineda had come to their table, Demetrius Eastwood had handed a paper bag to Bill McGee. "Go ahead, and open it. You seem like a man who might like a good cigar now and then. And if not, I know you know someone who would appreciate a fine stogie."

McGee opened the bag, looked inside, and saw two boxes of cigars. Brown box, fancy gold foil across the top. *My Father The Judge,* handmade in Nicaragua. Twenty-five inside each fancy box. Made with savory premium-aged tobaccos and wrapped in beautiful dark Ecuador *Sumatra*. Two hundred and fifty bucks a box, if you can find them. McGee could spot a fine *robusto*. Now he had two whole boxes of them. *Eastwood must want something really bad.*

"You are a gentleman and a scholar. Thanks, Dory." McGee smiled as he returned the box to the bag.

Eastwood stalled on the point of his presence and what he wanted from the old Navy SEAL. He asked, "What do you normally eat here?"

"*Two* chicken *chimichangas*. No *pico*, no guacamole, no sour cream. Cheese sauce. Rice, beans, lettuce. Extra cheese. Extra salsa."

"That sounds great! I'll take what he's having." Eastwood interlaced his fingers and placed them on top of the table. His lunch partner quickly dunked a still warm tortilla chip into the overlarge bowl of chilled salsa and shoveled it into his mouth.

Bill McGee swallowed and said, "Thanks, Letty." As the waitress walked toward the kitchen, McGee said, "The food is fantastic. It's all good." He noticed the television was snowy and adjusted the output of the Growler until the interference was gone and the television broadcast an image again; some Univision *novella* with beautiful, busty, dark-haired Latino women with their assets spilling out of their low-cut, mid-thigh mini-dresses.

Eastwood said, "I haven't been here in years. My folks would make the trip from San Antonio to Hondo just to have a real Mexican dinner at this place, only it wasn't this place. This is…much *bigger*. Newer. Things are usually smaller than what we remember as kids."

McGee smiled broadly. "My father used to bring the family here as well. He was stationed in San Antonio. Randolph Air Force Base. He said that one of the greatest inventions in the world was Mexican food. Chips, salsa, burritos, enchiladas. Margaritas. *Chimichangas!*"

Eastwood laughed at the way McGee said, "*Chimichangas!*" in that deep bass. He said, "Colonel Tracy McGee. One of the original Tuskegee Airmen."

McGee was impressed and nodded. "That's correct. I never thought many people knew that little bit of family history. When you're a SEAL, those things are kept fairly quiet, for obvious reasons." The men knew the history and achievements of the Tuskegee Airmen, the popular name of a distinguished group of African-American military pilots who fought primarily in Europe during World War II. Some flew the P-51 Mustangs, propeller-driven fighters with red painted tails. The Tuskegee Airmen had distinguished themselves in combat and in uniform after the war.

"Thanks for seeing me, Bill. I hope you and your family are doing well." The men engaged in small talk. They caught up on families and work. McGee had mentioned he had read Eastwood's articles and seen his television specials. He half-heartedly admonished him, "You keep your shit up, and little black helicopters will swoop down on you and haul your ass off, never to be seen again."

Eastwood laughed as he rubbed his eyes with his napkin. It was an old joke among former members of the intelligence community who bent their vow to never disclose the nation's old secrets still filed away in their heads. They stuffed more chips and salsa into their mouths. "Well, it's a fact that some of the folks from the big sandbox have tried to stop me, but they haven't been very successful. And you know they'd have to land on top of a skyscraper to try and find me now." The Growler's dull flashing light kept tempo with some oldies music from Herb Albert and The Tijuana Brass playing in the background. McGee happily noted that the Growler's lower-power setting didn't influence the jukebox.

McGee's found the salsa a little spicier than normal. A tear finally leaked onto his cheek, a sure sign that the habaneros were a tad hotter than he was used to. Maybe someone had slipped in a ghost pepper or two. He wiped the tear away and asked, "The Hummer doing ok?"

Eastwood nodded. He admitted he didn't drive it much, even though it was a magnificent machine. He meekly reported that he took renegade unlicensed cabs to the train station or to the network office on Times Square to avoid a street assassin. There was still a *fatwa* on him issued by none other than the late Osama bin Laden. The old terrorist might be dead, but his *fatwas* only expired when the targets were long buried.

Duncan Hunter and McGee had seen to it that the war correspondent was provided with an extensively armored Hummer H2 from one of the custom shops of one of Hunter's specialty companies. One armored vehicle had saved Eastwood and his driver from a bomb near Eastwood's house in Connecticut. The Hummer had been its replacement. An occupant would be expected to live if the Hummer came into contact with an improvised explosive device or an assassin with a high-power sniper rifle.

"I take it you're still in the office?" There was an impish quality to his question; of course Eastwood was still using the office.

"Yes, thanks to you and Duncan. What are you doing these days?"

"A couple of things. Our latest project in Texas is training law enforcement and teachers to engage shooters in schools, or churches, or even mosques. It's a special combat course with facsimiles of children as some of the detractors. You don't want to be the guy who shoots a kid by accident. America doesn't realize that we are living in a different world. These are not Kennedy's Democrats. Now we have kids with personality disorders going after kids in schools. Gun Free Zones. A fifteen-year-old who should be on the mental illness spectrum gets pissed off and steals a weapon and becomes a domestic terrorist hell-bent on making everyone's lives miserable while believing he'll achieve some level of notoriety."

Eastwood was confused, "I rarely hear that the kids and adults who shoot up schools and their places of work had mental illnesses. You think there is some correlation?"

"I do. Like DOD, the schools can't screen for sexual or personality disorders or mental illnesses anymore. Boys who say they're girls can't be kicked to special ed anymore. The schools have too many undiagnosed kids with problems and they're not getting treatment or counselling."

"Are you saying DOD is recruiting youngsters with sexual and personality disorders and mental illnesses, the category of people with a built-in stratospherically-high suicide rate? That if they aren't killing themselves at crazy rates then they are exhibiting violent behaviors that are off the charts?"

"That's exactly what I'm saying. But in the schools these problem kids are different; the ones with mental disorders are being radicalized. And you can thank our liberal friends in Washington. Dumb lefty laws."

"I'm reporting on those, but I thought the left just wants to take our guns. I see your point though; they have poisoned these poor kids' already damaged minds. That isn't cool," Eastwood said with a thin smile.

McGee's smile answered the subtle implication. "The other project is we've developed an anti-drone capability for airports. One method is to knock down hostile drones by jamming their frequencies. Some of America's *jihadis* operating out of mosques are flying drones into airports and creating all sorts of problems. There have been dozens of airliners colliding with drones on takeoff or landing. We are able to neutralize them as soon as they cross the airport fence."

"Damn. Just like as if you pulled their power cord, I guess?"

"Exactly. The other method is to develop killer drones. That is a little more challenging but may be more effective." McGee allowed some of what he had said percolate with Eastwood and then changed subjects. "So you've become, I guess, somewhat part of the team. Duncan said you helped him immensely."

"I suppose I have. Maybe I did. It's been a little crazy since Duncan dropped off the grid. I'm sure you know he called me from the Philippines and asked that I report that the Qantas jet which made an emergency landing had only experienced an electrical malfunction. Lost my job for a month over that one. But isn't that what teammates do?" A guano-eating grin preceded another chip with salsa. The language of teammates. "I served my time in journalist jail, got a reprieve, and I'm back at work. At least, I think I am." He grinned and attacked the chips.

McGee said, "…doing articles and specials. Half of the passengers died on that Qantas jet. Duncan saved the other half. I'll let him tell you how he got off that jet and how his name got on the deceased passenger list. He's dead and off the grid in his own little safe house far from the crazies on the east coast." *Of course. Where are you going with this, Eastwood?*

The men took a meandering route to get the conversation back to Eastwood's line of business. The articles and television specials that kept him busy revolved around the former president, Maxim Mohammad Mazibuike, who hadn't been seen since he deplaned Air Force One in Hawaii. Eastwood said, "There were rumors he had met an untimely demise."

Bill McGee smiled and responded, "Is that right? Hmmmm. No great loss there." McGee knew the truth about the demise of the treacherous President Mazibuike. He remembered seeing blood on Hunter's flight suit and asked, "Yours?" Hunter had responded, "His." *C'est la guerre!* McGee thought through a wicked punishing smile. He wished he had been there to see Hunter exact revenge on the man who had tried to kill Hunter, his wife, and hundreds of people on the airliner.

The pilot of the Australian 747 became an instant hero when he landed the airplane, an international version of the man who landed a crippled, unpowered jet in the middle of Hudson Bay. Only a few people knew that a self-radicalized computer scientist had nearly succeeded in crashing a Qantas 747 with a single keystroke of his computer. He had sworn his undying loyalty to Mazibuike. McGee knew the truth and knew how Hunter had eliminated the threat.

"Every network had those idiots on the television telling the world that it was terrorism." McGee chuckled and took a drink.

"Duncan promised me he'd tell me the whole story. I did my part, and I'd like to talk to him."

McGee removed his rimless glasses and placed them on the table. He smiled as if he was the winning panelist on the old "What's my Line?" television show. "I hear that you did see him but you were too busy, ignoring him for some dark-haired goddess and a radio personality."

"*What?* What are you talking about?" Eastwood demanded. He didn't understand. McGee grinned. "What… what…? *Oh, shit!*" Then it dawned on him. *The grey haired man with the bigfoot beard and sunglasses at the Pumpkin Papers Irregulars Dinner?* "Are you shitting me?" Eastwood sat there, crushed, shaking his head in disbelief. *Hunter was there; I didn't recognize him and…and I blew him off. I blew him off! I'm such a dummy!*

McGee shook his head and strained to control laughter. "I had to laugh on so many fronts. You see, when Duncan and I were at the Naval War College, he wore these expensive black suits with the most outrageous Ferrari-red ties. He must have had a hundred of those damn red ties—plain, spotted, ribbed, textured. All kinds. He said he had dressed for the occasion, hoping he'd run into you. I'm sure it about killed him to wear a dull grey suit and an orange tie."

Eastwood continued to shake his head at the missed opportunity. "I swear, I didn't recognize him. He was disguised very well. I thought I recognized the voice for a second, but that beard and nose totally threw me off. That nose was so hideous that you didn't dare look at it. Which, I suppose, was the point!"

McGee nodded. "I understand you also had an eyeful of Russian brunette. You could have been on fire and you wouldn't have noticed until the smoke obscured your vision.…"

The men laughed heartily. The noise from the table caught Letty's attention. She came over and refilled their glasses.

"So, Dory, if you think you're going to report on what really happened to that aircraft.…"

Eastwood continued to shake his head. "I wouldn't ever do that. We're teammates."

"Good. I think you need to drop that. You probably missed your opportunity to talk with him for a while. Was that the only reason you wanted to talk to me?"

"Bill, full disclosure. There are a couple of reasons why I came out here. I told my producer I thought I might be able to get the most highly decorated SEAL on camera. You could be a positive role model for African-American kids."

McGee grinned at the compliment. "SEALs avoid cameras and reporters like someone with an immunodeficiency avoids an Ebola clinic. No way; no how. Other than that. Bullshit."

Eastwood smiled at the gentle rebuke. He tried to stroke his ego a little. "Yours is a great story. You're a hero."

"That's only a rumor. Dory, little black kids would never watch a show like that. Great idea, but the black audience is busy looking the other way. The left feeds these kids and their parents stupid reality shows on music or sports stars. It's hard to get a black kid into uniform."

"Okay. Strike one. Maybe my coming out here was just a pretext to talk to you, get some real Mexican food, and get a message to Duncan."

McGee felt a little bad for snapping Eastwood's head off. He sighed and said, "Well, maybe I could give you a little background. I know all about you—you seemed to have been researched, poked and prodded like a lab specimen. Your guts were displayed in *Time* magazine, at the very least."

"That's true." Eastwood sighed at the old thoughts.

"Unlike you, Naval Academy grad, I was a prior enlisted guy—like Duncan. Classes at night. Too smart for Harvard, no poison ivy league for me, like Duncan. Got a commission through an enlisted commissioning program—also like Duncan. The Navy gave me a chance to prove myself—like the Marines gave Duncan. I had to become a great swimmer if I wanted to be a SEAL. As you probably know, not many *men of color* in the SEALs."

"Three officers, less than twenty enlisted, last count. I checked."

"Sounds about right. All junior guys."

Eastwood nodded and fast forwarded to, "I'm sure, when those jets hit the World Trade Center, you got a call."

"I did. My team and I left that night on the mission of our lives. We were going to avenge all those Americans who were killed by the Muslim murderers."

"Like the sailors and Marines dispatched by President Jefferson to go to Tripoli to avenge those who were killed and taken hostage by the Barbary pirates. So what happened?"

"Short story—we couldn't find him. Bad intel. Al-Qaeda had been paying attention. They expected a response, a small seek and destroy assault force. They used simple countermeasures to throw us off the path. We used billions of dollars' worth of satellites and surveillance aircraft, but Bin Laden was long gone."

"But when I say 'bad intel.' CIA.... CIA knew it was bad intel from the get-go, and they covered their ass. I barked at them for being feckless incompetents, and it pissed them off."

Eastwood said, "But they always called you. I mean, the SecDef or the SOCOM Commander always called you. What you're saying is that...the CIA...."

"We haven't always played well together. There's a long history. As Duncan would say, 'some days chickens, some days feathers. You didn't know from day to day which CIA turd would show up." McGee was matter of fact. "Interagency rivalries exist. Sometimes it's a matter of the wrong chemistry, the wrong people. Sometimes you have competing missions, competing personalities. Men with attitudes. But usually it was a matter of competing egos. They thought their shit didn't stink because they…the NCS had the intel. They wouldn't share. They wanted to use their guys. They wanted the glory. They wanted to celebrate, and we didn't give a shit what they thought. Wannabee Ivy League pansies with their cosmopolitan partners."

"Some days chickens, some days feathers…." Eastwood grinned, scribbled down the phrase, and then leaped to the next subject. "I would've thought you would've gotten a call to find 3M."

McGee grinned. The Growler flashed. McGee chose his words carefully. "3M. Ah, yes. Money, Marx, Murder. Or maybe Muslim. Four Ms…. The four horsemen of the Islamic apocalypse."

"President Mazibuike. Why didn't they call you to find him? Was it because you were retired? Or…."

McGee's smile telegraphed his answer.

"Or…they already knew where he was. Maybe he was already dead." Then without thinking, Eastwood blurted out, "If you weren't called, then they called Duncan!"

"You're very perceptive, Colonel Eastwood. Now, file that away and forget it, and never utter those words again to anyone. *Ever!* Change the subject."

Eastwood was nonplused. "Okay. I also wanted to say, to share…." He gestured with his open hand, "…that I think there's something else going on…. You're knowledgeable. I need a reality check."

"Shoot! My middle name is reality."

"There's something I've been working on…in the background. I need some help, and I seek your guidance and sagacious counsel. I'm also looking for some validation that I'm not chasing snakes down rabbit holes."

McGee smiled broadly as he pulled out his decrepit BlackBerry and typed in a message. He reached over and shut off the Growler before sending the text message. A few seconds later, the little green device was again flashing, a beat every five seconds.

Eastwood waited quietly. He knew McGee's basic story through unofficial channels, his contacts in Special Operations Command. The rest he extrapolated from experience. And now, Bill McGee had confirmed what he had long suspected. Within an hour after the first aircraft hit the World Trade Center, U.S. Navy Captain William "Bullfrog" McGee was in a cargo jet leading SEAL Team Six into

Afghanistan to find and kill the master terrorist, Osama bin Laden. After six months of chasing goat herders, goats, and ghosts, McGee and his SEAL Team were unceremoniously pulled out of the field. For the first time in a very long time, there would be no medals for anyone on the SEAL Team. Before the week of debriefs was over, McGee was ignominiously forced out of Special Operations Command and reassigned to the Naval War College, first as a student, then as an instructor. He retired a year later after an almost forty-year career.

Bill McGee had been one of three men awarded five Navy Crosses. U.S. Navy SEAL William McGee had been nominated repeatedly for the Medal of Honor. Confidentially, there was much angst in the Department of Navy about awarding a black sailor the Congressional Medal of Honor. And there was intense speculation whether, after a fifth nomination, the Navy brass would push institutional racism aside and do the right thing to honor their most courageous and most fearless sailor. But McGee wouldn't be awarded the Medal of Honor. It didn't matter. He had just done his job—leading SEALs against the enemies of America. He had failed to find bin Laden, but that effort never really had a chance of success. He didn't want to relive that part of his life.

"I sent Hunter a text message that you'd like to see him. *Again*. Now, what exactly do you think is going on, Colonel? And what have you been working on...in the background?" The questions preceded a grin being wiped away by more chips and salsa.

McGee nearly choked when Eastwood said, "For starters, in one of those boxes of cigars I've given you, are the complete archives of the Democratic National Committee. I can't possibly do anything with them, but I think Duncan might."

22

November 6
Andrews Air Force Base, Maryland

The sleek blue-trimmed Gulfstream G-550 with a white tail taxied into position and shutdown. The squall line that had dumped a couple of inches of rain had blown out over the Atlantic. A steady breeze remained after frontal passage and moved the lighted "T" to indicate the wind direction. The lawns in front and back of the Operations building were wet and the ramp was dry.

A lone man in jeans, light khaki bush shirt, polished black Lucchese caiman cowboy boots, and a black Stetson *El Presidente* hobbled down the jet's built-in airstairs. He carried a couple of black bags, a black backpack, a dark brown flight jacket, and a white Yeti cooler. A large revolver was slung from a black shoulder harness. Even at a distance, people could tell the weapon was heavy with a long barrel, unlike the smaller pistols the Secret Service carried.

The Director of Central Intelligence was momentarily slack-jawed as the man stepped from the jet. For several long seconds, the DCI didn't recognize his best friend under the cowboy hat and behind the dark sunglasses. The salt-and-pepper hair, caveman beard, and long wavy mustache seemed to be an integral part of the hirsute ensemble. His bushy, severely-raked eyebrows gave him the look of an axe murderer. But the two-tone Rolex Submariner covering a hideous circumferential scar on his wrist was where it was supposed to be. Duncan Hunter closed the aircraft's door. He pulled on the flight jacket to fend off the humidity and November chill.

Lynche never carried a gun. He didn't have to. He didn't wear body armor; it wasn't required for a person of his stature. He had a security detail to do the heavy shooting for him when it was necessary, and so far, no return fires had been necessary. Seeing Hunter with what he knew to be his favorite revolver strapped under his arm sent a signal to let people know he wasn't one to be screwed with. Lynche recalled what some Marine Corps general once said, "Be polite, be professional, but have a plan to kill everybody you meet." Hunter always sized up the men he met. His plan was to use the six-inch Colt Python if he had to fight his way out of trouble. But they were on the ramp of one of the largest and best protected air bases—Joint Base Andrews—on the East Coast. Colts, body armor, and laser sights weren't necessary.

After gathering his belongings, Hunter turned and saw Greg Lynche hurry away from an Army general and a man in a dark navy suit standing by a pair of black Suburbans. There were two women clad in full-body, khaki-colored, flame-retardant flight suits standing near an Air Force C-17, 90° and fifty yards away. Friend, spook, family.

Greg Lynche quickly closed the distance to Hunter and said, "You look like the hairball my cat threw up this morning." He eyed the man's disguise for its totality and effectiveness. "And, you're limping."

Hunter noticed the DCI's flight suit was straight out of the bag. Creases in the funniest locations. Shiny new black flying boots completed the picture. He said, "Nothing some Flexeril, 2,000 mg of Bayer, and a half-dozen lidocaine patches can't squash. Good to see you, too. Don't go racing off; slow down to a canter, and I'll be fine." Nothing suggested Hunter was still pissed at Lynche, and Lynche acted like nothing had ever happened between them. Hunter followed his comments with a familiar grin and he stole a peek at the women near the big jet.

"It's not like you to show your age, *Mav*. What are you now—sixty?" Lynche was a little concerned. Hunter used to play racquetball competitively; he had the stamina of an Ironman triathlete. Now he was limping. And if Hunter was limping, then he was hurt badly. Lynche couldn't help but think, *If he can barely walk will this mission be scrubbed before we even get off the ground?*

Hunter ignored his best friend's sarcasm. "Look who's talking. You're so old they have discontinued your blood type." He let out a sigh. "This 'getting old' shit isn't for sissies. I'm still vertical and on the right side of the turf. I'm just glad I wasn't welcomed like a North Korean dictator's latest out-of-favor uncle. But your timing was good— your call got me out of a prostate exam." It wasn't a fake smile; his eyes smiled too.

Lynche snapped, "I'm sure I did. No one would think about putting a finger in your *arse* wearing that cannon. That can't be your real hair." Hunter winked. The two men exchanged grins. He matched Hunter's uneven stride and wondered what new injury his best friend was trying to hide or if Hunter's body was finally reacting to all of the punishment it had received from tournament racquetball and other physical sports he used to excel in.

Lynche was aware of the long-ago repaired Achilles and Hunter's recently reattached hand surgeries. He knew Hunter's orthopedist had told him, "You're going to need a new knee in about fifteen years." And even that had been over twenty years ago. He knew Hunter would push through the pain until it impacted his performance in the air. Only then would he think about doing something about it. After a few steps Lynche asked, "What do you think?"

"I don't like your tie." Hunter grinned deviously.

Lynche wasn't wearing a tie, he was wearing an open collar Brooks Brother dress shirt under the flight suit. He shot back, "I meant the beard."

"Facial hair will get you there. You told me to grow it, I needed a disguise, remember? The first week was horrible and I couldn't stand it. I shaved and traded it for something from the House of Beards. I do follow orders."

Lynche patted Hunter on the back, "Thank you for following orders…for the first time in your life. But don't you think you could have gotten a larger one?"

Hunter said, "I think it's the model of beard what the snowflakes call 'excessive toxic masculinity.' Welcome to the non-binary world of today's Democrat. 58 genders and counting—how many bathrooms does the CIA have now?"

Lynche sighed heavily and shook his head at Hunter's caustic wit. He noticed that Hunter wasn't carrying his body armor. With his shirt showing under his jacket, it was obvious that he wasn't wearing it either. Maybe it was in his bag. It was a reasonable assumption—if you're going to land on the air base from which the President of the United States flies in and out on Air Force One, then it should be safe enough to go without it. Hunter rarely went anywhere without his body armor or his pistol. He had been shot at too many times.

The genetically-engineered spider silk was a miracle in engineering, the latest in lightweight and effective body armor. The spider silk vest weighed ounces and was many times stronger than the best commercially available Kevlar bullet-proof vest. It was a product from one of his research companies. And it could easily be folded into a helmet bag. Lynche knew Hunter carried weird things with him all the time; things he called "stuff." Doorjammers, extendible clubs, speed loaders, Buck pocket and Bowie knives, light bending material—the next generation in camouflage—and sometimes drones. Lynche learned not to ask, he knew that some of Hunter's "stuff" had saved his life.

About halfway between the Gulfstream and the Suburbans, Hunter stopped. Lynche stopped, questioning his friend's action. Hunter asked, "Do you know what you said to me twenty years ago today?"

"You are the one with the memory."

"Twenty years ago you called me and told me that the first lady had seen the budget for the Border Patrol that they'd received a fifteen million dollar earmark for three surveillance aircraft. She told the Immigration and Naturalization Commissioner to reprogram the money—that as long as she was in the White House, the Border Patrol would never conduct surveillance on Americans."

Lynche grinned. "I remember now." Greg Lynche viewed Duncan Hunter as a flawed character, not a drunkard, or a wife beater, or a philanderer, but something worse, a conservative Republican. Talented, smart beyond measure, and handsome—but his political views could be thought of as 'extreme' if you were a Democrat or an unclassical liberal.

Hunter popped off, "You know we weren't surveilling Americans but trying to find illegal aliens, drug smugglers, and *coyotes*. Now that woman is running for president? She violated the Espionage Act, how many thousands of times? She should be in jail."

Lynche ignored Hunter's comments and urged his friend to start walking. He recalled that period in his life. He had retired from the CIA and had first met Duncan Hunter when he was working for the U.S. Border Patrol and running a part of their aircraft operations. He still remembered the sales pitch, "Well, let me show you what we brought for today's demonstration. This is your basic Schweizer SA2-37B two-seat, single-engine, low-noise profile airplane. It's optimized for low-altitude surveillance and reconnaissance. This one has a suite of infrared and electro-optical sensors to covertly monitor activities on land and sea. Endurance about 14 hours."

Hunter had broken out in a huge mischievous grin. "She's beautiful—sleek, conformal antennae. I expected more of a muffler system like the YO-3A. Our pilots will munity if they hear they could be airborne for 14 hours—they're old and have to piss every few hours. It better have a relief tube!"

The Del Rio Sector Border Patrol Chief Patrol Agent had invited to the demonstration the area's U.S. Congressman and the other Border Patrol Sector Chiefs who were responsible for the southern border. After the presentation and demo, the chiefs and the congressman huddled with Lynche and promised an earmark for a few systems. Then the Democrat first lady killed the program. Not to be deterred, Greg Lynche drafted Hunter to fly another spy aircraft for Agency missions. Twenty years later, they remained the best of friends and Hunter was still flying that particular airplane for the CIA.

Lynche and Hunter marched to the pair of polished black Suburbans with blacked-out windows and a forest of roof antennas that were parked nose-to-tail, idling in the light of the parking apron floodlights behind the general and the civilian. Hunter didn't recognize the civilian, but he knew of the Army officer.

Introductions were made by the knocked-kneed Director Lynche. Hunter was introduced as *Maverick*. Resting just under his God-like beard was a black patch with embossed gold Naval Aviator wings. Under the wings was *Maverick*. Hunter dropped his bags, turned, and informally saluted the man in uniform.

Maverick? Could he be that *Maverick?* The Special Operations Commander, U.S. Army General James Runyan, held out his hand with reverence. His dress uniform was adorned with a neat black and white nametag and nearly every medal, ribbon and badge known to a combat Army soldier. He carried himself like a hardened warrior who had seen much death and action in the most hostile and remote locations on the globe. The creases at the corner of his eyes, deep and rutted like those of a professional golfer, spoke of many hours in the sun. His hands had never been manicured; they were cracked and scarred from secret battles on four continents. He had shown lack of emotion before the greeting but that disappeared when he heard and saw the name, *Maverick*. The crushing grip squeezed his frown into a hard thin smile, and the apparently glabrous Runyan offered Hunter a hearty and sincere handshake. "That looks a lot like the Stetson the 2nd Cav wears."

Hunter was instantly impressed with the man. He smiled and said, "But without all the regalia. Don't want to be accused of any *stolen honors*. I wear it as a tribute to the 2nd Cavalry rescuing the Lipizzaner Stallions from being lunch for starving Russian soldiers. I understand General Patton made it happen."

Lynche was both surprised and not surprised at Hunter's comment. He knew Hunter to be a historian of some repute, albeit aviation history. *Black Stetsons? Lipizzaner Stallions? Starving Soviet soldiers? Shouldn't he be wearing a white hat?*

As a man who knew the importance of time and schedules, the general nodded and continued, "*Maverick*, that was quite an effort in Liberia. Hopefully one of these days — over a beer — you can tell me how you did it. We still don't know." He looked at Lynche to express a shred of displeasure.

With a trace of a grin, Hunter said somewhat conspiratorially, "Well, sir, I just happened to be in the area and thought I'd drop in." Lynche rolled his eyes and turned away. Hunter had made what he had done sound so trivial.

The grin was returned. The general nodded. "It was a good thing you did. Is that a Colt Python?"

"Yes, sir." Hunter smiled at the general.

"Apparently, you like to have an edge. Thank you again, *Maverick*, and God speed." General Runyan reached out to shake his hand.

Hunter was surprised to have surreptitiously received a special challenge coin in his palm during the handshake. He immediately smiled and nodded a *Thank you, General.*

Runyan had newfound and instant respect for the man in the caiman boots. Over a year ago, an unknown man in black "coveralls" and a black pilot's helmet had somehow rescued a Nigerian Airlines jumbo jet from a squad of hijackers who forced the jet to land in Monrovia, Liberia. Some of the people freed from the airliner sang the praises of *Maverick* live on Al-Jazeera television. Special Operations Command first disavowed and later denied any knowledge of the rescue operation while quietly and cautiously taking credit. Everyone in SOCOM wondered who was this *Maverick* in the black *Nomex*®? Now General Runyan knew, and he had given Hunter a rare, heavily engraved and enameled challenge coin from his personal collection in thanks for his service.

The words of gratitude were Hunter's first clue that he might not return from wherever he was going. Lynche hadn't yet briefed him and Hunter had little idea what he had signed up for. Not wanting to show his concern he said in his best gravely Charlton Heston voice, "Whatever I can do, sir." He put the coin in his flight jacket pocket. "Thank you."

The next person in the impromptu receiving line was the Deputy Director of Operations and the Director of the CIA's National Clandestine Service, Steve Castaño. Typical of a man whose occupation was the art of espionage, he hid his eyes behind dark glasses. His thick black hair swished off to one side with nary a strand out of place, a man so upright that he combed his hair every hour. He was Carlos Santana's body double; his black bushy mustache was thoughtfully trimmed, something more suitable for a senior intelligence service executive than one of the rough and tumble hirsute men from Special Operations Group. He looked at the excessively bearded Hunter, long and hard as if he had met him once. *Maverick!* Maybe it was the barely visible revolver tucked under his arm that intrigued him. *Who wears a six-shooter and pilots a jet?* There was no recognition between the two men. It was hard for Castaño not to fixate on the revolver instead of the man. *This shithead is Maverick? Finally!*

23

November 6
Andrews Air Force Base, Maryland

Hunter's hackles were instantly raised; Lynche had betrayed him. *I said no spooks from the NCS! And this turd is all NCS! He even smells like old stale cigars.* Hunter strained to control his anger and not turn and glare at his boss. He remembered, *Be polite, be professional, but have a plan to kill everybody you meet.* He inhaled and finished his thought, *I'm going to kill this turd one day.*

Like the special operations general, Castaño knew of the *Maverick* in the black coveralls from the well-televised African aircraft rescue. But he had also heard about him from his former boss, the previous Director of the Central Intelligence Agency. Castaño knew of him as "the pilot," but he had never been given a name. Now it was more than likely that "the pilot" was nicknamed *Maverick.* The Special Operations Command (SOCOM) denied any knowledge of the rescue operation. The only other group of specially trained counter-terrorism experts capable of pulling off such a feat at a remote airport in Africa in the middle of the night immediately after the hijacked aircraft landed was the Special Activities Division or the Special Operations Group within the CIA's National Clandestine Service.

Castaño recalled standing in the center of the Operations Center at CIA Headquarters as the Nigerian Airways hijacking was underway, planning an interagency assault on the aircraft. Then the pilot of the Airbus 380 broadcast to the world that his aircraft was again airborne and headed to Lagos because two men in black coveralls had killed all the hijackers. Everyone at the Special Operations Crisis Action Center and in the CIA Operations Center had been confused at the turn of events. The NCS Director had spent an hour calling his contacts at the Israeli, British, and the French intelligence services. No one had any idea what Castaño was suggesting. They were even more confused and stood transfixed as, hours later, the Al-Jazeera television network broadcast interviews from deplaning passengers who were singing the praises of the *Maverick,* the white man in the black coveralls who rescued them.

Castaño had asked the heads of SAD and SOG, "Who the hell is *Maverick*? Is he one of ours?" *He left a calling card? No one leaves their name in this game!* No one on any of the continents knew. SOCOM denied they had anyone in the area who went by the handle *Maverick*. NCS likewise denied anyone in their organization had been part of the rescue. Which left the intelligence community without a clue who the two benevolent rescuers could be. Did they just parachute out of the sky or something? And if there was no intel on the two men, especially the *Maverick*, was it worth trying to find out? That was the day when *Maverick* became a legend in the Special Operations community and a target at the National Clandestine Service. And now *Maverick* was standing in front of him.

Castaño had suspected. Now he knew. It was right there on his flight jacket. U.S. Naval Aviator wings of gold. Not Air Force. Not Army. *Maverick. Finally!* He still didn't know how *Maverick* rescued the Nigerian aircraft and probably never would know. Al-Jazeera reported a white man and a black man were on the airplane. A pretty red-haired girl called one of their rescuers "*Maverick.*" Castaño recalled the video report, *The white man raced to her arms. And here is Maverick! And that's my little red-headed pilot going with him. She was on that Nigerian jet too. And they're together again? Oooh, isn't that just too coincidental? Maybe it's my lucky day!*

Hunter read the body language of the CIA senior executive. There was struggle and awareness, but little else. Beard fragments on Castaño's light Louis Vuitton shirt suggested he used an electric razor. The uneven scars on his face probably made shaving an adventure in bloodletting. Hunter searched for more clues behind his sunglasses, but he stopped his scan when he noticed Castaño's hands were severely scarred, likely burns from an accident in childhood. His ears were scared and his earlobes were fused to the side of his face.

Hunter had seen burns like that before on a Marine helicopter mechanic who barely escaped the burning wreckage of a chopper crash in Vietnam. He had scars over every visible part of his body; he told the young Hunter, "Call me Gunny Crispy." Hunter refused and respectfully called the man by his real rank and name.

Hunter gripped the CIA man's damaged hand firmly and sought some validation from eyes he couldn't see. No hidden coin in this man's palm. Castaño's hand felt like a foot, the product of skin grafts taken from the soles of his feet. Hunter felt neither sympathy nor gratitude, just a growing rage. They were like two desert bighorn rams with buckets of testosterone coursing through their veins, wary of each other before charging.

By process of elimination, Hunter ascertained the man was the Director of Operations. The head of the NCS. The lead dog of the dens of spies, masters of disguise. He was probably the Chief of Disguise at some point in his career. When they could get away with it, under the rubric of *political interference*, they'd assassinate an enemy of the United States or plan the assassination of a truly meritorious international criminal of the Castro or Andropov or Carlos the Jackal variety. There was a deputy director of the CIA, but the real number two at the Agency was standing in front of him. And there was no doubt Lynche had betrayed Hunter. *Why would Greg do that?*

Castaño returned the pressure with a thin, callous and conspiratorial smile. His accent and inflection were like that of a Tijuana used car salesman. Castaño said, "I too have heard about the mythical heroics of the *Maverick* from the passengers in Nigeria. If I'm not mistaken you saved one of my operations officers that day." He waved at the women near the large aircraft indicating that that operation officer was also on the tarmac. "It's an honor to meet you. One of these days you will have to tell us how you accomplished that incredible feat. Like the general, I hate to admit we still don't know how you did it. We do know al-Qaeda and the Islamic Underground slapped *several fatwas* on you; notified their networks to find you. You are probably the most wanted man in the Middle East." Castaño completed his thought. *Yeah, they put out fatwas on your ass, to find you and kill you!* "Thank you for your service, *Maverick*. Anything we can do to assist you, we are at your service."

However deferential, Castaño was also quietly furious. There was no reason for him to be excluded on this mission. Being able to meet the cowboy wasn't good enough. Some of the men on the other end of the mission were his guys. He was excluded while one of his gals was going! But somehow, someone who wasn't affiliated with the mission.... Nazy Cunningham apparently got to go because *she* was the NCTC Director. Or maybe she was going just because she was nice to look at and it was going to be a long flight.

Why was the CIA Director going, taking a personal interest in this obviously very special access program? Why was Cunningham going? The girl I might be able to understand; this Maverick dude is some kind of special pilot. She's an agency pilot. Maybe she's a backup pilot—the guy is obviously a cripple. But Cunningham? It makes no sense. Castaño had tried to weasel his way onto the jet. He was NCS, the head spook, the head spy of all spies. Two of his men had been captured. He should be there, succeed or fail. But Lynche wouldn't hear of it. *The lecherous DCI would have her all to himself.*

Castaño struggled to contain his fury and embarrassment. He wanted to lash out as a means to force Lynche to see things his way. He had done that once before and was nearly removed for cause. *Why are those two spending an inordinate amount of time together in the DCI's office? Could it be the reason the DCI excluded him was this Maverick character?* Castaño paused and changed vectors. *There's no way this Maverick could even begin to suspect that I hated him for what he did to me and my guys.* He shook his head almost imperceptibly. *We were minutes away from taking three billion dollars in gold from a terrorist and that asshole Maverick brought the Marines!*

As he was apt to do, Castaño instantly changed his focus. He glanced over at the two women near the C-17. One was his ginger haired operations officer. *Now this Maverick is in the picture. What are the chances he knows her, too? And what is it about this Maverick dude? He wouldn't even look at them. Everyone on the ramp is trying to steal a long peek at the tall woman, even when she was covered up from her neck to ankles in coveralls. But this Maverick ignores her like she wasn't even there. She's impossible to miss! If he didn't even try to look at her, then the dude was probably gay. Liked dudes. Or something….*

Hunter had been trained in the art of reading micro-expressions and was distracted by Castaño's complex body language. He couldn't see his eyes and that was a problem. It was as if the man was refereeing the little devil on one shoulder and an angel on the other, or maybe it was just the demons in his head. He assumed the sixty-plus, maybe five-eight, smarmy and oleaginous NCS Director had more to hide behind the *Maui Jims* than the lifts in his thick-heeled shoes. But Hunter didn't have time for soapbox analysis. Lynche was nudging him with a sense of urgency. Hunter was being herded away by an overbearing sheepdog in a Brooks Brothers shirt hiding under flying coveralls.

Hunter's curiosity was running wild. *Thank you? What the hell have I done? Why did I have to meet these guys, especially the spook? What the hell have I gotten myself into? And why did you do this, Greg? I don't trust him!* His eyes turned to Lynche who was welded to his shoulder, pushing him away from the men and their rolling black armored monstrosities that would make environmentalists weep for Mother Earth. Hunter imperceptibly raised an eyebrow. *Why did you bring these men, Greg? What purpose could this meeting have served? I don't like that asshole; I know I'm going to have to kill him one of these days.*

Lynche said to Runyan and Castaño, "We have to go." Hunter didn't salute the NCS man. The general and the spook stepped aside. When the women noticed the CIA Director pushing Hunter their way, they picked up their bags. They remained close to the gigantic jet as the men finished their goodbyes.

Lynche led Hunter to the nearby U.S. Air Force C-17 Globemaster III. He pretended to be talking; with hands full Hunter gestured toward a squadron of grey Marine F/A-18 Super Hornet fighter aircraft.

Mingled with the refreshing, dewy petrichor of the earlier rainstorm was the heavy scent of burning jet fuel from departing airliners painted up as military aircraft. He loved being on a military base with dozens of aircraft of every size and capability. He marveled at the engineering required to transport a president across the globe, from the chief executive's jumbo jet to the flying fuel trucks that could make such a trip possible. Hunter reflected on his time at the lectern, teaching an "aircraft and spacecraft development course" for Air Force instructor pilots. Reminiscing, even for a few seconds, was enough of a diversion to put his anger in check. *Give the old guy the benefit of doubt and don't say something you'll both regret. Cool your jets!*

To break the tension Hunter said, "I'm certain you have more time in one of those than I do," a clear reference to the time Hunter orchestrated a ride for Lynche in one of the highly polished blue and yellow F/A-18s from the U.S. Navy's Blue Angels Flight Demonstration Team.

Lynche smiled and nodded at the memory. He gave another look at the continuously limping Hunter. "I half expected to see you crawl out of an F-4 *Corsair*. Maybe bring the *Starship*. I didn't expect that thing on your face."

"Have you ever cranked up an eighteen-cylinder radial? Me either. I'd have brought one of the Howard 500s. But you said to hurry. That meant the G-550. I'm still in negotiations to buy a *Corsair*, by the way. Not many available. You do know we're rebuilding warbirds in Elmira?"

Lynche gave an abbreviated nod to confirm. He hadn't heard of a Howard 500; Duncan would probably tell him later what kind of airplane that was, he was sure. He didn't offer to carry any of Hunter's gear. Even with him limping, Hunter wouldn't hear of it.

Hunter said, "One Howard 500 is flyable but it isn't that fast, with radials and all. The *Starship* is also in Hondo, fresh out of an overhaul. New cockpit. New avionics. It's optionally manned—that's something you'd never believe I'd even think of doing. Greg, it's a nice airplane. I know you'd feel right at home in it."

"I would love to fly a *Starship*. I've always been enamored of them but...I've never seen one in person. But optionally manned?"

"I may have to jump out, one of these days."

Lynche rolled his eyes. The comment brought a huge toothy smile from Lynche. Hunter and his retired U.S. Navy SEAL sidekick, Bill McGee had jumped from one of Hunter's spyplanes and parachuted onto the back of a hijacked Nigerian Airways jet. Hunter's engineers had modified the Lockheed YO-3A to be optionally manned, and over the airport in Liberia he had programmed it to land at their alternate airport once he and McGee left the cockpit and skydived onto the back of the airliner. But making the *Starship* optionally-manned, that was thinking so far out of the box that Lynche shook his head in amazement. *That's a lot of airplane to turn into a robot. That's just a beautiful airplane.*

Beech Aircraft Corporation had built 53 of the futuristic-looking twin-turboprops. The eight-passenger *Starship* was noteworthy for its carbon fiber composite airframe, canard design, lack of centrally-located vertical tail, and pusher engine/propeller configuration. Hunter owned one of the last remaining operational *Starships*. Virtually all of the others had been repurchased and destroyed by the manufacturer.

Lynche patted Hunter on the back as a gesture of thanks and understanding. Hunter still had his hands full or he would have reciprocated. Another peek at Hunter made him smile. He wasn't used to seeing his old flying partner in a cowboy hat, or in a beard fit for an Amish elder with wrap-around sunglasses. His old sailor eyes with their deep creases showed disapproval. Cowboys and farmers weren't high on his list of the urbane or brilliant. He called them roadkill-eating rednecks, although affectionately. He disliked men with pickup trucks, Stetsons, and beards with a passion.

Hunter was the exception. When Hunter wasn't driving a sport's car, he drove a pickup, wore a cowboy hat, and was one of the smartest men on the planet, and that was according to the old intelligence officer at his shoulder. But he was also Lynche's political opposite which oftentimes torqued the jaws of the fiscally conservative—socially-liberal spook. Still, Lynche loved his prodigy like the son he never had, except when Hunter wandered off the plantation and brought up politics at the most inopportune moment. The discussion of politics was either taboo or substantially different at Lynche's level, just as news and information were different from classified intelligence, like the difference between what a doctor knew and what a patient felt.

Runyan and Castaño watched the small group walk away toward the big jet. Runyan couldn't tear his eyes away from the callipygian women in their flight suits. Castaño's eyes never left Hunter's cowboy hat, his back, and the accoutrements he was carrying, especially the specially-made black helmet bag. His mind raced with things to do while his boss was away with this *Maverick. And Cunningham.*

Castaño bid the general goodbye with a wave instead of a handshake. He turned and opened the rear door of his CIA Suburban with his left hand. He slipped across leather seats, careful not to touch anything with his right. With his left, he lifted the top of a square black plastic case and inserted his right hand and then closed the lid. He marked time on his rubberized Casio for the appropriate duration. Designed for capturing DNA from an unsuspecting donor, the inside of the container was sterile oobleck, a type of non-Newtonian slime with the properties of both liquid and solid. It enveloped his hand like raw watery latex. Top and bottom. After 45 seconds, Castaño told his driver he was ready to go. He opened the lid of the container and extracted his hand. The moist concoction had solidified. No residue remained on his palm. The Suburban began to move. He closed the box and pulled the corners of his lips back in an evil smile. Castaño didn't even look back at the diminishing view of the gigantic Air Force jet.

24

November 6
Hondo, Texas

Eastwood caught the old SEAL's not-so subtle body language. Bill McGee was being put on the spot. And he didn't like it. McGee didn't want to talk about DNC archives. He didn't want to know how Eastwood acquired them, although he had a suspicion. He looked at the bag with the boxes of cigars. *Supposed boxes of cigars.* McGee leaned forward menacingly and growled, "*Do not tell me you gave me a box of cigars that aren't cigars?*"

Eastwood thought he was going to die. He whispered, "The top box has cigars. The bottom box has flash drives. I wouldn't do that to you."

McGee sat back in his seat. *You owe me another box!*

Eastwood knew he had overshot the runway by announcing he had the DNC's archives. Intelligence officers worldwide wanted to be "the guy" who found or acquired the enemy's most sensitive records. Was the DNC really an enemy? Who knew? Eastwood looked at McGee for a sign that all was well—that he wasn't going to get shot. McGee had a pistol.

Now he knew what was going on. Eastwood had also lived through a sudden and traumatic end of his career. Demetrius "Dory" Eastwood had graduated from the U.S. Naval Academy and had served as an infantry officer with multiple combat tours in Vietnam, earning a Silver Star and four Purple Hearts. After Southeast Asia, he had been assigned to various "high visibility" tours in the Marine Corps before being assigned a job with the National Security Council. With no experience in the world of top secret security clearances and special access programs, he was a quick study organizing and running multiple counter-intelligence and counter-terrorism operations against primarily Islamic radicals and terrorist targets. He had risen quickly to the rank of lieutenant colonel. Then virtually overnight, he had been forced to resign from the Marine Corps. An FBI indictment charged him with conspiracy to defraud the United States by channeling profits from U.S. arms sales to fund anti-communist rebels in Central America. He was running top secret CI and CT operations against Islamic targets, not commies in San Salvador or Tegucigalpa or Santiago.

Like McGee, Eastwood had risen to the top of his profession only to fall utterly, completely, and spectacularly. The collapse was difficult to comprehend. They'd both been doing their jobs and could have accepted responsibility for their actions had they been causal to the failure of the mission. But they had been accused of activities for which they knew nothing about. Someone behind the scenes had been the real culprit for mission failure and had been able to flip responsibility for failure to them.

After being released from the Marine Corps, Eastwood became a pariah. He couldn't investigate who had orchestrated his downfall. But he knew the DNC archives could start a whole new career, a new life for him. He shook his head and looked away for a moment, then back at McGee, who was boring a hole through Eastwood's head.

McGee broke eye contact, checked his watch, and said, "Maybe *Maverick* will call. Maybe he won't. Don't expect anything soon—you know he'll get in touch on his terms. Teammates shouldn't expect a full debrief until the briefer is ready. And I'm not going to repeat what you just said. Something like that could get someone killed."

"It already has." Eastwood thought of the late Tommy Larrabee and his grieving mother. He told McGee where he got the archives.

"I can believe that. OK. I'll get the package to Duncan and see what he wants to do with it. Fair enough? Time to change subjects to something less lethal."

He nodded his appreciation. "Thanks Bill." More chips and salsa were enjoyed in silence, then Eastwood asked, "How did it happen to you?"

"What? Bin Laden? Becoming a terminal Captain? That's ancient history. Why the interest?"

"This is all related, I think. Ya' see, I've received countless letters from family members of Russian defectors and other political deaths who say their loved ones didn't commit suicide, or that their accidental death was actually a murder. Healthy men spontaneously had fatal heart attacks. Vladimir's former media tsar was probably murdered in Washington, DC, on the eve of a planned meeting with the U.S. Justice Department. Official cause of death was blunt-force injuries to the head, neck, and torso due to a series of drunken falls after days of excessive alcohol consumption."

"These deaths are suspicious; the government uses its awesome judicial power to close these cases. The police don't investigate. This leaves the families to ask the question, 'What just happened to my child or spouse?' They've begged me to investigate. I think these are casualties of political warfare."

McGee ignored the comment on "political warfare." He chomped on another chip. He glanced at the bag with the cigars. "I suppose you get a lot of those."

"I do, but there's a group of these cases that are a little different. Individually, they're just a family tragedy. But when viewed as group, something pops up. Every one of these special cases has a political component. Their loved ones had documents or information detrimental to Russia or the Democrat Party. The men and women who approached me are rational, accomplished, dedicated parents or spouses. They know they've been caught up in something they don't understand. And when their loved ones come up dead and the police rarely investigate, I'm wondering if it isn't political warfare."

"Politics...." It was both a question and a statement. Politics alone wasn't enough to pique his interest. Maybe if he used less generalities. Eastwood continued as McGee put his hand around his water glass and listened.

"There was the family of a certain Democrat lawyer who had worked in the White House. They found his body in his car near Fort Marcy Park. Five investigations concluded it was suicide."

McGee said, "A stone's throw from the CIA. You know Himmler became too high-profile of a person to be allowed to live after the war. He and the guy who released 3M's file...are probably in the same category."

What an odd observation thought Eastwood. He nodded and continued, "Another family, the family of a Democrat Party executive who was gunned down on the streets of Washington D.C.; he was the one who had the DNC's archives."

"It's Washington, D.C. That shit happens all the time. Don't you know gun control works wonders there? There are people throughout history who were so high-profile or knew such extremely sensitive stuff that exposure or disclosure couldn't be tolerated. Look real close. Did he have an agenda and something to share?" McGee leaned in the direction of the bag of cigar boxes. "Of course the answer is, yes."

McGee listened as Eastwood continued his list of suspicious deaths. As he spoke, Eastwood opened his notebook and wrote, *The guy from DC provided the archives of the DNC to his mother who gave them to me. If I'm found with them, I'm a dead man.*

McGee took the pen and notebook away from Eastwood and wrote, *"Now I have them?"*

Eastwood nodded. "For safekeeping. For Duncan. No one will

screw with you. Anyone who tries to screw with you and your SEAL network will be dead men soon." McGee shut his eyes for a few seconds.

The two men dropped the issue of archives as Eastwood cited dozens more examples of the untimely demise of political figures. McGee was startled when Eastwood mentioned General George Patton and an unfamiliar name, Whittaker Chambers.

Eastwood continued, "Then there was the family of a Marine Corps colonel, a pilot, who had officially committed suicide."

McGee's eyes narrowed. He quietly scraped more salsa onto a chip and said, "The wife found him. The Agency was flying into and out of the El Toro Marine Corps Air Station." He nodded as if he could have written the coroner's synopsis of the event.

Eastwood replied, "We're only given the official government-approved version of what happened. But you seem to know that there's a completely different story...."

"Some things are better left unsaid, Dory. It's hard to put the genie back in the bottle once you say the magic words." *I have the entire archives of the DNC! Some things are better left alone....* "No one speaks out of school when SAPs are or may be involved. Folks can die."

"Yes, sir. I know. I've been giving it a lot of thought with what little I know of your situation."

McGee said, "My situation is old history. It's not related in any way to this discussion. I'm serious."

Eastwood added, "I go back to my original thought—there's something going on, and I think there's more out there than just a silly conspiracy theory. It's like some are able to clearly see the numbers in a color blindness test, while those who are color blind cannot. The right sees things one way; while the left sees it completely differently, if not purposefully so."

"That's a good analogy." McGee chuckled. "That's probably the reason the loony left is so crazy. They can't see what is in front of them."

"There's a spectrum of events from murder to the actions that I call 'do not result in death.' I was indicted for something I did not do. You were relieved of command. We weren't *killed*, but our careers, our livelihoods were. We were dead to our bosses. My question is, 'Do you think someone orchestrated your downfall?' One day you're a hero, and the next you were gone, like a candle being snuffed out leaving nothing but darkness."

McGee's chin puckered like the pointy end of a football. He stopped eating chips. He stared at the old Marine. He didn't want to have this discussion.

Eastwood let his eyes casually wander across the other patrons in the restaurant just as Letty burst through the kitchen doors carrying two large plates in oversized oven mitts. He swung back around and said, "It took me while before I began to understand that, in my case, I was made to take the fall. With all the atmospherics surrounding September 11th, I think the same thing happened to you. You came home empty handed and you were poison, which was an unusual response. You were like the FBI—you always got your man. Someone made failure happen."

McGee showed no emotion at the remark while Letty placed the hot-out-of-the-oven plates in front of them. Melted white cheddar cheese with colored peppers covered the *chimichangas*. She cautioned the men that the plates were very hot and left them to attack their food.

When McGee and Eastwood had first met, fleeing Islamic terrorists on the road to the Tripoli Airport, the old SEAL had urged the war correspondent to evacuate with him to Algeria. But Eastwood demurred; he had a story to run down. Days later the men did join up at the U.S. Embassy in Algiers, just a few hours before radicals sympathetic to al-Qaeda and the Islamic Underground attacked and overran it. The radicals had bombed the walls of the embassy, stormed the compound, and kidnapped the CIA's Acting Chief of Station, Nazy Cunningham, who just happened to be walking across the compound. Eastwood had sprung into action to help McGee rescue Hunter's wife from the group of Muslim savages. That night they became undisputed teammates but they also frequently looked back at the timing of the radicals' attack. Were they just after Nazy Cunningham?

They were evacuated by helicopter to the *U.S.S. Eisenhower* in the Mediterranean Sea. Eastwood recalled seeing and filming a most incredible sight later that night. A WWII-era biplane had landed on the massive aircraft carrier. Duncan Hunter had emerged from the eggplant-colored Beechcraft Staggerwing. Hunter said he had "killed the guy who shot him out of the sky and stole the bastard's ancient airplane to escape the African continent." *The last of a Marine's Marine.* When McGee delivered the news about Nazy, the two former Marines and the former SEAL Team Six commander became more than friends.

The two men ate quietly until Eastwood changed the subject and blurted out, "I saw you and Hunter enter the White House last summer. It looked like Nazy had recovered from her ordeal. You did good work patching her up."

"You were essential, as I recall. Yes, that was quite an evening in Algiers." McGee lowered his eyes, pushed thoughts of Algeria to the side, and recalled that his wife and Hunter's had been well dressed for the occasion Eastwood mentioned. The president had awarded McGee and Hunter the Distinguished Intelligence Cross that night in a secret Oval Office ceremony. Later they'd been the president's guests at a State Dinner. It was the last time the old SEAL had worn a tuxedo and if McGee got his way, it would be the last time ever.

It was time to quit giving Eastwood a ration of shit. Show a little respect. He was part of the team. *And he gave me the archives of the DNC. Holy Moly! They have to be a thousand times more explosive than the Islamic Underground's national archives.*

Eastwood watched McGee adjust the tiny round spectacles on his face. McGee was massive and the size of his glasses was incongruous, considering the size of his face.

"So you think something is going on? In what way?"

Eastwood answered, "I do. I know this sounds a little 'out there,' but we live in a world where what's going on beneath the surface is overshadowed by what we see on top…. Like there's another world behind the curtain of top secret clearances and special access programs that normal people aren't allowed to see. Look at how congressmen enter the Capitol building as poor lawyers still paying off their student loans, years later they leave as millionaires. Multi-millionaires. They're getting paid off somehow. President Mazibuike demanded his cabinet members, generals and admirals to be aggressive with 'Muslim outreach' programs. Those that complied got rewarded with Gulfstream jets; those that balked or refused didn't just get fired, they got set up and were destroyed in the eyes of their families for sexual trysts or charges of espionage. Or for things even worse."

"I remember even right-leaning generals and admirals walking the plank. They refused to facilitate the infiltration of Muslims, with no experience or history, to bypass long-standing security measures and regulations. They quit and retired."

"What we see is the end result of someone's planning. I reported on a terrible protest a week ago. The protesters' signs all carried the red fist of the Communist Party of the USA tucked away in the corner. Was that the invisible hands of a puppet master at work?"

McGee nodded. "There's an election. That shit happens all the time, but those radical Islamists and commie clowns are in the minority."

Eastwood nodded before taking another bite of his *chimichanga. Clowns…. Always clowns….*

McGee continued, "There's no doubt the left or the communists orchestrate fights like those. Their surrogates aren't there to protest; they're there to provoke. They have an agenda. Sounds like you want to blame the commies, but I thought the commies had been defeated."

Eastwood said, "They're called something else now. Progressives or socialists or some such bull. They're emboldened by the political support of the left. They'll do anything for their handlers."

"The DNC." McGee nodded and smiled his concurrence. "I'm probably one of those guys—or at least I used to be. When I was sent to Afghanistan to find OBL, the CIA loaded up my team with their most unique equipment, or I should say I had a spook attached to me who was the keeper of the 'gizmos.' We called him 'the Geek.'"

"Gizmos? Like what? Big assed-bullets with glass noses? Lasers? Jetpacks?"

The last guess made McGee raise his eyebrows. "No need to know, Dory. But I'll say they have shit that's 20-30 years ahead of anything industry is working on, or what DARPA or IARPA and their contractors can produce. Maybe even fifty years."

Eastwood nodded. *Maybe now we can get somewhere....*

McGee relaxed more and shifted gears. He asked, "Ever had someone use the phrase, 'No harm will come to you or your family?'"

Eastwood stiffened as if he expected to be cold cocked by the massive black man with the huge fists and tiny glasses. He nodded tentatively and glanced at the Growler, which was still killing their conversation with electronic noise.

"This goes no further. Like a lot of SEALs and Special Forces, I was temporarily assigned to the CIA in the late 1990s. Near East Division. I was in the cafeteria when this dude, who I'd never seen before, came and sat at my table. I could tell he was probably former SF or NCS just by the way he carried himself. I thought I was being recruited by one of the bubbas."

Eastwood put down his fork and listened.

"Wasn't too surprising. We had some…there were very few SEALs and Army Delta who had cross-decked into the Agency. It was a normal, expected pitch among friendlies, the *bubbas. Dudes!* Because, as you can imagine, SEALs couldn't be pitched—not by the Soviets, the ChiComs, drug cartels—no one, not even the Agency. I told him politely I wasn't interested in becoming an intelligence officer for Langley."

This was one of the few times Eastwood had heard McGee put more than two paragraphs together at the same time. He recovered and responded by shoveling the remnants of a *chimichanga* into his mouth as he continued to listen.

"I could see why some guys did it. They were tired of all the Navy's BS; no more bullshit PFTs, ridiculous mandatory training for the craziest of reasons—human relations classes, be nice to your local black dude—that kind of crap. The pay was horrible for what we did, and we had to worry about our own government killing us."

"I don't understand." Eastwood had screwed up his face like a *sharpei*.

McGee unconsciously stretched his neck as if he could feel the strain of the old training. "One example, we had guys break their backs sliding off a speeding Zodiac. I can assure you that hitting the water at 60 mph is like falling from a truck and smacking concrete. And those were just training exercises. Going to the CIA meant your feet could heal. SEALs have the worst feet. We're always in the water in places that I still can't pronounce. Unknown funguses and parasites would make your life miserable in ways that are hard to comprehend. Ninety percent of us were on experimental drugs; the docs couldn't get rid of any of those bugs. I still have to take pills."

Eastwood frowned in compassion and understanding. Marine infantry troops also operated in some of the nastiest conditions when they were deployed. But they had it relatively easy compared to the extreme conditions the SEAL teams encountered in secret places where Marines in large numbers didn't tread.

"And going to the Agency meant double, maybe triple pay. I sure wouldn't have been deploying every time some North Korean nutcase threatened to invade his neighbors. So I was more than a little surprised that I hadn't been approached before. Maybe it was because I'm black. But then…I *was* approached. It was the CIA where everyone was white. Not many 'men of color,' as the liberals would say. There were absolutely no Muslims and damn few blacks. It was a very special club. I rarely thought about it, but when I was assigned to the CIA, like being a SEAL, I realized I was a black man in a white man's world. I've always operated in that environment and really didn't have the problems that some have claimed they had. White liberals are horrible; they treat you like you're helpless, a slave. White conservatives treat you like a human being. That you're part of the team. You can do many things if the racists or the left aren't part of the equation."

Eastwood nodded sympathetically and encouraged McGee to continue.

"Anyway, the dude wanted to see if I'd be interested in making a little money on the side. I've thought about this for a long time, and I'm convinced he thought I was a stereotypical black man who had repressed feelings and animus toward white men."

"A lot of these Agency guys had tours in Africa where the racism against whitey is blatant, a way of life, so some of that crap was understandable. Surprisingly, Africans don't like American blacks either. So maybe I could be turned to kill a white man, I thought, 'overseas' for a few bucks. Strange discussion." McGee shook his head at the old thoughts. "I asked, 'What are you looking for?' This dude pushed a Roi-Tan cigar box in front of me and whispered, 'Wet work,' like I was a Soviet flippin' Union exterminator. An assassin. I've killed the enemies of America in the course of my duties. But those were overseas. This was insanely different."

Eastwood frowned curiously.

McGee continued, "I figured it was probably a contract hit. A political hit. One time good deal. Murder some dude for us, and you walk away a rich man. I figured I'd be protected by the CIA, but there was no indication that would be the case. I can still see him tapping that cigar box with his deformed little finger. I assumed whatever was inside would be mine for the job. So I opened it and there was a stack of bills."

Deformed little finger? "A single stack of bills isn't worth much but....." Eastwood tried to do mental math. "A hundred $100 bills are only $10,000." *Not worth the effort. That's crazy.*

McGee smiled and said, "Bad assumption, GI Dog. You don't know with whom I was dealing. Those bills were 1934 United States Gold Certificates. $10,000 denominations. Like they'd just printed them out and put a little gold-trimmed wrapper on them. A million dollars. They've been out of circulation since 1964. I know less about the currency in my wallet than I do 1934 Gold Certificates. Reportedly, all of the notes were recovered and destroyed except for a few on the collector's market. However, some are *still* legal tender at a Federal Reserve Bank. Some serial numbers were never cancelled. They were issued on the condition that when they were presented for redemption, they'd be paid in gold coin or bullion. They're worth much more than their face value today, maybe ten to forty times as much on the collector's market."

Wide-eyed, Eastwood cocked his head in disbelief and whispered, *"Shit!"*

"The history of those particular bills isn't well known. The U.S. government used them to conduct large-scale business transactions. Not securities. Gold certificates. We bought Alaska...."

"Seward's Folly?" Eastwood interjected.

"Yeah. $7 million. Supposedly we paid the Russians for it with Series 1865 $10,000 notes. Seven stacks of 100 bills. They'd fit nicely in a cigar box. Over the years, Russians asked to exchange their gold certificates, and we complied. There's still over a billion dollars of unredeemed gold certificates 'out there.' It's apparent the Agency was using these large bills for clandestine transactions with foreign governments. If you knew what the NCS does, it would make perfect sense."

Eastwood laughed, "You've got to be shitting me."

McGee got noticeably quieter, which was difficult because his deep Barry White baritone voice resonated in the surprisingly superlative acoustics of the *Azteca*. "I could barely hear him. He said, 'You do this for us and this is all yours. If you decline our offer, I must insist you never mention this conversation. Ever. With your silence, you acknowledge you will never speak of this ever again. In return, I'll assure you that no harm will ever come to you or your family.' I shuddered and thought, '*Are you friggin' kidding me*?' I was in the middle of CIA Headquarters; this guy looks like he's giving me a friendly box of cigars. At first I thought it was a joke. Commit murder? Pull one over on the dumbass black dude from Texas. Then I thought I was maybe dealing with the mafia, not an intelligence officer."

McGee unconsciously shook his head, as if he still couldn't believe the vicissitudes of the strangest episode in his life. "I researched those transactions while Duncan and I were at the Naval War College. They have Secret and TS libraries. If we asked the right questions, we could get just about anything from the other federal institutions' secret archives. *As students we were researchers!* I always wondered if those bills were real. Found out they were."

"So those bills may still be on the books and still redeemable for gold? Incredible."

McGee nodded and grinned. He had wanted to tell someone that story for a very long time.

"So, you were offered a million for a single hit? In 1990? That's just...*incredible!* Did he tell you who they wanted you to....ah, ..." Suddenly Eastwood was at a loss for words.

"I know. I was curious and asked about the target? I didn't think he'd tell me, but I guess he sensed I might be interested if the target was the right guy. He gave me a clue so I could decide."

"*Really?!*" Eastwood was nearly bouncing in his seat with anticipation, thinking, expecting the target of assassination had to have been a significant political figure. *A million dollars. 1990...the up and coming Governor of Arkansas? The President of Israel? PLO Chairman? Someone way up the food chain.... Congress? Castro? Who?*

McGee looked at Eastwood with dark dead eyes and said, "He said it was a Marine Corps colonel. Someone who knew too much." McGee shrugged his shoulders that were as solid as a British castle and blessed with brutish power. There was a hard malevolent quality to his whisper. "Dory, you'd been in the news. You'd been pulled up before Congress. You took the fifth. You were on the cover of *Time*. I'd watched the TV, and these excuses for reporters said you'd overstepped your bounds, that you'd lied to protect the president. That you were the Marine who knew too much. I thought the target was you."

25

November 6
Andrews Air Force Base, Maryland
The two women on the parking apron hadn't been part of the official welcoming committee. They had watched with amusement as the men from the black government limos and the bearded wonder engaged in a hurried and sycophantic "meet and greet."

Hunter obviously had not been pleased with the DCI's shenanigans. The women had been briefed, they knew the drill not to acknowledge Hunter until Lynche gave the signal. They complied and had enjoyed watching Hunter being manhandled and corralled by their boss.

Nazy Cunningham's black hair was pulled back tightly like a Robert Palmer dancer, then elegantly knotted in a long and segmented waterfall braid that extended well past her buttocks. Her face was flawless, like a Rembrandt painting. Kelly embodied the sultriness of Veronica Lake, she was a curvy red Testa Rossa keeping pace with a black Ferrari GTO. By comparison, the elegant, strong, and confident women faced two trucks, an ancient broken down Jeep and an old rusty Dodge Power Wagon with a flat and a cluster of tumbleweeds in its grille—Lynche and Hunter. Despite the lack of family resemblance, Kelly Horne was Duncan Hunter's only child. Within the CIA, only Director Lynche and Nazy knew the familial connections.

As they walked toward the women, Hunter scanned the ramp across the runways, but the C-17 now filled his field of view. Air Force aircrewmen spilled out of the big jet and took the women's and Hunter's belongings. They passed them inside the massive jet. The aircrew knew the upcoming mission was going to be unusual, it was unique to see anyone carrying a revolver.

Hunter didn't need to help the 73-year-old Lynche board the aircraft, nor his daughter who followed. He held onto Nazy's hand as long as necessary to convey he had missed her. She ignored him and his beard for the moment. She'd maintain a professional demeanor up until the moment she could let down her hair and rip that thing off Duncan's face.

Just as when he had first seen the diamonds on the wedding band, he grinned again when he saw them on her hand. Her wedding ring setting encompassed the most remarkable set of perfectly cut diamonds he had ever seen—they dazzled like a Fourth of July sparkler—and since they'd been the only setting that caught his discerning eye, he had to have them.

Once aboard, he exchanged a quick look with his wife. *Those eyes. The most beautiful eyes in the world.* He had questions and wanted some answers, but her eyes said he'd just have to wait. She always made him wait.

When he had first seen those eyes, Hunter had been chasing a ball on a racquetball court. He had looked up for a fraction of a second and locked eyes with a dark-haired woman sitting in the viewing stands. His normal hell-bent game plan, a strategy of powerful kill shots and running dives for seemingly impossible return shots, came to a sudden and catastrophic stop.

She was breathtaking, and he instantly forgot he was defending a point in the middle of a game. He swung at the now out of reach ball—grossly missing as if he were a neophyte. The over-torqueing of his body flipped him over and he landed on his back. The landing sounded like a box of books crashing onto the floor. He lay there, taking inventory of any possible injuries and thanked God he hadn't broken his neck, or his back, or a leg. The only casualty was his pride. He was a world-class athlete and embarrassed himself in front of a goddess.

Even after years of marriage it was like that for Hunter every time he exchanged glances with Nazy. As for Nazy, she preferred Duncan on his back.

No one but Hunter and Lynche spoke until the cavernous cargo jet was at cruising altitude. The lights in the aircraft cargo hold turned from white to red. The cabin crew's work was done; they settled in for the administrative phase of the flight and moved to the front of the aircraft to find a place to sleep. Once the aircrew moved forward, the CIA crew—the three spooks and the contract pilot—moved to the rear of the jet. Hunter fetched water bottles from his cooler and handed them out. He was about to give Lynche an ass chewing he wouldn't soon forget, but first some housekeeping. Hunter removed his flight jacket and gave it to his wife to keep her warm. He slowly peeled off the facial hair and the prosthetic cheeks and nose. Nazy, Kelly, and Lynche approved the old look with smiles. Kelly sighed heavily and yawned as if she hadn't slept in days.

Everyone could see he was limping more noticeably this time, as if the simple exertion of retrieving water bottles spiked a nerve in his hip to the point where he struggled to move his leg. Hunter popped a handful of pills with his water.

Lynche allowed Hunter to sit before he spoke formally. "Six Navy SEALs and two men from SAD, Special Activities Division, were captured by ISIS several hours ago." Hunter glanced at Nazy who pinched her lips and nodded.

Lynche continued, "We believe our men will be executed at first light in a manner that's only limited by ISIS' murderous imagination." It was painful for Lynche to admit that all of their efforts could easily be for naught.

Hunter inferred that he and his quiet airplane were needed to find the missing men. No one needed to say it. It wasn't necessary. All the pent up anger and frustration within him dissolved. ISIS made al-Qaeda look like Romper Room.

"How did they get caught?" Hunter asked over the susurrus of air screaming over the C-17's airframe.

"An RPG round was fired through the building where they were meeting some resistance fighters. The upper floor fell on top of them. Two other SEALs were killed and pulled from the rubble. ISIS ensured they and the rebels were dead."

Hunter understood. Each dead SEAL received two bullets to the head. Double tap just to make sure. ISIS wouldn't waste a bullet on a Muslim resistance fighter. They'd use knives. But capturing a number of the legendary U.S. Navy SEALs was a bonus in terms of intelligence and propaganda value. America would pay dearly to recover their finest professional warriors, but the propaganda value of captured Navy SEALs outweighed any monetary reward. The Al-Jazeera network would run their execution *gratis*. Stimulate the radical *jihadis*. Motivate the Muslim masses. Recruit more warriors for the *caliphate*. The live execution of Navy SEALs would cause ISIS' recruiting efforts to skyrocket.

Nazy said, "Before the dust had settled on the collapsed building, ISIS fighters dragged the injured out of the building, they handcuffed them and then moved them to a nearby safe house. Predator video recorded the event until it was chased off by a surface-to-air missile. Our men were immediately surrounded. They never had a chance to evade capture."

"You sure they're still alive?" Hunter asked.

Lynche nodded. There was some additional information he wasn't going to tell Hunter unless he absolutely had to.

"Sounds like it was a trap. Or a bad RPG. You can't trust that old Soviet shit. I assume it was old Soviet crap."

Lynche frowned, nodded, and said, "Maybe. We don't have all of the intel on that operation. We have satcom on this jet. If there's any change in the intel…we'll receive it."

"So we think they're alive. Do you know where they are?"

Lynche pursed his lips and nodded. "Yes and no."

"Chips? Low-power proximity…."

Hunter was more intuitive than Lynche gave him credit for. "We used some of your quiet UAVs to determine their coordinates. Insufficient data. We believe you should be able to pick up their signals from the Yo-Yo. We brought a chip detector." Lynche pointed to an orange diplomatic bag among a pile of black and green backpacks and bags. Everything was dark or black for night operations. His Yeti cooler looked pink in the red cabin lighting.

Hunter nodded pensively. *His quiet UAVs were in a combat zone? Why shouldn't they be?* They were technological marvels of aerodynamics, acoustics engineering, and the latest improvements in battery technologies. Hunter's companies operated more as a well-funded secret research laboratory for the "intelligence community" contracts, especially for the Intelligence Advanced Research Projects Agency, IARPA.

Built on a CIA contract from the in-house laboratory of Quiet Aero Systems, the sixteen electrically-driven propellers allowed the unmanned aerial vehicle to take off and land vertically. Tiny acoustic sensors on the aircraft picked up and compared the frequencies from the alternating counter-rotating propellers. Signal processors continually monitored and adjusted the frequencies of adjacent propellers which cancelled out the undesirable noise-making harmonics to achieve quiet flight. A human couldn't discern the noise profile of the two-foot by two-foot rotorcraft, even from just a few feet away.

Hunter didn't say that his company's quiet UAVs could also serve as a mothership, able to carry a half-dozen of their latest tiny lethal rotorcraft. With shaped charges. In a few minutes they could be changed from picture takers to murderous weapons with tiny bombs designed to blow up in a person's face. DOD couldn't put artificial intelligence (AI) into weapons, but that's what Hunter's labs had done for the CIA and no other agency.

He changed subjects. "Why the welcoming committee? I didn't need to meet those two. That obsequious oleaginous little creep with the nice shades and bad haircut—I'm supposed to take him seriously? I think I've seen him in an episode of *Star Wars*. Bar scene. Ever talk to someone so stupid that they make you squint? Like he's a real spy or something because he's the NCS Director? He seems to have the intellectual capacity of a jerboa. That's a desert rat with funny ears. What's the psycho's name again?"

Lynche sighed. "Steve Castaño."

"How long has he been in *that* position?"

Lynche was put-off a bit. He hadn't expected the interrogation but answered his friend anyway. "He's been either the Deputy Director of the NCS or the Director for the last ten years. He's been 'with the service' since the late seventies. Expert in impersonation and psychological operations, and he taught courses in *political interference….*"

Hunter didn't like the Agency's wordplay. "You mean assassinations." The CIA wouldn't use a word unless they could obfuscate.

Lynche smiled at being caught fudging accuracy and continued, "…and cover and concealment. He was Chief of Disguise." He looked at Nazy. "He's also interrogated some al-Qaeda and Taliban. He was on the ground in Afghanistan directing bin Laden and al-Qaeda interdiction operations. He's somewhat of an intellectual."

Hunter quipped, "He's something of an ass, if you ask me." The reference to political interference and assassinations intrigued him. Hunter assumed they described the same function where one term was the "official term," much like how "spying" was never used in CIA headquarters but "surveillance" was the official term. Hunter said, "My definition of an 'intellectual' is someone who can listen to the William Tell Overture without thinking of the Lone Ranger. I thought you guys don't do wet work. Executive order and all that." Assassinations notwithstanding, the mention of the failed CIA operation to find Osama bin Laden immediately after the World Trade Center towers fell got Hunter's attention. The CIA blamed Captain Bill McGee and the Navy SEALs for failing to find the master terrorist in the Afghanistan mountains. "That was a *goat rope* of the first order. I'm certain they screwed SEAL Team Six's seek and destroy mission six ways to Sunday." Hunter's internal bullshit detector went off the scale. "He's been in on it, too. I can already see we are going to have a day of reckoning with that guy. He'd look better in a Gestapo uniform with a red arm band." *I can see I'm going to have to kill him.*

More braggadocio. Empty threats. Working with a conservative is a pain in the ass. Lynche said, "Better hurry—he's retiring in a few months. The coursework on *political interference* was for training foreign operations officers. It wasn't considered assassination when it comes to killing terrorists. They're legitimate combatants in the war on terrorism."

"I'd think he'd be considered to be your replacement if that woman you're going to vote for wins." Hunter deployed a devious grin at the direct poke at Lynche's previous Democrat political proclivities. *Lynche didn't want to talk politics. It was going to be a long flight.* "And what is it with that voice—he talks like he's a dying vampire. I have to say the Peter Principle is definitely strong with that one. That guy stinks of corruption; you can tell from satellite photos." Hunter pinched his nose and *val salvaed*. His ears popped. He yawned to complete the procedure, grateful for the equalization of pressure in his ears.

Nazy observed the interaction, Kelly was horrified that her father could be a horse's ass regarding her boss, and Lynche frowned at the cutting ad hominem attacks on one of his most trusted intelligence officers. He said, "If you can't say something nasty, don't say anything at all." He didn't know if Hunter was joking or what. But he was going to take it as a joke.

Over the years Lynche had endured much good natured kidding from Hunter who never missed an opportunity to poke at him for voting for the Democrat candidate for president who turned out to be a fraud. *You still a Democrat, Greg? God bless you. I hope you get well soon.* Lynche had voted for Senator Maxim Mohammad Mazibuike for president when Duncan was shouting from the rooftops that the man was dirty—no, he was more than dirty. He wasn't the man he claimed to be. He was a real life Manchurian candidate. *Greg, you really didn't smell a rat? You really didn't? Were you in a coma during the Mazibuike years? Had your brain been vacuumed out of its skull? If you had two brain cells to rub together and you hadn't been in a coma during his time in office, I'd expect you'd see the same thing I see. If you do see it, and it doesn't make an impression on you, we have to get you help.*

Hunter was right then. And the former attorney general running for president, Eleanor Tussy, was also dirty in Hunter's eyes; she was dirty in the ways only a director-level senior executive in the intelligence community could be. But Lynche wasn't going to say anything to Hunter; he'd let him think what he wanted to think. They'd work to do and talking politics siphoned off his energy. But Lynche had one bit of information to share before he returned to the mission. "He might have been interested in my job at one time but what he was really interested in was yours."

Hunter and Nazy looked confused. *What are you talking about?*

Lynche said, "Director Castaño came to me with a white paper, an unsolicited proposal to mount the TS2 sniper rifle on an airplane. He had even flown to Tucson, the Pima Air Museum to look at the YO-3A suspended over their SR-71 *Blackbird*. He thought that mounting the sniper weapon on a quiet aircraft would be the ultimate capability for the National Clandestine Service. An aerial sniper that could perform infil and exfiltration of defectors and NCS personnel. That operating overseas, it could be open season on terrorists." Lynche finished with a curious smile.

Hunter wasn't impressed but suspicious. "Isn't he's about twenty years too late? You said he was working to find bin Laden in the Tora Bora? Is he the one responsible for totally screwing Bill McGee and his SEALs? McGee should have received the Medal of Honor for his actions in the *Hindu Kush* but got fired."

"You know I had been retired for six years when that all went down, so I don't really know. What I do know is Castaño's and Runyan's guys in Syria were well past the front edge of the battlefield. Behind enemy lines. They, SOCOM and NCS, knew no one could rescue their guys; that they were lost, likely dead men. They'd be tortured, likely dismembered, and we'd never recover their remains. They didn't want their men to suffer. The president wondered if you could find them. I suggested to President Hernandez that we could give you a shot, and if you were somehow successful at finding them, then maybe a rescue squad could parachute in to secure them. Getting in is probably the easy part."

"I think the trick will be to find them and somehow save them." Hunter looked at the floor when he said it.

Lynche continued, "I briefed the National Security team on the concept of operation without divulging the capability of the airplane. Or you. If anyone could find them and actually do something to help facilitate a rescue, I said we had a very special guy. You always find a way."

Hunter rolled his eyes as he lifted his head; he stifled a grin and said, "So instead of blowing them up with the mother of all bombs, I get a shot at trying to find them? Anything, Anywhere, Anytime, Professionally." Hunter repeated the CIA's old Air America slogan, trying to be flippant. It was a huge weight on his shoulders. *When the Navy's greatest U.S. Navy SEAL was called to find and kill Osama bin Laden but failed, the Navy shit-canned him. Wonder what will be my punishment if this goes south? Greg already killed me off; buried me. Forced me to retire. Maybe I'll get a real bullet…from one of his NCS guys now that they have seen me. Maybe that bastard had a camera.* He looked up at Lynche. *I'm so mad at you; I can't believe you put me in jeopardy like that.*

Lynche clasped his hands and nodded. Nazy nodded as well. Her green eyes and smile flashed at Hunter like a beacon. Hunter recalled researching *green eyes* and finding that only about two percent of the world had green eyes. *But not like those green eyes!* They were as unreal as they were incandescent.

Hunter tore his away from Nazy's and turned to his daughter. Almost sarcastically, he asked, "Where do you come in?"

"I'm your eyeball. You're the shooter." Kelly used the terms from Hunter's fighter pilot days. Her voice wasn't high, jarring, or grating like some twenty-somethings working at Starbucks, but it was as forceful as it was naturally strong, soft and smooth, like suede.

He was an old Marine Corps fighter pilot; she had been an Air Force jet pilot training student pilots. As the "eyeball" she'd locate the targets using the sensors aboard the aircraft. If there were terrorists, *technicals* — *tangos*, in the vernacular, Hunter would be the trigger puller. Then, *Hold it! Just who the hell am I supposed to shoot?* suddenly banged around his head like a ball bearing in a short-circuited pinball machine.

Hunter shook his head. With a glare that could knock over an elephant, he hissed, "No deal. I can do this alone." He wouldn't look at Nazy or Kelly but stared at Lynche with venom and vituperation. *No deal!*

Lynche had known this moment would come. The main reason he brought Nazy along was to coax him onto the jet. He had then waited until they were airborne to brief Hunter, so that he couldn't easily back out. He didn't want to have the situation whereby Hunter would walk away, return to his jet, and leave after he was told of the impossible mission.

Hunter didn't want to be associated with failure, and he resented being put in an unimaginable situation where failure was expected. More like guaranteed. And wasn't one of the possible outcomes that he could die with his daughter? Parents don't put their kids in danger unless they're desperate refugees. Of course, Hunter would refuse. And Lynche knew Hunter would be furious at him for even suggesting placing his daughter in the most dangerous mission of Hunter's career with the CIA. If they were shot down over ISIS-held territory and lived, then their lives would be cut short in the most gruesome way by bands of murderous Muslims. The two best friends locked eyes. *How did we ever get to this point?*

Hunter had been the owner and operator of the YO-3A, codenamed *Wraith*, for over one hundred contracted missions for the CIA. For more than fifteen years there had been no other pilot in the aircraft. Now, with Hunter semi-forcibly, semi-retired, Kelly had two poppy-killing missions in Mexico under her belt, but she hadn't ever deployed the .70 caliber gun. It sat in the belly of her *Wraith*, folded like an origami dragon, collecting dust.

Lynche had no issues with Kelly using the four-head, ultraviolet laser to irradiate opium poppies in the middle of the night, but he drew the line at her "being the eyeball," targeting and killing terrorists. Or watching her father, "the shooter," kill men.

With the YO-3A, Hunter as a solo pilot had eliminated over 100 of the top international terrorists over a 15-year period, then Lynche had suspended Hunter's contract and semi-retired the special access program, *Wraith*. Now Lynche needed more than a favor. He needed Hunter, his daughter, and one of the quiet airplanes to fly over ISIS-held territories to find the missing men.

There were questions of course. Could Hunter locate them? Would they be dead? Alive? If he could find them, would he be able to disable or eliminate those that held the American hostages until the good guys could rescue them? How do you do that from an airplane? Was that the plan? It was all they had. And time wasn't on the side of the good guys.

With virtually every mission, Hunter had proven he could do the impossible. Hunter's antiquated airplane and its bevy of sensors could find all the rabbits in the field at night, and could do it without alerting them that they were being watched. The trick was to sneak up on the rabbits so they could be snared easily or to wound them sufficiently that they could be captured or eliminated. Under normal circumstances, Hunter wouldn't think twice about doing a mission for Lynche or the president. Lynche had always been able to count on Hunter's unquestioned commitment and loyalty. An unexpected outcome from Hunter's last mission had driven a wedge between the two best friends that was a mile wide.

Lynche and Hunter hadn't spoken to each other for months, until the DCI resolved that only Duncan Hunter and his airplane might have a chance to find and rescue the missing men in Syria.

There was understandable tension. Hunter wanted an apology, but Lynche was too arrogant to admit he was wrong. Although the magic words hadn't been uttered, Lynche was calm and matter of fact. "No, you can't do this alone, and you know it. Even if you are able to find them in time, we have no idea how many *technicals* will be on the ground in the area. The gun has a cyclic limitation; I know you can't get off more than six shots in a minute. Bill McGee wouldn't be able to reload the weapon as fast as you can in that cramped cockpit. I need you to assess the situation, manage the battle space, prioritize the targets, and not get task saturated. Kelly can fly the airplane. You'll be too busy targeting bad guys and reloading the gun. If it comes to that."

Hunter's mouth turned suddenly dry. It was one thing to be an airborne assassin for your country. It's another thing entirely to drag your daughter along when there was a possibility of slaughtering humans, if the evil men from ISIS could ever be considered "human." He glanced at Nazy, then Kelly, and then at Lynche. He put his head in his hands and started to focus on how he was going to do the impossible.

26

November 6
Hondo, Texas

"…you were the Marine who knew too much. I thought the target was you." Bill McGee grinned and tossed another salsa-laden chip in his mouth. A stunned Eastwood couldn't close his.

There was more talking than eating. After a sanguine minute, both men appreciated the interlude to feast on the chips and salsa. McGee continued, "Dory, you see, every time I see you or one of your TV specials I always remember of that time in the Agency cafeteria. I can still see it clearly. The rows of tiny ponytail palms that lined the windows of the cafeteria. The courtyard where the smokers congregated, even when it snowed. Someone thought you needed to be silenced because you knew too much. Someone wanted or needed to take you out. But it wasn't you, obviously. I would've read about you being dead. Someone would have probably made it look like a heart attack or a suicide. That's what I would have done."

Eastwood whispered, "Why didn't you do it?"

McGee hit the beer and said, "I didn't think it was real. I was a relatively new lieutenant commander and thought they were just screwing with a brother, ya know? Big bills no one has ever seen? Could have been Monopoly money for all I knew. It had to be some bullshit psychological test. They were always testing their guys for a variety of psychological issues. Polygraphs."

Eastwood finally recovered sufficiently to say, "If it wasn't me, then it had to have been Emory. Colonel John Emory. He committed suicide. People heard a colonel had killed himself and assumed it was me. Like you said, I'd been in the news. Same timeframe."

McGee shrugged and offered, "The medical examiner's report ruled it a suicide but never explained how or why the back of his head was smashed in, as if someone had taken a baseball bat to it. The family disputed the suicide findings. There were *five* separate investigations."

Eastwood frowned. *Five?* "So you know about Emory?"

"It's more than that. I know what precipitated his death."

"What? How so?"

He checked the Growler before he spoke. "Emory tried to blow the whistle on a bad CIA op. They had some bad actors smuggling heroin into the country in an Agency C-130."

"That's what you think?"

"That's what I know. Good credible sources, my guys. What was I supposed to think? I get pitched for a hit. They showed me the money. I think it's BS. Colonel Emory shows up on the blotter that same week. The following week, there was a tiny innocuous article in the *Navy Times*."

"O-6s…Marine colonels don't kill themselves. They're stabbed in the back so they can't make general. Or in this case, someone shoved a shotgun into his mouth."

McGee nodded. "I agree. And his teeth were broken. I quietly asked around—some of my SEAL bubbas in Coronado had hitched a ride—they called them 'milk runs'—to Honduras, Guatemala, Peru, Ecuador, El Salvador, Colombia. They moved all kinds of crap from household goods to armored cars for ambassadors. It was easy to get into country in one of the Agency's cargo or small passenger airplanes."

"A couple of SEALs mentioned to their skipper in Coronado that when they boarded the aircraft to go back downrange to Colombia, they could smell heroin on the airplane. The C-130 could be full of weapons and ammo heading to Colombia, and even over the smell of jet fuel that cargo has its own distinctive aroma of concentrated gunpowder, but they could still smell the overpowering odor of fresh black tar heroin."

"Seriously?"

"You know how that shit smells?"

Eastwood said, "Actually, I don't. Marijuana yes. Coke, heroin; nope."

"I'll tell you a story. I was out in Tucson, Arizona and the Border Patrol was going to give us a demonstration of how effective their drug dogs, their money dogs, and their people dogs were in the field."

Eastwood downed more chips and salsa and waited for the rest of the story.

"I went with some Border Patrol Agent to retrieve what they called, 'operational test pieces, or OTPs.' We rounded the corner of this warehouse and from a hundred feet away, I could smell it; whatever the hell 'it' was. The agent said the stuff continually outgasses, just like how C-4, dynamite, and explosives outgas."

"I've heard that smugglers think coffee, dead fish, stuff like that will confuse a dog."

McGee was agreeable. "They used anything that had an incredible stench. But those dogs surprised me. They were nearly perfect in a matter of seconds no matter what the stuff that was hidden in."

"So your guys thought because they smelled black tar heroin, that the Agency guys were moving the stuff around? Like bringing it into the U.S.?" Eastwood was flabbergasted.

McGee nodded. "The Agency guys wouldn't let any SOF return on the big cargo aircraft when it was coming home empty from Central America. New Air Branch policy. Under normal ops, it should have been no problem to hitch a ride home. The head of Air Branch changed the policy allowing us to fly with them. It was so odd as to be suspicious, obvious. My guys knew what was going on. They were smart not to say anything."

"So what happened to Emory?"

"The story I got was that Emory was flying a Beech King Air, a C-12, late at night on an approach into El Toro when the Agency's C-130 asked for an expedited landing. They used some nonstandard language to indicate they had a problem, and the air traffic controller asked if he wanted to declare an emergency. Emory was in front of the C-130. He got on the radio and told the control tower he'd 'go-around' to let the aircraft with the faster airspeed land. The Agency pilot wouldn't declare an emergency. He told the control tower he had it under control."

"So the pilot had an emergency but...."

"He didn't want fire trucks or firefighters anywhere near his airplane when it landed. Right."

Eastwood began to chuckle. "Okay...."

"The Marines had someone sitting at the approach end of the runway where they have landing lights that shine straight up, so the dude at the end of the runway can tell if the aircraft has his landing gear down or not. He's called the 'wheels watch.'"

"Sounds like a punishment job."

"Probably. Rumor had it Emory heard from the control tower, who heard it from the wheels watch that the gear was down, but two engines on one wing were out on the four-engine cargo airplane. Emory was so pissed at the Agency pilots for not declaring an emergency that when *he* landed, something like fifteen minutes later, he jogged over to where the Hercules was parked and was going to chew their ass for being so incredibly stupid."

"Sounds like something a Marine colonel would do."

"It's almost midnight; the flood lights were off in the area where the Agency aircraft was, and Emory got close enough to see guys removing what are obviously packages of some kind of dope from the belly of the aircraft. They probably hid the stuff under the floorboards. He was so close that if he had a little downwind breeze, he could have smelled that crap."

Eastwood said, "Makes sense." *The CIA was running raw black tar heroin into the country? Where have I heard this before?*

"Emory backtracks. Tells his big boss in the morning. Then after a day or so, some Marine Corps one-star tells Emory he's under investigation for misusing an aircraft. Emory called his buddy three-star on the east coast. By the end of the week, he's found in the backyard of his house on base. The wife found him; the coroner said he put a shotgun in his mouth. They ruled it a suicide. And just to be clear, that was later the same week I was pitched."

At that moment a pair of Texas State Troopers sauntered through the doors of the *Azteca*. All eyes panned to the men in their "Texas tan" uniforms. Their badges were reminiscent of the Texas Rangers' famous "star-in-a-wheel" badge. Shoulder patches featured the Texas Highway Patrol crest. They didn't remove their grey cowboy hats until they sat down.

Eastwood and McGee acknowledged the highway patrolmen's presence with a friendly nod and returned to their conversation.

"It's always good to eat where the law visits. So that was the same week you were pitched. All I can say is, 'Wow!'" Eastwood sat in stunned silence as Letty cleaned the table and presented the check. McGee let the bill sit until Eastwood recovered it. He fished out two relatively new $100 bills and told Letty, "The food was great. Nice job, Letty." He lowered his voice and nodded in the direction of the two State Troopers. "And, I'm buying those troopers' dinner. Keep the change."

"You'll spoil her!" warned McGee playfully.

"Like you haven't!"

Letty flashed a Hondo Homecoming Queen smile and thanked the men as she pushed away from the table.

"So, who do you think did it?"

"What, Emory?"

Eastwood nodded.

"We have a Presidential Executive Order that prohibits assassinations. With that said, my money has always been on that dude with the bad hands who wanted me to kill Emory."

Eastwood thought, *NCS. National Clandestine Service. The CIA's real spies. Operational undercover guys — operations officers. The best special operations training in the world. Handpicked for the most sensitive missions. When I was with the National Security Council, I heard that they have amazing access to amazing amounts of money. Like 1934 United States Gold Certificates?*

McGee continued. "I've given it a lot of thought. I don't know who else could do it. In Afghanistan they bought the services of the local militias to help them fight the Taliban. They buy intel. They buy muscle. They buy services. They buy loyalty. They bought horses! They know how to do it. They took tubs of cash to start the war on al-Qaeda and the Taliban."

He pointed to himself and said, "Guys like you and me have no idea how to get tubs of money. To them it was like getting a pad of paper from the wall locker in the Admin Office. I'll tell you, their cash saved lives. Their cash made the impossible possible." McGee snapped his fingers when he said, "…like that. They can do something like that on a moment's notice. We have to get orders well in advance of an operation. We live in the real world, not on the dime of the dark state."

Eastwood stopped breathing. *Did he just utter "dark state?"*

McGee turned his head toward the Growler and continued, "But when some dude with really bad hands and mirrored sunglasses, someone who's obviously NCS and is deathly afraid of having his picture taken, flashes a stack of rare large ones, you get the hint really fast that—assuming they were real—they have plenty more where that came from. Their little special access programs means they have special access to funds and special access to James Bond-type equipment—stuff that's twenty, thirty years ahead of anything you can conceive of—to do on the book jobs and apparently, off the grid jobs. And if you cross them, they'll bite you on the ass like an alligator on acid. Or jam a shotgun in your mouth and break all your teeth."

Eastwood shook his head and said, pensively, "Or get whacked in the back of the head with a baseball bat? So the dude had bad hands? Like how? Arthritic?"

"No, burned. Burn scars probably up to his forearms. Oh, and his ears were also burned. He wore his hair long to cover up his ears. Vain son-of-a-bitch. And sunglasses. Even indoors. Couldn't see his eyes. And he had a tic. Weird sucker."

"Bill, if you were at CIA headquarters, how would you have gotten to the west coast where Colonel Emory was? I would think they would've had you avoid public transportation. If you were to go to Dulles and jump on a jet, that would leave a trail."

McGee shook his head gently and said, nonchalantly, "I'm surprised you don't know. They had…*have* their own little airline. Emphasis on 'little.' I don't know if it is still in play. Small planes; twin engines. Like Sky King, the television show. I'm sure they have Agency pilots to move their agents around the country and the globe. Maybe the NCS guys are all trained pilots. But maybe they have contract pilots too."

Eastwood nodded and took a drink. "Just like in the 70s and 80s when the Navy and the Marine Corps had a couple of DC-9s that moved troops from one coast to the other." *They had their own little airline!*

McGee said, "Yes, there were too many bad guys out there willing to put a bomb on a commercial airliner just to kill an American or a British spook. PanAm had a 747 blown out of the sky over Ireland — someone squealed, probably a defector or a spy, that Agency guys were aboard the jet. So the Agency stopped the practice."

"Now Agency execs move around in jets; lower-level guys move around in smaller more discrete Air America airplanes, I suppose. They stay off commercial flights. Anyway, all those aircraft were run by Air Branch. Time sensitive travel can be contracted in a matter of hours." McGee thought of how he and Hunter raced to South Africa on a moment's notice.

Eastwood asked, "Weren't some of the Air America guys accused of doing exactly the kind of things that we're talking about?"

Suddenly McGee was quiet. Another glance at the Growler. He conceded. "I think you're correct. There were stories within the IC. But that was well before my time. All I do know is that once upon a time they were a huge part of the intelligence community and they were a tight-knit group. They could keep a secret when they had to. Which is why I learned early on that you must not cross them. We never had this conversation."

Eastwood swept his thoughts aside for the moment and nodded. "You can probably make the case that rogue CIA types knocked off Emory, but how would you account for these... *others* — the democrats, republicans, liberals, commies, conservatives? Sometimes I'm convinced the deaths of defectors are a piece of the puzzle. There's a whole lot of fake or manufactured suicides going on. Are they related? Someone has to be the ultimate decision maker. Someone has to be the belly button who determines who, what, when, where, and why to do one of these."

"I don't know who that person could be." McGee shook his head and shrugged his massive shoulders. He considered the alternatives for a few seconds and gave up. No one person could possibly be *the One*.

Eastwood said, "I used to think it was 3M."

McGee demurred. Shook his head slightly. "He was nothing until the dhimmis and the media created him. No, this shit has been going on for a long time. Well before that turd showed up on the scene."

A wicked thought entered Eastwood's head: *Has it been going on since before the CIA was created in 1947; maybe even before the OSS?* Eastwood offered, "Then again, maybe it's the Democratic National Committee."

McGee smiled smugly at the solution. "Crap! Maybe now you're getting somewhere. The kid that was killed? You said he worked for the DNC. Dirty tricks machine; they've been at war with the Republicans since Lincoln took their slaves away."

Eastwood nearly bit off the tip of his finger at McGee's comment.

"This isn't that hard, Dory. Look at who they have running that place."

"Zhavrazhinov?"

Eastwood had composed himself. "Yeah. The Democrats...*the DNC*—they make the Gambino crime family look like a charitable organization. They're in charge and they get away with *everything....*"

"Could it be him?" Eastwood laughed and almost choked. "I have to admit I don't know anything about him other than he was the spawn of some Russian expats and a law professor at Harvard. Taught little Tommy Larrabee and curiously, one former President of the United States, Maxim Mohammad Mazibuike."

"I know a little—he has an interesting past. And an interesting accent."

"But he doesn't really have an accent, does he? His grandparents were Russians who escaped the Bolsheviks. Supposedly he was born in America."

"That's what I mean." McGee looked away and then came back with, "Maybe he grew up American but if you're in the intelligence community, he speaks like he is a graduate of the KGB's language school. I'll bet his document history is all fake, bogus. I'd bet old-school KGB. Deep plant and maybe even runs a sleeper cell. Or two. Or twenty. And, you know, that would explain...." McGee was struck with a case of lethologica until he found the right word. "Much."

Eastwood almost whispered, "Yes. Much. Fake documents like Mazibuike's."

McGee nodded. He took a drink and watched Eastwood squirm as his brain did somersaults.

Eastwood liked McGee's analysis and his understanding. *I think we're simpatico.* "I have this notion that you and Duncan Hunter know a whole lot more than you let on. That you're operating at a level or two or three above my level of strategic thinking and understanding. I no longer have my clearances. I think you are operating in something that parallels that undefined entity you called the 'dark state' but on the side of good, not evil."

McGee laughed at the suggestion and grinned like he was holding something back.

"Maybe you and Duncan were behind the incident at the Burj Khalifa, the severed heads, and '*those girls*' being rescued from the UAE. And 3M is still nowhere to be found, although there's a curious rumor on the dark web that some part of him was found at the base of the tower. All of it smacks of some…that some of my friends have very interesting jobs. Lead very interesting lives."

McGee popped another salsa-dipped chip in his mouth. He tried to curtail a grin while he chewed. Sometimes a person not admitting to or denying an accusation leads the accuser to infer guilt. McGee just relished the remainder of his chips and salsa as he ignored Eastwood's fishing expedition.

27

November 7
Hondo, Texas

Finding no hint of validation in McGee's eyes, Eastwood attacked another tortilla chip and pressed a little harder by referencing one of his television specials, *Escape From The Devil's Hole*. Almost three hundred women and girls had managed to escape an underground prison and the centuries-old sex trade in the United Arab Emirates. A white man in black coveralls rescued them from their underground prison and led them to freedom.

Eastwood asked, "Is this something you did? As a SEAL?"

"What?"

"Political warfare. Domestic…assassinations."

McGee acted as if the question was absurd. "We killed the enemies of America. Overseas. We didn't conduct what you call political warfare in America. That's called 'murder' in a court of law. No normal person can get away with murder in the United States. At least not for long."

Eastwood pinched his lips in disappointment.

McGee looked hurt. "That's why you really wanted to talk."

"That's part of it. I keep stumbling into you and Hunter, a couple of old retired grey-haired guys popping up in the strangest places. Like on the U.S.S. Eisenhower. Like on the runway in Liberia. Dubai sounds like a Hunter-McGee op. And then there's this." Eastwood fished a thumb-sized bullet with tiny fins from his shirt pocket and handed it to McGee. "I dug that up in northwestern Nigeria a few nights after you and Duncan rescued us on that jet. It was obvious some Boko Haram leaders were killed from an aerial platform. Apparently lions dragged their carcasses off into the jungle. I reported on a couple of dozen Nigerian girls who were rescued from the clutches of the murderous Boko Haram. The girls said something interesting, that 'the sky flashed' and 'God had saved them.'"

McGee barked at Eastwood in hushed tones and wagged his screwdriver handle-sized finger. "That's another thing you can't say out loud, even when we have a Growler." The little green device kept flashing its green light to show that it was working. McGee handed the projectile back to Eastwood with an impassioned face. The bullet head had been fired from the one-of-a-kind special weapon in Hunter's airplane. McGee was curious. *How in the hell did he figure that out?*

Eastwood returned the glass-tipped, spaceship-shaped bullet to his pocket, apologized, changed the subject, and asked, "So were there any other reasons you didn't take the money? In hindsight, should you have?"

"If it was real and I took it, I'd have had to leave the SEALs. You just don't run off cross country because someone pushes a cigar box full of money at you and expect no repercussions. On one hand, I loved being a SEAL and wasn't ready to leave, even with all the Navy's BS. I was also just—as Duncan would say—becoming 'politically aware.' What impact politics had on me and my job. Who pulled the strings to make me do things to neutralize threats to the country. On the other hand, we learn to be very suspicious of Greeks bearing gifts. The Trojan horse wasn't just an ambush. What they giveth, they could easily taketh away. Know what I mean?"

Eastwood nodded; his face lit up as if he had seen an angel. "They could come after you. How can you trust an unknown entity?"

"Exactly. The NCS dude wasn't arrogant or cavalier. He apologized and said his intel was wrong. That maybe I could be pitched when I obviously couldn't be. Then he said, 'We never had this conversation, Lieutenant Commander McGee. Say nothing and no harm will come to you or your family. If you change your mind later, return to this spot and bring a cigar box like this one—Roi-Tans—and someone will come get you.' Then he walked away."

"That's strange."

"You think that's strange? The only cigars my father ever smoked were Roi-Tan Bankers."

McGee stared at Eastwood. The old Marine got the hint. *They must have vetted McGee and his family pretty thoroughly to find that tidbit of information. It was another way of saying 'I know all about you.' You can run but you can't hide.* Then Eastwood had an epiphany, *'You can run but you can't hide' probably applies to most Russian defectors. Whittaker Chambers was able to defect and hide—what did he do that the others didn't?*

McGee continued, "In a way, the good colonel wasn't worth my time. If I was going to knock someone off for money, it had to really be worth it. Colonels for a million bucks weren't worth it."

Eastwood nodded. Listened. *It was worth it to someone....*

"It would mean I would be out of the game...."

"*The game...?*"

"You know when you first sign that SF-86, get your clearance, you're a member of the intelligence community. A very special member. Yale may have had their Skull and Bones but there's no better secret society than the IC. And within the IC there are enclaves. The left, the right—opposite ends—are the main players on the board. Each one trying to gain control of Intel—the three letter guys—and Justice and the FBI. Every once in a while someone gets too far over their skis and has to go. They take damaging information with them, knowing they need a bargaining chip. I think this is what your Larrabee found himself in the middle of."

Eastwood concurred.

"Tomorrow we have an election. If that termagant doesn't win, there will be war. They'll try to start a race war, at the very least—which is what 3M tried to do. He did everything in his power to promote Islam and Marxism. In so many ways he was worse than that murderous African dictator Mugabe."

Eastwood had to agree and he said so. Then he shifted gears. "Bill, I've one more thing. For the last twenty years I've tracked the top 100 or so international…global terrorists. A kind of 'Who's Who" of master terrorists. And you know what? Most of them have either disappeared or died under mysterious circumstances. Yambo Griot, the murderous leader of Anwar al-Islami, the Light of Islam in Mali, the guy who couldn't keep his face away from a camera, was found dead outside an ancient mosque while earth-moving equipment sat idling. He was the first. You and Duncan show up in Liberia and whack what, eight hijackers, and then in Nigeria most of Boko Haram's top leaders go missing. There are some amazing things that happen to the world's worst terrorists when you and Duncan are *'in the area.'* Can I say that? And the list goes on and on."

"So?" McGee's grin was infectious. "A hundred is just a starter set for the two hundred forty-one Marines they killed in Beirut. They dumped Petty Officer Robert Dean Stethem's body on the tarmac in Beirut. Three thousand for the World Trade Center. Many thousand more in Afghanistan and Iraq."

Were those revenge killings? Eastwood thought. "So, I think the USG, specifically the Agency has been using Hunter and you to find and whack those moles and put them out of business."

McGee suddenly yawned as if he just got off the red eye from Washington.

"I was thinking if any or all that's true, that these are kind of *right-leaning*…uh, activities. Why can't there be a similarly capable, maybe offsetting…left-wing *service* for lack of a better word, to eliminate those who have committed political sins against say, lefty interests? Maybe they're funded by lefty billionaires. *Dark state* billionaires. I've given this a lot of thought. If POTUS or the DCI use you and Hunter to eliminate high-profile *tangos* overseas under a black program, a distinctly super-secret right-wing—some may call it patriotic—activity then wouldn't it make sense if the liberals, Democrats, progressives or whatever they're called this week used or had access to a similar capability that they would? But they don't use it to eliminate the enemies of America. They use it to eliminate the enemies of the left. The Democrats' enemies; the enemies of the Communist Party. Their enmity isn't confined to Republicans and conservatives and God-fearing people. They also include liberals and others who defect from the party and who know too much."

"...those who are a threat. Like you!"

"Yes, I'm a threat. Like my contact was in the DNC."

McGee stretched his neck, scratched his temple, pulled his nose, and rubbed his face all in an effort to dismiss such an outlandish idea. Another yawn. Suddenly he had more tics than an Iowan farm dog. Once the tics ran their course, he looked at Eastwood with hard eyes.

Eastwood continued, "According to his mother, he may have considered leaking some of their most sensitive information to one of those websites that specializes in making public, ah...censored or restricted official materials involving spying and corruption. And she indicated that he was so infuriated with the Democrats for actively laundering money for terrorist groups, conducting espionage for the Russians, and facilitating the employment of Islamic Underground men and women in federal service, that he felt compelled to defect from the Democrat Party. Maybe go to work for the Republicans. In any case, he was defecting...."

McGee waited for the real news.

Eastwood obliged. "I was on my way to meet him."

"Your informant?"

Eastwood was a little embarrassed. "Yes. He was my informant. He was murdered just yards from where we were supposed to meet. He had something of value to give me. His mother and I talked. At the time, I didn't know what he had or its importance. Now I do. He gave the archives of the DNC to his mother. He probably had the latest batch of information on him. So his death...it's sort of personal."

McGee said, "Shit happens when you play with the big dogs. I'm sure he had no training in counter-surveillance. I'm sure some clown figured out what he was doing and popped his ass. Was he a computer guy?"

Eastwood was shocked still and his eyes bugged out at the mention of "clown." He recalled the scene from the rear of the bus as a clown stepped into the light. He said, "Yes. He was the head of the DNC's opposition research department. They spied on Republican congressmen and senators, businessmen, general officers and admirals, and the right-leaning Supreme Court Justices. And the NRA. He told his mother that he had so much information, he didn't know if he could capture all of it, top secret information that was stolen from congressional offices by DNC tech staffers and sold to the Islamic Underground and Russian intelligence. There was even special access program information in the files. The DNC Chairman Zhavrazhinov and their presidential candidate were in the middle of it. Some of the info could have been used to blackmail underperforming Democrats at the state and national level and every anti-communist Republican member of Congress. He told her all of it. It may have put their lives at risk."

"And their contacts.... You know there's been a rash of journalists being murdered for exposing corrupt cops in Mexico. Moscow. London. Actually, journalists across the world are being killed."

Eastwood nodded. "And their families, too. Yes. I think he — Tommy Larrabee — had more information. He told his mother that he was saving the best for me. After his death nothing popped up on that leaky website, at least not immediately."

"Someone got to him first. Somehow his comms were tapped. If they weren't surreptitiously surveilling his computer with some special monitoring software, then you popping up on his screen probably got him killed. Or there may be other reasons." McGee pinched his lips one final time. "They're like the Kremlin. Anyone who could testify to a crime incriminating the DNC must be silenced. Your connection with him could put you at risk. *Again!* Definitely his parents. I'd worry about that. At the very least, you need to warn them that they could be targeted. Killed."

Eastwood pointed at the bag he had given McGee. "The rest of it. Maude Larrabee handed me that cigar box full of flash drives, ah, USB memory sticks. Inside are the complete archives of the DNC. Financial records. Everything but the most recent stuff. I told his mother she needed protection. She told me to kill the DNC; find who was responsible and tear that place apart. She's convinced they killed her son."

"Is she right?"

Eastwood mashed his lips and nodded quietly. *Without a doubt; I just don't know how or who would order the hit. I don't know who would come for her, but I'd start with the DNC Chairman.*

McGee wasn't surprised and grunted. "Any others?"

Eastwood pondered the question for a moment. An issue of relevancy. "It depends on which way you lean. Three men who eviscerated the DNC and 3M and were contributing authors for a conservative blog were found dead; officially of self-inflicted gunshots. They all wrote and published investigative stories about the true life and crimes of Maxim Mohammad Mazibuike and his ascent to the presidency. They were nobodies, except to their families. Their families contacted me. Tommy Larrabee had also done a law school research paper on 'what makes a natural born citizen.'"

Shit! There you go! McGee suddenly donned his cowboy hat and slid out of the booth, leaving Eastwood with his mouth agape. He retrieved the bag with the cigar boxes and tucked it under an arm. His non-shooting arm. McGee's actions were an unmistakable signal that he had had enough. It was time to go.

McGee pocketed the Growler; they walked out into the cool dry Texas night air. They walked along the sidewalk to their vehicles, stopped and shook hands.

Eastwood asked one more question. "I'm trying to chase another rabbit down a hole. In all of your travels and experiences with al-Qaeda and the Islamic Underground, did you ever see any connections with the Democrat Party and the SVR, the old civilian affairs office of the KGB?" Eastwood didn't expect a response.

McGee thought: *What an interesting question. I've thought the same thing…I don't know how many times….* "Beside all those former senators from Massachusetts? You know, Colonel Eastwood, questions like that could get a guy in trouble when he least expected it, like going for a ride in an Oldsmobile to the little town of Chappaquiddick or taking a stroll along a towpath of the Potomac or asking questions after your informant was knocked off. I'll bet your Tommy Larrabee had transferred a document or two to that website."

"Whistleblowers?"

"Yeah. Maybe he wasn't robbed of his wallet—I hear smartphones and fancy watches are the prime target for D.C. robbers. But you know, whatever he wanted to give you, it wasn't on his body when they found him."

Eastwood lowered his head and checked his shoes. Things that men do when they're out of thoughts or ideas. *Yeah, they didn't take his wallet, cellphone, or the fistful of expensive cigars in his shirt pocket. Maude Larrabee said Tommy's Tag Heuer watch, the one he received for graduating from law school, wasn't on his body when police found him and it wasn't in Tommy's apartment. Police didn't report it was stolen but it was missing.* Eastwood nodded, "McLean is likely involved. Guys with bad hands."

McGee scrunched up his face, telegraphing *"maybe; probably."* He said, "Thanks for an entertaining evening, Dory. You be careful and watch your back."

McGee scanned the wide road fronting the *Azteca,* and the nearby crossroad. No apparent tails. No apparent trouble. He patted his pistol on his hip just to make sure he hadn't accidently left it in the restaurant. Another vicious thought entered his conscious: *Duncan once quipped, "Washington Democrats and liberals must have little red prayer rugs with a finding compass so they can pray in the direction of London's Highgate Cemetery or Moscow and bang their heads in obeisance to Karl Marx or Lenin. But no one has ever been able to discover the connection. They were just lefties with Marxist proclivities." Riiiight. Nothing like the "Islamic Underground's secret strategic plan to infiltrate America." Could the Democrats have something similar squirreled away somewhere in America? Not likely. Maybe the focal point is the DNC. The CIA? An intersection of the DNC and CIA? Hmmmm.*

Eastwood watched McGee as he resolved some internal question. When McGee returned to the present, Eastwood asked, "You mean, 'watch my six.'"

"Well, Dory, whatever you do, I think I'd find a topic less *controversial* than those. Take the Hummer. You make great TV specials. I know there has to be money in those. I'd stick to those and not play detective." McGee realized his feet hurt and his head was pounding.

"So you think there may be a connection?"

McGee checked his surroundings again and energized the Grower in his pocket. "Maybe you need to do a thought piece on tactical level thinkers. When I think of 3M, I'm thinking of Marx, Mao, and Mazibuike. Those guys were strategic. And they have convinced scores of people to do their killing for them just so they can keep their hands clean while they collect millions. Billions. So the *dhimmis* in DC can stay in power. It's all about power. It's all about the money."

"Dory, do a little research on *General Plan East* then try to find the secret *General Plan West.* Maybe it's in the National Archives, if you know the right person and ask the right questions. As I understand it, *Plan West* was the Nazi's plan to retaliate against the United States through infiltration. Stalin got a hold of *Plan West* and used parts of it to great effect to rally American liberals and Democrats in the 40s and 50s. The Soviets got black America, who loved and were dedicated to the party of Lincoln, to switch parties with a well-designed plan to use the media to paint white Americans as racists. And they have controlled the American media and the Democratic members of congress for years."

Eastwood nodded and said caustically, "I always wondered how a congressman or a senator who makes less than 200K a year leaves Congress as a millionaire. They make the rules and enrich themselves...."

"While doing work for the Party. Espionage is much more lucrative than smuggling elephant tusk or rhinoceros horn, and definitely less bloody than blood diamonds. They can keep their hands clean. At least most of them. Larrabee and Emory were obvious professional hit jobs. No doubt in my former military mind." McGee exhaled in exasperation. "Pros know who to hire and how to cover their tracks. I'm certain there's a group doing...*doing that kind of work*. You lost your informant. That wasn't an accident. It could be a message. It's possible that clown didn't get a good look at you or know who you were, but I'd be very careful."

The men were interrupted by the sound of a low flying airplane approaching from the north. They turned toward the noise and looked up. By the sound of the engines, the men surmised the plane was still at takeoff power, suggesting it had probably just taken off from the nearby Hondo airport. The lights of the City of Hondo reflected off of the white wings and belly, giving them enough definition to make out its basic configuration; twin engine, tip tanks, retractable landing gear.

McGee looked for green paint and the telltale signs of a FLIR ball on one of the CIA's green aircraft but saw nothing. It was too dark to see the sides of the airplane. It was a "slick" airplane. Probably a Cessna. He knew from experience that the U.S. Border Patrol flew aircraft at night, but they focused their flight operations mostly along the border, not a hundred miles from it. They flew singles, not twin-engine airplanes. When the aircraft was no longer in sight but still audible, the men turned to each other and raised their eyebrows. No FLIR meant they hadn't been caught out in the open and surveilled by a thermal sensor.

Eastwood continued. "I plan to be careful. I used to think it was some lefty cartoonish billionaire Bond villain living on an island in a hollowed-out volcano who would come after me. Now I'm thinking it may be someone within the DNC or associated with your guy with the cigar box. It has to be someone pretty close to the top who orders a hit. Your guy with the bad hands was essentially asking you to do that. He'd be part of a group of pros. But I don't know who that key person could be, or how I'd begin to penetrate that group. Needle in the haystack problem."

"I'd drop it. No good can come of that."

Eastwood asked, "You don't think there could be an ultra-secret cell?"

"It's more than that. Political parties are secret societies, and they have access to money. They have more resources than you; they probably have a group of professional assassins "on call" who would kill you for free. And if they think you're investigating them, well.... Remember, your informant was deep sixed. I'd turn and walk away. Remember the warning, 'no harm will come to you or your family.' Let that sleeping dog lie, Dory. Good night and Semper Fi, GI Dog." McGee pulled the Growler out of his pocket and turned it off.

"You too, Captain McGee. Duly noted. Thanks for a wonderful evening. Be safe."

"Me be safe? We give you an armored vehicle, and you don't even use it," McGee said, half-heartedly.

"Didn't need it here."

"Never assume *'here'* is safe either. Weren't you and Duncan attacked not far from where we are standing? Didn't he, or probably Carlos, come get you in an armored vehicle? Heed the wisdom of a guy who was given a peek behind the curtain and lived to tell about it. Be safe; straight to Randolph. No roving by the light of the moon. And thanks for the 'cigars,' Dory. I'll make sure they get to Duncan." McGee pressed the button on his key fob to remotely start his vehicle, then turned and walked away to his truck. A big white Chevy Silverado.

Seventy years old and he scolds me like I'm seventeen. Eastwood grinned at the thought as he watched McGee drive away. He stood there, reflecting on McGee's actions, in the context of their conversations. *He still thinks he could be targeted. That someone could have placed a bomb under his truck. Effective streamlined assassination. Remote start is the countermeasure. I stopped looking under my vehicles a while back. I need to get back in the habit! Who places a bomb under a vehicle in America? Besides al-Qaeda, the Islamic Underground...and now Democrats? And I'd forgotten that Hunter and I were attacked not far from here. Motorcycle dude with a MAC-10. Hunter's fancy defensive driving saved the day*

28

November 7
Hondo, Texas

Demetrius Eastwood stood on the wide concrete sidewalk for a long minute. Breathing the cool clean Texas air was invigorating, not like the depressing miasma that hovered over the congested New York City or Washington, D.C. and their millions of vehicles.

While standing and filling his lungs with the nearby atmosphere of the "hill country," it occurred to him that there were categories, demarcations. Some people, like him and McGee, didn't fall into the special category of "knowing too much" and so didn't need to be quieted through extreme means.

Then there's the category of people who crossed some imaginary threshold, someone who not only "knew too much," but also did something that indicated they could give or would say something to someone not authorized to know the information, like defectors running away from the Communist Party where purloined secret information was their ticket to freedom. Those had to be silenced quickly. There was no time for planting bombs or planning ambushes. Would a presumed suicide or a chemically-induced heart attack require greater planning? If it was a hit man doing spontaneous wet work…he might only need one opportunity. Knock on the door—stick a gun in his face. Spray or drop something lethal in the area. Control the situation. Dead people who knew too much didn't need the services of a phalanx of lawyers at a legal defense fund. *Blame the dead guy!*

Then the obviousness of it all hit him. They had to have knowledge of extremely damaging, potentially explosive, political information *of the dark state*, like the names of deep cover spies in the government. The time with McGee had convinced him of that. He had to consider if he could be a legitimate target. *What if there was more than Islamists after me? The DNC? Someone with bad hands? Who could possibly be the head guy, the one who determines who had crossed the red line? Who's the guy who determines who should live or die?*

Eastwood wrote down in his notebook and said, "Legal defense funds. Foundations. General Plan West. I have my homework cut out for me."

He looked forward to the drive to San Antonio and the front gate of the huge military base. Eastwood had secured a room in one of the interbellum distinguished visitor quarters at Randolph Air Force Base. Covered *saltillo* tile porch. A nice bed. Ceilings fit for a giraffe. Antique fan overhead. A shower built for two. Off the grid of commercial hotels but still excellent accommodations. A safe place to stay for the night until he travelled back to Washington D.C. to cover the outcome of the election.

But first, he got on his hands and knees and thoroughly inspected the underside of his rental car. Finding nothing that could hurt him, he brushed the *caliche* from his worn out knees, slipped into the car, and headed east on Highway 90. He smiled at Hondo's local "Welcome" sign on the north side of the highway: *This is God's Country. Please Don't Drive Through it Like Hell.*

He slowed down going through the speed-trap town of Castroville. A Texas State Trooper was parked in the shadows of the Exxon station and kept his beady eye on the rental. Passing the speed limit sign on the edge of town, Eastwood bumped the accelerator to 70 and checked his rearview to see if that trooper was coming after him. He wasn't, so Eastwood engaged the cruise control and let his mind wander.

McGee has the DNC's flash drives. It seemed to make sense to put them into the hands of men who are obviously well up the food chain and "inside the wire" of the intelligence community. Patriots. There really isn't anyone else I can think of who would take them and use them properly. The FBI has become a joke. Maybe the CIA Director, but I'd never get a chance to see or talk to him.

Merging onto Interstate 410, Eastwood was mindful of the speed cameras on the freeway. Didn't need a ticket. Traffic was light, and the stars were obscured from the bright lights of metro San Antonio. He took the I-410 bypass to I-35, the interstate that split the State of Texas down the middle.

As he left the Interstate, a trap of state troopers, their cars flashing red and blue lights, were shunting traffic to one side of the two-lane. Voluminous columns of smoke suggested a car fire. He could hear approaching sirens but couldn't see the emergency vehicles. Being forced to slow down only to get funneled into a natural choke point, a narrow defile without any avenue of escape put him on alert. His old SERE training kicked in. *The classic situation for an ambush.* And he was without an armored vehicle. Or a weapon. Adrenaline spiked his veins. But the policemen weren't interested in him and robotically waved him onto the road's shoulder and past the car in flames. Eastwood's heart pounded; the adrenaline that flooded his system made him tingly all over, and not in a good way. He made out the unmistakable shape of a Chevy Volt. Front half on fire, the back half a pretty metallic red. *The last time I saw one of those on fire was in Algeria. Didn't anyone pay attention to history? There's a good reason we moved away from electric cars a hundred years ago! A battery is a chemical bomb. Discharge it too quickly and it'll overheat and go off. Some idiot will find out the hard way if they build a battery-powered motorcycle or find a way to make flying cars with propellers and batteries. Yep, it'll not take long before one of those things run out of juice and fall from the sky.*

With the incinerating car behind him, he returned to unsolved cases and murderous scenarios in his head. He said aloud, "The pros know how to cover their tracks." He slowed to a crawl over the relatively smooth railroad crossing and passed through the front gate of the Randolph Air Force Base, showing his ancient retired ID card to the uniformed gate guard, who didn't recognize him or his name. Eastwood tapped the steering wheel and muttered an observation as he drove away from the gate, "Be aware of old men in a profession where men usually die young. McGee's running a training compound that caters to the special operations community. That McGee—he's still more badass than I'll ever be."

He had changed subjects in his mind without a segue. Then he thought aloud, "They just don't send their screw-ups to some island of misfit toys. They kill 'em. If the DNC is a killing machine, then it'll take somebody like McGee or Hunter to expose them, hunt down their leaders, and defeat them. Hunter's a pro's pro…. So is McGee. But I don't see them getting involved."

After Eastwood got to his room he fired up his computer. He couldn't sleep from all the activity of the evening. As he was wont to do under the circumstances, he had time to write one more article.

29

November 7
McLean, Virginia

NCS Director Castaño took his chair and rotated his head as if he had a cramp in his neck. Maybe his Tourette's was acting up. The operations officers around the conference table knew that when the boss was off his meds and got "that way," neck stretches and random twitchings, they were in for a collective ass-chewing for something that was beyond anyone's control. Even without the occasional Tourette's outburst, the pressure and vicissitudes of counterespionage and counterintelligence work was like that. High blood pressure, headaches, and bottles of aspirin. It looked like it would be another meeting from hell. Maybe this time he wouldn't throw his laptop through a window.

Castaño stopped stretching and massaging his neck, but one hand continued to finger an imaginary pimple in his hairline. His attention turned to the men at the table.

Galvan Fässler, Chief of Counterterrorism (CT); Jarvis Bomarito, Chief of Special Activities Division (SAD); and Bennett Troxel, the former Chief of Air Branch and current Chief of Special Operations Group (SOG) were all in their mid-60s, fit and athletic with full heads of grey hair even as they burned shoe leather working toward retirement. Each of them had received waivers to remain on active duty past the CIA's mandatory retirement age. Each of them wore the same style clothing—navy Ralph Lauren suits, black Rockport shoes, and boring ties off the clearance rack at Macys.

The NCS boys took their fashion cues from their leaders in much the same way as Soviet KGB leaders mimicked the dress of Stalin and Khrushchev. Only Steve Castaño pushed the boundaries set by CIA leaders before him. He shopped at Saville Row and always wore white fitted Brooks Brothers shirts. The other men wore unmanly pastels and earth tones. The rule of thumb, heterosexual spooks don't wear expensive suits like those worn by rich gentlemen—no Base London brogues or ostentatious Italian ties. You wanted to look good, but you'd better not look better than the boss. That also meant no earrings or tattoos. Wedding bands and watches were optional. Breitlings and Tag

Heuers were marginally acceptable; garish gold Rolexes weren't. Wear a Rolex President or drive a new Jaguar F-Type convertible to work and you'd be investigated like Aldrich Ames and sent for a random polygraph. Or two or three. Once you were "on profile," the only way to get off was to go to jail or die.

The four men had all been born into multi-language families of significant means and international connections. Galvan Fässler was born in Switzerland of American parents. For a time his father had been a Swiss Air pilot, and the young Fässler had learned to fly his father's private Cessna in Europe. He was on the short side of average height with sloping shoulders, one higher than the other, but had the fortune of looking like his father who was often mistaken for a young Errol Flynn with flyaway hair. He had perfect white teeth, a husky voice that women loved, and a good sense of humor about life, which he developed by walking away from a half-dozen bad landings that totaled the aircraft he had been flying. He felt he was very lucky, and he'd often say he was the luckiest person he knew.

Jarvis Bomarito was the oldest of six children from the wealthy suburbs of Philadelphia and New York. One of his brothers told the officer conducting his background investigation that their youth was "conventional upper-middle class, well educated, well-traveled, interested in good schools and airplanes. Our social lives centered around the country club." Bomarito was compact and powerfully built. He bumped five-foot nine with a face and voice that were made for radio—lovely to hear but with an overly hawkish nose and steely slit eyes he wasn't much to look at, although he had little trouble attracting women.

Bomarito had his father's sense of humor and was fascinated with airplanes and fast cars. He did everything he could to barter rides at the local airport. He owned his first aircraft, an ancient Schweizer sailplane, and attained his glider pilot's license before he was old enough to drive. Most people looked at him with fear, especially when he looked from under his brows and scowled. People didn't find him likeable. He mumbled; he could be surly and taciturn and seemed to lack the charm and social skills of a senior intelligence service executive. He was full of himself, and it showed in his brazen swagger typical of the graduates of special operations training as well as in the fast cars he drove and collected. Bomarito believed his stable of rare Jaguars, Porsches, and Ferraris was his retirement account. He hid them in an aircraft hangar with a bevy of red airplanes, a Beech Staggerwing and a Fokker Dr1. His prized possessions were a red 1954 Mercedes-Benz 300SL

Gullwing and a BMW 507, million-dollar show cars.

Bennett Troxel was schooled at military academies in France and Germany and became fluent in both languages. His voice was rough and gravelly when he spoke German. He had the conventional good looks of a Hollywood movie star—slicked-back hair, wide toothy smile, and a caustic sense of humor when conversations turned dull. Short, medium build and muscular, he loved to tinker with anything mechanical. Not many kids owned four different bicycles at age 14, but he did, and they were immaculately maintained. His family moved to America, to Shaker Heights near Cleveland, Ohio, where he was no longer able to tinker with bicycles, so he was forever getting in trouble looking for new opportunities for excitement. His background investigator was told, "He's somewhat of a screw-up. He'd screw up a date with Japanese twins." Fifteen-year-old Troxel had stolen several single-engine airplanes from an airport a few miles away from his house, crashing the first two and walking away unhurt. He taught himself to fly in an airplane he stole from an airport east of Cleveland. He attended the aviation high school adjacent to Lake Erie, and by the time he graduated, he had both a private pilot and an airframes and powerplant license. He was a mechanic and a pilot. A great combination if you were prone to steal airplanes. As an aircraft owner, Troxel hid several rare "bent-wing warbirds" in a hangar not far from the 9/11 memorial in Pennsylvania.

Castaño had graduated from James Madison University with a major in world literature and history. His master's thesis was a treatise on the assassinations of world leaders. Before his accident he was class president and head of the school newspaper. He was voted "best politician," "should go to law school," and "most likely to succeed as a mob boss." He would have surprised his classmates with his politics, which he kept close to his vest. He was fascinated with presidential assassinations and frequently attended socialist and communist gatherings and with his facial scarring and burned hands, he was always fearful of being recognized. He learned how to hide his defects with makeup and rubber prosthetics and became a master of disguises.

The four men hid their politics from their families. Background investigators questioned friends and neighbors on the men's political leanings, but were met with indifference or ignorance. Not one of the CIA candidates had verbally expressed a political leaning which helped expedite the men's applications.

Their orbits first intersected in the corporate offices of Air America a few months before the CIA front company was sold off piecemeal to foreign entities. They were unceremoniously dropped from the

Agency's rolls. For the next four years they took whatever work they could get; at first none of it was glamorous or profitable. Then came the drug lords and the arms smugglers and the black market work put bushels of money in their pockets.

With their top secret security clearances close to expiration, Castaño contacted some of the people at the Agency with whom they had flown during the latter stages of the Vietnam War. He had flown assassination teams into and out of North Vietnam and other countries. He found that he could make more money flying drugs, contraband, preteen girls, and the occasional warlord and was rewarded handsomely for his work as a pilot who could keep his mouth shut. He made several close personal contacts with members of the special operations communities and the connections paid off; Castaño and his friends were soon back with the CIA. The infamous Farm. Paramilitary operations. They all had a lengthy stint in school learning the tradecraft and other skills necessary to be an operations officer. They were *experienced* and multilingual, and although they were shorter and older than the other trainees, they were leaner, meaner and a little brighter.

When Castaño's knowledge and expertise of political assassinations became known, he was pushed into instructor duty. He wrote secret case studies on John Wilkes Booth and Lee Harvey Oswald for the CIA's research board. Being an expert on the kinds of men who planned, attempted or killed politicians was considered the kind of useful knowledge that must be shared with new members of the NCS executive leadership.

Fässler, Troxel, and Bomarito found themselves working for Steve Castaño, Chief Pilot, Air Branch. For more than twenty years, Castaño dispatched the trio to the winds, flying missions on six of the seven continents. In private settings at the NCS training facility, he trained them in the art of assassinations. In the beginning, they privately called themselves *Werewolves*. One day they'd been "just pilots" driving small flying trucks from one East Asia hellhole to another. The next, they were transformed into lethal badass spooks, just as the mild-mannered Lon Chaney found himself being transformed into a vicious wolf during a full moon. When they were on the hunt for defectors or radicals, Castaño and his friends only worked under the cover of darkness.

It was over a card game at Castaño's house one night that he asked the men if they were interested in doing some work for an "unnamed customer." They'd be offered a significant incentive for what Castaño called "wet work." Would they be willing to use their skills to conduct domestic political assassinations on an as-needed basis? Not quite believing the nature of the work or the remunerations they were told they could expect to receive, they cautiously agreed. *They were a team.* As experienced operations officers, they knew how to make a killing look like an accident, a heart attack or a random murder or suicide. They knew how to cover their tracks. At the Farm they'd been personally trained in advanced assassination techniques by the *Top Gun* of wet work, Steve Castaño.

Bundles of American currency facilitated political removals—no questions asked and no records kept. If necessary, they'd leave evidence which would convict a locally known undesirable. Whenever they could, the men used local proxies to assassinate political targets, terrorists, and politicians.

Over the years this team of NCS men developed into competent professional assassins. They improved their skills by killing the enemies of America overseas and the enemies of the Democrat National Committee. The pay was astronomically better than their GS salaries. The targets never saw any of the NCS men coming. One second a target could be walking along a Potomac River path, the next they'd be on their face with a bullet to the back of the skull.

The three men had seen all of Castaño's tics and outbursts over thirty years. Some days were worse than others. Yesterday had been just a normal day at the office until two intelligence officers from SOG were captured by the Islamic State. ISIS.

There was fury behind Castaño's blinking eyes, but instead of the usual expletive-filled rantings of a psychotic with a neurological disorder, he was strangely composed. He was seething, but he was confident and unruffled. This was the first time any of the NCS leaders had seen him like that. His scarred hands settled into his lap, formed a teepee as venom dripped with every word, "We are in the middle of a *Great Game.* That asshole Lynche is running an op 'off the books.' Cunningham is read-in, obviously. We are not. I'm not. Just like the last time when she spearheaded that op in Dubai, and we were cut out. I was cut out. It was just she and Lynche…and they *just piss me off.*" He pounded his fist on the table to convince his men he was more than just ticked off; he was livid.

Up until that moment the men hadn't known why they'd been summoned to the NCS Director's office. The last time the three of them had been summoned for an urgent mission, they immediately deployed to Abu Dhabi to interrupt a meeting on the top floor of the world's tallest building, the Burj Khalifa, in Dubai. That day they'd been disguised as janitors, but didn't find *the pilot* that they'd been sent to kill. They were too late. It was as if their quarry was always one or two steps ahead of them. Instead of killing *the pilot*, as the on-scene intelligence called him, they butchered the dead men on the floor and left their heads, the heads of seven old Arab *emirs*, the financiers of international terrorism, on a conference room table. Their actions were meant to flush the unknown pilot into the open. Expose him. *Expose the pilot.* Find out who he was. So they could kill him. But the pilot remained unknown and out of sight.

The mention of a "great game" in the context of the Director of Central Intelligence running an independent counterterrorism operation outside the awareness of the Deputy Director of Operations wasn't just incredible; it was utterly unbelievable. All clandestine operations were run through the NCS. All. That was, until now.

The term hadn't been used inside the Agency for years except in a historical sense. Still, Agency intelligence officers all knew the history and the connotations associated with *The Great Game*. It was the term used to describe the political and diplomatic confrontation that played out between Great Britain and Russia in the nineteenth century. The confrontations weren't between soldiers from the opposing armies, but rather between the intelligence officers from the opposing intelligence services. They waged intelligence battles over Afghanistan and the neighboring territories in Central and Southern Asia. Whose spy was best? Which spy got the best intelligence? The smartest men in the military with the best education were pressed into spying for their country. Britain was fearful that the Russian Emperor would add India to his vast Asian empire and thus secure an unencumbered sea trade route from Moscow to the Indian Ocean. *The Great Game* was truly the purview of the brilliant: the best spies of competing countries engaged behind the scenes in political combat in a test of minds.

The three career operations officers at the table were shocked. They waited for the eruption that would surely come. Fässler consumed cans of Coke. Troxel ate tiny Milky Way candy bars he hid in his suit pocket. Bomarito chewed gum and waited for the boss to calm down.

Castaño was due a little respect and a little latitude, even if it meant covering up for him from time to time. Eliminating Russian defectors no one in the IC wanted to talk to or cared about had made them rich beyond their wildest fantasies. They owned aircraft and homes and other trinkets of wealth that they hid in adjacent states, under different names, the properties of front companies. Castaño covered their tails when their travel claims came under scrutiny. Since just about anything could set him off, they wondered what it really was this time. It had been weeks since he railed at Lynche for not supporting his proposal to arm an obsolete Army surveillance aircraft with the experimental sniper weapon. They wondered what had shaken Castaño this time.

The Great Game? Was Castaño in the middle of an undeclared fight, like a contest between a SWAT team and a gang, good versus evil? Was the undeclared rivalry between the NCS and the NCTC? Maybe the conflict was between the DCI and the NCS Director. Something more than professional envy, a spat between the Agency's number one and number two senior executives? Was it over that woman; the NCTC Director, Nazy Cunningham? Repeated rejections from that women seemed to drive Castaño over the edge. That might make more sense. But for Fässler, Troxel, and Bomarito, one thing was certain, this meeting was sure to become more interesting.

30

November 7
McLean, Virginia

Steve Castaño said with contempt, "I met…*Maverick*."

Uttering the word, *Maverick* raised their eyebrows. They knew of the near-mythical exploits of the man. *Maverick* was considered a threat, not a hero. He had screwed them.

Fässler asked, "What did you think?"

Evil welled in Castaño's eyes. "All I could think of was how do I kill him? I think when we find out who he is, he'll be easier to find where he hangs that damned cowboy hat and kill him." There was a faint shudder as he spoke. "We have an operations officer by the name of Kelly Horne. You know her?" Eyes ricocheted around the room. They knew Castaño fancied Asian girls, the younger the better. If he shook any more he'd look like he was riding the paint mixer at the Home Depot. When Castaño took a handful of pills, Fässler and the others were grateful.

All three men nodded. She had the kind of beauty you find yourself involuntarily taking a moment to marvel at in mid-conversation. Troxel offered, "She's mine. She's the redhead with the bangs and three feet of orange hair, and drives that old black Jag XKE. Hard to miss or forget; her or the car." Nodding at Bomarito, he said, "That car should be in your collection."

Bomarito nodded and said, "Oh, yeah. Oh, yeah, the Bangles chick. Oh, yeah, that Jag." He referenced one of the singers of the rock and roll band famous for lots of hair and hairspray.

Troxel said, "Yes. She's an eyeful. She makes freckles positively sexy. Pilot…. She's been on the Director's staff as his personal aide going on a couple of months now. She'll be there through the election. I haven't had a need for…her piloting *services*. ISIS, Al Qaeda, and Boko Haram are quiet this time of year. SOCOM is on the job." He smirked at the implied double entendre. In his younger days Troxel had a thing for women with boobs, bright eyes, and long hair. Redheads were in a different category. Now that he was old and on the verge of retiring, the closest he could get to a beautiful young woman with ginger hair was to hire them and force them to come to one of his meetings, make them stay afterwards, then watch them walk away. He'd fondle himself under the conference table throughout the encounter.

With enough meds, Castaño's tremors finally abated. He continued, "I want her file. And I want everything we have on this *Maverick*. I think he's *the* bastard who cheated us out of a couple of billion in gold in Algeria. I'm sure he's the same guy who killed the seven sisters in Dubai." The reference to "seven sisters" was a clear and disparaging innuendo to the seven old Muslim men, major financiers of Middle East terrorism, who were found dead on the uppermost floor of the Burj Khalifa and whose corpses were decapitated by the three superannuated NCS executives, sitting around the table. "Today, this asshole flew into Andrews on a Gulfstream. By himself. Have any of you ever heard of such a thing?" As he spoke Castaño shook his head and made wild gestures that would have made a spider monkey proud. Troxel wondered if Castaño was on the verge of having a breakdown.

"I still don't know what he looks like. Asshole was decked out in a beard, mustache, and wild hair straight out of my advanced disguise course. We need to find out all we can about him and that jet." Castaño flipped a business card to Fässler. "That's the jet's N-number. See if it's on *Tailwatchers* and if it isn't, contract for information."

"This might raise some eyebrows," offered Fässler quickly, nearly spilling Coke down the front of his suit. He looked at the card closely as if he was a magician and could tell who owned the jet just by the aircraft's serial number. Fässler sucked air before he answered, hoping the boss would calm down. Going to the Russian-operated website for intel was fraught with peril. The National Security Agency actively monitored *Tailwatchers* users.

"I'll do what I can, Steve." The three subordinate executives knew that saying his name over and over, like a hypnotist, calmed him down.

Castaño wouldn't be deterred. His voice shot up an octave and was sticky with contempt. "I know you can find out, '*quietly.*' That pilot must have a badge to get into this place. Maybe *used* to have. But if *Maverick* is Lynche's boy, he probably runs with an alias or is completely external to the Agency. He wears a five thousand dollar cowboy hat. Two-tone gold Rolex—it's one of the rare ones. First edition. Not everyone flies a Gulfstream like that. The curious thing is that he closed the door—to me that asshole just had to be the pilot of that damn airplane. I've never seen anyone fly a jet that big by himself. It's a two-man airplane. Looked as if it wasn't chartered. Maybe it's new. But maybe not. I'm not the expert in friggin' *Gulfstreams*…. He landed, and then he and Lynche left on a C-17. He's no Tony Stark, but the head of SOCOM and the DCI sort of treat him like he's damn close to it. Find him. *Tailwatchers* has to have something on that jet. I want to know who he is—a full workup and profile. Find out everything you can to include which airport that asshole flew from. Anything that might give us a clue."

Fässler nodded. "Maybe we can get some of the Air Branch guys to look into it."

Castaño nodded and then pointed at the Chief of Special Activities Division, Jarvis Bomarito. "So the real reason I wanted you here. I want a full surveillance package on Cunningham and Horne. No one else can be part of this op. Clear your calendars for tonight and be free tomorrow. Understand?" He pushed a black plastic box the size and width of a stack of twenty long-play albums toward Bomarito. "Get this over to one of the labs and run this for a DNA match. Let's see if we can find out who this *Maverick* asshole really is."

Bomarito didn't like the trajectory of the conversation, but it wasn't his job to like it. He nodded without showing he was a reluctant stooge. "Steve, I think we have to be careful with this one. If the DCI is personally running this *Maverick*, there may be safeguards in the system to set off an alarm if he's queried or if there's a chance he could be unmasked. I think we'll need a backstop story. Something…"

Troxel interjected, "…like there's a file on him from our MI-6 cousins? I could work that—I need to cash in on a favor with one of my buddies before he retires." Troxel had been a beat cop going to night school when one of his professors turned him on to a man who worked for the CIA. Interviewed and polygraphed, he had turned his passion for flying into a seat in the Agency's dummy corporation, Air America. He had flown executives across the country and Agency personnel all up and down coastlines of the Far East, the islands of Malaysia and India. He worked closely with British Intelligence services and often shared intel, a drink, and a cigar with "the cousins." Usually in that order.

Bomarito barked, "What did you have in mind? Pedophilia? Tranny sex?"

"If we can't kill him, I was thinking something a bit more explosive, something like blame him as the guy who leaked President Mazibuike's file. Expose him and then the media and the DNC can hound his ass."

Troxel said, "If we can find him, we can kill him and he'll never see it coming. I'm not sure a long campaign is the right way to handle this. This guy has to be a pro." The other men agreed.

Bomarito continued, "As I was saying, no one has ever found out who released Mazibuike's file, and the Democrats want that head on a pike. Before Lynche, we could have had S&T generate a bogus paper trail on him, and then expose him like that asshole who exposed Mazibuike. But S&T doesn't approve extracurricular work anymore without Lynche's knowledge and signature. I agree it would be better if the media found him and exposed him. Someone on the left. He'd be a dead man in days."

Troxel said, "Steve, that will definitely put you in good standing with *The Judge*." He pulled a brown paper bag from under the table and placed it on the table. Everyone knew what was in the bag.

Bomarito said, "*That* is very good. Genius."

Castaño's eyes bugged like a surprised Peter Lorre. "You are undeniably frickin' demented. And I love it. Make it so. Do you kill him now or make him suffer from a thousand cuts?"

Fässler had been quiet but interjected, "I'd rather kill him, quick and fast. You don't want to wound a guy like that. He'd be that torpedo that came back around and killed all of us." The turn of fate from *The Hunt for Red October* was understood.

"*Maverick*…. He's always popping up when we least expect it. I'm tired of dealing with his shit." Castaño waved a bony scarred finger.

Bomarito and Troxel nodded. As an afterthought, Troxel said, "*Maverick* is a pilot. Would it be to our benefit to know what kind of aircraft he's using? Not the Gulfstream of course, but whatever it was that was put on that C-17? Didn't the support guys in Dubai say that he used some James Bond jetpack and not an airplane?"

Fässler cautioned the group. "We need to be very careful if we try to kill him with paper. The FBI got caught with their pants down around their ankles trying to make a blackmail case on President Hernandez."

Troxel paraphrased a quote from an essay Emerson wrote on Plato, "If you try to kill the king, you better not fucking miss"

Fässler continued, "They missed badly. Now nearly all of the FBI executives are being fired with charges pending. You saw that it was a bloody massacre when the Repugs in Congress found out the FBI's blackmail effort was manufactured. Looks like the FBI's whole seventh floor will be implicated. Fired. You can bet someone from that crowd will talk or kill themselves in order to avoid jail time. All I'm saying is, we are rushing into a spontaneous operation and we need to be careful."

Castaño had stopped trembling. He nodded, waved bony scarred hands, and smiled. "Good catch. That's your area. Let's get back to the asshole with the jet. Put someone on it. Maybe we can triangulate his ass with whatever aircraft he's using. Could he be using an unmanned system? Fly it remotely, or is he really the pilot? Figure it out. Find out." *Could he be using something like a quiet airplane like that YO-3A at Pima?* He sighed at the thought. "They called on him to try and save our guys and the SEALs—that's a hopeless case. ISIS has them, and when they start to filet them on camera, their beheadings will be on every TV in the Middle East and on the front page of every friggin' Arab newspaper. Mark my words! There's no way this *Maverick* can rescue any of them. Now…back to our girls. I want to see if this *Maverick* is in their lives. If you can get Cunningham and Horne in the shower I'd like to see that too. *Kompromat.* Splatter their pictures on the web. That will teach Lynche he can't screw with me." *And it will teach that bitch not to reject me.*

Troxel said, "Revenge porn. Ruin them, run them out of town on a rail. I think we'd all like to see that. So, full package? Cameras in smoke detectors, shower heads, the vacuum cleaner, lightbulbs, and heat registers. Microdot cameras and microphones—those are impossible to find unless someone is specifically looking for them. The full Monty? Everything we got? Even the new stuff from S&T?"

Castaño nodded vigorously. "Everything! Whatever it takes."

Bomarito asked, "Do you want a camera in her car?"

Troxel asked, "The Mercedes? Look up her skirt?" Nazy used to drive an immaculate red SL 380. It turned heads whenever she drove it into the CIA parking lot. Then the assassins came for her and the director assigned a permanent security detail to protect her. Driving a red convertible anywhere was out of the question.

Castaño thought long and hard on what he'd say next. "I'd like you to install something *special.* Remotely detonated. If there are other vehicles in her garage, the same treatment."

The three men were shocked that their boss wanted bombs planted in any vehicles. This was an escalation they didn't anticipate or bargain for. It meant a trip to the hangar for materials.

Fässler interrupted the men's fantasies. "You're convinced there's a connection between Cunningham and this *Maverick* dude. If they know each other…*intimately,* then we should be able to manage her. Trap him."

Troxel asked, "What if you don't find that he knows her? You still want to kill him?"

Bomarito, Fässler, and Castaño nodded. Castaño said, "Yeah, that's the goal. If we have to snatch her to get to him, that would be great. Seems like this *Maverick* parachutes in when he's needed. Like a *contractor.…* Hmmm.… We'll see how it all works out. For now, I'd like to hear what they're saying—no NSA at this time. But above all else, I want pictures! I want to see what she has been hiding under those long-sleeved blouses, long skirts, and yoga pants." Laughter swept the table. Before Castaño dismissed his men with the back of his hand, he asked Troxel if he had any problem "finding the cigars." Troxel shook his head and followed the others out of the office.

When he was alone, Castaño fantasized about raiding Cunningham's panty drawer. *See what she wore under those tight suits.* He was fully erect. He smiled at the thought of rummaging through her hamper to sniff her soiled panties. *Take one of her bras as a trophy.* He'd leave a calling card that would be unmistakable. He stared out of his office window. Thoughts of a nude buxom Nazy Cunningham made him leak into his trousers.

After Castaño's little fantasies, he locked his safes, shutdown his computer, and ran out of the office. He had a plane to catch.

31

November 7
Newport, Rhode Island

The three-bladed Hartzell propellers of a very pristine Cessna 310 chugged to a stop. The twin-engine airplane was bright white and offset with lines of trim of the same dark metallic green paint made famous by Schwinn's Pea Picker Krate bicycle. A mechanic could look at the aircraft and tell it had always been hangered, out of weather and out of the sun. Considered in aviation circles as one of the most beautiful and graceful light twins ever built, the white and green Cessna 310 was fitted with two 310hp Continental turbocharged intercooled engines. Thirty-five of the specially-modified 310s had been initially produced for the CIA's Air Branch.

The aircraft's unique N-number—N2001F—wasn't a tribute to Arthur C. Clark's novel *2001: A Space Odyssey*, but it wasn't just another of the FAA's random tail number assignment either. It had a purpose and a history. The original N-number traced its lineage back to an Air America Dornier Do-28A; the aircraft was lost after the Vietnam War. It was still assigned to the Air America aircraft, and the CIA's Air Branch saw to it that that particular N-number was "used properly."

After a terrorist's bomb blew apart PanAm Flight 103 over Lockerbie, Scotland, the Agency had to find another way to move its intelligence officers around the country and the planet. Chief Air Branch proposed expanding their long-standing programs of providing Agency aircraft at airports across the Americas, the Middle East, and Africa. A contractor bought every available Cessna 310s and had them flown to a private airport outside of Harrisonburg, Virginia, for overhauls and modifications. Members of the National Clandestine Service were trained to fly the aircraft. Twin-engine pilot certification was added to the already extensive skill set of the expert spy. Air Branch was constantly on the lookout for additional aircraft to add to their Cessna 310 fleet, now sixty strong. The international *Air America* had been reborn and now it was a top secret domestic program with an N-number that would defeat any curious communist *Tailwatcher*. It would be easy to hide sixty identical airplanes with the same registration number: N-2001F.

Steve Castaño waited for the pilot to slide out of his seat. Once the pilot was out of his way, Castaño stepped out of the aircraft and onto the non-skid strip on the wing. He carried a stuffed computer bag and a brown paper bag with hemp handles. He steadied himself with his hands as he negotiated the two fixed steps to get comfortably onto the tarmac of TF Green Airport.

The flight from Manassas had been through clear blue skies with light turbulence that had gently bounced the aircraft. No queasy stomachs or sealed air sickness bags. The pilot remained with the aircraft; Castaño in his ubiquitous dark sunglasses walked toward the flight operations building. Castaño held the different-sized bags in one hand and pulled on his suit coat with the other, as he strolled into a stiff below-freezing breeze that blew across the tarmac.

Once inside the terminal building, the National Clandestine Service Director was ushered to a private booth in the corner of O'Brien's Pub and Grill. He placed the computer bag on the floor beside the booth and the paper bag on the table. He didn't say anything to the man sitting across from him perusing a menu. A swarthy waiter with jet black hair demonstrated his talent by pouring water into a goblet from three feet above the glass and not spilling a drop. The waiter announced the specials, took their drink orders, and left.

Castaño pushed the computer bag to the other side of the table with his toe. He withdrew a "Growler" from his suit pocket. He looked at a scrap of paper that was thrust across the table for him to view; after a brief moment the paper was withdrawn. Castaño rolled his eyes and sighed as he slid a business card across to the grey-haired former Harvard law professor, "I have a candidate; someone who I think might have outed 3M. It's purely circumstantial at this point."

Scribbled on the back of the business card in India ink was the word *Maverick*. "He's completely off the special activities and special operations grid. Everyone has heard of him, no one knows him at all. No one but the DCI. I've no idea who he is but I met him. He may be a contractor. As the number two person, I'm in the loop on everything that goes on at my place, except this program; I should know this man's identity. There's obviously an unusual relationship between him and the director. I should know something about him soon. DNA testing can take some time."

The man from Cambridge, the sitting Democratic National Committee Chairman, smiled broadly as he reached down and patted the computer bag. The names and photographs of intelligence agents from different intelligence services working in Europe and Russia, as well as the engineering drawings and operation manual of the Agency's latest lethal secret weapon, the Terminator Sniper System, now lay at his feet. Then he looked at the brown paper bag and smiled. "For me?"

Castaño returned the smile. It was going to be a glorious day. He said, "*My Father The Judge*. Your favorite."

The DNC Chairman oozed the words like whipped cream, "Pressed and blocky, these big *robustos* are topped with a three-seam cap. Bits of chocolate and gingersnap play off each other with hints of red pepper and almonds. An exquisite cigar. Thank you, Steve." He could smell them and wanted to light one up.

"My compliments, sir." *The Judges for The Judge*.

Then Dr. Zhavrazhinov was all business. "It would be a tremendous benefit if I knew who this man was—I've...*plans* for him." He slid a thin black Moleskine notebook across the table. Castaño opened it and thumbed through the pages of letters and numbers. Codes and ciphers. Access codes to bank accounts and cryptocurrency accounts abroad.

Castaño pocketed the thin notebook. The transaction was complete. The last time he had visited the DNC Chairman he had provided a fistful of flash drives and a laptop computer, the evidence of Tommy Larrabee's treachery. And he provided a working knowledge of the top secret Terminator Sniper System. Zhavrazhinov wanted more information on the weapon and its special ammunition, and another box of his favorite cigars.

The effeminate man in the three-piece suit said, "Thank you for the great work, Steven. That little nugget of intel is worth this meeting. *Maverick*. For the longest time we have been frustrated, unable to identify this criminal." He put the card in an inside pocket of his suit coat. "I think you need to add him to our list when you determine his identity. Highest priority, you can expect a special invite to our little place in the sun...and three times the reward for...."

Zhavrazhinov checked himself. He had been livid at the CIA's and FBI's inability to identify the man who had singlehandedly and completely disrupted the DNC in its effort to maintain Democrat Party control of America. The DNC had been so very close to achieving a tipping point. The release of the Mazibuike's file had identified sources and methods, and the extent that the U.S. media had participated in the conspiracy.

He took a long drink and said, "We're in a difficult phase with this election.... I don't want you doing anything until after the election, of course. We'll all be excited when she's elected. We don't want to do anything that would interrupt...your *next* assignment. *Capiche?*"

Castaño hissed meekly, "Of course." Of course, once she's elected all of the secret information operations against President Hernandez would be covered up like a cat covering a stinky slimy turd. No one in America would ever know what the leadership of the three letter agencies had done, or how they'd contributed to her election. She'd pay, of course, with political appointments, ambassadorships, and such. DCI Lynche would be one of the first to resign. Castaño would become the next Director of the Central Intelligence Agency.

Dr. Zhavrazhinov said, "I have one more for after the election. Are you familiar with the correspondent Demetrius Eastwood...an ex-Marine Corps officer?"

Another Marine? "I am." Castaño clasped his hands on the table. *This could be interesting....*

"He's written a series of articles on our candidate. His network turned his last vile article into television special. It was a—how do you say—a punch to the gut?"

"I saw it. *Was it Espionage?* That one?" He thought, *Oooh that was devastating reporting.*

Zhavrazhinov nodded, hate in his eyes. "I want him too. Quick and simple. He has hurt our cause...." He shook his head like a man defeated. "We can't take any more of his reporting. Polling suggests he's making an impact that we can't afford."

"Consider it done, sir."

"As soon as practicable. Now, on the zero-chance she doesn't win...*tomorrow*, we can't let *him*...we cannot let that happen. But we have to be prepared.... Regardless of the outcome, he must be first. And it must be quick. First opportunity. Disrupt the nation. There will be riots in the streets. We'll see to that. It'll be payback for the loss of Mazibuike and if the unthinkable occurs, the loss of Eleanor Tussy." Zhavrazhinov quietly clasped his hands in front of his face and sighed. *If she loses, I don't know what will happen to me.* Another sighing heave. *Oh, yes I do....* Zhavrazhinov didn't want to think about failure anymore.

Castaño said, "Of course she'll win. I fully understand; we have a contingency if there's a November surprise. I promise we'll take care of it. I assure you. First opportunity."

"Within 48 hours?" Zhavrazhinov's breathing was calming down.

The ultimate assassination is to kill a sitting head of state. Castaño gave the head of the DNC an evil sneer and said, "He won't win. The polls are on our side. So it's an easy agreement. Forty-eight hours? I'll guarantee within twenty-four hours. Whether he wins or loses, he'll go to Camp David, to celebrate or lick his wounds." Castaño snapped his fingers as if the dirty deed could be executed instantaneously.

Castaño stretched his damaged hand across the table, a social *faux pas*. Zhavrazhinov didn't mind since they agreed. The NCS Director said, "Please don't worry. We now have a very special tool."

Zhavrazhinov nodded and released Castaño's damaged hand.

If the election didn't remove President Hernandez, then the Special Activities Division had the plan, the ways, and the means. And they'd be swift. They'd been planning for this for a couple of years, beginning when Javier Hernandez left his position in Congress to be appointed to the Office of the President of the United States of America. Everything the DNC had worked to achieve had vanished in an instant when the Chief Justice of the U.S. Supreme Court administered the Presidential Oath of Office to the stunned Congressman from Texas who learned that President Mazibuike had resigned in disgrace and the Democrat vice president had committed a murder-suicide in the vice president's quarters.

While Zhavrazhinov could conceive of a Hernandez win if all of the variables, the swing states, aligned perfectly, Castaño couldn't conceive of such a possibility. President Hernandez wouldn't even come close to the requisite number of electoral votes. Numerous polls reported Mrs. Tussy held a double-digit lead going into Election Day. Turnout was expected to be high. They'd worked in the background for her election for years; Election Day was nigh. He couldn't win, so it was an easy promise. A standard verbal contract. The challenge would be finding the home of Demetrius Eastwood. Al-Qaeda had found him once and tried to kill him, but an armored vehicle saved him. Others had tried to find where the journalist called home, but all attempts to follow him had failed.

Castaño thought, *If not a double tap from behind, then a sniper's bullet for the former Jarhead too. There was no sense of urgency for that. The election is tomorrow. If he wins, POTUS would be first. Eastwood second. Maverick would be next. A political trifecta!*

Secret assassination operations carried out by the National Clandestine Service of the CIA weren't subjects openly discussed, but the DNC Chairman, like Stalin and Khrushchev, and the DNC Chairmen before him, had long adopted targeted political assassinations as a way of life. The only real stipulation was to never ever keep a record. Castaño despised recordkeeping and easily agreed. Zhavrazhinov was a "do as I say, not as I do" kind of man. He managed multiple programs that necessitated keeping meticulous records. One day those records might be needed as barter to save his life.

Castaño knew that some problems were best solved by erasure. Eradication. Zhavrazhinov preferred "neutralization." Like the men before him, Castaño and his men removed the egregious and the potential troublemakers from the political playing field. Russian defectors. American reporters. Like Kennedy's mistresses. Like Tommy Larrabee. Like Associate Supreme Court Justice Oliver Marcelli. Like the reporter Eastwood. Like President Hernandez. Like *Maverick*. After the election Castaño would throw another one on the chopping block for free. For himself. His nemesis, the CIA Director, the soon-to-be-*former* CIA Director, Greg Lynche.

The DNC Chairman sighed and said, "Well, Steve, I think congratulations are in order. I propose a toast to the next Director of the Central Intelligence Agency." He held his water goblet high; Castaño matched it and tinkled them together.

Castaño smiled and asked, "So what are you having?"

"I'll have the lobster bisque!"

"Let's make that two!"

32

November 7
Over the Atlantic Ocean

"There are only 60 rounds; six ten-round magazines. You are proficient enough to operate the gun and change the magazines when you need to. Kelly can laser designate the targets if you cannot." The Director of Central Intelligence had it all figured out.

Nazy held his hand. She could sense her husband was in turmoil. He was wrestling with the images of previous interdictions from the *Wraith*. Men targeted on the ground never saw him coming. The old weapon featured an electronic-targeting constantly-computing impact point system, and boasted a probability of kill of 98% at three miles. The new system on the YO-3A was so accurate that the projectile would hit within an inch of the laser designated target at ten miles.

Hybrid propellant within the projectile—a combination of black powder and a tiny solid rocket motor—reduced the severity of the G-load on the electronics and the tiny lens in the head of the massive bullet. Once the .70 caliber bullet left the muzzle, a solid rocket booster would ignite and hypersonically accelerate the projectile to its target. A minor drawback of the disruptive technology weapon was that the initial flash and the exhaust trace from the tiny chemical rocket motor was visible at night.

Lynche offered, "It's all moot if ISIS kills them before you get over the target."

Nazy asked, "Duncan, can you do both?"

He slowly shook his head. He knew what was in the art of the possible. It was reasonable to expect dozens of people in the area of the hostages. The weapon's cyclic rate was simply insufficient. More than six targets and he'd lose situational awareness. Once the firing started, people would scatter like roaches when the lights are turned on.

Hunter said, "I'm probably not going to know until I get there and see what we are dealing with. So you know basically, where they are? GPS, but no photos?"

"Clouds." Lynche indicated satellite photographs were unavailable but he sensed Duncan was warming up to the idea. That he'd do it. He still didn't know how Hunter would do it, but Hunter "was in." Afterwards, Hunter might not ever talk to him again, but war is hell. This situation was special. It wasn't a favor between friends. Sometimes it sucked to be the boss.

"We can get you within a grid square with 90 percent certainty. With you overhead that should quickly approach 100 percent. You know how to find them. You always know how to find the little bastards who don't want to be found. What does the Border Patrol call it? When they're hunting humans?"

"Cutting sign."

Lynche nodded. "You know they all leave some clues as to where they are, or where they're going, where they've hidden them, or what they've done to them."

Hunter wasn't liking any of it, but the mission was too important to let his feelings get in the way. He was sucking wind like a vacuum cleaner thinking of ways to protect Kelly from witnessing him killing men. *The huge spent-uranium rounds were devastating. An explosion of flesh and bone. My little girl…. This isn't for you!*

Lynche could almost guess what Hunter was thinking. He had a response. *She's no longer the daughter that you have to protect. She's a big girl now. She has work to do. Sometimes it sucks being in the CIA.*

Hunter knew killing a man with a bullet was much more personal. With a big enough bomb, you could destroy a factory to get at a single man or group of terrorists. With a missile you could target an aircraft, a vehicle, or a house to kill your target. But a gun capable of putting a single bullet the size of one's thumb through a man's skull at three miles wasn't only precision, it was intimate.

Knowing he'd likely be killing many more terrorists than ever before, Hunter envisioned scenarios that he'd likely encounter; for every situation there was a simple solution. This one reeked of being infinitely more difficult. But some of America's greatest warriors had been captured, and that demanded a concomitant response.

Hunter leaned into Nazy and stuck his hand into his flight jacket pocket. He pulled out the SOCOM commander's challenge coin. He flipped it around to view the obverse side then the reverse side. The red lighting in the cargo jet wasn't conducive for deep inspection. Nazy asked, "What's that?"

Lynche and Kelly leaned inwards to see the coin. The brass coin was etched and scalloped around the edges. It was enameled glossy black with a three-dimensional, stylized brass arrowhead pointing north, straight up. The words Special Operations Command arced below. On the reverse was a red flag with four white stars and the SOCOM commander's name. Hunter handed it to Nazy who passed it to Kelly, who seemed to be struggling with staying awake. Lynche smiled for a moment when it was his turn. They'd all seen the variety of the special coins before, but rarely did they ever receive one from one of the generals or admirals they met. In the military, coins went to junior enlisted and officers as "spot awards." Lynche and Nazy and the other senior executives in the intelligence community each had challenge coins they gave to agents or others who performed exceptionally well or well beyond expectations.

Nazy reached for her backpack, fished around inside, and brought out a single magnificently detailed coin. Dark blue background, the emblem of the United States of America was centered. In gold letters arcing across the top it read *National Counter Terrorism Center*. As she handed it to her husband she said, "Don't say I never gave you anything."

Lynche jumped on the opening. "That presupposes you've done something worthwhile to get a coin. You haven't done anything...*yet*."

Nazy smiled, but Kelly didn't like the spicy banter between her father and her boss. She viewed Lynche's comments as more caustic than comedic. She never had the benefit of seeing her father and her boss discuss politics. If she had, she would have seen that the two men loved and respected each other like close brothers.

Hunter took the coin with a smile and asked, very sensually, "Did I do something good?"

She pursed her lips and said, "You're here, aren't you? We really do need you."

Hunter turned to Lynche and said, "You might be on to something—I've flown for the CIA for twenty years and no one ever gave me a single coin, until now."

Lynche grinned, "When was the last time you did something good?" There was a red twinkle in the old man's eye from the red lighting of the aircraft's cabin.

"Do you really want me to answer that?" Hunter shrugged away the distraction of coins to return to the task at hand. He shifted in his troop seat to get more comfortable. When Hunter found a spot to his liking he asked, "What if we get there a tad too late to make the intercept?"

Lynche hung his head. Hunter knew the answer but was going to make his boss say it. So he did. "No one is expecting you to find them and rescue them. We know who we're dealing with. Timing is everything and our clock is out of ticks. If they are still alive, we might have this very narrow window of opportunity to do something before they separate them and we lose them. I'm under no illusions there's a road to success. If you find them you may not be able to do anything about it. But on the off-chance that the conditions line up and you can actually see our guys, you are authorized to do whatever you think is necessary. You are the ultimate decision maker, and no one will question your actions. We are at war with this evil."

"But you questioned my actions in Dubai. You thought I'd wandered off the reservation."

When Hunter brought up his last mission the color in Nazy's lips drained away as if she were about to faint. She held her hand to her mouth. Kelly yawned, she didn't know what they were talking about. The twenty-year best friends locked eyes.

Lynche was immediately conciliatory. "I did. I admit I thought that you weren't being truthful with me. That you'd snapped, and were covering up what you did. But I was wrong, dead wrong, and I apologize. I know you but I didn't believe you, and I should have. For that I'm terribly wrong and very sorry, Duncan."

There was something more than pain in the Director's eyes. For a moment Hunter thought he had seen the man's soul, his pain, his shame. Hunter reached over with a fist and the two men fist-bumped. All better. Hunter looked at Lynche hard. *That's not what I expected. It's like he was apologizing for something he did long ago.*

Nazy nearly cried and made little clapping gestures to telegraph her approval. *Finally!*

Kelly was so tired she was afraid she had missed part of a discussion. Her jetlag from her previous mission made her yawn every minute. She didn't know what her father had done to get the CIA Director so mad at him. Then she realized, she didn't want to know. She wanted a sleeping bag and sleep.

Lynche continued. "The FBI is conducting an investigation into who's responsible. Who came behind you. They're just getting started. But now we have to focus on this mission. You need to find our guys, and you need to take care of them. If you can."

Hunter understood the DCI's dictum to "take care of them" and said, "Let's hope it doesn't come to that."

No one wanted to kill their own troops. But to prevent the SEALs and the CIA officers from being tortured and dismembered on camera and having the act of their decapitation splashed on Al-Jazeera as a recruitment tool for more wannabe *jihadis*, it was a necessary evil. Hunter had killed scores of *jihadis* and *tangos* under an Executive Special Access Program called *Noble Savage*. Never in his wildest imagination would he ever have found himself in this scenario. He wouldn't kill "a friendly" unless he absolutely had too.

Neither the president nor Lynche had ever expected *Noble Savage* or the quiet airplane to be used in such a manner. The physiological toll on anyone put into that position would be devastating. Although Lynche had thought Hunter had lost his mind, he had to admit Duncan hadn't really shown any of the usual signs of mental breakdowns or fatigue after killing over a hundred of the world's worst terrorists. Normally such indifference was the hallmark of a psychopath.

Lynche began to understand that the amazing abilities of the man he had called his best friend was rooted in Hunter's inner strength, and that his own liberal upbringing likely geared him to see Duncan Hunter, the cowboy hat-wearing conservative, as a faulty man. For the first time in a very long time, Lynche felt shame for doubting his remarkable friend while at the same time feeling shame for old memories, old missions, old decisions.

"We'll just have to get there first." Hunter turned to his best friend. "Greg, you convinced them that this was the only way to do this?" Unspoken were the promises SEALs made to each other when operating in one of the world's shitholes. They promised that they'd prevent the capture of their injured friends by first killing them before turning the weapon on themselves.

Lynche lifted his head to speak. "It was the president's idea. That you were the only guy who gave us a chance."

Hunter faced Lynche and said, "War is hell."

Lynche pinched his lips and nodded. "You'll be the on-scene commander. We'll have electronic countermeasures aircraft in the area just in case the Syrians have acquired a Russian anti-aircraft capability. There will be an AWACS overhead following you, as well as a couple of C-130s with Special Forces ready to parachute in. A flight of F-18s will be on station to kill any anti-aircraft missile battery in the area. If you can somehow disable the enemy, make the call and the para-rescue team will land and take over the situation; the hostages. Army special ops helicopters will dash into the area if their guys leave their airplanes. The parachutists don't leave their airplanes and the helicopters don't fly except on your command. The air cavalry will be standing by on the Jordanian border. We don't need another group of hostages so deep in enemy territory."

Hunter nodded, deep in thought. He had done it before, found hostages who had been squirreled away out of sight for years and then provided top cover for a rescue force of U.S. Navy SEALs. He looked at Lynche and said, "I'm in."

Lynche offered his hand and Hunter took it. He mumbled something unrecognizable to Hunter, but Nazy and Kelly seemed to understand the discussion was over. They stood as if on cue. Lynche disentangled himself from Hunter and patted him on the back. Lynche reached inside his flight suit leg pocket and withdrew several packets. Hunter and Nazy could see they were passports. The DCI handed Hunter and Kelly one packet each, their emergency passports if, for whatever reason, they had to bail out of the YO-3A, or if they crashed and help wasn't on the way.

The other packets contained twenty, one-ounce, gold Krugerrands, emergency currency and tickets to buy freedom. Lynche said, "Technically, I'm giving you some coins—when we are done, I expect these back. Consider yourselves Canadian archeologists working at the Masyaf Castle ruins. I believe, Duncan, you consider yourself something of a geologist."

Hunter smirked, "I know the difference between gold and coal, silver and aluminum, and diamonds are a girl's best friend." He pronounced "aluminum" in his best Cockney, with the emphasis on the wrong syllable. Hunter's mock British accent was always horrible. Nazy playfully chided as she laughed at him. He wasn't done with Lynche and asked, "Where do you get...maybe it's better to ask, how do you get these? Suddenly, I'm curious."

"My initial answer is to tell you have no need to know. But I think it's okay. The NCS, that you so caustically revile, manages the currencies they need to operate in different countries. Think of the NCS Director as the James Bond of money. He funds operations. He manages fronts, like the old Air America. When I ran it, for example, I managed one front company, an import-export business that became the largest currency and precious metals firm in the Western Hemisphere, if not the world. We bought Russian titanium for our newest aircraft. Your labs in Texas were once Agency front companies. Today, we can't just accept bags of money or bullion from dictators like we used to. We were the world's money and metals experts." He reminisced for an unprotected moment. "We handled the most amazing currencies."

With barely concealed awe, Hunter said, "Damn, you are full of surprises!" He cocked his head and said, "I wrote an article."

Lynche's frown said he wasn't amused. "*You did what?*"

"Well, I wrote it and Dory Eastwood published it under his name."

Lynche looked at Nazy to verify her husband's story, but her eyes and expression said she wouldn't play.

Hunter said, "It was the '*Was it Espionage?* article. That was me. I know you read it."

"You are supposed to get anything like that cleared with the Publication Review Board."

"But how was I supposed to do that? You killed and buried me! I know you read it because it attacked your girl. It wasn't under my name and the agency wasn't even mentioned. I just wanted you to know."

"Why would you do that?"

"The media's greatest power is their power to ignore. They completely ignored Tussy's criminal behavior. She was conducting espionage and the FBI wouldn't even talk to her or her little Islamic acolytes. They gave her a tongue bath. A foot rub. And you guys don't do domestic issues very well. Jurisdictions, and all of that."

Lynche harrumphed at his best friend and grabbed one of the sleeping bags from the pile of bags.

Hunter suddenly remembered he was going to miss being able to vote. He said, "I don't suppose we'll be back in time to vote."

Lynche looked at his friend for a few seconds and said, "That's what early voting is for." He sighed heavily, more from fatigue than frustration. "We might be back." At that moment, he had enough of Duncan Hunter for one night. He chose a length of the troop seats, unrolled the bag, and plopped on top. He noticed the other members of the *Wraith* team on the other side of the Globemaster, two mechanics and a flight doctor from Special Operations Command. They were experts in managing the jetlag they'd experience after landing. They were already in sleeping bags wearing sleep masks and noise-canceling headsets.

The mechanics were Hunter's longtime YO-3A support crew, "Bob" and "Bob," Vietnam veterans who had kept the tiny fleet of YO-3As in better than pristine condition for the past twenty years. Bob and Bob worked under the cover of darkness. Only one of the black coated YO-3As had ever seen the light of day. Too much secret technology would be on display if the nighttime-only aircraft were ever operated during the day.

Hunter pulled his girls in close, one on each side. Pride and love swelled inside him. His "number two girl," as he called his red-headed daughter, was a devout Christian. She always wore a James Avery gold ribbon cross around her neck and a gold Rolex President on her wrist. Presents from her father. His "number one girl," as he infrequently but affectionately called his wife, Nazy Cunningham, had renounced Islam and survived many attacks on her life. Like Kelly, she was now a Christian and wore a delicate Cartier gold cross around her neck and a gold Rolex President on her wrist. Again, presents from Duncan.

Hunter rarely removed his two-tone Rolex Submariner from his wrist. He had a thing for finding and giving old rare watches to his friends and nice jewelry for the women in his life. And cars. Kelly had received a black Jaguar for her birthday and Lynche received a *concours-restored* Porsche 930 Turbo finished in *Diamant Sarah*. Hunter had stolen Nazy's Mercedes from the Islamic Underground imams who had sent Nazy to spy on him. He had the SL 380 towed from Newport, Rhode Island and transported to Texas where it was painstakingly restored.

Hunter turned to Kelly and apologized, "I always thought I'd ruin your life if I let you come to work *for this place*," clearly intimating the Central Intelligence Agency. "I'm not so sure about you going on this mission. The father in me is screaming, 'Don't let her go. This one could be too crazy, too dangerous.'"

Kelly yawned, smiled, and leaned into him. "Dad, I love it. Really. I wouldn't miss this for the world. I know you'll take care of me. I'll be okay." He wasn't convinced. He turned to his number one girl. "I think we're ready for some shut-eye." He kissed Kelly in the middle of her bangs and Nazy gently on the lips. He said, smiling, "I really have missed you two, but I think we all need to get some sleep. It's a long flight, and we have a stressful day ahead of us, and the jetlag will be painful. A good night's sleep will be a great band aid for the bumps and bruises that I expect will come tomorrow."

The women nodded as Kelly stifled a yawn and offered to say a prayer before sleep. Standing between the YO-3A's container and a line of troop seats, Nazy, Kelly, and Hunter held hands and bowed their heads. The agnostic Lynche, who had overheard them, stood and took Nazy's and Duncan's hands.

> *Lord, I have passed another day*
> *And come to thank Thee for Thy care.*
> *Forgive my faults in work or play*
> *And listen to my evening prayer.*
> *Thy favor gives me daily bread*
> *And friends, who all my wants supply:*
> *And safely now I rest my head,*
> *Preserved and guarded by Thine eye.*

Kelly left her father and Nazy alone after she got a big hug. Hunter unbuttoned his shirt revealing a grey haired, muscular chest, puffy pectorals, overdeveloped trapezius, and cobblestone abs. He was a magnificent tanned specimen of a multi-sport athlete. Kelly was immediately embarrassed that her father was outrageously good-looking and muscular like a Chippendale dancer. Nazy smiled at her half-naked husband as he stripped to his shorts. He had the chiseled thighs of a speed skater although one was discolored from an injury. They looked as if they were as hard as concrete. The scar on his cheek and the appearance of his body gave the impression that he was as tough and fearless as he looked.

Hunter folded his shirt and slacks and slipped them inside his flight bag. He was unembarrassed to be standing at the rear of the big jet in just his black Mack Weldon skivvies. He pulled out a two-piece black body suit from his flight bag. He explained to Nazy that the thin material was a conductive carbon fiber grid designed to block the electromagnetic signature emitted from the human body. "I don't know if I'll need it, but if I do, I should be able to walk through a junkyard and their guard dogs can look right at me, but they don't even know I'm there. It's essentially a Faraday cage that keeps your electrical energy field from getting out. Our guys developed the concept for Navy SEALs because we found out a wearable Faraday cage screws up a shark's senses too. Sharks bump right into a diver and turn away. Stuff's incredible. And it keeps me warm in a cold cockpit."

Lynche was watching the Hunter family interact, he realized, for the very first time. *They're never together. And here they are. One big happy family and I may be responsible for blowing it up.*

Lynche nodded to Kelly and pointed to a vacant spot near him. She spread out her bag, head-to-head. Sleep was near. She knotted her bright orange hair as they made small talk like an old instructor counseling a student after class. Lynche regaled her with some of the old *Wraith* missions before the gun was installed on the YO-3A. He talked about how he and Bill McGee had prevented her father from being killed by a sniper.

Her jetlag was a memory. She was suddenly alert and asked, "I've heard the story but not the details. How did you do that?"

Lynche told her, "We were hunting for a sniper who had been suspected of killing Navy SEALs. Predictive analysis—we assumed this sniper would target McGee next and set a trap for him. Duncan was on the ground and I was airborne in a Yo-Yo when your father stumbled on the sniper's hide. We had radios, so I screamed at him to back up; he was almost standing on the sniper's rifle. The sniper pulled a pistol and hit your dad twice. Center mass. Wicked bruises the size of dinner plates. Cracked ribs."

Kelly looked as if she had seen the ghost of her father. She whispered, "The body armor worked...."

Lynche nodded. "It did, and what happened next freaked me out. It looked like the sniper was in slow motion as he disentangled himself from his hiding place, kind of like how the *Alien* monster unfolded itself from its hiding space in the rescue pod. I knew he was going to finish your father off. I didn't have a lot of time to think about the problem, so I tried to distract him with the laser—you know how a cat will chase a laser. I knew we could display letters on the ground with the laser designator—like a laser show at an NBA game. It's one of the many functions of *Weedbusters* system. You know, the YO-3A carries different lasers, visible, IR, and UV for different applications. Your father showed me how the system was capable of doing that—so I typed BANG on the control panel and in red letters BANG was projected on the ground between where the sniper stood and where Duncan had fallen."

"The surprising thing was that it worked—he figured that the letters had come from an airborne platform and slowly looked up. That gave me the time to switch the systems so I could focus the *Weedbusters'* four UV lasers at the killer's eyes. When he looked up at the sky, I activated the laser designator to aim the UV lasers. I figured I'd just blinded him temporarily, as the UV laser isn't eye-safe. What I found out the next day was that, with less than a half second of dwell time, those invisible laser beams shredded the sniper's eyes as if a hundred razor blades had raced across the man's face at the speed of light."

"Oh, my God."

Lynche nodded. "*Weedbusters* was one of the CIA's most successful weapons we have ever developed."

"And now I get to use that to kill plants." Kelly was wide-eyed at her boss' narrative. She was surprised at the many capabilities of the laser systems installed on the YO-3A. Her jetlag was back with a vengeance. With one final yawn, she thanked Lynche for the bedtime story, told him good night, and snuggled into her sleeping bag. She was asleep in seconds.

Like most large aircraft at altitude, the cargo jet was especially stable. The noise from the wind rushing over the airframe at 600 mph was loud—loud enough to camouflage other sounds. Hunter pulled Nazy close to kiss her. She felt like her heart would burst just like the first time she had kissed Duncan. He reached up and playfully tugged on the zipper of her flight suit to telegraph he wanted to free Nazy's girls from their *Nomex*® constraints. He was having flashbacks to the last time they were together, unzipping her little black zipper dress. Duncan had a thing for zipper dresses and zipper blouses, and Nazy had a rack full of them. When they were together, she'd rip his shirt off and he'd slowly unzip her and her girls out of her clothes.

Nazy playfully slapped his hand. Flashing eyes told him to behave. Whether she looked at him or smiled at him, it always hit Hunter like an earthquake. He left her zipper alone and they kissed like teenagers in the back seat of a 57 Chevy convertible on Lover's Lane.

33

November 7
Bethesda, Maryland

Multiple seismic sensors sensitive enough to pick up the individual footsteps of four men approaching the house triggered internal transmitters and sent a signal to a receiver in the house just as the neighborhood experienced a significant electrical power failure. The security system's computer in the safe room logged the four-man incursion, sensed the power outage, triggered an alarm, and remained connected to the uninterrupted power supply in the basement. The five-foot tall stack of cellphone and deep-cycle batteries ensured the security system and other essential equipment in the home could remain energized for days.

The hard hits on the seismic sensor grid triggered artificial intelligence software and automatically placed the security system into DEFENSE Mode. Algorithms prompted by the "seismics" sent commands to the security system network to shut down non-essential security systems throughout the house—lights on timers, strobe lights, alarm speakers—first to save power and then to mask normal operations. Smoke detector status lights were extinguished while the detector remained operational and video recorders were set to RECORD. Electrical power to the refrigerator and freezer was put on an alternating schedule so neither appliance had power to it at the same time. The HOME ASSAULT subprograms queried microwave sensors throughout the house to detect the tiniest movement; the sensors were sensitive enough to detect the rising and falling chest of a sleeping person or a roach scurrying across the room.

Once the microwave system determined that there were no movements of anything larger than a cricket and there was no human activity inside, voice auto dialers and text message warnings broadcast an impending threat on the house over cable internet to the owner and to the police department. Dead bolts slammed home, securing and isolating the safe room. Wireless alarms powered down. Glass break window alarms deactivated. Cameras outside and inside remained activated, although as long as they weren't directly checked for electrical power, an external cursory inspection would indicate they were de-energized.

The thermal imagery from four forward looking infrared and low light television sensors imbedded in the trunks of trees at the four corners of the property recorded men getting hung up in hidden bundles of chicken wire, unexpectedly impeding their progress. Once free of the snares, the men continued on their march toward the back door of the house. When one man withdrew a hockey puck-like device from his pocket and depressed a switch, all cameras and sensors in the house and outside failed.

34

November 7
Jordan

As soon as darkness fell at Mafraq Air Base, the YO-3A was airborne. An AC-130 had finished refueling at the Al-Azraq Air Base. Parked next to the *Spectre* gunship, two U.S. Air Force C-130s had been refueled and waited for parachutists from the 1st Special Forces Operational Detachment-Delta from Fort Bragg, North Carolina to re-board the aircraft. Each man wore a camouflage version of their Halo Master Airborne Paratrooper Badge. Average age of the men, 35. No rookies in this group. They were seasoned combat-hardened troops with multiple tours in Afghanistan, Iraq, and unmentionable and unpronounceable places in Africa. For an occupation that killed young men by the score, the lethality of the old survivors of Special Forces wasn't to be taken lightly.

For the first time in his illustrious career at the CIA, Hunter wasn't in the front seat of the old spy plane. Kelly performed all of the administrative duties as the pilot-in–command. She took off, trimmed the airplane for its maximum speed at their cruising altitude, and confirmed with Hunter what vector they'd be heading. Transitioning from the front seat of his 600 mph jet to the back seat of the 200 mph propeller driven airplane made him feel like he was in the middle of a Bourbon Street funeral procession.

The landing gear, FLIR, and gun were all retracted into the fuselage to achieve the best dash speed to the Syrian border. Inside the aircraft it was very noisy in this configuration. Propeller speed, governed by the engine-mounted reduction gearbox, was at its maximum. The dual exhaust ports couldn't contain the exhaust gases of the engine at cruising speed and crackled on one side of the airplane near Hunter's right ear. The propeller tips created supersonic shockwaves as it spun at 2,000 rpm. The night air was calm; the clouds that had obscured much of the ISIS battlefield earlier had blown east. Visibility was CAVU—ceiling and visibility unlimited. With no moon it was a perfect night for flying a spyplane. Except for the noise.

Hunter busied himself in the rear seat. He talked to Kelly frequently, basically wargaming or projecting what he thought they might find if and when they located the hostages. Noise-canceling headsets facilitated their discussions over the roar of the multiple drive belts of the reduction gearbox.

Kelly was mesmerized by her father's stories. He was all transmit; she was all receive. His deep commanding voice sounded much deeper than normal over the interphone system. She was surprised that despite sleeping on the cargo jet, she felt extremely fatigued. She wasn't going to mention it to her father. She convinced herself she'd be fine once the adrenaline kicked when the shooting started.

"I've located over two dozen separate hostage sites in the last fifteen-twenty years. They were all different, but they were all the same. Some were in the mountains, some were in the jungle. But in every case there were guards. An overabundance of guards. Hostage takers rarely leave their hostages alone. Hostage are too valuable to take for granted."

Hunter flipped night vision goggles over his eyes and scanned the horizon, right and left, looking for distant light sources which would pop up as bright points of light. Then he pushed the NVGs up away from his eyes and let his eyes readjust to the red cockpit lights. "Sometimes, in the mountains or in the jungle, I'd be able to get a head count of the missing, using the FLIR. I'd crank up the gain to catch the basic thermal images of the hostages through thatched roofs. Our guys are HVTs, high value targets, and very dangerous if not restrained, so they'll be shackled and heavily guarded wherever they are, either inside a building or out. So for starters, we'll look for guards. And guards come in various shapes and sizes."

Hunter looked over his glare shield to see Kelly's helmet nodding. It was the nod of assent, not fatigue. She clicked her microphone twice to acknowledge she heard him. He continued, "Then there's activity. Everyone who's anybody in ISIS will want to see them and have a piece of our guys. The SEALs are deadly; I don't know much about our NCS guys. I assume they have the same basic level of training and skill set as the SEALs. So as long as our guys are alive, there should be great activity near where they're being held."

"Dad, fifty miles. Palmyra's on the nose." Kelly started to breathe hard as the excitement built up. Now anything could happen.

He thought he might have detected a bit of nervousness in her voice. Perfectly understandable. He again flipped night vision goggles over his eyes. Hunter looked out of the canopy across the void of eastern Syria. A few spots of green light dotted the blackness out to the horizon. "Roger. I've a few campfires to port. Goats and shepherds. Lots of encampments and activity starboard. But no fighting; no bullets flying about. That's good. But it's also time to slow this puppy down and set her up for quiet flight. They may have listening posts, and we want to sneak up on them. When we get to the quiet range, I'll lower the FLIR and the gun. And I'll check the laser designator, run the helmet-controlled gun aiming system, and fire up *Weedbusters*. We don't know what will be useful if, or when we make contact."

The helmet-controlled gun aiming system was from an attack helicopter system. It took precise, three-dimensional helmet positioning and mirrored that position with the aircraft's gun's movement. When the pilot moved his head to the right, the gun would move to the right.

Kelly found her father's firing up of the illegal drug crop laser, affectionately called *Weedbusters*, utterly bewildering. She had questions, many questions, the kind of questions that can't be asked with other people around. She finally had her father all to herself, but they were working. One question wouldn't hurt. "Dad...."

"Yes...."

"What was Director Lynche apologizing for? There seemed to be some friction, and then it was gone."

Hunter looked at the back of Kelly's helmet for a long second and then resumed scanning. "Greg and I go way back. To the very early days of this program when it was just a white paper concept—a quiet airplane and a FLIR, and we would just find drug labs, narco-terrorists, and kidnappers. Then the Agency provided the gun. The very next mission, I used it to eliminate bin Laden's buddy, Ayman al-Zawahiri. During the flight Greg decided he didn't want to do those missions anymore. On the same mission, we'd gotten into a huge jam—a gearbox chip detector light over Yemen. It was a very long way from our base in Djibouti. He thought we weren't going to make it. I think he almost had a nervous breakdown that night. He quit but was always there to help me with the CIA leadership to continue funding the program."

"Now that he's the leader of the CIA, he sees things from a different perspective. I've probably gotten harder, more cynical, in my old age; sometimes I think he's gotten softer, but he's a remarkable, smart man. I know there are days when he thinks I've turned into a death-dealing, blood-crazed Republican who wakes up every day just hoping for the chance to dismember my enemies and defile their civilizations. He thought I had dismembered the men at the top of the Burj Khalifa and I hadn't. I told him so, but he didn't believe me. After a bit of reflection, he realized I hadn't lied to him then and never had. So he apologized. I knew he'd get to that point one day." He laughed, "It's hard for a Democrat, even a recovering Democrat to say they are wrong. We're ok;

we're cool."

That was more information than she thought she'd get and said, "Thank you. I just wondered." She looked in her canopy mirrors to see her father smiling. It calmed her.

A few seconds of silence passed until Hunter came back up on the interphone. "And, I tell ya, I'd love to be able to tour the old city, see just how bad ISIS destroyed Palmyra's Arch of Triumph, the amphitheater, and the Tetrapylon. I don't know if you know this, but the ruins have been demolished by ISIS. Off to the west is Masyaf Castle, one of the most famous historical sites in Syria. It was the homeland of the Assassins. They captured and inhabited several mountain fortresses throughout Persia and later Syria. They were trained in asymmetric and psychological warfare, and weapons, much like what our special operations forces do today. Experts in all known weaponry. But we just don't have the time to screw around and sightsee. If I recall my history of this place, Palmyra, the 'Pearl of the Desert,' was once a refuge for travelers on the ancient trade route, the Silk Road. Roman temples and fluted columns have stood in Palmyra for thousands of years."

Kelly said, "It's hard to believe I'm here. I never thought I'd be here, flying with you." She looked into her mirrors with a smile.

Hunter smiled back and said, "I think it's time. We'll make a great team."

"Roger." At that moment a bucket load of adrenaline flooded Kelly's veins. She retarded the throttle and slowed the aircraft. She pushed the throttle into the QUIET detent, engaging the proper reduction gear with a thudding downshift that sounded like a mallet pounding on a thick steak. The increase in cabin noise and vibration levels were good indicators that the drive belts were doing their job, converting medium engine speed to a slow propeller turn for quiet flight.

She looked into the canopy mirrors to see her father. The vibrations were too pronounced to tell if he was relaxed or concerned. When the FLIR and the gun deployed into the airstream and locked in placed with a *thunk*, she knew the game was on. And somehow the vibrations in the cockpit ceased. Kelly hadn't been in this position before, undetected in a true combat zone. Every sensor and weapon they had were hanging underneath the aircraft. Would any of them make noises? Give their position away? Trepidation and fear crept into her thoughts. She knew altitude was her best friend in a quiet airplane and wanted to climb slightly just to make sure they couldn't be detected.

•   •   •   •   •

It took Hunter an hour of searching the Devil's hellish backyard to find what he was looking for. Children. Women. Dozens of children and women in a line, walking around an abandoned hotel. The children should have been asleep long ago, but they were being used as human shields. *Guards of a different color.* Hunter said, "These guys are well aware of our rules of engagement. The liberal media would eviscerate the occupant of the White House if Special Forces or unmanned aircraft purposely targeted women and children in an area where they suspected high level meetings were taking place or high-value targets were being held. A phalanx of lawyers, hovering over the remote pilot flying an unmanned aerial vehicle, would never authorize launching a Hellfire if there were women and children in the immediate vicinity."

"What about snipers?"

"Snipers are a different problem, but also offer an easier target. If they're not on a rooftop, then they're usually in the top-most floor. Well back from a window. They call it a 'hide.' The YO-3A is quiet. The thermal imagery of the FLIR and our shallow slant angle will allow us to find them. As we investigate this place, notice that it's isolated. It looks as if reinforcements are several miles away, and the good news, they're not moving. This place is special in its own way. Few visible armed guards and few high-value vehicles. The leaders drive the best trucks. One more thing, the basic rule of engagement for us is, if they have or are holding a weapon, or they're threatening someone with a gun or a machete, then we are cleared hot."

"Thanks, Dad." All of the "engaging the enemy" talk made her stomach flip. Her nerves were almost shot. She tried to calm herself.

"You're welcome. The rest of it is that the government, officially, never tries to kill innocent people. Not civilians. Not children. Not women. Only combatants. FLIR images of women and dead children as collateral missile damage would be splattered on Al-Jazeera—the carrier of the banner of Islamic revolutions—and the mental institution that's the Communist News Network and their proxy, the Russia Television Network, as well as on the front pages of the *New York Times* or what I call America's *Pravda*, the *Washington Post*. Images like that would be leaked. So they're to be avoided at all costs. The liberal media would be especially brutal to a Republican president. If given the opportunity to portray him as a murderer of children, even the children of terrorists, they'll go out of their way to make it the worst possible crime. Call him a war criminal. Our Democrats are looking for any excuse to attack him; they'd like to impeach him. Dead kids on Al-Jazeera would do it."

He snorted in disgust, "The *Post* and the *Times* are about as filthy a publication as ever existed. The truth gets no coverage at all; they wouldn't know the truth if it fell through the ceiling tiles and landed on the desk in front of them. They prostitute themselves by doing whatever the Democrat Party tells them to do or whatever will sell copies. They're worse than tabloid mags now."

Kelly acknowledged Hunter. She changed subjects and said, "I'm trying to pick up a signal, but this chip detector thing is useless. Either this little black box isn't working...."

He finished her sentence, "...or the embedded electronic chips in the arms of the SEALs have been neutralized." ISIS had had plenty of time to find the locator chips embedded in the SEAL's arms and remove and smash them. He dashed any thoughts about selective dismemberment. *It's ok if you find them, asshole, just cut the little things out and leave their arms alone.* He knew the ISIS terrorist group would turn their most sadistic torturers loose on the captured Navy SEALs or CIA officers. Like attempting to escape, having a low-power locator beacon embedded in one's arm would be a capital offense. Torture by knife until death was the punishment.

Hunter wouldn't tell Kelly that torture in a Muslim land had always been a blood orgy. For a thousand years, the ancient jewel-encrusted Arab *khanjar*, as well as knives and swords of varying lengths and curvature had been the favorite tools of the torturer. If the Islamic torturers didn't immediately saw a prisoner's head off, they'd take their time slicing off enough body parts to bring about a long and painful death. *Death by a thousand cuts.*

Hunter doubted the men who were captured would be allowed to live very long. They wouldn't be given lectures about the wonderfulness of Islam, about Islam being a religion of peace. They wouldn't be interrogated under bright lights, or subjected to loud music, or be made to stand for long periods. No, the captured men would be interrogated under the knife and then, at the very least, their heads would be cut off. Punishment for shooting Muslims in Muslim lands would be death, a bullet to the back of the brain.

Since Hunter wouldn't tell Kelly about the many ways in which they could die at the hands of an Islamist, he changed the subject and said some things about quiet aircraft that she didn't know. "Let's change the subject—I'm betting you don't know all that much about these little airplanes."

"You mean there are more than one type?"

Hunter scanned the buildings and structures with the FLIR as he talked. "One of these days we'll go to Elmira and I'll show you. National Soaring Museum and all that. In the meantime, these babies—the YO-3As—were disposed of after the Vietnam War. A couple found their way to London where the police used them to detect rooftop crime."

"*Rooftop crime?*" Kelly was bewildered. She had never heard of such a thing, but then again, a year ago she hadn't heard of the YO-3As either, and now she was flying them.

"Yes. There are plenty of London Bobbies on the streets, and they're quite the deterrent. So the 'breaking and entering' type of criminal looks for the weakest link in rows of buildings and businesses. In London, buildings are very close together. If you can gain entry to one from the roof, you can get on top of all of them—sometimes for blocks. Regular airplanes and helicopters are too loud and alert burglars. That allows the bad guys to hide and take shelter. There were no Schweizer motor gliders available to do the work. A couple of Yo-Yos were offered, and the last of the YO-3A pilots being discharged from the Army trained the British police pilots how to fly them. A couple of months later, the YO-3A crews completely eliminated rooftop crime in London."

Hunter continued, "Two other aircraft went to the FBI. They followed hostage takers. Two aircraft went to the Louisiana Fish and Game. Those pilots busted poachers by the hundreds. No one ever heard or saw those airplanes. Same pilot trained all of them before he was discharged and went off to fly for Eastern Airlines. The leaders of the FBI, the Fish and Game, and the London Police called those airplanes 'magical.' The only problem was they put guys out of work."

Kelly said, "I don't understand."

"One of the unintended consequences of all that success in London was that in very short order all the rooftop criminals were arrested, locked up, and policemen were sitting around doing nothing—they became 'excess.' The police leaders thought they could reduce their overhead, their 'excess' police force, detectives mostly. The London Police unions screamed bloody murder that they were losing positions, jobs, to an airplane, if you get my drift. The next thing you know, we were told to come get those airplanes."

"That's how you got them? The Yo-Yos?"

He nodded. "Kinda. So much for history. Now let's see if we can work some magic in Syria

35

November 7
Syria

Hunter contacted the AWACS aircraft on the encrypted frequency to announce "probable contact." Using the call sign *Greybeard*, he transmitted the structure's coordinates. As the small spyplane circled about 500 feet above the ground, the airborne combat air controller experienced extreme difficulty tracking the YO-3A on radar. Plotting its intermittent position on a moving map display was nearly impossible.

The sudden radio burst from *Greybeard*, galvanized the other controllers to jump from their positions and race to her console. E-3 controllers normally monitored their assigned area of the battlefield, detecting, identifying, and tracking airborne enemy forces far from the boundaries of NATO countries. It was another intolerably quiet night over Syria, and neither the Syrians, the Russians, nor the Iraqis were flying. That only left *Greybeard* whose radar blip uncharacteristically faded in and out, a product of radar waves bouncing off the propeller. A pair of C-130s laden with parachutists, and an AC-130 gunship following in loose trail high above the altitude of shoulder-launched anti-missile range.

The controller tried every setting she could to get a continuous positive lock on *Greybeard*. When nothing worked she gave up and relayed the new information to the three Air Force Special Operations Command Hercules aircraft. She thought, *What kind of slow-moving airplane can be nearly invisible to our radar? We can see and track anything that moves.*

Delta Forces in the C-130s were given the word to "standby." They loaded the coordinates of their target into the mission information system computer on their forearms. The wearable computer system kept them on course during night jumps. Now they waited for the green jump light to illuminate in the cabin, signaling they were in the appropriate jump cone to intercept the ground target.

At three o'clock in the morning, it was Grand Central Station at the Palmyra Hotel south and west of the old city. In the FLIR, Hunter watched several dozen children and large heaps of laundry he assumed were women in *burkas* walking or staggering about the grounds of the hotel. Herding exhausted children in a racetrack course was guaranteed insurance against an American missile attack from the high-flying unmanned *Predators*.

Hunter directed Kelly, "Bring us in a little closer, and let's drop down to 200 AGL. Any reinforcements are miles away." FLIR video of the hotel compound filled both screens in the cockpit. Hunter switched imagery to the thermal signatures of the hotel and its adjacent structures. After three orbits of the position at a mile of slant-range, Hunter began to think he may have been fooled into believing the hotel was a command post for some other high value target bedding down for the night with a wife or a rack of prepubescent girls stolen from an overrun village. Then he detected the thermal signatures of men in a covered parking area.

The imagery was distinctive, the product of the latest developments in forward looking infrareds. Seven burly men with hoods over their heads and their arms behind their backs were led out of a side door of the hotel's main building. Men on each side of the handcuffed prisoners forced the men to their knees when they were forced into position. The hostages were kicked and shoved to arrange them in a line, like a row of headstones.

Hunter barked, "*Bingo!* Get as close as you can. Things could go south in a few seconds." Kelly's skin tingled from the sudden rush of adrenaline as she pushed the control stick and hard turned toward the hotel. She added a few rpms to maintain airspeed. She could hardly believe what she was witnessing on the FLIR repeater-screen.

"Lower. Closer." Hunter was so focused on the imagery that he didn't blink and nearly whispered his directions.

Kelly made tiny corrections to avoid deflecting control surfaces which could make unwanted noise, usually a whistle. Her heart was pounding like a jackhammer.

Hunter continually assessed the situation under the pair of awnings used to shelter vehicles from the desert sun. He expected vehicles to be parked under the sunshades. It was odd and incongruous that some Toyota Hilux Surfs were parked adjacent to the awnings. The YO-3A's low altitude and less than a half-mile of slant range provided a crystal-clear and very detailed thermal image.

"Slip it to get us a little closer. Maintain altitude."

For the moment, the captives didn't appear to be in danger. The guards manhandling the captives had slung weapons or holstered pistols. The prisoners were secure. Hunter checked the status of the laser and the gun. Green status lights on the multi-function panel validated that the systems were armed and ready for use. A pictorial representation on the multi-function displays showed the *Wraith's* gun position. Hunter moved his head to the left and right to ensure the aiming system of the gun was working.

He counted and recounted. There should have been eight hostages. One man was missing. As the underside of the opposite awning came into view Hunter was relieved that there were no firing squads, only dozens of onlookers. In the middle of the awning there was a camcorder on a tripod and a man attending to the camera, making adjustments to the lens. A man who appeared to be the commander gestured rapidly and forcefully to the handlers to ensure the captives were in a straight line under the opposite awning.

Hunter said to Kelly, "See where they are; they're invisible to satellites, and high-flying UAVs with limited slant-range capabilities can't see them either. They know we are looking for them. This is exactly why we were...." He stopped in mid-sentence as seven other shapes suddenly emerged from the hotel marching in single file. Pistols were held near their ears and were pointed into the air.

Under his breath, Hunter yelled, "*Aaah shit!*"

Kelly stared at the FLIR image. She couldn't move.

At first Hunter couldn't resolve what was out of perspective. Then he realized the seven images with pistols were children, half the size of the men. They marched like little soldiers and then, one by one, stopped and took a position behind each of the kneeling captives.

Kelly was horrified. She had heard of the beheading videos ISIS proudly posted on the internet. After a couple of years the beheadings had lost their impact and ISIS began to use children to murder hostages. The propaganda value for the terrorist organization was incalculable.

Again Hunter said, "*Shit!*" and acted without thinking. The aircraft was in a turn with the nose pointed away and nearly perpendicular to the line of hostages; they were in a disadvantageous position moving to an impossible one. Seven children with seven guns stood behind seven hooded, kneeling men. Hunter watched as the children lowered their pistols near the back of each hostage's head. Two-handed grip. Hunter realized he had one opportunity to do something before he lost sight of them under the approaching overhead awning.

Kelly Horne was mortified at the scene in her FLIR scope. She couldn't tear her eyes from the imagery. *That...can...not...be happening....*

Hunter moved his head to put the laser designator on the skull of the closest kid behind his eye and "tagged" that point for the targeting computer. The gun's software swung the big-bore rifle to the designated target. Another green light on the multi-function display and a tone in his headset indicated the target was acquired, the gyro-stabilization system was engaged, and the projectile was ready. Hunter pulled the trigger on the control stick. The FLIR image was washed out momentarily as the exhaust gasses of the projectile left the barrel.

Kelly jumped at the sound of the bullet leaving the gun barrel. She was shocked at the sight in her FLIR screen. For a single second, the white hot bullet traced a path directly to the laser designated spot, the temple of the nearest child. She stopped flying the airplane and was no longer functioning as the pilot. *Those...are...children....*

Hunter felt the aircraft wobble in pitch and yaw and barked out commands. "Maintain altitude! Give me a flat turn! I need a 180! 180! 180!"

Kelly didn't respond. She was frozen in her seat, staring at the FLIR screen.

No longer able to see the hostages on their knees or the children with pistols, Hunter moved his head and the FLIR's sight picture to the dozen or so men under the opposite awning. He felt the aircraft dip its nose. He grabbed the control stick and yelled, "My airplane!" Hunter lost sight of the bullet's impact just as the opposite awning's overhang obscured his view. He didn't know if the spent uranium bullet had torn through the pterion below the frontal bone of the first child. He hoped he had been able to line up the targets perfectly.

Hunter immediately transferred his attention to using the laser of the *Weedbusters* system contained within the FLIR ball turret. He had over fifty solo missions from the front seat where he coordinated the use of the *Weedbusters* laser and gun systems, but he had never targeted dozens of people on the ground. He trimmed the aircraft for level flight, and set the laser's power to MAXIMUM.

When the supersonic crack of the bullet shattered the night, the bystanders under the awning all jumped. They were hardened, experienced fighters, so it only took a split second for them to realize that they were under attack. Hunter didn't waste any time. He squeezed the laser firing trigger and flooded the area under the opposite parking awning with high-energy UV. The invisible lasers swept the area under the awning hundreds of times per second. The slant range of the powerful, four-head, fiber optic laser was inside of a half-mile; too far away for the beams to be an effective cutting tool but inside the window for mass irradiation.

All of the men under the shelter jumped at the supersonic shock wave of the bullet, they were wide-eyed in surprise and were instantly blinded by the multiple laser beams. Ultra violet radiation seared their optic nerves; now all the men could see was white, as if they'd been caught looking directly into the flash of a welder's arc or the sun. The natural response was to blink their eyes shut. When they opened them again, they got another dose of UV. Hunter mashed the laser firing button; he was relentless in destroying their eyesight.

Convinced they'd been blinded and would remain so for some time, Hunter watched for their reactions in the FLIR scope. Hands flew to faces in an attempt to push the invading white beast away. Being struck blind fully immobilized the men and turned them into sitting ducks at an arcade.

Hunter ignored Kelly in the front seat as he killed a man every six seconds. He chastised himself for not firing at the camera sooner; he placed the LD on it and one round obliterated it. He reloaded the weapon as more people poured out of the building. Hunter trimmed the airplane between magazines. More irradiation; more blinding light that instantly incapacitated the new men running to an enemy they couldn't see or hear. Men fell to their knees and screamed. Some rolled around on the pavement, some tried to run only to stumble and fall like they'd been subject to a Dizzy Izzy. Others tried to crawl to an imaginary safe location. The ISIS soldiers may have had a natural urge to flee, but they could only drop and roll around aimlessly, like a child throwing a tantrum in a department store.

With the autopilot engaged and the *Wraith* trimmed and flying smoothly in the night sky, Hunter calmly targeted and killed the ISIS men, until he could no longer detect any movement in the FLIR. The cockpit smelled of the ammunition's exhaust gases. He overrode the autopilot and flew "Lazy Eights." His positioning in the sky was such that he was directly over the awning where the SEALs were being held and had yet to see if the seven hostages had been shot by the children.

With the immediate threat disabled, Hunter transmitted to the AWACS the code word to "let the angels fly." Within ten seconds, fifty parachutists were in freefall, plummeting toward their ground target.

Hunter had a magazine left and one partial load in the gun. He had spent 45 of the special, rocket-propelled, laser-guided rounds. No more *tangos* spilled out of the hotel to investigate the sounds in the parking lot. The women and children who had been walking around the old hotel had run from the supersonic cracks in the parking area as fast as they could.

It was time to check on the hostages.

Kelly was still unresponsive. Hunter looked over the rear seat's glare shield and her helmet didn't move. He accelerated and turned the aircraft to overfly the sun shelter and got the view he desired. When the aircraft's thermal sensor was finally able to detect the thermal signatures under the opposite parking lot awning, Hunter counted seven children as seven unmoving heaps behind the seven hooded men still kneeling. The imagery of dead children didn't affect him. He could only think, *Kneeling is good Maybe we got lucky*. He tried again to raise Kelly to no avail. He set up an orbit over the hotel ready to kill anything that moved.

He tried to talk to Kelly when the AWACS controller informed him vehicles were inbound. He panned the FLIR and scanned the area out to a distance of fifteen miles. The thermal images of some half-dozen ISIS vehicles were moving in his direction at a high rate of speed. Hunter powered up the *Wraith* and climbed, and set a course to intercept the trucks, head-on.

As U.S. Army paratroopers were landing near the hotel, Hunter engaged the first ISIS truck in column at ten miles. One truck after another, he put a round into the vehicles' radiators and engine blocks. The ISIS soldiers knew they were under fire when a spent-uranium bullet slammed into their vehicles and the sounds of the bringer of death echoed in their ears. They abandoned their disabled trucks and scattered in the night. The YO-3A pitched off and cleared the area just as the AC-130 gunship swooped in with Gatling gun blazing and eliminated the fleeing ISIS fighters.

Three minutes after touchdown, a squad of Special Forces entered the hotel parking lot to find dozens of dead ISIS men piled up under one awning. Another squad checked the condition of the seven kneeling men, and one by one raised a "thumbs up" to indicated the men were alive.

Hunter contacted the AWACS aircraft to tell them he'd remain on station. The E-3's combat controller responded "playmates inbound" to indicate that helicopters were on their way to extract the Delta men, the SEALs, and the CIA agents. Hunter raised his head and swung the FLIR around to pick up a squadron of helicopters coming in from the south. He powered up the engine and climbed to a safe altitude to deconflict their arrival.

As helicopters landed near the hotel, Hunter turned the *Wraith* toward Jordan. Kelly wouldn't speak to him when he tried to get her attention. Their interphone system wasn't kaput, nor had she been hit by a stray bullet. He had to believe she was in shock.

There was nothing he could do except speak to her in the most compassionate of tones. Hunter tried to comfort her with words of encouragement and love.

The sun started to rise in the east as Hunter lined up the YO-3A for final approach. Kelly finally "came to" and spoke in subdued tones. She offered to land the airplane. She whispered between deep breaths, "I'm okay, Dad. Really." She looked to the side of the canopy. Her tone and inflection suggested a little girl in great emotional turmoil. Hunter landed the aircraft and taxied it to their hangar. He couldn't do anything for her until he cut the fuel to the engine and helped her out of the cockpit.

A small cheering crowd waited for the black airplane to stop moving and the propeller to come to a complete stop. They expected the aircrew to jump from the airplane and share in the celebration of the mission's success. The propeller hadn't stopped when Hunter threw the canopy open, climbed out of the back seat onto the wing, and rushed to Kelly.

Hunter struggled to get his footing on the wing of the aircraft. From being in the cockpit so long, his hip was giving him some major grief, and he nearly stumbled and fell off the wing. He helped Kelly to remove her helmet. That was the moment when Nazy, Greg, Bob and Bob, and the C-17 crew knew something had happened to the pilot.

The flight doctor was the first one to reach the strange black shadow of the aircraft.

36

There was no time for celebration. Inside the cargo hold of the Globemaster, Nazy Cunningham cradled Kelly Horne like a mother holding a very sick child in an emergency room. Kelly would have little to do with her father or Lynche but found shelter in the arms of Nazy. Psychological wounds weren't the flight doctor's specialty. He checked her over and could only find that she was exhausted, as if she had run a marathon. He gave her a sedative and stayed by her side. The mechanics, Bob and Bob, determined this was a situation that they couldn't fix, so they retreated to their sleeping bags. With nothing else to do, Duncan moved to the other side of the jet and debriefed the mission with Lynche. The DCI reported that the Special Operations teams recovered all eight missing men alive. There were over forty dead ISIS men and seven male children, and an obliterated videocamera.

Hunter yawned and lamented, "She locked up when the kids took a position behind the hostages. She knew I was going to kill them, and she just shut down. I should have had her turn off the FLIR repeater in the front seat so she couldn't see what I was doing. They were so fast getting into position, I didn't have time to anticipate their next move. I...just didn't think it through. I was a little startled that they'd march kids out. I had this diminishing sight picture.... I knew that in a few seconds we were going to fly right through my window of opportunity to save them—if I could save them. It could have been a ploy or a practice execution but I couldn't take the chance. I had one chance. A very narrow window. So I shot the nearest kid and hoped the laser designator remained on the tagged spot so the bullet would somehow pass through all of them. Apparently, I was lucky."

Sarcastically, Lynche said, "You *are* the luckiest guy on the planet." Then he was serious. "Are you okay?"

Hunter said, "I don't feel like it. I put a bullet through their video recorder but I took too long to kill that camera. I was overcome by events and when I saw it again in my field of view, I blasted it. It was the best I could do."

Lynche said, "It was more than anyone could have done." Lynche didn't want to dwell on the possible live feed from Al-Jazeera transmitting pictures of an American bullet killing innocent Muslim children in order to save American men. He would deal with it later. *But the children....* The children were collateral damage. The consequences of war in a war zone. Hunter yawned, nodded, then Lynche nodded toward Kelly curled up in Nazy's arms and sleeping peacefully.

"She'll be ok, Duncan. We didn't know what you were going to find when you got there. When you have to shoot, you shoot. You did what you had to do. We knew they have used kids as executioners before. Hamas and Hezbollah have done it for years. I didn't expect it. I thought their guys would have fought each other just for the privilege of killing a SEAL or one of our guys."

Hunter nodded. He had wanted to slug his boss for putting his daughter in such a position, but with the element of time and distance, Hunter had worked through his anger and accepted responsibility for being distracted and not killing the camera sooner. He beat himself up because he should have seen the potential, just like a parent of a two-year-old should move the glass from the edge of a table. It's not the kid's fault you were dumb enough to put a glass where the little urchin could get it.

He should have known as soon as he saw those kids marching out of the hotel. Hunter admonished himself. *I should have known. I should have seen it coming. I did see it happening, but I didn't want to believe it. But there was no other way. A bullet to kill the camera would have certainly resulted in our guys getting shot. I thought I had to let the situation play out. The priority was neutralizing the threat to our guys. I made the right choice.*

It pained him that Nazy was the one taking care of his daughter. Time should heal that wound too. He hoped.

As Hunter stared at his family across the expanse of the cargo jet, Lynche could still not believe that Hunter had been able to disable nearly fifty ISIS fighters and facilitate a rescue while also having to fly the airplane. Lynche thought, *He really could have done it by himself—he just would have had to pilot from the aft cockpit, and in the end, that is exactly what he did. Just when I think I'm the smartest guy in the room, Duncan proves to everyone he's the real genius.* It momentarily put a smile on Lynche's face. He shook his head in wonder and thought, *Damn! Frigging genius.*

Hunter moved across to sit with Nazy. He spoke into her ear. "I love you."

She pressed against him. "How are you doing?" Nazy asked quietly so as to not interrupt Kelly's sleep.

"I'm fine. It was just too much for her. My fault."

Nazy caressed his face with her free hand.

Hunter said reflectively, "She grew up in a church-going family."

Nazy squeezed his hand and kissed it.

Hunter continued, "I inflicted our wicked little world on an innocent. Now she knows dad is more than someone who can handle a gun; he's someone who can kill because that's his job. He even kills kids. Will she...can she ever trust me again?"

Nazy gripped his hand. "Do not beat yourself up. She's not six or eight or ten. She's a woman and an operations officer."

Lynche had joined them and chimed in, "Yes, the culture teaches that violence traumatizes children—even adults. But Kelly is a smart girl. She's just come face-to-face with the hard reality of this work. Duncan, your work is righteous—murderers were about to kill our guys. They were hostages about to be executed. And you saved them."

Lynche said, "I'm sure Kelly will come to know that when you counter unjust violence—like the near execution of our guys—to save a life, it's a righteous act to fight and stop evil; it's the act of a moral person."

Hunter smiled, but he didn't feel much better. His hip throbbed. He said, "I had to kill children to save them." He pulled back to look at them; to receive their opprobrium for his wholly un-Christian deed.

Lynche said, "I know. Duncan, you did what you had to do tonight and in Dubai. What you did was an honorable and righteous act for most Americans. I apologize for doubting you about Dubai. You are a very moral person." He bounced in his seat a bit. It wasn't easy to admit his mistake to Duncan, but he meant every word.

After initially showing her concern, Nazy smiled, and nodded her concurrence. Then she relaxed and thought, *We've had enough of this heavy conversation. Time to get on with life.* She looked at Kelly, gently stroking her hair and murmured, "I have no idea how people are born this beautiful."

Hunter rubbed his eyes to wipe away the tears. *Says the woman who's a goddess in her own right...*

A minute passed before Nazy could look at him because of the tears running down her own face. She wiped her eyes with a tan cuff, leaned into his ear, and said, "Those were no longer innocent children. They'd been trained to be killers; devils in children's clothes. In this part of the world, people aren't of equal value. You had to do what needed to be done to save good men. You aren't to be blamed. Kelly will be ok. Always remember you're an incredibly good man, Duncan Hunter."

Then she kissed his ear. When he turned toward her, she placed her forehead against his. Hunter squeezed her free hand. They remained like that for several minutes, affirming their love.

Lynche observed the lovers. He had been wrong to doubt the tenacity and integrity of his prodigy. He tried to recall the conditions and circumstances that had led him to believe Hunter had lied to him about killing the leaders and financiers of international terrorism. And he drew a blank. It had to be his own liberal viewpoint that contributed to his distorted feelings. He loved Hunter as if he were his own son, and it had been troubling him that Hunter had a different political viewpoint than his. He had feared Duncan was drifting into the passing lane of extremism.

Hunter had debriefed Lynche about the Dubai mission. Just as terrorists targeted CIA agents by blowing up airliners, 3M tried to kill Duncan Hunter in a Boeing 747. Duncan had escaped the deathtrap set by a self-radicalized computer scientist and had hunted down the man who ordered the hit. The former Democrat president had begged for his life, he had tried to bribe Hunter, but could only scream *Allahu Akbar* as Hunter hammered a Bowie across the back of his neck and defenestrated head and torso from the top floor of the Burj Khalifa.

Lynche had determined that what Hunter did with his hillbilly samurai sword could never be considered a normal response. *Was that Hunter's right wing extremism or was that simple murder? Or was it something else, like an eye for an eye? Was it revenge? Mazibuike had tried to kill Hunter, trap him in a jet and then send it to Davy Jones' Locker. He remembered thinking, If you try to kill Duncan Hunter, you better not fail. 3M failed.*

Hunter's actions hadn't been sanctioned by him as the Director of the CIA or by the president. But with the benefit of time and distance, and a little more information, Lynche began to understand why Hunter did it. *He cut off the head of the snake so it couldn't do any more harm. It also sent a message. It may not have been a legal act, but it was definitely a righteous act against a former president who was pure evil. If someone breaks into your home and threatens you, what do you do? Mazibuike tried to kill hundreds in order to destroy Hunter. He deserved to die.* Lynche allowed an indelicate thought, *That would have been something to see.* The former president had crossed the line and suffered the consequences of having a pissed off Marine on his ass.

37

November 8
Over the Atlantic

Hunter put an arm around Nazy and kissed her hair. They sat quietly, connected, in the moment. Hunter helped reposition Kelly from Nazy's lap onto her sleeping bag. After ensuring Kelly was safe and secure in her sleeping space, they wandered over to the other side of the aircraft. Lynche followed. Each took a cold greasy pizza wedge and ate in silence. Hunter pointed at Lynche for remembering to get pepperoni with jalapenos. "You're a god."

Lynche winked. *Your welcome.* Then he remembered Duncan had wanted a favor. They hadn't talked about it yet, so he asked. Hunter told him in one sentence. The request surprised Lynche and Nazy. It wasn't personal; it was for a friend. Lynche reached across and shook Hunter's hand. "I'll see what I can do."

"Thanks, boss." Hunter finished another slice of pizza and made eyes at his wife.

After a wordless clean-up, Lynche broke the quiet between his two favorite people. "I don't suppose a drone could do what you did tonight."

Hunter stared at his boss for a good long time, then shook his head in mock disgust. "Impossible. On so many levels. First, you couldn't begin to do that with this soupçon of a logistics footprint. Second, you know that I'm able to spare the women and children. Drones…for every ten to fifteen people killed, you might get one bad guy. My way, I find the guy and take him out—not bomb the whole friggin' grid square back to the Stone Age.

Nazy looked on and let the men talk. She wasn't a pilot and had little comprehension of the challenges of flying a low-flying aircraft while shooting at a target. She used the time to unravel her braids and brush her hair. The men stopped for a second to watch her. It was the most calming thing they'd seen all day and it was mildly erotic. Of course, Nazy could have been flossing her teeth wearing a burlap sack and Hunter would have found something completely erotic in her movements.

Lynche peeled his eyes away from the woman. He wasn't going to give up on his line of questions. "Swarm?"

Hunter turned from his wife to the DCI. Business. "Greg, no. This wasn't some division of labor, an equation where you could send a dozen gun drones and a dozen laser drones to achieve equal success. This was spontaneous and creative. Your planners would never have considered using *Weedbusters* to blind and disable. It would have never been considered in theaters of operations. They always have a simple binary solution, find and kill. They assume that if a bomb can't be used then automatic weapons can—a linear equation. We have a prototypical single-shot gun, limited in many ways, firing transformative ammunition with tiny seeker heads and wings that guide on the spot of a laser beam. Those bullets are prohibitively expensive."

"A thousand dollars a pop. They're miniaturized missiles."

"Your lawyers would have a fit—you can't use a weapon to blind your adversary because of the Geneva Convention and you can't kill them with terminator ammunition. It's ok to blow them up, kill them all with twenty 5.56mm, and let Allah sort them out. But disable them…what I did back there required on the spot imagination. I knew we had the capability but would something like that work on a crowd? It's something we have never tested. If you're too close, you shred their eyes; if you're too far, they get dazzled by the laser. To a lawyer, what I did was illegal, but necessary. Just like when you first used it to save my sorry ass. That time you were surprisingly vicious."

"I did save your sorry ass—and look at the thanks I get!"

"I got you a pretty red Porsche for your birthday! I learned from the master." Hunter lightened up and smiled at Nazy brushing her princess hair. He then turned back to his boss. "I sometimes forget just how brilliant you really are. You took the idea, kill drug crops with a laser, and got the *company* to fund and advance the necessary technology to build a demonstrator. I know I give you shit sometimes because you are a stable genius despite your liberal leanings; I'm hoping you'll come around one of these days and reject the dark side. I'm telling you, there's no good to be had playing *on that team*."

Lynche laughed then shook his head, first at Nazy then at Hunter. *I did reject the dark side…. That was a long time ago….* He was more animated as the heavy topics had been lifted from the debriefing. "Yeah. While I was retired, I got the Agency to bring in the best scientists to solve the engineering problem of solid state fiber optic lasers. It was disruptive technology. Amazing mathematics and engineering. Cray computers and all that jazz. Industry would need decades to do what we did in a few of months. And look where they are today. Commercial off-the-shelf fiber optic lasers." He smiled at how far they'd come. He said to Nazy, "All of the available space under the Yo-Yo was taken up by the first *Weedbusters* system. Now we're on version four, and it's one quarter the size of the original and four times as powerful. And now we have a gun which has also shrunk in size with more capability."

Hunter interjected something about limits and transmissivity tables but neither Nazy nor Lynche knew what he was saying. Lynche turned from Nazy to Hunter and asked, "Is there anything good about drones?"

Hunter shrugged and said, "Drones won't be late to briefings. Drones won't start fights at happy hour. Drones won't destroy officer's clubs or total your favorite sports car. Drones won't try to seduce your buddy's wife or girlfriend. Drones will never purchase big ass watches like Rolexes or Tags. Drones won't jump on a bar table and insult the other services, or dance on tables, or pinch girls' asses. Drones won't do all of the other things that we know win wars! I see no future in them, other than what I'm about to show you."

Lynche was amused but wasn't amused.

Hunter added, "Seriously, now we have a gun with CCIP and a FLIR and an LD. That magical gun from S&T. There's virtually no room for anymore acronyms or anything else but a handful of drones." He paused for several seconds before adding, "I'm not sure drones and swarming technology are the next answer for your purposes. They might be. If they are, then some university or research lab will show you what's in the art of the possible, such as using drones with LIDARs to map tunnels and subways. Stuff like that, stuff a troop might encounter underground. Above ground, we should be able to teach killer drones how to defeat other drones."

Hunter turned to Nazy and patted her hand as he moved to his black helmet bag and rummaged through it as if he were looking for something at its very bottom. He was distracted…he admired her nails, always manicured; he was especially fond of her nails lacquered with Mary Kay's *Cherries Jubilee*. He composed himself when he found what he was looking for. "What was disruptive of noisy airplanes was quiet airplanes. Old stuff with new capabilities."

Nazy hissed, "*Wraith*?" like it was an evil word.

Hunter half-nodded and continued, "Yes, Baby. The *Wraith*. DOD wants drones, and everyone thinks they're the cat's meow, the best thing since sliced bread. I disagree—they're very expensive and require a ton of manpower or they are cheap and disposable and don't do much but be toys for boys. Whenever I fly a Yo-Yo, I disprove the marketing idiots, just like windmills can't power a ship or solar panels can't power this jet. There's a thing called *limits* in mathematics. Some things are optimal, perfect feats of engineering just by their being, like the *Concorde* and the SR-71 Blackbird."

She hadn't heard the complete story. As she continued to brush her hair, Hunter explained, "No one thought to do testing on animals to see if the laser would blind them. We just wanted to kill plants. And we did. We found the trade secrets to kill cocoa, poppies, and *the marijuana*. Each plant required a discrete combination of wavelength, power, and dwell. That required a lot of testing." Hunter laughed out loud. "We had to grow illegal plants! Under any other circumstance, we'd have gone to jail."

Lynche grinned at the thought and added, "It was good to have a DEA agent with us. Once we had a prototype system we did some of the most secretive tests we've ever done."

Suddenly Nazy was curious. "How did they do that?"

Lynche answered, "We, meaning the CIA, leased a warehouse near Elmira, New York. Brought in the equipment and laser scientists and botanists and thousands of baby plants. Sixty days later we had answers and a working model. Burned up a truckload of special-coated mirrors, if I recall. The program manager just knew they weren't going to be able to solve the mirror problem until Duncan said, 'The smartest glass guys on the planet are at Dow Corning, which is just down the road.' We brought in their glass experts, and they found a clever solution. They were still expensive to make, but now we could go twenty hours before we had to swap out the excitation and aiming mirrors. Before we brought in the experts, we burned up a set of mirrors in two minutes. That was the limiting factor. Now we have astronomy-grade mirrors that last forever."

Hunter said, "And we killed tiny baby plants while the darlings slept in their beds. So Greg, to replace me — technology and engineering are limiting factors. It seems to me that if you want to replace me, you need a suitable replacement. Someone with a good hip. Dig the Yo-Yos out of the museums, like SOCOM did while I was at the Naval War College, and turn them into what we have here. Optionally manned. Remember the laser only works at very low altitudes because of the UV wavelength. Once they're briefed, I know Air Branch and Special Ops Command will scratch each other's eyes out to have this capability. Then the lawyers will tell everyone 'you can't do that!' You'll find you really won't need me anymore. And then, *Wraith* will have been totally exposed and no one will have the capability."

Lynche grinned. "Oh, now that the word is out, there will be immense pressure for me to 'give you up' for other missions. The SOCOM commander, General Runyan, and the Joint Chiefs will want your YO-3A for the really tough guys like the bin Laden types who know how to defeat the satellites and the high fliers. Predators. Reapers. Next-Gen crap."

Hunter grimaced as he repositioned in his seat. He hadn't taken his pain killers in hours. He needed something to knock the hip pain back a bit. As he went for his backpack he said, "If you take me out of the cockpit and try to solve the multiple equations, you'll need to fund a program equally challenging as the effort to bring *Weedbusters* on line. Are you really going to put up a thousand tiny drones? We are supposed to get in and get out without anyone knowing. You'll have a trail of dead, damaged, and disabled drones that will lead back to your seventh floor office and the White House." Hunter found and swallowed his meds with bottled spring water.

Lynche wasn't convinced. "Think about it, *Maverick*."

Hunter nodded and said, "I have thought about it." He opened his fist to reveal a tiny four-rotor aircraft. Lynche's eyes bugged out of their sockets in surprise. Nazy also registered surprise and curiosity. Both spooks leaned in. Hunter asked Nazy to retrieve her computer tablet.

Lynche asked, "Is this what you used in Iran?"

He said, "Yes, sir. We used a handful of these to take out the last guys on the Matrix. I couldn't get a clear shot."

Nazy said, "But you found a way...."

Hunter nodded. "It was a unique opportunity. Greg, what I'm thinking is that if you give the *Wraith* capability to the Army and Air Branch you won't need me anymore. Maybe that's a good thing. I can ride off into the sunset. Take that vacation I've been promising Nazy. But this is what I was talking about." He pushed a button and four arms sprang out from its BlackBerry-sized body. He flipped the tiny device into the air, and it instantly came alive, rotors unfolding, spinning, and immediately stabilizing itself into a hover. A green light indicated the little aircraft was operational. The drone moved at shoulder-height; its tiny camera lens pivoted to look at Lynche, then Nazy, and then returned to look at Hunter. "It's determining if we are in its database."

Nazy was surprised at the lack of noise from the device and said, "You can't hear it."

"We're not Quiet Aero Systems for nothing." Duncan nodded and received the tablet computer from Nazy. He found the program he was looking for. After touching several icons a live video of Hunter filled the tablet's computer screen. "But maybe with this and hundreds more like them, maybe thousands, you just might be able to keep them away from my airplanes."

Lynche said cautiously, "Remotely piloted vehicles flew hundreds of missions with great accuracy and proficiency."

"Remember, billions of dollars for tens of thousands of large drones were also destroyed just to get to where they are today. With money you buy reliability. You can't take those things they sell in the mall and put them to work in a hot zone. But this is new. This is a huge deal in the state of technology."

First he disparages drones, and then he showcases one — is he on crack? Lynche was confused but mesmerized as Hunter seamlessly moved into instructor mode. The screen was awash in head-up display symbology with a reasonable image of Duncan Hunter still framed in the screen.

Lynche asked for clarification. "This is what you used to eliminate Hammadi, Mohammed Al-Yacoub, Abdullah Ahmed Abdullah, and Jibril?" *What am I missing?*

Hunter said, "Yes, sir. Maybe you've seen something like these in the mall or in the lab." Lynche nodded while Nazy was entranced. The video wasn't perfect, like a 1960s television black and white picture. Flashing bars formed a broken frame around Hunter's face. A white bar with black letters appeared: PRIMARY TARGET.

"It just recognized that I wasn't another target in its bad guy database. I'm in the good guy database." Hunter told Lynche, "Try and swat at it. Try to catch it." An amused Greg Lynche tried several times, and every time the device with the whirling rotors moved away as if it could sense the aggressive maneuver. Hunter continued, "I'm not flying it. That's all AI — artificial intelligence. It's flying itself. Its processor and tiny radars can detect motion and react a hundred times faster than you can. Faster than any human. The stochastic motion is a counter-sniper feature."

Hunter then held out his hand. On the screen the words PRIMARY TARGET changed to NAVIGATE TO TARGET. The tiny device landed in Hunter's open hand — perfectly in the middle of his palm. Lynche's mouth hadn't closed since Hunter had thrown the device and it had activated itself.

Lynche just mumbled, "How...."

Hunter said, "Like any cell phone it has tiny cameras and sensors. It can distinguish facial features through facial recognition applications. And it can carry about three ounces of a shaped charge."

Lynche and Nazy were shocked when the explosive words were uttered. *Oh my God!*

Hunter held up the little helicopter and scrutinized it. "With the good AI, it can ID a target on its bad guy database, fly to that person's forehead, and detonate an explosive charge. Twenty-four grams is sufficient to trephinate the cranium and destroy what's inside. Hammadi, Mohammed Al-Yacoub, Abdullah Ahmed Abdullah, Ahmed Jibril. One, two, three, four. I sent eight of these to hunt them down. These are a whole lot cheaper than our guns' ammunition or a Hellfire missile. And no swarm."

Nazy rocked back against the troop seat, put her hand to her mouth and blurted out, "You used *lethal* drones?"

Hunter nodded. "I did. The targets in the wedding compound moved around too much, as if they knew the protocol of avoiding a long-range sniper. I couldn't put the gunsight on any of them to get a lock for any length of time. If I got lucky and tried to shoot one, the others would have disappeared. So I programmed the eight drones we had to *only look for the four terrorists*. I flew over the compound and released them. News reports that those terrorists are dead means the drones found them. If the reporting is true, after identifying the terrorists individually from their bad guy database, they went on the attack. When they caught them, shaped charges poked holes in their skulls and took them out."

Lynche said, "That's incredible."

"You gave me four targets and provided their pictures. Programming was easy. Technically, we can gang them together, dozens or hundreds, and take out bad guys by the score. No longer is it theoretical. I taught them to be individual hunters. The hard part is programming. It's AI—they can be trained to act as a team—what you call a swarm—or function as a single entity. A swarm will sound like a locust invasion at ten miles. These are silent. They can penetrate buildings, cars, trains, doors without alerting anyone aurally. They can fly inside something silently—silent flight is the key and the discriminator—they can evade people who detect them visually and try to swat them out of the sky. Try to shoot them, and they can get out of the way. They're very difficult to detect and can't be stopped unless they run out of juice. They have a subprogram to 'remember' where the powerlines are and fly to them to recharge. And here's something else. They can be trained to *wait* for their target to appear. If they get damaged before they discharge their little explosive, we have a time delay capsule of acid that will prevent its reuse. If someone does knock it out of the sky, there's a shock switch that'll turn our best demonstrated and available technology into a plastic blob. The bad guys can't reuse our technology and they have no proof other than a wad of gum that we were ever there."

Lynche remembered Duncan was one of the foremost experts on aviation security and the terrorism committed on commercial airliners and airports inflicted by the Islamic Underground. He asked, "I saw your proposal, your strategy to keep commercial aviation safe from Islamic Underground suicide drones at airports. You want to deploy these killer drones at airports? We're looking at a lot of ideas but killer drones...."

Hunter nodded. Nazy smiled painfully. Lynche asked, "Could you have used these in Syria?"

"First, I only brought this one to show you. Even if I'd brought a hundred, I would've needed enough time to train them to do what I wanted. I had time on the C-130 to program eight on our way to Iraq. I had the bad guys' pictures. In Syria, with the *Wraith*, I didn't know what scenario I'd find. And I didn't have anyone's picture. No can do.....*today*. Tomorrow maybe. We might have been able to program them to not attack our guys, using their pictures, and say kill the rest. The problem in Syria was our guys were marched out with bags over their heads. I'm afraid our guys would have been killed with the others. You have to be careful with these things. We really are on the edge of the technology and you have to be smarter than they are."

Lynche asked if he could hold the flying device. Hunter placed it into his hand and said, "Throw it or drop it—it'll recover itself. They have limitations. In the hunting mode or when they're armed, they'll maneuver like an expert and kill anything that moves. With hostages like we had tonight, I think using them would have been too great a risk. I'm sure they would have killed the bad guys but I couldn't guarantee they wouldn't kill our guys too. I don't think the AI...I don't think with the numbers of men on the ground that they could have distinguished the good guys from the bad. They're not rocket scientists with ESP. These are about as smart as a dog, a Dalmatian, and I only say that because those beautiful canines are supposed to be dumber than dirt."

Nazy said, "We've been working on autonomous weapons for some time. I was in a brief where S&T thought the deployment of AI in these autonomous weapons would be feasible within a few years."

Lynche pointed at his best friend and said, "You have one and it's operational. Mission tested. That's incredible. And they can be used at airports to protect airliners against Muslim kamikaze drones. Why didn't you tell me?"

Hunter shrugged and said, "We weren't talking."

38

November 8
Over the Atlantic

Lynche lowered his head and nodded. Nazy smiled.

"The guys in Texas are doing it on our own dime. We took apart the smallest drone we could buy and loaded it with sensors. Then they miniaturized everything. But we did something that was off the charts."

"Yeah, what's that?"

"We found out that there's 'good AI' and there's 'bad AI.' Feed an AI computer *Leave it to Beaver* or the *Nancy Drew* series and what comes out is a functional yet passive drone. Feed an AI computer with concentrated evil like Hitchcock's *Psycho* or *The Clockwork Orange* and you have a horrific, amazingly destructive and punishing machine. It immediately became uncontrollable and wouldn't do what we wanted. We had to run that evil drone through a shredder. *We couldn't trust it!*"

Lynche shook his head. "Sounds like what happened at a Chinese lab. They developed an 'evil' AI lethal drone and it killed everyone in the building. It didn't stop until it ran out of ammo. Don't repeat that. Need to know."

Hunter nodded in understanding.

"We have developed a new generation of *Weedbusters*-like lasers. And S&T updated the air and ground versions of the sniper Terminator system. A million dollar effort. Ten mile effective range. Essentially, we now have the ability to wipe out multiple threats in a short time, out to ten miles. Optics are the key. We upgraded the guns in both YO-3As. The new gun wasn't radically different from what you were using before. But the computer and the targeting system. You have CCIP. Constantly-Computing Impact Point."

Hunter harrumphed. "I know. I ranged and targeted ISIS vehicles at ten miles, straight-on, and disabled them. I'd never fired at targets outside five miles before. I was so busy that I wasn't surprised but impressed."

Lynche said, "The new software allows the Yo-Yo to be able to target moving vehicles, drones, people. Aircraft.… Mortars in flight. A couple of circuit boards, gyros, and transducers, and a software update and bam, now you can target moving vehicles out to ten miles with the same probability of kill. The things you can do with bullets with wings."

"Well, DOD will want that capability too. I'm not so sure they're ready for these killers." Hunter frowned a bit as he juggled the drone in one hand. "When you indicated that one solution was to kill our guys so they wouldn't be able to be used as propaganda material, maybe this thing is what you were looking for or thinking about. But the hostages had hoods on, so even these killer drones aren't the perfect solution. Something for your lab rats to think about."

He told Lynche to keep the potentially deadly plastic critter. "One last thing, you can knock these out with a Growler. Acts as a mini EMP."

Lynche nodded. "Thanks, Mav. You've done enough—more than most, more than anyone could ask."

Hunter asked, "You think it's time?"

"You have the fake beard for it. If you had jeans and a red tartan Pendleton shirt you'd look like a mountain man." Lynche grinned and yawned.

Nazy said, "I find it very *sezy*." She reached up and stroked Hunter's bare chin. She remembered the last night they were together, and it made her smile.

Lynche frowned at the made-up word. Hunter smiled; it was their special word, usually reserved to describe the indescribably sensuous Nazy Cunningham. She was so far past mere *sexy*.

Nazy shut down the tablet computer. Hunter stretched and yawned. Lynche returned to the present. "I'll protect you for as long as I possibly can. We may have a new president soon. The Democrats have been hounding him for his anti-terrorist actions, and they have pulled out all the stops to defeat him. Every week they threaten to impeach him. And the Democrats just want you found dead. Head on a pike and all that. I have no idea which way this election is going to go. And they're still in my chili every time I go to the Hill. Somehow what you did is my fault."

"Well, you did hire me!" Hunter grinned an alibi.

Lynche laughed for a moment.

"Ah,…the dhimmis….." said Hunter, using the disparaging word for Washington, D.C. Democrats. An indelicate thought materialized, hundreds of congresscritters running for their lives while being chased by thousands of tiny silent four-rotor machines armed with shaped charges.

Lynche continued as if he hadn't heard Hunter. "If he loses, then I'll be gone by inauguration day and you and Nazy will be at the mercy of a new DCI who will, most likely, not be as supportive as POTUS and I are of you two. You have no more tangos on the Matrix. You have nothing else to prove. All contract must come to an end someday. I think it's best to shut down *Wraith* before the inauguration. You, plural, are at risk. I'm thinking it's time for you to retire. Maybe both of you. Shut it all down. Leave town for good. I'm going to Florida."

Nazy asked in mock horror, "You mean we'd have to live *together?*"

Hunter looked at Nazy impishly and laughed, "You make it sound like a bad thing. Anyway, I'd love to be able to live with my wife, *fulltime.*" Nazy smiled at her husband. He said, "The president will win. The Democrats think they have him on the ropes, but he'll surprise them. Eastwood's article and special are going to be magical. And when we get back, we're heading to Bora Bora or someplace we can call home. We'll be ok." He squeezed Nazy's hand, careful of her nails.

Lynche read the papers daily and checked the polls. He knew the score: *President Hernandez will be crushed.* He frowned and said, "Think about it. I'm thinking it's time for some sleep. I'm finally off my adrenaline high. You know…you about gave me a heart attack." He looked down toward his feet. His change of demeanor was palpable and evident. He had said he was finished with Hunter and Nazy and it was time for sleep, but his body language screamed that he wasn't finished talking.

Hunter didn't move. He turned to Nazy and asked Lynche in the oblique, "What do you have Nazy doing?"

It was one of those questions that's never asked within the intelligence community, and one that never gets answered. Lynche was mortified. Hunter wasn't read on. "You can't tell me? Seriously?"

Nazy said, "We recovered some old Nazi and Soviet files. Scientific things. We have a team going over content, context, applicability. Reality."

Lynche could have stopped her, but he let Nazy talk. By the letter of the law, Duncan had no need to know. Nazy telling him was a security breech. Lynche would never think of punishing her, because Hunter could keep a secret. Besides, he had a big gun nestled under his arm.

Lynche added, "The Nazi's brought together some of the greatest mathematicians and induced them to create, develop, experiment."

Hunter said, "Mengele was one of the insane ones, especially on children."

Lynche wanted to control the conversation. Nazy sat back and let him. "Mengele was nothing but a pervert, a hack, a criminal. The math geniuses were another thing entirely. Some got into atomic bombs, aircraft, and atomic energy. They'd conceived things that we are just now able to develop."

Hunter said, "The Nazi scientists had designed weapons that were so advanced and unique that, at the time and maybe even now, there were no counterpart in the American or British laboratories. There were hundreds of designs for special weapons. But the first challenge was getting those projects funded. The secret sauce is in the engineering. The Nazi's didn't have anything like what today's engineers have on their laptop or in their machine shops." He interlaced his fingers, plopped them in his lap and said, "Greg, what's really bothering you?"

Lynche yawned wide and said, "So you also know the Nazis developed atomic weapons?"

Hunter said, "I understand, several. You had me 'read in' after we found the Nazi gold and the Russian artwork under the runway in Germany. I know terrorists turn to the dark web's crypto-bazaars, social media channels and e-commerce sites to buy more coveted military equipment than the usual rocket launchers and AK-47s in the traditional black market. I understand the digital black markets allow terrorist organizations from Algeria to Yemen access to an assortment of goods and services, like firearms, atomic weapons stolen when the Soviet Union collapsed, and bomb-making expertise from the comfort and anonymity of their home computers."

"Terrorists learned how to take down power grids, targeting anything from a neighborhood to the entire eastern seaboard from info extracted from the dark web. I wouldn't be surprised if the dark web is where an old Nazi nuclear weapon came up for sale. You didn't tell me what happened to them. Maybe I didn't have a need to know. But it might be a case where your memory card is going bad."

Lynche laughed inside. "You did not." He sighed and said, "I also didn't tell you that hundreds of gallons of radioactive waste have gone missing. While you were over Syria, I got some intel. FBI is on the job, and they may need some help."

Nazy and Hunter looked at the old man with unbelieving eyes. He nodded and said, "Well, we saw that monster Nazi jet in that cave. I said then that it could only exist for one purpose. Huge bomb bay doors meant they either had or were developing an atomic bomb."

Hunter made reference to an underground aircraft manufacturing factory he had discovered as a kid in Germany. The Nazis had turned it into a makeshift storage bunker for the treasures of the Russian Empire.

Lynche continued, "It was a Heinkel that had a range of 7,000 miles. They exploded a test bomb inside Poland. Killed 400,000 Jews. Slave labor. Two more were reportedly built, but if so, they have never been found."

Weren't we talking about radioactive waste? Hunter interrupted. "They probably don't exist, maybe they're buried in the desert next to all those MiG-25s Saddam Hussein buried before the Marines stormed Baghdad. Have you tried to buy them off the dark web? I know you have guys who do those kinds of things....play in the background of the dark web. I wouldn't be surprised if the IC isn't running the dark web." Hunter smirked at him.

Lynche frowned at Hunter, then nodded.

Hunter added, "Okay. You know for an effort that size, they needed tens of thousands of centrifuges. They needed to have something on the scale of Y-12 to enrich uranium."

Lynche shook his head. He recalled the Y-12 facility was the World War II code name for National Security Complex in Oak Ridge, Tennessee. It was part of the Manhattan Project and was used to separate isotopes for enriching uranium for the first atomic bombs. In the years after World War II, Y-12 operated as the manufacturing facility for America's nuclear weapons components. He replied, "No. They found another way to enrich uranium 235. Reportedly, they used a photovoltaic method, which I might add, we still don't know how to do." He looked at Nazy for confirmation.

She said, "U.S. troops captured the scientist who was the brainchild behind their secret photovoltaic method. He was one of several scientists who wanted to talk and were being held until American physicists could interview them."

Hunter surmised mischief. "And something happened to him."

Lynche nodded. He was always impressed with Hunter's ability to see what wasn't obvious. "He was in a holding cell and was found dead. The official report indicated he had fallen. But it was obvious he died due to blunt force trauma."

"Baseball bat or nine-iron?" Hunter was ignored.

Nazy said, "Some of the latest Soviet Union archives suggest an assassination team from Moscow was dispatched to kill him. That's a fascinating archive."

"They killed him. Obviously." Lynche was emphatic. "The KGB was famous for their *wet work*. Infamous."

Hunter's head swung from Lynch to Nazy and back to Lynche.

Lynche asked Nazy, "And you are still going over the KGB archives?"

She nodded. "And Nazi archives. And the diaries."

Hunter jerked when Nazy said, "Diaries." He allowed that word to bounce around in the big jet, then he said, "You need to focus on the archives of the Islamic Underground. They're insidiously bad. I'm convinced 3M was their titular head."

Lynche agreed. "Hitler's plans for their atomic weapons was to load one on a U-boat, sneak into the Hudson River, and detonate it in Manhattan. He wanted to destroy the Brooklyn Bridge, the George Washington Bridge, and Manhattan. Apparently it was lost at sea. Hitler couldn't get another bomb built."

"So he evacuated?"

Nazy said, "He evacuated. You flew over his compound in Peru earlier this year. Last year. He died an old man."

Hunter turned to Lynche. "I thought you were joking."

"I don't joke about Hitler and the technologies the Nazis developed or envisioned and spirited out of Germany."

Hunter was incredulous. "Do you really think someone has an old Nazi A-bomb? In America?"

"We deal with the intelligence we have or what our allies may have on a particular subject."

"Like what?" Hunter turned to Nazy then back to Lynche. No one was going to answer. "Ok. Well, there's no way that old thing could go off. I know a little—damn little—and that thing has to be too old to do anything but go *pfffft* when the main charge goes off. Like a chihuahua with gas. Isn't the half-life of enriched uranium about 57 years? That's like 72 years ago. That thing, if it exists, is now nothing more than a paperweight. But I shouldn't talk—not my area. You should be able to get an expert to give you a brief."

Lynche nodded and said, "There's been some chatter. The Heinkel's target was New York City. So was the U-boat's. Al-Qaeda's main target was also New York City. World Trade Center. If Hitler's a-bomb is rusting away at the bottom of the Atlantic, that's not all bad. But with all this missing radioactive material, someone may want to try and explode it externally, and spread radiological hell over the city. The chatter suggests New York City and Washington. Islamic Underground chatter. They're excited. We're studying it. I had been expecting something before the election."

Hunter said, "More disruptive technologies. Hard to vote when your city has been bombed with radioactive waste. Whose side are these guys on? And I suppose the FBI is all over it. Why am I not impressed?"

Lynche harrumphed.

Hunter asked, "So what do you want me to do? We have the storage facility at the BWI airport, but that's just for us to be able to move the *Wraith's* container expeditiously. We can't fly a normal flight to New York. I don't have a hangar or anything around New York City. Elmira isn't that far away though, to conduct some operations in New York. If the chatter focused on Washington, we could use the strip at Camp Perry or the Marine base in Quantico. The Marines have a hangar that can accommodate the Yo-Yos."

"Virginia?" asked Nazy.

Hunter said, "Yes. Greg. What's the rest of this crap about missing radioactive materials?"

Lynche said, "Over the past several months we've had several radiological waste shipments go missing. Noteworthy amounts."

"That's the FBI and the Energy Department's problem."

Lynche shook his head. "I'm afraid if it's not the Islamic Underground, then it's al-Qaeda."

Hunter rocked his head from side to side and emphasized, "You mean, *again?*" Duncan referenced a secret volume of the 9/11 Commission Report that found over fifty men and women, associates of the Islamic Underground, had infiltrated contracted airport security companies across ten airports across the United States. When the White House shut down the airspace over America, the Islamic Underground members who had worked for the airport security companies left their jobs never to be seen again. The government created the Department of Homeland Security, federalized the passenger screening process to ensure the Islamic Underground, al-Qaeda, or any other Islamic extremist group and their supporters could never again infiltrate airport security and let suicide pilots and their weapons pass through the airport security checkpoints.

Lynche nodded. "You and I found some missing radiological material before it could be smuggled into the U.S. This could be the same thing, just on a larger scale."

"We did. The S&T had developed the sensors that made all that possible. I just flew the airplane while you picked up the radiological emissions."

"And lots of it. I remember. The problem is, this is domestic work in an urban environment. We could hide a lot of problems in the Arizona desert. We could hide the airplane—it's dark in the desert. In DC or New York, you'd be seen. What little cover you have left will be gone the moment you takeoff or land at an airport."

Hunter said, "The good news is the *black* coating we have on her can't be detected from the ground. We could repaint her—maybe even use that computer-generated wrap stuff—to look like the NASA bird. Say it's on the airshow circuit. But I have to say that I'm very reluctant to use that stuff. I've tried it before and two minutes into flight it starts to peel off. Buses and trucks are ok. Not good for race cars or aviation applications. But I'm willing to try."

Lynche smiled as if he were holding a winning lottery ticket. "How long will that take?"

"I don't know—couple of days. Maybe if I called Bill McGee, he could work some magic. But in all reality, it's still days away."

"Let's see what he can do."

"So something is up? Kelly can fly those missions."

Lynche turned to the sleeping CIA pilot, yawned, nodded and shot Hunter and Nazy a half-hearted smile. "Maybe that will work if she's cleared. It isn't kinetic. I think there are multiple targets just like on September 11th."

"She'll be ok."

"We'll talk more when we get back."

"In that case, good sir, I think I'm going to take my bride to the bridge and show her how the big dogs fly this jet. You did say they have a satphone up front?"

Lynche nodded.

"I'll see what's in the art of the possible with Bullfrog. Don't expect miracles."

"You performed several in Syria; this should be easy for you."

Hunter smiled, turned to his wife and held out his hand.

Nazy nodded, put her brush away, stood, and smiled. She shook her hair as it cascaded down her back. "Maybe they'll let me sit in the front seat." Lynche thought, *How could anyone say no to that face? To those eyes?*

She hugged her boss and patted his cheek affectionately. Nazy checked on Kelly sleeping and took Hunter's hand as they walked to the cockpit of the Globemaster. Lynche slowly brought up the rear like a dirty old man at the mall following the prettiest woman with the shortest skirt.

39

November 8
Over the Atlantic

The C-17 took the great circle route over Israel and Europe, passing just south of the southern white tip of oxymoronically named Greenland. Crew and passengers moved to the starboard side of the jet to view a uniform sheet of white ice and snow jutting to the south in a "V," like a paper snow cone cup. Blue sky above, blue ocean below, white acute triangle in the middle, stretching to the horizon, an inverse vanishing point. No icebergs anywhere.

The U.S. Air Force Globemaster aircrew were blissfully unaware of the mission into Syria, but the somber mood of the Agency personnel as they emplaned had warned them to go about their business of aviating, navigating, and communicating. The headwinds picked up significantly as the coastline of Nova Scotia came into view.

Hunter, Lynche and Nazy took in the sights from the cockpit. When Hunter decided to leave the crew alone to do their business, Lynche and Nazy followed. Hunter nibbled on the remains of cold pizza, looked at Lynche, and asked, "Are we going to have a new president?" Nazy frowned, curious about where Duncan's mind had wandered.

Lynche said, "I don't think it looks good for President Hernandez. The media and the Democrats are killing him on every issue. He's down in the polls — double digits; that's not where you want to be on Election Day. She'll be the next president."

Hunter said, "I think 'dumbass' has morphed into a species. Do you think an op like this…ah, would it make a difference? Help him?"

Lynche had been in Washington for years. He knew the pulse of the city, Virginia, and Maryland. All run by Democrats. He said, "Too timely, too cute, too much of everything. They'd find a way to drag him through the mud for that too. They'd blame him for the SEALs getting captured and for the way they were freed, if Al-Jazeera has good video."

Hunter smiled and asked, "What if it was leaked?"

Greg Lynche got very serious. As he thought about it, he shook his head. "I don't think so. No. Who do you have in mind?"

"Eastwood."

The name raised Lynche's eyebrows a foot and contorted his body and face. It was body language for *Absolutely no way!* Once he stopped twitching, like a whitetail buck in the last moments of its life after being hit by a truck, he said, "I don't think it'll make a difference. Too little, too late. And, I think if Al-Jazeera has video. they'd get it to American or British networks just to muddy the waters."

Nazy asked, "Why is that?"

Lynche said, "The media and the Democrats are screaming at the top of their lungs trying to convince Americans that Hernandez has been guilty of a conspiracy and complicit on everything from crusading against Muslims to colluding with the Russians. A tape of children being executed would cause an international and domestic, though *faux*, outrage."

"*Those Russians....*" Hunter added, "The left completely ignores Tussy's obvious crimes conducting espionage."

Lynche said, "What really infuriates them is that the president's been aggressive, undoing the outlaw policies of Mazibuike."

Hunter said, "That's bullshit and you know it. Say something."

"You know, I can't. What could I say that would make a difference? That the former president injected some 30,000 Muslims and radical liberal lawyers into the government? That the heart and soul of the FBI is totally compromised; that they're in the tank for her? The FBI exonerated her of espionage. At this level, we're supposed to be politically impartial."

Hunter exclaimed, "That's BS, too. The FBI has not been politically impartial since their inception. And when she wins she'll undermine our democracy, and her crimes will be covered over like fresh cat shit. Just like the media and the attorney general covered up Mazibuike's history."

Lynche said, "FBI deputies have their fingerprints all over it. They're going to need a shipload of lawyers if President Hernandez is elected. But if she's elected, I agree, everything will be ignored, covered up—like it never even happened. I'm powerless to do anything. And no good can come of anything I say. The DNC owns the media."

Nazy asked quietly, as if she couldn't believe she was asking the question, "*Are these Mazibuike's guys?*"

The DCI nodded. "Some, most, all. Don't know. Americans don't care that she's corrupt. It's over. He's behind double digits, nationwide. You cannot make up that much ground."

Hunter asked, "How did they do it?"

Lynche suggested, "When Hernandez was sworn in, the Democrats screamed bloody murder—I'm up on the Hill every month answering the same question—who released President Mazibuike's file? The DNC raised billions of dollars from the release of his file. You can buy a lot of media influence with that kind of money. But they were also at work finding ways to attack him, force him to resign for cause or for something improper. Remember he has survived dozens of impeachment attempts. They'll never give up."

Hunter held Nazy's hand. They nodded in unison.

Lynche said, "I understand the DNC's opposition research department is their go-to guys who make things happen. However, Hernandez was so squeaky clean, their *oppo* research couldn't use their normal bag of tricks. Their challenge was to remove him as soon as possible which meant moving the plan to opposition operations. I stopped every attempt by S&T to manufacture a file—a list of phony or presumed peccadillos, prostitutes, and perverted friends; the more the merrier. Destroy him. We can create a photograph of Mother Theresa giving the Pope a nude massage on the altar in the middle of the Sistine Chapel, and experts would swear it was real because the quality of the photo would be so good. Manipulate one pixel at a time then run it through a photographic processor. The Russians have the same capability."

Hunter said, "Seriously?"

There is so much you do not know. Lynche nodded, "Photographic evidence in an election… something like that is hard to overcome. Remember, the Russians removed Beria from official photos like he was never there. They're experts. They can create several false scenarios, false histories, encounters with prostitutes and homosexuals, the typical blackmail protocols, just like we can. We do it to turn a source overseas. They're doing it to Hernandez to kill him politically in the eyes of voters."

"That's BS, Greg. Who initiated it? Better yet, who paid for it?"

Lynche said, "Do you mean, do I know who paid for it?"

"Yeah."

"To do something like that, you have multiple sources. I'd look at the DNC's opposition research department. They have contacts in Moscow who can create the histories. Something like our S&T. That's how it works."

Nazy said, "I understand they have a whole office dedicated to opposition research. They might have up to a hundred people in that office." Nazy turned and meekly asked her boss, "Didn't they have one of their staff members murdered recently…in D.C.? Donny? Manny? *Tommy!* Tommy Larrabee was his name."

Hunter barked, *"What?"*

Lynche nodded to Nazy, "You're correct...."

Hunter sighed then said, "Knowing all this, how could you ever vote for that...anyone in that *party*?"

Lynche took his time answering. It made Hunter squirm, which was the intent. Finally he said, "I won't be this time. President Hernandez is an honest and humble man; he was thrown into the firestorm *you created*. On one hand, you've made his life miserable. On the other, he can't thank you enough for giving him the opportunity to reverse the radical policies of 3M—now you have me calling Mazibuike, '3M.' They'll kill me if I do that in front of Congress."

Hunter smiled and impishly said, "You are so welcome!"

Lynche admonished Duncan with a finger and a menacing wave. "I've seen that look before. No leaking for you, either!"

"I'm not the FBI. I was only going to say she was corrupt to the marrow of her bones."

"I don't know what you are talking about. We never had this talk." Lynche smirked. Hunter grinned. Nazy terminated the discussion with a smile and changed the subject. She wanted to go back to the cockpit.

The jet stream was strong coming over North America. The remaining ride was unusually bumpy until touchdown.

At the rear of the aircraft, Hunter, Nazy, and Kelly had traded their flight suits for more appropriate civilian attire—polo shirts, jeans, running shoes and dark sunglasses. Kelly had brushed out her hair. Her sad face under long bangs and straight hair made her appear as if she was in mourning. Hunter had stuffed his flight suit into his helmet bag and changed into soft cargo pants and his cowboy hat. As they waited for the aircraft to come to a stop, Nazy and Hunter fired-up their BlackBerrys. Immediately, they erupted in a series of vibrations and ringtones. With heads down, they scrolled through missed emails and text messages. Nazy was the first to lift her head and nudge Hunter. She showed him one particular email.

With no fanfare or marching bands or even a Follow Me truck, the Globemaster taxied into position and shut down. The discussion in the rear of the cargo jet was animated. Lynche wanted Kelly to be admitted to Walter Reed Medical Center for observation or even taken to the world class John Hopkins School of Medicine in Baltimore. Hunter looked up from Nazy's BlackBerry and reminded his boss that having Kelly admitted would kill any chance of a career with the intelligence community. If she had a documented psychiatric episode, it would be sufficient grounds for loss of clearance. When you lose your clearance at the CIA for psychiatric reasons, you are out of a job. Terminated.

Lynche acknowledged Hunter's logic. He wanted what was best for one of his best young intelligence officers. Nazy removed an Apple iPad from her bag and fired it up. As Duncan applied finishing touches to his fake beard, nose, and cheeks, he encouraged Lynche to allow Kelly to go home with Nazy. Before deplaning the aircraft, Lynche relented. Nazy remained seated, head-down staring at her iPad. Lynche collected Kelly's and Hunter's packets of passports and Krugerrands.

The plan was for Hunter to leave Nazy and Kelly on the ramp with Lynche. He'd take the Gulfstream and return to Wyoming. Although he didn't feel safe in Washington, it wasn't right to abandon his wife and daughter when they needed him the most. There would be much consoling and caregiving for the next few days at Nazy's house, which was a fortress. While Hunter had made it so, the house was still an assassin's glory hole. If someone from the Islamic Underground ever saw Hunter entering or leaving the home on the Potomac, it would be attacked. It was best that he never got near it. It was always safer for Nazy and Hunter if he just got a room at a secure hotel.

As they'd done countless times on the Navy side of the air base, the *Wraith's* mechanics, Bob and Bob, supervised the offloading the YO-3A's shipping container and helped guide it onto a waiting tractor-trailer combination rig. Once the shipping container was bolted to the trailer, the old guys and the truck driver left the base and headed for the Baltimore-Washington International Airport. They'd lease an aircraft from the BWI executive terminal and overnight in Memphis so they could have the best Mexican food in Tennessee at *Los Reyes*. Three locations. No waiting. The old guys had their priorities.

Lynche had been on his cellphone with his deputy director for an update from the Operations Center. He was to drop the duo off at Nazy's house then swing by the White House for a private debrief with the president. But Nazy was transfixed in her seat. She called for Greg Lynche. "Look at this." Kelly hadn't been invited, but like a good intelligence officer observed at a polite distance, over Nazy's shoulder.

Nazy had received several messages that the security system in her house had triggered a series of alerts. Nazy had queried her security system and accessed the sensor recorders and system activity history.

Kelly was intrigued; she had never seen anyone query the status of their home security system before. She didn't have anything that approached the level of home security she was witnessing.

Lynche asked Nazy, "All okay?"

Nazy said, "Actually…no. My system had an uncommanded reboot. It seems there was a power outage in Bethesda. MacArthur

Boulevard to my street was without power for a couple of hours yesterday. Last night." Annoyance and concern leaked from her lips. "But now everything seems fine...."

Hunter squinted at the implied problem and said, "But you have an UPS." Uninterrupted power supply. He reached for her iPad. He wanted to see the tapes. Hunter's beard got in the way of looking at the electronic device and he tamped it down. Nazy and Lynche leaned in. There was an ominous quality to all of the activity at the rear of the C-17. All the cargo had been taken off the jet. The Air Force aircrew didn't think it was their place to shoo the Agency people off their aircraft, and so they waited.

When Hunter had bought the house for Nazy, he had installed the finest security system available to the intelligence community. Low-light television cameras (LLTV). Thermal imagery. Seismic sensors. Everything within the legal bounds of security, which meant no lethal deterrent. If it was good enough for the CIA, it was almost good enough for his main girl.

Fifty seismic sensors were buried around the perimeter of the house. The system was so sensitive that cats, squirrels, and raccoons continually set off the sensors at the most inopportune moments, which drove Nazy to bark at Duncan, "*It's too sensitive!*" A few tweaks to the system and an artificial intelligence (AI) interface between the LLTV and thermal imagery would first determine if the intruder was feline, rodent, or canine. Humanoids in the sensors and cameras would trigger AI algorithms and set off lights and the alarms.

An uninterruptable power supply in the safe room inside the house and an external generator tucked in the garage ensured electrical power was always available in the house, powering the security system and creating a positive outflow of the air handling system in the bedroom's safe room. After a minute, Hunter found the imagery he was looking for. The two women, Lynche, and Hunter exchanged concerned glances.

The silence was deafening. Then Lynche shot out of his seat, left the aircraft, and rushed to his limousine. He commanded the driver, "Activate *Acrobat*. White House." The driver got on the radio and alerted the rest of the security detail following behind the Director's Suburban that there had been a change of plans, and the DCI had ordered a full decoy multiple-vehicle operation. Lynche also pocketed a handful of challenge coins from a box on the rear seat. He told the driver, "I'll be right back." Two armed agents escorted him back to the jet.

The small screen of the iPad was alive with the images of people moving through a wooded area, getting tangled in unseen chicken wire before rushing the corners of Nazy's house. Hunter couldn't believe what he was seeing. Nazy gripped Hunter's arm a little firmer as she watched. Lynche reentered the jet. Kelly was becoming anxious. Hunter explained to Lynche, his voice expressed a level of defeat. "Seismics and thermals set off the system. Nazy received voice auto dialers and text message warnings while we were in Jordan. The thermals are all over the place; the imagery goes in and out, in and out. I've never seen anything like this. One second the pictures have four ninjas trying to enter her house. Then nothing."

Lynche stared at the screen in disbelief. He knew what the obvious clandestine movements of the men in the vicinity of the home meant. *It's like looking into a window of my past.* He composed himself. Somehow, someone had found Nazy's house. And while she was away, someone made a run on gaining access. Lynche was stunned and unresponsive.

Hunter didn't have time to notice Lynche's problems. Sometimes he'd get "that way." Duncan pointed to one set of images and expanded the picture with sweeping movements of his fingers. After several deep breaths, Lynche leaned in and scrutinized the camera shot and advanced and reversed the wavering image as it faded in and out until he was satisfied what he was witnessing: one of the intruders had pulled a Growler counter-surveillance device from a pocket. Lynche had seen enough. He shoveled the old memories aside and wondered, *How did they find her house?*

The actions of an active assault team were unmistakable. The fluctuating thermal imagery was caused by clothing designed to not only reduce the thermal energy but also to block the electromagnetic signatures which are naturally emitted from the human body. Used with a scent blocker developed by professional hunters, the special clothing could defeat deer, elk, bears, and guard dogs which wouldn't be able to sense that a person had penetrated their space.

Lynche was scrambling, he said, "They have a Growler. Light shifting camouflage. Maybe a backpack jammer to kill the power to the local grid." An Agency surveillance team had attacked one of his most trusted officers. He shook his head with a look of disgust that would break glass. No time for history; special access program type of history. History covered by non-disclosure statements and buried in the Director's personal vault. He didn't answer Hunter's accusing eyes. Lynche turned toward his troops and said, "And they use the same technology you have under your flight suit. Nazy, you can't go back home. You and Duncan need to get out of town. Disappear. We'll talk tomorrow. Or not."

Hunter was livid and strained to contain his temper. "I know your guy Castaño did this. He's behind it. If I ever see him, he's a dead man."

Lynche bit his lower lip and stared into the face of rage. He had been there too, once upon a time. He oscillated a finger at Hunter and cautioned him to think about the consequences.

Hunter flipped to a new problem. He read Kelly's mind before she or Nazy or Lynche could articulate the question. *"What about Kelly?"*

Lynche crossed his arms and determined that the threat was directed at Nazy, not Kelly, but he couldn't be sure. He could have the Security Chief determine if there had been an attack on her house. But that would take some time and probably involve the FBI. The CIA's Director of Security had ways and the means to determine if an officer's abode had been penetrated and bugged. "She can come with me. We'll go back to the office. Worst case, I'll take her home, and she and Connie can play tennis or play with the cats. She's still my aide. No one would think twice...." Hunter suggested Kelly go with him.

Hunter jumped as his BlackBerry went off. He nodded at Lynche's comments and saw that Bob Jones was on the other end of his cell phone. Neither Bob had ever called unless there was an emergency. While Lynche, Hunter, Nazy, and Kelly remained on the jet, the Bobs and the Air Force aircrew had quickly offloaded the CIA's spyplane in its container and had departed the Air Force Base. Hunter opened the encrypted connection and listened without interrupting. Bob Jones said, "We're being followed."

Hunter pushed a button to activate the speakerphone. "Bob, you're on speaker. Say again for Greg."

Bob Jones repeated, "We're been followed. We'd just left the base when Bob spotted the tail. Could be an unmarked G-ride." Undercover government Crown Victoria.

Lynche spoke first. "Bobby, take the circuitous route—50 to 97; don't go up 295. I'll have Homeland Security interdict. I'm going to give them your number. Let me know, let us know when the Calvary comes, and your girl's safe in bed." Since there were no women traveling with them, Bob Jones knew the DCI was talking about "his girl," the *Wraith*.

Hunter mumbled something about, "Watching your six," an aviation term to "be careful and always check behind you." He told Bob he'd call him soon. He was leaving town.

Bob Jones promised he'd relay any news from the Baltimore-Washington airport to Lynche then Hunter via satellite telephone.

The DCI looked up at Hunter and his family. The timing of the incursion into Nazy's house was noteworthy. Having the *Wraith* clumsily tailed wasn't just curious, was it another piece of a larger puzzle? The two men shared their thoughts without speaking. *Who knew we had an operation going on?* Lynche didn't like the answer banging around his skull. Hunter pulled a vertex pen from his shirt pocket and wrote three letters in the palm of his hand. He showed his work to Lynche, who momentarily closed his eyes and turned his head, refusing to believe the blasphemy.

Lynche said, "As Joseph Heller once wrote, 'Just because you're paranoid, doesn't mean they aren't after you.'" When Lynche looked at Hunter, Duncan got the answer he knew to be true, but without the DCI's validation, it was just an unfounded opinion.

Hunter said, "It's not paranoia if they're really out to get you. That's what we have here. The real thing. Very dangerous."

Nazy pulled Hunter's hand to her face and read: NCS. The National Clandestine Service. *No! Please, God, No!*

Lynche said to Hunter, pointing at the Gulfstream, "File your flight plan and get out of here. I wouldn't go to your home plate. You have an alternate where that thing can disappear?" Lynche nodded in the direction of the G-550. The swept wings, oversized engines, and paucity of external markings made it the perfect transcontinental getaway vehicle. The only problem was it left amazing fingerprints of its being; flight plans, radio position reports, landings reported to the FAA, fuel purchases. You can run away in a jet but you can't hide its carbon footprint.

Hunter nodded. He was already several steps ahead of the verbal Lynche. Duncan asked Kelly to file a flight plan to Corpus Christi, Texas. He'd preflight the jet. Kelly nodded and raced into the Navy's Base Operations building to file and receive a weather brief. Nazy powered down her iPad. Hunter gripped Lynche and expressed his concerns for his wife and daughter's safety.

Lynche assured Hunter he only had his, Kelly's, and Nazy's best interests at heart. Hunter turned to the business jet to make it ready for flight.

Once Hunter unlocked the Gulfstream's door and lowered the airstairs, he scrutinized every inch of the sleek aircraft, ensuring that the tires were properly inflated and there were no leaks, or cracks, or missing pieces. But most importantly, he ensured that no one had wedged an explosive device into a dark corner of a wheel well or in between control surfaces and the wing. He quickly returned to the C-17 to help Lynche and Nazy gather all of their belongings. The three stepped from the rear of the Globemaster and walked across the parking ramp to the Gulfstream. Hunter moved the bags from the tarmac to the jet. Lynche noticed Hunter's limp was more pronounced. Hunter could barely walk but wouldn't say anything about the pain.

The DCI glanced over to his waiting limousine then to Hunter and Nazy, now wrapped in Hunter's flight jacket. Kelly reappeared from the base operations building and raced to the G-550. Lynche bid Hunter and Nazy goodbye with hugs. Hunter said, "Hey, Boss. Don't forget to vote."

Lynche shook Kelly's hand and pulled her close, whispering something into her ear. He returned to the C-17 crew as Nazy, Kelly, and Hunter climbed into the G-550.

The CIA Director shook every U.S. Air Force aircrew member's hand, handing each of them a CIA Director's challenge coin. He told them they did great work and he was particularly appreciative of their efforts and professionalism. "This mission hasn't been completed, so don't repeat what you've seen or heard. National Security and all that. And try not to tell anyone where you got those coins, ok? One of these days they might become collector's items."

40

November 8
Andrews Air Force Base

Duncan Hunter closed the aircraft door, helped Nazy to a seat, and directed Kelly to sit in the copilot seat of the Gulfstream. Kelly was confused and questioned the rationale of being invited back to the flight deck of an airplane after her failures in Syria. Her sedative had worn off, she wasn't overly tired, and the cockpit beckoned. Pausing to consider her options, she didn't refuse her father's directions.

The normally calm and composed Nazy was nearly apoplectic. She couldn't comprehend why her husband would do such a thing as direct his daughter back into a cockpit. After the mission over Syria, Nazy believed Kelly was in a very fragile state, but he was treating her as if the previous evening's event over Palmyra hadn't happened, like Kelly was just another pilot on another flight.

After closing the airstairs, Hunter doffed his hat and moved his bags and cooler to the middle of the aircraft. Nazy was lost and shadowed him like a puppy following its mother. She wanted answers. Even as Hunter winked at her, Nazy was confused by his actions. She was a detail-oriented person and needed details, and her husband was focused on another mission. Before Duncan stepped into the cockpit, he blew her a kiss as if to say *I love you and I'll be right with you just as soon as I get this jet airborne*. She calmed down, walked to the front of the cabin, and found a seat with a view. Every chair had a view outside, but not every seat had a view of the cockpit. Nazy wanted to monitor what happened between Duncan and Kelly. Reclining in the overstuffed white leather seat was like lounging in an air-filled cocoon.

Kelly had been in the cockpit at the controls of the large corporate jet once before. She had sat in the seat opposite her father, but at that time, there had been no intention of going flying. As she waited for her father to enter the cold cockpit, she scanned the instrument panel and center console and contemplated how difficult it must be to fly the aircraft from the left seat. The pilot's seat. Solo. The G-550 wasn't like the sleek little supersonic training jets she had strapped on when she was an Air Force instructor pilot. Those you could fly by yourself. As she studied the cockpit layout further she saw that the Gulfstream's cockpit was very well laid-out, comfortable, and ergonomically designed that a single pilot could fly the aircraft with minimal assistance from the copilot. The pilot had a Head's Up Display. She suspected that her father flew the $60 million jet by himself when he needed to travel in a hurry.

Hunter removed his bogus beard and entered the cockpit with a head of steam. Before stepping into the empty seat, he reached up to the overhead panel and tripped switches which immediately brought the APU to life. While the auxiliary power unit spooled up at the tail end of the jet, he rushed to buckle his lap and shoulder harness. Without the use of a pilot checklist he ran through the steps necessary to provide electrical power to the cockpit. The cockpit was awash in lights and alarms. He ran through the before engine start procedures in his head and then started the number one engine. Once the Rolls-Royce turbofan approached idle, Hunter asked Kelly to call for their clearance and departure. By the time the second engine came up to idle and operating parameters, ground control had provided taxi instructions and the altimeter setting.

Kelly had strapped herself in, put a headset over her ears, boom microphone near her lips, and marveled at her father's command of the aircraft. She was more intimidated than awestruck. He asked if she wanted to do the takeoff. Adrenaline filled her veins. She looked at him long and hard, as if it were a trick played on her by a Charlie Brown character. She took the bait and nodded politely. *Of course.*

She positioned her seat, fore and aft and up and down, to ensure her feet were comfortable on the rudder pedals and her hands were resting firmly on the yoke. Hunter made all the radio calls, he taxied the aircraft to the runway, and as directed, he "held short." When ground control directed Hunter to "position and hold," he complied. When ground directed him to switch radio frequencies to the control tower, he complied. He transmitted, "Tower, November eight zulu yankee, with Romeo."

Nazy leaned forward in her seat to get a better view. She was mesmerized by the activity in the cockpit.

"November eight zulu yankee, cleared for takeoff. Runway one niner right. Remain this frequency."

Over the interphone system, Hunter said to Kelly, "You have the jet."

Kelly said, "I have the jet." Hunter then took his hands and feet from the controls. Now that they were cleared for takeoff, he talked her through it. She might not have known where everything was in the cockpit, but she knew what to do when given control of a high-performance jet aircraft. She ran up the throttles; Hunter pointed to the engine gauges and confirmed they were operating within parameters. She expertly used the rudder to track the aircraft down the centerline of the runway. Hunter called out airspeeds and told her when she should feel the nose was ready to lift off.

When she sensed the aircraft was ready to go flying, she gently applied pressure and pulled on the yoke. In seconds, pilot and copilot felt the landing gear struts fully extend with a thump. They were airborne.

Hunter raised the gear and the flaps at the appropriate speeds. Kelly trimmed the aircraft and flew the published departure and waited for radar vectors to clear the Washington airspace. Kelly turned when directed and climbed when cleared to another altitude. She was surprised that the Gulfstream was incredibly nimble and a dream to fly. Hunter continued to handle all the communications and assisted in navigating. Once Kelly leveled off at 35,000 and engaged the autopilot, Hunter changed radio frequencies again, patted his daughter on the shoulder, unbuckled shoulder and lap belts, and left the cockpit.

Nazy was surprised to see Duncan coming toward her. He sat in the chair directly across from her. He leaned forward and explained that when pilots have to eject out of high performance aircraft, the goal is to get them back into the cockpit as soon as possible, if they're physically ok. The operations officer or the commanding officer assures them that whatever they experienced, "was just an anomaly," that they're still a great and competent pilot, and that they're absolutely ok. "Yes, it's a confidence maneuver, but more than that, it's a physical demonstration that I trust her, that I believe in her and that I'm not going to hold her accountable for her little brain fart… brain *freeze*."

"In golf they call it a mulligan. In the air, before we get to that point, we call a 'knock it off.' She was so overwhelmed at observing what I was doing she couldn't call the 'knock it off,' and I was too busy. I think she's ok. It wasn't a seizure. She wasn't shaking like a paint mixer. I think she'll be ok and be able to put it behind her. She's talking to me, and she can still fly. The lesson here for you and Greg is absolutely no more kinetic missions for her. She's not wired for those things. I should have been more forceful and shouldn't have allowed her to be put in that position."

Nazy smiled at him like she had the first time she laid eyes on him. *He's so smart.* "Do you really think she's ok?"

"I do. It's like getting back on a bike after you fell off. I think she'll have some issues with me for what I did. Maybe. Probably. We'll talk about them. She's a good girl. She'll be ok."

Nazy pulled her hands into the sleeves of his flight jacket. She was cold. The cabin *was* cold. She nodded at Hunter's explanation and knew he was probably correct. She had underestimated him, underestimated just how aware and thoughtful he was of Kelly's experience, of her mental state and his acceptance that he was the one most responsible for putting her in that position. Nazy had to defer to Duncan's judgment that he was right to get her back into the cockpit. A significant distraction like flying a jet would force her to push the bad thoughts away and replace them with the challenges of high-speed, high-altitude piloting.

Hunter slipped out of his chair and knelt on the floor in front of her. He coaxed her legs apart which caused Nazy to look over his shoulder toward the cockpit with sudden embarrassment. He unzipped the flight jacket, sending cold air where there had been warmth. Her nipples were instantly erect. She placed her arms over his broad shoulders. He cozied up to her, crushing her breasts while sensually and slowly kissing her. As Hunter would do from time to time, he evacuated the air from her lungs and filled his. When he pried his lips off of hers he said, "I've been wanting to do that.... Kissing you is like kissing a bolt of lightning...."

"Uhhuh...." She nodded and gently bumped her forehead with his until their noses touched. Breathlessly, "That's probably the most absolute perfect kiss...the kiss to end all kisses...."

Duncan tried to say something but Nazy interrupted him with her lips. She arched her back, pulling him closer and kissing him harder. Nazy wanted him to take her right there; Hunter could see it in her eyes. Make him roar like a stag in rut. But he responded with a malevolent smile. One of them wanted to be bad that very instant, but one of them had to behave.

He said, "I probably need to get back up there. Want to sit up front?"

No! She was visibly disappointed at his lack of spontaneous amorous fervor but brightened quickly with the thought of again sitting in one of the pilot seats. She frowned, playfully pushed his nose with the tip of her finger, and then smiled. "I'd thought you'd never ask."

41

November 8
Washington D.C.

Greg Lynche departed the White House lost in thought and looking glum. He was like a cell phone user immersed in the moment until he found himself tumbling into an open elevator shaft. The debrief with the president, the vice president, and the Chairman of the Joint Chiefs was a fairly one-sided affair. When Lynche entered the Oval Office he was struck by how unusually quiet the room was. A smile from the CIA Director and the room became instantly alive. President Hernandez expressed his gratitude for the CIA's timely response to the crisis in Syria; the VP and the chairman wanted to know more about the unique capability the CIA employed to facilitate the rescue of the men from Special Operations Command and the CIA's Special Activities Division.

The men were polite and differential, and they wanted more information. They knew their place in the pecking order and waited for the president to announce, "A few months ago Greg and I agreed to retire *Maverick*; this was a one-time good-deal to save our guys from certain public murder. We didn't know if he'd be able to do anything. I understand he arrived in the nick of time?"

One nod from Lynche. "Yes, Mr. President. Scores of women and children were marching around the hotel as protection from aerial attack. Literally, the moment he found the location, our troops were marched out of the hotel and positioned under—I'll call it a sunshade for parked cars. You see them in car lots in Phoenix and Tucson. *Maverick* indicated he thought it was curious that there were vehicles parked in the vicinity of those sunshades but not under the sunshades. He knew there had to be a reason. ISIS is very aware of our strategic capabilities, and they wanted a place that was out of the view of our satellites and unmanned surveillance systems. *Maverick* flies low and slow and can look under those anti-satellite countermeasures. He found dozens of ISIS men and a camera on a tripod."

The Chairman of the Joint Chiefs expressed his surprise that the CIA had resurrected the old Army strategy of flying a quiet aircraft low and slow over the jungles of Vietnam where jungle canopies obstructed the cameras of fast moving reconnaissance aircraft. He had expected something more technologically advanced. "We've spent billions in alternative fuels, battery power, unmanned technologies, and you used an obsolete gas-guzzling aircraft?"

"The aircraft is unparalleled in its effectiveness." Lynche continued, "Remember, Osama bin Laden had a huge overhang which masked his windows for just that reason. *Maverick* knew what he was looking for and he was in the only aircraft that could have gotten him into that position." The VP and the chairman crossed their arms and their legs in anticipation of the details. "After our men were marched into position, children with pistols were marched behind each of the hostages."

President Hernandez and others were shocked and asked for clarification. "Children?"

Lynche continued with the diversion. "Yes, Sir. At that point they were combatants. Germany is just the latest intelligence agency to issue a warning that the children of Middle East jihadists pose serious security risks as a home-grown, new generation of Islamic radicals. They're brainwashing children to make them as deadly and ruthless as their Islamist fathers; they're a significant threat. One of the first steps in their training is to have them execute *Amerikis; yanquis*. Usually these are tourists or businessmen or clergy."

The Chairman of the Joint Chiefs said, "That would have made tremendous propaganda value for ISIS to have their junior warriors execute America's finest. Kind of like a Masai youngster killing a lion to prove his manhood."

"And it may have been transmitted live." Lynche pinched his lips and explained, "*Maverick* employed a weapon prototype to eliminate the threat posed by those children, and then he used a laser to blind those under the opposite sunshade. They had slung weapons and were surrounding the camera. A reasonable expectation is that the group of ISIS soldiers would have killed our men if their plan was interrupted. Al-Jazeera may have been programed to transmit the executions live."

"No 'may have' about it," said the vice president.

"In the spirit of full transparency, once *Maverick* disabled the ISIS men under the sunshade, he obliterated the videocamera. The camera could have captured the children being killed."

The vice president and the Chairman of the JCS looked at each other and shared an indelicate thought: *He used a laser to blind them? Things the CIA can get away with while DOD cannot.* The president asked, "Greg, when will we know if Al-Jazeera had captured that scene?"

"I would expect soon, Mr. President. I would expect it to be released today via RTN or the BBC to inflict the most political damage. My judgment is, if the Russians and the Brits haven't received something from them, then I believe *Maverick's* actions were *fortuitous*."

The JCS Chairman pulled out a BlackBerry from a pocket and texted a message. The VP hawked the television monitor to see if he would be staying or leaving the administration.

The men turned their heads to the television inside the Oval Office was tuned to Fox News. Broadcasters were going through the election results. It was still too close to call several states. Everyone in the room stole peeks at the TV at various times. No one had mentioned a videotape of children being killed in Syria.

The JCS Chairman looked for a text message that did not come. "The initial field report indicated all ISIS fighters and the kids '*under the sunshade*' had been killed. They didn't say how the threat had been neutralized. They didn't know. The captives were hooded and couldn't see what was happening around them. They never heard ISIS fire a shot from a Kalashnikov but heard the massive cracks of heavy, high-velocity rounds hitting close to their position. They wondered what was being used to neutralize the enemy to the point where they couldn't shoot. An A-10 can't fire singles; your airplane fired single shots according to the men on the ground. They heard screaming and moaning, and then after about forty or fifty rounds, all was quiet."

"Then Special Forces arrived. We were told, 'they didn't see or hear the telltale signs of any aircraft in the area. No sounds, no lights. Whatever was used, they were glad he's on our side.' I see how this aircraft could lay the groundwork for possible clandestine counter-terrorism missions in countries where Islamic militants are active. Countries where Special Operations Command have not previously tried to find, or kill, or capture them."

President Hernandez nodded. "We have done that. For the last, correct me if I'm wrong Greg, almost twenty years."

The chairman and the vice president were shocked into silence. The men shook their heads in disbelief. *Twenty years?* Once the vice president recovered his composure, he asked why a laser was used. Lynche looked to the president for permission to divulge aspects of the *Weedbusters* special access program. A quick nod and the Director of Central Intelligence provided the high points of the laser system, its primary mission, as well as how it could be employed for "special situations."

Lynche explained, "It's not a cutting tool, but more of a trade secret, a perfect combination of power, dwell, and a discrete wavelength that enables us to kill illicit drug crops, specifically opium poppies and the leaves of *Erythroxylon coca*. I've learned to say that properly because not all coca plants are the same, and the laser is tuned for the specific species. But more importantly, *Weedbusters* needs a special platform from which to operate. And the only platform that could be used was an old Army aircraft."

The Chairman was nearly indignant, "I still cannot believe it's not an unmanned system." *It must be!* He was sure the CIA Director was lying to them. DOD and the CIA had spent billions on developing unmanned aerial vehicles and related technologies. With the current state of technology in the United States, the claim that an obsolete airplane was employed was so absurd as to be unbelievable.

The president shook his head, took a look at the television, and chimed in. "When hunting the world's worst terrorists and their drug-making enterprises, we have found you have to bring out the old stuff. Isn't that right, Greg?" The DCI nodded, and President Hernandez continued. "Old planes. Old guys. Very small footprint, logistically." He raised a finger and continued, "One cargo jet. State of the art lasers and weapons. We know the best SEALs and Delta are old guys. Their average age is what, 36? Greg's guys probably average well over sixty. This isn't work for the young, despite what the authors of thrillers and the makers of action movies want us to believe. A very special old airplane; a very special old pilot. But not as old as us!" The men laughed as the president prepared to adjourn the meeting. The VP and the Joint Chiefs Chairman had received a little intel and wanted more.

The JCS Chairman's BlackBerry went off. He read the message and reported, "The Al-Jazeera camera was a videorecorder with a tape. Incapable of transmitting live video. What was left of it was recovered by the rescue force."

Lynche broke out into a massive smile. *The best news I've heard all day!* President Hernandez said to "chalk one up for the good guys! That's fantastic news."

The vice president was glued to the television like he was in a trance. He was witnessing history. He pointed to the monitor like a mime giving directions.

The networks were reluctant to forecast a winner of the election. Apparently, no one wanted to be first to confirm the election results. Surprisingly, President Hernandez was within a hair of having the requisite number of electoral votes with several states—several *red states*—still counting. One reporter voiced her concern that the Colonel Eastwood special was cited as the main reason for the high Republican turnout and the apparent rejection of the Democrat Party's candidate.

President Hernandez could see from the anxious faces on the network talking heads that he was about to hit the magic number in the Electoral College. *They thought it was impossible. I thought it was impossible. Our men were rescued and now this!*

Lynche was aware of the energy building in the Oval Office. He was near-exhaustion, jet-lagged, and was ready to leave. To the surprise of everyone in the room, the election wasn't going the way the Democrats or the pollsters believed it would. He asked the president for a private moment.

President Hernandez nodded to join him behind the Resolute Desk. Lynche asked a question and received the response he had hoped. "I'll see what I can do." *It* was something the new president could do.

Then the television erupted in a stunningly unexpected announcement. The vice president smiled broadly and said, "Congratulations, Mister President, we must get to election headquarters." Lynche returned to his place with the VP and the Chairman of the Joint Chiefs. President Hernandez turned to his VP and said, "When she calls to concede, then we'll roll."

The president turned to the CIA Director and said, "Greg, we have one more thing to discuss. As you know, waste management offices across the country have reported to the DOE that several trucks containing radioactive waste have gone missing over the past few weeks. The FBI recently updated that in addition to the missing containers, the drivers and their assistants are also missing. What you may not know is that the FBI believes the missing men are likely of Muslim origin and may be members of the Islamic Underground. Based on the chatter, the FBI believes these men have moved into our area and New York City. It's not really a time to celebrate. We could be in great danger."

Lynche looked at the president and asked, "*Maverick?*"

The president nodded. "If anyone can find these containers, these men, I think he can. Whatever we have to do, pull out all the stops. The FBI Director can give you the particulars. I don't know how much time we have."

Lynche said, "I've pre-briefed *Maverick* on the basics. He'll do it. Whatever is necessary. He'll do anything for you, however, I'm afraid he's halfway to Texas. I'll get him back."

"Fellow Texans." The president grinned at his DCI.

The telephone atop the Resolute Desk rang. President Hernandez moved to the desk and scooped up the receiver without trepidation. The vice president, chairman, and the DCI stood when the president stood. The three men remained standing and listened. President Hernandez accepted the Democratic Party opponent's words of concession with no apparent emotion. He was gracious and thoughtful.

After a quiet minute, he returned the receiver to its cradle. He stepped in the middle of his closest advisers. "Okay, *now* I *have* to go. I hope my speechwriter knows what I'm going to say."

Lynche held out his hand. "Congratulations, Mr. President."

The president shook Lynche's hand and pulled him close. They walked to the door, connected by an extended handshake. With their backs to the VP and chairman, the president whispered in the voice of a close confident, "Tell *Maverick* not to pack his bags. Not yet. We still need him. And his airplane." The president gripped Lynche's hand more firmly, as if he were falling and only the hand of the CIA Director could save him.

The CIA Director sighed heavily and nodded. *I sent him cross country to escape the NCS. Probably wasn't one of my finer decisions.*

The president slapped Lynche on the back with a smile, and departed the room with the vice president, the JCS Chairman, and Lynche in tow.

The Oval Office was quiet once more.

42

November 8
Washington, D.C.

CIA Operations, in concert with the Department of Homeland Security, validated that there wasn't a hint of surveillance on the Director's motorcade. Leaving the White House was facilitated by the Secret Service who allowed the CIA Director's vehicles to depart before the president's motorcade. By the time Lynche slid into the rear seat, he was near exhaustion. It had been a stressful, turbulent forty-plus hours for the septuagenarian, and the jetlag made his fatigue even worse. He needed sleep and would have nodded off, but his mind was still at work. Without Hunter to poke at or the breathtaking Nazy Cunningham to surreptitiously look at, the drive from the White House to McLean was made in silence.

There was something he had overlooked, and knew it was important. The election outcome was the furthest thing from his mind — as if it was someone else's dream, and he wasn't invited to share. Decoy drivers didn't detect any surveillance on their vehicles as they wound through downtown to the George Washington Parkway. Lynche's driver had anticipated the DCI's need for solitude and raised the screen between the front and rear seats of the big limousine. If the boss needed to sleep, he could.

With the afterglow of the presidential debrief in the rearview mirror, it was time to look at the sequence of events which had occurred while he was away personally overseeing the emergency reactivation of Hunter and the *Wraith*. Lynche ran through the sequence of events again when the *Wraith* mechanics had reported a tail on their transporter as they left Joint Base Andrews. He had called the Secretary of the Department of Homeland Security and requested a DHS counterterrorism team to interdict the trailing vehicle.

Within minutes the DHS Deputy Secretary had reported, "Director Lynche, the vehicle was stopped as requested. It was an undercover, dark-windowed, Crown Victoria registered to a U.S. government organization. Two uniformed members of the Secret Service were in the vehicle. The Secret Service Agents presented their identification cards and badges and informed the DHS agents that they weren't tailing anyone; they must have been on a coincidental parallel path with the other vehicle. They didn't know what vehicle had reported them. The Secret Service Agents had been relieved of their detail at Andrews Air Base and were heading for the Baltimore-Washington International Airport to retrieve another agent. They wanted to take the quickest route, but it was blocked by an accident. They took a more circuitous route." Then the DHS Deputy Secretary informed Lynche that his men had no reason to detain the Secret Service Agents any further and let them go without incident. Lynche was initially embarrassed for his apparent overreaction and thanked the DHS Deputy Secretary for his indulgence. Now he wondered if it was all a coincidence or something else.

It was as clear as Swarovski crystal that while he was away from the CIA's flag pole, several someones from the Agency had sabotaged the local power grid and entered the house of one of his most trusted agents. *Why would they do that?* As for the tail of the *Wraith's* container, it was simple case of mistaken identity. *Wasn't it?* As far he knew, no one had yet taken a page from the old KGB and tried to backtrack the route of Hunter's Gulfstream. *I was in a hurry to get him here. I thought I'd taken sufficient precautions to protect his identity, with the sole exceptions of introducing Duncan to the SOCOM commander and the NCS Director. And those shouldn't have mattered. Two of the most trusted men in Washington.* Those concerns were vaporized with the pressing problem of who had found Nazy's home and broken in. And why.

It had been a secret known to only a few people outside the Agency; within the CIA only Lynche, the Director of Security and Nazy's security detail knew where Nazy spent her nights. A handful of people. The Agency's senior intelligence executives might have had her BlackBerry number for official business, but not her home address. When Nazy wasn't camping in her office, she often spent weekends at the Agency's conference center or in Annapolis with Lynche and his wife, either at his house or on their boat. A personal security detail half the size of the DCI's escorted her whenever she wasn't with Director Lynche. She could no longer drive her own car. *Maybe the security detail was compromised?* Lynche rolled his eyes at the possibilities. *They had to be and they told someone at the NCS.* Lynche called the Director of Security and asked her to meet him in his office.

When Nazy was at work, she was protected by three layers of security. If she needed anything more, she'd have to be removed from the Agency, transferred under cover of darkness to some obscure location, and put into a witness protection program. Or dispatched on Hunter's jet. Lynche knew Hunter had a few hundred locations where the two of them could disappear on jet-capable runways without control towers.

Handling multiple problems was normally not an issue for the CIA Director but fatigue was impacting his thinking. Lynche suddenly realized he needed Hunter to find the missing radioactive materials. He promised the president that Hunter would be a player. And if there were actually two locations the terrorists had planned to detonate a bomb and spread the radioactive waste, that meant Kelly Horne would be needed to fly the other YO-3A. He was sure Hunter's backup Yo-Yo was in Texas. It would be quicker to fly it to the east coast than to arrange a pickup. Picking up passengers could be done with a phone call. Picking up a shipping container required calling in a favor and time to organize an aircrew that can keep their mouths shut. Lynche thought it through: *Duncan wouldn't be able to protect his wife while he was engaged in finding the radioactive materials. Ergo, Nazy was needed back at work where we can protect her. She can camp out in her office until we find out what is going on with the NCS.*

The NCS! He was breathing hard and was too warm in the back of the limo. He ran his fingers through the remnants of his hair. *I think that leaves only two options, either call out the Marines or call Bill McGee. McGee was a SEAL and… they… have… a… network. But he'd have to drive.* He patted his leg unconsciously as he thought. *It'll take a few hours even to dispatch the Marines. Hmmmmm.*

Greg Lynche reminded himself that Nazy Cunningham had been the subject of several kidnapping and assassination attempts. A target had been placed on her back time and time again. She had interrogated and broken the most hardened Islamic terrorists in the world, al-Qaeda, the Taliban, as well as other Muslim extremists held at the inescapable detention facility at Guantanamo Bay, Cuba. Having a woman speak to the terrorist masterminds infuriated them as she scolded and ridiculed them. To them, a free woman's voice was a form of torture and blasphemy.

Lynche looked across the Potomac River, in the direction of Nazy's house. *The CIA takes care of its own. Nazy's house has been compromised! And there's no doubt in my former NCS mind that my old group is responsible. Strip away all other possibilities and I'm left with only one conclusion, somehow Steve Castaño or his friends learned the whereabouts of Nazy's place and had some reason to break inside. Duncan would just kill them. I have to say I'm coming over to Hunter's side of the issue. I'm so angry I could kill Castaño!*

He rubbed his face in an attempt to erase the pernicious thoughts flooding his jet-lagged mind. He didn't want to believe: *They carried a Growler. My guys. The National Clandestine Service Director, Castaño and his bunch. And I brought him to the airport to shake Hunter's hand and express his gratitude.* Lynche's heart was beating faster than it should. His face was flushed and he felt ashamed. *Just how stupid are you, Lynche!?*

The east coast staging location for the Wraith is also likely compromised. And Hunter's jet is likely on the international tail watchers websites. Bells went off in Lynche's head. He pulled his BlackBerry from a pocket and drafted a text message for Hunter: *They may be pulling in favors from the family to find your horse.* Hunter would get the meaning of the gently coded message—one or more members of the intelligence community may have unwittingly been tasked to find and track Hunter's jet, his ride, his horse.

Lynche felt physically ill. The penetration of the home-fortress wasn't the work of the Russians, the Chinese, al-Qaeda, or the Islamic Underground. No. What he saw from the few seconds of thermal imagery taken from a well-hidden sensor was the work of professionals. Americans. They didn't carry M4s or AKs; instead they carried CIA-issued holstered pistols and bags of equipment. And a Growler. The penetration team knew the target was away, and they wouldn't meet trouble while installing surveillance gear.

Hunter had warned the DCI multiple times over several years that he suspected someone very well-placed within the National Clandestine Service was somehow involved during specific *Wraith* operations. The NCS didn't have a need to know of the capabilities of the *Wraith* or its crew, and under DCI Lynche's leadership, the special access program had remained an Eyes Only program. It remained a secret even from the most trusted executives in the Agency. However, someone at NCS was driven to determine what was hidden in the *Wraith's* container and likely, who the enigmatic *Maverick* was. And they were likely resolved to determine if there were any link between *Maverick* and Nazy…and Kelly.

Lynche asked the driver to pull over at the next available cut-out. The request was relayed to the security details, leading and following. As the three armored vehicles pulled to a stop a few miles from CIA headquarters, Lynche lifted the receiver of the satellite telephone and dialed a special number.

43

November 8
Over Memphis

Duncan Hunter jumped when the sat-phone buzzed next to him. Few people knew the number; fewer people used it. Nazy surmised correctly who would be calling them at 35,000 feet. Hunter lifted the receiver and answered with his best Clark Gable, "O' mighty wizard, how may I help thee?"

The Director of Central Intelligence came right to the point, "I need your number one to return to home plate. And I also need you for some more work, *ASAP*. Number one has to go underground for the interim—the problem is I have some very special, some critical work I need her to do."

Hunter replied, "I can turn around and drop her off at...say the conference center? Your strip?" He referenced the runway at Camp Perry, home of the CIA's "Farm," but it was in the middle of NCS country and was likely a very bad idea. Any unusual aircraft movement would be relayed to the NCS leaders.

Lynche dismissed those ideas with a sigh and a yawn. "I don't think any of those are good; I've reason to believe the jet has been compromised. It needs to disappear, not double back. Not land anywhere on the coast."

Hunter nodded his understanding. "You think the *Tangos* were alerted." It was a statement, not a question.

"I do. I'm afraid they could be on the lookout for and will report your tail number if you dropped her off at any local airport here. You're headed to a place where you can land in a secure location. I prefer to maintain the advantage I have with her, ah, *on assignment*. Is that something Willy could help with?"

Hunter turned to Kelly and said, "Call Center and change our flight plan for..., um, Fredericksburg." He leaned across the center console and punched buttons on one of the pilot's multi-function displays.

Kelly wondered at the change of destination, but she complied. Nazy watched Duncan's face intently as if she knew they were talking about her.

Lynche sought validation that Kelly was sufficiently composed to be functional. He wasn't sure Duncan could fly either, but the irascible Hunter told him, "I can fly, I just don't walk real good." Lynche said, "I've this vision of her flying the jet while you and your best girl are making out in the back like a couple of teenagers." Then he asked, "She's ok, isn't she?"

Hunter smiled reaffirmation. He placed a hand on her shoulder. "She is. Back in the saddle. Who do you think is flying this beast? Where are we at, boss?"

He spoke in an easy code without having to name names. "I don't think number two is the target, but with you and number one in close proximity, she may also be at risk. I should have figured it out before, but I don't believe she's in any immediate danger as long as she's with you. For the moment, I need your number one to return. Do you think Willy can drive her to the conference center? At least get started. My next call is to ask the Marines for some help. But that will take several hours. Are you getting close to your place?"

"Another hour. Nasty headwinds. As for Willy, I can ask. He'll say yes, or if he can't, he'll have someone trustworthy drive her. Network work."

Network work. Lynche batted the words around in his head like a volleyball. "Good. I don't want to take any chances with her. For the time being, she needs to be off our grid and on another network. I need her back no later than…24 hours."

"That's about what it'll take to drive that distance. Minimum. Unless you get help."

Lynche said, "Let's do that for starters. Get some vehicles moving in the right direction."

"Okay. Roger and Wilco." Then Hunter said thoughtfully, "You have a plan. You figured it out."

Lynche responded, "Yeah. And more. Plans may change. One thing is certain, I don't think you can continue to wherever the hell you were planning on going."

"Copy all. The plan was to see Willy anyway and catch another ride. I have spares. We'll change airports when we get close." Hunter's eyes never left Kelly, who was looking at her father over her shoulder. Hunter and Lynche used "Willy" as code for Bill McGee, retired Navy SEAL extraordinaire.

In the cramped cockpit, Hunter *val salvaed* to equalize the pressure in his ears and then noticed competing perfumes; Nazy's cinnamon and Kelly's vanilla. *When did they have time to put on perfume?* He shook his head in exasperation. Muslim women, even former Muslim women, tended to wear their perfumes strong while Kelly opted for more subtlety, an intriguing scent. Nazy had always been coy about where she got her perfume, leading Hunter to believe when she wasn't driving terrorists insane at GITMO, she was some kind of mad scientist, aromatic brewmaster. Kelly wasn't coy about wearing *Loant Lovann* made from Bourbon, Tahitian, and Madagascar vanillas. With the mixture in the cockpit all he could think of was fresh cinnamon rolls and vanilla icing. He returned to the satellite phone and waited for Lynche's next ridiculously coded missives while he calculated where the closest Cinnabon store might be.

Lynche sounded less tired than he was. "There are lots of things I don't like banging around in my head. I know I'm missing something, and I've much to do. Why do you always hand me a shit sandwich when my hands are full?"

"It's what I do. I'd use gloves, boss."

"Listen, they'll want to debrief number two. I can probably hold them off for a couple of days. I need some time to poke around their stuff. I'm afraid when I pull the trigger they'll bolt for the door." He paused for a few seconds and then added, "Or something worse."

"Understand. Can you say you are just going to keep her for mentoring? If it comes to it, maybe you could say you've reassigned her. Your old job?"

"My old job?" For a moment Lynche was confused. He had held every minor and major position at the CIA during his 35 years.

Hunter nodded absentmindedly and said, "Afterburners." The A-B code between them was for Air Branch.

Lynche understood and said, "Wilco. I want you to know that if you are right with your three letters, this is very bad."

"I do. And you know I'm right. You have to clean house. I don't envy you. I think that could even be dangerous for you and yours. While I'm getting number one to a safe haven, you need to get your best girl somewhere safe. More of everything. More Marines." Hunter nodded to Lynche hundreds of miles away. Lynche unconsciously nodded back to his former flying partner. Sympatico and synchronicity. Always looking out for the other.

Hunter understood the scenario Lynche was trying to portray. He took issue with one of Lynche's assumptions, the issue of Kelly and NCS's desire to debrief her. "I don't think you've thought the whole thing through."

"Speak."

"If we just disappear with number one and two to places unknown, won't that send an unmistakable signal that their ninja activities were detected? You can say my number one went directly to Bali Bali on assignment, on vacation or something; that she never planned to go home. That might work for a few days. I know where *I can hide her*. I don't know where *you* can hide her."

"I've plenty of spaces."

"Roger. I'm also leaning to your thinking. Number two's place has also been compromised. She was also on that jet. He saw her; she even works for him when she isn't assigned to your office. It's not that they didn't have time. They had to go there too. Low hanging fruit. Numero uno's house was a tough nut to crack. I agree they're trying to find me, too. They don't know who they're dealing with. Yet."

Nazy listened intently. From her understanding of the one-sided conversation, Lynche was advocating splitting her and Hunter up for safety reasons. She didn't want to be separated from him. She was becoming concerned and anxious. Her face said it all.

Hunter's heart was quickly sinking. He was beginning to believe Nazy wasn't the primary target; the situation had pivoted like a weathervane in a gust of wind. *Was the penetration of Nazy's house just to prepare the battlefield to see if I would visit? Am I the real target? During the power outage, they had to have installed cameras. Microphones.*

The multi-million dollar house was well-beyond the means of a senior intelligence officer's salary. It was more of a house expected of someone with a Gulfstream in the garage. If the NCS made the connection between Nazy and Kelly going on the mission with *Maverick* and installed capabilities to document Hunter entering Nazy's house, then they could kidnap her or re-enter her house when she was there, and hold her hostage, and force Hunter to expose himself or give himself up.

Hunter's head hurt. He thought he had figured it out. Nazy would have to go into hiding far from him. Hunter reminded himself of the old saying, *The eagle who chases two rabbits catches none. Divide and conquer. Split up and rendezvous at a later time and place.*

Hunter relayed his thoughts and concerns. Resignation was in Lynche's voice. "I think that's a good catch. No one is going to like it. I want you to know I made several mistakes today. I need her here and I need you back here with a pair of Yo-Yos ready to go to work."

"You said Madam Curie's revenge might be on the loose. I take it's the latest crisis *du jour*." Hunter knew enough about the missing radioactive material that he felt confident Lynche would decipher his poor excuse for a code.

"*Tally ho!* We do need to do that. That reminds me, the tail chasers on your number one beast was stopped. Bad guys were questioned, but they were just a couple of *sierras* on their way to the airport."

Sierra's were SS and not Nazi Stormtroopers. Secret Service. Number one beast, in this case, obviously meant the YO-3A, the *Wraith* in her container. Hunter appreciated Lynche's use of another descriptor. Although he could have kept up with his real "girls" and his airplane "girls" if and when Lynche flipped and flopped back and forth, the new term alleviated that problem.

Hunter asked, "What were the *sierras* doing out there? I know you got validation." *Are you sure?* "I still say it's your guys. Somehow."

"I still don't know if it's my guys, and that makes it my problem. I'm working it." Lynche was scribbling notes between yawns like a madman who wanted to sleep but couldn't because he had work to do.

"Apologies, good sir. They'll not like it, and everyone will be in danger. Constantly check your six." Hunter ran his fingers through his hair, smiled at Nazy, and waved a finger at Kelly to do some "aviating." Check instruments or something.

"It looks like Madam Curie's revenge is going to be accelerated into a full-blown program if the fibbers have trouble hunting them down."

Hunter knew "fibbers" stood for FBI while "Christians in Africa" was the CIA. He looked at the two women in the cockpit and saw their confusion. The coded language confused them only for a moment. They realized Lynche was referencing both of the operational YO-3As. The *Wraiths.* Hunter calmly said, "Number two is with Willy. Fresh paint, an annual, and all that. That's where I'm heading to get my tail resprayed." No one called Bill McGee "Willy" except Duncan when he was talking to Lynche. It was a term of endearment Nazy and Kelly hadn't heard Duncan use before.

Nazy and Kelly looked at Hunter, unable to understand what was meant by getting "the tail resprayed." He made a mental note. Once he was off the phone he'd explain that his aircraft repair and manufacturing company in Fredericksburg had "production N-numbers" for new aircraft. The Agency had a couple of others on the FAA's database to be used when an Agency aircraft needed to "disappear." This was just such an occasion.

Lynche said, "That's good. Meet in twenty-four to recap? I gotta go. Unless you need me, I'll call you. Be safe. Out here."

Hunter said, "Good sir. We are outta here."

Hunter and Nazy traded places after he replaced the handset and the satellite phone connection was severed. Hunter killed the radio to ensure no cockpit conversations could be accidentally transmitted. The three CIA employees talked over Lynche's understanding of the problem, his challenges, and his plan.

Nazy learned information that Duncan hadn't previously disclosed for fear that she'd think he had lost his mind. She couldn't find any fault with his logic that the NCS *ninjas* could be using her to get her husband. Hunter had a history of believing certain intelligence officers from the National Clandestine Service had been acting "extracurricularly," doing things which weren't mission-related. He was convinced they were using the power and instruments of their very unique position in the intelligence community to enrich themselves and somehow Hunter had suspected or discovered their activities.

The more Hunter thought about the NCS' capabilities and possible treachery, he envisioned situations where they could easily be involved in political assassinations. They were the only group of spies trained sufficiently to penetrate the best defenses the CIA employed at their facilities. They were masters in the art of cover, concealment, disguise, and penetration. And now they were probably after him.

Hunter assured Kelly the DCI wouldn't let anything happen to her. Nazy was convinced Duncan would take care of her. He exuded confidence that he could be trusted totally. He had been her guardian angel and only lover for fifteen years, husband for five.

He switched the aircraft's radio back on and confirmed the Gulfstream was cleared "direct Fredericksburg." Kelly continued to fly the jet. Hunter sat back and watched his daughter's growing confidence handling the corporate aircraft. Nazy sighed, nudged Hunter and lamented, "Is this going to be another night without you?"

Hunter hung his head. He couldn't look at her. He said to the floor, "Or it could be much longer."

Kelly quipped, "Don't you two have something better to do, like find my dad's missing cufflinks in the cabin?" Nazy's green eyes went to Hunter's Levi shirt cuffs. *He doesn't have cufflinks on his shirt.*

Nazy blushed and covered her lips with her fingers. Hunter lifted and shook his head and said somewhat sarcastically, *"Children."*

Nazy and Hunter left the cockpit. They sat together on one of the bench seats and kissed for a long minute. Then he told her what Lynche wanted to do, that he needed her to do some special work. Nazy didn't like it, but concurred.

Minutes later, they were back in the cockpit much to Kelly's surprise. Hunter sat in the jump seat and was on the satellite telephone again. The women couldn't hear what he was saying so they stopped trying to listen. When he disconnected, Hunter told them he had talked to McGee. He kept to himself that McGee had something for him. "Something special. Right up your alley."

Hunter didn't even try to figure out what McGee could possibly have that would be "right up my alley." Hunter thought, *I stopped bowling years ago!*

There's only so much a passenger can see from a side window of a jet. But the view from the cockpit on a clear winter night can be stunning. You can actually see everything, from the lights of cities below to the stars and dust clouds of the Milky Way above. No lights or haze to obscure the view. No thunderstorms or clouds to interfere with the lights shining from the cities and towns and highways below.

Passing through 33,000 feet MSL and descending, nighttime Memphis sparkled east of the winding Mississippi River. Hunter pointed out the big FedEx jets departing the Memphis airport. Interstate 40 raced in a straight line to the lights of Little Rock on the nose. Nashville disappeared off the right wing, Jackson, Mississippi off the left. Soon, Texarkana came into view, then Austin. The bright lights of Dallas and Fort Worth dominated the horizon. Interstate 30 rolled out underneath the jet all the way to Big D. Hunter pointed out Waco, Fort Hood, New Braunfels, San Antonio further south. Kerrville and tiny Fredericksburg.

After the final legs of nighttime sightseeing were behind them, Nazy and Hunter exchanged places. Hunter radioed Air Traffic Control and cancelled his flight plan. He instructed Kelly to divert to the Kerrville airport. He talked Kelly through the approach to touchdown. She flew the jet like a typical rock star former Air Force jet pilot. Hunter beamed like a proud papa.

Hunter taxied the Gulfstream to one of the company's hangars. He expertly positioned the jet in front of open hangar doors. He chopped the throttles and ran to the cabin to open the airstairs. Hunter handed the women several bags, his cooler, and his hat before he limped down the aircraft's stairs.

Outside and adjacent to the hangar were Bill McGee and a pair of black Hummer H2s. Nazy gingerly stepped down the airstairs and raced to McGee's arms; he hugged her gently and playfully told her, "I swear you get better looking every time I see you. I wish this was under different circumstances. Ready for an adventure?" Once Nazy uncoupled herself from the big man's arms, she nodded. Kelly and McGee renewed their acquaintance and shook hands professionally. Kelly knew him as the owner of the Full Spectrum Training Center and manager of her father's businesses.

The three of them watched Hunter limp around the jet, inspecting the exterior like he had done countless times before. He wouldn't break the old habit just for the sake of saving a few minutes. Airplanes aren't like cars. There's no telling what you might find after you landed. Hunter had told McGee about the time when one of his squadron pilots was flying in the number two position in a section of F-4 Phantoms. When the two aircraft landed to refuel, one of the pilots discovered that the twelve feet of the airframe that covered the afterburner was missing, as was the afterburner and half of the stabilator. The aircraft was so big and heavy that the pilot hadn't felt a thing in the air. It was an important lesson why pilots look over their aircraft after every flight.

As Hunter hobbled around the Gulfstream inspecting the landing gear and control surfaces and their hinges, Kelly walked over to view a number of vehicles stored in the hangar. In one corner of the well-lit building she recognized her father's maroon motor coach and smiled at its size and color. She was also astounded by the number of rare and old sports cars parked along opposite walls of the hangar. She recognized her father's black Aston Martin Vantage and his yellow Corvette racing car on a flatbed trailer. Several cars were covered with grey car covers. She recognized the distinctive shapes of Corvette coupes and Jaguars. She pointed to the car cover that was closest to her. The sleek shape under the grey cover didn't resemble any sports car she was aware of. It was brutish even under a car cover.

Duncan was under a wing, checking the landing gear and brakes, and saw her ogling the unique shape and told her, "It's a black One-77. Aston Martin. Hypercar. I haven't even driven it yet. Maybe when this is all over, you and I can take it out for a 200 mph-spin on the banked track of the Texas Speedway."

Kelly nodded, smiled, and before she let her father continue with his work she asked, "What's it with all the sports cars?"

In a moment of mischievousness, Hunter said, "Because no *real* girl ever said, 'Take me for a ride in your Prius.'" Kelly laughed so hard that Nazy and McGee noticed. Hunter resumed his limp around the jet.

Bill McGee took Nazy's bag. She reflected on the special relationship she and McGee had. He had rescued her from some murderous Algerian men. For two years, she had cried whenever she saw him, unable to put into words her gratitude and respect. Now that event was a distant memory. She still repaid him with a hug and a kiss on the cheek whenever she saw him. She was comfortable in his big strong arms. He always gently hugged her in return, a demonstration of love, as if she were one of his daughters. A person whose life was saved treats their rescuer with love and appreciation.

Duncan ended his inspection of the jet and closed the airstairs. He placed his Stetson on his head and tossed McGee the keys. Hunter raced inside the hangar, started a bright yellow towing vehicle and drove the TUG to the nose of the aircraft. In ninety seconds, the Gulfstream was safely inside the hangar surrounded by vintage sports cars on either side of the wings. Another three minutes, the lights were out and the massive hangar doors were closed. All was quiet on the airport.

The men talked out of earshot of the women. McGee gave Hunter a box of cigars, which he politely accepted even though he didn't smoke. Nazy and Kelly were involved with saying their goodbyes.

After a few minutes, Hunter moved his bags, to include the G-550's flight bag filled with approach plates and maps, from the ramp to one of the Hummers. He told Kelly to put her things in the same vehicle. The box of cigars went into his Hummer, too.

Nazy watched the goings on, knowing that all the activity was for her, to get her someplace safe. She felt alone. She knew what was coming. Hunter was leaving her. Kelly was leaving her. And it was breaking her heart.

As Hunter finished loading his vehicle, McGee sidled up to Nazy and handed her a large red arrowhead-shaped piece of brass. It distracted her for a moment from the pain of being pulled away from her husband. She looked at the obverse of the big brassy piece. In the light from a distant airport tarmac lamp, the profile of an Indian chief looked back at her. In raised brass letters at the bottom were the words *The Tribe*. She fingered the three-inch black brass arrowhead like a talisman. She turned it over to see the Roman numerals VI overlaid by the eagle, trident, anchor and pistol of the U.S. Navy Special Warfare insignia, the "Trident," one of the most recognizable military badges of the U.S. Navy.

Hunter hobbled back to Nazy. She held the very heavy SEAL Team Six token with one hand and wrapped her arms around Duncan and kissed him for all she was worth.

McGee and Kelly watched for a few seconds and wondered when husband and wife would be reunited. They were a little uncomfortable with the public display of affection; they turned away and looked at each other. Kelly opened her arms and McGee gave the lithe, winsome, ginger goddess a hug too.

Seconds after Nazy and Hunter uncoupled, Nazy was gone. She and McGee raced off the airport in one of the Hummer H2s. Hunter hobbled to the other armored vehicle where Kelly nervously waited in the passenger seat. They took off on a southerly vector for the little town of Hondo.

The contents of McGee's cigar box wasn't far from Hunter's thoughts.

44

November 8
Fredericksburg, Texas

After five quiet minutes of driving, Hunter reached over and took Kelly's hand. Hunter said, grinning, "Your mother loved to ride and drive my Corvette. She would say pilots with sports cars are more fun and exciting than guys who drove VWs or Subarus."

Kelly was amused and smiled.

Hunter continued, "The way you wear your hair makes you look like your mother. She was an incredibly beautiful woman, and so are you." She squeezed his hand, meekly smiled, and thanked him for the compliment. While he had embarrassed her, it also cheered her up.

Hunter gave Kelly a rundown of the capabilities of the Hummer. She thought he sounded like an instructor. "One of our businesses is to find and buy, primarily, Hummers. We do other vehicles too, like Yukons and BMW X5Ms. We take them from their standard configuration and modify them to shield all of the occupants from the mayhem of bullets and bombs. We have about a thousand pounds of armor-piercing bullet protection surrounding us and state-of-the-art technologies to protect us from explosives. All the windows have been replaced with 40mm bullet-resistant multilayer polycarbonate glass."

"With the exception of the BWMs and Mercedes, our mechanics fit a very large supercharged Corvette motor under the hood. It's also armor protected. The engine is specially tuned to deliver maximum horsepower to allow us to escape trouble, on or off the road. On the four corners are 'run flat' tires which enable us to run at high speeds for long distances, even when punctured multiple times by bullets. The 700 horsepower motor with 700 foot-pounds of torque allows heavy-footed fathers to do four-wheel burnouts. As long as the beefed-up drive shafts don't break; I can nearly climb a telephone pole in an emergency." He grinned and continued to drive.

Kelly laughed; she didn't quite believe her father's bombast. He continued, "The fuel tank is reinforced with quarter-inch ballistic steel making it both bullet-resistant and blast-proof. Plus, this thing has many of our quieting technologies built in. With a flick of a switch I can make the sound of the exhaust diminish to that of a frog fart. Proprietary noise cancelling technologies. Night vision capable cockpit—I can drive at high speeds in pitch black darkness with NVGs. IR lamps are mounted above and below. It's an absolute brute; a tank and a rocket. We modify about six Hummers a month and sell every one we build. But the best part, this truck drives liberals nuts, and there's a foghorn that scares the living crap out of the Prius drivers with 'coexist' bumper stickers."

She didn't believe the part about the horn or scaring Prius drivers. And she told him so: *So you don't like Priuses!* Hunter hit the air horn and Kelly nearly bumped her head on the truck's roof. Now she knew even a horn could be used as an offensive weapon as well as not challenge her father. *Maybe someday he'll explain his antipathy towards Toyota's little hybrid.*

•　　•　　•　　•　　•

Bill McGee told Nazy they'd be going through Memphis first. She'd be safe in the armored Hummer on the way to Virginia and a CIA facility. From the console he handed her a lightweight Kimber model 1911. "I know you know how to use this." She nodded, smiled, and accepted the pistol, grip-first. She went through the routine safety procedure. She pressed the magazine release and removed the full magazine. Then she racked the slide and locked it in place. Nazy checked to ensure there wasn't a round in the chamber. Then she returned the magazine, released the slide, and chambered a round. She walked the cocked hammer home and set the safety. The .45 was locked, loaded, and ready to go. She casually slipped the weapon in a pocket.

"There's a sleeping bag in the back seat," McGee said.

Nazy said, "My jetlag isn't too bad. I just don't think I can sleep, Bill. Thank you. When I'm ready, I'll let you know." She held up the SEAL arrowhead token. "This is quite impressive."

"It's our equivalent of a challenge coin, but with a twist. Those particular arrowheads are loaded with a ton of technology. Try to find the USB port and the handcuff key. They're very well hidden."

After a couple of minutes in the dark of the Hummer's cabin she found both. He said, "That's pretty good. Most people wouldn't even look at the obvious."

"We have a guy in S&T who's a master of hiding a seam. In metal, in wood. Plastics—it doesn't matter. But he lets us know what to look for. So I guess I could be guilty of cheating." She smiled.

McGee said, "When I gave one to Duncan he said it reminded him of the very first satellites. The Soviets put up a basic tin can that beeped while we put up a satellite with a spy camera. If Americans were going to do something, it would be for a purpose." He then went over the features imbedded within the arrowhead. She listened intently; she hadn't seen or handled anything like it. "It has several chips embedded to include a couple of gigs of memory, and an incredibly bright flashlight—it'll blind anyone close; it doesn't discriminate. There's a powerful laser beam, strong enough to blind a driver or a pilot for a few days. And it also has a spike that turns this benign looking thing into a weapon. You found the handcuff key. Plus these things are matched."

"Matched?"

"Yeah, when you get two of them together, there's a chip that senses the proximity of the other, and then it'll illuminate the red glassy part of the arrowhead. Only SEALs who are part of our little underground railroad, our network, have these. If you show it to a SEAL, he'll try to match the arrowheads. If you're a legitimate SEAL, he'll take you wherever you need to go, do whatever you need done, and protect you with his life. So don't lose it."

Nazy smiled and held the SEAL Team VI arrowhead close, marveling at its beauty and construction. It was a real challenge coin, designed to be kept on one's person at all times, not just for beer challenges. She asked, "Bill, what have you been doing since the last time...."

"...we were last together?" McGee pulled a cheek back in a friendly grin. "That was the State Dinner at the White House. Duncan and I got medals. You and Angela were in gowns that were breathtaking. I was in a tux that about strangled me."

Nazy nodded and smiled. *Let the men talk,* she could hear her mother say. "What are you doing now?"

McGee returned to the present. "Mostly conducting threat assessments for churches and schools in Texas, Oklahoma, and Louisiana. We are trying to protect kids from liberal nut jobs with guns. I know you've heard about all these killings in Europe when Islamists rent a truck and barrel into a crowd. Businesses, schools, and churches have been forced to consider barriers for protection from vehicles— bollards, concrete Jersey barriers, mostly. Boulders are cheap bollards."

Nazy said, "You can't trust anyone from a mosque anymore. Nearly every Muslim leader who offered their help to DOD or the FBI or the IC are in jail for their ties to some terrorist organization. Very few Muslims are willing to help. We don't see Muslim defectors whose information would be invaluable. I'll wager only one percent ever has intel we're interested in. The others are just looking to get into the intel community. But they cannot pass a polygraph."

McGee gritted his teeth and nodded. "I know. All I can say is that the information from defectors is sometimes incalculable. When I was in Afghanistan, the Muslim men we had as interpreters were solid citizens and provided us intel we would have never known. We tried to get those guys to come to America. Some made it, some didn't. Anyway, those things are history and well beyond my control. What we can do locally is inform and educate. The most effective barrier is an armed cop or an open-carry parishioner at the door to meet and greet their people. We're doing defensive work, planning work. Deterrence. What about you? You still in that NCTC job?"

"Greg keeps me 'hopping,' as Duncan says. Do you know what Duncan did this time? Did he tell you?"

McGee shook his head with a look that was something between concern and hurt. He rationalized that since Hunter hadn't called him to go on another adventure, it must not have been anything important.

Nazy shared with him, everything. The reconciliation—Duncan and Lynche were back on speaking terms. How Kelly flew the airplane while Duncan managed the sensors, lasers and the weapon system to free some of his friends—U.S. Navy SEALs—as well as a couple of Agency men from the NCS. She mentioned Kelly's difficulties in the air that forced Duncan to take over the flying duties while he targeted ISIS killers. "He used the *Weedbusters* laser to blind them."

He said, "He's the best. A genius. I wouldn't have thought about that. That man is so smart!"

"He used the aircraft's weapon system to…kill ISIS…."

"What is it, Nazy? Was there something else? You know I'll get the complete story from him, so it isn't necessary to tell me everything. I just want to know if he was successful."

Nazy smiled, composed herself, and took her time responding. "Yes, your friends were rescued. He was successful." She told him an expanded version of why Duncan and Kelly were flying airplanes back to the East Coast, and why he was taking her back to Virginia. Nazy told him what Lynche and Hunter thought the men from the NCS did once they entered her house in Bethesda, that Duncan had been right about some of the men in the National Clandestine Service.

With McGee caught up on the rationale and logistics of the impromptu rescue mission, he said, "I think we're going to be fairly safe out here as long as I don't hit a deer or a wild hog or have some texting and driving idiot run into us. Out here in the hinterlands there are no facial recognition cameras. But if you want to sit up front, glasses and scarves please. From what you've told me we can't trust the Agency or the FBI at this point, the long knives may be out looking for you and we can't take for granted that they're on our side just because they're in the intel community. Bad guys are always escaping the torpedo nets."

Nazy nodded. She figured out his meaning about "torpedo nets." She was occupied with other thoughts. Like a trained lawyer, she used the fewest words possible when in a discussion. McGee wondered if it was a holdover from her upbringing as a Muslim girl in Amman, Jordan, being told to only speak when spoken to. Or maybe she was still a little intimidated by the thought of this huge black man in close proximity to her. McGee was in control of the situation, in control of the vehicle. In a way, in control of her.

McGee thought she might be very uncomfortable being alone with a man who wasn't her husband. He knew Islamic customs forbade a woman from touching a man who wasn't her husband. But she didn't have any issues with hugging him and kissing him on the cheek. Maybe it was because he had seen her at her absolute worst—naked, unconscious, bleeding, half-mutilated and on her way to death. He had saved her life. *Maybe she was eternally grateful. And just maybe, she was thinking about work.* Then he realized how little he knew of her. He had saved her life, but he really didn't know that much about her. So he asked.

Nazy was taken aback. She pondered the question and said, "I was born into a non-practicing Muslim family. My father had official duties as a justice on the Jordanian Supreme Court, and I'd only been exposed to a moderate form of Islam. Muslim girls generally aren't even supposed to be seen. Some other families in Jordan, in Amman, practiced and went to mosque. It wasn't an issue at my house. My family was completely westernized. My mother didn't wear a headscarf unless she went to a formal dinner. I can't remember either of my parents forcing Islam down my throat. We wore western attire more than Arabic clothes."

"I really didn't know what 'real' Islam was until after the Ayatollah Khomeini returned to Iran. My mother was born in a town outside of Tehran and was a cousin of the Shah Pahlavi Reza. That's where I get my green eyes. She was worried about her relatives. Khomeini had them murdered. I was a little girl, but it was then that I started to see what I thought was the 'true' Islam."

Bill turned his head and smiled at her. He nodded as if he knew what she was intimating.

"You have to understand that during that period, the time of the

Shah, Jordanians, Egyptians, Iranians, and others in the Middle East practiced the type of Islam that was peaceful. The people I knew didn't practice Islam hardly at all. In some ways it didn't even exist. Living in Jordan, it wasn't really a part of our lives. There was a spirit of being westernized. We looked toward America and Europe and all of the things that those societies provided. Air travel, beautiful vehicles, and beautiful clothes. All across the Middle East, we attended the American Universities. At college graduations, the women wore dresses and the men wore suits."

"As I got older, I got caught up in the Islam the Ayatollah Khomeini introduced in 1979. I think it was my rebellious youth. My parents sent me to boarding school in London. I wasn't very happy with them. I met other girls from the Middle East who thought Islam was good." She paused for a few moments before continuing. "When Islam came under attack I became a Muslim apologist."

"Islam casts a huge shadow on everything in life. I quoted verses from the Quran that were written in the early days of the Islamic movement, when Muhammad lived peacefully in Mecca. When you read those passages they make Islam appear loving and harmless as they call for love and peace and patience. When I'd graduated from law school, my father forced me to return to Jordan. My activism bothered him greatly. He didn't want to believe his daughter could fall for *the deception*. That's what he called it. 'The deception.' He said one of the reasons he sent me away was for me to become well educated, become a free thinker. I had failed him greatly."

McGee listened intently. It was quite a story.

"He lectured me, told me I was gullible. He was so disappointed with me he sent me away. I was forced to marry because he would no longer support me financially. My husband was an uneducated and lazy lout from a well-respected family. When I wasn't being abused by him, I turned to my mother. She responded wonderfully. She said that Islam is now being led by Khomeini and his evil minions. That Khomeini used the Iranian treasury to fund imams across the Middle East to teach the verses in the Quran that embrace an evil Islam, and they'd force this type of Islam down everyone's throats. She blamed Khomeini for everything, even after he died."

McGee looked straight ahead and said, "I'd blame Khomeini too. The Middle East was at peace before he left France, I believe, and then he set the world on fire."

Nazy nodded. "Those later Quranic verses nullified the earlier verses which were rendered void by later passages that incite religious intolerance, killing, decapitations, and terrorism. I know now that Khomeini completely funded a radical Islam. It was a corrupt ideology imposed on a sophisticated, tolerant and free people by the ignorant and evil. Women became subservient property. Radical, terroristic men imposed this new ideology with a sword or a bomb."

McGee had nothing more to say. They drove in silence for some time. Nazy looked out the side window seeing only a blurry darkness. After an hour on the road, McGee tried to start another conversation. "We'll only get food through the drive-throughs. If you have to go the little girl's room, I'll escort you. I'd like you to be fully covered like we're an Islamic couple. They can look at us all they want, but they won't see you. We really can't take the chance of you being seen by a security camera. The NCS has many friends in all the wrong places."

"Thank you, Bill."

"There shouldn't be any issues. No harm will come to you—I'll ensure no one will bother you. You have a pistol and the token. If for some reason we are ambushed and we are separated, your weapons are your last line of defense. There's virtually zero chance of that happening. We'll just get you back to McLean, or wherever your boss wants me to take you."

Nazy smiled and nodded appreciatively. She tried to hide a yawn.

"I was going to have my SEAL network take you back, but Greg Lynche thought it would be best if I drive you to Virginia myself. Greg seems to think he needs both YO-3s to find some radioactive materials."

"Thank you, Bill." She was well past tired, heading toward another unlady-like yawn. "Greg has work for me. He wants me to dive into some archives to see if I can find the reason why the NCS is seemingly out of control. Some of them are no longer working for the country but for themselves. What happened and why?"

"I had a feeling it was something like that. Hard to do research from Duncan's basement in Jackson Hole." As Nazy yawned for the third time he told her to hit the rack in the back.

She nodded, touched McGee's muscular arm, and crawled into the back seat. She put the Kimber .45 pistol in an opposite pocket so she could get comfortable. In a few minutes she was asleep.

Soon McGee stifled a laugh. *How could such a tall, thin woman snore like that! I'm not going to worry about falling asleep.*

•　　•　　•　　•　　•

"Dad, seriously? Do you really think you need something like this?" Kelly was somewhat mortified to see the impish almost juvenile qualities in her father. Having the oversized sports utility vehicle for protection, she wondered, *Protection from what?*

Hunter glanced at Kelly for a second. She could see the seriousness on his face in the glow from the instrument cluster. "Yes, I'm serious. Armored vehicles like this one have saved my life several times. Nazy's too, and Bill McGee. They have saved the lives of the people who bought them."

"Here? In America?" She didn't believe him. It was too impossible to believe.

Hunter nodded. "We built and gave one to Colonel Demetrius Eastwood for when he worked in New York City. He was part of the group who rescued and saved Nazy. He and I survived a mad Muslim on a Ninja motorcycle with a machine pistol, a MAC-10, not far from the old house outside of Fredericksburg. Bullfrog delivered a level six armored...I think it was a Yukon, to New York City. Days later, when Eastwood was leaving his home in Connecticut, he and his driver survived a bomb blast and was able to drive away. Yes, in America. It was either the Left or al-Qaeda or the Islamic Underground. In Bogotá, Nazy and I escaped another motorcyclist with an AK-47—an armored vehicle saved us. There are very few places I'll go without one. That's because there's still a million-dollar *fatwa* on Nazy and me." He added with a grin, "Although, I'm officially dead."

Kelly couldn't find words to speak. Finally she said, "Dad, I think after this op I'm going to want a Hummer, too. Do they make one with red seats?"

Her comments were the spark that Hunter needed. "Can do easy. Maybe a Black Widow Yukon or a BMW X5M would be more suitable for you. You reminded me that these seats are also armored—the Hummer is a level seven and will stop a .308 or a .300 magnum rifle bullet." He had calmed his emotions sufficiently with talk about armored Hummers and Yukons and BMWs so that he could brief Kelly on the mission ahead. But first he needed to be sure she understood that what he had done in Syria was necessary to save good men.

He asked what she thought. Kelly said she was more embarrassed than disappointed with him. After a lengthy back and forth discussion, she told him she just wanted to forget it even happened. It wasn't going to ever happen again. She whispered as she told him she couldn't believe what he had done. That was something she couldn't do. He gently disagreed with her. "If the conditions are such, yes, even you would and could. People are put into situations where they have to choose. There are rules for those situations. Once those kids held the pistols in their hands and stood behind those hostages, they became combatants. Their ages became irrelevant. We are at war with an evil army. Any blame belongs with the ISIS adults there."

She looked at her father for a long time, thinking through his argument. She sighed and acknowledged that he was correct on all counts and she was just a foolish young woman.

Hunter continued, "The real world is a crazy world. The more I've thought about it, the more I'm convinced I was wrong to think you shouldn't have gone. I couldn't have saved our guys alone."

"Dad...."

"Sometimes you just have to do whatever you can to save a life. It was a freakish situation. I didn't think about it as I was doing it. Taking a life to save a life. A handful of guys survive a crash on a mountain top. No help arrives and there's no food. What do you do? You do what you must in order to survive. To live."

Kelly nodded and took his hand.

Hunter thought their discussion had gone better than expected. It was incomplete, not fully explored, and she might want to revisit it later. But now it was time to move past the old mission and onto the upcoming mission. "Nazy needs to investigate some of the leaders of NCS. Greg suggested she should return to the D.C. area on the SEAL's underground railroad, their network. It's operated and maintained by active and former Navy SEALs. And it's safe. Sometimes they have men who have crossed a biggie, a very bad hombre in the terrorism world, and they need to hide themselves and their families like in a witness protection program. There's no official *fatwa*, but the community knows their men are marked for discovery and elimination. I don't know when we'll see her again, but with Bill, I know she'll be safe. My main concern is to ensure that your boss won't be able to get to her. Or you."

45

November 8
Fredericksburg, Texas

Kelly turned and looked away. "Were you serious about killing my boss, Steve Castaño?"

Hunter said, "I'm sure he has targeted Nazy and me, and likely you. He may have been, once upon a time, a patriot working in the best interests of our country. But as sure as I'm sitting here, I'm certain he's no longer on 'our side,' that he's gone over to the dark side. Whatever the hell that means. Greg thinks he was in the video at Nazy's place. If true, he's violated the one of the cardinal rules of conflict—if you have a problem with me, then you fight me. I won't go after your family and you don't attack my family. Castaño knows the rules and broke the deal. He's a wild card, he can't be trusted. He'll kill you and me if he gets the chance. I intend to not give him any chance. I'll do whatever it takes to kill him even if I have to hunt him to the ends of earth."

Kelly was stunned. She couldn't believe what she had heard. She asked her father if he was joking. "My boss?" She looked at her father quizzically.

"Yes, your boss. Castaño."

Now she was more confused. *Another conundrum. He wouldn't explain any further. He'll tell me when he feels it's the right time.* Kelly blurted out, "Why do *you* do it? This kind of work?"

"Like what did we did in Syria? I stopped the murder of our troops. You…we drove the getaway vehicle. Who wouldn't want to do that?"

"You didn't have to do it."

"No. The president asked if I could find them and rescue them. I'm of the school of thought that you don't say to the president, 'No sir, I'm not interested saving Americans when it may be in my skill set to save them.' That's not how it works, 'at that level.' There's a level of patriotism and professional pride. You texted me you were in trouble somewhere in Africa. Bill and I rescued you in Liberia. We jumped out of a YO-3A. I killed the guy who was seconds away from raping you. I wasn't there to give him or his fellow hijackers a back rub or a foot massage. They crossed the line and would have raped and murdered all of you. Yes, sometimes you have to do whatever you can to help people, especially the ones you love."

That's interesting.... Kelly said, "I texted you we'd been hijacked and about an hour later the lights went out on that jet, and when the lights came back on, there you were. I didn't know...."

"Bill and I flew over the field and parachuted onto the back of the jet. There's an emergency hatch near the front of that jumbojet which leads into the aircrew's sleeping quarters. Sounds fairly simple just talking about it, but it was full of danger. I overshot the jet, but Bill caught my chute and hauled me up the side of the fuselage. He's a master parachutist and as strong as a bull elephant. Bill thinks I'm just lousy bad."

She push aside all thoughts that her father was a potential murderer. There was a lesson of life in his viewpoint. He had killed evil men to protect Americans in distress. She sighed and laughed at the vision of her father dangling over the side of an Airbus and McGee with a handful of parachute nylon trying to rescue the rescuer.

"Dad, it was simply unreal. The lights go out on the jet, the terrorist who had been molesting me is…dead in the aisle…the lights come back on, and there you are."

Hunter nodded. "It would have taken *days* for SOCOM to organize something—and they still wouldn't have figured out how to get into that jet. A rescue operation that complex would probably have failed— no one ever thought of parachuting on the back of the jet. And not every aviation expert knows about the escape hatch for the relief crew area. Not every jet has those."

"At night, no less." Kelly squeezed his hand in gratitude for rescuing her. She didn't remember much about that night but she recalled that she was confused and wasn't unhappy that her father killed the man who was seconds away from raping her. She just didn't think about it.

Hunter said, "But when they introduced you into this operation, I almost said no."

"You did say no."

"Greg knew I wanted an apology. I wouldn't really say no, not to him or the president even if it meant putting you in danger. He knew I'd find a way to do both, do the mission and to protect you. He knew I'd bring you home."

"I really screwed up. I was no help."

He shook his head. "I'm assigning all the blame to me. I could have pulled a knock it off—it's too dangerous. Told you to turn off the FLIR repeater in your cockpit. But I was too arrogant to think I could do both while I ignored the dynamics of your upbringing."

"My grandparents were pacifists. They were terrific parents." Then she remembered her grandmother keeping the information of her father away from her until after her death. Kelly rubbed her temples with her fingers.

Hunter nodded. "They raised a fantastic woman. And we managed to get away with our lives. There will be no next time. Greg plans to shut me down and it's probably for the best."

Kelly stared at the profile of her father for a long time. Bumps in the road made her turn away. They drove for several silent miles until he broke the silence. "There were two things I wanted in life. To fly and have a family. I lost your mother. I'm so grateful you came into my life. I'm so fortunate to have you and Nazy. I wouldn't want it to end on a bad note."

Kelly squeezed her father's hand again. He drove on. They talked about family. She learned that her father attributed much of his tough guy attitude to his father, who was a muscular man with a few conspicuous tattoos. He smoked cigars. Hunter said, "I was with my dad, going deer hunting. My dad and his peers, who were all outdoorsmen, had an incredible work ethic. As a group, they impressed me. If this is what it's like to be a manly man, then I wanted to be like them. They were the kind of men I wanted to be when I grew up. Except I hated cigars. And I wasn't big on alcohol. Or dope."

"I was pretty boring. I worked three jobs and didn't have time for my friends who ran around smoking weed and getting drunk. I think that reality formed me politically. I spent my money on a car, nice clothes, stereo and records. They had memories of getting high or drunk; those that are still alive. Years later I said to myself, 'They must be Democrats because they're a bunch of freeloaders.' I looked at my dad and his friends, guys that worked their butts off and did great things like work on cars and trucks and jets and said, 'Well, they're Republicans, and I must be one too.'"

Kelly was quiet for several minutes before asking, "What was my mother like?"

Hunter had been prepared for the question a couple of years ago. He tried to recall what he wanted to say. When he found the words; they flowed from his mouth with care and tenderness. "Kim was just so beautiful, I was instantly smitten. I didn't know that kind of love-at-first-sight existed. She made my chest hurt. It was incredible. You know how we met from your mother's diary. My view was a little different."

"I was in a flight of two out of Kingsville, Texas, two instructors with students. The field was closed at El Toro in California—we couldn't make the last leg because of headwinds. So we landed in Phoenix, Williams Air Force Base, and checked out the Air Force's student club. We were tired, but when we walked in everyone got quiet as every eye fell on us. We'd interrupted a huge party."

"My knees were shaking and your mother came up to me—I'll never forget what she said. 'You Navy?' I stared into her eyes and probably shook my head a little and said, 'Marine.' Then she turned into a little playful imp. She said, 'Too bad, I have a thing for sailors.' And then she turned and went back to her table, which was now laughing more than they should. I thought I'd just been visited by a red-haired, green-eyed goddess who made my heart go crazy. We couldn't keep our eyes off of each other, so I went to her table and asked her to dance. We swing-danced and close-danced. I'd given the disc jockey $50 to play *Unchained Melody* if I got Kimberly on the dance floor. And we didn't leave the floor until she said, something like, 'My guys are making bets whether you take me home or I take you back to my place.'"

"Seriously?" *Maybe this was more than I asked for....*

Hunter nodded and smiled at the old memory. "You read your mother's diary. My heart was bouncing around in my chest, and before I could say anything your mother said, 'Do you believe in love at first sight?' I told her, 'I do now. Feel my heart slamming in my chest!' right about the time the DJ kicked in the Everly Brothers. She said, 'Mine too,' and took my hand and put it on her heart. I told her something from an old Oliver and Hardy movie, 'Here's another nice mess you've gotten us into.'"

"We promised to stay in touch with each other. Two weeks later I drove from Texas to Phoenix and we went out for dinner."

He didn't say he stayed with her. "In your Corvette?"

"Yes, the old Yellow Peril. It's an old 1967 coupe—it's my racecar now. The exhaust was so loud we couldn't talk. I got a newer yellow convertible with a quieter exhaust system and we drove all over the country with the time we had. She loved to drive that car fast. Kim went on to fly students—she stayed in Phoenix, and I was transferred to Hawaii. Having a Marine and an Air Force officer so far apart was a challenge. We jumped on MAC flights whenever we could. I took her to Kawai and the fern grotto and walked around the mountains. She took me to Flagstaff and we went skiing. Whenever we were together there were sparks—much like what you see when Nazy and I are back together. Absence does make the heart grow fonder. Then I got orders to a carrier. When I deployed, your mom stopped writing."

"She had cancer and was pregnant."

"I didn't know. My heart had broken. I never knew what had happened until you found me in my classroom and I read Kim's diary. I'm the luckiest guy on the planet."

Kelly knew the rest of the story from her mother's diary. She looked out of the window then asked, "Was your voice always that low? I just don't remember any of the cadets at the academy having that...."

"Deep bass?"

She nodded.

"No. It's not something I think about. Girls would say I had a sexy voice, but my ear hears a squeak. So I thought they were just being polite. No, no. My friends tell me it has gone down with age. I can't imagine it's going to go much lower. Bill McGee really has the low voice. He sounds just like Barry White."

By the look on her face, the name *Barry White* meant nothing to her. Kelly thought about asking more of her father's life, but after a few miles on the hilly and curvy road, he said, "Back to work. I need to teach you how to use the gun. Tell you how accurate it is. How it works. You may need to use it. Maybe even protect yourself. A guy shot at me with a surface-to-air missile. I shot back. If someone shoots at you, you're either going to be scared or you're gonna to be pissed. If you try to run you'll be blown out of the sky. If you want to live you need to be able to shoot back. Then I can show you how to turn the laser designator into a writing tool and then turn *Weedbusters* into an offensive, debilitating weapon."

"Like in Syria?"

Hunter nodded, he shifted in his seat and drove.

My father's here...that means the guy who tried to shoot him down is probably dead. Kelly couldn't find the words. Any words. She nodded as if she had been asked a question that she understood and concurred. But she was immobile, unable to comprehend that her father had long been the target of terrorists. *He's still here, and that means they're gone. Doesn't it mean something? If murderers are after you, don't you have to protect yourself and your family? Kill or be killed?* Her father talked shop while she focused on something else.

Hunter explained how to turn the system on, how to deploy the gun, and how to load the gun. "If I'd been by myself last night in Syria, I wouldn't have been able to save our guys."

Kelly returned to the present. She looked confused. "Why's that?"

"For starters, I modified the original airplane so I could fly it from the front seat. The gun's magazine only holds ten rounds. Spent uranium bullets. In all of my missions we assumed I wouldn't need to reload, that I would be ok with ten rounds. Normally I go after a single terrorist on the most wanted list. More bad guys mean more capabilities."

"Like the drones?"

"Exactly. So in the Yo-Yo, you change magazines from the aft cockpit. Having you in front forced me into the back so I was able to change magazines quickly."

"Fortunes of war?" she asked.

"Yes. Some days you're the windshield, somedays you're the bug."

He explained how each bullet has just enough gunpowder to get the bullet out of the barrel without excessive Gs harming the electronics and the tiny glass seeker head on the tip of each bullet. He said, "Once the bullet is out of the barrel, then tiny fins pop out, and the solid rocket fuel is ignited. The bullet flies to the laser designated spot. The gun is electronically slaved to where the sensor was pointed. And it's unbelievably accurate. You control and hold the LD on a target with the coolie hat on the control stick. One squeeze—the first detent—of the trigger 'tags' the spot you want tracked. The computer will track the spot as you fly the airplane. Pull the trigger to the second detent and the gun fires. The bullet will hit your spot within three inches at three miles. At ten miles the 'probability of kill' drops a bit. You only have to hold the LD on the target a few seconds. It's over in a hurry. There's nothing like it. Product of S&T."

Kelly shook her head. *Sounds simple enough.*

The lights of Hondo broke over the horizon. Hunter said, "Break, break, new subject." Hunter glanced over to his daughter. She smiled.

Duncan shelved any further discussions of guns and sensors. He told her the rest of the story of how Castaño and likely senior members of the NCS had penetrated Nazy's house while they were in Syria. "They likely broke into your apartment as well, and installed cameras and microphones. I'm afraid you'll have to move; if the place isn't booby-trapped, at the very least it won't be safe to take your clothes off or take a shower there. I'd feel a lot better if you'd let me find you a house where I can install a state-of-the-art security system." Hunter felt he was forgetting something. The feeling left him uneasy.

Kelly was stunned. The very training she had learned as an intelligence officer for the National Clandestine Service had been used against her? How did he know? It was a bitter pill to swallow. *What proof?* She wanted to challenge her father, ridicule him for his outrageous conspiracy theories.

Hunter continued, "Greg agrees that it isn't safe for you to go home. He wants us to tackle a domestic problem while he runs down the truth and sends a team in to see if our assessments are on target. He wants to see whether Castaño is the lecherous traitor we think he is."

"What does Director Lynche want us to do?"

He briefed their mission until they arrived at the Hondo airport. Hunter waved a white plastic card with an imbedded RFID tag at a sensor near the airport's security gate. There was a delay, as if a computer had to wake up and send the "open" signal. Then the gate jerked alive, trundling along a guide-bar on the ground until there was enough of an opening for the Hummer to pass through. Once the vehicle passed an optical sensor, the gate reversed and closed automatically.

He drove to the north edge of the tarmac. He knew where he was going, one of two hangars at the north end of the field. There were no ramp lights but the Hummer's headlights provided plenty of light to illuminate the front of one hangar.

There was an aircraft on the ramp adjacent to the hangar that could have been white but it was too dark to make a definitive determination. It resembled an airplane, but Kelly had no idea what it was. It could have been an alien aircraft that escaped from the infamous Area 51 but it wasn't other-worldly. It did cast a shadow that was ominous and unnatural. Then Kelly found the right word, *futuristic*. There was wonder in her voice as she asked, *"What's that?"*

Hunter opened the Hummer door and answered, "That…is a *Starship*. Max speed, about 400 knots."

Hunter entered the hangar and turned on lights. Kelly stared at *Starship*, now bathed in the diffused light of the hangar. It looked like something from the mind of Burt Rutan or the long-dead German aircraft designers, the Horten Brothers. It resembled an oversized VeriEze with swept wings at the rear of the fuselage and vertical tails at the wing tips. With twin engines and pusher propellers with sweeping tails on the wingtips, it looked like it could go like a bat out of hell.

She got out of the Hummer and walked around the *Starship*. Hunter had returned to the vehicle and parked it inside, along a wall of the hangar. He unloaded the Hummer and placed bags outside the building's large doors, Kelly returned to her father to say something about the *Starship* when she spied two large twin-engine taildraggers in the hangar. One was in a corner and appeared to be ready for flight. The other was in the opposite corner, on jacks, in a state of overhaul. She didn't know what they were. The long-wing black YO-3A took up the middle of the building. With a smile she thought, *My Dad has the most interesting airplanes. And cars….*

After all the bags had been transferred to the outside the hangar, the pain in Hunter's hip was back with a vengeance. She walked and he hobbled into the hangar at Duncan's pace and pushed the YO-3A out of the building.

Hunter said the airplanes were the last flyable Howard 500s. "In their heyday, they were the ultimate piston-driven bizplanes. They were flown by professional pilots, not just rich guys who flew Staggerwings and smaller things." Kelly nodded. She kicked off her shoes, stripped to her underwear, and donned a black t-shirt, a black flight suit, and flying boots. She thought *If my dad doesn't have qualms with me seeing him in his shorts I guess I don't have many qualms with him seeing me in mine either. It's not sexual. We are in the flying business.*

Hunter limped around the YO-3A preflighting the aircraft. He checked the oil level and the tire pressures. After he completed his circuit of the aircraft, he showed Kelly how to load the gun and gave her a quick lesson on the proper switchology to deploy, activate, operate, and retract the weapon. He showed her how to make the laser designator write letters wherever it was pointed. He helped Kelly strap on a parachute and strap into the aircraft. He was all business. He handed her helmet and asked, "Ready for an adventure?"

Kelly nodded enthusiastically. She put her helmet on, and Hunter climbed off the aircraft very gingerly. He didn't want to aggravate his hip with a sudden jump to the ground. He was going to pay for all the extra movement as it was. When Kelly was airborne, he'd find his bottle of painkillers.

He grinned and shouted, "Courage is being scared to death and saddling up anyway. We're just moving the airplane so our guys can install sensors. Ok? Let's giddy up, girl."

She spun two fingers to signal "starting engine" and the Continental 360 fired off after five turns of the propeller. On any other aircraft the engine exhaust would have shattered the calm and quiet of the night. The YO-3A exhaust system was unique. A series of mufflers coupled to a specially designed exhaust system ran down the starboard side of the fuselage and over the wing. The noise that came out of the exhaust system was about as loud as an infant passing gas. The quietist piston-driven airplane in the world was ready to go flying.

Hunter favored his right leg as he saluted her. She taxied off. Then he withdrew his BlackBerry and sent several text messages. He didn't expect answers. He shunted the pain in his hip off to some dead spot in his brain. He didn't have time for discomfort. Taking the Howard 500 would have meant the trip to Washington would take too long. He didn't have time for a slow airplane. The *Starship* wasn't the fastest in the stable but no one knew he had it and it would escape the notice of the communists at *Tailwatchers*. He had work to do. Hunter transferred his cooler and baggage from the Hummer to the aircraft. He climbed aboard the *Starship*, closed the door, fired up the turboprops, and was soon airborne. After he engaged the autopilot, he washed down a handful of aspirins.

46

The Director of Central Intelligence's heels clicked across the grey granite and stainless steel emblem on the floor. An oversized art deco clock high above the Security counter indicated it was nearly midnight. He sped through security and swiped his badge to log in, the waist-high, barrier optical turnstile opened. His two personal security men followed at a safe contact distance. The old man could walk fast when he was in a hurry, and today he was flying.

When Lynche looked up, his security detail also looked up. Suspended from the ceiling of New Headquarters Building's glass-enclosed atrium were matte-black models of the Agency's most famous aircraft: U-2, A-12, and D-21 reconnaissance drone. During the time the CIA developed and operated spyplanes to collect imagery over the former Soviet Union, the U-2 was the first of the high-flying surveillance aircraft followed by the supersonic A-12. The aircraft were built by the Lockheed Aircraft Company under the eye of legendary designer, Kelly Johnson. The A-12 derivatives, the SR-71 held speed and altitude records that remain unbroken. The D-21 drone had extended the A-12's capabilities into high-threat areas over China.

He took the down escalator to the ground level; the model aircraft display disappeared from view behind him. Lynche knew a YO-3A model should be hanging up there with Lockheed's best known spyplanes. It would be in good company, but it would never happen. The *Wraith* special access program was an Eyes Only project, many times more secret than any of the other Agency-inspired aircraft, and would never be declassified.

The lift to the executive suite was one of the fastest in the city. However, tonight Lynche was convinced it couldn't move any slower. When it finally opened, the lights on the seventh floor were on, as were his office lights. He rushed into his office just as his turn-of-the-century, black onyx, Tiffany desk clock chimed twelve bells. It was officially midnight and Anna Comstock, the CIA's Director of Security, was waiting for him as directed.

There was no preamble. The DCI told Anna what he wanted. What he needed. She took mental notes and scribbled detailed directions. She asked a few questions and cautioned the DCI on certain aspects of his understanding of the situation and his plan.

"If it was NCS that you saw and there were four of them, then I'm not surprised. The three division chiefs and their boss. They have been on my shit list for years. They're too cool for school. We haven't been able to get a good polygraph out of any of them. I'm talking about '*derogs*' on Fässler, Bomarito, and Troxel. Castaño vouches for them. He won't hold them accountable."

Derog was the in-house Agency term for derogatory comments in an unfavorable evaluation, especially for security violations. If you received a couple of *derogs*, you'd most likely be asked to leave the CIA. Escorted off the property. Have your clearance pulled. Drop your badge in the basket. Never to return. Any history of your presence would be erased. Security called it the *Beria Treatment* after Lavrentiy Beria was removed from power as chief of the Soviet secret police and had every image of him in photographs erased, like he had never ever existed.

How's that even possible? Lynche thought. Then, "How so?"

"Whenever the interviewers get to the direct espionage questions, such as, 'Have you ever given classified information to someone not authorized to receive it?' They just laugh. They exclaim, '*That's my job! Talk to Steve.*' The last polygrapher to interview them reported many adverse reactions to their poly. For the last five years they have been together in the top jobs, covering each other's ass."

"Why is that, Anna? You know something." Lynche finally sat in his chair. He made a teepee with his fingers.

"You're a pilot. Former Chief Air Branch. I thought you'd know that they go way back. Way, way back to the good old days. I think that at least three and maybe all four are former Air America pilots — Fässler, Bomarito, and Troxel, for sure. They got into the airline at the tail end of the war. As I understand, so did Castaño, but he was part of the management after the airline was sold."

Lynche knew Agency history. The CIA offered some of the Air America pilots work within Air Branch. But when the pilots learned they'd have to be trained as intelligence or operations officers, few took up the offer. Most of the pilots just wanted the freedom to fly for an airline. Lynche recalled he was on the other side of the world, in Australia learning how to fly Cessnas. Air America pulled out of South

Vietnam and a few years later it was dissolved.

Anna said, "It was only a rumor that Castaño was also a pilot—no one really knows how his hands and face were damaged. Some think he was in an old helicopter that was shot down, caught fire; only he escaped. Someone told me the scars on his hands and ears resemble the scars from burns from magnesium fires. It's not something anyone talks about. It's just Steve. As for Stevie…and the boys…. Let's just say that after the election, we expect them all to be gone, retired. They received waivers to extend their mandatory retirement age. I really expected them to go before the election but for some reason they're hanging around."

It took a long time for that bit of information to sink into Lynche's head. *Why would they want a waiver? I couldn't wait to get out….escape.* "I didn't know that. For whatever it's worth, they never worked for me at Air Branch. And I don't ever recall meeting them when I was over there. So I'm under the impression they went straight to NCS, either Special Activities Division or Special Operations Group. Maybe Ground Branch. I don't remember any of them well from the days when I ran that place either. They were probably assigned to an embassy. Anyway, I'm not sure how any of that's relevant." He flipped his fingers at her. "More on their polygraphs."

"Every examiner who worked them stated that they demonstrated deceptive answers to some questions, but they passed them anyway. They're NCS." Her voice shot up an octave, "*It's their job. They're the most trusted operations officers in the service.* If there was any problem, the examiners received Castaño's assurance that they were just doing their job. Everything they touch is SAP-related. Everyone else had a need to know. That excluded polygraphers."

"Espionage is a two-way street." Lynche waved his arms around, trying to emphasize something. "I can't boot them for that."

"No one took the polygraph deviations seriously. They're NCS." Anna Comstock's curiosity was growing and she was getting frustrated. "Well, then all of them have a tendency to procrastinate in submitting travel claims. I'm being generous when I say 'procrastinate.' It's always been a bear for accounting to reconcile their claims. The Finance Office filed several IG complaints."

Lynche strained not to roll his eyes. This was a petty complaint. "So the Inspector General looked into their travel, their transactions?"

She nodded and added, "Mostly their travel. They're spooks. When Castaño feels they need to go, to travel, it's always immediate, travel first, paperwork last. They charter jets and…."

"They've chartered *jets*?" Lynche exclaimed. He rubbed his face for a second. *Sure, they have the authority for mission-related work, but….*

"Specifically, Castaño chartered the jets for them. Yes, sir." Anna was a little surprised at his interruption, his outburst. *Of course they charter jets…. Spies have to have a way of travelling without getting the whole damned airplane blown up by all the terrorist organizations the Agency has pissed off over the years. Where have you been, Director Lynche?* "Yes, sir. Missions call for it…I suppose. Sometimes their claims aren't filed on time, nor do they indicate who they meet. That's the part that infuriates me. They're almost exclusively, not 'security-friendly.' But I know that's the nature of their job. Immediate response to a crisis in crazy places. And then don't tell a damn soul who they talked to, because that opens up means and methods."

He was confused, *But they are NCS executives and the exces don't do field work anymore! This is crazy.* "Do you know to where they chartered jets? And when?"

She thought, *What an odd question. Questions.* "I do. Ah, as I recall, there have been several recent ones. Anything older and I'll have to check. There was one to Tunisia before the Algerian embassy was overrun. It was shortly after the ambassador to Libya was killed. There was one to Amman. And the most recent was one to Abu Dhabi."

Lynche asked, "Not Dubai?"

"No, I'm sure it was Abu Dhabi. They had to buy fuel. Pay landing fees. If they had business in Dubai it's only about sixty miles away. Always someplace in Middle East. They're always going to Africa. I know it's a hotbed of activity over there, if you read the Early Bird. But they're NCS. They are above reproach."

Lynche nearly fell out of his chair. *The NCS four were at the intersection, in the immediate vicinity of Wraith operations. Shit! I hate it when Duncan's suspicions are right! But having an NCS officer involved in any parallel operations which crossed over into our special access program was absurd.* He recovered his straight face and asked, "They had to incur expenses."

All 250-pounds of Anna Chapman nodded. "Full disclosure. They eventually submit their travel claims, and they're always clean. Late but identical, like they xeroxed the form and changed the name. Nothing extraneous like five-star hotels or special maid service. I can only imagine what 'maid service' is in the Middle East. But we all know they have tubs of cash." She shrugged. "Castaño's justifications are always the same. 'Immediate response required for SAP.' The finance officer was just happy that there were no unauthorized or extravagant expenses. And their cash holdings are always *copasetic*."

"But you think they abuse traveling by…private jet?"

"Those are separate issues. Castaño always signs off on those. Immediate secure travel when DOD couldn't provide an aircraft. Before you arrived, normal ops was to ask for a charter jet and run it up the flagpole for signatures. That could take days as you guys on the seventh floor are very busy. They're NCS and sometimes didn't want to get the Air Force involved. When it is mission essential and time sensitive, they can override, charter first and promise the paperwork will follow. The only reason I know anything is that I'm friendly with the finance chief. He always has issues with their books. It's not cash that they've asked for; they have plenty of that in their SCIF. It makes sense for those guys to need quick access to aircraft and money if the mission calls for it."

"Anna, I can probably guarantee you that for some missions, we can't have the Air Force involved. If there's misuse…a problem, I'll have to reconcile those myself. Is there anything else? We need to find them. If they're in their offices, then we need to pull their badges and keys, get them out of their offices, and off the property. At this moment, I'm not interested in frog-marching them out of their building in shackles. There will be an investigation of their activities."

An investigation into what? She was confused.

He read the question on her face. "They need to go, tonight."

"It's after midnight, Greg. They shouldn't be in their offices. And I think this is their card night." She looked at her watch one more time as if the darkness outside the director's office windows wasn't to be believed. She shook her head and walked to the office's windows as if she could see the NCS men in their offices in the Old Office Building. The OOB was black. Lights out. She turned and said, "I know they aren't there." Anna was growing frustrated with the DCI's lack of candor. She never suffered fools well and wasn't about to start now. "Greg, sir, we go way back. You and me. I know you're on to something, and you don't have to tell me. But you are right. There's something about those Musketeers and their leader. I've tried to find something to hammer them for breaking the rules, but Castaño is always there to bail them out or cover for them. I'm PNG over there." *Persona non grata.* Not wanted.

Lynche frowned.

"They routinely travel to the same training venues or locations together, and they used Air Branch assets almost exclusively. Domestic SOP. When they have to. International is a different ballgame. They love those business jets."

Lynche encouraged more information with hand gestures. "Details."

Anna Comstock was more than eager to oblige. "Before you came to us a couple of years ago, three of the four spontaneously traveled overseas. Always chartered a jet." She snapped her fingers. "This was after the ambassador was murdered at the consulate in Benghazi. The three amigos went to Tunisia. I recall it because it was so odd since Director Rothwell was also out of town, and Castaño was out of town. We never have the DCI and the DO out of town at the same time."

"Rothwell took one of our jets or military?"

"Are you kidding? Under President Mazibuike, the Agency received a pair of new Gulfstreams, the *Gulfstream Express*. Maybe you didn't know that 3M authorized the Agency to purchase a couple of jets. He authorized new Gulfstreams for all the cabinet members."

I knew that…. Hunter told me and I didn't want to believe it. Lynche scribbled a note. Comstock continued, "I found out later by accident that the four of them were in the same immediate area. Rothwell was enroute to Germany, I think, but diverted to Italy. Miss Cunningham had been evacuated, and he rushed to be by her side."

"I've heard the story."

"Well, the finance officer was hot again that the three amigos took another jet and never got Rothwell's or Castaño's signature. It normally takes a couple of days to contract for that scale of airlift. Without the approvals, that's a financial violation, but Rothwell dismissed them as 'mission essential.' And I never received their contact disclosure forms. That's a security violation. The rule book doesn't apply to them. At least, not anymore. They're on the *road*." Retired on active duty.

Why are Agency executives from the NCS flying business jets? Am I the only one who sees this is a problem? "Do you know what happened?" Lynche knew only because Hunter told him "the rest of the story" from his perspective.

Comstock answered, "I understand the Ops Center informed Rothwell that Ms. Cunningham had been evacuated from Algeria to an aircraft carrier and was later evacuated to a navy base in Italy. Probably Sigonella, if my Marine Corps memory serves me."

The mention of Nazy being evacuated to Italy was met with indifference, as if Lynche had no previous knowledge of the event. Comstock watched his actions; analyzed them, cataloged them, dismissed them. She said, "I asked, several times. Castaño said, 'SAP,' and that was enough to put a kibosh on any further questions. Apparently, chartering a jet by NCS was mission essential. The Algerian Embassy had been under siege but they went to Tunisia. That's close but I didn't understand. The Navy was able to evacuate the ambassador and the embassy staff, but they were in Tunisia."

Lynche asked, "And they were not part of the embassy evacuation?"

Anna shock her head. "No. Finance went ballistic. $40,000 for the pleasure of flying Hollywood Class; roundtrip. I was unaware of any SAP or mission to that part of Africa, but then the embassy gets overrun, and I naturally thought they knew something in advance and maybe they were racing there to help evacuate the embassy, like we did recently when South Africa started killing white men. But all the bills indicated they went to Tunisia and they did not claim to be involved in any part of any evacuation. I know it's not my place to know everything but the question I had was, so what were you doing there? I guess you can kill any question from an investigator by uttering the three magic letters, SAP."

Lynche asked for more.

"Okay. You may not know this. Sort of old news, before your time. Don't think any of it is relevant. Castaño's inattention to detail led him to be charged with two major security violations. These were after you retired, well before you became the director. He left a briefcase of classified materials on a chartered jet somewhere in the Middle East. Rothwell only gave him a verbal reprimand. Then there was a huge incident at a diplomatic reception in Abu Dhabi. Castaño got into a loud, drunken argument with a Russian official and put his cigar in the middle of the Russian's chest. Again, the Ambassador was furious and kicked him out of the country. Rothwell only slapped him on the wrist—no *derog*. *Like it never even happened.* I received a blank contact form and couldn't matrix anyone at the party."

"Are you saying Rothwell was dirty too? Someone should have caught this. The IG?"

"Sir, Rothwell had problems with pretty girls. He chased them like bull elk in the rut. He had a massive hard on for Miss Cunningham and she volunteered to go to Algeria just to escape his advances. Ever since President Mazibuike disappeared, the IG has been overwhelmed with congressional inquiries to determine how the president's file was leaked to the media and public. And if you look at what has been going on at the FBI with their top brass, you see that they've been out of control too and got caught trying to remove the President with false documents."

"Let's not go there right now."

"Greg, they were able to hide what they were doing under the auspices of special access programs. They are out of control. Who do you go to when the leadership has been completely compromised?"

47

November 8

CIA Headquarters

Anna Comstock continued, "The other three—Fässler, Bomarito, Troxel—have a Chinese menu of security and personnel violations. They have a thing for the foreign ladies, affairs with the cultural attachés at the Peruvian, Colombian, and Ecuadorian Embassies. They've been caught dead to rights in compromising positions with CIA informants. Women. Videos. That kind of stuff. No *derogs* for those either. When I went to see the Inspector General he wouldn't even talk to me. Frankly, I wasn't sure who to talk to. I began to think that if I pressed to hard I would need to fear for my life."

Lynche pinched his lips and asked, "Any contact with Russians?"

Comstock shook her massive head and said, "I'm not aware if any of them have had contacts with Russian or Chinese or their embassies. As for any one-on-one contacts, they're notoriously remiss in submitting accurate contact disclosure forms. That's the only way we would know, unless someone came in and filed an unauthorized contact form against them. That hasn't happened. Their financial disclosure statements, the most recent were done last year, indicate there were no rare Jaguars in garages, no summer homes in the Hamptons, no offshore accounts. But after Aldrich Ames, anyone spying for the Soviet Union or Russia learned their lessons. No one openly meets a Russian handler in Washington. No one flaunts their wealth."

"But we have NCS executives taking Air Branch aircraft all over the country and private jets to the four corners of the globe with no oversight, only Steve Castaño's signature."

The words struck Comstock silent.

Lynche said, "It's not rare Jaguars in garages or summer homes in the Hamptons but it does look like someone is flaunting the government's wealth. In other words, this isn't the typical mole profile. There're pilots. They could be meeting Russians at small airports that don't have control towers, for example. They could hide their wealth through front companies. And they know how to set up a front company. How much money are they sitting on?"

Anna struggled to find her tongue. "I...I really have no idea. A hundred million? They have a SCIF with a bank vault."

"Yeah, when I ran the place we called it the *black vault*. Shrink-wrapped bricks of used twenties, fifties, and hundreds from the U.S. Treasury."

Anna said, "I know it's inventoried every month."

Lynche frowned a bit then added, "Overseas contacts and sources won't touch new bills. Think they're fake. Treasury gets certain serviceable bills that are destined for destruction from the Federal Reserve Banks." Lynche suddenly shuddered.

Anna asked, "But they're not?"

"It's cash removed from the national inventory of money for special projects. They're removed from circulation and become free of government scrutiny. We need to be responsive, have fallback options. Like when we invaded Afghanistan. We needed a ton of money to buy—let's call it 'help'—and it would take weeks for the Fed to separate the good-enough bills from the truly trashed which are shredded or incinerated; they send the good stuff to us. We can use them."

Anna Comstock rubbed her hands together. "I haven't been over there in months. I kind of suspected that was what we did. I didn't know NCS ramrodded that....*sport*."

Sport. What a good word. Lynche asked, "How about drug tests?"

"They're SIS. Exempt based on their position. We are in that category. Just like them. I've one more thing you might want to consider."

"Go."

"Everything I've told you is what I've heard. With the exception of missing travel claims and late authorizations for charter jets, there's not a lot of documents on them." Comstock waved a finger in front of her face for emphasis. "But you need to know, the moment we or the IG tries to interrogate their computers, their BlackBerries, they'll know something is up. They have their cigar-smoking friends in all the right places."

Lynche nodded, almost in defeat.

Anna continued, "They're 40-year guys. Not 30-year guys. They have friends everywhere and everyone wants to be their friend. They're NCS and they don't give out their special challenge coins to just anyone."

Challenge coins, again. He laughed.

"Now, I think I can get the IT dudes to block them, but if it's the wrong IT geek, he might squawk when I'm not looking or when I leave and sound the alarm. These guys are slick. When they want or need something, they hand out boxes of cigars like Santa Claus handing out candy canes at Christmas. A few gals want their challenge coins for their kids; most of the guys just want the cigars. People will do anything for them."

Lynche continued to absorb the woman's observations.

"That might be enough to set them off. Nearly all the guys in the Ops Center have worked for them. They get hurt, get old, and move out of the field and to a desk. My movements in the building at night probably terrify some people. Someone in Ops sees me coming, they'll alert them. And assuming this office isn't bugged, if you are going to make a move on them it'll have to be a secret."

"You can't keep a secret in this place," Lynche lamented.

"Who knew?" Comstock was enjoying the back and forth. She was unprepared for what her boss had to say next.

"I've reason to believe members of NCS broke into Nazy Cunningham's house, and possibly Kelly Horne's home, and planted eavesdropping and surveillance equipment. Furthermore, I believe Castaño is behind it. There were at least four men who attacked Nazy's house, two-by-two, frontal assault, and they employed security and surveillance systems countermeasures consistent with equipment and methods exclusive to NCS. I haven't figured out why or who came up with the idea. And I don't know if Nazy's is in any real danger but...I couldn't take the chance. I dispatched Nazy away.... For the moment she's in hiding."

"*Again?!* Shit, boss!" The night just got interesting. Now she understood the cat and mouse. "How can you be so sure it's them?"

Comstock realized that Director Lynche might not know that Nazy Cunningham had been the target of other surveillance teams and had survived several assassination attempts, mostly from al-Qaeda fanatics. Anna had assigned her a large security detail.

Lynche said he was appreciative of her thoroughness but he already knew of Nazy's after-hours security detail. He shifted topics and told her what he had seen from Nazy's laptop, from her home security system. "I didn't need facial recognitions systems—they wore masks too. I saw the video of them. Classic two-by-two progressive assault. But they underestimated the level of security at Nazy's house and neighborhood, and one of them was caught pulling out the unmistakable shape of a Growler. We haven't shared that technology with the FBI, DIA, or anyone. And of course, as soon as that thing was energized, the recordings of the house's security cameras and thermal sensors' transmissions ceased, just like an EMP bomb went off over

Bethesda. Nothing but blank screens on those recorders thereafter."

Flippantly, Anna Comstock said, "I hear that using that thing will sterilize a bull. Our *ninjas* really attacked Nazy's house? Could it have been a test? Tradecraft training exercise?"

Lynche was emphatic. "Anna, I'm certain they sabotaged part of Maryland's power grid that provides power to her neighborhood. Then they leveraged the power of a Growler to kill any surveillance systems that may have still been operational with an uninterrupted power supply or an emergency generator. They were just a little too cavalier making their approach. If they had energized that thing ten seconds earlier, Nazy wouldn't have had any clue that her house had been attacked, penetrated, and probably bugged by…the CIA."

"They don't know…that we know they killed everything electrical—known or suspected—in the neighborhood and around that house. They don't know that we know they got into her home. We have the advantage in taking them into custody."

"If they are on the property, but they are not; I can almost guarantee it." Anna thought, *Oh my God, this cannot be happening. They'd know how to do it! Jammers. They have everything a spook needs to penetrate a target's home or business or power grid.* She couldn't believe what she was hearing. *Intel officers don't attack other intel officers.* She composed herself enough to say, "Maryland did have an extensive power outage a day…couple of days ago? Out for a couple of hours during the evening. Of course, while you were away. Shit, this is bad. Do we really have that capability?" She looked at the floor and shook her head in disbelief.

"Precision directional jammers powerful enough to interrupt a power transformer? Of course. Anyway, I want to know who they are working for. I cannot believe this is one of Castaño's bright ideas. The FBI doesn't have Growlers, and they wouldn't run him to do something like this without me knowing. There's no conceivable reason or rationale for these actions…." He thought, *Yeah, there's no conceivable reason or rationale for these actions…other than to checkmate Duncan Hunter. Find him, pin him, blackmail him using Nazy as the bait. Then they'd kill him. Just like Duncan expected if they ever found out who he was.* Lynche wasn't happy with himself but didn't have time for self-loathing. "I want you to know formally, neither the president nor I authorized those actions. And that was no test or training run."

She nodded. "Now I understand. What outcome do you want to see?"

"Besides handcuffs and shackles?" Lynche pounded his finger on the desk, deep in thought, trying to answer the woman's question. He scanned his desk for some magic words, a one-time pad with the answer to the ten-million dollar question. *Who's the belly button behind this? Maybe it's just an NCS op; maybe Castaño's just infatuated with Nazy. Rothwell went mad because of her. Maybe, maybe, maybe....* He finally looked up at the huge woman who was speaking.

"...with any of our regular problem children, we usually do one of three things. If you pull their clearance and send them home, they fight the charge. Lawyer up. Go on the national news to claim the Agency is trying to frame them for some minor security breech. Next, they resign in a fit of pique; especially if they're close to retiring. They throw their badges at me, but only after they drop their papers to quit or retire. They destroy their computers or offices if they get the chance. When we get wind of what they're doing, my guys escort them off the facility."

"But not necessarily in that order." Lynche thoughtfully asked, "What about any special software that can remotely lock down computers in their offices, for example, if they were raided by the FBI?"

"We have systems overseas that a user can change passwords, remotely log out workers from a computer and even switch off machine so data couldn't be collected. It's possible they have such a system on their machines. But I have to say that doesn't seem to be their style either."

"We rarely have to march anyone from NCS off the property. It's usually a contractor. Even with all their issues, up until this hour I always saw them as patriots. Wildcats. Patriots with an asinine attitude at times, guys who always smells like an ashtray, guys who drive me and everyone who doesn't smoke cigars a bit crazy now and then for bending the rules, but still guys on our side. Honorable trustworthy patriots. They're NCS."

Lynche said, "Great cover for an enemy." He rubbed his eyes and face, trying to drive away fatigue and the jetlag. He had work to do; sleep would have to wait.

She shrugged. "Lastly, depending on how and when they're notified, if they're not arrested immediately, they run. If they're able, they take as much information as they can carry to be used as a bargaining chip. They can't transmit information from their office computers, so they'll destroy the hard drives so as to prevent us from seeing what they were doing on their computer. They have a disintegrator in their SCIF."

Lynche said, "But if we want to...."

"You're back to the Aldrich Ames model. If we suspect they're moles or spies, then we and the FBI begin an intensive counterintelligence (CI) investigation of each on them to include electronic surveillance. The FBI will open a criminal CI investigation. It's what they do for a living. They'll comb through each one of their trash cans, hack their computers, and if possible, place a tracking device on their cars. When we are trying to catch a spy and don't have anything but a good hunch, they're kept under virtually constant physical surveillance. We even use these great newfangled quiet drones to monitor their movements. Then, normally, something occurs—a deviation from their daily routine. When they alter that routine, the FBI will think one of the subjects under surveillance may have made the tail, that kind of stuff. Then the FBI is forced into a corner. If they're unable to arrest his contact, they just move in and arrest the guy. We get warrants to look at his office and files and home."

Lynche yawned, checked his watch, and then his shoes. He looked up at Comstock and said, "You know, Anna, I used to be the DO. Ran the NCS."

"Yes, sir. I know that."

"I've a hard time believing what I saw. And I know if we try to make a move on them—even just notify the FBI what we suspect—they're going to know—*that fast*—and they'll bugout." Lynche snapped his fingers and balled his fist in frustration. "To the four corners of the globe. They must have a dozen passports with aliases. I certainly did. I had my network. Castaño has his network. And I always had tons of cash on hand. There's lots you can do with a hundred million dollars in cash." Lynche was frustrated and pounded his fist on the desk lightly.

"Why would you have tons of cash at NCS, if I may ask? You said you needed money to buy help?"

"Usually we need to quickly finance non-governmental assistance or buy loyalty and sometimes weapons and vehicles. Maybe we would have to pay for newspaper articles. Sometimes it is to buy silence. Airplanes carrying weapons crash in Central America. Minutes after we were notified of the crash, NCS is gone with tubs of money and buys the silence of the locals to cover our tracks. We didn't want the Russians or the Cubans to know we were supplying arms to their adversaries."

"And you know, it's been in all the newspapers that after September 11th our guys parachuted into Afghanistan, bought horses, and a mounted cavalry. Untraceable worn cash was given to warlords to buy their assistance—in the form of freedom fighters—for fighting the Taliban and al-Qaeda. Sometimes our guys need to be able to finance bogus documents, dossiers, passports, as well as push money to the local media. Some things are time sensitive. You'd be amazed at how much destruction a well-placed $25 article can do to a third-world politician. It's like dropping a bomb on them."

"I had no idea, Greg. In the hands of the wrong guys, they could start their own war."

"Sometimes that was the goal. Finance warlords to fight Angolans, Cubans, and Russians without getting our hands dirty. I'm now wondering if those guys were using NCS contingency funds to buy influence with our own media. *Christ!* That would explain much." He thought, *When I was running the place, I had tens of millions of dollars in contingency funds including hundreds of millions in bogus bearer bonds. Even old gold certificates.*

"Sir, we can try to interdict. Have you been over to their place recently? Serve as a diversion? Put a tracking device on their vehicles while in the parking lot?"

There was that evil thought again. *What am I missing?* Lynche shook his head. "They're trained to check their vehicles. They know what our trackers look like and where we hide them. They're the masters. It's their purview. They have installed dozens on other vehicles. They'd bolt for the Caribbean. No. I don't think we have a winning hand."

"What are you going to do? What do you want me to do?"

"I think we need to see what they did and sanitize Nazy's house, but that isn't the priority. First, I think we need to see where they are. If they're here, then arrest them. If they're off the property, we have to call the FBI. If they're off the facility, you and your guys can make that permanent. Pull their badges, then triage their offices and see what's there and what's missing. Then see what damage they have done. See what kind of pain they can inflict. If we have to pull our covered guys from all across the globe to safety—recall them if we have to—wherever they may be, we'll do that. We need to do that first. They can be vindictive. I don't want to do casualty calls."

"Is that where you want me to start?"

Lynche got up from his chair and walked over to his window. He stared out over the grey leafless trees and found nothing to interrupt his thoughts. He turned around and asked, "Are you familiar with submarines and radars?"

Comstock thought Lynche had lost his mind with the non sequitur. She was confused, but shook her head. He continued. "There's a scene in *The Hunt for Red October* where Captain Marko Ramius, Sean Connery's character, is looking through the periscope when the American submarine transmits a Morse code asking, 'If Ramius is defecting, send a single ping.' Of course, Captain Ramius is looking through the periscope and is astonished. He said to his radarman, 'Give me a ping, Vasily. One ping only, please.'"

"You think a single 'ping' will get them to move?"

"I do. Before we do anything, let's notify our guys overseas to retrograde to safety. One of them will ask Steve and company what happened. We're still dealing with the fallout of that Snowden character. We can say it's related to his disclosures."

"Sir, that is an exceptional 'ping.'"

"We have much to do to get started. I'll notify the duty officer to notify the embassies and chiefs of station."

"Well, I can check my computer to see if they're logged into the building. If they're not, we can assume they're in town; playing cards, maybe even watching the election outcome."

Lynche said, "The president won, if you didn't know."

Comstock broke out into a smile. "I was hoping for that outcome. That's great!" *Halleluiah! Halleluiah!*

"I need their personnel files. Operational history. From day one and their Air America days. Need to see what it was that made them tick; need to see what it was that made them traitorous."

Anna Chapman smiled and nodded. "Files and history I can do in minutes. I'll block them all from entering any of our facilities when you give me the signal. SCIFs. Everything. I'll kill their badges. Then if they're not on-site, I'll try to locate them with *StingRay*."

"*StingRay*?" Anna waited as Lynche called the Operations Center duty officer and spoke with him for several minutes. When he hung up he asked again, "*StingRay*?"

"Cell-site simulator. We can identify and track a cellphone or other cellular device even while that device isn't engaged in a call. It doesn't ring them, it just interrogates the cell phone's signal. We can triangulate its location and pin-point their ass."

"*StingRay* their ass." Malice rumbled in Lynche's voice.

"When the duty officer starts the ball rolling, I'll ping their ass with the *StingRay*. If we get good positional data of their location, I'll have the FBI put out an arrest warrant for them. That will allow me get into position with my guys; I can raid their offices. Get their hard drives. Check their phone records. Open their safes. You'll want the FBI to get into their homes. Home computers."

Lynche grinned. "Girls are so smart."

"Give me ten minutes, sir." Anna Comstock, the former Marine Corps drill sergeant and military policewoman, waltzed out of the office. It was probably "hurry" for her. She shouted over her shoulder as she crossed the entrance boundary, "Also, you'll have to call the FBI Director."

I'm not calling that…communist…unless I absolutely have to. He nodded and promptly forgot about calling the FBI. He had other more pressing concerns. *This can't be happening!* It was very unusual for the DCI to take such steps, but he'd be remiss if he didn't do something. He had seen enough of the evidence to suspend the clearances of the leaders of the NCS without going through the Agency's attorneys. Suspects have rights. Wrongful dismissal. Arrest without evidence could be a huge political and intelligence community blunder. Lynche didn't hesitate. He raised his head to shoo her out of his office, but she was already gone.

All was quiet on the seventh floor. Comstock's footfalls had faded away. A squirrel had been let loose in his cranium. He tapped his foot and his hand.

Lynche spun around in his chair and looked out into the night and thought, *It's time....*

48

November 8
Washington, D.C.

Demetrius Eastwood wandered the ballroom of the JW Marriott waiting for the president-elect to make an appearance. Signs and banners were everywhere, even on the floor. The crowd was intoxicated with excitement that the president would get four more years in the White House. A reveler came up near Eastwood and shouted to no one in particular, "He wasn't supposed to win! He wasn't supposed to win!" Eastwood smiled and nodded as the half-inebriated man stumbled off. *The polls had him losing badly. And now he's the president-elect! What does that say about lefty polls?* Then someone with a megaphone announced, "President Hernandez is ten minutes out."

Eastwood went off in search of a beer. He reflected on the president's background for an article he had been thinking about. *Will President Hernandez indict Tussy?* He checked his BlackBerry for messages since it was so loud he wouldn't be able to hear the ring tones. He barely felt the cell phone vibrate when a message came through.

The text message made him smile. He had received a message from Duncan Hunter, congratulating him that the president had won the election. The night just couldn't get any better. He stood, hands in his pockets, very un-Marine like, and waited for the president to arrive.

Javier Hernandez's rise to Speaker of the House had stunned everyone in Washington D.C., especially the establishment Democrats. They underestimated the good old Spanish-speaking Texas boy who favored black ostrich boots, black alligator belts, and black John Wayne War Wagon cowboy hats from Sheppler's.

He had attended Yale Law School and was a member of the Young Republicans at a time when the Grand Old Party was reviled and most right-leaning students and faculty had transferred to safe conservative bastions such as Texas A&M and Southern Methodist University. The joke on the Connecticut campus was that the last remaining Republican Yale professors had been ushered into an underground bunker for their own safety.

Hernandez clerked for Supreme Court Justice Oliver Marcelli, a legal scholar and "Constitutionalist" who favored hunting deer over defense arguments. Marcelli loved stalking antelope and aoudad in the rough hill country of West Texas near the tiny town of Marfa. Together, judge and clerk chased a few whitetails, Barbary sheep, and an occasional antelope by day, and by night they sipped local craft beers under the Milky Way with their feet propped up on a fire pit and on the lookout for the Marfa lights.

On his first attempt at elected office, Hernandez won the Office of City Prosecutor in San Antonio. His passion was politics, conservative politics. Texas law. Hernandez was featured on the local nightly news as a no-nonsense guy who supported the military, the police, and the U.S. Constitution. He was hard on criminals and illegal aliens, and was profiled on *Texas Monthly*.

Then he won the congressional seat for the 23rd District, a seat that had been in Democratic hands for two generations. He reversed decades of democratic malfeasance at a time when congressional earmarks were *in vogue*. He acquired more manpower, facilities and equipment for the U.S. Border Patrol, the U.S. Customs Service, and the local Laughlin Air Force Base. He was fearless and successful. Several Congressional re-elections later, Hernandez became the first Latino-American Speaker of the U.S. House of Representatives. When President Maxim Mohammad Mazibuike suddenly resigned and the vice president was found dead from an apparent self-inflicted gunshot wound, Congressional Democrats went ballistic as Congressional Republicans formed a protective barrier around Javier Hernandez until the Secret Service arrived *en masse*. Javier Hernandez was hurried to the Supreme Court by a phalanx of U.S. Secret Service Agents, and under the 25th Amendment to the U.S. Constitution, was sworn in as President of the United States of America.

He was a president with his own agenda—he vowed to protect Americans wherever they were and to kill or neutralize budding terrorists before they could become the next Osama bin Laden. Unknown to most of the country, Javier Hernandez had lost his baby sister, a Trans World Airlines flight attendant, when an unknown terrorist attacked a Boeing 747 off the coast of Long Island. The press reported the jumbojet suffered a severe electrical malfunction while Congressional leaders sought remedies to ensure no terrorist could blow another commercial airliner out of the sky with a surface-to-air missile.

As a tribute to his sister, on the day he took the Oath of Office,

President Hernandez vowed he'd take the fight to the terrorists, whoever they were, wherever they were.

•   •   •   •   •

When Secret Service Agents flooded the JW Marriott ballroom, Eastwood knew the president was in the building and would be on stage soon. The ballroom had been loud before; now it was positively pandemonium. In the back of the room, network commentators from every political bent were reporting the results of the election; many looked as if they were about to burst into uncontrollable sobbing. Their favorite old screeching termagant of a candidate had lost to a good ol' boy from Texas. No wonder they were miserable.

He was shoved and nearly fell. When he regained his balance and composure, Eastwood found himself nose-to-nose, chest-to-chest with Viviana Vaslakova. She had been pushed into him, at least that was how it looked to the strangers surrounding the pair. Eastwood maintained his balance while catching her before she was totally knocked off her stilettoes. She apologized as did he. She pushed mounds of hair from her face and said, breathlessly, "I missed you at the Pumpkin Papers Irregulars Dinner. I raced over here before you got away again. I wanted to talk to you and invite you for an interview. I'm Viviana Vaslakova. RTN; Russia Television Network."

Eastwood was so enthralled by the woman's dark and silky voice and natural beauty that he had to force himself to pay attention to her words. He was distracted by her long, thick, black hair which was now swept back over her shoulders. He struggled to keep his eyes from dropping to her bust, which was heaving from her alarming near-fall and was well-covered by a fashionable green turtleneck sweater and a fluffy avocado scarf.

His defenses were down. *The exact time to get pitched.* Beautiful, forty-something women can do that, even to a 70-year-old-man.

He stuck out his hand for a more formal greeting. "Well, *Viviana*.... I've heard of you; you've developed a good reputation. Fair, balanced. Every time I'm flipping through channels, I stop on RTN to see if you're there. Your special on the 4,000-year-old underground Chinese village was a masterpiece. The camera isn't your friend. You are so much better in real life." He wasn't convinced the run-in was unintentional, accidental. Anyone working for the Russian network had to be an agent. That would make her a spy operating in the open. Those are the rules and that's how the game is played.

He gulped air by the gallons. He recalled, *Russia Television Network — that network is run right out of the Kremlin. She has no Russian accent — another graduate of a KGB language school?* He said, "You made quite an entrance at that dinner. And then — bang, you were gone. Everyone's head turned when you came into the room, even the women. I was surprised that the anchor of RTN would even cover that little get together. I regret I didn't get to talk to you."

"You are too kind, *Colonel* Eastwood…thank you." Her voice was melodic. Unique. Sensual. And there was a quality about it that aroused him.

Her beaming smile lit him up, and he struggled not to hyperventilate. He calmed himself by talking. *It's amazing how puerile you can find yourself acting over a girl, even when you're almost twice her age.* "I'm glad to finally meet you. I suppose the U.S. election was significant news, big enough to bring the best reporters from around the world to cover this story?"

She took the professional compliment with a disarming smile and a nod. "Is it not reasonable that the biggest networks, newspaper chains, and wire services saw fit to assign their best reporters to cover the biggest news story of the new century? This night is history-making. We can't get close to the president for an interview, but I think I have the next best thing."

There was that smile again; it made him squishy.

Given the evidence of her skill sets and his sobriety, he grinned. He was soft-spoken, extremely polite, with a very recognizable drawl in his voice. "So, Viviana, you really want an interview?" *Yes sir, the only reason to watch RTN is to see you.* "I might be interested, but I just don't see what you could possibly want from me?" He pointed to the empty lectern. "The only real news for the next week is up there. The president is the winner. I'm old news. Just a journalist now."

Eastwood's antenna was shaking like a palm tree in a hurricane from the vibrations the woman was giving off. And it wasn't all because she wanted an interview. Her voice was European, dark, deep and creamy — too smooth and too perfect for a Russian reporter. He returned to what he knew. *Those Russians.… Was this the opening salvo to being pitched? Why would she want to pitch me — I know nothing anymore!*

She said, "But your television specials are excellent, as are your articles. You are hard on your former president. He was …*loved* by significant numbers of Americans. And your most recent article, I think it may have played a major part in this election. Your readers listen to you. *You have stature.* That makes you an interesting public figure." She punctuated her last words with a smile.

The crowd erupted in applause and whistles and screams. It was now impossible to communicate except through hand and arm signals. Eastwood and Viviana turned to see the president and the first lady and their family slowly making their way to the lectern in the middle of the dais. Eastwood joined in the revelry, clapping loudly and whistling like a bosun's pipe.

Viviana was unmoved by the spectacle. The newly elected president wasn't her target. She watched Eastwood with an amused eye. She slipped her hand into her coat pocket and withdrew the Morgan silver dollar.

Eastwood hung his head for a moment and said a silly little prayer that no one could hear. *O Lord, thank you for your divine intervention and wisdom. Thank you for ensuring that that woman will never be president.* His prayer was over, but he had an addendum to his thoughts. *We dodged a bullet. Maybe the North Koreans can use her voice as an air raid siren. Maybe she can return to the mothership in Russia.*

Among the spinning confetti and falling balloons Eastwood pumped a fist as he stood there grinning like an inebriated old fool at a wet T-shirt contest. He smiled at Viviana; he noticed she wasn't wear a wedding band, and she wasn't applauding, so he nudged her and encouraged her to clap, which she did after returning something to her pocket. She was eager to please him.

President Hernandez thanked nearly everyone in the room. He took some time to tell the audience that he had received a telephone call of concession. The party faithful exploded into a frenzy. Viviana exuded a façade of excitement as she watched the old war hero pinch his lips together; he had become a little emotional. No tears or misty eyes, but he had the look of a man struggling to hide his less-than-manly emotions. Their shoulders touched naturally in the crush of the crowd. She fingered the silver coin and waited for her chance.

The president-elect said, "These are not ordinary political times. This election made it clear that America isn't engaged in politics as usual. We are in the midst of a political war." The throng of supporters roared with every truncated line of his speech. "As you know I didn't seek this office. I was happy as a congressman from Texas, representing my constituents when someone released the file on President Mazibuike. The contents of that file showed that the Democrat Party and their friends in the media conspired not only to elect an ineligible person as president but someone who was the very antithesis of what it is to be an American; a radical, a communist, and a member of the

Islamic Underground. Someone who was on the side of Marx, Stalin, Mao, bin Laden. Some patriot released that file. He resigned and fled the country like the cowardly criminal he was. You chose me to be your president. I am humbled by your support and faith in me."

There was little celebration as President Hernandez spoke. The crowd had been quietly listening to the story of how a congressman woke up one morning and by the time most people were getting to their offices, he had been sworn in as the President of the United States. Few knew what had actually happened behind the scenes and now the American public was getting the rest of the story that had been hidden by a fake media and a vengeful Democrat Party. The men and women in the ballroom erupted in more cheers and applause, whistles and *yahoos!*

"And as we have seen, the Democrats, their friends in the fake media, and holdovers from the Mazibuike administration engaged in a conspiracy to subvert the Constitution and remove a sitting president. My real sin began when Mazibuike's file was released and the Democrats' 'chosen one' was removed from office. Your real sin was preventing Eleanor Tussy from being elected. This was, essentially, a campaign that asked the questions, 'Are we going to allow the corrupt Democrats and this media complex to run and ruin America?' Whose country is this?' You said this is your country, and your country has been on a rocky road to hell with corrupt communist politicians, and you said you weren't going to take another damn minute of it!"

The crowd roared its approval. Some people were delirious. Confetti and balloons fell from the rafters.

"I'm very aware you, by yourselves, cannot do what's necessary to turn this situation around. Please know, I'll be your tool to rectify the wrongs of the former administration. I promise I won't let you down. There's much to do. But the first thing we are going to do is celebrate our victory. Freedom loving Americans are back in charge!"

Men and women screamed; their hands hurt from the continuous clapping, and they weren't close to being done for the evening.

"They tried to steal your jobs and send them overseas and you stopped them. They tried to steal your country and you stopped them. We'll hold those in the Washington media and the Democrat Party accountable. America will never become a socialist country! We are going to drain the swamp."

The throng erupted in cheers and burst out in a chorus of "Drain the swamp! Drain the swamp! Drain the swamp!" The crowd roared for two minutes as the president absorbed the accolades.

"We needed a change, and you took the biggest gamble in the history of elections. I'm humbled by your support, and together we'll accomplish great things. America is the greatest of all nations. With a hostile Democrat Party and corrupt media complex, changes that benefit Americans aren't going to come easy. The Democrat Party has been taken over by radicals and communists and criminals; they'll never give up on their totalitarian ideals; they cannot be allowed to attain power again."

"Meaningful change won't come overnight. There's an entrenched dark state that thinks they're still in charge, and they'll do everything in their power to keep that power. We'll rid our government of these embedded saboteurs and replace them with Americans, with patriots who'll work for the benefit of all Americans, men and women who are dedicated and loyal and unabashedly proud to uphold and defend the Constitution of the United States against...all enemies...*foreign and domestic!*"

The throng of supporters were delirious with joy and pride. Chants of, "*USA! USA! USA!*" shook the ballroom walls as if a small earthquake had rumbled through downtown Washington D.C.

Then the woman from RTN nudged Eastwood and slipped the silver dollar in his suit coat pocket. She took his arm and looked up at him longingly. Eastwood hadn't ignored her; he didn't mind getting bumped by her. He didn't bother to roll his eyes at his own stupidity, he just felt a bit foolish. Again. *Beautiful women can do that to an old guy.*

Viviana was smiling. She shouted over the din and nodded. *Success!* Her voluminous hair went everywhere. "I assume your prayers were answered; the president will remain in the White House."

Eastwood recovered, smiled, and nodded. "The left believed Tussy would save them from the Hernandez revolution. She should have been charged with more felonies than that cigar-smoking Al Capone. The Democrats tried to assassinate him, politically. He promised to drain the swamp of Mazibuike's holdovers." He scrutinized her face. *She probably didn't know who Al Capone was.* Viviana wasn't forty, closer to fifty. She was definitely curvy with a nose that was so perfect Eastwood was convinced she had to have had one of Beverly Hills' finest plastic surgeons on her Christmas card list. He thought, *The interview has begun!* He asked, "So you want to interview me. When do you have in mind?"

"Tonight?"

Eastwood thought he smelled sex in the air, but it was only her *Giorgio.* "Sorry, Viviana, I have a previous engagement." He smiled broadly. She frowned like a petulant six-year-old.

She asked, "Work or...*pleasure?*"

He loved the way she said, "...*pleasure.*" He said, "Work. I'm leaving town immediately after this. I don't know how long I'll be gone. Probably a day or two. Are you staying in town? Can I call you when I return?" He withdrew a business card from a shirt pocket.

She was taken aback for a microsecond. He didn't go for his suit pocket; the coin was safe for the moment.

They exchanged business cards, and he promised to get in touch with her soon. She nestled in close to him which could have been purposeful or incidental since the election mass, the great unwashed, the deplorables who cast aspersions at the Democrat Party were insane with happiness. There was no space in which to move or maneuver; they were witnessing history. She held on to him to prevent a current of people from separating her from him.

Eastwood couldn't get past the media's narrative that, *President Hernandez wasn't supposed to win!* He returned his eyes to meet hers.

Viviana was happy when he looked at her. She hit him with sultry eyes and said, "I thought she was going to win. I believed he didn't have a chance. The polls were.... The DNC Chairman assured the country.... I don't understand."

He put his face into her hair where her ear should be. He said loudly, "First, you can't believe the Democrats. Nearly all the networks and papers in this town are run by left-leaning owners, editors, pollsters, and journalists. Today's American media is really the propaganda wing of the Democrat Party. Tonight every newspaper in the country will parrot what the once world-famous newspapers, papers that no self-respecting fish would be caught wrapped in, the *New York Times* and the *Washington Post* had to say. Not that the American people spoke and gave him the win, but that those Americans who voted for him were sexist, misogynist, homophobes, deviants, deplorables, you name it. Everyone on the right is wrong about everything."

"Every network will report the stunning turnaround of fortune, that he was down double-digits yet won an unexpected number of 'solid blue' or Democrat stronghold states thought to be safely in the vault for his challenger."

Viviana nodded and listened.

"These are the trials and tribulations of a two-party system." *Not like the one-party Russian model,* he thought. "I think they believed the media, their own propaganda, and quit politicking. Hernandez was working and politicking right up to the last minute."

He extricated his face from her hair, her perfume, her space. He could get used to that thoroughly sweet and creamy gourmand fragrance. Eastwood checked the time on his BlackBerry quickly, then stuffed his hands in his pants pockets. He took his eyes off of her, turned and stared right through the people on stage.

Viviana motioned she had something to say, he leaned over so she could speak into his ear. "Will they blame Russia?"

Eastwood narrowed his brows at the interesting question. He shook his head, then into her ear he said, "What could the Russians have done? I think the Democrats ran a bad campaign, she assumed some states would go for her and never visited, but he campaigned there and won them. Then they threw every bogus charge and conspiracy that they could think of, short of an assassination attempt, to remove him from contention and office. In true Nietzschean fashion, what didn't kill him, apparently has only made him stronger."

She nodded as if to say, *You're right. What could Russians do to an American election? What they can do is what they always do; they can foment resentment toward the candidate they do not approve of. Develop and spread lies about one candidate they do not approve of. Create an unfavorable impression in the eyes of the citizens of the candidate they do not approve of. Create and release adverse materials to the media. What Russians…what communists have been doing to democracies for a hundred years.*

Demetrius Eastwood and Viviana Vaslakova listened to the rest of the president's acceptance speech. "…these are the useful idiots that we were warned about decades ago. They hate America. They hate our troops. We have liberated people—the United States of America—our troops and soldiers…. Our armed forces are the only forces in the history of the world that when the population sees our army coming over the hill, they don't run away in fear, they cheer! Why? Because they know that we are there to do away with despots and dictators: the Japanese Empire, the Nationalist Socialist Worker's Party, the Union of Soviet Socialist Republics—all of which were united by force under the treads of tanks and all of which was ultimately defeated by American and allied forces!"

The congregation of Republicans went wild. Eastwood could no longer hear the president. Confetti and balloons continued to fall from the ceiling like a heavy snowstorm. Paper detritus covered their shoulders like multicolored epaulets. He was afraid to look at the Russian woman after his president had just slammed her country. He found his courage and looked at her anyway. She was simply stunning.

Viviana's question rang loudly in another part of his brain. Eastwood's thoughts weren't being driven by the woman at his side or the historical moment of the night, but by a mature and healthy dose of fear. The question wasn't *What could the Russians have done? Isn't a better question, 'What are the Russians going to do now?' Their candidate lost and lost spectacularly! There will be no follow-on friend in the White House like the communist Mazibuike now.*

The frown on his face said it all. *Neither the Left nor the Russians will take this loss laying down. This was her time to win, not to lose. They'll continue to attack Hernandez and throw every phony and scurrilous charge against him — and the media will gladly run any lie as if it's true — if they can find a way, they may even try to change the election results. Accuse him of some heinous crime. Try to negate the election. Somehow they'll try to disqualify him. It's been done before…just not at the presidential level. There'll be impeachment talk before he's even sworn in. The House Minority Leader is screaming that they can't have him serve a full term. This is only the beginning; the opening salvo against a legitimately elected president.*

Another check of his watch and he knew it was time to go. He didn't want to leave the ballroom just as the president was taking his bows, and he was reluctant to leave the lovely Viviana. He bade her goodbye, but she offered to walk out with him.

Like salmon swimming against the current, they strained against the people still trying to enter the ballroom. She took his arm as he tried to lead them out of the room. Side by side passage was impossible, so they dissolved their connection for single file efficiency. He led and held her hand so that they couldn't be separated.

Once they were outside the hotel they came face-to-face with clumps of young men and women in black bandanas carrying red signs. A small band of anarchists were trying to organize a spontaneous demonstration against the election results. It was a slapdash and half-hearted effort since the Washington D.C. Metro Police Department wouldn't allow any large protest to form. Arrests were made quickly. They pushed the wannabe demonstrators away, the rowdy ones were tossed into unmarked paddy wagons.

Eastwood could feel Viviana stiffen when she saw the protestors. He didn't like them either. You can't trust a mob. He knew that in seconds, a reporter could be completely outnumbered, overwhelmed, and beaten, or worse. Female reporters across the globe usually found out the hard way what uncontrollable dynamic they were getting into. Some were raped, some were killed, and all others were physically abused to the point of requiring hospitalization.

The weather was cool for early November. No rain and no wind, but they could definitely see their breath as they chugged along the sidewalk. Eastwood chatted lazily with Viviana, no longer on his arm. She made him forget about the potential of an ambush; no time for *fatwas* when one-half of your brain is in the gutter and the other half has no idea what it's doing. They walked briskly toward his network's D.C. headquarters across from Lafayette Square. Eastwood talked about the election. She talked about Eastwood's letters to the editor, his articles. He didn't realize his most recent articles and letters had been published. Viviana had questions about his charges that the defeated Democratic presidential nominee was guilty of espionage. She asked, "Will she be charged, now that he's the president? That he's been elected?"

He shook his head and muttered to himself, looking over to the brightly illuminated White House and sighed audibly. "I doubt it. Let's just say that 'No good can come from kicking someone when they're down.' Tonight the Democrats in the Congress and in the networks, and let's not forget the DNC, were given a swift kick in the teeth. This election is going to hurt for a long time. Republicans by their nature are afraid of retaliation."

He signaled a taxicab. He opened the door for Viviana and helped her inside as he bid her goodbye. No cheek kiss, which would have been welcome in Europe. Best to keep it professional, but it was going to be difficult. Smiles, a handshake, and a promise to get in touch with each other later.

Once inside his network building, Eastwood took the elevator to the top floor and walked out onto the balcony. Only then was he able to begin to shake the heavenly vision of Viviana Vaslakova from his head. He could still smell her, her scent penetrated his suitcoat. He sobered up and replaced the image of Viviana with Eleanor Tussy. The transition from Red Queen goddess to communist termagant made him shudder. *Tussy! She's the only person in the world who can take a $5,000 designer coat and make it look like a Mao Nehru jacket that's been slept in for a month.*

Eastwood had said in the "correct company," that Tussy's voice made his teeth hurt—it was nothing like the smooth-as-silk voice of the RTN reporter who made his skin tingle and his blood scream wildly through his carotids. Few people were brave enough to mention Tussy's voice—it was high pitched with an intermittent horrible billy goat, rat-a-tat speech tic that was exacerbated whenever she spoke without using a teleprompter. *A-a-a-a-a-nd…. So-o-o-o-o….* Eastwood grinned impishly, shook his head, and then shuddered. *It's a time to celebrate!*

In his office-away-from-his-New York office, he pushed women from his thoughts and reflected on the election. The man of the hour. *The fight for the Oval Office was so intense. Will we have a recount? The president won the electoral vote; she won the popular vote. I'm sure he or his family will be targeted. Lawsuits. Investigations by Democrats. The left was so spun up over this election, it was just crazy. I just hope they're not murderous. I hope the Secret Service is up to the challenge.* He glanced over his shoulder toward McLean. CIA Headquarters. Of course he couldn't see it; he just knew where it was. Then he looked back at the brightly illuminated White House. Behind it, the Washington Monument stood tall in a ring of floodlights and American Flags. Thousands of people were on the mall celebrating. All that was missing was fireworks and the Marine Corps Band.

The Democrats won't take this lying down. I hope I'm wrong. I could write an article. But that would be rubbing salt in their wounds. Maybe this isn't the right time.

Eastwood needed sleep; he yawned and rubbed his eyes. He checked the time and called the network's limousine service. Eastwood couldn't believe Muslim assassins would be up so early but if they were, they'd have a tough time finding him in the back seat surrounded by reflective black opaque windows. When a Lincoln Town Car pulled up to the network's door; Eastwood ran to the limo, and settled in the back seat.

The driver was given the location: The BWI executive terminal. The driver didn't speak and chose not to leave the city via the most direct route, New York Avenue to Highway 50 to I-295. Downtown Washington D.C. was clobbered with celebratory people, protestors, and the flashing lights of hundreds of emergency vehicles.

Eastwood didn't care. He was fast asleep in the back seat and dreamed of the lovely Viviana.

49

November 9
New York City

The drizzle had turned to rain as the temperature hovered just above freezing. It was a crappy night to lose an election. When you win, the weather doesn't matter. Life is wonderful until the next crisis waltzes through the door.

Dr. Nikita Zhavrazhinov couldn't get away from election headquarters fast enough. His candidate threw an ashtray at him and blamed him for her failure. She refused to admit defeat. He knew she was distraught; he had done all he could. It didn't matter he had accomplished a miracle of sorts when she won the popular vote. The loss was especially painful as the president won the Electoral College by a landslide. The popular vote didn't matter. Tussy screamed at him that it should.

The DNC Chairman walked gingerly through throngs of mourners inside the Javits Convention Center, many in utter despair just as the contest was called for President Hernandez. Some wailed uncontrollably at the announcement of concession, as if they had watched in slow motion the family dog being mangled by a car. His candidate and the Democrat Party had been hit by something they hadn't expected or envisioned, and it was a bloodbath. States thought to be firmly for Eleanor Tussy had voted for the incumbent, President Javier Hernandez, and other Republican candidates. The election meant Republicans retained both chambers of Congress and the presidency. Soon the knives would be out for him. Someone always has to take the blame.

For the moment, Zhavrazhinov wasn't worried about losing his life, but others should be. His first response was to blame others. They'd failed spectacularly. As the head of the DNC, he had facilitated a spectacularly great campaign. Tussy just didn't win. He couldn't be blamed. But he knew who could, and a growing fury made him shake.

He had controlled the primaries and the election, and helped elect socialist and communist candidates masquerading as Democrats. The next president would have been a world-class politician, a centrist, a woman. A Communist in Democrat Party clothes, like his protégé, Mazibuike. Zhavrazhinov had controlled the message, the media, everything except the deplorable voters who inexplicably voted for a *Repug*. Nothing made sense. The polls had given her the election before the first polling booth closed. No one could overcome her double-digit lead.

But President Hernandez did. He won, although the outcome wasn't officially called for hours as the media struggled with the shifting paradigm and would not, could not call the race. The Democrats and the media's world had just been upended.

Eleanor Tussy was supposed to win…*easily*, but that reporter…. *That despicable and disgusting reporter, Eastwood*…. He could hear the voices of the Russian president and the leadership of the Democratic National Committee: *How did he win? Hernandez wasn't supposed to win! He must be stopped. Find a way!* Dr. Zhavrazhinov stormed away from the Javits Convention Center.

He could blame others to make himself feel better, but he knew better; failure had never been an option. An incredible amount of funds had been raised and paid to countless politicos and media figures to ensure the DNC's narrative dominated the media, the newspapers and the airways. He never realistically considered that Eleanor Tussy would lose.

That reporter…Eastwood…. He killed her with his article.

He played the last hours of Election Day in his mind. On every major newspaper's editorial page, American voters were informed that the Democrat candidate for president had been caught at and was, in all probability, conducting espionage. She could have been a spy for the Russian Federation and she could have been an apologist for the Islamic Underground. An FBI investigation by low-level functionaries uncovered her treachery, but the FBI leadership completely ignored the evidence. Americans may not have trusted their media or the Federal Bureau of Investigation, but they trusted old Colonel Eastwood to tell them the truth.

Now he has killed us all…. Zhavrazhinov hung his head as he raced across the conference center parking lot. He was recognized and was mobbed by a throng of reporters demanding a comment.

He inhaled deeply to gather his thoughts. His statements came out like bullets fired from a Kalashnikov. "The American people have elected a tyrant. Americans ignored the fact that we starve children to death, that we bomb the houses and buses of children for no reason. The election of President Hernandez ensures tax breaks for billionaires. And

Colonel Eastwood's article was unfair and inaccurate, and was nothing more than a Republican dirty trick. The DNC will use every breath we have to oust this president. We will formally demand a recount in the morning. Good night."

Zhavrazhinov pushed through the crowd and walked as fast as he could up the incline toward his hotel on Times Square. His mind raced with the possibilities and probabilities. Someone at the highest level in the Party would be held accountable. Nikita knew who that was going to be, who would be first in the queue. The brushfire would start with him and work its way up through the Kremlin leaders as a raging inferno. Would he be allowed to live to see the funeral of that Colonel Eastwood? *Would Castaño make it look like an accident or a suicide? Or would he just be shot like the traitorous Tommy Larrabee? An assassination sends a signal!*

• • • • •

Viviana ran from the taxi and into her network offices. After a speedy application of makeup for the television camera, she took her seat behind a clear blue table and waited for the producer's countdown and mark.

"This is the Russia Television Network in Washington D.C., Viviana Vaslakova reporting. Much of America is shocked by the stunning upset win by Javier Hernandez over his challenger, the former U.S. Attorney General, Eleanor Tussy. Republicans in this city are overjoyed that their candidate pulled out a stunning come-from-behind win."

"Democrats across the country are devastated that, although their candidate won the popular vote, she failed to win several crucial states. America has an Electoral College system to select their chief executive, a process that goes back to their founding documents. President Hernandez exceeded the requisite electoral vote count and was declared the winner. Some have called his victory a 'landslide' but the number of actual votes cast indicate it was a very close election."

"The Chairman of the Democratic National Committee, Doctor Nikita Zhavrazhinov, wouldn't take our questions as he left the DNC's election headquarters in New York City but he did make a statement. Dr. Zhavrazhinov laid the blame of Ms. Tussy's defeat at the hands of the war correspondent, Demetrius Eastwood. He said, 'Colonel Eastwood's article was unfair and inaccurate and was nothing more than a Republican dirty trick.' We hope to interview Colonel Eastwood soon. This is Viviana Vaslakova, reporting from Washington, D.C."

The taxi ride to her hotel was made in twenty minutes. In her room, she kicked off her boots and shed her coat as she set up and turned on her laptop computer. A piece of black electrical tape covered the camera lens at the top of the computer frame. She inserted a transmitter for a tiny portable wireless mouse, and after a brief warm-up period, Viviana selected a tracking program which filled the screen. Dory Eastwood was on the move. *Let's see if you are a reporter or an intelligence agent.* Viviana frowned a bit. *His article was obviously problematic. I hope I don't have to kill him.*

She logged in to visit the world's largest on-line auction to find a particular item for sale at an unconscionable price. She selected "Comments from the Seller." When she deciphered the single encrypted line in the Comments box, she was buoyed. Dory Eastwood would live another day. Another man would not.

He'd likely be emotionally crushed and susceptible to suggestions. Viviana crossed her bare legs and punched the numbers into her smartphone. She waited for the line to connect.

•   •   •   •   •

Nikita Zhavrazhinov barely had enough energy to make it to his hotel. He sat on the edge of the bed, in a lump, exhausted and shattered. He hung his head in despair and wept. Zhavrazhinov wanted to escape New York City and the carnage of the evening. He had made his mind up that in the morning, he'd leave the monumental failure of the campaign behind, sneak out of the hotel, and flee to his home in Massachusetts. But he knew that no matter what he did, he couldn't run away from *them. From her.*

And they would find him there. It would be the first place they looked. Losers are creatures of their environment; they do not *fight or flight* but they do lash out, forsake life, and give up.

Zhavrazhinov removed his jacket, tie, and his shoes. He needed a drink. He dispensed with a glass and took a long powerful swig from a bottle of *Tovaritch. Russia's finest vodka.* Much alcohol would be needed to assuage the pain of the string of failures that he had experienced the last few hours. Turning on the television would only reinforce the trauma of losing the election he thought he had won. Left-wing pundits were likely already eviscerating him on national television. He didn't want his failures thrust into his face again. He took another long pull of the *Tovaritch.*

He had a few coherent thoughts. No matter how bad Eleanor Tussy was as a flawed candidate, she wouldn't be held responsible for the election failure. The Eastwood articles may have been a factor but Zhavrazhinov resigned himself to one unmistakable fact, that while there may be others in the orbit of the Democrat Party universe who contributed to Tussy's failure, he'd be the only one held responsible. He put the bottle down before he dropped it. He gulped air by the buckets, he was on the verge of hyperventilating. He strained to compose himself but failed again, and broke down.

Few ever achieved the lofty position or stature of Chairman of the Democratic National Committee without being an elected official. But Dr. Zhavrazhinov had been brilliant; in classrooms and courtrooms, in organizing and campaigning. The DNC saw in him the leadership the Democrat Party needed so desperately to lead them to victory against an onslaught of strong, powerful, and accomplished Republican candidates. He had succeeded in getting an unaccomplished junior U.S. senator elected president, but somehow, someway the Republicans had built a thick file on the man they wouldn't call "President" and disrespectfully mocked him as "3M," as if he were some flimsy red paper product. The evil Republicans exposed Mazibuike as a charlatan, a Communist and a Muslim and a Brit, and chased him from office.

He knew what his future entailed unless he did something to avoid a team of assassins who would hunt him down like a wounded animal and kill him. *She wouldn't do it.* A momentary smile for the first time in hours. He ran fingers though his white bouffant hair and shrieked. *She won't do it.* He wiped tears from his face. He had gotten so close; so close. *That damned Eastwood!*

Nikita had also failed *Him.* The Russian president. *He* had been counting on him, grooming him for the day when he seized control of the American Democrat Party. Medals awaited him in Moscow; but not now.

A sense of urgency had built up in Zhavrazhinov. He felt that he had to leave if he wanted to live, but he could barely move his feet. He felt hopeless. They'd come for him. *She would come for him.* He wouldn't be able to run and hide in America; Zhavrazhinov was too well known. If they didn't find him and she didn't kill him, he'd be recalled to Russia. That outcome was no better. Being recalled to Russia just prolonged the inevitable. Hanging. Firing squad. Gulag. That is, if they allowed him to live. *They may force me to ingest a polonium pellet and have my guts set on fire from the inside.* He wept and wailed and rolled into a ball on the bed. *Her way was the best.*

After several minutes, he sat up. The vodka was working. Again Zhavrazhinov cussed the journalist Eastwood for his untimely article. *He has killed me. He has killed me.* Zhavrazhinov was convinced that that single article had turned Americans away in sufficient numbers from electing what should have been the history-making first woman President of the United States. She would have been able to implement Moscow's secret agenda.

He jumped when his cell phone rang. He ignored it at first, but it continued to buzz and vibrate. He stared at the noise until it stopped. It rang again. Zhavrazhinov recognized the ring tone and sighed like a man defeated. He retrieved his smartphone and looked at the screen: Russia Television Network. Dr. Zhavrazhinov recognized the caller. *It's her.* He nodded for several seconds. He had used her many times over the years. She was one of his best resources for eliminating hard-to-find Russian men who escaped the former Soviet Union and were terrified of being discovered. She had the perfect cover to find and neutralize the most difficult defectors and other undesirables, as well as American reporters.

Maybe she's reporting that she made contact. She was probably calling in her official capacity as Moscow's reporter in America. He had given her a special coin with which to track the detested American reporter. *If she's calling about that, she's very fast.* Zhavrazhinov could give her a few minutes. He wiped his mouth with the back of his sleeve, composed himself, and made the connection.

Her voice was soft yet forceful and encouraging. He brightened immediately and listened intently to her. They'd known each other a very long time. She understood him. She felt for him. The challenges of his work. He began to relax and breathe deeply. For the second time all evening he smiled. Zhavrazhinov found himself being spellbound by the woman's voice and her command of the Russian language. He was comforted by her sympathy and understanding. His eyes flickered, open and closed. He was exhausted and relaxed, completely comfortable by the sound of her voice. After one long inhale, filling his lungs, he exhaled and nodded off.

She had suspected the DNC chairman would be very susceptible to suggestions, and he was. He was distraught, in despair. Probably had some vodka to relax him. He was completely hers. Then she barked, "*SLEEP!*"

Zhavrazhinov's eyes slammed shut. He could still hear that melodic, sing-song voice amplified with every beat of his heart. He was asleep but aware. He couldn't move but he could hear. His chin rested on his chest. Zhavrazhinov became more relaxed with every second. Then he heard, "It's time to escape, Nikita. I'm going to help you escape, Nikita."

After a minute of instructions, Dr. Zhavrazhinov put down his cellphone, opened the door to his room, crossed the eight-foot hallway, and climbed over the guard rail. He leaned over and let go.

After a minute of silence, Viviana Vaslakova disconnected the line and closed her laptop. She was spent but found the energy to turn on the television and check on the networks' coverage of the election and their post-election comments. Anything to divert her attention from the late Dr. Nikita Zhavrazhinov.

The New York City RTN reporter claimed she hadn't been able to get the DNC chairman to make a comment, but another reporter from another network was successful. Cameras panned to heartbroken and bewildered Americans, crying and wailing at Democrat Election Headquarters inside the Javits Convention Center. On every channel on every network, American media figures were in a state of disbelief. When they had come on the air, they had been cocky, now they were in shock. A press of a button and the TV was silenced.

She took her time removing her clothes and lingerie. She wouldn't let the DNC chairman enter her thoughts. She wanted to think of someone else.

Viviana admitted to herself that she hadn't wanted to leave Eastwood. He was very good looking and stirred feelings inside her that she hadn't felt in a very long time. *How long has it been since a man interested me? Too long. But work is work. That's the one thing they have never directed me to do. I never volunteered to do....other men, Russian men are just puerile or slobs, rarely thinkers or doers. Demetrius Eastwood is different in so many ways. I can see why he threatens them.*

She surprised herself with her next thought. Smiling, she stepped into the tub; the shower pressure was full, like a firehose as she shampooed her hair and soaped her breasts and legs with very warm water. She paid particular attention to her toes. *They need polish.... There's never enough time to do them, and there hasn't been anyone interesting enough to motivate me. Now...maybe there is....* When she finished shaving her legs and underarms like an American, she closed her eyes and played with herself, thinking of Eastwood, tickling her, titillating her, and tantalizing her with an experienced tongue. After a long minute, Viviana slammed the water off and stood there gasping for air, legs trembling, nipples erect, skin quickly cooling. She stepped out and sat down on the edge of the tub. She had enjoyed her time with Dory. *Even his voice was sexy, and when was the last time I met a man in journalism whose voice didn't sound like a prepubescent teen?* She toweled herself dry, shut off the lights, slipped into bed, and hoped to dream of Demetrius Eastwood on his back and not Nikita Zhavrazhinov falling twenty-two floors.

50

November 9
Vienna, Virginia

Galvan Fässler placed the huge *Cuban Corona* in an ashtray and waited for Troxel to take a seat before he dealt a hand. Bennett Troxel had just returned from one of Castaño's more lucrative missions. He waved at "the boys" and gave them a "thumbs up." He took his time getting food and a beer before taking his seat. He had already pushed the thoughts of the quick hit from his mind, since he had gotten away easily with no eyewitnesses. He had left no traces of his work, his very last mission. Nothing really to talk about. Hiding a couple of Claymore mines on a sailboat was child's play.

He cut the tip and lit the Dominican *La Gloria Cubana No. 6* that he took from his shirt pocket and glanced at his watch. He puffed on the short, thick cigar like an old Southern Pacific locomotive shooting puffs of smoke out of its stack. A billowing cloud enveloped him for a few seconds. He glanced at Castaño and gave him a wink. *Mission accomplished.* The successful mission put the others around the card table in a better frame of mind.

Troxel asked Fässler how his mission went.

"No one thinks a clown will hurt you. I'm ready for some cards." At a bus stop near the Galleria Mall, Fässler left a Russian defector and his daughter gasping for air after dropping a Coke bottle in a trash container. A tiny vial containing concentrated poison gas had broken inside. He made his getaway by walking into the wind. A hundred steps upwind, he looked back to the bus stop to see the defector and his daughter in death throes, jerking spasmodically, foam oozing from their nose and mouth. Poisoning the defector would stop him from informing the Federal Bureau of Investigation's counterintelligence agents that the DNC Chairman was a deep Russian agent.

Castaño had been on one of his tears ever since leaving the office. He had started making caustic comments and yelling at the television when election results started coming in. He frequently consulted the television as the left-leaning reporters agonized over the poor performance of their candidate. Every minute was another minute in hell for the reporters as well as the NCS division chiefs.

He had been promised the Office of the Director of the Central Intelligence Agency. He had been teased nearly every day that he was going to be the next DCI. Lynche was a political appointee and would be resigning soon; if he didn't resign then President-Elect Tussy would dismiss him "with dispatch."

Castaño asked Troxel if there had been any problems with booby-trapping the CIA Director's sailboat and prized Porsche Turbo with the "whaletail." Troxel shook his head to the first; nodded on the second. "Couldn't get close to that car. It's at the dealer, in the showroom. I couldn't tell if it was on loan or if it was for sale." Castaño's frustration and evil frown was contagious as it bounced around to everyone at the card table.

Jarvis Bomarito ignored Castaño and rolled the big thick *Romero Y Julieta* from one side of his mouth to the other just as the BlackBerry on his hip went off. He ignored it. He was off, playing cards, and he wasn't going to let work interfere with cards. And he wasn't letting election results interfere with his winning either. He was having one of those nights when the cards came his way, and there wasn't anything the others could do about it.

Bomarito couldn't see Castaño as the CIA Director under any circumstance. Not now, not ever. If Castaño had to face a Congressional hearing, Bomarito knew it would be a disaster. He looked up to the television to see the latest returns and then at Castaño. The reporters and pundits could barely function without sobbing on camera, Castaño was about to scream. *He had been so close.*

The networks refused to report President Hernandez had won, hoping for a miracle that wasn't going to materialize. *They'd booed God at the Democratic National Convention; what did they expect?* With every second it became more apparent what the networks were hiding: *He's winning.* Bomarito couldn't say it, but he could think it: *Hernandez is winning and Stevie boy, that means no DCI for you!*

The four men sat at four sides of the six-sided green felt table so they could all watch the election results. They couldn't view each other's cards, and the size of the table was sufficient so no one bumped elbows. Election reporting was preferred over some pornographic channel for this evening only. The results were streaming in.

Steve Castaño smashed his eyes closed; the fresh addition of competing aromas and smokes stung his eyes. He favored a long thin cigarillo, the kind you'd expect to find hanging from the lips of a used car salesman in Tijuana. The game room was so smoke-filled the men could barely make out the images on the wall-mounted television. He placed his cigarillo in a Lucite ashtray made of colorful cigar bands and picked up his cards. He spat tiny pieces of tobacco off to the side when the network finally called the election for President Hernandez. An audible groan from the card table overpowered the stunned silence from the TV. Some reporters cried and some were in shock. *Sometimes your candidate wins, and sometimes life's a bitch.*

The men stopped playing for a moment; Castaño wouldn't be the next DCI. And the realization of that fact was written across their boss' face. They would retire immediately, as they were on a waiver and past their mandatory retirement date, and there was no reason now to stick around. *No more easy million-dollar wet work.*

Castaño furiously threw down his cards in disgust. *No DCI!* They'd planned on quietly celebrating the Democrat candidate's victory and by extension, Castaño's victory over the old man in the seventh-floor corner office.

Troxel asked, "She had been up by double digits—what happened?"

The Great Game had an unexpected winner, just not the horse they were betting on. They'd brought beer and pizza and a new box of cigars, the best of the embargoed Havanas. The four of them had taken a day of personal leave and weren't expected to be in the office the following day after their long night partying. Since there had been no reports about why their candidate for president had crashed and burned, maybe it was time to call it a night. Things would look better in the morning. They could begin their retirement paperwork. Go on terminal leave. Maybe take a jet to Amsterdam one last time. But no one moved, pretending that they were more interested in playing cards than elections, ascensions, and the end of all the lucrative wet work.

Card night at Castaño's was normally an event not to be missed. A five-thousand dollar six-place card table with luxury furnishings, detailed inlays, and intricate carvings on the sides and legs sat in the middle of the dining room. Hundreds of empty cigar boxes mostly made from cheap wood or cardboard and colored in the brown tints of various tobacco leaves were stacked to the ceiling along one wall, an accent wall as if they were a complicated *art nouveau* project, a puzzle. No one would dare to pull a box from the middle for fear of toppling the stack. Framed oversized prints of Cassius Marcellus Coolidge's oil paintings of illegal gambling and poker-playing dogs hung on the walls. *A Friend in Need, Dogs Playing Poker, Poker Game,* and *Pinched with Four Aces.* They were soiled from the residue of thousands of cigars smoked in the room. Lamps made from fancy bourbon glass bottles stuffed with cigar label bands sat on several footlocker-sized Buck Cigar shipping containers. A pair of display cases were filled with old and rare cigar bands. The room was a tribute to exotic and unique cigars.

Persian and throw rugs from across the Far East covered the hardwood floors, souvenirs from markets found outside the remote airports, where *Air America* pilots landed and shopped. A distressed sign of a pair of wings and a shield reading *Air America* hung over the door. The white had turned yellow, the red was a darker shade of mahogany, but the blue was nearly black and the sign was sticky from twenty years of tobacco smoke. Pizza and snacks covered the table in the kitchen; empty beer bottles filled the trashcan. A box of *Fuente Fuente Opus X Lost City Piramides* was open as were others. For those who wanted them, the handcrafted cigars had been brought out to celebrate the election results. Now, their cigars had lost their taste.

The house was a dun-colored two-story with a two-car extended garage. Two-car garages were exceedingly rare in delightful Vienna, Virginia. Vienna was established in 1890, if the welcoming signs were to be believed. Chain Bridge Road, Highway 123, ran through the middle of town and eventually led many to their place of work: CIA headquarters.

Vienna was the town of choice for the upscale senior intelligence officer. In the seventies you could buy real estate in Vienna at a reasonable price. By the year 2000, junior intelligence officers couldn't afford to live close to CIA Headquarters. Homes that sold for $25,000 in 1965 became million-dollar properties thirty years later.

Vienna was also the place where Castaño had been pitched by a raven-haired princess from Turkmenistan, one of the 'Stans' from the former Soviet Union. Her English, with no discernable accent, was the product of the Dzerzhinsky Higher School of the KGB. Men had difficulty keeping their eyes off her chest. She had a wicked thick scar from open heart surgery that ran from the top of her sternum and disappeared deep into her bra.

She had taken her time recruiting him. If she was at the bar when he walked in, she'd move to a private booth. If he was at the bar when she walked in, he'd do the same. She wore a thick vanilla-based perfume that Muslim women favored; he reeked of cigar smoke. At the end of a month, he asked her what she wanted. She didn't want secrets or documents spirited out of the SCIFs at the CIA. No, she wanted some very special men for "wet work," as assassins killing Russians on an as-needed basis. Being one of the few men educated in assassinations and trained in making a death look like an accident or a suicide, he was the perfect specimen. If only he could be pitched and turned. He taught the course at the Farm. He thought she was kidding; he was intrigued. She didn't mind his scars, he didn't mind hers.

During his early days in federal service, Castaño didn't make a lot of money. He made a decent salary as he was promoted to GS-13, 14, 15. Making Senior Intelligence Service had maxed out the pay scale. Remuneration for an hours work eliminating a Soviet defector or a high-level embassy functionary was ten times his annual base pay. Some events, one million dollars. Uncle Sam's retirement program couldn't compete with the gold bullion, or coins, or the woman's body. He refused cash from the Russian—their money was all counterfeit. He preferred Krugerrands until the U.S. Mint began making gold coins again.

For several years he'd wander into the bar, see her, and get assigned a mission later while they wrestled between the sheets. Within a week of any of their meetings, the media would report of a foreign national who had died suddenly of a fall or a previously undiagnosed heart condition or had committed suicide.

Castaño and his men knew how to make it look like someone else was responsible. They knew how to kill at a distance; they learned how to use chemicals to kill someone within a few seconds. Political deaths often occurred across town while he was engaged in a Vienna bar with dozens of witnesses. It was an art to create the perfect alibi. Lethal toxins and gases were tricky to use; the real challenge was how to make them. During just such an experiment in high school, Castaño's concoction had burst into flames and had burned him from his navel to his ears, including his hands.

There were so many spies in the Washington D.C. area; there were so many who took the walk, heard the cries, and stopped working for the Soviet Union. Those that ran, those that defected would be hunted down and made to pay the price of treachery. Sometimes the target would be a reporter, someone who knew too much, someone who received sensitive intelligence from defectors.

With his newfound wealth, Castaño began buying houses in the name of a front company. He looked for the "right" place to call his own. Several places, actually. The place he thought would be perfect for him was owned by another Agency officer. By the time Castaño closed on the custom home, the intelligence officer had retired and left the area for a house on a golf course in Annapolis.

For the first time in his life, Castaño had a real home. It was more than a place to get away from the crazies and craziness at work. A thousand times better than the shacks or hotel rooms he lived in when he worked for Air America. His home was unique in the area in that it had a two-level basement. The entrance to the sub-basement was cleverly hidden. And it had what all intelligence and operations officers desire when the enemies of America find out where they live, an impenetrable safe room. The previous owner had installed a wine cellar and a walk-in humidor.

Trees were everywhere in the neighborhood, oaks and maples and evergreens and lots of grand and impressive crepe myrtles. The number of trees meant that no snipers would have a clear shot into a bedroom or living room window. It was a place to kick back and slam a few Heinekens or sample international beers and IPAs. A place to decompress in the hot tub on the deck without interruption, without anyone realistically discovering him, targeting him, or shooting at him.

Troxel was the daring one and said through the cigar in the corner of his mouth, "I thought she was supposed to win. Polls said it was a lock." His cigar had lost its taste.

Eyes tried not to shift toward Castaño. Everything he had worked for was gone, courtesy of the Electoral College. All he could do now was to drop his retirement papers and clean out his desk.

"She'll never concede. She'll demand a recount. Democrats know how to cheat and stuff ballot boxes; they always win the popular vote," said Fässler. Then, as an afterthought, "There's been nothing on the television. I think the bastards…the country is in shock."

Castaño pushed aside any thought of extracurricular work. He too had lost. He had been thinking only of "taking the oath" of office for the DCI. He changed the subject. He asked Fässler, "Have we heard anything from Cunningham or Horne?"

Fässler had anticipated the request and had checked the surveillance cameras they'd installed. *Still nothing.* He had also anticipated Castaño's reaction to the video and photos of the women in the buff. But with no women in their respective homes, there were no images to display. He replied, "Not yet."

Bomarito asked, "Is it just me, or is it odd that we haven't seen Cunningham and Horne? Knowing Lynche is back and not seeing them in the cafeteria, I'm getting a little paranoid that…."

Castaño snapped at him. "…that what?"

"That our little excursion may have been detected."

No one would second Bomarito's motion. Fässler discarded two cards and said, "Two." Bennett Troxel's attention was glued to the television.

Castaño wrinkled his nose. Not the answers he was looking for. He asked Bomarito, "Did you ever get the results of that DNA test?"

Castaño's Blackberry vibrated and rang an unusual ring tone. Only he understood its significance. He picked it up and read the terse text message, a dozen numbers and letters. His men looked up at him and wondered *Who could be so ballsy as to interrupt their game?*

Jarvis Bomarito rolled his eyes back to his cards and said, "No. Not yet." Then Bomarito's BlackBerry went off and nearly vibrated off the table. He studied his cards and ignored the phone.

In deep thought, Steve Castaño almost slurred his words, as if he were experiencing the beginning of a stroke. He pointed at Bomarito. "Your... Black... Berry... went... offfff."

"I'm not working. We're playing cards." Bomarito didn't look at his boss, who looked like he had been tasered.

Castaño sighed heavily. He was suddenly feeling like a ton of elephant shit had landed on him. He had been distracted because of the election results. He now realized he had committed himself and his guys for several jobs. Dirty work. Dirty wet work. He knew he would target the winner of the election. All that was necessary was to assign hits on the war correspondent, the CIA Director, and the unknown dude *Maverick*. One target for each man.

He was the DNC's insurance policy that would prevent President Hernandez from continuing in office. Castaño felt like John Wilkes Booth entering the Ford Theater, knowing that a quick kill would throw the country into chaos.

After a few blinks, Castaño returned to the present. *I can't conceive that The Judge would want a solution tomorrow. I have time. We have time. I need some time to recover. To think.* He stretched his neck uncontrollably. His face was a nightmare of tics.

Since Bomarito had sniped at him and deferred, Castaño knew he was holding something good. He drew one card, trying to hit an inside straight, but still didn't have a damn thing. "Ping that asshole who told you he'd have results today. It's tonight already. I fold." An agitated Castaño sighed heavily.

Bomarito tossed a few chips in the pile as his BlackBerry went off again. Then Castaño's pager buzzed. A second later Troxel's and Fässler's BlackBerries rang simultaneously. The room was drowning in a sea of competing ring tones from their special Agency-approved encrypted BlackBerries. The men dropped their cards and snatched their communication devices. *Something bad is going down in the Middle East? Egypt was a growing powder keg! Iraq? ISIS again? Maybe another international hijacking of an airliner.* Their devices presaged something was happening in the intelligence community. *That the Ops Center must be trying to get in touch with us.*

A television reporter had interrupted their election coverage to announce that the DNC Chairman, Dr. Nikita Zhavrazhinov, had fallen to his death. Suddenly, all of the BlackBerries and pagers in the room fell silent.

The Judge, dead? The men peeled their eyes away from the television and traded glances around the card table. One by one, they found safe haven checking their BlackBerries. Bomarito didn't ignore the news on *The Judge*. He put his cards down and opened the oldest message he had received and read it aloud. He said, "I got it, Steve. DNA test high probability (99%) Duncan Hunter, deceased USMC pilot. Pilot nickname, *Maverick*. Buried Arlington 28 July 2014. Hunter DNA high probability (99%) link to Agency OpsO Kelly Horne. High probability, daughter. Full report in the attached file." Bomarito raised his BlackBerry as if he had won a trophy. He ignored his other messages. The monkey was off his back now and maybe he could get back to his cards.

A string of text messages came across the ether; BlackBerries rang and vibrated, and then they stopped.

Castaño was unmoved.

Troxel and Fässler couldn't believe the messages they had received. Troxel said, "My buddy in IT just notified me that security killed my badge. I…I…I can't get through security now."

Fässler looked at his screen curiously and said, "Mine too."

Bomarito picked up his smartphone and found the message. He said, "Shit, mine too. What's it mean, Steve?"

Castaño checked his pager. He could tell by the string of zeroes that it was the DCI. *Lynche!* His private office number. He looked at the pager for a dumb second, turned away and stared at the mirrored wall. *I'm not calling him. He knows!!*

The BlackBerry rang again. And again. And again. With emerging fear in his voice, Bomarito shouted, "They might be pinging us with a *StingRay*."

A series of text messages punched through the encryption and firewalls. It was from an anonymous source within the CIA. Five fives in the "From" line. Castaño read, *FBI raiding your office.* He stared at the message. Two seconds passed as the warnings sank in.

Castaño pushed his chair from the table with difficulty, as if his shoes were nailed to the floor. He shouted a whisper, "*The FBI's raiding our office. We have to leave. Now! Out the back!*" He tossed the pager among the chips as the men ripped the batteries from their BlackBerries and threw the pieces into the center of the table with the chips and dollar bills. They ran out of the back of the house, single file. The men thundering out of the house sounded like a toilet flushing on a Russian train. The flurry of activity on the BlackBerries could only mean three things—their activities at Nazy Cunningham's place had been discovered, they were now wanted men, and someone was actively trying to find them.

Lynche knows!!! He's actively looking to locate…us! Before he closed the back door behind him, Castaño armed his home's security system. Afterwards, he snatched an unopened box of *Dunhill Aged Diamantes*, pulled the door closed, and ran across the back yard.

51

November 9, 2016
Washington, D.C.

Anna Comstock burst through the open door with a headful of steam and a handful of flimsies. She handed Lynche several paper copies of emails that had been intercepted real-time. She explained that within seconds of her engaging the help of a senior Agency IT technician to place the NCS quartet's—Castaño, Troxel, Fässler, and Bomarito—BlackBerry text and email accounts under surveillance, there had been an explosion of activity. The IT manager killed the four men's accounts and printed out the most recent correspondence. Anna Comstock was waving them in her hand. Lynche grudgingly took them.

One message was from some unknown functionary within S&T. Greg Lynche sat down in open mouth disbelief at the text message to Jarvis Bomarito, Chief Special Activities Division. He read it and couldn't believe what information was contained on the single sheet of paper. His head was about to explode. He looked at Anna and thought, *How did he get Duncan's name…and DNA?*

Comstock said, "They're not on the facility. *StingRay* located their Blackberries in Vienna. According to his emergency data information, it looks like it's likely Castaño's official residence, where he's supposed to receive his mail, but it could be a dummy. I blocked their badges and I told the duty IT (information technology) tech to shut down their BlackBerries. I was standing right there in his work station. I didn't trust that asshole…and if I find that he warned them.…"

"Someone warned them." Lynche believed he may have underestimated Castaño and his men.

"They can't use them to call or receive messages, but our BlackBerry servers are intercepting anything that's going to those accounts. One problem is they know what we can and cannot do with those BlackBerries even when the battery is removed. Gate security has been ordered to stop anyone and everyone—with the exception of an FBI investigation team. No one from NCS is allowed onto or off of the property. I have to personally clear them, and a security agent will escort them to their offices. The FBI is passing their tickets to our security team in order to enter our compound. I passed their info so FBI counter-intel can arrest them. Sir, have you talked to the FBI Director?"

Lynche shook his head and said, "I'm sure someone in the Ops Center warned them. If it wasn't IT."

"Yes, sir. At the very least."

"They're the least of our worries. And I pinged his ass. Castaño's pager. I should've done this sooner. If we don't get them, it'll be my fault."

Comstock said, "He won't call. And I disagree with you on your assessment about it being your fault. You more than anyone else, know that these guys are the best the National Clandestine Service has, and they're always going to be two or three moves ahead of the terrorists they're hunting. Now we're hunting them. They have been out of control, arrogant, and have taken advantage of their position. Being on the receiving end is something new for them."

Lynche said, "I think you're right." *They got Hunter's DNA, and now they know that Kelly is his daughter. She's in danger too. Maximum danger. Just like Nazy. I didn't see this coming.*

Anna Comstock said, "I also took the liberty of having FBI agents dispatched to your house. I didn't think it was such a good idea to use our security guys—too many connections with NCS. They'll…, uh the FBI…they'll have student agents on their way to your house. I'm not sure what they'll do, but at the very least, there will be an armed security force for your wife."

"Thank you, Anna. Good catch. My cats will run to the basement and hide with Constance. I may never see them again." He sighed heavily as if he had been defeated.

"Am I at liberty to ask who this Duncan Hunter is? I checked. We had him for years as a contractor with a green badge and a Level One Yankee White clearance—which is absolutely nonsense if not unique—and which makes absolutely no sense if he's dead and buried. In 2014 his badge was terminated."

Lynche frowned. "They'll run now. Let me call Connie and tell her what's going on. I want to know what their offices look like. As for Hunter…he's a pilot. Executive SAP. Officially he's dead."

"Officially? But not really? Got it." Anna's eyebrows shot up to her forehead as Lynche pinched the bridge of his nose and his lips and nodded.

She was beginning to see the outline of a very special program running off the books. *Executive SAP? What the hell is that? POTUS and DCI only? No congressional oversight? That could be a problem. And now the leadership of the National Clandestine Service has just been booted off the property? The DCI has been running a deep covert operation with a dead man. On election night! Wow!*

She recovered from the shock of being read-in on a special access program without actually doing the paperwork and said, "Okay Greg, I think they'll be pissed. Can't discount retaliation. But first, yes, they'll run. Are running. Whatever they were up to, you just put the kibosh on it. I need to go meet the FBI and open up their offices and safes. If you haven't already, you need to call the FBI Director and tell him what's going on. And tell him thank you."

What do you mean by retaliation? "I do. I will. Thanks for reminding me." He picked up the telephone receiver and asked, "Anna, what did you mean by retaliation?"

She stopped and turned around. "They're not the type that will just run to a New Zealand mountain or a Mexican beach. You have totally screwed them. They'll try to get even. They'll try to make your life miserable. Bomb your car, your house, your boat. Shoot you and your family. Maybe the cats. Just for starters."

She said it! Bomb your car! The DCI nodded and concurred. "Let me know what you find."

Lynche hesitated before he dialed his wife's number. He sent a message to the White House. Who knew when it would be delivered to the newly elected president? His mind raced with the possibilities. He was worried; he couldn't kill what he couldn't see. *Castaño will fight back. I agree, it would be completely out of character for him to just run away, never to be heard from again. He's an amazingly dangerous man. Not to be trifled with. I knew he coveted this job, but more than that, I kept him away from anything associated with the Wraith program. Not just once, but countless times. Drove him nuts. But that can't be all of it! Duncan was right, but I still don't know what's driving….what was driving Castaño.*

There's more here than just having his professional pride snubbed. He wanted certain info. Now he knows Maverick has a name, and Kelly is his daughter. I see him etching Hunter's name on a bullet. Kelly's too. Nazy also. Lynche breathed heavily as if he had been lifting weights for hours. *Mine? Connie's? Who's going to die tomorrow?* He pounded a pen on a thick file in frustration. *I wonder how long it'll be before Duncan's name is in the Washington Post, or Congress asks me about Duncan. They know too much! This could even derail the president. This is bat guano bad….*

He dialed his home number and as it rang, he realized he had made a tactical error. He scribbled down three names, two letters, and three words. Lynche spoke to his wife in bullets; told her, "Not to worry. Expect FBI agents. Text me when they arrive. I won't be able to answer the phone. I don't know when I'll be able to come home."

Lynche called the two letters on his paper. The Director of the Secret Service. He cursed when the connection went to a voice mail box. Lynche left a voice mail and followed it up with a text message: *Call me!*

52

November 9
Vienna, Virginia

They ran into frigid temperatures with no wind, a very low cloud deck overhead, and high misties; things pilots observe when they move from indoors to the great outdoors. Potential local flying weather is never far from the minds of aviators, even old pilots, and especially so if there was a chance they could be flying. Aviators had their own coded weather-related vocabulary. "CAVU" was the ultimate flying weather—clear with unlimited visibility. If a pilot said there was "high misties," it referred to that intermediate meteorological condition between fog and drizzle.

Castaño settled into the passenger seat of a frigid bakery van and began the process of altering his identity.

Troxel took the driver's seat and had already donned thick glasses and a fake nose. He switched on wipers to intermittently sweep away the heavily moisture-laden air which accumulated on the windshield. He pulled a golfer's hat over his forehead.

Bomarito and Fässler sat in the rear of the panel truck with several weapons stuffed in an oversized dark duffel bag. Troxel backed away from the front of a dark house situated behind Castaño's home. The Dunhill Bakery truck appeared to be on a delivery in the neighborhood.

Steve Castaño had known that he wanted it when he first saw the bakery truck; it was more van than box truck. As the newly installed NCS Director, Castaño had negotiated with the owner of the bakery, a retired CIA analyst, for the infrequent use of the box truck for tradecraft and training work. Sometimes the conservatively marked Dunhill Bakery truck made stops at the White House and the vice president's residence at the National Observatory, delivering sweet breads and pastries for catered events. Sometimes the truck would serve as a decoy, delivering NCS officers-in-training or dispersing intelligence officers in disguise to locations around Washington. When Castaño called to borrow the Dunhill truck, the owner, an older woman who had worked as a Near East analyst, always outfitted the front seat with a heavy pastry box filled with a range of goodies. Her bear claws and cinnamon rolls were oversized with enough calories to add ten pounds to a high school gymnast. Borrowing the truck and finding the hot bakery treasures had been standard operating procedure up until the moment Castaño purchased an identical box truck and had the vehicle painted exactly like the CIA's contracted Dunhill Bakery truck.

Tonight there were no pastries to be found inside, only pistols, assault weapons, and sniper rifles. Night vision goggles and several tubs of hard, very used cash filled the rear of the van. The inside of the van had yet to warm up appreciably, and the men's breath came out as little steam bursts. The heater blew cold air at max capacity. Wipers easily cleared the wet windshield.

Troxel eased out onto Highway 123 and headed directly to Interstate 66. They didn't expect trouble and didn't want to fight their way to the other side of Manassas unless they had to engage law enforcement.

The truck was a rolling armory with three dozen fully-automatic M4s chambered for .223 caliber. There were fifty loaded Magpul banana-shaped magazines. A pair of .50 caliber sniper rifles rested in hard cases. One oversized hard-shell case the size and shape of a chainsaw contained one of the latest products from the Science & Technology Directorate's laboratories, an improved prototype of a long-range sniper rifle.

The Terminator Sniper System wasn't aimed manually but by a very powerful spotting scope with an internal laser designator. A user only had to set the weapon on its electronic-driven plinth; movement of the barrel was synchronized with the movement of the telescope, much like the position of a fighter pilot's helmet was synchronized to control the position of the seeker heads on air-to-air missiles.

Everyone within NCS who knew about the TS2, the Terminator Sniper System, had been waiting for the opportunity to try it out in an operational setting. S&T scientists claimed a bullet from the TS2 could blow through brick walls; enemy snipers were no longer safe outside of two miles.

Castaño asked Troxel to check his disguise. A quick nod and then Troxel was back hawking the rearview mirrors to see if a law enforcement vehicle had slipped in behind them. Castaño pulled a laptop computer from his bag, and within seconds he was viewing a series of camera images in and near the house they'd just abandoned. He swept through all the camera views before announcing that there were still no FBI vehicles rolling into the neighborhood. He was sure it was only a matter of time. With every second it looked more likely they'd make it to the airport before federal agents rolled in on his home. The heater was finally blowing hot air into the truck.

Driver and passenger turned their faces down whenever they approached a bridge or a light pole on the interstate highway. Troxel and Castaño had practiced the "emergency egress" several times over the past two years. They knew the best, most direct route. They knew where the speed, license plate reader, and facial recognition cameras were located. They were very wary of the FBI's and Department of Homeland Security's facial recognition systems which could identify someone even if their face was covered. A classified briefing suggested the program was improving almost daily. DHS and the FBI had come a very long way after September 11, 2001, when every interstate highway on the east and west coast was outfitted with tens of thousands of high resolution cameras all tied into a matrix of the largest and fastest supercomputers ever built.

Facial recognition systems were just a piece of the larger surveillance system matrix, a sub-program called the Concealed Face Recognition Identification System (CFRIS). High-speed cameras and high-speed processors fed an artificial intelligence network that instantly mapped facial points, license plates, and road vehicles. An FBI agent in Quantico, Virginia could "load" the photograph of a suspect, and the computer program would "map" multiple points of that person's face. The program could capture a suspect's history and all of the suspect's movements for the past week. CFRIS could match a face with a vehicle; it could match a face with relatives and people they came in contact with frequently. The AI could estimate age, ethnicity, and gender; it could distinguish who you met, where, and when.

CFRIS was a constantly computing program that compared a photograph's data points and continually matched them within seconds when a face was photographed on the interstate systems. Over the years, the AI system had been expanded and enhanced to network with company security cameras from businesses, department stores, warehouses, convenience stores, and gas stations. CFRIS was initially designed as a means to identify terrorists at ports of entry. But now, the DHS and FBI's artificial intelligence system could find any nearby private camera system and link the additional surveillance cameras into the nation's security system for processing. Software designers ensured CFRIS could pick out professional criminals, terrorists, or anyone in the database, even if they tried to conceal their identity. The program could even predict where a suspect would travel based on traffic patterns. When the system was queried to find a person and the CFRIS recognized a face, the Operations Centers at the FBI and DHS received an alarm. Average intercept time in NYC and Washington D.C. was seven minutes. The system on the East Coast was housed in a football-sized warehouse on the far side of Fort Belvoir, Virginia; on the West Coast, in a warehouse near the former El Toro Marine Corps Air Station.

Scientists at the QAS Laboratory in Texas had developed CFRIS as an outgrowth program for travelling intelligence executives who believed their luggage, belongings, and other personal effects had been disturbed at hotels. Researchers found that a simple AI program "learned" to pick up and identify minute deviations from one set of photographs to another. A "before" photo was taken of the luggage and clothes in a room. When the executive returned to the room, an "after" photo was taken from roughly the same location. The special software was able to locate any items that had been disturbed or "accessed," or discern if a hostile listening device or cameras capable of color and clarity, even in very low-light environments had been installed by spies or housekeeping personnel. It was a simple matter of enhancing the software to capture and measure the data points of faces.

Troxel and Castaño wore hats, thick dark glasses, and scarves over their noses and mouths to foil critical facial data points. Intimate knowledge of the system allowed them to defeat it.

"If the FBI is raiding the office, they'll be at the house soon. It's only a matter of time. They'll be in for a big surprise." The men didn't laugh. When Castaño had armed the house security system, he had also electronically armed a number of anti-personnel mines strategically located in innocuous cigar boxes. Arming his house's security system had also armed a pair of binary weapons, also hidden in cigar boxes. Once given the appropriate electronic signal, two glass vials would shatter and the mixture would explode into a sticky fireball. When activated, the binary explosive would immolate the house and everything inside.

Castaño was counting on the FBI not having a Growler to neutralize the wireless signals on the Claymores and the binaries. He said, "So far there isn't any surveillance. We would have picked it up. We have a great shot of getting to the airport unmolested."

"Who could have found us out?" asked Bomarito.

Castaño said, "Has to be Lynche. I don't know how. But I think somehow, someway they traced us entering Cunningham's house. She hasn't been back to work since Lynche returned, and neither has our little pilot."

"Horne?" asked Fässler.

Castaño said, "Yeah. I didn't think anything of it. She's been the DCI's intern. I'm sure she hasn't returned either."

Troxel offered, "There was nothing, no info on that jet either. The serial number doesn't match with anything on the FAA's master list."

"Our aircraft aren't on that list either. Handshake deal with the Feds likely." Fässler continued, "This had to be a spontaneous decision. What was the catalyst? Cunningham's house?"

Bomarito offered, "That house must have had another layer of security. Hidden sensors." He remembered getting caught up in lengths of old chicken wire. Then he realized there shouldn't have been any chicken wire anywhere near a multimillion dollar home with manicured lawns and gardens. He felt like a fool.

It was apparent that in their zeal to plant cameras to strategically photograph Cunningham in the nude, they had underestimated the house's total security system. Castaño was disgusted with his stupidity, "Probably seismics, low-light TV, thermals…. And, uh, I may not have engaged the Growler in time."

Bomarito interrupted and shouted, "That bitch had chicken wire! Why would she have that much security?"

Troxel said, "She's been targeted by MB, AQ. That's why. That big-assed bitch in Security squirreled her away a couple of years ago on that mountain top…what's that place where they take defectors to debrief them?"

Exasperated, Castaño said, "Spindletop."

Fässler said, "That's right. The ones we never find. What did we leave in the safes?"

"A hundred million, *counterfeit*," said Troxel as he and Castaño again lowered their faces as they approached an overpass. "We still have over a hundred million *used* at the hangar."

Troxel said, "Still no tails."

Castaño said, "Easy with the speed. We'll make it okay."

Fässler said, "Steve, you cannot be happy with this. We've been forced to move. We have to leave the country."

"We have gotten away, otherwise they'd have been on us like stink on shit. We have work to do," Castaño said ominously. He turned his head away at the approaching overpass.

Bomarito spat, "Bullshit Steve. I'm done. We've discussed this. If we were ever uncovered we would head to the four corners of the world. I'm going to a place where there's no extradition and I can buy me a pretty young thing who will screw my brains out."

Suddenly agitated, Fässler demanded, "What do you mean we have work to do? Every law enforcement agency will be on our ass before we know it. Are you friggin' serious? I'm not sticking around either."

There was evil in Castaño's eyes. He wasn't sure what to do. *Zhavrazhinov's dead. The deal is off but it isn't off! All our plans for Lynche's boat and house will be discovered by the FBI. He's the one responsible for this.*

He will pay…. They will all pay. Castaño turned to the back of the van. He assured them that meeting a violent death wasn't one of the tickets he wanted to punch. "We are too good to get caught." He ended his brief with, "We have this one final thing to do. I'd do it myself, but we have multiple targets. We had to wait until the election was over. And once we have eliminated those targets…. The payoff's worth the effort." *Or we might find ourselves on the wrong end of an assassin's bullet.*

Troxel was no longer his usual cheerful self. Getting run out of the CIA had affected him differently than the others. "Steve, you've been right on nearly everything. You've gotten us out of jams that would have ensured we would have seen the inside of a jail for a very long time. Don't think I'm not appreciative. But this time I have to side with the boys. The time to escape the dragnet is when you can. Doubling back to complete unfinished work is a deathtrap. *The Judge* is dead. We're not on the hook for any more work and the paymaster is now a blood stain. If we stick around and try to take out your targets, they'll catch one of us or all of us, and they won't let us live. FBI sniper delivering a taxpayer's relief shot. I can disappear and live like a king in a Bogotá hotel. Dubai. We have enough for all of us to take a plane, and in a matter of minutes, be airborne, over the beach, out of reach. This weather will help us escape."

They had talked about "this day" for more than twenty-five years. No more cover at the CIA. The CIA was their livelihood, but it was more of an operating base than a work place. All of the important decisions came from Castaño. He was the unequivocal leader. And while he was judge, jury, and prosecutor, they knew Castaño received the off-grid missions from an unknown decision maker. They speculated who it could be. They determined the ultimate decision maker was the DNC Chairman. They confronted Castaño who called him *The Judge.* And his favorite cigars were a box of *My Father The Judge.*

The Judge provided the taskers and decided who would live or die. With Castaño pulling strings like a puppeteer, Bomarito, Troxel, and Fässler were willing marionettes.

While Castaño had made them rich, he had failed to see that his men would walk away from the lucrative wet work with the death of *The Judge.* Zhavrazhinov's death changed the dynamic. If they were serious about leaving him, Castaño knew he'd be forced to make a decision he didn't want to make. *The Judge* would have concurred. When men knew too much and were no longer dedicated to the cause….a signal had to be transmitted in a language that was unmistakable.

53

November 9
McLean, Virginia

Greg Lynche's telephone suddenly had two, three, four, five calls waiting. The Agency's Operations Center, the FBI Director, the White House Situation Room, the Secret Service Director, and Duncan Hunter. No National Clandestine Service Director. No Steve Castaño. That one he would definitely not call.

Lynche punched the line for Hunter and barked, "I'll call you in a few" without even giving Hunter a chance to acknowledge. Then he took the FBI Director's call.

They were on first name basis, as everyone at their level in the government was. But the old FBI Director wasn't a fan of the relatively new CIA Director and vice versa. Lynche viewed him as a communist; Vincze viewed Lynche as a defector from the Democrat Party, that he was a "Democrat in name only." They were both registered Democrats, they were of the same age, mid-seventies, and their politics were supposed to be agnostic, but in actuality they were in opposition, Lynche acted more like a Republican than Vincze's Democrat. When they were forced to deal with one another their dealings, outwardly, were strictly professional. The FBI was almost 110 years old and could investigate the younger CIA, and like a younger brother tormented by an older brother or a like a mule in a hailstorm, all the CIA could do was take whatever was thrown at it.

Lynche knew his counterpart at the FBI was on the verge of resigning or being fired for what could only be described as facilitating "Democrat Party dirty tricks." The FBI Director had allowed the FBI to become a weaponized tool against political enemies. Lynche could hear Hunter's opinion on the closet communist FBI Director as he waited for the connection to be made: *He couldn't be trusted any further than my grandmother could throw a Studebaker.*

During the election primaries, newspapers and the networks had slipped and reported that the FBI Director had once voted for the presidential candidate of the Communist Party of the USA. The media suppressed or ignored any further discussion on the topic of a former communist being allowed to remain in office under a Republican president.

He had been fairly equal, professional, and apolitical up until the day when the *Whistleblowers* website published incredibly damaging information on the Democrat Candidate for president. The FBI conducted an investigation. He had called a press conference and laid out the case against the Democrat presidential nominee, Eleanor Tussy. But to the surprise of both political parties, even though there was compelling evidence that she had committed numerous felonies, the least of which was that she had conducted espionage and transmitted hundreds of classified documents to a home computer, FBI Director Vincze refused to prosecute her. The Democrat nominee for president had clearly violated the Espionage Act of 1917. In one article after another she was a labeled a "modern day Alger Hiss." For his failure to act in accordance with the law, FBI Director Vincze was labeled a "modern day Aaron Burr" by conservative media outlets while the rest of the media simply yawned.

For years, the American public had believed the FBI was as apolitical as it was independent. It wasn't true. The secret in the halls of the FBI Headquarters was that the FBI leadership had always been "loose as a goose" with respect to political secrets and rarely took the side of a Republican administration. Then President Mazibuike, a lawyer himself, flooded the halls of FBI headquarters with Democrat partisan attorneys and CIA Directors had to keep their wits about them lest they become the next victim in the political parties' propaganda wars.

The FBI Director was on his way out. Andrew Vincze looked like a Stalin-era Soviet colonel, overweight, crusty, with the bulbous red nose of an old alcoholic. Right wing reporters had uncovered the ugly truth that Vincze and his staff had been caught conspiring with the Democratic National Committee to remove President Hernandez from office using cleverly crafted but bogus documents from foreign intelligence services.

However bad it was going at the FBI, with Ms. Tussy being defeated and President Hernandez being elected, Lynche remained cordial. He expected some pushback from Director Vincze for leaving the interagency coordination work up to the CIA's Security Director. Vincze had a right to be pissed. Lynche hoped to diffuse the personal slight in protocol. He was a bit too friendly as he said, "Hello, Andy. We're having a hell of an evening. I hope yours is somewhat better."

The anticipated animus wasn't there. "Hello, Greg, I guess you have your hands full with some...."

"Yes, sir. Seems the heads of my NCS team have wandered off the plantation and over to the dark side. It goes without saying, we never saw this one coming."

"One rarely does."

Lynche remained professional and brought the FBI Director up to date. "We believe they're on the run. I've barred them from the property. Last known *StingRay* contact was Vienna. Likely Castaño's residence. I understand they frequently have a card night."

"My guys are enroute to Langley, Castaño's place, and your house. I hear you have a sailboat at a yacht club. We'll check it out too. And your vehicles. We're moving on the intel your security director provided. It's a bad evening for this to occur with the election and all."

"It could be very bad. Yes, sir. I know. Thank you for your help. Your counterintelligence team is vital. If they need anything, I'll personally ensure they get it."

"Thanks, Greg. That's helpful, but that's not what I called for."

Lynche was surprised. He spun around in his chair. He had rolled over like a lapdog for nothing? "Oh?"

"We got a bead on those boys."

Now Lynche was confused. *Which boys are we talking about?* He crossed his fingers and said, "That's great—how did you do it so quickly?"

"The Terrorist Screening Center picked up two teams, which I'll refer to as the A Team and the B Team. Team A is in New York and Team B is here. We have positive hits and positive IDs. Your Ops Center has the particulars. The DOE Counterintelligence Field Offices have been notified. This was the break we've been looking for."

Lynche breathed a sigh of relief. *The stolen radiological materials.* "You have hits. Do you know where they are?" *And the big question: Is there an old Nazi bomb in the picture?*

"Roughly. We identified them through CFRIS, the Concealed Face Recognition Identification System. We know where they are to a couple of grid squares. A few city blocks. We have special agents moving to those areas."

"Is this going to interfere with your guys looking for my missing fire team?"

"I understand your security office transferred head-shot photographs of your band of misfits. We'll index them and set CFRIS to find them as well. I take it all data goes to your Ops Center."

"Andy, that will work. Again, thank you for your rapid response."

"No factor."

The FBI Director could be heard sighing heavily, as if he were exhausted. Lynche suspected his days were numbered. He said, "I assume the Containment and Emergency Response Teams have been activated. No indications of a special weapon?" Lynche made reference to the missing ancient Nazi atomic weapon.

"Rolling out of Quantico this very minute. The other team is on their way to the Manassas airport to fly to New York. And nothing on any special weapon. If we get any new intel, I'll let you know immediately."

"Thanks. I could offer up my jet...."

"I think we have it covered. But thank you. I was briefed the last time your place helped with one of these smuggling cases. I understand you had some special purpose aircraft that was able to pick up radioactivity? Maybe it could help us pinpoint the hot material's locations?"

"I may have something that might help, two aircraft, but it would be several hours before they could arrive on site. I've pulled them all out of bed. We need some time to install the detectors."

"At this point, all we can do wait for them. Greg, I think you know what a single grain of polonium 210 did to Alexander Litvinenko. If they get those materials into the water supply millions could die."

"Yeah, I know."

"Okay. Anything else I can do for you?"

Lynche was getting vibes that the G-man was ready to terminate the call, but he had other things he needed to relay. "Andy, if it was anyone else but these four men, I wouldn't ever say what I'm about to say. I don't think they'd sabotage their offices with explosives and binary weapons, there are just too many chances for an accident to occur. However, I'd be cautious to the extreme when you go to their homes. I don't trust them. I'd be very wary of booby-traps. They have had access to some of the finest weapons and CT equipment our labs could produce for the last twenty years. They're NCS. They have been above reproach. Consequentially, there's no telling what they have been able to squirrel away."

"Thanks for that, Greg. I'll pass that along. We'll send in the robots. Evacuate the area. In the meantime I'm certain the White House will be calling you."

"I took your call first. And I need to put a couple things into your agents' hands. They might be very helpful."

"What are they?"

Lynche didn't want to give the FBI the technology. Especially, the FBI Director. He may be executing the duties of his office at the moment, but the CIA Director felt he couldn't trust the FBI Director with knowledge of the device, but Lynche felt he couldn't put FBI special agents at risk when he had the power to protect them. "We call them Growlers—hand-held jammers that can provide a sphere of electronic interference which can kill electronic eavesdropping measures and wireless signals.... They are very powerful and perfect for your field agents."

The FBI Director had heard the technology to shrink the counter-IED devices to a hand-held was ten years away. *Disinformation operation from the CIA.* He shook his head in awe and asked to confirm, "And signals to IEDs?"

The CIA Director said, "Especially signals to IEDs. Yes, sir. Crush them like bugs."

"Yeah, we could use those. I thought they were just rumors. Next generation stuff under development."

"No." Lynche leaked a grin. "DOD troops in the field have vehicle and backpack units. Ours are the size of a donut. Apparently, we can keep some secrets."

"I'm jealous of your S&T labs. Okay. Thank you again."

"I'm afraid it's going to be a long night, Andy. Thank you and good night." Lynche thought, *I just hope the thing doesn't end up in a diplomatic bag headed to Moscow.*

"You know the old Chinese curse—'May you live in interesting times.'" The FBI Director mumbled a laugh like an evil Vincent Price character, and then Vincze was gone.

Lynche took a moment before throwing himself onto his sword and answering the White House Situation Room. *This could quickly spin completely out of control, and then that commie turd will be investigating me. I doubt being a fellow Democrat will carry any weight. Especially on a night like this. I'm sure his girl will be pulling in favors now that she lost the election. Retribution is never a good thing. Can't think about that now. I've calls to make.*

Lynche spoke to an underling in the White House Situation Room. He received a polite but obvious statement, "Director Lynche, the president is very busy."

"I'll call back later if he doesn't call me."

"Sir, you might want to send him a text message. He'll have to look at his BlackBerry sometime tonight. If not him, then the chief of staff or his communication director."

"You guys excited?"

"We didn't think he'd win. We're so delighted that we can't think straight! We are still celebrating!"

Lynche tried the Secret Service Director again. On the second ring,

R O Gates answered. He asked several questions. Paramount was, "Can you find out if two of your agents were stopped by a DHS counterterrorism vehicle near Andrews Air Force Base a couple of days ago?"

"Greg, you know something…."

"It's better said, I suspect something."

"What's that?"

"My complete NCS leadership has wandered off the rails. They're on the run. I think a couple of those turds may have disguised themselves as two of your guys, complete with uniforms and IDs. Maybe even a dummy Crown Vic with a duplicate plate from your fleet."

"Ouch! Okay, I'll see what I can do. We are so friggin' busy, you wouldn't believe. I really can't spare anyone at the moment. I'll get back to you. I gotta go."

Lynche said, "Thanks, R O. I owe you one."

"Thanks, Greg."

Before calling Hunter he called Anna Comstock. "Anna, I need you to get the following guys in here now and set them up for a rigorous polygraph. ASAP." He stabbed the air with a finger for emphasis.

"Ready to copy."

"Duane House and Bob Marsh are NCS. The S&T guy, I think, is Fred Saldanã, a comm expert. All from the Covert Communication Group. Then I want everyone that is or has been on Nazy's security detail. One of those guys talked and told Castaño where Nazy lives. I'll have more specific questions I want asked. You can read them their rights when you're hooking them up to the polygraph. No lawyers. I want them to know this is no time for bullshit. They screw with me and I'll personally put them in orange jumpsuits, send them to GITMO, and throw away the keys! Maybe I'll send them to the Egyptians or the Jordanian Mukhābarāt and the Saudi's secret jails. *I'll make them…*" He caught himself before he let the vulgarities fly. "I'll make them…*disappear!*"

Comstock smiled broadly. She had never seen the Director so fired up. "Got it; will do. Anything else?"

"Not right this moment." Lynche severed the connection and dialed Hunter's number. *What the hell does Duncan want?*

•　　•　　•　　•　　•

The satellite telephone and STU-III caused a minor disconcerting hum over the line. It wasn't enough to stop Hunter from poking at his best friend and boss. "I can't believe you voted for that criminal over our president."

"Oh, shut up." Lynche wouldn't be goaded into politics. He had too much to do. "I didn't have time to vote. He won anyway. Where are you at?"

"Enroute to Quantico. I've picked up Bob and Bob from Memphis— *no Los Reyes*. Bob Jones will help Kelly when she arrives. Smith will go with me to BWI. We'll bring the airplane to Quantico in its container. I assume you'll have a place for us. What's the status of the bad guys?"

Los Reyes? Hunter and his Mexican food. Lynche said, "The Commandant of the Marine Corps is making arrangements for you to use one of their hangars. As for Mrs. Currie's guys, the fibbers have identified them, and they're in town. Here and New York City. We don't think we have much time."

"Meaning we aren't going to be able to wrap the Yo-Yos. We needed a couple of days to print them out and apply the film. Just so you know we'll be flying black birds. Kelly's going to be landing a black bird in the daylight."

"Yes, I know. The day came that we even had to unwrap the SR-71, B-2, and the Stealth Fighter. All good things must come to an end someday."

"Okay, George Harrison, what are we dealing with and what's the plan?"

Lynche told Hunter that the senior leadership at the NCS had disappeared and the FBI was raiding their homes and offices. Hunter uttered one of his more brilliant analysis. "Well, that sucks. You need to find him. Them."

"First things first. When do you think you'll be operational?"

"We have the sensors and mounts. Kelly's aircraft has wiring and can be up and running a few hours after we land. Our number two girl in Baltimore is going to need a little more time. I'll get it to Quantico for the mods. Do we know what we're dealing with yet?"

"One hundred, twenty-gallon barrels of Class 7 are missing."

Hunter believed Class 7 was the DOE's category for radioactive waste. He shouted, *"Tally ho!"*

"The fibber's facial recognition system positively identified the four men who were involved in taking some of the missing materials. They were the drivers, assistants in the last two local cases. Two are in New York, and two are here in the D. C. area."

Hunter frowned. *There's more than that.* Not the answer he was looking for. He wanted more specificity. "So you know where they are?"

"Sort of. The fibbers had tracked them to a city block and then they disappeared."

"I don't suppose that facial recognition system is tapped into the surrounding buildings."

"You're not supposed to know that stuff! Anyway, they're working on it. Maybe by the time you're airborne they'll have better information. Maybe they will get lucky and find them. We need a break."

Hunter understood implicitly. *There's only so much one can do.* "What do the DOE and fibbers think is in the art of the possible? What can these turds really do with this stuff? I don't think we're talking about one of Adolph's missing projects to spread the material, are we?"

"Chatter has always been about contaminating the water supply."

"That's bad enough."

"*Mav*, you have no idea. A single grain of polonium 210 in his tea was sufficient to kill Litvinenko in just a few days. Imagine what would...."

"I got it boss. This is bad juju."

"Call me when you land in Baltimore. I've got my hands full dealing with the fibbers and my guys on the lam. I need to go."

Hunter was left with a severed connection. And no idea what he'd be doing other than flying grid patterns. The situation was similar to another, virtually no-notice radiological emergency that he and Lynche had responded to in the summer of 2003.

That was the time al-Qaeda was aggressively trying to smuggle a large quantity of radioactive Cesium-137 and release it into the air of major cities and deposit it into their drinking water supplies. The FBI, the DEA, the Department of Energy, and the U.S. Border Patrol intelligence agents working the case had expected the materials to be smuggled into the country via one of the drug cartel's tunnels in Nogales, Arizona. The National Reconnaissance Office and the National Security Agency had tracked "the package" from Iran, across the Atlantic, and into Mexico.

The "Feds" didn't interdict the shipment. They allowed the materials to move so they could smash the cartel and send a signal. *America's reach is long, and if you threaten us, we'll find you and crush you.*

Sensor operator Greg Lynche had detected something "hot" at the proposed transfer location in Mexico. Two hours later, the *Wraith's* sensors picked up the load in Nogales, Arizona. Thirty agents from FBI and DEA and Department of Energy took down the houses on both sides of the border and the vehicle with the radioactive load. Lynch had recorded the takedown of the houses on both sides of the border with the forward looking infrared.

That night, the men and women of the law enforcement agencies and the DOE intuitively knew some kind of aircraft was employed to help them but they never saw or heard the *Wraith* even as Hunter flew it directly over their heads.

54

November 9
Baltimore-Washington International Airport

The sun was rising through a fogbank, and in the ever increasing light, the aircraft drew a gaggle of onlookers. Demetrius Eastwood had never seen such an aircraft. It was as if someone had broken an airplane into pieces and then all the pieces were given to a madman or a five-year old-to reassemble while blindfolded. All the major parts seemed to be there, but they were distributed much more radically than he was used to seeing on airplanes. Long wings swept back at a radical compound angle and had been shifted all the way to the rear of the fuselage. The horizontal stabilizer, which was normally found at the rear of the fuselage and under the tail was now bolted to the front, just under the pilot's feet. There wasn't one, but two miniature tails, but who had ever seen an airplane with tails sprouting up from the wingtips? And then who but a juvenile delinquent would think of gluing the engines on top of the wings, then mounting them so unconventionally—they pointed to the rear of the airplane in a "pusher" configuration?

The *Starship* drew a crowd wherever it landed. When it did, the men and women of fixed based operations, executive terminal operators, and maintenance facilities informed everyone who could be interested in the unique airplane to "come take a peek." They appreciated the unique and futuristic lines of the out-of-production business aircraft.

Hunter's *Starship* had some favorable attributes not afforded to standard business or corporate jets. Primarily, the *Starship* wasn't on any of the international *"Tailwatcher's"* lists; no one bothered to add the *Starship* to the "be on the lookout for" aircraft. It had propellers. Since there were so few survivors of the original fleet, no one paid attention to the aircraft except the people at the executive terminals. *Tailwatchers* had a reputation of focusing on the large cabin corporate and business aircraft which provided a steady income for tail watchers with their massive telephoto lenses and ignored superannuated aircraft deserving of a spot in a museum or a boneyard. Hunter counted on the *Starship* to possibly catch the eye of a tail watcher, but they'd likely dismiss it as a relic and not receive a dime if they tried to report on it.

Signature Flight Support, better known around the airport as the executive terminal, was a bustle of activity. It wasn't the reception Duncan Hunter was hoping for. Although it made him look like a cross between a movie star and a fool, Hunter maintained a modicum of anonymity behind dark wraparound sunglasses and a beard made for Moses.

Eastwood thought Hunter looked like he was from central casting, a bearded civil war general or a male model for the Outdoor Channel. All he needed was a plaid flannel shirt, big silver belt buckle, and a shotgun. Hunter wore a ridiculously expensive black Stetson that seemed to be pressed and turned in the right places to accentuate his face and build; it had been tailored for him in a little hat shop in San Antonio. Eastwood shook his head. He was mildly shocked that he still didn't recognize him right away; it was no wonder that he had missed Hunter at the Pumpkin Papers Irregulars Dinner. It finally came to him that Hunter had to have done something additional to alter the look of his face. *Was it the nose? Cheeks?* At his first opportunity, Eastwood would ask, *What makeup do you use?*

Two older gentlemen laden with dark bags and a white cooler stepped from the aircraft. An orange and lime-green, on-field airport taxi pulled alongside of the *Starship*. The driver took his time getting out of the vehicle and opened the rear hatch. Hunter and the older men stashed their bags in the rear of the multi-passenger van. Hunter waved at Eastwood who was standing in front of the Signature Executive Flight Services operations building.

As Eastwood walked to the van, Hunter bounded inside the building and paid for a few maintenance services—fuel and other services necessary to operate large aircraft. High on the list was a secure building area where the aircraft could be hangered for an extended period. A credit card was presented for all services and remained "on file" for "Dante Locke" of QAS, Inc. Quiet Aero Systems, Incorporated, out of Fredericksburg, Texas.

Once Hunter had taken care of his airplane, he hobbled out of the executive terminal as fast as a one-legged man at a track meet could and encouraged Eastwood to join him.

Colonel Eastwood secured his bag in the van and boarded the vehicle. Hunter crawled inside but completely ignored him. The old men were all the way in the back of the van with ball caps over their eyes.

Hunter gave the driver directions then settled in his seat, slipped the Stetson over his face and feigned sleep, as did his partners. Eastwood caught the drift and didn't say anything that the driver could overhear. Neither Eastwood nor the van driver could tear their eyes away from the sleek unusual spectacle that was the Beechcraft *Starship*.

The driver took a service road around the approach end of runway 15R, well past the cargo-configured jumbo jets of Atlas, FedEx, and UPS to the airport cargo processing docks. The drive was made in silence until Hunter woke up from his phony nap and asked the driver to "let us out here."

With arms full of bags, luggage, and the cooler, they walked to a loading dock. One of the men produced a key and unlocked the door of the corner unit. Eastwood saw several other doors with the corporate markings of their businesses. Gold letters, QAS, on a dark red panel. The four men moved inside where there were two identical shipping containers in the cavernous space and a black Hummer H2.

Hunter said to Eastwood, "We're going to need some help—are you up for a little physical labor?"

"Whatever you need." Eastwood was eager and curious—*what are in those boxes?*

Hunter and his wild Forrest Gump hair and beard turned and said to one of the Bobs, "What do you need us to do for you?"

"You two can ensure the lift jacks at the four corners are locked and pinned. I'll get the tractor and trailer from the parking lot. Bob will take the Hummer to Quantico and then, uhhh, we need to get the pins out of the refrigerator." In a flash, the old man raced out the door as fast as an excited, sleep-deprived 80-year-old could run. Hunter motioned to Eastwood to walk with him. Hunter explained how the jacks worked and how to check that they were fastened to the corners of the shipping container. One Bob raised the oversized roll-up garage door and drove the Hummer out of the building.

By the time Hunter and Eastwood had checked the hardware holding the floor jacks to the container and pumped up each corner with a hand pump, Bob Smith had returned. He smiled because, with Marine Corps-like efficiency, Hunter and Eastwood had achieved in getting the shipping container off the floor and level. Hunter smiled at the new big rig with the AeroCab sleeper; the trailer was parked neatly against the bumpers of the shipping dock, and the Kenworth's engine idled like a lazy diesel. Bob reeled out a long steel cable from a winch and attached it to the container. He asked, "Pins?"

Hunter grinned at Eastwood and hobbled over to retrieve the Yeti cooler. As he limped into the Spartan business office space and approached a full sized refrigerator, Hunter asked Eastwood to open the cooler. Hunter extracted four obviously frozen metal cylinders from the freezer, two large and two small. He called them "pins" but they looked like metal cylinders that had been precision turned on a lathe. Duncan placed them gently inside the cooler and covered them with blocks of dry ice. Eastwood strapped the cooler lid as the last few feet of the shipping container was dragged out of the building and onto the trailer.

Hunter told Eastwood to "get in" the tractor cab as he labored in closing the doors of the building and setting the alarm. Bob Smith had walked around the trailer and secured the container to the trailer with safety locking pins. When Hunter finally entered the cab, Bob put the running big rig in gear and they departed the cargo terminal of the airport.

Eastwood occupied a seat in between Bob and Duncan. He was simply bewildered. He asked, "What's that thing in back?"

Hunter yawned and smiled and said, "No need to know, sir."

Eastwood turned to Bob for an answer, but all he received from the grey haired old guy was a smirk. He turned back to Hunter, his eyes questioning everything.

Hunter continued, "I know I owe you some answers about that Qantas jet. When I called you, I felt it was terribly important to maintain the fiction that it just had an electrical malfunction. I felt we needed some time; we didn't want to alert the terrorist group who had been able to *electronically* hijack the jumbo jet."

"We, meaning the CIA." Eastwood asked to be sure.

Hunter nodded and squished his face as if he were in pain. He said, "Catholics in Africa." *Of course. You know that, you big dummy!* He leaned forward so Bob could hear what he had to say. "I'd offered Colonel Eastwood a deal for 'the rest of the story.' He needed to go on national television and pass a fiction—the aircraft that had made an emergency landing in the Philippines with half of its passengers and crew dead had simply experienced a severe electrical malfunction."

Eastwood noted, "And I did that." He had barged into an on-air panel discussion and told the panel that he had just received information from the copilot that the Qantas 747 which had landed in the Philippines had suffered a very severe and complex inflight emergency. It wasn't terrorism. Bad wires or something. The fiction had allowed Hunter to assume the identity of the Qantas copilot, fly to the United Arab Emirates on a Qantas jet, and pursue 3M, the former president, in Dubai.

Hunter said, "I was on a mission and your timely announcement, I'm convinced, took the pressure off of my target to run and hide. He didn't get spooked, I was able to complete that mission, and I thank you very much. But I can't tell you any more of that story. We've been shot at once before—you don't want to become a greater target just because of information."

Eastwood thought about the implied warning and the mechanics leading up to it. He stared at Hunter. *So I'm going to assume you killed the missing President Mazibuike in Dubai. Your mission was to find and assassinate the former president, and you did it. That's just incredible.* He allowed some time to pass before asking, "So where are we going, and what are we doing?"

"We're going to Quantico. We are going to modify what we have in the container...."

"An airplane."

Hunter scowled at him. Bob Smith laughed half-heartedly. Hunter said, "...so we can detect radioactivity. We hope to stop—what we think—is a terrorist group which has been able to commandeer radioactive waste materials. Our best intel is they'll likely dump their radioactive materials in the water supplies of New York City and Washington D.C."

Eastwood was stunned into silence. After several seconds, he asked, "How's that possible?"

Hunter asked, "Do you want the short answer or the long answer?"

"All of it, I guess."

"I think what we'll determine is that the Islamic Underground or al-Qaeda has infiltrated the handling, security, and transportation systems of the radiological hazardous waste stream. At the very least."

"What?"

"It's no different than what they did to American airport security—those terrorist groups infiltrated the airport security companies across the country which led to September 11. Very simply, the government federalized airport security because the bad guys, al-Qaeda and-or the Islamic Underground, were able to infiltrate the contracted airport security providers at the major airports in the country. They were major players who were in on the 9/11 attacks. X-ray screeners allowed weapons to pass through the x-ray machines. And now they've weaseled their way into the contracted radiological disposal business."

Eastwood was flabbergasted. "Sorry. I just never had anyone put those two events together so precisely. Wow. I had no idea; I want to scream *No!* but it's the only thing that makes sense and...you are correct. I don't know what else to say."

"Why do you think the feds federalized airport security? Just so the TSA could molest ten-year-old girls and fondle little old ladies?"

"So, those nineteen hijackers…. They had help?"

"Yes. That was what I just said." Hunter frowned at Eastwood. "You are a real reporter, aren't you?"

Eastwood smiled, nodded, and asked, "How?"

"Mosques are used for purposes other than worship. You know…you even did an article on the subject, *Is Your Neighborhood Mosque a Sleeper Cell?*' The dude that tried to kill you and me—what was it, a couple of years ago—he was out of a mosque in San Antonio."

Eastwood said, "They say that their mosque is *their helmet*, their cover, their staging area."

Hunter continued, "Not all of them, of course, but those that receive…ah, special handling—they should be on the FBI's radar scope. Once upon a time they were. But now they're not. Remember 3M exposed the program and pulled all the FBI surveillance out of those mosques with the anti-American imams. President Hernandez tried to re-institute that policy only to have it derailed by some traitorous holdovers from 3M's reign of terror. Liberal circuit courts are always issuing stays of President Hernandez's orders." Hunter then remembered, "I understand you went to the *Azteca*. You gave Bill a token of your appreciation."

Eastwood smiled at the memories of his visit with McGee in Hondo's *El Restaurante Azteca*. It seemed a lifetime ago. He looked outside as they came to the Wilson Bridge and the newly constructed MGM Grand Hotel at National Harbor. Halfway across the bridge he reminisced, "They make the best *chimichangas*."

"West of the Mississippi. One of these days I'll take you to Memphis for the best *chimichangas* on this side of the Mississippi."

"Memphis?" *The home of BBQ? BB King. Beale Street?*

Bob Smith announced, "Yes, sir. Memphis. Yes, sir."

Hunter laughed and said, "Dory, tell me of your little find."

Eastwood patted the souvenir bullet head in his shirt pocket. When Eastwood first saw it, it was like nothing he had ever seen before. He dug the .70 caliber projectile from his pocket and showed Hunter. He said, "And you can't tell me about this either, I suppose? Missing Boko Haram leaders? Rescued Nigerian girls?"

Hunter smiled broadly. He shook his head and said, "Nope. But you can tell me about how you acquired the DNC's archives."

Eastwood nodded and talked nonstop for the next hour.

"I have an idea what to do with them. Dory, this crap can get you killed in a microminute. Bullfrog says you've been investigating political deaths. Political murders."

"Yes."

"Like who?"

"3M, for starters. I think the CIA killed him." *I think it was you but I don't have any proof, like my spent bullet.*

Hunter repeated the party line. "You know, officially, assassinations aren't in their charter. Executive orders and all that. So, I wouldn't go there; I know there are more bona fide examples."

That sounds exactly what a polished politician would say! Eastwood was convinced Hunter had killed the former president. Hunter couldn't ever admit he had executed Mazibuike. Eastwood decided he'd play along and if Hunter really had assassinated 3M, his secret was safe with him. He asked, "You are talking about the Russians?"

Hunter said, "Seems like somebody is knocking off Russian defectors every week, here and in the U.K. Here and New York City. I don't know why. Who doesn't love those awesome Russian fur hats and trendy Soviet pins on their lapels?"

Eastwood tried to stifle a laugh and failed.

Hunter continued, "Interesting, no Chinese. It's open season on Ruskies but not Chinamen or anyone from the Islamic Underground. All I know is that when the Russians lose one of their most trusted intelligence agents to defection, they would move mountains, as my dear old grandmother would say, to find him and have him returned...."

Eastwood said, "I think they try to kill them."

"You mean wet work?" Hunter sighed and squinted his eyes as if they'd seen something he shouldn't have.

Eastwood nodded.

"I'll leave that alone for the moment. The Russians arrest a U.S. tourist in Moscow on an espionage charge. The American intelligence community knows the citizen isn't a spy and protests. All this time I thought the Russians just wanted their defector back. To punish him. To send a message."

"The way it's supposed to work is that when the FBI catches a Russian intelligence officer engaging in espionage, he's arrested and maybe declared *persona non grata*. The Russians sometimes reciprocate by entrapping and expelling an American intelligence officer with diplomatic immunity. Or there's a spy swap, the Russian intelligence officer for the tourist."

Hunter said, "All chapters in the Great Game. It's been part of a shopworn gambit that dates back to the early days of India and perfected during the Cold War. The citizen learns a valuable lesson and the defector walks into the FBI or CIA and sings. Tell me about this wet work."

Eastwood said, "After several dozen Russian defectors had been killed in Washington and the law enforcement community wouldn't touch those guys, their families contacted me. I started looking into their murders. Then Tommy Larrabee, former DNC staffer, was killed."

"That's how you acquired their archives?"

"Yes. He was their head of opposition research. I never got a chance to meet or speak to him. I don't think the DNC knows I have their files."

"Dory, if they thought you had them, you'd already be a resident of a morgue, on a slab of granite with a toe tag. So what happened?"

Eastwood relayed the story of how Larrabee's mother contacted him and set up a meeting and how the meeting didn't materialize. He relayed information from the police report, that it had been a botched robbery. That Larrabee's wallet and house keys were on his person, but his watch was missing.

Hunter asked what kind of watch Tommy Larrabee once had. Eastwood told him and said that his mother had it engraved to commemorate his law school graduation. Hunter asked about the *Whistleblowers* website. Did they receive anything? Did they leak anything?

"Well, so far, the *Whistleblowers* website hasn't let on that they'd received anything, and they haven't leaked anything either. But they're a cagy bunch. I just knew I was sitting on a time bomb, that it would take someone who knows the tradecraft to see that these archives are used, ah, *appropriately*."

After exiting the interstate, Hunter had Bob pull the big rig off to the side of the road. Two black Chevy Suburbans were also on the side of the road leading to the main gate of Marine Corps Base Quantico. Hunter bid Eastwood goodbye and told him that the limousine ahead was to take him to the Army and Navy Club. Hunter handed him his card key and told him "to enjoy the room." He apologized for terminating their talk. Hunter said he had work to do and that maybe when it was all over, they'd be able to meet someplace for breakfast or lunch before he departed for his home in the west.

Eastwood didn't want to leave; there were so many questions he wanted to ask. He was grateful for what he had received. He could tell Hunter was focused on something else. So it was time to go.

Hunter stepped down from of the truck and when Eastwood's feet hit the dirt, he shook Eastwood's hand. Hunter's hip was killing him. Painkillers would have to wait. Then he tapped his temple with his fingers in an improper informal salute that would have sent a Marine

Corps drill instructor into a spitting screaming rage. Eastwood returned the compliment before he turned and walked away. The driver of one Suburban opened the rear door for him. Seconds later, the black vehicles drove off.

With Hunter grimacing back inside the metallic Turkey red and gold trimmed Kenworth, Bob Smith pulled the tractor-trailer up to the main gate. After Bob and Hunter showed their ID cards to the gate guard, who saluted the retired Marine Corps officer with precision, Bob pulled the truck onto the base. Hunter crawled into the sleeper and found the stash of aspirin in a first aid kit.

Hunter put his head on a pillow and intended to close his eyes for only a minute....

55

November 9
Warrenton

Steve Castaño handed Troxel a white card for the airport gate card-reader. With a beep and an indicator light change from red to green, the airport security gate rolled slowly on a dirty track. Seconds after they drove through the opening, the chain-link gate reversed its direction of travel. There was a light overcast but no ground fog at the airport.

This was the most difficult part of their escape plan, and they knew it. A Dunhill bakery truck had no reason to be on the airport property. When they stopped at one of the small hangar doors, Steve Castaño, Galvan Fässler, Jarvis Bomarito, and Bennett Troxel bailed out of the van and hurried to open the hangar door. Castaño was the lookout. Troxel knew where the trip wire of the booby trap was located and disabled the anti-personnel mine. Once the door had reached its maximum opening, Troxel returned to the driver's seat and drove the van into a corner of the hangar. Then the men pushed two blue and gold-trimmed twin-tailed Cessna Skymasters, one after another, out of the hangar and onto the ramp of the Warrenton-Fauquier Airport. Floodlights at the corners of the T-hangar did a poor job of illuminating the two multi-engine airplanes but it was sufficient for the men to transfer boxes and bags and weapons into the two airplanes.

Steve Castaño lost the argument to stay and fight another day. Bomarito, Fässler, and Troxel had had enough of Castaño's entreaties to complete the new missions; missions that they would never be paid for. Once on the airport property, Castaño quietly capitulated, which struck the three men rather oddly. Their leader wasn't one to take 'no' for an answer, even when he was on his meds. Castaño acted like a defeated man and helped load bags aboard the two Cessnas. Bomarito, Fässler, and Troxel continually encouraged him to leave with them. They were a team. He had nothing else to prove. The only mission they had now was to escape; the sooner they disappeared the better.

Troxel implored him, "Steve, anything you do is a suicide mission. Let those crazy politicians beat themselves up. They're not worth dying for. They'll kill you. Come with us — we're begging you. I'm begging you."

Castaño's head swayed from side to side. He repeated that he had a job to do, that he could do it alone. "And, that's that. Go on. I'll be okay. We've been in worse situations and come out of it smelling like...."

Bomarito tried to put a positive spin on things and interjected, "...money!"

Castaño remembered the intoxicating scent of Nazy Cunningham and countered with, "...cinnamon. Don't worry about me. I'll catch up to you at the rendezvous point."

In minutes, the rear seats and the small cargo holds of the aircraft were full of materials from the hangar. Aircraft batteries were connected. No one checked to see if the aircraft tires were properly inflated. A swift kick to each tire persuaded the pilots that they were "hard enough."

For Bomarito, Fässler, and Troxel there was a sense of urgency to escape. They quickly climbed into the Skymasters. Bomarito would fly solo. As soon as electrical power was applied to their airplane, Fässler said to Troxel over their headsets, "That's not Steve; that's not our Steve. He's scared shitless and not thinking straight."

Bomarito started his airplane. He couldn't help but think the mercurial Castaño was too calm, too cool, and too rational, as if he had overdosed on his meds or was high on meditation or marijuana. His actions weren't real. Maybe they were seeing the first signs of a stroke.

Castaño stepped from the hangar and returned to the ramp as the two Cessna aircraft taxied away. The airplanes quickly took the runway and departed to the south-southeast. Once they were airborne and the takeoff lights were stowed, the airplanes disappeared into the low cloud deck. Castaño stood outside with his hands in his pockets. Although he could no longer see them, he could hear the unmuffled engines and the supersonic shockwaves spinning from the propellers.

At the point where he could no longer hear the Skymasters, Castaño removed a smartphone from his pocket with a snappy motion. He never blinked as he swiped and tapped a few commands on the screen. At the page he selected there were two options: yes or no. He tapped "Yes" and looked up toward the horizon. Seconds later he saw two immense explosions in the distance. Castaño didn't blink and very businesslike, pocketed the device into a shirt pocket. He turned away without expression although a small tic returned to menace his face.

Castaño walked back into the hangar calmly. Among various boxes, barrels, and racks and racks of parts and tools and consumables within the hangar was a reasonably new, 24-foot Air Stream trailer. Castaño remembered how Fässler had expertly parked the trailer against one wall of the hangar, leaving just enough room for a mouse to squeeze by. It could be entered or hooked up easily and driven away without any problems. But the trailer wasn't ever going to be used for over-the-road ventures. He stepped inside.

He walked over to a mirror mounted over a desk. As he stared into it, Castaño's anger began to erupt like a Hawaiian volcano; he berated the mirror, "*You should have stayed with me. No one likes a coward or an ingrate!*"

Castaño opened a large makeup case and began to transform himself into someone even his mother wouldn't have been able to recognize

56

November 9
Marine Corps Base Quantico

Getting the shipping container off of the trailer looked to be more complicated than it was. Bob Smith was an expert with the winch as the container slowly moved until nearly half of the container was hanging over the edge. The cable was taut as the container over-centered and pivoted at its midpoint. Steady pressure on the winch joystick controlled the lowering of the container until one edge was resting on the tarmac. It took about a minute.

Hunter had awakened when the big rig stopped. He dismounted the truck and watched the offloading evolution with arms crossed. He marveled at the old man's command of truck, trailer, winch, and container.

The *Wraith's* container was offloaded beside a decrepit hangar. For a secret operation there were plenty of Marines in uniform, with sidearms, eager to help. Some of the Marine officers were awestruck at first the sight of the black spyplane as it landed on the runway. Now that they were closer to the aircraft at the rear of the building, they could not believe what they were and were not seeing.

The Commandant of the Marine Corps had said the building would be demolished in 24 hours, the CIA Director had promised the CMC that his folks would be out of it well before then.

Modifying the two top secret YO-3As in a location where the level of security was crucial for maintaining the security classification of the program was an utter failure. The CIA's facility "down river" was considered inadequate for the work as it couldn't accommodate the two long-winged YO-3As and the hangar doors of the Marine's obsolete hangar had been removed for demolition, exposing the operation to anyone on the flight line. The only good news was that no one coming from the access road could see inside the old hangar and there were several Agency personnel on scene with non-disclosure agreements to ensure any Marine who saw the secretive aircraft would promise never to divulge what they'd seen.

Under Hunter's guidance and direction, five men and a woman

from Marine Corps Helicopter Squadron One, the squadron responsible for the transportation of the President of the United States, helped to guide the extraordinary black-coated airplane out of the offloaded container and into the adjacent hangar.

The fuselage of the *Wraith* was moved in tail first, as most tail-draggers were. Deep inside the old unilluminated aircraft hangar was the YO-3A that Kelly Horne had flown from Texas. Bright yellow chocks were placed fore and aft of its main landing gear tires. Both airplanes looked more like black shadows, two-dimensional silhouettes, than real aircraft. Such were the visual illusions the aircraft's coating played on the eyes.

Hunter advised the Marines what to do for the next phase. He entered the LED-lit shipping container and the Marines followed. The long nanotube-coated wings gave the Marines pause. They'd never seen anything like the long glider-like wings that did not reflect light. Not only were the wings spooky, they were disorienting. Hunter explained it was the same special coating used to protect the Presidential helicopters against laser-guided surface-to-air missiles, but only in black. Hunter tossed strips of white bedsheet over the wings so the wings would actually look like wings, something the Marines could handle and not be freaked out trying to handle some eerie bottomless black hole with no definition.

The Marines lifted the cloth-covered wings from their cradles as instructed, and carried them out of the container, one at a time. Hunter gave directions to follow him as he and Bob Jones carried the wing cradles into the hangar. Once inside, Hunter placed the cradles where Bob Smith suggested and the two Bobs helped the Marines guide the long glider-like wings into them. Kelly emerged from an office; she waved at her father and yawned from her cross country trip.

Hunter thanked the helpful Marines and pressed a $50 gold piece into each of their palms when he shook their hands. He began to nod as he slyly suggested, "I know you'll forget whatever you saw this morning." Once he received a chorus of "I've no idea what you are talking about, sir" he dismissed them with a smile and a salute made for Hollywood soldiers.

After the Marines departed, he turned and yawned heartily. He rubbed his hip unconsciously and he asked Kelly, "How long have you been here?"

"I landed about an hour ago. Mine should be finished soon. I understand after they install the sensors they need some time for the sealant to set up. We don't want the sensors blowing off at the worst moment."

Bob Smith walked up and said, "Duncan, we should have both aircraft ready before dark." He saw that the two pilots couldn't stop yawning and said, "I think you guys should get some sleep."

Through the open hangar, Hunter said, "And food! I didn't stop at the *Azteca* and pick up a dozen chicken *chimichangas*."

One Bob tried to activate the mercury vapor sodium lamps suspended from the hangar's ceiling but they didn't work. Hunter told Bob that the hangar was being demolished and the electricity was probably cut. He turned and hobbled to the hangar's entrance and whistled at the Marines walking back to their hangar. After a minute of explaining his problem, the Marines retrieved a pair of light units which lit up the interior of the hangar as well as any overhead lighting system.

The men and Kelly stood their ground and stared at the dark shapes of the YO-3A fuselages sitting in the middle of the hangar. The Bobs were always impressed by the black nanotube coating on the YO-3As. Every time they saw the fifty-year-old *Wraith* aircraft coated with the latest in cutting-edge technology, they tried to describe the paint anew. Today Bob Jones used "other-worldly." Bob Smith shook his head and said, "Still inadequate." Kelly wrapped her arms around herself and stayed close to her father.

With Kelly in tow, Hunter walked over to the fuselage of one of the YO-3As. He said, "The black coating on this airplane—it has a trade name, but it escapes me right now—has some properties other than sucking all the light that photons give off. The nanotubes absorb any wavelength of light to include collimated light—laser light." Hunter unholstered the Python under his arm, depressed the switch on the grip for the laser sight to illuminate, and pointed it at the airplane. He put his hand up to show the size and intensity of the red laser dot, then he pivoted the revolver to the fuselage, and the dot disappeared. Hunter pushed the gun until it nearly touched the airframe and still there was no laser light.

Kelly remarked, "That's incredible."

"And as an extra bonus this stuff also contributes to having a very low thermal signature; of course the aircraft's exhaust can be acquired by a heat-seeking missile."

Kelly was confused when Hunter said, "Some people had to be shot down over Algeria to get that message. But the main thing is that it's virtually impossible to acquire with radar or laser-guided weapons. Heat-seekers are always going to be a problem; the shoulder-launched, anti-aircraft missiles are the worst because of the altitude we fly. We can install countermeasures. Flares. When we are flying, we're the hottest thing in the night sky. If we are acquired and hit, there's not enough time to get out and get a parachute inflated. Let me correct that—I got one swing in the chute. I was lucky."

Kelly asked, "Is that because the laser beam scatters and there's nothing for the seeker head to acquire?"

Hunter nodded. "At least that's what we've found in our little trials with lasers. I didn't check to see if this was true for all wavelengths, but if DOD is confident this nanotube coating will completely defeat an LGM, a laser-guided missile, shot at the Marine One helicopters, I'm confident too." Another "something" triggered his mind to consider other missiles, but what other missiles were there? He knew there was something else, another type of laser-guided missile, but it was so obvious that he couldn't come up with it. He was running on sheer adrenaline and needed some sleep to help his brain reset. A ten-minute nap was insufficient.

As the two Bobs worked on the two aircraft, Hunter walked outside with Kelly to watch a Marine helicopter turn up. She surprised him with a question. "Dad, will anything change with the election of President Hernandez?"

Hunter looked at her and said, "Oh, there will be a response. The Democrats hate him. Congressional Democrats have been pushing him to fire Lynche for the 3M leaks. Not because they want justice, but because they're still pissed 3M was removed as POTUS. Now that the Red Queen, Eleanor Tussy, will never be president, they'll be even more livid. They'll scream it's a constitutional crisis or some such BS. It's not a constitutional crisis, but if the Democrats say it is, then the media will go along."

"Then the media-Democrat complex will cry for impeachment, which was their ultimate goal up until the election when they thought that their girl was going to win. But now the Republicans have majorities in both houses of Congress. The Dems will be marching and crying in the streets. They thought they had won but those were the thoughts of the insane. I think that there'll be some kind of political attack on President Hernandez."

Kelly asked, "Like what?"

Hunter shook his head almost imperceptibly and almost whispered, "I've never seen it so bad. I think someone will try to kill him. They have worked themselves up into a frenzy. There was the guy who tried to murder Republicans practicing for a softball game. They're so hostile to the cabinet and their families; they can't even go to a D.C. restaurant for a meal without some partisans or protesters threatening them and their families. Look at how they treated the Supreme Court nominee. I'm surprised that, so far, no one else has gotten hurt. But I'll tell you, they're out-of-their-minds crazy."

Kelly turned her head and rolled her eyes. Hunter stared out over the runway and continued, "It's gotten absolutely crazy and dangerous. Twenty years ago when I was with the Border Patrol, an agent could stop an illegal alien and tell him to get in the back of the truck. He was peaceful. Not a threat. Five years later I had a Border Patrol Agent in my class who said that when he was on patrol, the illegals and the drug smugglers shot at him with automatic weapons. Today's political environment has experienced a similar shift and is absolutely dangerous. We've had crazy Democrats escape the radar net and fly Cessnas into The White House. Someone is always jumping over The White House fence. Every day it's something new. We haven't had, to my knowledge, anyone use a suicide vest in America, but I'm afraid those days are coming. I blame 3M because he let in hundreds of thousands of people who will not assimilate and who hate America."

Hunter filled his lungs and said, "It's obvious someone will be sacrificed for failure. It won't be Eleanor Tussy, it won't be the DNC Chairman, it won't be...." Hunter stopped his soliloquy. After a full minute of silence he said, "The Democrats will not try to destroy their own, at least not immediately; they'll declare war on the president and try to force him to quit. They tried to kill him politically after 3M abdicated the Oval Office. Starting today, they'll say he stole the election—she won the popular vote—and the media will have it on the air, twenty-four, seven, crap like that. Or they'll make it so difficult for him to govern, he'll be rendered ineffective. To them it was never a matter that he shouldn't have won but that he should never have been president. The media and the ruling class in Washington picks the president, not truck-driving rubes from middle America."

Kelly said, "Won't they seek other ways to…damage him? There's a difference between the crazies in every party and those in elected leadership positions trying to do harm."

Hunter nodded his agreement, *in theory*. He asked, "Which is what they're trying to do. Where did that come from, Kelly? You've been bouncing that around in your head for a while? I'm programmed to think a certain way, and sometimes I don't see too clearly. Where did that come from?"

Kelly said, "The previous CIA Director, before Director Lynche,…ah, Dr. Rothwell, said during an assembly in the Agency's auditorium that one of the priorities he received from the president was that he was to help boost CIA recruitment efforts in Arab and Muslim communities."

Hunter closed his eyes to purge the thought of a CIA Director boosting CIA recruitment efforts in Arab and Muslim communities, an open door for al-Qaeda and the Islamic Underground to infiltrate the intelligence community. He was aware of 3M's policy. *Too bad they couldn't pass the polygraph!* Hunter said, "I talked to Colonel Eastwood on the way down here. Same subject. He said, 'Since President Mazibuike disappeared there has been more stuff come out. Some people may not know his administration officially extended a welcome to the Islamic Underground at the White House. Their star was rising and they became a partner in the Mazibuike White House. The crown jewel of Islamic Underground influence was the fall of the Egyptian president during the 'Arab Spring.'"

Hunter added, "I'll say I was surprised the Egyptian president wasn't assassinated—he must have had too much protection. I recall it wasn't reported until after the fact that 3M's White House fully supported the Egyptian Islamic Underground candidate for president. 3M threw our ally under the bus, as they say. But with Hernandez in office, the Islamic Underground wasn't wanted and immediately fell out of favor. The Egyptians didn't want any part of the Islamic Underground either. Their military staged a coup and now the Islamic Underground-backed former Egyptian president is out of office and in jail. It's all old news, now."

The Bobs had moved to modify another set of wings. Kelly said, "I suppose that's the essence of presidential power politics. Not for the timid."

Hunter said, "Unless they're trying to kill you and your family."

Kelly nodded. She wondered what other new revelations she'd learn.

Hunter said, "My conversation with Eastwood was enlightening. You know Attorney General Tussy's right-hand woman… uh…Amal Torabinejad and her family have strong ties to the Islamic Underground; her family has always promoted a hardline Islamic ideology. We know she edited a radical Muslim publication that blamed the U.S. for September 11, 2001. Her father outlined his Islamic Underground view of sharia law, and how it's the Western world that has turned Muslims 'hostile.'"

Kelly was nearly floored. "Are you serious, or is that some right-wing conspiracy theory?"

He wagged his finger at her. "This is really 'need to know' material. You can check it out on Al Gore's amazing internet."

Kelly frowned and nodded.

There was quiet for a substantially long time as Hunter and Kelly pondered the insider information. Hunter said, "I suppose President Hernandez's election means the Islamic Underground will also be pissed. Eleanor can scream and throw ashtrays at her husband all she wants, but the bottom line is 3M vacated the Oval Office, and President Hernandez has stopped whatever infiltration momentum the Islamic Underground had or thought they had."

He continued, "It may not have been a good idea to tell you everything, my darling daughter. The left is crazy. They want to find and crucify the person who released 3M's file." Hunter chuckled to himself and thought, *And they'd go batshit crazy if they knew that the same person who released 3M's file also has the DNC's archives.* He sighed, *I'm not sure what to do with them yet.*

"Dad, I just wanted you to know that I'm quite aware of the history of the Mazibuike administration, that it's rife with connections to or with the Islamic Underground and the preferential hiring of Muslims 'for the top jobs.' Nazy has been a remarkable teacher. They pushed an infiltration agenda. There have been some other leaked documents stating that sensitive and top-level government positions in the U.S. and British governments were to be filled by Muslims. Would these people have unquestionable loyalties to the United States? Britain? I don't think so."

Hunter couldn't find the words to express his admiration for his daughter.

Kelly said, "I could see that the election of Miss Tussy was to be the third and fourth term of President Mazibuike, as he and his minions worked tirelessly to fulfill the dictates of the Islamic Underground's strategic plan to infiltrate the American government. What's more 'fundamentally transforming' for the United States than an open door policy for the unfettered immigration of uneducated and dissatisfied Muslims, or the infiltration of radical Muslim extremists in the government? One look at what's happening to France is a look into our own future."

She's really becoming a chip off the old block. He finished, "If it hasn't already been done, I think we'll see President Hernandez reversing Mazibuike's policy of removing the FBI's surveillance on mosques. I'm sure he will reverse all of 3M's strategic work to 'transform the United States of America' through 'Muslim outreach' or 'Islamic engagement' programs, as well as to announce the public eradication of the Islamic Underground's strategy of phased infiltration of Muslims into government. I know our CIA Director announced that the Islamic

Underground is a terrorist organization. Everyone at the three letters and the State Department has to get new expanded polygraphs. The roaches are leaving in droves."

Kelly offered, "You have to admit you have a problem before you can begin to fix it."

Hunter yawned and said meekly, "How'd we get on the topic of politics? Did I start that ball rolling? I'm so sorry."

Kelly smiled and concurred. "Nothing to be sorry for. That was great."

Hunter said, "We should have had McGee here. He has some strong opinions on 3M. He's glad that man is gone, too."

"You have more, don't you?"

Hunter nodded with a sizeable grin. "We haven't talked about the Russian connection."

"Russians too, huh?" Kelly knew there was more. Something was eating at her. She finally pulled all the loose ends together and asked, "To change the subject only very slightly, do you have any idea who could have released 3M's file?"

Tactfully avoiding an answer, Hunter glanced at his Rolex and said with a yawn, "I think it's time to get some shuteye."

Kelly frowned and was stunned at the turn of events. She was beginning to see her father in a different light. *My father, Maverick, can seemingly do anything, no matter the difficulty. He virtually rescued those men in Syria…singlehandedly, He's been flying missions with a gun for years. Targeting terrorists.* The topic of *who released 3M's file* crept inside her head. She thought, *Could it have been…..? Nahhhhhh.*

57

November 9
Texarkana, Arkansas

As the sun broke over the Texarkana Regional Airport, a dark and odd shape appeared in the distance. Bill McGee shielded his eyes from the yellow dwarf star that sustained life on Earth. Nazy Cunningham had also turned her head away from the brilliant new rays of sunshine climbing over the hills and racing to all points west. In minutes, custody of the National Counter Terrorism Center Director would be transferred from the retired sailor in the Hummer H2 to the active duty Marines in the shiny dark green MV-22 *Osprey* from Marine Corps Base Quantico. Nazy said her goodbyes to McGee with a gentle hug and several thank yous. He didn't say anything but smiled, and with an informal salute he waved her away. Then he turned and walked back to the Hummer. McGee would get a room at the Red River Army depot and sleep.

The CIA Director had changed the pieces on the board again, dispatching a fast rotorcraft to bring the trusted NCTC Director back to Headquarters as quickly as possible. The White House Military Office, Airlift Operations, expedited his request. They called the Marines. The Presidential Helicopter Squadron had been on standby in Anacostia to provide lift support. None of the Marine aircrew imagined they'd be racing cross country to retrieve an intelligence officer of the CIA.

With new intelligence, Lynche needed specialized help and he needed it fast. Nazy was uniquely qualified for the new task. She was needed. She had work to do.

She was given a headset and was escorted aboard the aircraft as if she held a Level 1 Yankee White clearance, which she did. Nazy was one of a handful of White House staff members who work directly for or had direct contact with the president or the vice president. As she took a seat and buckled in, she felt severely underdressed in her jeans, shirt, and boots. She wasn't dressed in the uniform to give the President's Daily Brief, but it was sufficient in which to travel *military air*. The aircrew took notice that she wore an old, rugged, brown G-1 Navy flight jacket with a patch with the embossed wings of gold of the Naval Aviator. *She looked more like a model than any Maverick.*

Her previous rides in government aircraft had been for official business, and at a minimum she had worn business attire. In jeans and a shirt she felt more than a little out of place. And she felt cold, even bundled up in Duncan's flight jacket. She felt safe with these Marines. Nazy patted her pocket to ensure the Kimber .45 caliber pistol was in an inner pocket where it was supposed to be.

The aircraft lifted off like a helicopter, and within a minute, the Rolls-Royce Allison engines and rotors began their synchronized tilting action until the propeller-engine combination rotated 90°, effectively turning the helicopter into an airplane. The pilot accelerated the aircraft to 275 knots, and the *Osprey* performed like any nimble twin-engine aircraft, its engines delivering power to the propeller's gearboxes. The order had been to expedite the NCTC Director to CIA Headquarters. The pilots pushed the *Osprey* to within a few percent of redline limitations.

The change in altitude made her positively shiver until she emptied her backpack and put on everything she had. One of the two aircrew members in the cabin mentioned the discomfort of their passenger to the pilots, and one of them selected cabin heat and cranked up the BTUs.

Nazy and the crew chiefs soon sweltered in the cabin. The heat pouring from vents was tinged with the smell of burned jet fuel. The pilots fiddled with the heater control until they found a neutral setting for the comfort of all.

Nazy fingered the SEAL arrowhead until she noticed one of the Marines was watching her. She slipped it into the flight jacket pocket and smiled.

After a few hours airborne, a female Marine aircrew member walked to Nazy, bent over, and told her they'd be landing soon. From her backpack, Nazy fished out a half-dozen National Counter Terrorism Center challenge coins. Nazy climbed into the cockpit to tell the pilots and the other aircrew 'thank you' for coming to get her. She handed a coin to each of the Marines in flight suits. The Marines were surprised yet grateful.

Once Nazy returned to the cabin and buckled in her seat, the lone female Marine found it hard not to stare at her. She thought *My God, she must be the most beautiful woman I've ever seen without makeup. Her looks must sometimes be more of a handicap than an advantage. What a problem to have.*

The pilot commented to the copilot, who was gently fondling the large dark blue enameled coin, "I'm going to go out on a limb and say she's from the NCTC and is pretty high up the food chain to hand these out. She might even be the director. Who knows what she does, but I'll bet it's not as fun as flying."

The copilot just smiled and nodded.

•   •   •   •   •

A few hundred miles away, Lynche was distracted by other events. He had the Marines delivering his NCTC Director. He had the FBI investigating the apparent treachery of the leaders of the National Clandestine Service, including their director, Steve Castaño. By the direction of President Hernandez, he had activated the special access program *Wraith*, and his two pilots were safe on deck in Quantico where their aircraft were being fitted for radiological detection flights. And he had Anna Comstock rooting out the rest of the Rothwell rot at the NCS.

Lynche's office was being buffeted by the winds of change with the election of President Hernandez. Embassies across the planet dispatched the rumblings of the host nation's left-leaning diplomats—many didn't like the current right-wing president. Learning that President Hernandez would be president for four more years was more than many could stand. Liberal Democrats, both foreign and domestic, stepped up their attacks on the man, and several internationally renowned assassins were making their voices heard through the deep dark side of the internet, letting it be known that their services were available at fire sale prices. Chiefs of Station at U.S. embassies around the globe reported that assassination chatter from their sources was unprecedented.

Lynche had dispatched the Security Manager, Anna Comstock, to go by the Cunningham abode and pick up a few outfits for Nazy. She noted the FBI electronic surveillance detection teams were still busy finding, disabling, and removing surveillance equipment in the living room, bedrooms, bathrooms, and appliances. Every bug that was found or neutralized represented the best the CIA's S&T laboratories could produce. The FBI team knew what to look for since they also knew where their agents liked to place similar surveillance devices.

Anna told Lynche, "The FBI counter-surveillance team used a special signal detector device to find and removed hidden microdot cameras and microphones. They didn't forget to check the appliances and the vacuum cleaner, and I understand they found cameras there too. Steve Castaño and his boys used every gizmo S&T had in their bucket of surveillance tricks. Even developmental stuff."

The FBI special agent in charge reported to Anna that they'd not only found tracking and explosive devices in both vehicles, they'd also found all of the devices on the house's installed security system. They removed the tracking devices and the remotely-controlled detonators hidden in a Mercedes and Hummer H2 vehicles, and they'd imaged the walls with other specialized detectors and found nothing of interest. "They said they'd restored the original system to manufacturer's specifications. As such, it was again operational."

After all of the FBI technicians departed the house and returned a pair of Growlers to the Agency Security Chief, Anna wandered around each of the rooms. She doubted the owner would ever return to her home. Once a residence had been penetrated, it was psychologically difficult for anyone to feel comfortable in their own home. *It had been violated.* One would always wonder if there was some camera or microphone that had been overlooked.

Anna had been to the Cunningham residence before when Nazy had been the target of Islamist hit teams, likely the Islamic Underground. Comstock remembered they were relentless then. Now, nothing had changed except the bad guys. It was still difficult to accept that Castaño's NCS had targeted one of their own. *And they had planted bombs.* Comstock shook her head in disgust as she went to Nazy's bedroom and retrieved undies, casual and work clothes, again. She picked up a couple of bras and couldn't help herself from checking the size. She raised an eyebrow and grimaced, *Good God!* Anna also found the yellow sweatshirt with CORVETTE stenciled across the front. During that episode of personal protection for Nazy, Lynche had indicated that Nazy always slept in the oversized sweatshirt. Comstock wondered how he knew that private bit of Cunningham's habits. Personal information like that should have been way too intimate for a CIA Director to know.

Anna was in and out of the house in under ten minutes.

• • • •

Tracked FBI robots with cameras, arms, and drills attacked the four walls of the residences of the CIA's Chief of Counterterrorism, Chief of Special Activities Division, the Chief of Special Operations Group, and the NCS Director. They quickly determined that the homes of Galvan Fässler, Jarvis Bomarito, and Bennett Troxel weren't booby-trapped and were safe to enter.

That left Steve Castaño's house, and it was a hot mess. Holes had been drilled through the walls and windows. Fiber optic cables with fisheye camera lenses were pushed through the openings to determine if there were any explosives, booby-traps, trip-wires, laser traps, or antennas to trigger a device by remote control. After hours of preparation time, electronic snakes were turned loose on the residences. As the tiny robots slithered into the rooms with their high-definition cameras, one member of the National Explosive Task Force, Explosive Ordnance Demolition (EOD) Team shouted, "Claymore!" With the discovery of at least one anti-personnel mine, the structure penetration operation was terminated. It was time to move back and reassess the situation.

Questions spewed from the EOD Team leader. Was the robot able to determine how the M18A1 Claymore mine had been armed? "Yes, it has a microwave activated trigger. We may be able to clip the antenna or jam the signal. We have a jammer in the truck, but the boys upstairs will want to know if I considered other methods. I have to say we expect that there's more here than a single Claymore."

The EOD Team Lead asked, "Are we sure it isn't a dummy?"

"You can't take a chance in these situations," the senior FBI on-scene commander said. "If these guys have access to anti-personnel mines there's nothing to stop them from using them in the manner intended." Heads nodded in obvious agreement.

"Look who we're dealing with," offered the EOD Team Lead. "If HQ is correct and the owner of this house is a member of the NCS — a senior member no less — then I'm surprised it's still standing."

The FBI Special Agent in Charge said to the EOD Team Lead, "If I was on the run, I would have burned it down — but not until everyone in the neighborhood was evacuated. They could have set multiple traps — I'd have done that, just to keep an EOD team locked up all day."

"Which is what we're doing."

The National Explosive Task Force huddled with the Explosive Ordnance Demolition Team and the FBI Special Agent in Charge. Now fifteen demolition experts strong, the questions came rapid fire. They wanted an assessment from the robot operators. "What else are we dealing with here?"

The operator with the best video of the anti-personnel mines in the house responded, "I think they have tried to create confusion with something that would frag us when we entered. Give them some time to get away safely. I think we need to rethink the problem, broaden the scope. I'm not willing to send my guys in close under these circumstances. For example, look on either side of the house, there's a bunch of trees in the front, on the sides, and a couple in the back. We haven't trained in an urban environment like this. I suggest we go slow and be as methodical as necessary — we aren't on the clock."

The other FBI Special Agents agreed with positive nods. He continued, "I suggest we consult our EOD Notes. I recall guerillas in the Angola bush war would pack two Claymores back to back and mount them into trees along avenues of approach. Isn't that we have here? Trees and avenues of approach?"

The EOD technician said, "That may be so, but no one in his right mind would expose Claymores, real Claymores in a residential area with kids and pets? I can't believe it."

The supervisor made a decision. "I believe we need to clear the whole damn area with the robots. If they established layers of mine protection, then we also have to consider IEDs and why not land mines. It could take us a couple of days to clear the yard and the house in order to enter it, kill any emissions so an electrical firing signal can't penetrate a well-hidden IED. And I don't want anyone stepping on a mine."

The FBI Special Agent in Charge crossed her arms over her chest. "We need to clear the block. Evacuate the neighborhood." The woman thought, *I'm beginning to think CIA officers make lousy neighbors!*

"Yes, ma'am. The guys we're dealing with won't make it easy on us—they know every trick in the trade just like we do. I'm of the opinion that they left us one of the most impressive and highly complicated traps we've ever encountered, and it'll be very risky to clear with conventional methods. The director needs to know he will not get a quick answer."

Motorola radios on belts came to life. The FBI Special Agent in Charge (SPIC) answered the call. A member of CIA Security requested to see the SPIC; she had something to give her. A tall, lithe African American woman with intricately braided hair and a blue CIA badge introduced herself and handed over three Growlers. She said, smiling, "These should help. And I won't leave until I get them back when you're done."

58

Sunshine branched out through leafless grey trees and spilled into the dirty windows of the office of the NCS Director. Director of Security, Anna Comstock picked up the land line on Steve Castaño's desk and pinged the Director of Central Intelligence. He picked up at one ring.

"Good morning, Director Lynche, I'm certain they didn't know we were on to them. The FBI cleared the offices of any booby-traps. Safes are all buttoned up and locked—we're getting the combinations to see what they have and what they don't have."

"What about their computers."

"Not so good."

"What do you mean?"

"It looks like they used a program to remotely lock their computers. Nonstandard stuff. Our IT guys will have to try and get in—otherwise we might have to take them to the FBI. I'm not sure which one of us has the better data extraction subroutines, but my vote is they do more forensics than we do. I didn't think they were the kind of men who would do that, but the intel from the FBI field team is that Castaño's house is booby-trapped. Big time. It's obvious he was at least thinking about it. Planning for the day."

"So they knew you were coming?"

"I wouldn't say that, but it just seems to me that they were prepared. They didn't know when the day would come, but they left a major shit sandwich in Vienna. They knew it would."

"Let me know when you know more. I'll be here all day."

"It'll be one of those mornings. There's one more thing, Greg."

"What's that?"

"When we searched their desks we found something interesting. They threw their paychecks into the bottom drawer, unopened in those pre-direct deposit days, because I suppose, they didn't need them."

Lynche didn't respond to her comment and signed off with, "Later."

• • • • •

Lynche was startled when the telephone rang. He hadn't remembered falling asleep at his desk. The caller identification number looked familiar, but he was still in a haze. He would have tugged on his tie to compose himself, but it had been dispatched to a corner of the desk. He answered, "Lynche," and as he had done for forty years, he picked up a pen and was ready to copy. These weren't social calls. More the type where someone would throw a dead monkey on his desk hoping someone at his level could do something to solve an earth-shattering problem.

He listened as the FBI Director spoke nonstop for several seconds. No dead monkeys this time. Lynche wrote furiously. The call was terminated at the other end, and the DCI looked at his notes, hoping that his hand and fingers had awakened sufficiently to keep up with the transmission just received. The FBI Director had been succinct and terse; no animosity, just bullets of information. Surprisingly, it was mostly good news.

FBI — located and retrieved all missing radioactive materials. 1 NYC, 1 DC. No spills or releases. 4 arrests. No one is talking. Perps ID'd by face recog sys. No ID on the NCS 4. 3 of 4 houses breeched — nothing.

Castaño — house booby trapped. Area evacuated. Growlers on site. Are there other houses or structures that they own?

Director Vincze had indicated the perpetrators of the radioactive material theft had been located through the use of wearable facial recognition systems that could have been easily been mistaken for eyeglasses. Dozens of FBI Special Agents had combed every floor, every room of every building until one of them received the information they needed to effectuate an arrest.

Lynche looked at his notes and was thankful the terroristic plan was intercepted in the earliest phase. A good news story that won't make the nine o'clock news anywhere, unless there was another Mark Felt-like creature in the system to leak information to the media. He looked up from his notes just as Anna Comstock burst through his open door.

"How much bad news can you tolerate at this hour?"

"What? No 'Hello?' I just got good news and you want to spoil it. Shame on you." His eyes encouraged her to let him have it.

She frowned and said, "You look horrible, sir. If I may say so."

"You may not. What do you have?"

"Good news first — Miss Cunningham is ten minutes out if you want to meet her at the landing pad. I have her clothes."

Clothes? What's that about? Then he remembered. He said, "She knows the way to the office. I mean, can you bring her here? I really can't leave. I have my own good news."

"Like what?" she cautioned.

"The radioactive materials have been found and secured, and the men have been arrested." He started scribbling notes as to what he needed to be doing for the next phase. First, he needed to call Hunter and tell him his services and the YO-3As were no longer needed. Second, he still wanted Nazy for some research. It was more important for Comstock to bring Nazy to the office than to provide an update to the Security Officer. "And you have....?"

"The bad...."

"Seriously? I'm all ears, Anna. Shoot."

"Your boys have been very bad. They took a few things with them apparently. S&T didn't have a firm date when they were supposed to return the gun. So they have had it for a while."

"*The gun?*" Lynche was more confused than ever. *Maybe I'm not fully awake,* he told himself.

"Sir, S&T gave them a 'TS2' Terminator Sniper System to evaluate. I received the brief that four systems were built and the director, who I assumed to be you, directed two of them to be shipped to Texas. I presume those two are with *Maverick*. S&T has retained one and one went to NCS for test and evaluation. They—NCS—have not brought theirs back, and it's not in their building. I hope I'm wrong, but I assume our bad boys have it."

Lynche was recovering sufficiently to understand. It still took him a few moments to articulate a response. *These guys aren't going into an on-call sniper business. There's only one reason to run away with a ten-mile weapon, and that it to use it against high value targets.* He thrummed his fingers on his desk looking for words to say. Suddenly, the possibilities horrified him. He uttered the words of a man in despair, "No, I'm not and I wasn't the approving authority for those systems—they were developed before my time. However, yes, there were two airborne systems, and yes, I know that two were transferred to Texas for test and evaluation, and that's where they remain. They're installed equipment, and I can attest that they're accounted for." He shrugged and nodded and said, "*Maverick.*"

Anna smiled in admiration.

"So NCS has one of the ground systems and it's missing?"

Anna nodded. She crossed her fleshy arms. "I understand it has the latest in AI; artificial intelligence decision trees that can enable it to fire remotely or when a target is in optimal range or other targeting parameters."

Then it hit him. "*Shit*, Anna. That's not just a fire and forget weapon, but one that can be programmed to fire...."

"It also has facial recognition technology...." Her eyes widened at the implications. Both CIA officers then glanced at the wall with the former Agency directors and the president's photographs.

Lynche heaved a sigh. "That's not good." He reached for the telephone. "What else? I know there's something else."

"There *is* something else. Minor stuff. The FBI picked up on it in their offices; they were sitting on a hundred million dollars of what looks to be counterfeit cash."

Lynche said, "Counterfeit cash? That's impossible. Those bills are direct from the Treasury. They screen for counterfeits before we get them."

"Well, maybe they should tell you what they found. What I know isn't sufficient. They told me it looked as if it—all of it was counterfeit."

Lynche knew he had the telephone receiver in his hand. The problem was what to do about it. He looked at her quizzically. "Counterfeit? How? How much?"

"Maybe all of it? One, two, maybe three hundred million dollars. It's in large tubs and I'm not a good judge of what even a million dollars looks like."

His head hurt. He closed his eyes and tried to make sense of it all. "It depends on the denominations."

She was confused. She counted hundred dollar bills in her head. *One hundred stacks of a bundle of $100 bills. They'd probably fit in a briefcase.* She asked, "What's the problem?"

"Forget the money for now. You don't know anything more about that weapon?"

"Not really. From this evening's capabilities brief—it's a level-seven IRAD program. Internal Research and Development. Maybe one or two outside laboratories were involved. But totally in-house. Need to know."

Lynche nodded. "The basic weapon was an experimental gun, with revolutionary ammo. The ones we initially put on aircraft had about a five mile effective range in the air. But these are next-generation prototype weapons. If I recall correctly from the capabilities brief, it has an integrated tripod, the barrel is electrically-driven, and the airborne and ground versions can hit moving targets out to ten miles."

"*Theoretically?*"

"No, really. The ammo...the bullet head is laser guided and is propelled by a tiny rocket motor. The fuel is the same as they used for

Space Shuttle solid rocket boosters. The good news and bad news is, if the electronics survive leaving the barrel, you can't miss."

"What do you mean, can't miss?"

"It has, theoretically, a probability of kill approaching 100%." The telephone earpiece was at his ear as he explained, "Both systems have a very powerful telescope with a laser designator and night vision capabilities. Put a laser designator on a target, and it'll hit the spot on the target within an inch or two…I'm aware that the airborne system is effective out to ten and maybe fifteen miles because the targeting system runs through gyroscopes, rate gyros, and other onboard sensors, then outside of that, the bullet gets squirrely because it's difficult to hold the laser spot as still as the system requires. But mounted on a tripod at five or ten miles the laser spot is very stable. Probability of kill…still in the high 90s, approaching 100% P sub-K. Depending on crosswinds. The magic of the system is that it removes the natural ballistics curve of a regular bullet; this is a 'smart bullet,' and it flies flat like an airplane and directly to point of illumination and impact—it's a rocket-propelled bullet with wings. Put a gyroscopically-stabilized laser dot on a target and the spent-uranium bullet will guide on it until it hits that infrared illuminated target. It's the ultimate sniper or counter-sniper rifle. Blows through metal and brick. Enemy snipers can't hide behind a brick wall."

"And if the targeting system is coupled with AI and facial recognition…. Director Lynche?"

"Hold one second, I'm calling the Secret Service Director. As long as those clowns are out there and that gun isn't accounted for, President Hernandez and the VP have to be sequestered. Protected. Families too."

Now it was Anna's turn to utter, "*Shit!*" *That's why he's the Director — thinks of things that are way over my head. Talk of bogus money can definitely wait.*

As he waited for the Secret Service Director, his other line rang. Lynche asked Anna to answer it at the secretary's station. By the time he got off the phone, Comstock had returned with a message. "Miss Cunningham has landed. A couple of my guys are bringing her here."

"The morning is getting better by the minute. The President is staying on, the radioactive materials were recovered, and Nazy is here. Anna, the rest of the *Wraith* team will be coming here too. Marine helicopter. Do what you can to accommodate them. *Maverick* will need a computer and an office. He might have a badge, but now that I think about it—he's dead, so he'll need a new one."

"Do we have a name for *Maverick*, since his alter ego is dead?"

Lynche didn't have time for humor, otherwise he'd have offered the names Azzam Mohaned Bakkar or Buck Naked or something *smashing* which would dig at Hunter for years. He rubbed his eyes as if to extricate all the bushels of sand from his eyes. "Anna, I gave him a couple of working passports; aliases, use one of those names. I'm sure one of them is *Dante Locke*. That will do."

She said, "Can do easy. I can put him downstairs, or *Maverick* can work out of your conference room."

"Downstairs will be fine. He's a Marine. Just give him a field desk and a trash can, and he'll be happy."

Comstock was confused. "Why a trashcan?"

There wasn't an impish quality to his voice. "He needs a place to sit."

Anna waggishly said, "I'll make sure he has a chair. We have chairs. We don't really have any space for a *Maverick*, but we'll find some. Sir. What level of access for *Maverick*?"

"Director level. Anyplace, anywhere, anytime. Any problems? He still has a Level One Yankee White clearance." Lynche sighed as he thought about all the complications bringing Hunter back into the CIA with a new name. "He'll need a new NDA as well."

She shook her head as she pursed her lips. Lynche raised a finger to "hold that thought." So she did. It was obvious he was deep thinking. And when he got that way, Lynche needed quiet. So Anna sat still until the boss gave her his final instructions.

Lynche pounded the desk with a finger—a habit over the years that made the tip of his finger flat—and then suddenly picked up the telephone, consulted a list of numbers, and dialed one. He was blunt. "Hello Bill, where are you? I really could use someone with your talents. I can send a jet or maybe mil-air for you."

The man on the other end of the phone asked a couple of questions. He told him he was in Texas, at least twenty hours out by car, and he had a few hours of sleep. Lynche offered a plan. McGee agreed and told him what he needed.

McGee wrote while Lynche talked.

"Great—we have other problems, and I need some help I can trust. I take it you don't have your badge and you have weapons? Weapons you have. Ok. I'll pass along your numbers. Do you know what airport is close? Ok. It'll take a couple of hours to get there, a couple more to get here. We'll have a car and a Security Officer escort you when you arrive. Anna Comstock will help coordinate your travel. She'll pull your vitals from the system and get you another badge. I'll text her numbers and yours. Thank you, and be safe."

Anna nodded at her new orders and said, "We still have our fruit loops from NCS running lose with a gun that can shoot ten miles. I'll cool my jets until we recover that damn thing. Or them. I have my orders." She shook the floor as she ran out of the office.

Lynche called the Secret Service Director. There was no time for preamble. Lynche said, "R O, Greg. One more thing."

"Shoot."

Bad choice of word. "R O, those four operations officers.... I think we caught them running a hostile op. The FBI is on the case. But the timing is horrible, with the election...."

"Go on."

"Well, I think...my concern is that they might...*retaliate*...in some way. They may run but...."

The pitch in his voice dropped an octave. "Greg, what are we talking about?"

"You know my NCS officers have access to the latest weaponry to come out of our labs and industry. I know of one that's probably not your radar—it's a ten-mile sniper rifle. Experimental, revolutionary ammo. Nearly 100% P sub-K, probability of kill."

The Secret Service Director slammed his eyes closed for a moment. *Are you friggin' kidding me?* "One hundred percent, P sub-K? Holy shit! Ok—well, I'll try to get the counter-sniper teams up to speed if you can provide me with some technical data on that weapon. We'll recheck our plots. So we know what we're dealing with. Every nutjob in town is on the warpath; apparently, they didn't like the elections results. They've gone berserk and we have everyone pulling double shifts. This isn't good news. But I'll find someone to help."

"A thousand apologies. I'll have the tech data sent over. Any news if you had guys stopped by DHS?"

R O Gates was suddenly depressed and said, "Not yet. Good night, Greg."

Lynche held a dead phone. He didn't have a chance to thank the Secret Service director. He smiled for a moment and thought, *Who would name their kid R O?*

•　　•　　•　　•　　•

Marine CV-22s were getting a workout during the early morning hours following the historic election. One departed Marine Corps Base Quantico to transport a group of men and women to CIA Headquarters. Another *Osprey* had begun its early morning mission into Arkansas. Annotated in the aircraft's Yellow Sheet, the pilot wrote: *Retrieved & Delivered a devastatingly beautiful DV.* Due to his lack of professionalism, the pilot's candor would likely get him into a little hot water with his commanding officer. Another Marine *Osprey* was enroute to Texas to pick up a retired U.S. Navy SEAL.

At Joint Base Anacostia, a trio of VH-3D *Sea King* "white top" Presidential helicopters and aircrew were on standby, ready to take the newly elected president to Camp David.

• • • • •

From his *dacha* overlooking the Baltic Sea, the President of the Russian Federation turned away from a single television monitor. The outcome of the American election wasn't what he had expected, not what he had planned for, not what he had been promised, and not what he had paid for. One of several telephones on his desk broke the silence.

The head of the Federal Security Service informed the president, "RTN is reporting that Comrade Zhavrazhinov is *unwell.*"

Disgusted, the Russian Federation president hung up the telephone. He moved to the fireplace, stared into the flames. He lifted his head to view a dark and foreboding portrait of Joseph Stalin over the mantle.

The Americans have done it to us again. All that we've worked for, gone.

59

November 9
CIA Headquarters

Nazy had thanked Anna Comstock for retrieving some clothes for her and applauded her choices of dresses and suits. Before Duncan was scheduled to arrive, Nazy had showered in the fitness center's locker room and changed out of jeans for something more appropriate for staff work. The men fell silent when she entered the DCI's office in a cream-colored dress with a huge colorful Hermès scarf that obscured the outline of her bosom. Blue heels left marks in the carpet.

As soon as Kelly Horne and Duncan Hunter entered the director's office, they walked to the NCTC Director and softly commented, "Good morning, Miss Cunningham, so good to see you again." Kelly and Hunter took turns gingerly embracing Nazy as if they were business associates about to attend a meeting. He was still limping and ignoring the discomfort; Hunter knew better than to expose Nazy's cover.

Lynche's office was active, the DCI was on the phone and had no time for small talk. Anna Comstock observed the interaction of the new man with the women; it was obvious they knew one another. She wondered if he and Nazy were married.

With Duncan in the room Nazy unconsciously checked her scarf and dress, and turned her voice down an octave. With Anna Comstock in the office, it was a time to be professional, so they both behaved. The two women stood off to the side and talked in low voices.

The handset plopped loudly in its cradle as Lynche announced that Bill McGee would be joining them later. He had been able to send a Marine Corps *Osprey* to fetch him. Lynche motioned for everyone to move around his conference table and for Anna to begin a video presentation. Like a college professor lecturing a small intimate group, Lynche said, "The four men seen in this video, assaulting Nazy's house, I believe, were the four leaders of the National Clandestine Service. They're Galvan Fässler, Chief Counterterrorism; Jarvis Bomarito, Chief Special Activities Division; Bennett Troxel, Chief Special Operations Group, and the Director of the National Clandestine Service, Steve Castaño."

Anna added, "These fugitives are practiced, successful killers. Not only with guns, but also with explosives. Our fugitives have demonstrated their mastery to use them in a wide range of environments, using multiple methods of delivery and detonation. The FBI reported Castaño's house in Vienna is wired for anti-personnel mines, at a minimum. That's another way of saying that you must inspect your vehicles before you insert a key into a door lock or ignition. These men are the best covert killers the CIA could produce. They may be at retirement age but they're very clever and very lethal." She passed 8 X 10 photographs of the men to Hunter for his perusal. Hunter knew only Castaño from his meeting on the ramp at Andrews AFB.

Lynche narrowed his eyes at something the security woman had said. He allowed the ugly thought to bounce around in his cranium. He continued, "I've reason to believe they have been responsible for—let's call it *extracurricular* activities—while on active duty. They're on the run, and they're armed with a very special sniper system that has a maximum effective range of ten miles."

Hunter turned his head to Lynche. There were alarms ringing in his ears. He knew the calculus of ammunition and ballistics, and his mind was doing arithmetic. He said, "Sounds like my gun."

Lynche nodded and said, "It's an enhanced ground version of the *Wraith's* gun."

Hunter rolled his eyes and said, "That isn't good. Now I know why you wanted us here."

"You're the smart guy—tell me why." Lynche smiled at his best friend.

"The short version is you want us to find them, if we can. The FBI found the radiological terrorists; you found out you have your own band of terrorists, and now you have a job for…Ms. Horne and me."

Lynche smashed his lips together and nodded. "And Bill McGee, if we need him. I asked Nazy to do a little research for me. Us. Nazy?"

Nazy stood and said, "The actions of Fässler, Bomarito, Troxel, and Castaño didn't make a lot of sense. Director Lynche wanted to determine if our four missing men could have been involved in something more nefarious than just breaking and entering and installing surveillance systems at my house and Kelly's. They also installed trackers and explosives in my vehicles."

Hunter closed his eyes for a mere moment. *I'm going to kill that guy….*

Kelly was horrified that her apartment had also been penetrated with surveillance equipment. Lynche interrupted, "Anna, you confirmed surveillance equipment and explosives were found and removed from Nazy's vehicles but not Kelly's?"

Anna announced, "Correct. We weren't able to find Miss Horne's car." Lynche looked relieved for the first time in several hours. Kelly answered the question of where her car was, "The Jag's at the dealer." Hunter was disappointed until Kelly said the car was just in for servicing. He calmed down for the moment.

Nazy continued, "While you were at the Marine base, I had some time to use the AIRRAID tool to try and get a sense of direction of what precipitated such actions. Where their allegiance lay. I researched their travel records as well as their attendance records, as recorded by the access entry portal in every CIA building and all the other three-letter agencies. I wanted to see if there were unusual intersections. Vectors. Links."

"*Air raid*?" asked Hunter meekly as he was confused. The CIA generated horrible nonsensical acronyms and special access program names.

"I'm sorry. That's A I R R A I D for Artificial Intelligence Rapid Retrieval and Analysis Interface Device. It's an AI-based assistant or a 'tool' for analysts accessing not only the Central Intelligence Agency's operational files and archives but all of the IC's other secret and top secret archives which are interconnected via a secure data link. Navy Intel. Library of Congress. British Intelligence. Bletchley Park. NSA's museum. Even the Naval War College's naval warfare and intelligence library."

Nazy continued, "It's used to conduct top-level and immediate intelligence research during periods of national and international emergencies. We can't have direct connections for security reasons. AIRRAID rolls around amongst the SCIF's servers to access the IC's separate archives."

Lynche added, "Actually, it moves around like a hyperactive cartoon character and plugs into the scattered arrays of compartmented mass storage devices, as needed. I like to call it 'a rolling brain.'"

Nazy finished, "It takes verbal commands and questions and rapidly processes information to support intelligence officers who are performing top level research work."

Lynche threw out, "AIRRAID can take the place of a hundred analysts. It condenses the output of thousands of neural networks and provides the requested information in a matter of seconds. Its reachback into the histories of the intelligence communities is unprecedented. Think having instant access to the full Library of Congress at your fingertips. Anything you want you just have to ask."

Nazy continued, "Thanks to its 'neural' AI network the greatest thing about AIRRAID is its interactivity. Not only does it learn and offer solutions to problems, but it also will challenge you to look at or consider tangential intelligence. The first thing I wanted to know is what *Maverick* has long suspected, 'Were members of NCS involved in the — I'll call it the 'Algerian caper?'"

Hunter smiled at the words *Algerian caper.*

Lynche interrupted again, "Even an analyst with unlimited research clearances couldn't do much more than just work through a schematic view of prescribed checklists and procedures — think of an archer only being able to shoot a single arrow. With AIRRAID, think of a Gatling gun being able to shoot from a thousand barrels arranged in a globe. Once loaded with a question, Nazy is able to direct and redirect questions to AIRRAID which can query millions of databases simultaneously. When it learns where a certain subject exists on one of the mainframes in the intelligence community network — and that includes our allies — it'll retrieve it, analyze it or ask if the information is germane to the research."

Nazy said, nodding, "We haven't had this *'tool'* that long and I'm really the only one who has used it extensively, which is why Greg wanted me back — he thought I could get Alvin, that's what AIRRAID calls itself, to see if there are any trails or hints of evidence out there on our four missing men. AIRRAID can detect trends. Humans are predictable and leave clues."

Hunter smirked and asked, "So does Alvin have a computer voice? Who does it sound like? HAL 9000?" He said mockingly, *"I'm sorry Dave, I can't do that."*

Nazy didn't know who or what HAL 9000 was, but smiled at her husband, shrugged her shoulders at his snarky comment, and in her best husky, cut-glass, British accent said, "You."

"Me? How's that even possible? And why would you do that? Could you do that?"

"I said, 'Alvin, you are to respond to me in Charlton Heston's voice, only an octave lower.' And it did."

"So you think I sound like Charlton Heston? I need to get my hearing checked." He loved seeing his wife in a dress at work; he was totally entranced by her command of the topic.

Anna Comstock again wondered, *Do these two really know each other...well? Intimate, maybe?* A glance at both of their wedding bands on their ring fingers only proved there were rings and not wedding bells. Anna got it, *They're married....*

Lynche said, "May we finish this?"

Nazy said, "I asked Alvin, 'Is there an intersection between special access program *Wraith* in Algeria and the travels of Fässler, Bomarito, Troxel, and Castaño?' In a couple of seconds, the information was displayed on our five very large screens. I had to input where you were, as your SAP wasn't in any database; *Wraith* is completely off the books, there are no records. In the case of the *Algerian caper*, Alvin determined three of those men had chartered a jet to Tunisia and leased a vehicle from the Tunis airport. His analysis was they were in the rural area of Algeria. They didn't make any contact with the Chief of Station in Algeria, nor did they attempt to help with the evacuation of either U.S. Embassy. They may have been on another mission and may not have known what was going on at the U.S. Embassy in Algiers."

Nazy said, "Colonel Eastwood, Bill McGee, and one other SEAL were there that night." The words could have made her momentarily emotional. She flushed slightly reliving the evening she had been kidnapped when the U.S. Embassy was bombed and overrun. She later learned that Eastwood was part of the group of men who chased down her kidnappers and rescued her. She paused, smiled, and forced herself to remain focused on her brief as she shoveled her memories of the aftermath of that night in Algeria into a deep dark hole. Hunter itched an eyebrow and nodded his support in how Nazy handled the imagery of when she had been blown up and assaulted.

Lynche pointed at Hunter and said, "Right off the bat, Nazy validated that three of the four NCS men were in the area of Algeria the night you were shot down and escaped to the USS Eisenhower. My predecessor was headed to Amman, Jordan in an Air Branch jet, and upon hearing that Nazy was enroute to a Naval Hospital in Italy, he diverted to Italy. Castaño, as the DDO, remained in D.C. Alvin placed the three senior leaders of the NCS in Tunisia. What do you think they were after?"

Hunter knew exactly what they were after. "*Gold! Billions in gold coin.* Almost twenty years of ransom was hidden in an underground vault." He looked at Lynche who nodded his concurrence.

Anna Comstock's eyes nearly fell out of her head. Her mouth was agape for minutes.

Hunter had always thought that the mission to find and eliminate the master terrorist, who had a vile and wicked history of using shoulder-launched anti-aircraft missiles to shoot commercial airliners out of the sky over America and England, had been compromised. The Algerian terrorist seemed to know where to look in the sky for Hunter's quiet airplane. Hunter had watched the man and analyzed his body language to see if he was looking for the telltale signs of an all-black aircraft—blacker than the night skies—and the linear masking and unmasking of stars as the profile of the YO-3A flew a couple of miles away.

Nazy said, "This was one of the very first executive SAPs. The president authorized the CIA to do whatever was necessary to prevent the unknown terrorist from shooting down commercial airliners. The United States paid a ransom every year. The NCS had been in charge of that E-SAP until the U.S. Embassy in Algeria received new instructions. The annual ransom was a new business jet with a hundred million dollars in untraceable gold coins. We believed we'd finally identified and located the master terrorist and sent *Maverick* to Algeria to confirm our suspicions."

Lynche said, "You were right, I was wrong. Again. Let's try not to make this a habit, okay, *Maverick*?"

Hunter smiled at the unexpected apology. He raised his hand with a "thumbs up." The smile was all it took to receive one from Lynche. It was obvious to everyone in the room that Hunter had tackled and completed very difficult missions. They weren't just implausible, they were impossible.

Lynche said, "I don't think *Maverick* has told anyone, but the President of the United States awarded him the Distinguished Intelligence Cross. Three times now, I believe." Nazy smiled proudly. Comstock and Kelly were stunned. The DIC was the highest medal awarded to a member of the intelligence community. It was extraordinary for a person to receive one DIC. Lynche had one. Nazy had one. For someone to have three was unbelievable.

Anna thought, *Maybe you can keep a secret in this place after all*. Kelly Horne couldn't look at her father. She was on the edge of choking up with emotion.

Nazy cleared her throat and said, "While we waited for you to arrive, I spent some time with Alvin and anticipated *Maverick*'s questions. I wanted Alvin to tell me if any other of *Maverick*'s missions had any overlap with any of the NCS four. Nothing solid before Algeria, but after Algeria it seemed as if they were everywhere where *Maverick* was in the area, as if they were trying to triangulate *Maverick*'s position. Three of the four were in Somalia when *Maverick* found dozens of hostages. Two of the four were in Abuja, Nigeria before *Maverick* rescued Kelly and a Nigerian airliner. Three of the four had taken a jet to Abu Dhabi and were likely in Dubai during that mission."

Anna wondered what "mission" that could have been. She was becoming aware that *Maverick* was a very special person in the Agency to have NCS apparently shadowing him.

Hunter said, "Then they were responsible for the seven heads on the table. I don't know how they got on the floor...."

Lynche said, "Someone from the comm team fed Castaño information real time."

Anna said, "That's fresh information. We just polygraphed the shit out of him."

Hunter's head was about to explode. His jaw popped open for a fraction of a second. *The NCS had an inside guy.... Of course!*

Lynche explained, "I had the men polygraphed who were providing technical support in Dubai. One talked; he had been with NCS before and wanted to get back. Castaño promised him the moon if he'd keep him appraised of what you were doing in Dubai. All of you."

Anna added, "One man from Nazy's security detail also told Castaño where she lived." She was embarrassed that one of her most trusted security officers had informed the NCS director of Nazy's residence. *It's getting so that you can't trust anyone.*

Lynche asked if AIRRAID could be used to help find the NCS four.

Nazy said, "I can try. I could use *Maverick*." She smiled. "We could have something useful in very short order."

Lynche asked Nazy if she'd inquire about the possibility of the NCS four being pitched by anyone from the former Soviet Union or the Russian Federation, and if "yes," when and where. "I don't want to tell this august group of patriots that as of this minute, I can't trust anyone in NCS. It's a professional embarrassment. I don't know if they've been pitched, working for Moscow, or are freelancers."

Hunter crossed his arms and couldn't believe what he was hearing. When Lynche began to talk of the FBI, Hunter nearly slipped out of his chair.

Lynche said, "We've seen what corruption at the highest levels of the FBI leadership can do to try and remove the president. Congressional Republicans are having a field day exposing the conspirators. The number of agents involved are off the charts. My hope is we only have a handful of...."

Hunter interjected, "Traitors!"

"...these compromised Agents to deal with. I'm afraid everyone at the NCS will have to be polygraphed again. I'll have to clean house. Until we do that, I need trusted agents. *I need you*...to find the missing four and neutralize them. For some additional trustworthy help, I asked Bill McGee to join us."

Kelly Horne could now see a little more clearly that the trite challenges she faced every day were nothing in comparison to the challenges of the top leaders. She had come to admire her boss greatly and now looked at him with reverence.

Nazy said she wanted to return to the SCIF housing AIRRAID to ask Alvin a few more questions. She sat in one of the chairs facing the DCI's desk and began scribbling notes. Questions for Alvin. Lynche made little hand gestures to Nazy to go, and she suddenly stood and walked out of the office. She smiled at Duncan as she passed him.

Anna's BlackBerry went off. She announced, "Mr. McGee has been picked up in Arkansas. When he arrives, I'll get him badged and brought up. I've much to do. If you will excuse me." Lynche was deep in thought and dismissed her with a nod. He directed Kelly to assist the security officer. She wasn't offended but pleased. Anna and Kelly turned and dashed out the door in single file. All eyes but Lynche's watched them go.

Hunter said, "Greg, what do you really have in mind?"

The Director of the Central Intelligence Agency ignored the question and said, "*Mav*, I need some privacy." Lynche picked up the telephone and Hunter was out the door looking for his wife.

60

November 9
Washington, D.C.

The tracking software appeared to have suffered a malfunction. Viviana Vaslakova couldn't comprehend the track of the transmitter embedded in the Morgan dollar coin. Washington D.C. to the Baltimore airport to Quantico, Virginia and then back to the greater Washington D.C. area. After she sent an interrogation signal to the coin in Eastwood's pocket, her eyes lit up like sparklers at a Fourth of July celebration. Her laptop indicated the tiny transmitter was near L'Enfant Square. Maybe the Army and Navy Club. At first she frowned then she smiled to herself. *You aren't acting like a spy.* Suddenly she became aroused at the thought of bedding him and asking him a question.

•　　•　　•　　•　　•

Demetrius Eastwood awoke with a start. *Where am I?* He looked around the dark room. Then it came to him; he was at the Army and Navy Club as Duncan Hunter suggested. Eastwood had been dreaming of Russian television anchors and murderous clowns with guns. The sheets of his bed were untucked and drenched, as if he had tossed and turned with a triple-digit fever.

He quickly forgot about the evil white-faced clowns in his dreams; she was still on his mind. Viviana. After a trip to the bathroom, he switched on the bedside lamp and found his clothes hanging over a chair. He searched his shirt pocket for her business card. He smiled and mused about what he should do or what he could say. Eastwood made his smartphone come alive with tappings of his index finger and sent her a text message: *Are you still awake?*

Seconds later came the response: *I am! Can't sleep. What are you still doing up?*

If she can't sleep.... A text message wouldn't be sufficient. Eastwood called her.

•　　•　　•　　•　　•

The RTN reporter cooed across the stainless steel diner table, "I wanted to tell you that your article on Eleanor Tussy's obvious espionage was very good, very powerful. It made a difference in the election."

Eastwood countered, "It should have been enough for the FBI to roll out federal criminal charges to indict her. But they didn't. Their ignorance and inaction were very curious."

Viviana Vaslakova asked, "Do you get your information from the FBI or the CIA?"

Eastwood was surprised that the woman could be so bold, so forward. He dismissed any concern and thought, *But fellow journalists are like that.* Then he had an epiphany and looked at her with a little more wonder. *Is she pumping me for information? So much for intimate talk....*

Viviana continued, "I can't get over the fact that she was up by double digits, your article is published, your television special was shown several times, and her numbers fell like a rock and she loses. The DNC Chairman, Dr. Zhavrazhinov, looked right in the camera and blamed you. Dory, it was incredible."

Eastwood wasn't prepared for her excitement. He wasn't sure what he was thinking other than the possibility of romance. Although it had been a long time for him, he still knew the signs. Early morning telephone calls had a romantic quality, but the thrill was beginning to leave since the Russian woman wasn't making long duration eye contact but only seeking answers to questions he didn't want to discuss. "Viviana, my answer is 'neither.' Some were from 'open sources.' Some were from on-line websites such as *Whistleblowers*. They sometimes receive classified information from leakers. Defectors."

"Defectors?" She smiled the most deviously curious smile. *Of course!*

"Yes, defectors. Most of the defectors are from..." He smiled. He didn't know if he could say it. "Russia...*ah, the Motherland.* Some of them say there's a high-placed spy extremely close to the seat of power. I'm not sure what seat or what power. All I know is those guys have been getting knocked off just as soon as they pop up on the grid. But I would think you would know that."

Americans and their sayings.... What's this grid? She shook her head. *Has it been that obvious? No more talk of defectors!* Viviana said, "As I said, I was a little stunned the DNC Chairman blamed you for Eleanor Tussy's loss." Her tone changed from serious to playful. "I think you might have to go into hiding, or leave the country at the very least." She smiled the smile of a sultry movie star for a glamour photographer as she said, "You'll have to hide that handsome face."

Eastwood broke out into a huge smile. He dumped cream and sugar into his coffee. As he stirred the jamoca-colored concoction, he thought, *That article was Duncan's article.* He'd tell Hunter the next time he saw him, that in some journalism circles, his article was credited or blamed for the presidential outcome. Eastwood grinned and chuckled on his side of the table until he put the coffee cup to his lips.

"You know, Dory dear, those Democrats could be hazardous to your health."

"You're telling me! If it's not al-Qaeda or the Islamic Underground, it's the Democratic National Committee. Is that what was keeping you up?"

She oozed sensuality. "Some of it."

He blurted out, "With all of this coffee, I don't think I'm going to be able to sleep now." He threw the first volley of romance across the table.

Viviana smiled and nodded. No return volley.

Eastwood hung his head for a moment and realized their little get-together was just coffee, and nothing more.

The sounds of a diner in the early morning hours intermittently interrupted Viviana's and Eastwood's talk of families and work and travel. Then their smartphones rang and vibrated. They picked them up from the table and thumbed through messages until they found what precipitated the interruption. The messages in the two devices were identical, clips from the Associated Press wire service sent to competing networks: *There has been an aircraft crash on Interstate 66 near the highway 15 Warrenton exit. Investigate and report.* Eastwood snapped his fingers to halt a passing waiter and ordered large coffees to go. Viviana called for a taxi.

They rushed from the Alexandria diner and headed toward the reported location of the crash site, east of Washington D.C. From the back seat of the cab they each talked to their producers. She had calmed hers down; his had been yelling that other networks were reporting the wreckage was still smoldering and too dangerous to approach and to be careful. Eastwood's producer relayed information that ammunition was "still cooking off" from the aircraft and law enforcement wouldn't even let firefighting equipment respond or let reporters get too close to the wreckage. Her producer confirmed that her film crew would meet her at the crash site. Eastwood would be representing the Washington branch of the network and reporting solo.

As the taxi entered I-66, Viviana leaned over and rested her head on her hands. *What an evening!* She was exhausted and would have gladly traded a little less excitement for a little more sleep. She lifted her head and avoided looking at Eastwood, who was typing furiously on his smartphone. It was dark inside the taxi which was a blessing. Viviana didn't want him to see tears welling in her eyes. Maybe she was just too tired for another investigation, even with Eastwood in tow.

She thought of her last mission and stared off in the distance. *I can't do this anymore! Poor Professor Zhavrazhinov. You had your mission; I had mine. You came very close.... You'd have been a hero of the Russian Federation.... They would have named streets and schools and a medal after you. But you also knew what waited for you if you failed. You'd have seen your intestines spilled out onto the floor in the basement of the Lubyanka. You would have watched your blood run into the drain as your life trickled away. I was your friend; I let you go. I let you go in your sleep. I didn't let them have their pound of flesh. I expect I'll be punished too....*

Viviana turned to look at Eastwood, who was head-down, typing something on his smartphone. She thought, *Communism is a vile and nasty woman. She'll cheat you out of your life if you let her. Don't let her. I won't let her anymore.* Viviana returned to her reverie, looking out the taxi's window and not feeling anything but fear. She wanted to cry.

I have to plan my escape. I know who'll help me.

Viviana wiped moist eyes dry with a hankie and looked over to Eastwood with a smile. Then she took his hand.

•   •   •   •   •

According to the press reports from the first responders, two aircraft had collided in a spectacular fireball and crashed into six lanes of traffic on Interstate 66. Immediately after firetrucks arrived to extinguish the multiple fires on the freeway lanes, hundreds of rounds of ammunition began to cook-off, sending low-velocity bullets in every direction. First responders found cover behind firetrucks and ambulances, hoping that nothing exposed would get tagged by a stray bullet.

Because of the ammunition aboard the two aircraft, the Department of Homeland Security and the FBI were notified. As the reporters were pushed a mile away from the wreckage, Viviana and Eastwood became instantly suspicious that there was going to be more to this story.

•   •   •   •   •

Cameramen moved from side-to-side, like competing hummingbirds scootering to different flowers, jockeying to find the best picture of the burning aircraft wreckage in the distance with their reporter in close-up, filling the rest of the screen. When they found the optimal sight picture and no overlap, the cameramen stopped and planted a tripod in the grass to steady their cameras.

Illuminated by powerful lights in front of the eye-level camera for the Russia Television Network, Eastwood watched the lead anchor, Viviana Vaslakova, prepare to deliver her report. She had fluffed her hair several times to give it some body before the camera was turned on. He found her movements sensual as he chuffed the cold air. He was panting like a hound dog, and that was probably not the impression he should be giving in the middle of an aircraft crash site. The ravishing Viviana was busy with her camera crew. He went off to interview some of the first responders.

•　　•　　•　　•　　•

Hours after the flames from the aircraft crash had finally died down and there had been no other ammunition "cooking off," firefighters were allowed to attack the fires. They had extinguished the numerous flaming pools of spilled fuel that had scorched the roadbed and the median. Once all the fires were out, firefighters and investigators cautiously approached the remains of the two aircraft. It would be several hours before the remains of the bodies were extracted from the wreckage.

As the on-duty coroner approached one aircraft, which appeared to have pancaked into the concrete of I-66, he noted a major section of the fuselage remained partially intact. The front engines from both aircraft had been ejected from their mounting points on the fuselage while the aft motors remained attached to the airframe. What was left of the occupants were still strapped-in their seats.

The lead coroner was astounded at what he saw when he first observed the victims. Blunt force trauma which pulverized torsos and craniums were the most common injuries observed in "sudden stoppage" plane crashes. But these victims had died in an unusual manner. He couldn't tell why the aircraft burst into flames and fell from the sky, but he believed the people in both aircraft had died instantly — shredded from the rear from the pressure wave and metal fragments of an anti-personnel mine. He observed many dozens of pieces of shrapnel throughout the victim's charred bodies, as well as the number of pieces of shrapnel imbedded into the metal structures of the aircraft and the remains of the instrument panel. He was able to pinpoint the location of the blasts; from the rearmost seat. The blast hadn't come from the rear engine; logic dictated that the cause of death was from something else.

The coroner extracted DNA samples from the bodies. He told the on-scene commander from the Virginia State Troopers, the laboratory would issue their analysis in forty-eight hours. The coroner's office said they'd issue a statement and submit a classified finding to the FBI and the Secretary of Homeland Security. The National Transportation Safety Board and the Federal Aviation Administration were notified by the on-scene commander.

Eastwood exchanged notes with the other reporters on the scene, what the first responders had found and what information the police were allowing on and off the record. As Viviana worked in front of the camera, he wandered off to a quieter location. He thought Duncan Hunter would be interested in the unusual findings. He pressed a shortcut key for Hunter and hoped the line would connect.

61

November 9
CIA Headquarters

Bill McGee walked directly to Greg Lynche and shook his hand. Anna Comstock watched McGee wave at the youngest person in the room, Kelly Horne and wink at Nazy. She gave him a 'thumbs up" like her husband always did. He pointed at Nazy and said, "You turn up in some of the strangest places." Hunter shook McGee's hand and asked if he had any sleep. A tiny scrunch of massive shoulders told the story. *Some.* SEALs always sleep when there is nothing to do. McGee said, "Greg, I know this has to be important to drag me away from Texas."

Lynche said, "I think so and I appreciate you coming. *Maverick*, can you brief Bill? I have some things I need to do."

Hunter nodded and asked, "Do you need us to leave?"

"Might be best—you can use my conference room. Bill, have you eaten anything?"

The big man looked around the room as if no one knew what food was. Everyone had a job to do but the director's aide; Kelly Horne quickly got the hint and said she'd make a raid on the cafeteria. Anna said she had to check on several security teams. Nazy said she had more research to do and needed to get back to Alvin. The three women left the Director's office as a most unlikely trio; tall, short, and wide.

Hunter's eyes followed Nazy's flowing dress and legs and sang the Hollie's lyrics to himself, *She was a long cool woman in a black dress, Just a 5-9 beautiful tall.... Time get moving.*

McGee frowned at Nazy's use of the term "Alvin" as Hunter led McGee to the conference room adjacent to the DCI's office. Hunter closed Lynche's door.

He plopped into the chair nearest the entrance; McGee took the seat opposite him leaving the space open at the head of the table for Greg Lynche, should he wander in. The former military men knew the protocol for pecking orders.

Hunter slid photographs to McGee. He told McGee what he knew of the NCS men. "Greg thinks these are the four men who assaulted Nazy's house. They installed surveillance equipment and placed explosives in her vehicles. They are...were the four leaders of the National Clandestine Service." McGee returned a hard cold face to signal his disgust. When McGee reached the last photo, he looked up at Hunter. He tapped a finger.

Hunter said, "That's the Director of the National Clandestine Service, Steve Castaño."

McGee recognized the man named Castaño. He pointed at the photograph. He shook his head. Words failed him.

Hunter narrowed his brows and asked, "You know him?"

McGee nodded with his whole body. He said, "I just told Eastwood a couple of days ago that there was a CIA guy who tried to pitch me for a hit job. He's the guy who ran the Agency desk in Afghanistan. He was the guy with bad hands."

Hunter said, "Scarred hands, like they'd been burned?"

McGee nodded and gave Hunter a point by point recollection. He told him of the cigar box, the stack of rare gold certificates, that he wanted a Marine colonel killed. "I thought he wanted Eastwood dead for some reason because Dory had been a media darling for weeks. I didn't think it was real. I thought it was some kind of test. I turned him down. Then a week later, in the *Navy Times*, there was a little blurb that a jet pilot named Colonel Emory had passed away. Suicide."

"Harriers." Hunter indicated the name of the jet. "The early models were called *Widowmakers*. Killed a lot of Marines. I think Emory had the most hours in Harriers than anyone."

"My buds at Coronado had good intel that some rogue dudes from this place were using an Agency C-130 to smuggle cocaine and heroin out of Central and South America and into the country, via the Marine base in California."

"El Toro."

McGee nodded. "The implication was that Emory tried to report what he saw to his superiors, but all it got him was an investigation. Next thing you know he's dead—supposedly he put a shotgun in his mouth and pulled the trigger."

"That usually makes a mess."

McGee looked at Hunter hard. He shook his head ever so slightly. "That's what you'd think, but there was no exit wound. Five investigations. Five times it was ruled a suicide."

Hunter frowned at the suggestion. "Who investigates a suicide five times? But you say there was no exit wound? The shotgun blast was...*contained*? How's that possible? That's unbelievable." Hunter became very quiet. He tapped his fingers together in a teepee. He said,

"That's probably one of the many types of ammunition the S&T or one of their labs developed. Nasty and lethal. Maybe some low-velocity shaped charge. Something that just bounces around a cranium without penetrating it. Federal Air Marshalls have ammo designed not to poke a hole in an airliner if they have to shoot someone."

Director Lynche strolled into the conference room. Hunter informed him that Castaño had once tried to pitch McGee to assassinate a Marine Corps officer. "I'm going to kill him if I get the chance."

The CIA Director shook his head and pointed at Hunter in disgust. "You're not going to kill anyone. You aren't a murderer. As for Castaño being tangential to some Marine's death, at this point nothing would surprise me." Lynche replied, "One of the things the National Clandestine Service is supposed to do is interdiction, find and neutralize the Russian or Islamic assassin who may try to eliminate one of our guys or an ally. They have license for that kind of work overseas, but not in the U.S. Interdiction work in the U.S. is the purview of the FBI."

Hunter asked, "Have you ever heard of an operations officer pitching someone for an assassination?"

Lynche frowned at the question, shook his head, and continued. "Not our guys. Political assassinations are usually the purview of Russians; the FBI views Russians killing Russians as 'Russian on Russian' crime. No one gives a shit. They're not going to spend any time on those cases unless it emerges into political warfare. Sometimes we have been able to do it—prevent the murder of a defector we are interested in."

Hunter asked, "Like the woman from Iran...."

"Something like that. Success is usually a function of the quality of the intel. I won't say we've been able to stop all of them. But those we do interdict, we try to turn them. When they disappear from the SVR and they show up at our door, it irritates their president."

McGee said, "*Screw Vladimir.*"

Hunter said, "*Vint Vladimir.* So the SVR can assassinate the enemies of Russia in the U.S. and the Agency still isn't authorized...."

Lynche cut him off. "We're not authorized to conduct assassination operations anywhere. Executive order. Of course, we're not supposed to blind our enemies either." Lynche refrained from looking at Hunter, and Hunter refrained from looking at Lynche or McGee. The one hundred plus assassinations Hunter had conducted against high-value *international* terrorists targets were "off the books." They were called something less lethal than assassinations, redefined as *aerial eradication operations* and were kept at the executive special access program level of secrecy. And they were all overseas where terrorists were considered enemy combatants and not a political figure. *No regime changes.*

Hunter's BlackBerry went off, vibrating and ringing. He checked to see who could be calling him. He looked at his two friends and connected the call. He said, "Good evening, Colonel Eastwood, how can I help you?"

Eastwood provided a synopsis of the night's aircraft crashes on the interstate. "Duncan, it looks like a pair of Cessna Skymasters with the twin tails exploded in flight, in close proximity, at the same time. It doesn't look like they collided as previously thought. There are three victims. Two in one and one guy...."

Hunter said, using the vernacular, "A solo pilot. Apologies for the interruption. Continue please, good sir."

"One of the reporters overheard the coroner say to a state trooper that it looked like the victims were killed by an anti-personnel mine."

Duncan Hunter scrunched up his face with the information and spun around to face McGee and Lynche. *What?* He asked Eastwood, "You mean, like a Claymore?"

The mention of "a Claymore?" got the full attention of McGee and Lynche. They stared at Hunter. Hunter was more confused than ever. *A Claymore? A Claymore. Would those clowns from NCS have access to Claymores?* After a few long seconds of ignoring Eastwood and processing his thoughts, he thought, *Of course, they would. They have access to everything and no one would question them for wanting them or having them. They're training aids.* He said, "You mean someone who knows what a frag pattern looks like? They say it looks as if they were killed by a Claymore." *While they were airborne? That information is intriguing but confusing. There is a solution set if you eliminate the impossible, whatever remains, no matter how improbable, must be the truth.*

Eastwood continued, "Correct. Apparently. It looks like they departed from, ahh..., the Warrenton-Fauquier Airport."

Hunter tapped his hand to his forehead. He rolled his eyes. *Of course! Low-key airport. They have excellent facilities and rows of T-hangars! Adjacent to other facilities. Jet capable. I should have thought of it; I should have checked my stupid smartphone.* "Nice job, Dory, and thanks. I'll get back to you."

Before Eastwood could ask his friend a question, Hunter was off the line, looking at his boss. He wanted to say, *Greg, I think three of the NCS dudes are out of the game. That leaves one still on the loose. And I'll bet you a new sailboat I know who that is. If I can find him....* But it was too early to conjecture on initial reports from an active aircraft accident scene. When he wore his aircraft accident investigator's hat when teaching the course, he scolded any student who conjectured on the causal effects of a crash. Hunter apologized for the interruption and continued his conversation with McGee and Lynche.

Hunter said, "We were talking about *aerial eradication operations* and Russian assassinations by the KGB. KGB is way more cooler, deadlier, nastier….than SVR. Foreign Intelligence Service for civilian affairs. SVR sounds like a goat fart or an abbreviation for some kind of video recorder."

Lynche continued without comment. "Former Russian foreign intelligence service agents disappear from the SVR radar scope in Europe. If they don't show up on an embassy door in the middle of the night or make contact with one of our officers, we send a jet for them; then transplant them with new identities. The majority already know English—the old KGB, now SVR trains them in technical and conversational English—so getting them set up doing work other than killing Americans or Russians has been a good thing. They usually provide a wealth of information and they have good intel, like Oswald was programmed by the KGB to kill Kennedy. Those sorts of things."

Hunter interjected, "I know some hundred Washington Democrats are in bed with *Vladimir*, but who isn't working for Moscow at State? Foggy Bottom is like an old Soviet college campus."

Lynche waited for an opening to continue. "When we turn them loose, we keep an eye on them, usually through a local police chief. Sometimes we think one of them has been discovered and eliminated. Some can't handle the pressure of being on the run, some can't handle freedom or vodka, and they take their own lives."

McGee mouthed, "Seriously?"

Lynche nodded.

McGee said, "Sounds like those that reportedly off themselves were actually tracked down and killed by the Russians. They made it look like suicides."

"I want to blame the NCS dudes," interjected Hunter.

Lynche frowned and continued, "You always wanted to blame the NCS dudes. It's well known that the Thirteenth Directorate is loose in America, Europe, England, and the Middle East, and they're at it again and even more so. They're even more aggressive today. After the Berlin Wall fell there was a pause… if you will. But the number of newly unshackled senior intelligence officers who wanted to escape Moscow went through the roof."

Hunter offered, "Pilots stole cargo jets and flew their families and friends out of the country. Some stole suitcase nukes."

Lynche wanted to throw something at his best friend. He sighed and continued, "The former intel officers knew where to go and whom to talk to; they overwhelmed our capabilities. We couldn't handle all of them, to discern who was a good guy or a plant. It remains a game of opposing intelligence communities."

Hunter said to Lynche, "Sounds like we're just the latest pawns in the latest version of the Great Game. It's been going on for over a hundred years."

Lynche added, "A hundred *and fifty* years ago. Rudyard Kipling's *Kim* was very accurate."

Hunter brought McGee up to date. "At this particular moment, these four are on the run. They have weapons. Including an upgraded ground version of the YO-3A's gun. Max effective range is ten miles."

Hunter thought, *And if we are lucky, three of them are now shredded wheat and burnt toast.*

McGee shook his head at the thought of a ten-mile sniper weapon that troops could carry. "Same ammo, I take it."

Hunter and Lynche answered, "Yes."

Lynche asked, "Are you going to tell us what Colonel Eastwood had to say?"

Hunter said, "Colonel Eastwood reported that two airplanes crashed on the westbound lanes of I-66 out by Warrenton. Ammunition cooked off as the aircraft burned. The coroner was overheard saying three men were likely killed by Claymores."

Lynche nearly jumped out of his seat and asked, "*Claymores?*" He knew who in his Agency had access to them. NCS trainers at The Farm. NCS executives.

Hunter knew what Claymore mines were, although as a long-time aviator there was no need for him to know anything more than the basics on how to arm and disarm one. He had a vague recollection of receiving Claymore training from his Marine Corps boot camp days in the early 70s. *I remember they were simple enough to setup and arm that even a pilot could understand.*

McGee was the expert on U.S. explosive devices and caught the two men's uncertainty. He said, "As you know Claymores are anti-personnel mines. At point blank range, one will shred a human so thoroughly you'd need tweezers to pick up the pieces and put what remains in a shoebox. There are a dozen ways to employ them, to include remotely. The usual way is by trip wire."

Lynche nodded and said, "They train foreign nationals how to use them at the Farm."

Just as I thought! Hunter said, "My bet is that three of the four NCS turds were on those airplanes."

McGee said, "Leaving one." The men exchanged glances. *Would this crisis solve itself with three of the four men being removed by Claymores in airplanes? That's a new one.*

Lynche rubbed his face and said, "Let's not jump to conclusions. We haven't heard from the FBI, so there's nothing official."

McGee understood the dilemma and returned to the tabletop exercise. He asked the question but knew the answer already. "Why do you think they'd take a ten-mile sniper system with them?"

Hunter said, "They want to take out the targets the Left, or the Democrats — but I repeat myself — want to eliminate. I'd think our newly elected president has to be a priority target."

McGee nodded and thought of other assassination candidates. *Lynche, Hunter, then the list goes on.*

Lynche was quiet. He contemplated what to say next.

McGee said, "They would only carry it for one purpose."

Lynche smiled and nodded. He knew; he already knew. *It's obvious.* "I talked to the Secret Service Director already, told him that the president is in danger. His family too. The radiological crisis has passed. Now I need Duncan to find them."

Hunter said, "It would be good to know that the missing ground TS2 wasn't in those airplanes. It would suck to find out it is still out there. Ammo cooked off. It would also be good to know what weapons were found on those aircraft." Hunter thought about the potential new mission. *Finding them and doing something to them is another thing. You want me to find them and not kill them? I don't think that's negotiable, Executive Order or not. They targeted me and my family.* Hunter broke his silence and said, "I still think we may have gotten a break, but we may have just been dealt a more complicated problem. Needle in the haystack stuff. I'll bet we only have one NCS dude to deal with now, and I think we know who that is. Subordinates rarely blow up their bosses. But it'll take some time before we know who's actually dead in those airplanes. For the moment, I need to see this Alvin gizmo and ask him what his intentions are with my wife." McGee was confused and Lynche sighed in exasperation.

Lynche walked Hunter and McGee to the SCIF that housed the AIRRAID tool just as Kelly and Anna Comstock brought food and drinks. They retreated to the Director's conference room where Hunter held the door open for food, family, and friends. Bags of food were torn open and consumed. Nazy smelled the food on the floor and joined the group, she sat next to Duncan.

After ten minutes of scarfing down burgers and fries, Nazy led Lynche, Hunter, and McGee to the SCIF. She gave the men a primer on the AIRRAID tool. Nazy said she had asked Alvin, "Is there a history of unresolved political assassinations within fifty miles of the Washington D.C. area?"

"Alvin asked me a series of questions to narrow my focus and differentiate between the layers of intel." She projected a graph from her computer, "As you can see, these four men were in the immediate area of some fifty political deaths ruled suicides, suspicious heart condition, or done by an unknown assailant. That's not the only thing that popped out at me. I expanded the database to include government, military, civil service, other intelligence officers. It's reasonable to assume they could be involved in another 50.… colonels, generals, admirals, senior executives, policemen. Noteworthy, all men. When the search was expanded to include women and political affiliation, I thought that the data were corrupted. I had used the generic intelligence officer. Alvin found nearly a thousand going back to before the Second World War. Mostly Russians."

"Islamists?" Hunter asked meekly?

Nazy shook her head. "Hardly any."

Lynche had expected the answer but asked anyway, "From what source did Alvin pull those?"

"Primarily law enforcement reports, the travel claims and performance appraisals from members of the IC, after action reports, embassy dispatches, and the Library of Diaries."

Lynche nodded; Hunter was confused but held his tongue. McGee watched the show.

Nazy filled the large monitors with Alvin's findings in spreadsheet form. Lynche and Hunter thought that the President's Disposition Matrix looked similar to Nazy's spreadsheet, but instead of listing the names of terrorists and their locations, it included listings of Americans, Canadians, and British who presumably knew too much or had become political liabilities.

McGee asked if there was an intersection with a Marine colonel named Emory, in California. Nazy consulted the spreadsheet and said, "According to this, Steve Castaño and Jarvis Bomarito were within 50 miles at the time and place of death. You are probably aware that Colonel Emory's death was ruled a suicide." She caught herself and asked Alvin to refresh the screen to include political deaths attributed to suicide.

McGee nodded. *Good idea.*

After two minutes the wall of screens were updated with new data points. Nazy located the Emory data line and said, "Mr. Castaño's travel claim and travel orders have him in the town of Oceanside for a meeting. He returned by Air Branch aircraft that evening."

Hunter said, "El Toro Marine Corps Air Station was just up Interstate 5. That's more than just being in the area."

"Purpose of the meeting? Do you have that?" asked Lynche. Proximity to the Marine base concerned him. There was an old rumor that an Agency aircraft had been used to move contraband from South America into the United States. It wasn't a sanctioned CIA operation.

"He met with another operations officer from SOG. Topic unknown. SAP." Special Access Program. "All of the travel claims have a purpose of 'temporary duty;' in almost all cases, the travel claim doesn't have sufficient granularity with which to make a determination. And I'm assuming that if our men are a reasonable distance away from one of these…assassinations…*suicides*…."

Lynche said, "Let's call them variously ascribed deaths or some such rot. I don't want to call them assassinations just yet. Ask Alvin to confirm an Agency aircraft operated out of the Marine base supporting embassies or operations in South America."

After a quick inquiry from Nazy, the little robot came back with an immediate response: Operation *Conchita*. SAP.

Hunter asked, "Embassy ops?"

Lynche nodded. He knew the answer to the bigger question. To the smaller question he said, "Ambassadors get armored cars. Those cars were built in Orange County. We moved their household goods to and from their place of duty. Weapons. Agency-specific equipment. Shredders. Disintegrators."

After a pause, Hunter nodded and asked, "So what do you want us to do, Greg?"

He told them.

Hunter scratched his head. "If Castaño didn't kill his friends, then it's easier to find four than a lone wolf. They have to be somewhere. Someone has seen them. They have to sleep somewhere unless they used Agency passports to get out of the country."

"Could they do that?" asked Nazy.

"They're pilots with tubs of cash and a ten-mile sniper system. If it was me, I'd run to the nearest airport and commandeer an airplane and get the hell out of Dodge as fast as I could. I'd disappear."

Lynche said, "You're not normal, Duncan."

"Same principle." Hunter smiled. "Shouldn't we think about what their next move might be? They're never going back to their houses or their old lives." Hunter paused and everyone looked at him. He said, "Greg, apologies for redundancies, but did you ask the FBI to check your house and sailboat for explosives."

Lynche looked defeated and nodded. He said his wife was probably making breakfast for the FBI agents at the house and the FBI Director was on top of all the possible bomb targets. Thoughts of being shredded by a Claymore distracted him. *They could take out Connie too. She never asked for any of this.*

McGee waved a giant hand. "If they have a TS2 weapon system, then they'll use it." He turned to Lynche and said, "If they're dragging this around, they have some unfinished business. You called them, spooked them, and they're on the run. They're not happy with you, sir. They'll come after you. At the very least, you and the president." Then he thought, *And if they're working for someone like the Russians, the Russians will want that weapon too.*

Greg Lynche nearly popped out of his chair. "*Me!?*"

Hunter blithely said, "You know Bill's correct."

McGee continued, projecting what he'd do. "Hotels have security cameras—they're not the right places to go in this situation. The roads are clobbered too."

Nazy found a spot to sit down and touched Duncan on the nose with her index finger and said, "They also know how to defeat them. The cameras. Facial recognition systems."

Hunter nodded. *If the disguise is good enough. And…the NCS dudes are masters of disguises. Crap!*

Lynche asked, "Are you suggesting they must have another place not too far away? Where would you go, Duncan?"

"I'm a pilot. They're pilots. I'd go to an airport. The closest one here is National. Then Manassas. There are some others. Bridgewater, Frederick. We used Easton to stage the YO-3A for several years until we got the space at BWI. That's a great airport across the Bay Bridge in Annapolis. But I'd say that one is too far."

Hunter allowed his thoughts to freewheel. "There are hangars to hide in. They're remote, have security, and…. They're absolutely some of the best places to stash sensitive things. Stuff. Thieves don't bother airports too much, unless you try to steal an airplane and unless you're a pilot; that's usually a fatal outcome."

Hunter expanded the scope of his thinking. "If they have squirreled away tons of money, and they're pilots, I'd think they had to have gone shopping for some very special airplanes…."

Incredulously, Lynche asked, "You mean like a warbird?"

Hunter shook his head and said, "That's a possibility, but they're boy scouts. Always prepared. No, the special airplane I'm thinking about is one that can carry what they need when they need to evacuate."

Lynche said, "Um, they wouldn't necessarily need to have one of their own. We have the green fleet. Cessna 310s. We have them all over the country for our guys to move around the country. Why couldn't they could self-evacuate?"

Hunter's body language dispelled the notion of using Agency assets. He said, "Using one of the Air Branch airplanes would send off alarms all across the National Airspace System. Pick up the phone and Air Branch could tell you where every one of their airplanes are. The FAA tracks the special N-numbers. No, I'm still back at airports. You say they're pilots. Flight currency isn't an issue—like riding a horse—you know that. I'm thinking airports. There's Bridgewater, Virginia, but it's a private field and requires a tilt-rotor ride to get there quickly. I'm sorry, any pilot worth his salt who needed to disappear quickly and quietly would get to the closest airport and either take his own airplane or steal one. In a situation like this I subscribe to *Occam's Razor*. Unless they have access to a helicopter, then all bets are off. If they had a Robinson they could operate from a backyard."

McGee offered, "And I'd take as much firepower as I could carry. I would not be giving up without a fight."

Lynche said, "Then it's either they stay in the local area because they have unfinished business, or they run for a safe haven."

McGee offered, "There's not much worse than having a pissed off special operations sniper with a ten-mile gun wanting revenge."

Lynche suddenly felt chilled.

Hunter blurted out, "Or they took the first boat to China or Russia or some anti-American country—where did Hitler go? Argentina? Peru?" Then Hunter thought of something which was mentioned earlier. *What did Lynche say? What did Nazy say about a Library of Diaries? What the hell is that?"*

Lynche rolled his eyes. He waved a finger at him for disclosing top secret information. The others in the room thought Hunter was just trying to bring a little levity into the discussion, but the CIA Director refused to play along.

Nazy came to the rescue. "I have another list of things I want to ask Alvin."

Hunter said, "Then I think it's time to ask Alvin some more questions."

Lynche nodded and made motions with his hands "to go." He asked her to "...run intersections of all political deaths of all kinds and politicians who committed suicide or had heart attacks with our four missing turds. Add military guys, law enforcement. It can do that in seconds, correct?" And then he said, "And run 'the diaries' for possible triangulation."

Nazy Cunningham said, "Yes, sir." Hunter smiled and wondered again what was meant by "…the diaries." Hunter knew if he asked, Lynche would shake his head and scold him: No need to know!

Lynche asked Nazy to use the diary database to see if past presidents had given the CIA or the OSS any assassination missions. "If the thing balks, don't press it. The diaries database has some unusual information that an analyst might not understand. It was just a wild hair…." Lynche stood to leave.

Nazy agreed and said, "I'll ask Alvin…."

"…or anything else we might think of." Hunter smirked, clearly suggesting mischievousness. McGee knew when he wasn't wanted and stood beside the CIA Director.

Before Lynche and McGee left the SCIF, Nazy finished her thought. "I was going to add, are there any other questions that Director Lynche or Mr. McGee might have?"

McGee shook his head to indicate he had none. He uttered, "You two behave. You know there's cameras in here.

Hunter frowned and said, "There are no cameras in SCIFs—what planet have you been on?" Nazy blushed and Lynche and McGee returned to the Director's office with huge smiles. Hunter leered at his wife.

62

November 9
CIA Headquarters

When Nazy asked her first question, the little round robot ran up and down the spaces between the mainframes and computer stacks. It freaked Hunter out a little. "It's AI with an IQ of over 400 and the programmers gave it an attitude. Alvin is very smart and can think like a human…actually like ten Einsteins all at once."

"Even the Chinese?" Hunter meekly asked.

"They're smart but have no advanced manufacturing capability. They're still buying jets from Russia, and trying to steal our trade secrets from every business sector. But you know that."

"I'm ready for the show. I have a couple of questions. And I want to know about the diaries. Greg said something about diaries."

She ignored his last couple of sentences. *Director Lynche shouldn't have mentioned those.* Nazy said, "Alvin, please say 'Hello' to Dante Locke. He'll be assisting me during this session."

In a voice that was strangely like Hunter's, Alvin began with "Hello, Dante Locke. I'm assuming this isn't your given name."

Nazy scolded, "No need to know, Alvin. Mr. Locke and I'll be asking questions. Are you ready?"

"You know I am, Miss Cunningham." Hunter gave Nazy a side-look of mock horror. *Could the electronic Alvin have a temper? Shades of HAL 9000! That's all I need…another damn computer shitting all over me.*

Nazy turned to Hunter for his first question. "Hello Alvin, I'm interested in the known histories of unresolved political assassinations. For example, JFK had an affair with a woman named Mary Pinchot Meyer. She was a direct vector to the president; her death is an unresolved political murder or an assassination. I'm interested in any of those similar unresolved political murders or political suicides that have any intersections with any of the leaders from the Operations Directorate to what's now called the National Clandestine Service. Also, any intersections between NCS members and any Russians or any of the intelligence officers of the former Iron Curtain." The diminutive robot didn't move.

Nazy spoke to Alvin and listed the names of the men from the NCS and their titles. "All NCS leaders or OSS equivalents going back to the creation of the OSS. Or if you determine an outside group's influence, I'd like to see that as well."

The round robot spun 180° and immediately shot down the wide middle aisle. Hunter lost sight of it. Alvin's voice was piped through a set of speakers on the workstation, "Murders, suicides, and unresolved or questionable deaths with the top men of the OSS and NCS. I assume you want both conditions in North America and in Europe. There are a significant number of the requested intersections in South America, Africa and the Middle East. May I assume you'd like to view these as well?"

Without lifting her eyes, Nazy said, "Correct. Prioritize North America and Europe. Then the others." She scribbled down the directions Hunter had given Alvin. Sometimes a note would stimulate other conditions or scenarios.

Alvin returned, sped up the center aisle, and said, "Your data are displayed on screen one through four. Monitors five and six cite the subjects and references in database format."

Hunter was dumbfounded as the wide six-foot monitors came to life. The first thing Hunter noticed was the list of over a hundred unresolved deaths of the terrorists he had killed from the YO-3A in Africa, the Middle East, and South America as well as the names of the NCS officers who were in the immediate area and provided information in dispatch to Headquarters.

He scanned the presented material and thought, *In nearly every case one or more of Castaño's guys was on the ground providing the intel for me to target terrorists. That's not the work of someone who had gone off the rails. What happened to these guys?*

Seeing Duncan struggle with the information Nazy held up her hand and wrote on a tablet: *Be general, no specifics that Alvin can use at a later date.*

He took the pen from her and wrote, *Alvin just listed, virtually every one of the terrorists neutralized by Wraith with the NCS officer who was on the ground observing the terrorists directly or receiving data or developing intel. Then they fed Headquarters with the details and on-the-spot intel in dispatch. Most of my targets came from intel from the NCS four, at one time or another. They probably didn't know they were working to develop the intel for me. That's how they could be so close to the action. NCS got a little piece of intel, over time put two and two together, and put their guys on scene. For glory or gold. Who knows?* Hunter smiled to himself. *That's how they knew who had the money or the gold or the antiques or elephant ivory. They developed the intel. They were there when I was there!*

Nazy nodded and said, "Good work Alvin. I'll need some time to process these. Please leave them on the screens."

The voice coming from the rotund computer was crystal clear and smooth. "Alvin can process and analyze for you. On screen five I've also listed the intersections of political deaths of all kinds, to include unknown with the name of the NCS officer who provided the intelligence as the on-scene agent. On screen one, Steve Castaño reporting the date, the location, and the names of the deceased." Alvin went on to repeat the same information for the other three NCS men on separate screens. "Total number of intersections: two hundred twenty-two. These are single reportings. Multiple reportings, where more than one NCS officer was present at an intersection, are as follows on screen six." The roly-poly robot stopped and waited for another command.

Hunter had written down a question for Nazy. She asked Alvin to investigate and cross triangulate *Stingray* data from the NCS men's BlackBerries with location of a political death. Three minutes later and the little robot refreshed the multiple screens.

Hunter checked the lists he had received from Eastwood and McGee. He found the names Larrabee and Emory embedded with dozens of politicians and generals and others, many with Russian or Arabic surnames. The *Stingray* confirmed that, within minutes of the police reports, both Castaño and Bomarito had been in the immediate area of where the bodies of Larrabee and Emory were found. Three of the men had been in the area of Algeria on the night Hunter was shot down. Fässler, Bomarito, and Troxel. No intersection for Castaño. Three of the men had been in Abu Dhabi on the night Hunter found and killed former President Mazibuike on the top floor of the Burj Khalifa in Dubai. The same three: Fässler, Bomarito, and Troxel. No intersection for Castaño.

Nazy wrote on the pad: *What about breaking and entering, like my house?*

Hunter took her pen and wrote: *Was your house ever reported? Did your system dial the police? Not sure the info would be good, since you live so close to their offices.* She said, "No."

Duncan scribbled out new instructions. *Can Alvin find out if they owned or leased aircraft and where those aircraft were hangered or based?* Nazy said, "Ask him." So Hunter asked Alvin a string of questions. One after another. Alvin answered some requests quickly. Others required the robot to reposition itself and plug into another computer stack.

Hunter had a dozen additional questions he was ready to pose to

Alvin. Nazy had other ideas. She spun Duncan's chair around, hiked her dress up, and straddled his legs. She crushed her breasts against his chest and kissed him until he was out of air. She whispered, "See...I missed you."

"I can tell." He kissed her back and gently ran his hands over her ass. She immediately uncoupled her lips, stood up, and pulled down her dress, then frowned at him. Apparently touching her hiney was the signal that it was time to return to work.

• • • • •

Hunter asked Alvin to look at the FAA aircraft registry database for any owners of aircraft under the names Fässler, Bomarito, Troxel, or Castaño or any of their first or middle names. Alvin reported that none were found. Hunter asked for the last time they had purchased any type of aviation fuel or gasoline with a credit card, or any payments for insurance, any payments for maintenance. Hunter then asked Alvin if were there any leases under the NCS four's names. After an inordinate period, Hunter asked for the sales records of Cessna Skymasters and any local purchases. Alvin reported that some aircraft had been purchased several years ago. Two Cessna 337s had been picked up in Florida and flown to Virginia. Alvin annotated the N-numbers of the two aircraft.

"Are there any flights associated with these aircraft, or are they holed up in a hangar being worked on? Who are the Skymasters registered to and do they have other aircraft registered under those names and their location." Hunter's voice became more demanding. Alvin listed the city-pairs from which the two aircraft operated. The Skymasters spent time crisscrossing Virginia and the New England area. There was a favorite airport: the TF Green Airport in Rhode Island.

"They're the masters of disguise, they have access to different identities. They know how to create and operate shell companies. If these guys are as bad we think they are, they'd never willingly put the other side of their life on display." Nazy agreed.

Then Hunter asked about the Agency's airplanes which were run and maintained by the CIA's Air Branch. Alvin told Nazy there were hundreds of entries for servicing fees at private airports and dozens of receipts for services rendered at military installations. Hunter asked Alvin to find intersections of these aircraft within a 75-mile range of a political death. *Bingo.* Hunter believed he now knew how NCS did it. He had had enough of Alvin. It was a marvelous tool. Intriguing. But it was also aggravating. He was ready for something additional to eat, like key lime pie or ice cream and he wasn't about to invite some machine that was preoccupied with his wife to join him.

Hunter had a few more questions for the little robot. Nazy looked them over and asked if they could wait. She was intrigued at the direction of thought Duncan had suggested with his questions. It would require analyzing the DNC's archives and a set of diaries she didn't know if the Agency had. "Low priority, Miss Cunningham. When you can get around to it."

Nazy sent Alvin to his recharge station. She took Hunter's hand and led him out of the SCIF.

63

November 9
Washington, D.C.

The lead special agent of the FBI's bomb disposal units investigating the homes of the CIA's NCS leaders, reported to the FBI Director that their investigation was complete. Several significant and sophisticated booby-traps involving active and de-activated M18A1 Claymore anti-personnel mines were found at one of the residences. He said over a speakerphone, "The Claymores jammed into trees and the corners of rooms were just plastic casings; the explosives had been removed. Since we couldn't trust anything they did, we used the CIA's jammers and saturated the area with RF energy—we jammed every signal on the spectrum. It allowed us to find and disarm their booby-traps. One of those booby-traps was a binary weapon."

FBI Director Vincze stopped placing desk items into a box. He asked, "Also hidden in cigar boxes?"

"Those bastards had a thing for rare cigars. Had that weapon received the appropriate detonation signal, the two glass vials would have shattered, and the mixture would have exploded into a sticky fireball. Think Molotov cocktail on an industrial scale. Our guys would have been fried. The CIA's little green jammers were instrumental in our safety."

The FBI Director sighed, thanked the agents in the field, and said, "Okay, good job to all. Great catch. You can stand down. Thank you for your quick response. I'll let the CIA know." He disconnected the call. He left a voice message for the CIA Director, his last official act as FBI Director.

Andrew Vincze signed his resignation letter and placed it on the middle of his desk. He replaced his pen inside his suitcoat pocket. The only things on his desk were two telephones and the single sheet of paper. He removed his service pistol from the top drawer of his desk. He withdrew it from its holster, racked a cartridge, stuck the barrel under his chin, and pulled the trigger.

•   •   •   •   •

Sitting in front of the dressing table, a clean shaven Steve Castaño wore a white t-shirt with the silkscreened image of a uniformed cop in a menacing clown face pointing a revolver. Only he and his men knew the significance of the image on his chest, a private joke. He worked for hours to disguise his face with prosthetics and makeup to alter his cheeks, and eyebrows, and the ends of his mouth. He was nearly finished with the transformation when a radio tuned to a Washington D.C. station repeated the announcement of the election of President Javier Hernandez and the death of the Democratic National Committee Chairman, Dr. Nikita Zhavrazhinov. The events seemed to be from a lifetime ago.

Castaño sat stunned in the chair for over an hour, not moving, just thinking the radio broadcast reminding him that *The Judge* was dead. Any arrangement he had had with *The Judge* was null and void. It was unlikely there was another member in the DNC who ran spies or men like him to eliminate problems. He debated whether it was worth his life to continue his final mission, for he'd surely be killed or captured. He convinced himself that he'd never be captured…alive. Special operations warriors across the globe knew that being captured while performing a mission on the battlefield meant a gruesome and painful death. The man who had risen to the pinnacle of the clandestine world would find it too embarrassing to be captured on the political battlefield to stand trial. Castaño turned off the radio and continued his preparations. He'd finish what he promised. Castaño was convinced Republicans were responsible for the unmasking of 3M, the failure of Eleanor Tussy, and *The Judge's* death. He would never become the CIA Director. He'd make them pay.

Castaño just needed to fool the facial recognition cameras between the airport where he was and his destination. His final act was changing into a black battle dress uniform, buttoning the last of the buttons to hide the crew neck t-shirt. Black boots with speed laces and an official black cap of a Secret Service Agent completed the transformation. Distinctive patches and special tabs on the uniform indicated he was a member of the Presidential Protection Service and a member of the Counter-Sniper Division.

He raced away from the airport in a black BMW X5M, an expensive German sport utility vehicle with a racing engine. It had the perfect getaway rubber on all four corners—run-flat tires—in case someone tried to shoot them or throw spikes in front of his vehicle. He also had the vehicle "up-armored to level-seven," in the parlance of the military. A specialty shop in Texas did all the modifications to ensure the BMW was impervious to armor-piercing rounds fired from a rifle. That body shop did custom armoring work for the rich and famous, as well as for law enforcement, politicians, and the intelligence community.

Steve Castaño settled in for the near one-hour trip down Highway 1 which paralleled the interstate. From time to time he looked in the side and rearview mirrors checking for marked and unmarked cars of the Virginia State Police. A check in the rearview mirror confirmed his disguise remained perfect. His mother wouldn't recognize him. With all the time on his hands, he quietly thanked the Agency women who trained him to disguise his looks and expertly hide the disfigurements on his hands and face.

He remembered their faces when they saw his hands. "There's not much we can do with your hands. Make-up won't work. Prosthetics will, but they have limitations — you'll lose all sense of touch, and they'll look waxy after a few minutes. I'm afraid that under all circumstances, you will have to wear gloves. If you want those things covered up, we're going to have to make up something resembling a glove. There's not much else we can do." He gritted his teeth, *Those things! Those things!* He amazed himself in maintaining his composure that day when the women called his hands, *Those things!*

He was taken back to the time he was experimenting with compounds during high school chemistry. He didn't know why some complex compounds smelled horrible and could be detected from far away. Castaño had been mesmerized, because the compounds with the more noxious fumes were, curiously, also the most chemically active. He had stumbled on how to make a tiny explosive from just the clear sweat formed on the test tube of something he threw together. He expected he could make something truly deadly from the rack of special compounds that were in a white steel cabinet behind lock and key.

Castaño wanted to see what would happen if he mixed up a larger batch of explosives, something with a little more "pop" than a cap gun. He assumed a linear reaction with an increase of chemicals. He didn't take static electricity into consideration as a source of ignition. He wasn't grounded and a spark ignited the volatile invisible vapors which surrounded his bare hands and arms. Safety glasses had saved his eyes, but the exploding concoction scorched his face and ears. Castaño had jumped up and turned to run out of the room as his hands and ears were on fire. The instructor knocked him to the ground and pulled coats and jackets from the backs of chairs to put out the flames. He awoke later in a hospital covered in white gauze. Skin grafts from various parts of his body covered his burns to make him somewhat "whole" again. The most painful surgeries during reconstruction were when the soles of his feet were removed to become new palms for his hands.

• • • • •

The airwaves remained saturated with the news that President Hernandez had won the election. Castaño punched a button for another radio station. The local conservative talk radio host was giddy, delivering the news with wit and humor and newfound zeal.

"The White House Communication Director announced President Hernandez will be traveling to Camp David this evening. In other news from the campaign offices of the defeated Democrat candidate, a friend of the family made a short announcement that Mrs. Tussy will be meeting with her advisors and will weigh all her options. A formal announcement will be forthcoming. The death of the DNC Chairman looks to be an accident, however, authorities have not ruled out suicide."

The talk show host passed the microphone to the traffic newscaster. She announced that "Interstate 66 is still closed to both east and westbound traffic due to an aircraft crash. Emergency responders remain on the scene. We'll bring you more information as this tragedy unfolds." Castaño shut off the radio.

As he approached the Wilson Bridge he saw his target at his one o'clock position. *Getting in* should pose no problem. *Getting on* the roof might pose an issue, but he thought he could bribe his way to the top of the building. He had a few challenge coins, and they always opened doors when money or cajole could not. *Getting set* would depend on when the president moved. *Getting down and away*—he should have enough time on the roof to weigh his options, surveil the area, and come up with an escape plan. *No one will think of jumping* kept rolling around in his mind. It was as if he had already decided that, come the moment of success, he'd be over the side of the MGM Grand Hotel's tower, strapped into a pilot's ultimate getaway device.

• • • • •

The sun would be setting across Washington D.C. soon, culminating one of the most remarkable days of American election history with an appointed president becoming an elected president. Most government offices were closing or had closed when the first of a series of telephone calls came through to the office of the CIA Director. The news was depressing. The men from the NCS had apparently escaped the intelligence and law enforcement nets. There was mounting evidence that they'd gotten away easily. It shouldn't have been a surprise. They were experts in disguise.

Of course they got away. The FBI and DHS had spent billions secretly developing the facial recognition program, and when it was needed the most, it failed to produce. The NCS executives were well versed in the capabilities and limitations of the system. The consensus from the CIA, the FBI, the DHS, and the Secret Service was that four of the most dangerous men in the special operations world knew how to avoid being detected by the facial recognition system and were still on the loose.

●　　●　　●　　●　　●

The once euphoric media had been reduced to a stunned blubbering maelstrom of confusion, pity, and disbelief as they covered the aftermath of the Tussy debacle and wished for something uplifting to report. The men and women of the visual media remained shell-shocked from the election results. Some reporters could no longer function as on-air commentators, yearning for something—anything to deliver them from reality of the Democrat Party losing the election in what some were calling "a landslide."

The late breaking news of the DNC Chairman tumbling to his death and a multiple aircraft crash weren't newsworthy enough to push the presidential election results off of the front page of newspapers or the teleprompters of news anchors.

64

November 9
Washington, D.C.

The Secret Service Agent carrying an oversized black duffel bag on his shoulder marched across the marble floor. He spied the concierge; his path did not waver. The manager was summoned before the man dressed in the black uniform reached the busy concierge's desk. Once the manager arrived, the man flashed his identification card and bona fides, but his eyes remained covered in the dark, wrap-around sunglasses favored by Secret Service Agents. He informed the manager that he was the advance security party for a significant visiting political figure. He apologized for not being able to forward the appropriate paperwork from headquarters because this mission was very fast moving, all very quiet, all because of the election.

When the manager spied the embroidered tabs on the man's shoulder and front pocket—Presidential Protection Service and Counter-Sniper Division—his demeanor changed from concerned to helpful, and the conversation between the two men became one-sided. The Secret Service Agent required unfettered access to the tallest part of the MGM Grand National Harbor and a room as close as possible to his overlook point. He'd be up there for a few hours or a few days; when he was on the roof he wasn't to be disturbed. "I'll view any approach as an attack on my position. I'll be in radio contact with my teammates. May I have your cell number?"

The manager's jowls bounced up and down as he agreed and spit out his cell number. He asked if this was in response to the president being elected and the Democrat nominee being rejected. "She was supposed to win. I don't understand it."

The Secret Service man's answer was predictable. He rested a hand on his holster. A Sig Sauer poked out from under his hand. "We stay out of politics as much as possible. We just protect 'em." Then the Secret Service Agent nodded a nonverbal assent, and the manager smiled broadly.

As they rode the elevator to the roof, the manager stated that he had only met a few Secret Service Agents, as they're rarely in uniform when they come through the hotel and casino. "You're probably the first." He offered to feed the man in black, "first class room service, courtesy of the house." Upon arriving at the top-most floor, the manager found the correct key and unlocked and opened the door to the roof access. The little man offered the key to the door. "I'm afraid of heights, so I'll leave you here. Just thinking about what's on the other side of that door makes me dizzy."

The government man's voice was silky smooth, as if he had been a radio personality in a previous life. It was a voice you listened to; a voice you obeyed. The voice was part of his disguise and an effective one gained through years of practice. He said, "This is a fast moving mission. Hopefully, I'll be out of your hair in a few hours. No more than a couple of days. Then, you never saw me. I'll ensure you are properly compensated. Thank you for your assistance in protecting our president and our diplomats." Then the Secret Service Agent pulled out a challenge coin and gave it to the manager. It was dull bronze and green with the "tip of the spear" and read: Special Operations Group. "These aren't for everybody. You can't say where you got this; this is our little secret. A token of my appreciation for your assistance to the Secret Service."

The hotel manager left the top floor clutching the enameled coin as a good luck piece. He never looked back. Steve Castaño dropped the large black canvas bag inside the roof access area at the base of the stairs. He didn't go up and open the door to the roof. He entered the hotel room adjacent to the roof access door, threw open the curtains, and surveyed his surroundings—it was indeed the highest point in the immediate area. Off in the distance stood the Washington Monument, 555 feet of white marble ashlar blocks. Castaño knew that behind it stood the White House. He removed a huge pair of binoculars from the parachute bag and confirmed he had a narrow but unobstructed view of the top of the White House.

He had previously calculated the distance and the bullet's time to target: *At 7.14 miles and a muzzle velocity of 4,000 feet per second means about a ten-second flight.*

•　　•　　•　　•　　•

Hunter walked into the Director's office like he owned the place. He walked to the wall of windows and closed all of the blinds and curtains. Lynche and the others watched with suspicion.

Hunter smiled at McGee as he encapsulated the corner office with closed curtains. McGee asked, "Has anyone asked *Maverick* what he thought of the election? I'm sure he has his own unique spin on how it came out."

Lynche threw up his hands in defense; he begged Duncan not to say anything. "We're having a serious discussion here; we have a crisis—let's not ruin it...."

Kelly Horne looked at each of the men for a moment. She was intrigued, cautious. She crossed her arms. McGee was just mischievous. Lynche put his hands in his lap and frowned. Anna Comstock scrunched up her face—she had no idea what was coming. Nazy had heard it before and laughed it all away.

Hunter obliged. "I think the whole thing with the Eleanor Tussy candidacy says a lot more about the Demo*crats*, who for decades supported this filthy, old, lying, four-flushing, disingenuous, money grubbing, influence pedaling, prevaricating, cold, calculating, deceitful, divisive, rotten Benghazi-bullshitting criminal business partner of the Kansas bicycle seat-sniffing trailer park troll, who was convicted of perjury, then impeached, and then disbarred. Anyone who supported her in the past and is now trying to distance themselves from this ugly, screeching Basilisk, needs to be frisked for their duplicitousness. They should be grabbed by the neck and have their faces rubbed in this pile of steaming poo and told, 'Look at what you tried to make President of the United States, you friggin' idiots!'"

Even Lynche broke up in laughter. Once he caught his breath he said, "*Maverick*, tell us how you really feel!"

Nazy asked her husband in all seriousness, "Did we dodge a bullet?"

Hunter paused and then said, "Oh, hell no. I think we dodged a meteor! If she had won, the Dems would have taken the House and the Senate. We would have seen the country change virtually overnight. Activist judges would have overseen the dismemberment of the First and Second Amendments—the whole Bill of Rights for that matter. She would have tried to confiscate weapons. They would have passed laws to force Americans to buy everything from electric cars to electricity from windmills. She'd have thrown open the borders—America would be like Europe after their *de facto* Muslim invasion. The EU is a dumpster fire; it is morphing into the Soviet Union. The transformation of America would have been complete, minus a new flag, a new anthem, and a new name. USSA. What the Russians and Stalin and Khrushchev had hoped to achieve would have been accomplished. She would have been a socialist hero in Europe and Russia. No, no, no. We escaped the end-of the world asteroid from Armageddon. We are so very lucky."

Surprising everyone in the room, Lynche cut to the chase and said, "That I can agree with." Nothing more needed to be said. They'd work to do and Lynche was back to giving directions.

Hunter passed a few documents to Lynche. He said, "Your AIRRAID thingy produced these."

Nazy continued with, "I asked Alvin several engaging questions from *Maverick*, such as what would NCS men on the run from the Agency do with a sniper rifle that has a maximum effective range of ten miles. Alvin responded, 'My initial concern would be the safety of the president, the vice president, and the CIA Director, and of course, their families.' Then, without asking, Alvin produced a map which highlighted the...."

Hunter jumped in. "...avenues of approach... unimpeded sniper lanes."

Nazy smiled — no offense taken. "Yes, unimpeded sniper lanes for a ten-mile weapon. Was there such a lane or a set of lanes in the vicinity of the White House? Yes there is, surprisingly. It's a Secret Service document."

Hunter pointed at Lynche and said, "The good news is that Alvin and the Secret Service concur that there are no possible avenues of approach or sniper lanes for the DCI. The bad news is there's a single, theoretical, almost eight-mile unimpeded sniper lane to the White House. The Secret Service dismissed it because...."

Nazy chimed in, "...as far as they're concerned, there's no such weapon as a ten-mile sniper rifle and there are no effective sniper lanes to the Oval Office."

Lynche nodded. Nods spread around the room. He asked, "So we don't have a problem, right?"

Some were shocked to hear that the president could still be in trouble. The thought was too radical to conceive.

Nazy continued, "Alvin indicated the Secret Service constructs similar threat condition maps — with sniper lanes — wherever the president goes, and the Secret Service puts counter-sniper teams in those places where a sniper could hide. They can't cover them all and there are gaps, but they're usually limited. They only go out to three miles...."

Hunter finished her sentence. "...which is well beyond the maximum effective range of all known conventional sniper rifles. The world record kill by a sniper is a little over two miles. But with a ten-mile bullet, powered by a rocket motor that doesn't follow a conventional ballistics curve but flies directly to the target illuminated by a laser spot, distance—once the advantage of the target—has been radically pushed in favor of the shooter. The game has changed. Few people are aware your ten-mile sniper rifle exists. I'm sure you'd like to keep it that way." He pointed at Lynche, "I haven't tried many ten-mile shots, if you were wondering. You have to hold the laser designator on the spot to be hit for a very long time. 4,000-foot per second muzzle velocity and that is, if I do my gazintas correctly, ten, twelve, fifteen seconds or so."

Lynche frowned at Hunter's made up metric. "I was not." He looked around the office. Nazy continued, "Alvin suggested we notify the Secret Service as an immediate action item. Restrict the President's movements."

Anna Comstock raised a finger like she was in eighth grade and said, "That's going to be tough to do since he was just reelected. He has places to go and hands to shake. People want to see him."

Lynche said he had already done so. He was grateful that someone else recognized the potential threat on the chief executive, even if it was electronic and theoretical. "That's why you closed the blinds and curtains."

Hunter nodded. "Just in case the Secret Service's mapping skills aren't in synch with their politics. Who knew the FBI could be so corruptible? Could be a disease."

"What did you just say?" The look on Lynche's face said *All I can see are trees. It's winter and all I can see is grey branches and twigs. So I'm not leaving my office. If I can't see anyone within a mile, no one can see me from ten miles. Why did you link the Secret Service's mapping skills with their politics?*

Hunter ignored the question as Kelly asked, "Is this seven-mile vantage point a secret?"

Nazy said, "If it was, it isn't now. It's the rooftop of the MGM Grand Hotel at National Harbor."

Lynche said, "I'll inform the Secret Service and the White House of the threat. POTUS must not walk in front of a window—even though they're bulletproof—unless the curtains are drawn."

Hunter made a face as if thinking was painful. He said, "Those bullets are spent uranium warheads that can tear through the side of a tank. I don't know what kind of bulletproof glass protects the White House, but I hope even uranium slugs can't penetrate them. Way out of my purview."

"You know this could turn into a suicide mission." McGee captured their attention as he continued, "If our shitbirds are looking to go there, they'll have the high ground. Even if it's only one person up there, he can be very effective. It'll be tough to get him off of there. If he has a team below decks, they'll waste a number of lives to protect their guy on top. We've seen how effective a lone sniper can be when he controls the high ground. Austin, New Orleans."

Lynche said, "That will be tough to defend for any length of time. I've seen that position—free base parachutists have wanted to jump from there."

McGee asked, "Didn't someone say these guys used Claymores at their homes? What if there are anti-personnel mines along the route to or at the door of the roof?"

"That would be ugly." Hunter turned to Lynche and said, "We need more information. I'd like to know if there's anyone up there now."

Lynche nodded. "If there is, I'd like to get *Wraith* up there."

Kelly Horne offered, "Maybe two?"

"Can't hurt," said Lynche. He looked at Hunter and Nazy for concurrence. It would mean returning to Quantico. No problem.

McGee said, "Shouldn't we let the FBI know what we suspect? They might be corrupt but they might also be able to capture them...him, if they're truly dumb enough to be there. Maybe Alvin's wrong."

Lynche nodded, but he wasn't about to say his AIRRAID tool was defective. Neither was Nazy.

McGee offered, "Now, I was trained as a sniper and I've been around several dozen in my years as a SEAL. If this guy and his murderous friends are as good as you say they are, then they wouldn't be caught out in the open. Snipers need a hide. A place where they can be effective without being seen so they can't be targeted. Maybe the roof isn't viable or accessible, but the floor below is good enough. Sometimes a roof is sufficient if you own all of the high ground around you, if there's no one else that can get above you or possibly see you. I'm certain that particular spot can be seen by incoming air traffic into the National Airport. I'll guarantee you they'll have something to hide...ah...their thermal signature, for starters. I think the trick is to get there first."

Nazy said, "But a commercial aircraft isn't targeting someone on a roof."

Lynche asked, "If there are one or two there, if they're there can we use a drone? *Maverick*, you have your little quiet drones. Is this a sufficient scenario to utilize them? Especially the lethal ones."

Hunter shook his head to indicate he did not. *I've one, and one drone without an explosive warhead is insufficient for a job like this. This would be a job for a swarm of lethal drones. Kill everyone on top of the roof.*

Nazy said, "Can I say something? With this talk, we are getting into all kinds of legal problems. The lawyer in me is suddenly very uneasy. We are in America and the CIA or its contractors aren't authorized to take direct action in America."

Nazy Cunningham had thrown a turd in the punch bowl. Now no one was happy.

65

November 9
CIA Headquarters

"I know the president's security isn't our problem but if we can, I want us to find *our problem children* and neutralize them." Lynche was emphatic.

Nazy said, "I understand that, Greg, but this time we aren't in the Middle East or Africa. We aren't out locating and eliminating terrorists. We can detect and provide guidance but this is a job for law enforcement. Secret Service. It'll keep everyone out of trouble. You don't want to be hauled up before Congress. The president would have to remove you. We don't want to be the rogue Agency out to eliminate one or two or four of our personal problems that should be handled by the FBI."

Hunter chimed in, "That's what the Democrats do. I hate to admit it, but Nazy's has a point. And for the record, I have no problem whacking any one of them. But I wouldn't like my chances in a court of law."

McGee said, "But if you go after them and someone brings the FBI into this after the fact, you are opening yourself up for a mess—federal grand jury, conspiracy charges. They'll send you to the basement of Fort Leavenworth where you'll never see the light of day again, and they'll feed you nothing but pizza and pancakes and potato chips." McGee gritted his teeth. *Maverick* could be in incredible legal jeopardy if he were unmasked.

Kelly asked an incongruous question, "Why pizzas and pancakes and potato chips?"

Hunter grinned, turned, and chimed in, "Yes, Bill. Why just pizzas and pancakes and potato chips?"

McGee smiled and said, "Because they're the only things that can slide under a cell door."

Peals of laughter were replaced by visions of Hunter in court on the stand, taking the Fifth Amendment. The idea made Lynche shudder.

Hunter said, "The FBI *leadership* hasn't been honest recently; they have gone all-in trying to destroy President Hernandez through fake documents, spies within the campaign, everything you can think of short of murder to ensure Eleanor Tussy was elected. They failed to remove him from office. Now they'll pay for their treachery. It'll take months, maybe years before their whole executive staff is implicated in that conspiracy. That thing is a Democrat-media-FBI goat rope. The CIA has been completely free and clear of that little nasty conspiracy. I don't think you want to go there...."

Lynche was suddenly quiet, solemn, as if something from long ago had just crawled back into his conscious.

Hunter noticed the change in his incredibly tired friend and asked, "What is it, Greg?"

Lynche regained his composure and said, "I'm sorry. Nazy and Bill are correct. It's a legal matter. The CIA is just not fit to protect the president from a sniper. That's not our job. I don't want to go to the FBI; that's not their job either. I'm afraid they have been working for the other side and may be part of a larger cabal. They have proven to be completely untrustworthy—we don't want to use them. This is the job of the Secret Service."

Nazy said, "Greg, we have to. We have to let them, and the Secret Service, in on what we found and assure them that although we have traitors on the loose, we aren't going to interfere."

Anna Comstock said, "We did use them, are using them, and all appearances they're playing ball. The rank and file FBI Agent is a good guy. The problem is…their leaders are Mazibuike holdovers who should have been removed after President Hernandez took the oath of office."

Lynche said, "I agree it's not the rank and file FBI agent who's the problem. Mazibuike removed hundreds of attorneys and replaced them with...."

Hunter said it. "Members of the Islamic Underground and others loyal to Democratic causes. Some in the media did their homework. All those guys were hand-picked by the DNC." Hunter tossed a pen onto Lynche's desk and said, "Boss, I think it's time to take our little airplanes and go home. It's an impossible mission, and no one in this office can win. Tell the Secret Service, tell the FBI, and hope that they can stop them if they find someone camped out on that roof. We're going home. Bullfrog, let's go. Kelly, you don't have to come unless you want to—I can get the Bobs to box up the Yo-Yos and trailer them to Texas."

Anna Comstock heard a new term, *Yo-Yos*, and was intrigued. Lynche frowned at Hunter for cavalierly revealing the nickname of the YO-3A to someone not authorized to hear it. Hunter looked at his wife, who was in a state of shock. He innocently dragged his thumb across his eyebrow. She recognized the subtle sign; she blinked wildly and said, as if she had rehearsed it, "My place is here with Director Lynche until this is resolved. It'll give me some time to work on the new archive."

Lynche spun around to Nazy. His face registered concern when she said, "new archive."

Nazy continued, "Thank you for all your help, *Maverick*." Then she took her little fingernail and scratched her eyebrow. *Message received.* Hunter pretended he didn't notice the coded message from his wife or Lynche's reaction to the mention of the DNC archive.

Lynche recovered and was apoplectic. "Just like that? You're running out on me?"

Hunter walked over and placed a hand on Lynche's shoulder. "Boss, you said so yourself, the CIA doesn't get involved in domestic matters. No domestic operations. It's the FBI, or the Secret Service or the U.S. Marshals. It's their show. No killer swarms in America. You'll have to do it the old fashioned way. Remember the famous words of Baltazar Gracian's *The Art of Worldly Wisdom*. 'Let someone else take the hit.' You will find a path; you always do. But our services are obviously no longer required here, so it's time for this crew to do something else and for you to go home and get some sleep."

Hunter subtly shook his head to stop Kelly from speaking, then winked at her. For a second, she was more confused than before. Then it dawned on her and she smiled and nodded at her father.

Bill McGee suggested he probably needed to get back to Texas. "I don't suppose you could get the Marines to take me back to my truck."

Lynche's eyes narrowed and shook his head. *Something's going on....* He said, "Probably not. It's one thing to ask a favor to get you here ASAP."

McGee said, "No factor, Greg. You're busy. I'll find a ride home."

Hunter asked Nazy, "Don't you have some big black ugly thing in your garage?" Everyone in the office was shocked to silence.

Anna was instantly alert. *He knows what's in her garage?*

McGee smiled and said, "I was starting to wonder if you were talking about me."

Hunter asked, "Sir William, do you live in a garage? I didn't think so."

Nazy took a deep breath and sighed, "I don't drive the Hummer. I prefer the Mercedes."

Hunter sighed and said, "That little red car is more lady-like. Then can we get the ever capable Ms. Comstock to give us a ride to Nazy's place? We are out of here. It was fun but not real fun. Good luck, Greg." Hunter stepped close to shake Lynche's hand and then hugged Nazy. He winked at Kelly and gestured for her to go before him. She didn't move.

Hunter started to shake Anna Comstock's hand but she pointed at the television and said, "It looks like the election has taken its second and third casualties. The networks are reporting that early this morning the Democratic National Committee Chairman, Dr. Nikita Zhavrazhinov, may have jumped from the twenty-second floor of the JW Marriott Hotel in Times Square. And this evening the FBI Director has committed suicide."

Lynche was stunned. Hunter smiled and said, in poor French, "*Vingt-duex*. The lucky number on the roulette wheel in *Casablanca*." He said the number again in French, then frowned and looked at Bill McGee and said, "So it begins." *And the DNC's archive is safe with Nazy. I'm certain that whatever she finds will be pretty spectacular.*

"And, so it begins. Another one's gone, another one bites the dust." McGee led Hunter out of the office.

Comstock didn't know what was meant by "So it begins," but said, "Excuse me, gentlemen, you're going to need me if you want to leave the compound. Positive control at the entry control point."

Hunter was gracious. "Please lead the way, Ms. Comstock. And thank you for all you have done for me and for putting up with my cranky boss."

As Lynche frowned at the emerging spectacle in his office, Anna Comstock said, "You are very welcome, Mr. Locke." She wanted to say, *Mr. Duncan Hunter* just to see the look on his face.

"I'm *Maverick* to my friends." He smiled. Everyone smiled.

Lynche ignored the goodbyes of his friends. He picked up the telephone and starting punching numbers from memory.

Before leaving the CIA Director's office, Bill McGee bumped into Hunter enough to get his attention and said, "Was there really a need to get Nazy, you, me...all of us here as soon as possible? Sounds like we are victims of a hurry up and wait scheme."

Hunter nodded and said to charge Lynche three times the normal rate. "Call it bonus pay. You were the one who got screwed."

Lynche ignored him and continued with his call. It was to a secure telephone in an office in 7 World Trade Center. When it connected, he spoke softly, "It looks like the DNC Chairman, Dr. Zhavrazhinov, took a dive from his hotel room. You need to find him and take possession of his things. If you can, of course. You know the drill. Thank you."

Hunter and McGee and the others were oblivious to Lynche's

conversation and had walked out of the office, past the secretary's station. McGee bantered and barked sarcastically, "The black dude is always getting screwed!" Hunter and McGee put their arms over the other's shoulders like brothers leaving a wedding and looking for a bar. Laugher echoed down the hallway.

Just as Kelly was about to say something to Anna, Hunter and McGee dragged her up between them so she was boxed in by her father and the old SEAL. McGee asked, "Are you ready for another adventure?" She nodded enthusiastically. Comstock was confused.

McGee said, "She's just a chip off the old block." Hunter tried to keep up but his hip refused to let him move as quickly as they could.

Comstock was thrown another confusing clue but had now figured out what all of the interactions and their banter meant. *She's the daughter.* Anna had work to do and called for the elevator.

They waited patiently for the elevator to come to the floor. Hunter said to McGee, "She's getting there."

Then Lynche called Bill McGee back to his office. Yelling from the desk in his office wasn't something he did, ever. Hunter looked at McGee; both men shrugged. McGee stopped, made a face, turned around, walked back to the Director's office and poked his head in the office doorway.

Lynche said he needed McGee for a mission. "No Duncan."

McGee nodded and turned, and said to the group at the elevator "Go ahead, I'll catch up later." He re-entered the director's office and took a seat.

Lynche explained what was necessary and what success looked like. McGee was intrigued and said, "I'm your guy, Greg."

66

Morning newspapers across the United States continued to report on the unexpected win of the incumbent president over his heavily favored rival even though she had led all polls and had won the popular vote by over two million votes. Most of the national media's websites and newspapers published tiny notices of the death of Dr. Nikita Zhavrazhinov, the Democratic National Committee Chairman and Eleanor Tussy's campaign manager and the FBI Director. The articles were all "below the fold."

The headline and article credited Dr. Zhavrazhinov with having run a brilliant campaign for Mrs. Tussy whose electoral fortunes grew to double-digit leads. The article also mentioned how the former Marine Corps officer and current war correspondent, Demetrius Eastwood, had singlehandedly turned the election to President Hernandez's favor with the timely publication of Eastwood's "hit piece," *Was it Espionage?* and subsequent television special. The Democrat Party-media complex accused Demetrius Eastwood of planting enough doubt in the minds of voters that Mrs. Tussy was no longer "the woman of destiny."

● ● ● ● ●

Bill McGee was intrigued as the CIA Director called the Chief of the Border Patrol and relayed a request.

Three hours later the retired Navy SEAL had changed into black battle dress fatigues and stepped from one of the Border Patrol's ultra-quiet MD-600 NOTAR helicopters. McGee entered the residence of the former Harvard professor. Heavily armed members of BORTAC, the tactical and special response arm of the U.S. Border Patrol, fanned out and surrounded the residence while McGee searched the premises.

He quickly found what he was looking for, a poorly hidden five-foot tall wall safe. He blew the door off with specially-shaped wedges of C-4. McGee took a moment to investigate the contents. He wasn't surprised to find Communist Party of the USA documents—lists of contacts, donors, secret cells, apparatuses. He removed all of Zhavrazhinov's papers, files and books, including the DNC's chairman's journals. He was about to leave a thick handbook when he decided to flip through the pages to see if it was anything important. When he realized what he held in his hands, he ground his teeth. He slipped the manual and journals into his shirt and moved the rest of the safe's contents into a duffel bag. He walked through the kitchen and turned on all knobs of the big gas range, then he tossed a lighted cigar into the sofa. By the time McGee and the Border Patrol special operations agents had returned to the helicopter and was airborne, the house was totally engulfed.

•   •   •   •   •

The White House Communication Director announced, "President Hernandez, his family, close friends, and administration officials will be traveling to Camp David this evening. After a long hard-fought fight for the Oval Office, the president will outline and establish his agenda for the next four years. The evening departure of Marine One taking the president to Camp David is expected to bring thousands of onlookers and well-wishers to the gates of the White House."

•   •   •   •   •

Lynche worked the telephones throughout the day, talking to the White House, FBI, Homeland Security, and the U.S. Marshals. Post-election activities had every department stretched to the limit. In downtown Washington D.C. near the White House, rabid masked anarchists were in an uproar, livid with the election results. The fascist anti-fascist groups were mobilizing for another round of violent protests and a night of destruction. The White House switchboard was shut down from threats of violence made on the President and his family. Various threats were made on the vice president and the cabinet members. Law enforcement and the Secret Service were helpless to do anything but double the line of protection on Pennsylvania Avenue for the newly elected President.

A text message from the office of the CIA Director worked when the telephone did not. An hour later the Secret Service Director called and apologized for not being able to respond. Lynche voiced his concerns over the missing secret sniper rifle.

The Secret Service Director hadn't known Lynche very long and didn't know him very well, but he knew enough to know that Lynche was a wine connoisseur. He thought Lynche maybe had had one bottle too many, either celebrating the president's win or drowning his sorrows at the challenger's loss. Lynche *had* to have been drinking—either that or he had lost his mind.

The Secret Service Director barked at Lynche, "*There's no such thing as a ten-mile sniper system! If there were, the Secret Service would know about it—I'd know about it!*"

The Secret Service Director wouldn't budge from his position; he wouldn't even give the DCI the courtesy of sending someone over to the hotel for a five minute check. Rioters were amassing from every corner. He had no time to pull a man off the wall of law enforcement and presidential protection. He dismissed Lynche with a bullshit promise to send someone to the hotel if he could and signed off with an exasperated goodbye.

Lynche was incensed. He tried the National Reconnaissance Office to see about reprogramming a satellite for a few flyovers of the hotel; the NRO Director flatly refused. "This isn't 1995 anymore, Greg; I don't have that kind of power and you don't seem to have enough justification. Just cannot help you. And besides, you're worried the president will be shot…well, I'm not real happy with him anyway. You know these things are false flags. Quit worrying about it and take Connie to dinner. Sounds like you might have been celebrating early."

Lynche was so incensed that he hollered at the NRO's most distinguished scientist, using questions he had never asked anyone before, "*Who the hell did you vote for? Did 3M give you that job?*"

Stung by an implicit accusation, the NRO Director reconsidered his position. "I'll tell you what, Greg, I'll see if we have had any recent activity. Hold on while I call up the data files for that bird." After a few minutes the NRO Director broke the hold and said, "You still there, Greg? Ok. It's your lucky day—we actually had eyeballs on the area in the last hour, we had an analyst look at the area. She verified we had good views of the rooftop of the hotel—and accounting for angles and shadows, clouds and even thermals, there was no one on the roof; there was nothing there but a flock of seagulls as of a couple of hours ago. One of 'our birds' very recently passed over the area but we need some time to analyze the imagery. If there's anything there, I'll get back to you."

Lynche thanked the satellite scientist. He replaced the telephone receiver feeling defeated. *The analyst confirmed there was no one on the rooftop. Does that help? No. What would I do if I was in that situation? I'd make sure I knew the satellite schedule, and if it happened to be overhead any time I was outside, I'd leave the roof for a few minutes. Castaño is a master in tradecraft and would know the satellite schedule and would remain in the stairwell or the hall or in a nearby room until the satellite passed.*

In a flash of insight, Lynche called the Capitol Police. He was handed off to their aviation division. He wanted to ensure the roof top of the MGM Grand Hotel wasn't harboring a sniper. The head pilot was in a joyful mood and looked forward to assisting the CIA. Within thirty minutes one of the Capitol Police's helicopters was airborne and headed for the hotel. They promised to add the hotel's roof top to their patrol and to relay anything of interest.

He called the U.S. Coast Guard Commandant and asked for one of their orange HH-52 *Dolphins* that patrolled the Atlantic seaboard and Potomac River to check out the rooftop of the MGM Grand. The admiral was eager to help and signed off with, "*Semper Paratus.*"

Lynche acknowledged, "*Coasties* are 'always ready.'"

67

November 9
Marine Corps Base Quantico
The driver asked, "Where do you want to go?" The older man said, "Quantico."

Immediately after being delivered by the CIA Suburban, Kelly followed Hunter to "his airplane" and watched him load the YO-3A's gun, the airborne version of the Terminator Sniper System. He opened the access door to the gun's receiver, removed a loaded magazine from his helmet bag, and shoved it into the weapon's magazine carrier. He mechanically chambered a live round, then closed and secured the access panel. He smiled at Kelly and said that was all there was to it.

For a moment Hunter thought about loading Kelly's weapon. She hadn't had any training on firing the weapon from the airplane, and her reaction to targeting terrorists in Syria convinced him it just wasn't a good idea. He told her, "If by some chance we find someone and they see us and fire on us, I can fire back. *And I will fire back.*"

Upon arriving at the old hangar, several of the Marines' VH-3D *Sea King* helicopters had taxied into a position into the winds. Hunter was familiar with the mission. The "white top" *Sea Kings* would depart for Joint Base Anacostia to provide decoys for the presidential lift as well as transport the president and his family from the White House to the Presidential Retreat at Camp David.

From the leeward side of their hangar, a dozen Marines from Presidential Helicopter Squadron One remained outside after their *Sea Kings* departed. As they had earlier, they watched the goings on inside the hangar scheduled to be demolished with a modicum of interest. The crazy black spyplanes were so unique as to be unbelievable.

A few people began milling around the two matte black aircraft inside, a sure sign there would be some activity. Some of the Marines wondered if the spyplanes were to be a part of the presidential lift, providing some kind of surveillance.

The winds were worsening and howled through the leafless trees forcing Hunter and Kelly to question their ability to taxi and takeoff without incident. Between the taxiway and runway, the lighted windcone was fully extended and indicated that the wind was running a steady 90°, perpendicular to the runway. Hunter knew that trying to execute a severe crosswind takeoff in a motorized sailplane would have been impossible, under normal circumstances. These weren't normal circumstances. He viewed the most pressing problem would be taxiing to the runway without gusts or high winds spinning the YO-3A around or flipping the light long-winged aircraft onto its back.

If the winds were bad on the ground in Quantico they'd be worse once aloft. Duncan Hunter had briefed a two-aircraft operation. The area where the hotel was situated at National Harbor was saturated with aircraft, commercial aircraft streamed into and out of National Airport; Coast Guard, Navy, and Marine Corps helicopters operated from the Anacostia complex, and the Capitol Police Hueys were a stone's throw away from the MGM Grand. Hunter felt he'd need an extra set of eyes to alert him from conflicting traffic and proposed a one-time, good-deal, two-aircraft mission. He considered aborting the two Yo-Yo solution and go it alone. But he'd need Kelly's eyes if he would be focusing on any rooftop activity.

Hunter said, "There's a thing called 'commander's wishes.'"

Kelly smiled and said, "I'm familiar."

"So he wants someone to go up and take a look. We won't tell anyone we're going to go up and take a look and ensure there's no sniper on top of the hotel before the president departs the White House. Stay above me, keep me out of trouble with any traffic. On the way to the hotel, follow me in loose trail. The winds are bad, but they should die down as the night progresses."

From the windward side of the other newer and massive hangar, Marines watched the spyplanes being prepared for flight. Hunter had a solution to safely move the YO-3As from the hangar to the taxiway in the strong winds. With a wave of his arm, again the Marines responded.

As the Marines jogged away from the Presidential hangar, they were met with and braced themselves against the buffeting wind.

In the decrepit hangar, between the YO-3As, Hunter and Kelly had stripped to their shorts and shirts and donned black flight suits and flying boots. Even protected from the wind, it was freezing cold inside the building and the two pilots hurried to cover their bare flesh. They placed their flight bags inside their cockpits.

As Marines in their camouflaged uniforms lined up in front of him, Duncan told them what he needed them to do. He directed the Marines to split into two teams, left wing and right wing. He walked behind them and showed them where to place their hands, and said that the wind will want to lift the aircraft. "You don't let it, just keep pressure on the wing—I know it looks strange but just do this by feel; keep pressure on the aircraft on the ground until the nose is pointed toward the taxiway, until the pilot starts the engine and powers away. With this wind this airplane will want to fly as soon as it is out of the hangar. You just push straight and let the pilot control the direction with brakes and rudder. Then come back and get me, and we'll do it all over again with my airplane. Got it?"

A chorus of, "Sir, yes sir!" rang out.

Hunter responded, "*Ooorah!* Let's go."

Kelly was up on the wing and stepped into the seat. She stretched her legs until they touched the rudder pedals and buckled her shoulder straps and lap belt. The Marines were at the ready. Kelly lowered the canopy. Bob Jones removed the chocks and shouted, "Let's go!"

Kelly fired up the engine, checked the oil and manifold pressure, and advanced the throttle. The Marines pushed the airplane for a few seconds and let go when it accelerated away from them. The winds were so strong that the YO-3A nearly leapt from the ramp after a run of twenty feet. At takeoff power, the airplane climbed like an Iberian ibex running straight up a cliff, gaining a lot of altitude with little forward progress.

Flying into the gale was a new experience for Kelly as she discovered one of the unintended consequences of flight in high winds—now she was bouncing around in her seat like a drunk on a mechanical bull at Gilley's Bar and Grill. Through all the updrafts and downdrafts, she handled the airplane expertly. She set a course for the coast where she'd rendezvous with her father.

After Hunter was pushed into position with Marines holding the *Wraith* against the headwind, he engaged the engine starter and the engine lit off after three turns of the prop. Like Kelly's aircraft before, the Marines were amazed that there were no exhaust sounds coming from the YO-3A. The turbine-powered helicopters that took off before the spyplanes were loud, generating well over 125 decibels, but the strange black-shaped motorized gliders were silent. Some of the Marines thought the aircraft might have had an electric motor that spun the propeller but the obvious, elaborate, multi-muffler exhaust system squashed those ideas.

Takeoff was uneventful until the aircraft popped up over the trees and was gobsmacked by severe headwinds and intermittent crosswinds. Hunter deployed the FLIR and found the thermal imagery of his daughter's YO-3A circling the beach.

They headed for Washington, D.C. using the standard course rules for VFR flying—out to the beach and then fly up the coast. They didn't want to be co-altitude with another general aviation aircraft going the opposite direction. The airspace around Washington, D.C. was some of the most restricted in the world and there shouldn't have been another aircraft in the vicinity. The Yo-Yos weren't detected by radar, hence, air traffic control wouldn't see them.

Hunter and Kelly bucked the robust headwinds from Quantico to National Harbor and the MGM Grand. The headwinds bounced them around like cats caught in a clothes dryer. After one extremely powerful gust, Hunter was thrown completely inverted with the nose pointing to Mother Earth. He transmitted, "Oh shit!" as he reduced the power to idle and deployed the spoilers to slow the aircraft and pull it out of its unexpected, unusual attitude.

Kelly, flying a few hundred feet off of Hunter's right side, missed most of the gust that upended her father. She watched as he expertly recovered from the winds. She was worried because the long sailplane-like wings of the YO-3A were flexing up and down at least five feet. She hadn't flown it in such extreme turbulence and hoped the engineers had built the wings so they wouldn't break off.

After ten minutes of fighting the winds and the aircraft's controls, Kelly was grateful the winds had calmed down as the two airplanes approached the Maryland shoreline from the south. Hunter radioed her to applaud her flying skills and told her when they got to the river's edge, he'd cross the Potomac River and overfly the MGM Grand Hotel "to take a look." As briefed, they'd come in from the northeast in the hopes that if there were NCS guys targeting the White House, they'd have their eyes focused on the South Lawn and not an aircraft approaching from their rear. The FLIR was awash in thermal imagery.

* * * * *

Three identical Marine green Sikorsky helicopters were in an echelon formation and inbound to the White House. Two of the decoys pretended to approach the South Lawn one after the other, but as they got close each waved off and set a return heading for Joint Base Anacostia. Even with gusting winds, the third VH-3D "white top" helicopter made a perfect approach onto the South Lawn; the pilot set the landing gear on the three large metal discs used to protect the grass, shut down its engines, and stopped its main rotor using the rotor brake.

* * * * *

His mission was *"a go"* when three Marine "white top" helicopters flew past the hotel room window, thundering up the Potomac River. Castaño was familiar with the procedure and knew they would be landing at the Navy base in Anacostia just a few miles upriver, waiting for the movement order from the White House to proceed for "the lift." He would see the helicopters again when they lifted off from their intermediate landing site and headed toward the Washington Monument. Then it would only be a matter of minutes before he aimed the "smart" sniper rifle, pulled the trigger, and killed the president.

He moved from the bright lights of his hotel room to the darkness of the roof access landing. Castaño stood and removed a computer notebook from his duffel and checked the program that tracked the positions of all satellites. As the system loaded on the computer he thought of the most famous of all presidential assassins, John Wilkes Booth, hiding in the president's box at the Ford Theater, waiting for the right time to execute President Abraham Lincoln. The irony was thick. Killing Lincoln at the height of the civil war decapitated the government and threw it into a state of panic and confusion. Assassinating Hernandez immediately after the election would crush the Republican Party and send the Democrat Party into delirium. *Maybe they could award Tussy the presidency since she won the popular vote. This is exactly what The Judge envisioned.* Castaño took a few deep breaths. *I'm on the cusp of entering history.*

As the last satellite had passed overhead according to the on-line satellite tracker, Castaño returned the computer into the duffel. Just as he started to crack open the door to the rooftop, he heard the district *wop-wop-wop* sound of an approaching helicopter. Then he felt the vibration of the aircraft in the door handle. He was shaken for the moment with the creeping idea that his plan may have been discovered. But he hadn't been outside, he hadn't set up his hide, so there was no evidence that anyone had been on the roof to prepare a shooting position. Castaño stilled his heart and convinced himself that he still had time as presidents are always late leaving the White House. *No factor! No factor!*

He checked the deadbolt on the door, paused, and reflected. If the helicopter stopped and hovered to inspect the roof, it could mean his mission had been compromised and he must consider aborting. *Then again,* he thought, *it could be nothing but a random flyby.* Castaño couldn't convince himself that an approaching helicopter was a random event. *The helicopter landing area is on top of the parking garage, not the roof!* He stood still as if in a trance. *The hotel is miles outside the sniper lane! How could they have found out? It's impossible!*

Steve Castaño pushed the heavy duffel bag with his foot. He was anxious and becoming more nervous by the second. He debated whether to crack open the door to see if the helicopter was just passing through on patrol or was inspecting the rooftop. His thoughts of a quick inspection were overridden as the increasing reverberation of the helicopter's rotor blades and the near deafening sound of its engines indicated the machine was definitely making an approach to the roof. He double-checked that the deadbolt was in place in case the helicopter landed and someone tried to open the access door. He pulled the stogie from his lips and held his breath for what seemed like an hour until the sounds on the other side of the door dramatically decreased, signaling the turbine-powered helicopter had departed. He checked his watch; luminous green dial markers indicated that if he was going to try the shot he didn't have much time, if the president was on time.

He threw open the deadbolt and opened the door. Castaño was greeted by an overpowering vile stench from several deep pools of fresh bird droppings, piles of bird *guano*, and dozens of dead birds. He retreated back inside, closed the door, and rummaged around his duffel until he found and withdrew a black tactical gas mask. He cursed himself. Pounds of bird poo were something else snipers sometimes had to contend with; places that are excellent places to hide are also outstanding places for birds to roost. And shit. And die. Roofs were the best locations for a sniper, but sometimes they came with problems.

Castaño stomped his feet on the concrete floor in a display of pique. He never liked wearing gas masks, but once it was on and checked that respirator filters were working and he could breathe, he stepped onto the roof. Breathing was hard, inhaling through the thick filters was laborious. All that was important was that the gas mask was working. He could smell nothing as a stiff ocean breeze buffeted him. Castaño avoided a few pools and piles of fresh and dried droppings as he crawled to the edge of the roof where he saw the red and green position and rotortip lights of a low-flying helicopter flying away from him, up the Potomac River. Even through the gas mask he recognized the distinctive shape of a Coast Guard *Dolphin*. He found that he was in the perfect place to set up the weapon and hide, and it was relatively bird shit-free.

As he looked around the whole roof he saw hundreds of rock doves and seagulls walking about, flocking, sleeping, and cooing. Castaño clapped gloved hands and startled a few birds. They quickly took flight and then, just as quickly, returned to where they'd been.

They won't be a problem. Game on!

He retrieved his duffel from the roof access. He set up the weapon, adjusting the legs and the receiver until the barrel was still inside of the building's safety rails. Castaño powered up the sniper system and erected his hide—a gray awning which quickly unfolded and reasonably matched the uniform color of the roof's waterproof coating but not the amorphous concoction of white and black bird droppings. He found the Washington Monument in the telescope and depressed a button on the control panel to activate the servomotors to make fine, incremental alignment adjustments of the barrel and the laser designator (LD). He looked through the gas mask and telescope as the White House came into view. Castaño continued slewing the barrel until the telescope's crosshairs rested on the side of the president's helicopter.

The Coast Guard's helicopter's approach to the roof had set him back a minute or two, but the sight picture in the telescope indicated that there was nothing to worry about. The weapon was set up and Castaño had the target in its crosshairs. If he hadn't been wearing a gas mask and the winds hadn't been so severe, he would have lit up a cigar. He craved the taste of the tobacco leaf on his tongue.

The roof was an industrial-sized petri dish. Castaño was cautious not to touch anything, glad he had the foresight to pack a gas mask and wore gloves. He repeatedly peered through the telescope looking for any deviation in the sight picture. He waited to get a glimpse of any movement from the ground crew that suggested the POTUS and his family were approaching the Marine One helicopter. He saw nothing yet, which was good. He popped his head out from under the awning to check on the helicopter again, but it was still on course, flying up the Potomac a couple of miles away.

Another check of the scope still didn't indicate any new activity at the White House. A fire truck was parked near the helicopter with firefighters in flame-proof bunker coats and trousers, holding gloves and helmets. Secret Service Agents in black uniforms and business suits stood around waiting for the president and his family to emerge from the White House. He slewed the telescope back to the helicopter and began taking cues from the big green Sikorsky on the South Lawn—the navigational and position lights were on, but the upper and lower anti-collision beacons remained off. Castaño rationalized that the Marine One pilot sitting erect in the cockpit was anticipating the imminent arrival of the first family.

In his zeal to set up the weapon and determine if the Marine One helicopter was running early or late, he had neglected to check the system. He peered through the telescope and engaged the laser designator. He depressed a button on the joystick controller which coordinated ultra-fine movements of the rifle barrel and telescope. Castaño didn't know what was wrong; he couldn't locate the red laser spot in the rifle scope. He depressed the LD button again to lase the target. But nothing happened; the laser designator wasn't working. There was no laser spot in the telescope's viewfinder. The crosshairs were lined up on the painted sheet metal, and that should have been the location of the LD. He panicked. He placed his hand in front of the LD to see if the red dot laser would display a spot on his hand, and when it did, he was flummoxed. *What the…. Maybe the scope and the LD have become misaligned.* He frowned and quickly panned the laser designator to another part of the aircraft—the landing gear tire. When the red dot appeared on the tire in the telescope's crosshairs, he realized that the LD wasn't able to illuminate a spot on the helicopter's paint. His mind raced through the possibilities. He thought about the radar absorption materials developed for stealth aircraft. Castaño smiled to himself; the aircraft was likely coated with a special material designed to absorb or scatter all wavelengths of light in order defeat laser-guided anti-aircraft missiles. *Smart guys!*

An evil smile came over his face. His hide was perfect. Castaño now knew what John Wilkes Booth had felt and seen when he realized he had defeated all of the government's countermeasures to protect the president from an assassin.

Again, he looked over the weapon toward the White House. The plan had been to shoot the president directly through the thin aluminum skin of the helicopter, but the lack of any reflectivity of the paint would prevent a sufficient lock-on. With no laser dot there could be no laser-guided bullet—it couldn't follow the laser to the laser spot. *But there was Plan B. There's always a Plan B and C and….*

He was feeling good about himself. He was just about over the deaths of the three amigos; Fässler, Bomarito, and Troxel. They could have been part of this. Part of history. But they ran. They left him alone.

Castaño placed an eye behind the telescope to target the pilots through their Plexiglas doors. The crosshairs and laser spot danced on the side of the head of the pilot, directly in the middle of the right ear-cup of the woman's headset. The artificial intelligence algorithms of the targeting system would maintain the laser-designated "tagged" spot for the laser-guided bullet. The massive spent uranium round would tear through both pilots easily. If he timed it perfectly, the bullet would kill the pilots and cause the helicopter to crash. *Who'd ever think about taking out multiple targets with a single shot?* Congress would never blame an unknown sniper; they'd blame the Marines for the death of the president, or the Secret Service for failing to protect the president adequately.

Castaño slaved the telescope to the right and up slightly and designated the side of the pilot's head in the right seat, which he could see clearly through the side window. When the laser designator generated a targeting spot, he depressed the switch and the "tagged" spot was loaded into the gun's firing computer. The fire control computer of the TS2 would hold the laser designator through gusts of wind or, in the case of the helicopter, when it lifted off and transitioned out of ground effect for flight.

He wished he had the ability to time the firing of the gun perfectly to hit both pilots, but the artificial intelligence was in control. It would complete the firing sequence based on the computer program. The best Castaño could hope for was to wait for the perfect sight picture and physically depress the trigger as the helicopter turned and try to time the bullet's strike when the two pilots would be in line. Success of killing the pilot in command was assured. Killing both pilots with a single shot was highly improbable but when the pilot's head exploded in a mess of bone, brains, and blood, how could any copilot remain steady at the stick? Castaño bet that if the bullet was unable to kill both aviators, no mere mortal could be functional after the cockpit was saturated with the remains of a dead pilot.

Even if he couldn't see them, he knew things would begin to happen when President Hernandez and the First Family entered the cabin. Once the president was buckled in, the pilot would turn on the anti-collision beacons, one on the belly of the helicopter and one on the tail. Once the uniformed Marine Corps crew chief verified the lights were on and rotating, he'd enter the chopper and haul in the stairs. The helicopter pilots would start the engines, the rotor brake would be released, and the main rotor engaged. Once the rotor was up to speed, liftoff was less than two minutes away.

• • • • •

Hunter slaved the forward looking infrared and zoomed in on the helicopter sitting on the South Lawn of the White House. *Still no beacons! Let's take a look at the hotel.*

Hunter turned his helmet to the front of the aircraft, the FLIR and camera ball slaved to the front. The low-light camera couldn't pick up the shape of anything human on the MGM hotel roof but when Hunter selected FLIR, the thermal image of a human with a short-barreled gun on a tripod filled the screen. He recognized the familiar shape of the TS2 and was shocked for a microsecond as he confirmed, *There's a sniper on the roof! And he's using a laser designator to target the president's helicopter.*

He mashed the transmit key and shouted, *"Tally Ho — Bandit! Bandit! Bandit!"* Kelly slewed her FLIR to the hotel.

Hunter immediately engaged the YO-3A's laser designator to "tag" the sniper. The spot settled on the back of the man's head. Hunter didn't wait for the Marine One helicopter to move; he had the sniper in his sights. He pulled the trigger to fire a bullet, less than three miles and closing. There should have been a recoil and hot gases escaping from the barrel, momentarily blotting out the imagery. But nothing happened. No recoil. No sound. No hot gasses to wash out the FLIR image. Nothing. Hunter looked at the multi-function panel and read the computer alert: MISFIRE.

Hunter had never had the gun jam before. There was no way to unjam the gun from the front cockpit, and Hunter couldn't crawl into the back seat to unjam it. He slaved the FLIR to the White House lawn just as the anti-collision lights illuminated and the beacons began to rotate. *Less than two minutes to takeoff! Shit!*

68

November 9
MGM Grand Hotel National Harbor
The gun was in autonomous tracking mode. The weapon's computer's laser designator would follow the "tagged" spot on the helicopter pilot's temple. The artificial intelligence system would determine the optimal sight picture and send a signal to initiate the firing sequence. Ten, twelve seconds later, the hypersonic bullet would strike the AI-driven, constantly-computed "tagged" spot.

Castaño popped his head out from under the tarpaulin as if he could find unadulterated air. It was work to breathe through the filters of the gas mask. At three miles, the U.S. Coast Guard *Dolphin* helicopter reversed course and flew lazily up the Potomac River opposite the hotel on the Virginia side; its course never varied an iota. *They wouldn't chance another encounter with a flock of birds.* He peeked over the side of the tower. No emergency vehicles gathering; no law enforcement personnel running toward the hotel. No one to stop him. It was evident that he was going to pull off the impossible. He slithered back under the awning and watched the show on the tiny monitor. One minute to lift off. Ninety seconds to trigger pull.

● ● ● ● ●

Hunter panicked. He shouted into his microphone to tell Kelly to "*shoot him, shoot him!*" only to realize she wasn't carrying a loaded weapon. He blinked wildly as if resetting his brain to solve another problem. One he couldn't fix.

His heart was pounding like a hummingbird's as he closed in on the hotel. There was only one solution. Hunter pushed three buttons on his automatic takeoff and landing system, programming the aircraft to retract all sensors and weapons, and return to the airport in Bridgewater, Virginia. He looked over the nose of the aircraft and through the propeller arc one last time to judge his distance and closure; the hotel was 'on the nose" but he was drifting westerly. He climbed and turned into the wind slightly. The ocean breeze would push the airplane back over the top of the hotel. A gust of wind tipped the wing. He was in the intercept window for overflying the MGM Grand Hotel. He transmitted to Kelly, *"I'm out of here!"* Over the Potomac River, Hunter jettisoned the canopy, unbuckled his lap belt, then stepped up onto his seat and jumped out into the airstream.

•　　•　　•　　•　　•

Castaño knew the President sat in his designated seat with the Presidential Seal on the headrest. He wished he could have shot him before the aircraft took flight, but the damn helicopter's paint wasn't going to allow it. *That's why you plan for contingencies. That's why snipers get into position early. This mask is killing me. I want a cigar!*

•　　•　　•　　•　　•

Kelly was shocked to hear her father's deep electronic voice say, *"I'm out of here!"* She tried to scream when she looked to her father's airplane as the aircraft's canopy flew off. She was stunned when her father jumped over the side of the YO-3A. She covered her mouth but could not scream.

•　　•　　•　　•　　•

With no altitude for freefall, Hunter deployed the parachute, which fully inflated and then set up a vector to land on the middle of the roof. Through the night vision goggles, his eyes moved from the intended green landing spot to the green sniper and back again. The intended landing spot was a dozen feet from the edge of the sniper's hide. He had to aim for the center — the winds were still being fickle. Hunter worked the risers and felt like he had a good glide slope. *Touchdown… about ten seconds.* He focused like a laser on flying the competition parachute to his landing spot. He fought the wind gusts until he realized he was pulling one riser so hard he might collapse the parachute.

Hunter struggled with the risers to turn to a more favorable and controllable angle. He constantly adjusted his position; his glide angle and height were looking better about five seconds from touchdown. Then a gust suddenly pushed him off his trajectory. His internal calculator told him he was drifting; he turned hard into the wind to stay on target. *Eighty-feet, four seconds to touchdown.*

His adrenaline spiked as he ballooned a bit when a gust hit him from behind; now his approach angle was too steep and he was too high. *Sixty-feet, three seconds to touchdown.* Then he got a whiff of something noxious, ammoniac. He didn't have time to think of what he could be smelling. He yanked the riser hard, then harder. He couldn't control the parachute in the winds. As the winds pushed him away, he realized was going to overshoot his landing spot. The smell increased with every second. It began to burn his nose and eyes. Then he realized he wasn't only going to miss his landing spot, he was going to miss the roof.

●　　●　　●　　●　　●

Marine One lifted off the South Lawn of the White House and settled nicely into a four-foot hover. The pilot performed a gentle pedal turn of almost ninety degrees and then centered the helicopter's rudder pedals. A final scan of the instrument panel assured her that the polished Sikorsky VH-3D was performing perfectly; the pilot in command pulled up on the collective stick to increase power and lift. She programmed the control stick slightly; she bumped the nose to start a gentle forward transition and the big green machine complied.

●　　●　　●　　●　　●

Blowing through twenty feet to touchdown, Hunter pulled the safety pin on his main parachute, separating him from his main chute. He clawed at the air like many first time parachutists do when they're pushed out of an aircraft. He tried to torque his body into a proper landing fall so he could land on his feet then tuck and roll right back to his feet like the professional parachuting teams do. But a single gust had a major effect on his falling body, and he fell at an angle. He'd land on his side if he couldn't regain control of his falling body. Then the vile stench punched him in the face like a supersonic shockwave. The air around him was gross and putrid. He was inhaling the breath of death.

●　　●　　●　　●　　●

Castaño couldn't wait to get off the roof and breathe some clean sea air. He looked through the eyepieces of the gas mask and telescope as he counted down; the computer perfectly tracked the "tagged" spot on the Marine One helicopter as it lifted off and gradually transitioned to fly toward the Washington Monument then left toward the U.S. Capitol. The gun's barrel made infinitely smooth corrections as new information was fed into the gun's computer. "Ten…. Nine…." At about forty knots and a fifty feet of altitude Castaño expected the aircrew would relax slightly. *Falling from a hundred feet in an out-of-control helicopter should be fatal for all inside.*

•   •   •   •   •

Kelly felt helpless and realized she was going to fail…. *I'm going to fail again…. Fail my father again!* She had no gun. She had nothing. She looked around the cockpit for anything that could be useful. Her eyes fell on the *Weedbusters* control panel. Then she remembered Lynche's words. Kelly rammed the throttle to the firewall to make some noise. The YO-3A lurched sideways.

•   •   •   •   •

From about 10 feet up, Hunter looked at his feet. They weren't perpendicular to the landing area; he was at an acute angle and couldn't get straightened out. If he didn't blow a hole through the roof, he'd crash land opposite the sniper's position near a retaining wall. If the landing didn't kill him, the odor certainly would. He realized it was birds. And he was going to land on some of them.

When the side of his feet plowed through sleeping birds and touched the hard roof, he tried to cushion his landing with the bent knees of a modified parachute landing fall, but the knees that would have acted as shock absorbers in the vertical didn't work in the oblique, and he fell awkwardly. He smacked the roof hard on his hip, then his chest and head, nearly knocking the wind from his lungs. Crushing a few birds did not cushion his fall and somehow his head remained in his helmet. In the first microsecond after touchdown, Hunter couldn't breathe and he couldn't see. He could hear the wingbeats of a hundred birds taking flight. He knew he was literally and figuratively in a steaming pile of bird shit.

•   •   •   •   •

With a sudden break in the wind, Castaño heard the sound of a nearby aircraft propeller at takeoff RPM; then he heard a sound like a duffel bag had landed behind him. He froze as he realized he wasn't alone on the roof anymore. Nearly the whole flock of birds on the roof took to flight and began spinning around the rooftop, trying to return to their roost. He spun around in the tarpaulin, pulling his pistol from its holster. The roof wasn't perfectly pitch black. He could see the vortex of birds and little else. The lights of the National Harbor provided some ambient light. He looked for a threat.

On the opposite side of the roof, between dozens of returning doves and gulls, up against the retaining wall, very vaguely he could make out the silhouette of a man with a helmet and NVGs. Castaño's brain couldn't process what his eyes suggested. He wished he had been wearing night vision devices instead of the gas mask.

The intruder's uniform seemed to merge with the color of the roof's sealant. Castaño tried to comprehend how anyone could have gotten onto the roof with him. He had a decision to make, and time wasn't on his side: Kill the interloper or kill the president.

He turned to the sniper rifle. A green light confirmed it was tracking its target. Castaño reached over and pulled the trigger. The AI software took command of the firing sequence. He cocked his Sig Sauer and turned to kill the man on the roof.

* * * * *

Kelly calmed herself and remembered what her dad had told her. She pushed six buttons on the laser designator panel and slewed the LD to the man near the weapon. She selected *Weedbusters* and MAX PWR. The sniper was wearing a gas mask. She didn't have time to wonder whether her plan was going to work. The LD scribed letters on the roof just as the man moved from under a tent with a weapon in his hand. She moved the *Weedbusters* joystick which moved the crosshairs of the eradication laser in between the eyes of the person's gas mask. She waited for him to look up. She prayed it would work.

* * * * *

Castaño stopped as the red letters BANG appeared in front of him. He was in such a state of agitation that he jerked his eyes up to the sky.

* * * * *

Kelly Horne had anticipated the man's reaction to the laser letters on the roof. It was a natural reaction. The *Weedbuster's* crosshairs perfectly split the man's gas mask. She mashed the aerial eradication system's trigger and irradiated his wide eyes with the UV lasers.

* * * * *

Hunter was on the roof but his hip had taken all of the impact. The suddenness and severity of his pain was a sure sign he had broken his hip. His brain told him not to move or breathe but he had too. He was damaged equipment; out of order. He took air through his mouth in order to live. It was a thousand times worse than the air in Kabul, Afghanistan.

He held his breath as best as he could. He knew whoever was on the roof with him probably had a gun and a temper; the penalty for intruding on an assassination in-progress was a short-range double-tap. He was going to die for parachuting into to heaping pile of bird shit where the air was nearly totally fecalized with the droppings of a thousand birds. A couple of bullets from a pissed off assassin with a gas mask would put him out of his misery.

Below the waist, nothing worked. Above the waist, he moved as fast as he could.

He felt as if his cerebral cortex had been bounced around in his helmet like a BB in a boxcar. The severity of the landing didn't dislodge his helmet and his NVGs hadn't flipped up and away from his eyes. Yet they were inoperative. Hunter reached up to the goggles and felt the battery cable had become dislodged. Sucking air through his mouth, he found the battery connector, inserted the plug, and energizing the photomultiplier tubes in front of his face. There was a man in a gas mask with a weapon coming toward him.

Hunter's pain was so intense that he knew he couldn't run or stand; he just needed to survive. He willed himself to move and found enough strength to torque his shoulders so he could get to his weapon. Hunter flipped over onto his other side, off of his throbbing hip. He pulled his Colt Python from his shoulder holster and placed the red laser sight on his target, in the middle of the man's gas mask. His brain demanded he breathe. With every beat of his pounding heart the laser dot bounced all over the man's gas mask. He heard Nazy's voice, *You can't kill him.*

He exhaled and held his breath; he dropped the red dot to the man's leg—the laser dot froze on the target and Hunter shot him in the knee, just as the man reached for the eye shield of his gas mask. For a fraction of a second Hunter thought his bullet had gone wide, but he saw the man's knee explode like bursting fireworks in the NVGs. When he inhaled, he nearly puked.

He couldn't tell who the man was; three of the four runaways from the NCS were clean shaven; Castaño sported a Carlos Santana-like mustache. This dude wore a gas mask, so it could have been someone entirely different. Hunter blinked twice; his eyes burned and teared. He struggled to see if he had stopped the sniper's advance. Hunter reached inside his flight suit and ripped his t-shirt from his chest, wadded up the ragged material, and stuffed it into his mouth. He breathed through the makeshift gas mask.

•　　•　　•　　•　　•

Castaño grabbed for his eyes just as his kneecap shattered. The hollow-point bullet tore through his patella and nearly amputated his lower leg. The pain was instantaneous and excruciating; he screamed. He stumbled and fell; his knee was on fire, his eyes burned as if acid had been squirted into them. He was surprised to find he was stilling holding his pistol after slamming it into the face of his gas mask, a reaction to his eyes being burned out of their sockets. He labored and raged and fired at the position he surmised the man on the roof might be.

His leg flopped around uselessly in a growing pool of blood. Castaño crumpled to the roof. He was in a panic and his heart was about to beat out of his chest. Blood poured from his knee.

•　　•　　•　　•　　•

Both men jumped as the sniper rifle erupted. It sounded as if a cannon had been fired. Hundreds of terrified birds took to the air. A tiny white fire shot out of the rear of the rocket-propelled bullet.

•　　•　　•　　•　　•

Hunter heard the sniper screaming inside his gas mask but he had to take care of that bullet. He forced himself to focus on the sniper rifle and the red laser dot from his weapon. The stuffed shirt in his mouth allowed him to breathe without gagging.

Seven miles in ten seconds. Eight seconds. Hunter placed the laser sight on the part of the barrel of the sniper gun he could see and ascertained where the rest of the weapon was under the tent. His heart slammed in his chest making the laser sight bounce with every beat of his pulse. *I can't do this one-handed. Five seconds.* He rolled to one side and used both hands to aim; he lined up the laser sight as steadily as he could. *Three seconds.* He took one breath and held it. His eyes watered from the concentrated ammonia. The laser dot finally rested on the aiming point. He locked his elbows and pulled the trigger four times. The swirling mass of birds departed the rooftop for a quieter location.

Fragments of the sniper system flew each time he pulled the trigger. Hunter thought his heart and lungs were going to burst.

A revolutionary sniper bullet had been launched downrange. Seven miles to the target. Hunter had done all he could for the president. He could barely move and the gases on the roof were killing him. Now he had to save himself.

The sniper had something he needed.

•   •   •   •

Castaño heard the heavy thumps of magnum rounds being fired and slamming into metal. Somewhere in the recesses of his brain he thought, *That bullet is gone! No factor!*

His eyes and leg useless, Castaño suddenly stopped shrieking, threw off the gas mask and screamed in the voice of a wounded madman, "You're too late!" He raised his gun and sobbed, "*Sic semper tyrannis! I've done it!*"

He wailed and writhed in his own blood. The ammonia from the bird guano caught up to him. Castaño tried to shout again, "*You're too late!*" but it came out in a croak. He waved his weapon, pointing aimlessly, trying desperately to locate the man who had shot him but he was blind, completely blind.

The rounds from the Colt Python had echoed on the roof and each fired bullet sounded like a balloon popping in the cooling tower of a nuclear power plant. The cascading echo made it impossible for Castaño to triangulate and locate the interloper by ear.

The gases had caught up to him. Castaño couldn't breathe or see. His brain couldn't register anything but white, and his eyes and nose and lungs were on fire as if he had been doused with acid. He dropped his pistol and tried to claw through the tacky pools of bird excrement, dragging himself and moving about a half a foot with every exertion. His blood pressure was failing. Although the pain was excruciating and he struggled to breathe, he focused on a single thought, *What's wrong with my eyes?*

•   •   •   •

Hunter knew there was no time for rest. Kneecapping a person was only fatal if the wound wasn't tended to. If it was Castaño, he wasn't doing anything to help himself. That man needed a tourniquet and he needed one fast. Hunter needed more bullets, but felt he needed the gas mask more.

Time might solve the problem of interrupting the assassin at work. The puddle of blood under the sniper was comingling with fresh droppings. Duncan ignored the dying man for the moment and looked through the NVGs for a sign that he had been successful in deflecting the assassin's bullet. But he couldn't get into a position to see over the ledge of the hotel roof. He couldn't even see the Washington Monument from where he lay. His lungs burned from the caustic bird guano. He surveyed the scene on the rooftop in shades of green. He saw the gas mask and it wasn't too far away. When the winds were strong, they helped Hunter breathe easier through the t-shirt material in his mouth, but when they died down, breathing through the t-shirt was totally ineffective and he choked. Hunter was afraid his throat would close up or he'd lose conscious from the concentrated ammonia that hung like a fog over the rooftop. He dragged himself toward the gas mask.

Hunter was certain the sniper was Castaño. He was bleeding out but he still may have had a weapon. Hunter couldn't see if the man was still armed, he had just one focus: reach the gas mask. Save yourself. Let that asshole die.

Hunter's upper body strength allowed him to quickly crawl through puddles of droppings, past the wounded man. He was becoming lightheaded. His hip and knee were excruciatingly painful; his nose and throat felt as if he had been forced to drink battery acid. His eyes were almost useless from the caustic air.

Hunter only had seconds before he slipped into unconsciousness. He was near death, asphyxiated, when he reached and secured the gas mask. He went through the motions to remove his helmet and don the gas mask. An old thought reminded him to clear the gas mask before taking a breath. Hunter collapsed atop a mound of bird droppings. And breathed.

Filtered air never tasted or felt so good. His eyes recovered incrementally as purified air filled the gas mask. Hunter rested for a few seconds breathing scrubbed air and exhaling the poisonous effluvia. *Thus always to tyrants? Really, asshole?* He took a deep breath, reached for his speed loader, reloaded the Python, and then turned to confront the sniper.

• • • • •

The emergence of a brilliant white-hot spot on the edge of her field of view, Kelly jerked left and followed the trace toward the Washington

Monument. She had seen the thermal streaks of the special bullets with rocket motors before when her father killed the ISIS men and children in Syria. Brilliant streaks of white hot energy. She was sickened then; now she didn't have time to feel ill; she felt completely defeated. With the bullet speeding to its target, her father had failed, too.

Kelly turned the FLIR away from the White House and Washington Monument and returned to the MGM Grand Hotel. She expected more failure and didn't want to see any of it. She didn't want to see her father killed on the roof or her president killed on the helicopter.

She couldn't bring herself to climb in altitude to better see what the FLIR imaged on the rooftop, so she turned and tried to find a fireball or any sign that the streaking bullet had hit its intended target.

●　　　●　　　●　　　●

There were no departing jets from the National Airport to drown out the sounds on the roof. Steve Castaño could only hear his own laborious and painful breathing as his life slowly slipped away. He could move no further. His brain told him to stop breathing.

Someone had interfered with his plan, interrupted his life. His strength ran out as blood trickled out of his knee. His head crashed onto the roof. Castaño's last rational thought was the answer to the question that began when a man fell onto the roof with him: *Maverick?*

●　　　●　　　●　　　●

In her periphery, Kelly noticed a pair of helicopters had changed direction and caught her attention; their rotor tip lights and anti-collision beacons were getting brighter by the second. One approached the hotel from the west and one from the north. She added power, programmed some aft stick, and climbed five hundred feet to get out of the way and hopefully, continue to avoid visual detection.

She slaved the FLIR from the White House to the helicopters, then to the roof of the hotel. When she saw the thermal image of a man falling over the side of the building, Kelly screamed and prayed. She stopped flying her airplane. When she felt the aircraft move under her, she snapped out of her trance and regained control of the YO-3A. Kelly timidly looked into the FLIR scope. Seconds passed as she flew over the topmost part of the MGM Grand Hotel. The FLIR showed the thermal image of a single human wearing a gas mask resting against the railing circumscribing the roof. She watched in rapt fascination as the man raised the unmistakable shape of a revolver to the sky with one hand and gave a "thumbs up" with the other.

Kelly had seen the sniper wearing the gas mask. She was crushed that she had failed. That she had failed her father. She tried to fly the airplane as she broke down and cried.

With tears running down her cheeks, she looked over the side of the canopy rail of the YO-3A to see the flashing and rotating lights of emergency vehicles converging on the MGM Grand Hotel. A Coast Guard *Dolphin* helicopter, with its shrouded tail rotor, approached the roof. A Capitol Police twin-engine *Huey* trained a spotlight on a body at the foot of the hotel. The thermal images of the helicopter engines were as bright as magnesium flares.

Time to wipe away her tears; her father was gone. It was time to go. Kelly turned east, engaged the autopilot, and collapsed in her seat. She continued to monitor the activity on the roof with the FLIR until it was physically impossible to monitor the hotel rooftop. She fought the ocean breeze headwinds until it was time to turn and fly down the Virginia coast. She retracted the FLIR and *Weedbusters* lasers, and gained a twenty knots of airspeed.

Kelly reprogrammed the autopilot to take her to the private rendezvous airfield. She pulled her BlackBerry from a lower pocket of her flight suit. Surprised she had a strong signal, she texted Nazy Cunningham with a synopsis of the events and where she was heading. She imagined Nazy reading her words and collapsing in grief. She tried to call Director Lynche at his desk.

The automatic takeoff and landing system would take Kelly to the runway in Bridgewater. She felt like she was the CIA's greatest failure. Maybe she'd try to land the *Wraith*. Maybe the winds would be better in the valley. Maybe it would be better if the ATLS did all the work. Maybe she didn't care to live anymore.

69

November 10
Washington, D.C.

The Army and Navy Club on Washington, DC's historic Farragut Square was more than an elegant "home away from home" for some of the most illustrious names in America's military. It was also a place where senior members of the intelligence community, if they were members, could find safe and secure overnight lodging. Members absorbed the Club's timeless elegance and atmosphere, fine dining, and delightful accommodations. While reservations normally needed to be made months in advance, occasionally there would be a cancellation.

The reservation clerk recognized him and handed him his key. She wished the old Marine a "Happy Birthday" as she surreptitiously looked over the woman who had entered the lobby with the old correspondent. She made a face as if she had seen her before on television. One thing was for certain, she knew the woman was a Russian. *Was she one of those beautiful Russian spies that the government was deporting?* She bid Colonel Eastwood a good night.

After Eastwood and Viviana had filed their reports on the aircraft crash site, the RTN reporter recommended they go to his hotel room.

Viviana Vaslakova was convinced Dory Eastwood wasn't an intelligence agent masquerading as a journalist. She killed the tracking device she had slipped into his pocket. If he ever found it he'd always wonder how he had acquired a shiny old Morgan silver dollar.

They held hands in the elevator and down the hall. Ever the deep cover agent, Viviana knew where the cameras were and hid her face from them with a flick of her hair.

The fact that Eastwood was taking the Russia Television Network anchor to his hotel room had put him ill at ease. He was excited and in a mild state of shock. He hadn't been with a woman for years. He wasn't an intelligence officer who had been trained to find hidden cameras in hotel elevators and corridors and was oblivious to the hotel's surveillance systems. Viviana noticed. He was a trained reporter and not someone who made his living in the tradecraft.

They lay curled up in the middle of a king-sized bed; the bedsheet was pulled up to their necks. After making love for an hour, Eastwood got up and turned the ceiling fan to "high" in a vain attempt to cool off the overheated lovers. The scent of their sex swirled under the fan's blades.

They lay in each other's arms, enjoying the high velocity air coming from above. He knew she wanted something; she knew he wanted something. It wasn't just sex. Sex was the medium to break the ice to be able to say what was really on their minds.

Eastwood began like a good old Marine marshalling ground troops for a frontal assault. "Viviana, you want something from me." More question than statement.

She was coy, a little embarrassed. She built up her courage with several nods. Viviana crawled on top of him, straddling him, and took his hands to emphasize she was unimaginatively serious, then finally said, "Dory, I'm a colonel in the Russian army. For the last twenty years I've worked in the Thirteenth Directorate of the SVR, the Foreign Intelligence Service of the Russian Federation, civilian and public affairs. I want to defect and work for the CIA. I think I can be of help to America. I know that when I disappear the Russian Main Intelligence Directorate will send out a team to find me and kill me. I want to defect, and I want to live, and I want to be with you. Is there something you can do?"

Dory Eastwood was speechless: *She really is an intelligence agent!* He didn't know what to say, nor could he remember what it was that he wanted from her. She crossed her arms over his chest, her eyes pleading, begging. He put his arms around her and drew her close. He rolled them over onto their sides.

He was in shock as he absentmindedly, almost mechanically kissed her. When their smartphones began to ring and vibrate, they separated and turned to find them, somewhere lost in heaps of clothing. Eastwood got up and recovered his, leaving Viviana still perspiring and sprawled naked on the bed. He looked at her admiringly. His eyes said, "Yes." He nodded and whispered, "I have a friend. I'll see what he can do." He read the new text message, looked up and said, "There's been a shooting at the MGM Grand Hotel. What do you want to do?"

Viviana said, "I'm done with that life. You don't have to do that anymore, either. I want you to come back to bed."

He shut down the offending cellphone and slipped back into the bed. They held each other close. No real thoughts of more sex. Viviana was restless. Something was bothering him. She wasn't through talking. He held her close and waited for her to say what was on her mind.

Just as she pushed away, rolled on top of him, and whispered, "I want you to tell my story" Eastwood figured out what was bothering him. As he untwined from Viviana, he moved to get out of bed and got dressed. She was confused and felt rejected. He said, "Viviana, I think we need to go to the MGM Grand Hotel. I've a hunch a friend of mine is in trouble there. I could be wrong, but I can't afford not to go and check. Can you tell me your story after we make sure he's ok?"

"Who's your friend?"

"He's the one who'll be able to get you an interview with the CIA."

Viviana scrambled off the bed and raced Eastwood to get dressed.

●　　●　　●　　●　　●

Greg Lynche took the call immediately. He thanked the person on the other end, hung up, and took several deep breaths. His intelligence officer in New York City had called to confirm he had completed his mission. Dressed in the uniform of a New York Police Department cop with an EVIDENCE vest, he had been one of many NYPD officers investigating the death of Nikita Zhavrazhinov. He had been able to work the crime scene and retrieve the dead man's computer, cell phone, and several Moleskine notebooks and placed them into an evidence bag.

Holding the transparent EVIDENCE bag out and away from him as if it was a stinky diaper, he passed through the doors of the JW Marriott, mounted a black NYPD Segway personal transportation system, and disappeared into the night.

It was quiet in the Director's office for the first time in hours. Lynche allowed his eyes to slam shut. He dreamed the nightmare of an exhausted man who headed the greatest intelligence organization in America and he had one mission and he had failed. His friend and president had died and he hadn't been able to stop one of his own from killing them. *Just like before….*

The distant ringing of the telephone jolted him awake. He picked up the receiver expecting confirmed death sentences. Lynche's heart rattled in his chest like castanets, the pressure on his chest felt as if an airplane had been dropped on it. He dreaded the call. He didn't want to hear the verdict but jumped to his feet, pumped his fist, and shouted when he heard the news.

70

November 10
Washington, D.C.

The Walter Reed National Medical Center was on lock-down. The President of the United States was visiting the wounded, awarding Purple Hearts, shaking hands with the recuperating, consoling parents and spouses of injured soldiers and Marines. He was directed to the Navy SEALs and NCS operations officers who had recently come from a military hospital in Germany. He complemented the hospital staff for their incredible work. He had wished injured Marines "Happy Birthday." It was the birthday of the Marine Corps.

When meeting wounded patients, it was slow going. The president told the injured and the recovering, "I'm so very proud of you, and I'm thrilled you'll be back on your feet soon. You have to come by the White House and let me know you've been discharged. If I can, I'll give you a tour. You are a great American and a patriot. Thank you for your service."

He pressed a president's challenge coin into the hands of each wounded man. For the men medically evacuated from Syria via a U.S. hospital in Germany, the president leaned over and whispered something into the ear of each SEAL and NCS officer.

The Secret Service detail cleared the next hospital room on the president's schedule. It would be his last stop for the day, and it was expected to be a lengthy visit. Everyone except the patient was standing in the room as the Secret Service men sidled out; then the president strode in.

President Hernandez ignored the sleeping patient for the moment and shook everyone else's hands after politely hugging and giving cheek kisses to the women. Although the weather outside called for wools and flannels, Nazy Cunningham was dressed in a long, flowing, floral sundress with a crew neckline and sleeves that hid her arms. Red lacquered nails poked out from black and white platform sandals. Kelly Horne wore something less ostentatious, a black chiffon, flower and butterfly maxi-dress with robin blue sandals. They made a colorful pair against the stuffy dark warm suits of the men in the room.

The women's choice of clothes was unexpected. Lynche had rarely seen Hunter's girls in anything but rock-ribbed Republican conservative business attire. He was sleep-deprived yet rationalized that both women must have had their homes cleared by security and were able to find something nice from their wardrobes. They were beautiful women even as Kelly Horne yawned uncontrollably every minute.

It was only the second time the President had seen Nazy in something other than a silk blouse and business suit. When she and Duncan had been invited to the White House, she had worn a stunning evening gown and lit up the State Dining Room with her megawatt smile. The ladies brightened up the drab and antiseptic-smelling hospital room with their attire and made all the men smile. It was a day to celebrate. Birthdays and life.

The men in the room had seen this show before. The president stopped before each one and said a few things, very warm and nice things. Greg Lynche was first; President Hernandez said he was going to miss him. Lynche dropped his head incrementally, in a bit of shame. It still stung a bit, but he knew he had made the right decision. He had given President Hernandez his resignation; the president threatened to refuse it until Lynche explained that it was for the president's benefit as well as his own. And Lynche suggested an outstanding replacement. "It's time for me, Mr. President...." He was interrupted by the patient who still had his eyes closed.

Duncan Hunter had been rushed into his room, nearly bypassing the recovery ward. His eyes were irritated and he didn't want to open them, even if he could. He snored and snorted as if he were partially anesthetized, then suddenly blurted out, in a slurry voice, "Heee wants tooo goooo...back tooo his old life.... Sail his booooat to the...Ba...ha....mas...." Hunter went back to drooling and snoring.

Lynche squeezed Duncan Hunter's toe, smiled and pled, "Guilty."

President Hernandez stepped in front of Bill McGee and shook his hand. Both men smiled as if they were sharing a dirty joke telepathically. The president nodded and said, "We'll see you and your family tomorrow."

Demetrius Eastwood was the new kid on the block and President Hernandez told him so. "You've done some remarkable work, Colonel Eastwood. You've been very helpful in ways that... um...." He turned to Lynche and McGee for the correct word or phrase. Eastwood had reported exclusively that a sniper had been stopped by a Secret Service agent on the roof of the MGM Grand Hotel overlooking the

National Harbor.

Lynche said, "…in ways that cannot be measured."

McGee said, "…would bring great credit to you and your country."

President Hernandez used both spontaneous yet militarily familiar lines and welcomed Eastwood to the team.

Then the president moved to Duncan Hunter's side. He looked past the patient and was impressed by a huge tubular multi-armed contraption suspended from the ceiling holding a number of drip bags, monitors and tubes which were attached to Hunter's arms, fingers, and chest. He squeezed Hunter's limp hand. "I don't know where to start, Duncan. The evidence is in that you took extraordinary measures…that you put the lives of me, my family, and the Marines flying Marine One over yours. We'll always be grateful. Thank you."

There were no nurses to pat his cheek to wake him. Hunter heard his name and lifted an eyelid revealing a sliver of a severely bloodshot eye. He tried to surveil the room. His voice was slurry from a damaged windpipe. He saw Nazy and tried to smile. There was another unintelligible outburst from him followed by a snort. He uttered something that was a poor use of the King's English. "….think heaven… missing… *an angel.*" It sent the group into peals of laughter and applause. He struggled to open both damaged eyes and croaked, "Who died?"

Nazy was very emotional. Her chin trembled, her throat was tight. She held his hand and scolded Duncan in her best British, "You almost did." *You jumped out of an airplane!*

Kelly said, "I thought he had died. After I landed in Bridgewater and Nazy told me he hadn't, I started crying again."

Nazy added to the assembly, "We are going to get away when he's able to walk."

The president said, "That's a good plan. He needs a vacation. I promise not to call. I should say, I'll try not to call." The men laughed, and the women smiled. He looked around the room and asked, "Does anyone have the whole story? What Duncan did last night?"

Hunter returned to dozing. Kelly Horne self-consciously raised a hand and gave an accurate accounting of her father's actions. "The sniper was where we thought he'd be. You could see the sniper using a laser designator in the NVGs. I thought Dad was going to shoot him but I think his gun jammed…."

With eyes closed, Hunter offered a guttural, "…*yuuupppp*…."

"I was about a hundred feet higher than he was. I had a good thermal image of him and a weapon on a tripod in the FLIR. Then the next thing I see is Dad's canopy flying off. One second later, he's up in his seat diving over the side. He deployed his parachute. He worked the risers, but the winds were terrible. Maybe they were affected by the MGM Grand Hotel and pushed him away from the landing area on the roof."

McGee offered, "He's not the best parachutist. But I give him credit that he landed where he needed to be."

Hunter tried to grin. Compliments from McGee were rare.

Kelly continued, "I was trying to fly; trying not to run into anything. But I couldn't take my eyes off of him. I don't know how he managed to get over the roof, I'm sure he jettisoned the parachute and crashed onto the roof."

Lynche nodded and said, "Breaking his hip; trashing his knee." *Killing birds, swimming through bird feces....* The thought made Lynche retch.

McGee chortled to himself. "Duncan Hunter can hit a racquetball at 130 miles per hour, run a three-hour marathon, and shoot the lights out at amazing distances with that cannon of his, but he's horrible with a parachute." The group laughed nervously. "But there's no one like him. He doesn't give up. Must be a major character flaw."

Hunter's sleepy time expression changed from nonplussed to smiling. He uttered a couple of letters—*M...C*—no one knew what he meant.

McGee added, "I'm sure he meant, *Mission Complete*." He squeezed Hunter's toes with pride. "I can also say that the great ones play hurt."

President Hernandez clapped a bit and nodded his approval. "You're right, Captain McGee, the great ones play hurt."

Tears ran down Nazy's cheeks. Lynche patted her back.

Kelly finished her story. "I saw the thermal image of a bullet heading for the White House. I almost died a thousand times when I saw someone go over the side of the hotel, knowing I'd lost my dad. The man who shot the sniper gun wore a gas mask. So I thought the man with the gas mask had pushed dad over the side...."

Nazy said, "She texted me what had happened. I couldn't believe Duncan had died. I called Greg, and he talked to the Capitol Police and the Secret Service. And here we are."

Lynche frowned and said, "He did it without authorization."

McGee interjected, "Commander's wishes." Lynche didn't look at McGee but he did bite his lip.

Kelly was suddenly aggravated with her boss. She continued, "It took about five minutes for the emergency responders to arrive. Helicopters began to converge on the hotel, and I had to leave."

Nazy said, "It was only much later when Greg received a report that they found Duncan."

Lynche said, "I told the Capitol Police to look for a man in a flight suit, shoulder rig, and a Colt Python. He's the good guy."

Nazy continued, "….and they found him; they took care of him. Got Duncan off the roof. I understand it took them forever…."

Lynche said, "…they needed a biohazard team…."

Nazy continued, "I couldn't talk to them; I was a wreck."

McGee said, "He doesn't give up easily."

Lynche said, "I was half-worried that if he was on the roof, they'd think Duncan was the bad guy. Shots had been fired. I was worried they were going to shoot him."

In the makeshift SCIF, where high-value patients could utter classified information while unconscious, Lynche said, "Mr. President, the man on the roof with the sniper weapon was Steve Castaño. The men from the aircraft accident on I-66 were his subordinates, Galvan Fässler, Jarvis Bomarito, and Bennett Troxel. We think Castaño placed anti-personnel mines aboard those two aircraft and detonated them remotely." At that point Lynche glanced over to Nazy and then to McGee.

Nazy said, "We believe one or two of the four planted explosives on Director Lynche's sailboat. The FBI EOD team found and removed the devices."

Hunter slurred, "Did they check… the Porsche?" Not everyone knew Duncan Hunter had given Greg Lynche a Porsche for his 70th birthday. Lynche indicated the car was ok, at the dealer, on display in their showroom, but Hunter had dozed off again.

President Hernandez crossed his arms and shook his head.

Bill McGee said, "Unbeknownst to any of us, up until just recently, Castaño had a very close relationship with the DNC Chairman, Nikita Zhavrazhinov. When the DNC had a problem with a particular person….*politically*…."

President Hernandez asked, "Castaño took care of them for Zhavrazhinov?"

Lynche said, "Yes, sir. Or one of his three minions. Documented. Zhavrazhinov kept a journal. Also, when the authorities found Castaño, he was wearing a bizarre t-shirt of a uniformed cop in a clown face pointing a revolver. They're looking into its meaning…."

Hunter sighed heavily, opened his damaged eye again, and scowled at McGee. He struggled against the anesthesia to utter, "…drugs."

McGee said, "Go back to sleep. You probably had this figured out all along."

Nazy dried her eyes and looked at her husband with admiration. She said, "Duncan has the best new hip and knee money can buy." Everyone in the room smiled and nodded their agreement.

McGee popped off, "I don't know—I'm sure they gave him the lowest-cost, technically-acceptable parts. He won't be able to go through an airport magnetometer without it blowing up." More smiles and gentle laughs. Eastwood smiled and took mental notes.

Nazy asked very timidly, "This may be a poor time to ask a question...."

President Hernandez said, "Miss Cunningham, please feel free." He looked into her eyes; it was much safer location than looking at her dress.

Nazy was reluctant to ask one not-so-obvious question: "I understand the sniper system fired a bullet. Do we know where the bullet hit? Duncan just wouldn't be able to live with himself if...."

The president smiled and said, "This morning, the U.S. Park Service reported one slab of Maryland granite on the Washington Monument was shattered by a projectile. They thought it might have been a meteorite that had struck the monument. The U.S. Park Service never had one of the granite slabs actually break and fall from a bullet. They tell me that the monument gets hit about five times a year by small caliber bullets. Those bounce right off."

Director Lynche explained that the Secret Service had calculated the flight window of the laser-guided projectile was a mere four inches. "A normal sniper's bullet could wander horizontally by feet in the winds. They thought it was impossible at ten miles with a conventional ballistic weapon. But it was possible with an unconventional bullet with wings. Duncan apparently upset or killed the laser designator just in time for the computer to break lock on the Marine One helicopter; the laser designator either illuminated a new spot or it was de-energized. The bullet likely drifted into the Washington Monument."

Bill McGee crossed his massive arms and said, "In other words, no one was hurt."

President Hernandez took Nazy's hand. "That's not correct. Duncan broke his hip in the fall—he never let a little broken hip slow him down. He saved my life, my family, and everyone on the helicopter. He's just amazing."

Lynche articulated a warning, "Not too many accolades, Mr. President—we still have to live with him." Laughter raced around the room.

Then Hunter shifted positions in his bed, smiled, slurred, and groaned, "Thannnnn you. Mr. President. I'm soooo sorry I did not stand…. I'mmmm becoming an old…dodardddd like Greeggg." Nazy leaned over with a tissue and wiped drool from his mouth in an attempt to prevent him from saying anything more. The men's eyes followed her bosom's every move.

President Hernandez slipped his hand in his suit pocket, patted Hunter's shoulder, then thrust the president's special challenge coin into the hero's hand. The show was over. When the President left the room, Lynche stuck his head out of the door and called for a nurse. When one arrived, McGee asked for more "happy juice" for the patient. "We're done with him. He needs his sleep, and we're going to get out of here and let him rest. Thank you." Lynche watched Nazy and Kelly follow the president. He realized he was going to miss that distraction every time Nazy came into or left the room.

After everyone had departed, it was suddenly quiet in the room. No distractions, no voices, no one pulling on his toes or taking his hand. Hunter relaxed and dozed lightly; he gripped the coin like it was made of gold, which it was. He thought he was dreaming. He heard the door open and there were feet shuffling in the room. He thought someone had come back to spend some more time with him. They'd have to wait. He wanted nothing more than sleep. A nice sleepy fog to avoid all the antiseptic smells and incessant noises of a hospital.

Hunter thought he heard a voice: "Who's he?" He thought he heard another voice say, "I think he's *Maverick*." Hunter opened an eye to see who was in his room and found eight men, apparently patients with IV stands surrounding him. Every man had a thick bandage covering a forearm. He tried to move and open both eyes as the sedative worked on him to put him out of action. Hunter thought one man stepped forward and said, "The President of the United States said you were the man who saved us in Syria. Sir, we'd like to tell you 'thank you' for your service."

Hunter didn't know if they were real or if he was dreaming or if he was still in a post-surgery fog. He was very sleepy. He struggled against the drugs, and raised a hand with an IV port and gave the apparitions the best salute he could muster.

71

November 11
Washington, D.C.

The men and women of the media went ballistic when a shiny red ambulance, emblazoned with Walter Reed National Medical Center arrived and was expeditiously waved through to the White House. Duncan Hunter, coherent but undoubtedly crotchety, was pushed in a wheelchair by a tall, slim Marine in a Dress Blue uniform who knew where he was going, through the side door of the White House and into the Oval Office. Hunter wasn't the man of the hour; it was Bill McGee's turn. McGee greeted Hunter with his usual line of caustic humor. "You should be in the hospital."

Hunter said, "There're some things you just don't miss, good sir." They bumped fists.

Nazy watched as Angela McGee leaned over and kissed Hunter on the lips. She said, "Hello." Hunter told her she was beautiful and squeezed her hand. Each of McGee's long-legged daughters got into line and gave Duncan a stiff hug. He kissed their cheeks and held the girls' hands for a moment before accusing them of getting bigger and more beautiful than the last time he had seen them.

He had watched McGee's girls grow up. He coached the pre-teen girls in racquetball and watched them become very competitive players in the women's divisions.

Hunter winked at Nazy seconds before President Hernandez entered the Oval Office and told a story how a kid from Texas grew up in the shadow of a great man and a patriot. "Of course I'm talking about Bill's father, one of the Red Tails, a fighter pilot, one of the original Tuskegee Airmen. A Silver Star winner. So it's not too surprising that the nut didn't fall too far from the tree. U.S. Navy Captain William McGee has won five Navy Crosses. Every one of those Navy Crosses was for extraordinary gallantry in the face of the enemy. A hero among heroes in the service of his country."

The president continued, "Colonel Eastwood's article highlighted that there have been only three men who have been awarded five Navy Crosses. The first was a U.S. Navy submarine commander, Roy Milton

Davenport. The second was U.S. Marine Corps General 'Chesty' Puller. And the most recent, our very own U.S. Navy SEAL, Captain William McGee, known in Special Operations Command as 'Bullfrog' to his friends and to his enemies, 'the Black Ghost.' For his actions in combat, Captain McGee was repeatedly nominated for the Medal of Honor."

"Thank you, Colonel Eastwood, for your timely article. Captain McGee was certainly deserving of our Nation's highest honor. I directed the Chairman of the Joint Chiefs to review Captain McGee's distinguished combat record. I wanted to know why Captain McGee hadn't been awarded the Congressional Medal of Honor. The Chairman completed his review…and determined that there was an outstanding recommendation for a Congressional Medal of Honor for him, for meritorious and heroic actions in Afghanistan. The reason we are gathered here today is to allow me the privilege and pleasure to rectify this oversight and award Captain William McGee the Congressional Medal of Honor. I'm also announcing today that the Navy will be christening their newest guided-missile destroyer, the USS William R. McGee, now being built at the Huntington Ingalls Industries shipyard in Pascagoula, Mississippi. The U.S.S. William R. McGee will be the first ship named in honor of the most decorated serviceman to ever wear the uniform in America's armed forces."

"Captain Hunter, please read the citation."

Demetrius Eastwood took official photographs of the president and McGee, standing at "attention." He avoided including Hunter in any of the pictures. The distinguished guests stood in sartorial splendor for the occasion. McGee looked spectacular in his white service uniform; he stepped forward and faced the president. From his wheelchair, Duncan Hunter barked, "Attention to Orders! To all who shall see these presents, Greeting: This is to certify that the President of the United States of America, authorized by Congress, takes pleasure in presenting the Medal of Honor to Captain William Randall McGee, United States Navy, for conspicuous gallantry and intrepidity in action, at the risk of his life, above and beyond the call of duty…."

• • • • •

After the ceremony, President Hernandez, Greg Lynche, and Bill McGee walked out to the South Lawn to a gaggle of reporters and camera crews. President Hernandez announced that he had accepted the resignation of the Central Intelligence Agency's Director, Greg Lynche. He then presented Captain William McGee, U.S. Navy, Retired, as his candidate to be the next Director of the Central Intelligence Agency. The ribbon of white stars on a light blue background, the Medal of Honor, was draped around McGee's neck. McGee's Special Warfare Badge dazzled in the sunlight.

President Hernandez exclaimed, "Captain McGee brings a distinguished resume which is unparalleled in the Intelligence Community. The first OSS Director, William Donovan, was a person who led from the front and was in most of the country's major invasions, including D-Day at Normandy. Major General Donovan was the only American to receive the country's four most prestigious decorations: the Medal of Honor, the Distinguished Service Cross, the Distinguished Service Medal, and the National Security Medal. Captain William McGee follows in the same tradition as Wild Bill Donovan. He's an exceptionally accomplished professional and has been awarded the Congressional Medal of Honor and five Navy Crosses for conspicuous gallantry and intrepidity in action in the defense of our nation. Captain McGee is the most decorated serviceman ever to wear the uniform of the United States of America. I expect a swift and unanimous confirmation from Congress."

● ● ● ● ●

Hours after President Hernandez announced his nominee to run the Central Intelligence Agency, outgoing Director Greg Lynche, incoming Director Bill McGee, and CIA contractor Duncan Hunter traveled to a remote location in the woods near Great Falls, Virginia. During the drive from the White House to "Annex Tango," Lynche provided a running monologue on what the facility entailed and what it contained. "Top secret information of such a nature that it can't be housed or accessed at or by the National Archives or other intelligence agencies. These are unique, one-of-a-kind, intelligence files. For the longest time we stored them at Ft. Knox. And you'll see why."

McGee wondered what kind of information was so sensitive that even the SCIF curators at the National Archives were prohibited from having access.

Hunter asked, "Ft. Knox? Seriously? What are we talking about?"

Lynche explained that the building was in a remote industrial park. "We own all of the buildings here. Most people have no idea what's back here. Those that do know tend to stay away. Which has been good for our purposes. The people who built the complex of a dozen buildings ensured this one would be totally isolated. In every way. It has dedicated air supply and exhaust ventilation with high-efficiency particulate air filters."

Hunter said, "Sounds like a bio-lab."

"It was. It used to be a research laboratory rated to biological safety level four. Nothing better. You had to completely change clothes before entry, shower on exit, and decontaminate all materials prior to leaving the building. The people who used to work here needed a full-body suit providing positive-pressure and breathing air."

"If we're going in like this, I assume it's safe. A decommissioned bio-lab?" Hunter's interest was piqued.

"Before I answer that, Bill, you'll have to oversee the transfer of these documents to another more secure facility. One is under construction near the NSA on Fort Meade. As for you, my somewhat indisposed friend, think of Admiral Canaris' or General Rommel's diaries. Goebbels. Ribbentrop. Molotov. Hitler. Amin al-Hussaini. As we know from the Nazi's munitions chief, Albert Speer, he wrote in his diary that Herr Hitler was an admirer of Islam and Jihadism."

"The list goes on. It was a time in history that people kept diaries. Depending on the person, their thoughts and writings could have been worth millions. One soviet general who ran the gulags to support a gold mine siphoned off billions of rubles worth of gold and hid it very well. After we received his diary we went after it and brought it back. That kind of information."

Hunter smiled and shook his head in amazement as McGee wheeled him up to the security checkpoint of the heavily guarded SCIF.

Lynche continued, "Annex Tango contains extremely sensitive information contained in the hundreds of thousands of diaries and journals from the lovers of politicians, the presidents and prime ministers, dictators and deviants, lawyers, doctors, admirals, generals, Indian chiefs. The diary and journal library has nearly half a million books, documents, and journals. We even have the private documents smuggled out of the Soviet Union after Gorbachev left office and documents from Iran years before and after the fall of the Shah."

Lynche pushed Hunter in his wheelchair through the security checkpoint and into a heavily guarded SCIF, then Lynche handed Hunter what he called, "Our first book." It was one of the private journals of William "Wild Bill" Donovan, the first OSS Director. Lynche continued, "In it, he described how Vice President John Nance Garner asked him to see if it was possible to interdict and neutralize an assassination team from the Soviet Union. This was the late 1930s. Before the OSS. You may not know that at that time, the Navy was the predominate international intelligence-gathering agency in the United States, followed by the Army. Since the Navy sailed the seven seas, they naturally acquired much intelligence. If naval officers didn't pick up diaries when they were at ports of call, then embassy personnel were charged with acquiring them. They were stored at Naval Intelligence for a while, then Fort Knox, then when the CIA came into being, we looked for a way to use them and maintain them."

Hunter opened the Donovan diary. It naturally opened to where a slip of paper was inserted between the pages. He read, "Whittaker Chambers." He thumbed through the pages as Lynche and McGee talked.

Hunter returned the yellowed paper to the pages of the diary. He came to grips with what he was witnessing, "So this is one giant-sized special access program. If any of these names ever 'got out,' there could be significant damage to a countless number of people and many governments, including ours."

McGee said, "So guys like Canaris, Rommel...."

Lynche said, "...Hitler, Eichmann, Goebbels, the complete Nazi leadership. Others that you have never heard of. Most of the diaries contain information on informants; spies that we used and they used. Agents. Contacts. Adversaries. Handlers. Alliances. Analyses. The location and combination of safes. Safe houses. Who was burned, who was turned. Drop off locations. Escape routes. Explosives and bomb making. And of course, experimental programs."

Hunter frowned and asked, "Of course, like anti-gravity devices?"

Lynche nodded. "Atomic weapons. Anything you can think of. Then we have the Russians. The Soviets killed the scientists who developed the mathematics. One of them knew that he'd be killed by the Soviets. He told a lowly Soviet guard that his diary was incredibly valuable and that the Americans would give him a reward and asylum if he gave them the book. He defected, gave us the diary, and we rewarded him. That guard died of old age on a farm in Iowa. We call diaries that unexpectedly fly into our windows *Bluebirds*."

"I suppose we buy them where and when we can?" asked McGee.

Hunter said, "If we can't steal them. It's always about spies, isn't it?"

Lynche nodded to both men, "It is. And money. *And sex*. It's an extension of The Great Game; it's just that the major players have shifted positions on the world stage. Once it was Great Britain versus the Russian Empire. Now it's us against the Russians, the Chinese, the Islamists, and so on. Through their private writings, we have the names of most, if not all of the players."

Hunter said, "So, when you have these diaries...."

McGee finished for him, "...then we know their private secrets."

Lynche said, "The OSS started the practice. Donovan enlisted a great cadre of men and women that embodied the United States of America. And he sought out other members, including foreign nationals and especially displaced individuals or defectors from the former czarist Russia, such as Prince Serge Obolensky and Rasputin."

Hunter tapped his wheelchair's armrests as if they were bongos, and sang,

Ra Ra Rasputin, Lover of the Russian queen
They didn't quit, they wanted his head.
Ra Ra Rasputin, Russia's greatest love machine,
And so they shot him till he was dead.
Oh, those Russians!

McGee frowned and sarcastically asked Duncan, "Are you through?"

Lynche, nonplussed, continued, "Through his sources, General Donovan had heard that the entire intelligence cadre at the Soviet embassy in Washington and the consulate in New York City had been recalled to Moscow. I suppose they were part of Stalin's *purges*. One-way trip to the Lubyanka. Anyway, something had happened in their world of espionage and there were few clues locally. While Soviet spies were being recalled to Russia, the CPUSA had been shut down. Donovan knew that the Soviets had moved in to the old Romanov mansion on the Chesapeake. His family had a mansion that was close enough to monitor their movements, and he would often monitor the comings and goings of older Soviet men."

Hunter said, "Intel guys...."

Lynche nodded. "He understood the Soviet intelligence chiefs from the embassy played cards there. Had parties with women in the evenings, parties with families during the day. When they left and the mansion was boarded-up, Donovan entered the building and came away with a couple of thousand diaries from people from all over the political spectrum. Those diaries were the seeds for this place."

Hunter was impressed and said so.

Lynche continued, "We have plenty of analysts with time in Russia and the old Soviet Union. The weak link has always been the Islamic countries. Nazy has been invaluable—transcribing the most sensitive diaries from Islamic leaders going back hundreds of years. The treachery of Amin al-Hussein...."

McGee wasn't familiar with the name. Hunter asked, "The grand mufti of Jerusalem?"

Lynche nodded and continued, "The major players and the bit players. Even the Ayatollah Khomeini and his generals' papers—by and large they don't keep many records. When we found papers or had them delivered, as was the case of the woman Duncan exfiltrated out of Iran, we pay for Islamic archives. Nazy knows Farsi and other Arabic languages. She's crucial to the success of this effort. All of the new Islamic leaders and terrorists discovered they need to keep a record for the same reasons that the Germans and Russians and Japanese kept records. Info on spies. Sources. Sleeper cells. Dead drops. Recipes for bomb making. You name it."

Lynche asked, "You know who Nikolai Ivanovich Yezhov was?"

Hunter said, "The head of the Soviet secret police?"

"That's him. I know this one will knock your socks off—in his papers he unmasked the sabotage of the *Hindenburg*. Stalin was not happy with *Herr Hitler* and American communists flew a remote controlled aircraft into the airship."

Hunter said, "I'm not surprised. I'll also bet Stalin's boys in the U.S., Communist Party members stole the plans...."

Lynche smiled and nodded. "They did. There's a bit of everything."

McGee nodded and asked about Mary Pinchot Mayer.

Lynche looked at Bill McGee a long time. Unnaturally long. Hunter was surprised at Greg's momentary impasse. Lynche finally recovered and said he knew the story. "I can tell you what I know, which isn't much. She was one of JFK's mistresses and was killed by a Soviet assassin to punish JFK for Cuba and the embarrassing removal of Soviet missiles. The FBI was tracking a couple of Russian nationals; they lost them and within an hour she was found dead. Russian caliber to the brain."

McGee said, "I read something where we had men on the ground trying to sanitize the crime scene while the counterintelligence chief broke into her apartment."

Lynche did everything he could not to overreact. He nodded pensively, "That's one of the dirty jobs of the DO. That's all true. Her diary is in here. Somewhere. And Bill, just think, after your confirmation in the Senate this will all be yours."

"I don't know what to say but 'thanks' seems a...."

Hunter said, "I think it's a gift and a curse." He wasn't done analyzing Lynche's odd responses and wondered what was going on inside that man's head. *That was a long time ago....*

Lynche replied, "I think the Chinese said it best: May you live in interesting times."

McGee said, "Are 'my' books here yet?"

The question caught Hunter off guard. He spun in the wheelchair to look at McGee. Lynche said, "They're being processed." Now Hunter was totally confused. It used to be him who was the interface. Now it was Bill McGee.

McGee rolled his eyes and smiled conspiratorially at Hunter. He let Duncan squirm in the pool of the unknown as he helped Hunter back into their vehicle. Then he let Duncan know that he had simply responded to Lynche's request to locate and recover the DNC Chairman, Zhavrazhinov's papers. He found them and handed them to Lynche, who turned them over to Nazy and her special intelligence team for analysis. Nazy's the Chief of Diaries."

Hunter shook his head in disbelief. *She never told me!*

McGee continued, "We just can't have the FBI help us. They have been fully compromised. In addition to the DNC, the Islamic Underground has infiltrated that organization. It's been that way for a very long time and it's a shame. The FBI Director resigned, and killed himself, and we can expect their whole seventh floor to be fired or indicted. They tried to take down President Hernandez."

Hunter asked innocently, "Will it ever be known the Agency's four horsemen of the apocalypse also tried to kill the president?"

The men frowned; McGee and Lynche shook their heads in synchronicity.

Lynche said, "A cursory review of Zhavrazhinov's diary has the names of defectors, spies, sleeper cells, apparatuses, as well as the names of FBI and Agency men who were pitched and worked for him. Like Vincze and Castaño and company." Lynche waved a hand and said, "Pages will be scanned for everything you can think of, including secret inks or laminated pages."

McGee thought Lynche would have discussed the other journals and diaries he found at the Zhavrazhinov estate, such as the diaries of previous DNC chairmen. Hunter would have loved the political dirt.

Hunter was quietly basking in self-aggrandizement; the DNC Chairman's journals would be in the house of diaries once Nazy was through with them. He asked, "So technically, hundreds of political murders and reported suicides could be solved...."

The McGee pointed a finger at Hunter and said, "I know what you're thinking. And I know Greg has been wanting to say this for a long time, 'Not your job and you have no need to know, Mr. Hunter.'"

Hunter frowned, and threw his hands in the air. "And so it begins, *again!*"

Lynche and McGee laughed themselves near tears. Then Hunter joined in.

Halfway back to CIA headquarters, Hunter asked, "Didn't I read where 3M declassified the members of the OSS?"

Lynche said, "He did. Against the wishes of the intelligence community. 750,000 pages, 35,000 personnel files which included applications of people who weren't recruited or hired, as well as the service records of those who served."

"Why would anyone do that?" McGee was confused.

Lynche said, "The Russians also have an extensive collection of diaries. They've been at it for a hundred of years. One of Stalin's bright ideas. The Russians, they're our competitors for diaries. So when 3M declassified the members of the OSS, the Russians were able to see who had been spying on them. When the National Archives released those documents, hundreds of men and women, the children and grandchildren of those who had worked with the OSS, were branded as traitors and became enemies of Moscow. They tried to escape Russia. Some were successful but most died. Those that didn't die were sent to the Lubyanka or the gulags." Lynche's voice trailed off as if he had had enough for one day.

McGee said, "That guy was a flaming piece of shit."

Hunter said, "He signed their death warrants. Mazibuike was a communist plant, but no one wanted to believe me."

Looking at Hunter McGee said, "Well, that asshole will never darken anyone's doorway again."

Lynche turned away and quietly stared through the darkened window of the Agency limo.

72

Kelly Horne could barely believe the responsiveness of the three-ton armored vehicle. She wasn't intimidated by the Hummer H2's size or its powerful motor. She had flown high performance jets; ground vehicles were poor substitutes for the rush and thrill of afterburning jet engines. The visibility was spectacular out of the windshield but turns were almost done "in the blind." Drivers had to hope and pray they didn't hit anything, especially turning right. The excitement of driving the big black beast would soon be over and then it would be time to get serious and tell her father what was really on her mind.

In the passenger seat, Duncan Hunter just smiled in between sentences. He was constantly on the lookout for trouble. *An odd habit* she thought. He had called her, and now they were on Interstate 66 from the environs of downtown Washington, D.C. heading west. They talked about airplanes and cars. She wanted to talk about work. He didn't. They drove by the remains of an aircraft accident from days before.

When Hunter said to "take the next exit," she complied as any chauffeur. Off the freeway and heading into town she summoned up the courage to admit, "Dad, I'm not cut out for this kind of work. I almost got you killed…*twice*."

Hunter disagreed. "Kelly, you saved my life. You paid attention to what the Yo-Yo can do. You dazzled Castaño's eyes and stopped him. You gave me a second chance to live, because he would have surely killed me had you not intervened and blinded him. I couldn't move; I really was a sitting duck. Don't beat yourself up. Kinetics, being a trigger-puller, may not be for you. I'm sure you'd be a different person, more comfortable running surveillance airplanes for Air Branch. Don't you think?"

"Yeah." It was a meek response.

He said, "Stick with surveillance aircraft. Whack poppies and coca. Find hideouts and hostages and drug labs."

She was relieved. "That I can do—and I think I can do that well."

"I'll tell you, that's plenty. Aren't you exhausted by the end of the mission? You have to be. I was and Greg and I did exactly that for years. Together. The technology has progressed what two old guys you did in tandem you can do solo."

Kelly appreciated the different outlook and support.

Hunter added, "But, darling daughter, if you stick with the Agency, you'll have to get very comfortable with a weapon. Not just for pistol qualifications. You have to be able to protect yourself."

As they rolled up to the aircraft owner's gate at the Warrenton-Fauquier Airport, Hunter continued, "When you hit him with the *Weedbusters* laser you saved my life. I was disabled, dying; couldn't breathe. That was good thinking. Saved my life."

"I listened to Greg."

"There was a part of me that wanted to see who it was. I suspected it was Steve Castaño. I had no doubt I'd win a shooting battle with him; he didn't have NVGs. I did, and I had a laser sight. But he had a gas mask. The roof was a Petri dish and the gases were killing me. I thought if I hit him center mass that he'd pivot right off the roof, taking my life preserver with him. I needed his gas mask."

"Why are we here?"

"I took Castaño's keys and wallet before I threw him over the side. I think your old boss and his buddies stored their getaway airplanes here. So we are spending this father-daughter time to and see if this opens the owner's gate." Hunter handed Kelly a plain white credit-card shaped key, similar to some of the upscale electronic hotel keys but thicker. Old school RFID.

Kelly was familiar with the airport security entry systems. She touched the access pad with the card, the gate came to life, and rumbled across their path. She was surprised and said, "Wow! You were right." She pulled forward and stopped.

"That's the easy part. We still have to find their hangar." Hunter held up a ring of keys. Once inside the airport property, the access gate rumbled closed behind them. "Now we have to find the lock that fits the key." He pulled a Growler from the center console of the Hummer and turned it on. He looked over the rows of hangars and selected the row where he would have wanted to store an airplane. Kelly drove close to one side scrutinizing the locks until Hunter asked Kelly to stop. He scrutinized the padlocks on the hangar doors with the Master Lock® key on the ring and said, "This looks like a good candidate."

Kelly helped her dad into a wheelchair. Hunter was worried about booby-traps and said so. He said he'd try the lock and separate the two-halves of the welded lock receivers to move the doors open only after he inspected all of it for mechanical and electronic booby-traps. He set the Growler in his lap, inserted the key into the lock, and it turned. *Tally Ho!*

He removed the lock, placed the Growler on the ground by the door and tied a rope to one of the doors. He got out of the way, and Kelly slowly pulled the door open. They repeated the process with the other door. Hunter noted there were no airplanes in the hangar, but there was plenty of interesting "stuff," beginning with an incongruous Dunhill Bakery truck tucked in a corner. He searched for trip wires with a powerful flashlight, and right about the time he was going to declare "all safe," he found a taut wire stretched six-feet inside about four inches off of the ground and spanning the width of the hangar. The dull wire was nearly invisible in the shadows but reflected some light when the flashlight beam swept across it.

The musty hangar smelled of oil and cigars. Convinced there could be more than one booby-trap, Hunter pushed his wheelchair at a snail's pace, parallel to the trip wire. He was slow and deliberate, and moved perpendicular to the shorter wall. He was surprised at the number of different shaped cigar boxes that filled one side of the hangar. He found a wire leading into one of the cigar boxes; it was the only one which rested on its long side with the top facing the middle of the hangar. *Clever. One box lost in a forest of boxes.* Hunter searched the rest of the hangar for similar wire traps and found none. Kelly remained hiding behind the armored Hummer as directed.

Hunter scrutinized the upright cigar box, the wire, and its surroundings. He checked the floor and found several footprints near the upright box. He thought he had figured it out. He opened the lid of the oversized cigar box exposing a Claymore mine. FRONT TOWARD ENEMY in raised letters indicated the mine was properly facing the inside of the hangar. His eyebrows bounced up and down like Groucho Marx' when seeing a pretty woman.

He didn't remember if pulling the detonator would disable the mine, or if there was some other procedure. He was a pilot; Claymores were an infantry weapon. He told Kelly, "There's an inspection mirror in the center console—it's on a flexible long handle. Can you bring it to me please?"

Kelly was shaking as she retrieved the mirror used to inspect the underside of the Hummer for explosive devices and handed it to her father. A breeze moved her hair, obscuring her vision. She bundled her out-of-control mane and quickly knotted it behind her. She watched her father intensely from the safety of the Hummer.

He maneuvered the mirror to view the backside of the mine and saw that there was nothing back there. He pulled the detonator from the fuse well and said, "That should do it." He continued to talk, "These mines contain a layer of C-4 explosive behind a matrix of about seven hundred BB-sized steel balls. If my memory serves me, they're set into an epoxy resin. Here's what they did. When they wanted to work in here, they de-energized the mine by turning it off and disconnecting the trip wire. Explosive ordnance disposal 101."

Hunter removed the trip wire and he gingerly removed the Claymore mine. He turned it around to face the wall; if it were to go off, it would shred hundreds of cigar boxes and the side of the hangar. Once his heart calmed, he spun his wheelchair around and rolled on into the hangar.

Hunter looked at the wall of cigar boxes. "They were definitely into cigars."

Kelly said, with all sincerity, "Didn't they know that stuff would eventually kill them?"

Hunter chortled. *Cigars? Claymores? Or CIA pilots?* He sighed. He took a mental inventory of the inside of the hangar as he rolled the wheelchair from one end to the other. He opened boxes, tool chests, peeked into drawers. He marveled at the insides of the bakery truck. With the exception of the cigar boxes, the inside of the hangar looked like a costume shop had collided with an old-time Army-Navy surplus store he had visited with his father in downtown Denver. There were shelves from floor to ceiling filled with a variety of military equipment and clothing. There were racks of uniforms, mostly Secret Service. Some were emblazoned with special tabs indicating the Special Services Division, or the Counter-Sniper Division, or the Presidential Protection Service. They had everything necessary to assume a synthetic identity.

There was a rack of several dozen clown costumes, masks in boxes on top of the clothes racks, and cases of makeup specifically made for the professional clown. The rubbery masks were state-of–the art latex head-coverings designed to fool the closest inspection.

The hangar was large enough to easily hold two Cessna Skymasters in the available floor space with sufficient space for a couple of large vehicles. An Airstream trailer filled one side of the hangar. Hunter found the chocks for the airplanes; he knew how the aircraft were parked when they were inside the building. There were gas cans, a gas-powered tow bar, a rack full of oil and a case of 5606 hydraulic fluid for airplanes. And boxes and boxes of spare parts for a Cessna 337. Then he knew. The two aircraft that had crashed onto the freeway had come from this hangar. Castaño killed his friends. *How crazy do you have to be to kill your friends? Don't make eye-contact crazy. They must have voted him off, leaving him. He punished them for abandoning him.*

Hunter opened opaque containers the size of banker's boxes and found wrapped bundles of money. There were parachutes, professionally packed and on clean shelves. There were chrome-plated tools, the best brand that money could buy. A set of keys opened two large gun safes. They were filled with OD green ammunition boxes and sniper rifles, foreign assault weapons, and night vision goggles. There were telescopes from Russia, binoculars and cameras from Germany, and *Hasselblad* cameras from Sweden. Scattered among the shelves were special assassination tools, devices, and unique weapons and their operators' manuals, and a variety of lock-picking tools from the S&T labs. Another key opened a locked door at the rear of the hangar. It was temperature and humidity controlled and filled from the floor to the ceiling with a diverse collection of antique cigar boxes.

Hunter opened one to find trays of gold and stainless Rolex and Tag Heuer watches, neatly separated in felt-lined compartments to accommodate the width of the timepieces. He removed one tray of Tag Heuers and picked up watches, one by one, and checked the back for engraving. Hunter was surprised to find the one he was looking for and slipped it into his pocket.

Several dozen boxes contained dairies. Several boxes contained rolls of rare U.S. gold coins. Hunter open another cigar box and recognized an 1854 Liberty Half Eagle. Others contained passports and stacks of international currency. One box was full of numerous badges—FBI, Secret Service, police. Several boxes, surprisingly, contained diaries. Hunter thumbed through a dozen books but didn't find any names he recognized; he knew McGee and the Chief of Diaries would probably be interested in them.

There was a shelf made of princely antique wooden cigar boxes, each wooden box was a drawer. What was inside took Hunter's breath away: Stacks of bright, pristine Series 1922, 1928, and 1934 Gold Certificates. $10,000, $5,000, $1,000, $500, $100, $50, and $20 denominations. Gold seals and gold numbers and the back side of the bills were also gold colored. It seemed every bill was crisp and uncirculated as if they'd recently come off the printing press. They were wrapped with slightly faded gold wrappers from the U.S. Treasury. He shook his head in wonder, *How do you acquire something like that?*

Kelly wandered inside and could barely believe what was in the structure. Words failed her and she could not close her mouth, she was awestruck.

Hunter searched for more explosives and found blocks of C4 still wrapped in dark green wax wrappers. *Leftovers from explosives training? Where are the detonators?* He looked inside another dozen adjacent cigar boxes and found several types of detonators.

The sun was setting which put the hangar in shadows. Hunter felt it was time to go, but a military-style backpack caught his eye, and he rolled over to investigate it. What he found under the backpack's flap confused him. He had heard of backpack jammers that were counter-IED systems, electronic systems to defeat improvised explosive devices used by terrorists to harass and kill American soldiers. But the jammers could be used for other functions, one of which was to interrupt and disable electrical power distribution networks. He thought, *They probably used this to kill the power in Nazy's neighborhood…. They thought of everything. They had everything they needed to interrupt the power control relays.*

After his cursory inventory and segregation of some items, he helped Kelly load what they could in the Hummer. Some of the expensive weapons were loaded as was the backpack jammer. Some things were left behind. Hunter would give the keys and the coordinates of the hangar to the new CIA Director. The boxes containing Gold Certificates, gold and silver coins, and rare Federal Reserve Notes were moved to the floorboard of the Hummer, right next to his feet. Dozens more filled the back seats. Kelly found some space in the back of the Hummer for the skin-like Chief of Disguise's masks and wondered why her father would want them.

After their father-daughter adventure at the airport, Kelly drove the Hummer to a private airport in Bridgewater, Virginia. Most of the contents of the H2 were offloaded into another hangar, a hangar much larger than the one near Warrenton. One with a pristine and polished U.S. Air Force C-47. Hunter kept a cigar box loaded with late American $50 gold eagles on his lap.

When Kelly drove through the tiny local college town, her father asked her to stop at the local IGA supermarket. A little old lady was ringing a bell, soliciting donations for the Salvation Army. Hunter handed Kelly the box of gold coins and asked her to deposit them into the Salvation Army kettle. She did; one hundred coins, one at a time.

•　　•　　•　　•　　•

The midnight release of the first tranche of the Democratic National Committee archives caught the nation by surprise. The rogue website *Whistleblowers* announced the release, a million documents, without further comment. Democratic leaders from Congress, K Street, and the governors of Democratic voting states dismissed the documents as blatant forgeries from the cast of usual troublemakers in the Republican Party.

Colonel Demetrius Eastwood was brought onto television talk shows for his thoughts. "We'll have to see what's in there. Millions of documents were released just today. The head of *Whistleblowers* indicated they're in possession of more than 100 terabytes of data — which is more than 50 times the estimated size of the entire print collection of the Library of Congress. Law firms, legal foundations, foreign embassies, and Republican members of Congress are pouring over the first tranche of documents, what some are calling the 'Keys to the Kingdom' of the Democrat Party. Resignations from some top Democrats have already occurred. More are expected as more documents are released and this 'treasure trove' is fully analyzed."

The television host offered, "The most damaging set of documents were released in the first tranche. If these released records are accurate, then the Democrat Party is in serious trouble. I can't see how they can survive this. For example, some of the documents detail how the DNC paid a tertiary front company $100,000 the day after the death of Tommy Larrabee, a senior DNC official who was murdered and whose murder remains unsolved. Other documents detail how the DNC and senior party leaders created and maintained what appears to be a sex trafficking ring in the Caribbean."

Eastwood added, "Some of the documents I've seen exposed the DNC Chairman as a deep cover Russian operative. The archives reveal the DNC's strategic plan to eliminate Republican leaders through voter fraud schemes and what some in Europe have come to know as 'replacement theory.' Flood America with immigrants, legal and illegal but hostile to assimilation. Their plans to disarm Americans through gun control strategies and infiltrate the branches of government with loyal leftist Democrats in an effort to overthrow the government should be chilling to all Americans."

"The election of President Maxim Mohammad Mazibuike was crucial to their plan, and the election of Attorney General Tussy would have sealed the deal. Every new file revealed a horror story. For example, the DNC maintained a special account that paid for hundreds of one-way airline tickets to Miami for men, women, and children of every age. There are several references to suggest that the women may have come from, ah, body painting competitions and modeling agencies. Apparently, private aircraft flew these men, women, and children to a private island where they were housed and maintained for parties. There had been rumors of this enterprise for years."

"And these people never returned?" The television host was aghast.

"I believe the FBI is raiding the island right about now. We'll see. I haven't seen any evidence in any of the documents released that would suggest these people ever returned to the United States. There may be evidence in other documents yet to be released."

The host had the final word, "The new attorney general and the new FBI Director are investigating. The release of the DNC's archives proves the Democrat Party was fully controlled by Moscow. While the media were fixated on the stunning election of President Hernandez, they completely ignored the number of Muslims who won democrat seats in the House and Senate. In a story that hasn't been fully told, it seems former President Mazibuike facilitated the infiltration of the Islamic Underground into the Democrat Party to such an extent that Muslims won nearly seventy percent of the Democrat Party primaries. The Democrat Party as we knew it may cease to exist. They may have to reconstitute themselves with a new name, a new charter. These new congressional members are already calling for the impeachment of President Hernandez, and they haven't even been sworn in yet."

●　　　●　　　●　　　●

Demetrius Eastwood was able to see former SVR Colonel Viviana Vaslakova one last time before she was absorbed into the CIA's defector protection program. He could still feel her lips on his. One day soon, he hope they would be reunited.

He returned to New York City via AMTRAK's Acela and went straight to his office in the 7 World Trade Center building. He had been up all night writing about the latest release of the Democratic National Committee archives and "Why the DNC Killed Tommy Larrabee." They would be explosive topics. The released tranche of documents were particularly revealing in that they catalogued the unexpectedly heinous conduct of the DNC staff, Democrat senators, congressmen, or governors.

It wasn't his best work, but it was a good start. He printed out copies of the articles, then saved and closed the files; he'd re-read and edit them in the morning.

He didn't know which of the newspapers would publish his articles, if any of them. Eastwood had become an overnight pariah when the DNC Chairman, Dr. Zhavrazhinov, looked into a television camera and blamed Eleanor Tussy's loss on him. His television producer didn't call him for investigative work. Being solely responsible for the Democrat's loss was apparently bad for the news business but not for the book business. Multiple publishing houses were offering book deals.

Eastwood started thinking about another article, along the lines of how a Russian intelligence officer and network reporter gained the confidence of and infiltrated the Russian defector network. *Maybe for another day….*

He looked over his latest proposal one last time before sending the article across the internet.

Submission for the Editorial Page

By: Demetrius Eastwood

Title: How President Mazibuike Facilitated the Islamic Underground's Infiltration of the Democrat Party and Created the Dark State.

73

November 21
Indianola, Iowa

On Highway 65, an ancient red-brick gas station from the 1920s lay ahead, a splash of wine in a field of white. A foot of snow had fallen the day before and had covered everything within eyeshot, including the leafless trees. Duncan Hunter gestured like an excited child and hollered at Eastwood to pull over so they could see the early Standard Oil station with a pair of visible gas pumps sticking out of the snow like six-foot tall, faded-red fire hydrants. Other snow-covered Americana, petroleum-related signs mostly, surrounded the structure. A historical marker was bolted near the door of the tiny building. The owner had thoughtfully shoveled the hard surfaces for visitors.

An obsolete gas station that no longer sold nickel gas wasn't something either man got to see every day and it was worth a few minutes of their time. They were ahead of schedule, they had a little extra time. Hunter cautiously got out of the vehicle so he could get a better look. Eastwood scanned the rolling hills of farm country and the highway winding through it like the path of an acrobatic airplane at an airshow. There were no straight lanes anywhere.

The corn and soybeans fields had long been harvested, now rolls of hay as big as Priuses rested in lines or stacks on snow-covered fields. The last time Eastwood visited, there were three hundred shades of green wherever one looked. Today, just snow dominated the landscape. Multicolored farm implements of every sort were stored in dilapidated shelters for the winter.

Shortly after they left the old gas station, Hunter had Eastwood stop their rental at the first sighting of a pair of bald eagles majestically flying in tight turns adjacent to the road. Several hawks perched in trees or on fence posts, other eagles fought like cats and dogs for the chance of feeding on deer carcasses that littered the snowplowed highway.

As they left dry pavement for a plowed but snow-packed farm road, Hunter said, "I never get tired of watching raptors."

Maude Larrabee offered the men fresh squeezed lemonade and warm banana bread from the oven. They sat inside a sunroom. She favored a little sun, while Hunter removed his hat and hogged the shade. Eastwood did most of the talking as the sun beat on the back of his neck. She was introduced to Hunter who gave her one of his cover names. "But you can call me, *Maverick*."

Eastwood told her, "There's no doubt that your Tom found himself in the middle of something he couldn't control. He was likely trapped and wanted to get free, just like many people from the communist bloc who worked a lifetime to be free. I've met a large number of these very special people who defected from the eastern bloc, from communism, or from socialist and Marxist countries."

She said, "I think Tommy found himself in the same situation as those who cherished and sought freedom."

Eastwood continued, "These people were forced to do work that was anathema to their beliefs and convictions, and they had to find a way out. Just a few years ago, many Americans thought our country was lost. If America succumbed to socialism and a communist president, then where do you go when the left has won and there's no more America?"

Maude Larrabee said, "Tommy was inspired by the nameless faceless patriot who released 3Ms file. If you love America you can see that whoever did that was a patriot."

Hunter interjected with a devious smile, "Someone chased him off."

"Thankfully." Maude Larrabee wiped a tear from her cheek and said, "Tommy thought he might have a chance of getting away and being able to live in peace if he had some form of insurance. That's why he smuggled the memory sticks out of the office and wanted me to give them to you. He trusted you. A great number of Americans trust you, Dory."

Eastwood thanked her for the kind words.

Hunter reached into his suit pocket and handed a watch to Eastwood, who handed it to Mother Larrabee. She trembled at the sight of the Tag Heuer timepiece. She knew instantly what it was. She broke down and cried in Eastwood's arms. When she recovered her composure, Hunter said, "Your Tommy was a patriot. Some guys are 'late to light,' a term from my fighter pilot days. They experience an epiphany, a political epiphany. Their eyes are opened. They see what has really happened to them. And when they finally figure it out, when they see how deep they're in, they work to extricate themselves, to free themselves. Some people stay, looking for the right moment to escape. Some are able to get away immediately. I wish I'd been able to meet Tommy. I know the type. They are my friends. He was a good man."

Eastwood said, as he prepared to leave, "I don't expect you to know this, but everything he gave to you he also sent to the *Whistleblowers* website."

Hunter said, "His office computer probably had a program that if Tommy didn't checked in everyday, it would download files. He left an unmistakable trail that he transferred files to that website. I'm certain that he was savvy enough to leave overwhelming evidence that he didn't copy them, he just transmitted them."

Eastwood said, "That was very smart on his part; it probably saved your life and mine."

She asked, "Do you know what's in those files?"

"Some. Some documents go back to the 1930s. I hear they'll release about a million documents a week. I can assure you, Washington, D.C. will never be the same. Singlehandedly, Tommy exposed the DNC for what it really is."

She sighed and looked off in the distance. Maude Larrabee said, "One of the last things he said to me was that he felt like that other whistleblower, Whittaker Chambers. Both of them returned to God, they realized they were pilgrims in the unholy world of the Communist Party and had to escape."

Eastwood said, "If I remember my history, Chambers succeeded in leaving and was able to leave a normal life." *It's a shame Tommy got caught*. Maude Larrabee sighed in sorrow and wiped away another tear. She stared at Hunter and debated whether to thank him or just kiss him for retrieving Tommy's watch. She lovingly looked at her son's watch for a long moment and asked, "Will anything happen to my husband? He's the executive director of the Iowa Democratic Party."

Hunter shook her hand and looked to Eastwood for an answer. Maude Larrabee took the opportunity to kiss Hunter's turned face. He politely embraced her and let her weep on his shoulder.

Eastwood stood quietly and let the moment pass. When everyone had composed themselves, he said, "I just don't know what will happen to your husband. It may depend on what's released from *Whistleblowers*. I'll hope for the best for you and pray for your family. Thank you, Mrs. Larrabee." He held out his arms and embraced her. They held each other tight.

Maude Larrabee reached out for Hunter and Eastwood's hands and led them in a short prayer. Duncan asked her if she felt like she was in any danger. He said he could provide some personal security if she felt unsafe, but she demurred. "My husband is a senior executive in the Iowa Democrat Party. They have a saying, 'no harm will come to you and the families of lifelong Democrats.' I'll be fine."

Hunter handed her a business card and mumbled something about leaving a message. He said his goodbyes and hobbled to the rental car. Eastwood stayed behind for a few private words, he held her hands, and said, "I'll keep you in my thoughts and prayers. If your security situation changes for any reason, you have my number. You can call us anytime. Mr. Locke has friends in high places."

They drove for almost an hour. As they took the off-ramp for the Des Moines Airport, Hunter commented, "I'm surprised they let her live."

Eastwood nodded. "The Democrats of the Midwest are farmers, businessmen, and hardworking people; they're not crazy like the Democrats of Washington, D.C., where politics is a blood sport. Political assassination is a funny business. The reason they leave her alone could be as simple as her husband is a committed Democrat...."

"...who knows where the bodies are buried...."

"...or who is just praying that the right document doesn't drop in the middle of the night."

74

November 25
Washington, D.C.

The librarian led Eastwood through a warren of shelves and desks in the National Archives. She stopped at a desk, and he took a seat. She cautioned him that he couldn't make any notes while he was examining the requested documents. She waited for him to don blue nitrile gloves and an allergy mask before handing him a long pair of forceps. Another librarian placed the thick document in front of him.

Eastwood began his research by turning the thick black cover of the National Socialist Party's *General Plan West*. After his allotted time was up, he left the building with a better understanding of the threats the United States faced. He was shocked to learn that *General Plan West* mirrored the strategic master plans of the Islamic Underground, the Democratic National Committee, and the former Soviet Union to overthrow the United States through peaceful means. Those documents were virtually identical in scope and method. It was understood that the United States can only be defeated from within with a president, someone who was anathema to the United States, someone who could facilitate the infiltration of key people into the top positions in government who would change public policy and undermine the country's laws until the U.S. Constitution was rendered useless.

Eastwood reminded himself that some scholars and politicians have viewed the Constitution clause, "natural born citizen" as nothing more than a relic of Eighteenth Century concerns that have little relevance to modern America. He remembered Alexander Hamilton explaining in the Federalist Papers, the requirement was placed in the Constitution to ward off "the desire in foreign powers to gain an improper ascendant in our councils" by "raising a creature of their own to the chief magistracy of the Union." Few Americans would have ever believed the former president, Maxim Mohammad Mazibuike, was never a natural born citizen but was an evil creature; a fraud, a product and puppet of the old Soviet Union.

That can't be a coincidence, he thought, sadly. *America is in a fight for survival and most Americans don't even realize it.* He thought, *Maxim*

Mohammad Mazibuike, Eleanor Tussy, the Russians and the dark state almost pulled it off. Thank God Duncan Hunter stopped them.

•　　•　　•　　•　　•

Kelly Horne and Nazy Cunningham stepped from the Agency Suburban and were escorted up the steps to the Federal Reserve Bank by two CIA security officers. They were quickly seated in an office of one of the bank directors. Kelly opened an old doctor's folding bag and extracted several ancient wooden cigar boxes. From one, she withdrew several stacks of pristine 1934 Gold Certificates. Each Gold certificate read: *This Certifies That There Has Been Deposited In The Treasury Of The United States One Hundred Dollars In Gold Coin Payable To The Bearer On Demand.* Nazy handed the Federal Reserve Bank director a three by five card with account numbers and directions on where to deliver the gold coins.

•　　•　　•　　•　　•

Hunter had wrapped his arms around Nazy and Kelly stood beside them on the pier at the Eastport Yacht Club. They waved goodbyes. Greg and Connie Lynche, and their cats, probably hiding in the belly of the beautiful blue and white fifty-foot Beneteau, silently motored from the dock and headed into the open waters of the Chesapeake Bay.

Hunter said, "They won't be back."

The statement startled Nazy. Nazy asked, "What makes you say that?" Kelly was confused, her eyes sought for an answer but said nothing.

"I know him. The last time he got 'this way' was when he stopped flying with me in the YO-3A. Something frightened him then, something is bothering him now. He couldn't wait to get away and start a new life."

Suddenly worried, Kelly asked, "But *you* will see him again?"

Hunter pinched his lips and turned toward the clubhouse to leave. Kelly and Nazy followed and once they reached the parking lot, Kelly hugged and kissed her father's cheek. Nazy's kiss was more sensual and lingering; as she was apt to do, she reached up and grabbed a handful of his hair when she thoroughly kissed him. Duncan's real knee got weak. The women stepped into the CIA limo and drove off. Before Hunter mounted a black armored Hummer H2, he withdrew a long-handle inspection mirror from a pocket and checked the underside for explosives. Before driving off he smeared the license plates with mud from a dirty puddle.

•   •   •   •   •

A black Hummer with dark windows and dirty tags parked several blocks away from Embassy Row in Washington D.C. The driver's door opened and a tiny black drone was tossed into the air. It sensed it was airborne, in the early stages of a ballistic arc, and turned itself on. The drone immediately unfolded and engaged its rotors, and flew away from the vehicle. As the Hummer drove off, the little aircraft gained altitude. It received GPS positional data from three satellites overhead. The drone determined where it was in the Washington, D.C. area and flew to the large house that had been downloaded into its memory. Its artificial intelligence programs guided it to land on top of a streetlamp adjacent to a multistory mansion. There it would remain alert, a tiny camera scanned the comings and goings of people walking in and out of the house, checking each target's face in the facial recognition database for the desired person to come into view.

75

December 7
Tetiaroa

"Why did he do it? I mean, he had to wait until I was under anesthesia?" Wearing a straw Panama hat, Hunter acted as if he was confused and slightly distracted. He swished the crystal clear ocean water with his hand. "The view is breathtaking. And I don't mean the scenery." He pulled his sunglasses down his nose to admire the features of his wife. He smiled and received a blown kiss in return.

The size of Nazy's floppy straw hat would have made a sombrero jealous. She checked her perfect crimson nail polish and continued to smile at her husband.

To him the view *was* spectacular. For fifteen years he had promised to take her to Tahiti. He had never said that Tahiti was just a stopover. They'd taken a small airliner, Air Tetiaroa, to get to the private island of Tetiaroa, where they were being pampered at one of the most remote islands from the luxurious *The Brando*.

He wanted to talk shop while there was no one to hear them. She humored him. "He told me he had to do it. When Steve Castaño found out who you were through DNA, you were no longer just *Maverick*, you had a name. Greg and the president knew it wouldn't be long before your name found its way into the Washington Post, or some member of Congress would begin asking about *Maverick*. If not *Maverick*, then Duncan Hunter. Greg suggested that having your name unmasked could even derail the election. It was a tactical move to protect the president and his executive special access program."

He said, "I knew that Castaño was bad the moment I saw him."

"No one knew if Castaño had shared your personal information. There was only so much the president and Greg could do—and remember this was just before the election. Things were crazy."

"I remember."

"Greg watched the Democrats on election night, and he saw one guy who ran away from their election headquarters screaming and crying like a little schoolgirl. It was Nikita Zhavrazhinov, but then he went dark. That was totally contretemps. Something drove him to try and escape New York. Greg thought he acted like he needed to hide from someone; that someone was either after him or would be soon."

"But who could that be?" Hunter was sarcastic.

"The Russian president. Of course, but Greg didn't know that at that time. It was an incredible leap in logic that he tied Zhavrazhinov with Castaño. He felt Castaño was probably taking orders from someone and somewhere in that marvelous brain of his, he extracted the DNC chairman as the likely decision maker."

"Greg thought his only real option to save you *and the president* was to intervene with Zhavrazhinov, to see if he had your name. Greg couldn't trust the FBI for much help. They did have a long file on him, but they wouldn't share with us—he was an American citizen. But before any agency from the U.S. government could get to him, he committed suicide."

"That was fortuitous. I mean for us." Hunter's devious smile wasn't ignored. Lynche had orchestrated the removal of espionage evidence from Zhavrazhinov's room and body.

She smiled at him and winked. "It was all of that, but more than that, it was curious."

"I agree." *I think....*

"In the end, Zhavrazhinov's diary didn't contain your name, nor was it in any of the DNC's files in the DNC's archives."

"That's good to know."

Nazy said, "On the odd-chance that you'd been unmasked, that Castaño made a call or left a text message for Zhavrazhinov on a phone we did not know about, Greg resigned to preclude a call before Congress. He had done everything the President asked him to do—he drained the CIA of its swamp creatures from the previous administration and eliminated the world's worst terrorists. Finding and eliminating the four from the NCS about gave him a heart attack. And as for you, he didn't want to lie about you. The president didn't like it, but he concurred. And Bill was the obvious choice to take his place. The president told Bill, "I think we still need Mr. Hunter's services. I'm afraid there are many more terrorists out there."

"I'm pretty sure I've eliminated them all. No more names on the Matrix. No more crazy ops. And no more using Kelly in bad places. *NO kinetics.*" Hunter shook his head and waved his finger from side to side to emphasize to *don't even think about it.*

Nazy's puffy lips agreed. "I think we concur. Greg's experiment didn't work out. So, it's already taken care of. She's assigned to Air Branch and will be doing the occasional surveillance but primarily

Weedbusters missions. She'll also move in with me."

"Are you going to be okay with that?"

"I am. It'll be a perfect fit for both of us. That house is huge and it will be ok. You'll have to do something with the Hummer if she is going to put the Jaguar in the garage." The way she said *Jaguar* and *garage* with her British accent just made him smile.

Hunter contemplated the possible pitfalls of Kelly's new residence. It sounded reasonable for a pair of intelligence officers to share a house. He asked Nazy what would happen to Viviana Vaslakova; could she be used as a double agent?

"We don't get walk-ins like her very often. We don't think she's a *dangle*, a fake defector with *cooked* intel. Distorted intel. No, Viviana volunteered she thought she could have Zhavrazhinov commit suicide before he could skip town, go into hiding. But she shocked us when she said she wanted to prevent him from destroying his records. That the Agency would want them and analyze them. But more than anything, she thought it would help establish her *bona fides*. They knew each other and she worked for him from time to time."

"That's incredible." Duncan shook his head in awe.

"She's adamant she wants to defect to help us, to move to a place where they can't find her, and try to live a normal life. She's convinced that if we try to double her, they'll know she's *burnt*, that she's exposed and they will kill her immediately. I agreed. Not worth losing an amazing resource."

Hunter shook his head in disbelief. "She could actually kill someone with the sound of her voice? Wasn't that what got Odysseus in trouble? The Sirens?"

Nazy said, "Not exactly. She's beautiful, an…odd girl with a unique voice—our psychologists call her a 'speed hypnotist.' Apparently she was very effective, especially with despondent and depressed men. Nearly every Russian defector drank vodka to excess and was depressed. She spent a career using her voice to encourage men who had encountered difficulties defecting from the old Soviet Union and Russia to kill themselves. Agents who were far from Moscow and the SVR who failed to complete their mission. They listened to her, they fell under her spell, and they did it."

"What a weapon. Don't piss her off."

"When she couldn't talk a defector into suicide, the DNC chairman contracted for an assassination."

Hunter said, "A hit!"

"She was a colonel in the SVR. Thirteenth Directorate. Assassins and Sabotage. And unknown to Zhavrazhinov she was Moscow's insurance if Zhavrazhinov failed or defected. She turned over her computer and cell phone to us. She had some interesting programs, one that could wipe a cell phone clean remotely. Another program could locate a cell phone—at her fingertips, if she had a telephone number she could locate a defector. The Russians have already filed a complaint. Officially, we don't know where she is at or what they're talking about."

"All part of the game, I suppose."

"Been going on for centuries. They'll soon kidnap a tourist in Moscow or a family in Leningrad, declare them spies, and try to negotiate a trade."

Hunter said, "I don't know much about that directorate."

Nazy summarized the Foreign Intelligence Service activities and actions since the Bolshevik Revolution.

Duncan nodded at the little history lesson. He thought of Viviana Vaslakova. He bit his lower lip. He knew the power of a woman's voice. He had fallen in over his head the first time he heard Nazy's. Her accent and timbre turned him into a blubbering fool. He was struck dumb by the way her voice resonated. Deep and dark and breathlessly husky like Lauren Bacall, but with a sugary British accent. "What are you going to do with her?"

Nazy had a surprise. "Don't know. Too early to tell. The Russian president even called President Hernandez and demanded we return her to Moscow immediately."

Hunter chortled. "Like that's going to happen."

Nazy was suddenly smug. "She's been granted asylum. Viviana said she wants to marry Dory Eastwood. Move to Montana. Drive a pickup truck."

"Dory? Seriously? He's 70! He could be carbon-dated." *No, he's over 70!* Hunter remembered he was about twenty years older than Nazy and stopped being pompous. After a few minutes of silence, he nodded then rolled over in the shallow water. He propped himself up on his elbows. "I'm not so sure it's a good idea to marry a girl who could convince a man to take a swan dive off a twenty-second floor balcony. *Vingt-duex, vingt-duex.*" Once he purged the imagery of an Eastwood and Vaslakova partnership from his frontal lobe, he asked, "What about you?"

"The president, Greg, and Bill think I should become the DO. There's a vacancy. I still have a few years before I can retire."

"The Director of Operations? That's mighty fast for anyone in the IC. Heads will explode in the Senior Intelligence Service. Does that mean Congressional approval? Do you have to come out of the shadows? I'm not sure I like that. The left will put you on their surveillance program. You won't be able to move without them watching you. Can I offer my veto?"

She nodded. She knew there would be problems. "No Congressional approval, but it's not a good fit for me. For us. At some point I want us to be able to live together."

Hunter smiled and said, "Sign me up for some of that!"

"But I'm a better analyst than I'm a manager. I'm not driven to be the DO. Men will do what I ask, but the senior women will always be a challenge. I've moved too fast up the organization. I like what I'm doing. I enjoy delivering the President's Daily Brief. Solving intelligence problems. Being the NCTC Director, the Chief of Diaries. Finding bad guys, as you say. Regardless, Bill has already assigned a much larger personal security detail to me. We know what they'll try to do."

"So when did that discussion happen?"

"When you went with Kelly out to the airport to find Castaño's hangar. All those old gold coins. Currently, I'm acting, holding both positions. NCTC and the NCS."

Hunter frowned.

"What do you think of that, my darling husband?"

"You know I think you'd rock in that job. Someone needs to clean up that mess. Polygraph them all and shitcan the losers. I know 3M was able to dump a bunch of his friends from the Islamic Underground into the Agency. It's what the FBI needs—3M put hundreds of jihadis in the DOJ in the form of law school trained brothers from the Islamic Underground. *Drain the swamp*, I'm sure some politician has copyrighted that."

"But you're frowning. You aren't happy."

Hunter said, "The lesson that Republicans must learn isn't just that Washington Democrats will stop at nothing to get their way, but that the Left is unstoppable. Republicans can vote for candidates who promise to 'drain the swamp' all they want. Democrats will ensure the swamp will never be drained. Their intention is to intimidate and demoralize Republicans, induce them to give up and get out of the game. The Democrats have taken a page from the caliphate rulers who display gratuitous brutality against their captive non-Muslim populations solely to intimidate and demoralize them, to reinforce the lesson that resistance was futile."

"So, the Democrats think they can get away with murder?"

Hunter nodded and looked off into the distance. "They can. And for a while, they did. Washington Democrats. The DNC."

Nazy took his hand and looked at him with compassion. "You were right, darling Duncan. I don't know how you knew." Nazy smiled and said, "We don't know yet how many or who all were involved. The older records were more challenging for Alvin to cross check."

Hunter asked, "Maybe Alvin will be able to give you a hint."

She smiled and thought, *I'll tell him later."*

Hunter said, "I don't trust that thing. You know Hal 9000 went crazy and had to be deactivated."

She laughed at her husband. She had a surprise for him!

"But weren't there scores of tangential political deaths that couldn't be explained away?"

She said, "We can't discount the Russians had some of their senior officers doing wet work out of their embassy, going all the way back to the 30s. They have such a vast network in Washington. The FBI thinks they may have a thousand spies."

A thousand? "Those Russians...." Hunter said, shaking his head in disbelief, "So we can say Zhavrazhinov managed and assigned...wet work, just like he was the head of the Thirteenth Directorate."

"Zhavrazhinov bragged that Castaño was his greatest accomplishment. Russia's greatest spy since Alger Hiss. Zhavrazhinov spelled out how he politicked Democratic senators and congressmen to put pressure on President Mazibuike to ensure Castaño became the head of the NCS. He'd have become the DCI if President Hernandez had lost the election."

"Incredible."

"We might have suspected something earlier had we paid more attention. They never cashed their payroll checks."

Hunter's face registered his obvious confusion.

"When we searched their desks, we found that they didn't cash their paychecks. In days before direct deposit they threw their paychecks into the bottom drawer. They didn't need them. They forgot them. Huge clue that they were dirty. But they were NCS. They were above reproach."

"Zhavrazhinov indicated Castaño was paid millions in cash and he was paid in gold bullion deposited in offshore accounts. Later he was paid in cryptocurriencies. So were Fässler, Bomarito, and Troxel, but they were minor players. Castaño assigned jobs and was the paymaster for his guys, and Zhavrazhinov didn't mind if he took a cut."

Hunter quietly asked, "Zhavrazhinov had Castaño kill Tommy Larrabee? One of them did it."

Nazy looked out over the ocean. She kicked her feet and splashed water. She sighed, nodded and said, "Yes. There's much to that story.

In his journal, Zhavrazhinov recorded that he had Larrabee install a private email server for Attorney General Tussy."

Hunter leaned over in surprise. Nazy continued, "He and Zhavrazhinov were given administrative rights to Tussy's illegal server. The SVR received a blind carbon copy of everything she received or sent. All of her missing correspondence was in the DNC archives. It was mostly Islamic Underground-related. She may not have been the ultimate Russian mole as Zhavrazhinov's power and influence over her wasn't total. He was Castaño's puppetmaster but not Tussy's."

Duncan smiled, looking very smug. *I knew it!* It wasn't going to do any good to revel on what he had long suspected. Tussy's treachery, NCS targeting him. It was time to change the subject. "Had he been to their little island?"

"Tommy Larrabee? No, never. Castaño, many times." She smiled as if she knew a secret. "Zhavrazhinov wrote in his diary that Castaño always wore a disguise."

Hunter thought of all the clown suits in that hangar, *A clown....* He said, "I bet he went as a clown."

She nodded, surprised at Duncan's perspicacity. Nazy continued, "That island. That's also code for the benefits package. Zhavrazhinov rarely used codes to mask names or places or amounts. Virtually every democratic leader in congress visited the island. They called it a convention. He kept a record of who came to the island. And photographs and videos and he kept a record of Castaño's activities and, by extension, the three from NCS. We think Castaño and company put some of the Agency's best surveillance equipment to use on that island. At Zhavrazhinov's direction, of course. The best blackmail information anyone could ever want. Zhavrazhinov had it all. Who was targeted and when, and the payout. Castaño apparently wasn't interested in the money and was rewarded with trips to the Democrats' secret island in the Caribbean."

"I understand he was sitting on a hundred million bucks."

Nazy nodded and looked at him conspiratorially, "Which is missing, by the way. Many of the patrons wore masks. Or gloves. Castaño had to. He was recognizable. At least his hands were."

She said she had read a DNC report on Castaño on the island. *He had been served a dinner of roast peacock while wearing nothing except a clown mask, gloves, and a bow tie. The waiter had a card around his neck: "If my services don't please you, whip me."*

She continued, "Zhavrazhinov was rarely at the same locus as Castaño, but they met frequently. Castaño typically used one of the Agency's Air Branch airplanes to go to a small airport in Rhode Island to meet Zhavrazhinov. No cameras. Used a Growler."

"General aviation, TF Green Airport. Did Castaño leave a diary?"

It wasn't such an odd question but Nazy didn't have an answer.

"It wasn't in any of the cigar boxes I found. But I didn't look through all of the boxes in that hangar."

"Greg and Bill and I had hoped you'd find it. We have crews who are still investigating. Nothing in any of the houses. Their other hangars had… operational equipment."

"There were other hangars?"

"You know there were." She smiled at his attempt of playing ignorant. She nodded while still looking out over the horizon. It was near high tide and ocean waves would soon begin to breach the lagoon's higher points. "Seems they bought and hid away some very rare cars and airplanes…. Three different hangars in West Virginia and Pennsylvania. They used front companies to hide their treasures."

"Really? Any idea what they are? The cars and the airplanes?" She had his interest, but she wasn't about to reveal the cars or the aircraft. He'd hound her for information. And she'd playfully demur.

After a long period of quietude, she announced, "They were transferred to Elmira. The president said we needed to reward you. What *was* an appropriate award for someone who saved the president? When Director McGee was appraised of those airplanes, he talked to the president and authorized those aircraft confiscated and transferred. I think they're supposed to be on loan from the Marine Corps Museum. Getting back to your question, had Castaño been to the DNC's little island? He went several times a year. Alvin…."

"That computer has the hots for you," he teased.

Nazy turned, smiled, and playfully poked at his nose. She said, "Alvin created a huge database which identified when he was overseas at work and when he was at their island. When his guys were dispatched to places like Algeria and Dubai, Castaño would run for an Air Branch airplane and spend a day or two down there." She turned her head. *Nothing but sex slaves there.*

Hunter wasn't surprised. He pulled Nazy's focus away from the island in the Caribbean. "What about guys like Colonel Emory?"

Nazy rolled her eyes. "Tip of the iceberg. Thanks to Zhavrazhinov's journal, we know the DNC Chairman, the Washington Democrats, and the Russians did everything they could to run drugs into the country. The Russians backed the Taliban and the opium trade and the Russians backed the narco-terrorists in South America and the drug cartels who produced 93 percent of the cocaine that makes its way into the U.S.

through Central America. So while the Iranian ayatollahs funded Islamic terrorism throughout the globe, Moscow and the KGB sponsored the drug trade in Europe and America. The Iranians and the Russians teamed up to destabilize our country. They believed the DNC's strategic plan and endgame held the greatest promise to defeat the United States. Flood the country with drugs and immigrants to 'replacement levels' and drive the Republican Party to extinction."

"One party rule."

"There is no other way to do it. So, it appears that Colonel Emory saw something he shouldn't have. What Zhavrazhinov didn't know was that Castaño was running a load off the books without Russian sponsorship or knowledge. He did that one and supposedly no more. Chief Air Branch at the time didn't know a thing. Anything for money, I suppose. Or in that particular case, gold coins. Bullion."

Her final comment made him wince. He said, "So we think Castaño killed Colonel Emory."

She nodded and said, "Alvin indicated a very high probability. It looks that way. Castaño was in the area. Zhavrazhinov was livid when he found out. That was in his diary. He threatened to keep Castaño away from the island, cut him off. Castaño begged for forgiveness. Offered to do other work *gratis*. His journal is a treasure trove of information."

"I'll bet Castaño knew Zhavrazhinov would blow a fuse and have him knocked off if he ever found out he had gone rogue. That's probably why Castaño pitched Bill McGee to do his dirty work. Bill rebuffed him, which probably forced Castaño to go to California as soon as he could to kill Colonel Emory himself. Some of his boys had to be overseas or something for him to have to do the dirty work solo."

"Some were on assignment in Colombia."

76

December 7
Tetiaroa

Hunter thought about what he'd say next. "It's almost unbelievable that four dudes at the NCS could work together, conspire to do something like a murder-for-hire outfit."

"Did Castaño ever share information with Zhavrazhinov?"

She said, "Apparently, all the time. He knew where the gaps were and exploited them. Copied material on a typewriter and carried it out the front door in a cigar box. Bill retrieved copies of the manuals for the TS2 sniper weapon. Much like the spy, Alger Hiss, at the State Department. I also know the DNC pulled out all the stops to find you, to determine who you were."

"But they couldn't. The president and the DCI held close the *Wraith* special access program. It was great cover." Hunter smiled at his bride.

"Tremendously. Your aerial eradication efforts kept them off balance. You and *Weedbusters* kept getting in their way. Zhavrazhinov and Castaño always knew someone like you 'had to exist,' but they didn't know who you were or how you were being funded. It drove them crazy. They searched everywhere. State, Defense, Homeland Security. DEA, FBI, CIA. The DNC's archives and Zhavrazhinov's diary outlined how he had Larrabee on the dark web looking for clues and names."

"But Castaño found a way."

"He did. The president suggested Greg invite him and the SOCOM commander to the ramp that day. He got you're your DNA. Your identity and your relationship to Kelly was transmitted to his BlackBerry right before his BlackBerry was killed."

"I shook his hand."

"That can do it. We have a certain...*process* that we can use if we need to establish a person's identity via DNA."

Hunter said, "I supposed your guys checked the dark web...."

"Duncan, darling, there was no information linking you to *Maverick* or Kelly. Subsequent monitoring suggests that data were never shared and all email and text traffic from those four were embargoed at the

Agency and destroyed. You are completely in the clear. They couldn't find you because you were completely off the grid — no NCS, eyes only-DCI and the president. I'm surprised they were able to keep you and the *Wraith* secret for, what, fifteen years?"

"Over fifteen years. Closer to twenty." He nodded. "Greg said we essentially took a billion dollars' worth of opium and cocaine off the streets every time I went out in Afghanistan and South America."

"That's an amazing capability. *Weedbusters*."

"So the Democrats' island really was like that old television show with Ricardo Montalbán and the little dude and the mysterious island? *Da' plane, da' plane!*"

She squinted her eyes as if in pain. She had no idea what he was saying. In her most officious British, "My dearest Duncan, I'm unfamiliar with any of those references. I assume that's from television. How do you find time to watch television?"

He smiled at her mild rebuke. "How's the president? Anything new from his daily brief?"

"I know you saw where Greg was in front of Congress and announced that the Islamic Underground and the Iranian Revolutionary Guard were designated terrorist organizations. There will be no more government sponsored 'Muslim outreach' or 'Islamic engagement' programs. The president signed an executive order to announce the public eradication of the Islamic Underground's strategy of phased infiltration of Muslims into government. You know the Democrats in Congress went crazy."

"Now we have dozens of Muslims in Congress. Of course. So let me get this straight, I screwed up the strategic plans of the DNC, the Islamic Underground, and the Russians?"

"All by yourself. Yes. You likely derailed the election of Eleanor Tussy and you made 3M leave the country."

"Makes me sound like a one-man wrecking crew."

As Duncan made faces at her, mocking the Democrats in Washington D.C., she was getting tired of the debrief. She wanted to swim, but she had a few more bits of intel to share.

"Remember the cigar boxes of old gold coins?"

"I do. I remember a Liberty Half Eagle stared at me like it had been lost, and now it was found."

"Well, that's exactly what you did. That particular batch of coins were stolen from the Du Pont family in 1967. Someone stole more than 7,000 coins, including the rare $5 gold piece known as a Liberty Half Eagle and a couple of family diaries. They were all returned to their rightful owners. You're a hero. They'd like to give you a reward."

Hunter laughed. *They'll probably offer me a lifetime supply of Nomex®.* He nodded and changed the subject. *Luckiest guy on the planet!* He rolled over and made eyes at his wife. "Baby, you are my reward."

She kissed him tenderly. "I think that wraps it up, Mr. Hunter. Nice work."

He looked at her longingly. She smiled at him. He asked, "What about Greg?"

Nazy was confused but mostly she was concerned. *"What about Greg?"*

"Wasn't he in the DNC's archives? His early days in the Agency."

For several moments she stared at him in disbelief. For a whole minute, she didn't like her husband. She believed he wouldn't have been interested in the DNC archives and the analysis of those records. He was more prescient than she believed possible. There were no secrets between them. But she wouldn't lie to him. Omissions weren't secrets. She had left out some crucial information. *How could he have known?* As if she had been backed into a corner, she looked away from him, out over the ocean with embarrassment, and whispered, "Yes, Duncan."

Hunter pressed her lightly, "Early to mid-sixties. When he was first assigned to the Operations Directorate. Before there was a presidential executive order prohibiting assassinations. He didn't want you to look into those records."

Embarrassed for her former boss, Nazy said, "He prohibited me from downloading the archives. He demanded they be destroyed; that they were domestic intelligence and the CIA does international. He believed I hadn't downloaded them; that I still had them in a cigar box. He took the box of USB memory sticks from me and dumped them into the disintegrator to ensure all traces of them were destroyed."

"You smelled a rat."

"Duncan, darling. I don't like that analogy. But you are correct. I asked Alvin to find any reference to a Duncan Hunter and Greg Lynche. There were things he did and said that made me suspect Greg had been on an early special access program and had possibly infiltrated the Communist Party. We didn't have a good diary from anyone from the Communist Party of the USA or the DNC who mentioned Greg Lynche. After Bill became the Director, I told him of my suspicions that Greg thought he may have been mentioned in dispatch in the DNC's archives and that information could significantly damage the Agency and the president. I had Alvin check the archives in memory and there was a significant history on Greg. From those archives, I learned that several men from the FBI and the Agency were handpicked for an assignment.

Bill asked me if there was a way to recover those files that mentioned Greg. From *Whistleblowers*."

Duncan Hunter smiled at his wife, not in any suggestive way but he beamed with pride. He chuckled, *Just like the Mazibuike file!*

"One of Alvin's capabilities is that it can use the NSA's tools to hack into just about any company website. So I had Alvin break into *Whistleblowers*. He extracted everything Tommy Larrabee had sent them that referenced our Greg Lynche."

"My, you are a naughty girl, Chief of Diaries. First 3M's file and now the DNC's archives. You are simply incredible. Is it any wonder I love you?"

Nazy was reluctant to tell the whole story. She tried to sum up what she had found. "Greg was assigned to infiltrate the Communist Party in the U.S. but he was already a member. Somehow he passed a polygraph or paid off the polygrapher."

Hunter said, "Rothwell and others just admitted to their polygrapher that they voted for the Communist Party candidate for president. They didn't advocate for the violent overthrow of the USG so maybe that's how they got in." Hunter was gentle but wanted answers. "I came to the conclusion that he was likely part of a team...."

Nazy said, "He and three others were on a special access program to find and eliminate political enemies, mostly communists who had defected from the USSR and the Soviet bloc. But he was a triple agent. While he took orders from the DNC for about a year, and the CPUSA for a little longer, he also worked the Agency trap lines to find and stop American communists defecting to the Soviet Union; primarily those who stole aerospace secrets. When the CPUSA wanted him to assassinate a defector, Greg offered his resignation to the CIA Director; he wouldn't work for them anymore; he wouldn't commit murder for anyone. Greg was removed from the program and transferred. The leaders of the DNC and the CPUSA were panic-stricken. No one knew where he had gone to. He and his family simply vanished. He was reassigned to Alice Springs in Australia. There he learned how to fly. Eventually, he was assigned to Air Branch."

Hunter said, "So that's how he did it. He never told me the particulars. He defected, just like when Whittaker Chambers left the CPUSA. He's my best friend. I'm sure when he learned the DNC archives had been compromised, that chapter of his former life would probably be exposed if there was anything there."

Nazy looked toward the beach. "I'm confident—there was no evidence Greg did any wet work."

Hunter said, "He's not up to any form of direct action. Remember how he nearly went ballistic when we interrogated bin Laden?"

She nodded. She was done. She wanted to go back in, have fun, relax, and forget Greg Lynche's past. The debrief was almost at its end.

"Castaño went rogue. Is that information still 'out there?'"

Nazy turned to Duncan and smiled. "No. I was able to erase Greg's history with the DNC and the CPUSA. I told Alvin that we were conducting an exercise and any and all records on the former director needed to be expunged. He purged those files at *Whistleblowers* and in our DNC server, and any saved reference to one Duncan Hunter. And when he did it and demonstrated to me that those archives were clean, I fed that little robot into the disintegrator."

Hunter whipped around and his eyes popped out of his head like a surprised Marty Feldman character, he clapped his hands and howled. *"You are so full of surprises! Wow!* Nice job baby!"

Nazy beamed. It excited her to see her man excited for her. "He always kept it a secret."

He said, "He never told me either and I only got a strong hint of his past when we toured that house of diaries. No one but an analyst is interested in old documents but it seemed the DNC trove scared the daylights out of him. There had to be a reason."

"Who knew our Gregory Lynche had such a colorful past?"

Hunter said, "He never told me any secret. I was never certain to what extent he was an actual Democrat believer, or if he was just an infiltrator, working undercover. There were little hints that he was a believer that he and a bunch of others 'in his year group' voted for the CPUSA candidate for president. So did the three previous DCIs. Maybe at that time, it was fashionable for Democrats entering the CIA who voted communist. But unlike the others, only Greg didn't go off and learn Arabic. Unlike the others in his year group, he didn't convert to Islam and didn't learn how to bang his head five times a day on a prayer rug pointing toward Mecca."

Nazy continued, "He may have been forced or was expected to do that. Those records were pretty thin. I couldn't tell if he did that to prove his fealty to the CPUSA or if it was something the Agency suggested. But if he was a believer, I'll always think he had come to see the light; that communism was a horrible system and wasn't the way of the world."

"Like Whittaker Chambers."

There's that name again. I'm going to have to read his book. Nazy nodded absentmindedly. She was slowly creeping toward the water. She was nearly finished talking. "I believe, to atone for his sins, he had worked and fought to be the best CIA Director the Agency ever had."

Hunter liked happy endings, especially when his bride was instrumental in destroying Alvin the artificial intelligence robot and Lynche's history. *She set me up and got me on that one.*

They looked at each other with huge grins. *That was enough about work!* Hunter said, *"Enough! Enough! No mas! No mas!* We're on vacation! On our own private island. Not even a plane in the sky. We are so remote, no one can find us."

Nazy smiled and splashed water like a five-year-old's first time at the beach.

He said, "You are incredible. And have I told you recently, you are very good looking?"

"About ten minutes ago. When you rubbed oil all over my body." She laughed at him for being silly.

"I'm slipping. I'm so lucky; I really am the luckiest man on the planet. I love you, Miss Cunningham."

She bit her bottom lip as if annoyed, and then she stood up, undid her bathing suit top and stepped out of her bottoms. Naked boobs are to a man what a laser pointer is to a cat. Hunter was immediately excited at the vision of his nude wife. He followed the sway of her breasts as she moved. She caught him ogling her and laughed at him. Her scars didn't matter. She splashed water at him with her foot. He stripped off his shorts revealing several new scars from hip and knee replacement surgeries and his runner's tan. His muscular torso and legs were brown, but his ass was as white as beach sand.

She returned to the dry part of the beach, laid down and rolled around in the sand until her body was completely covered. On her back, Nazy looked at herself, between her breasts to her toes and marveled at her sandy rolling hills. She wiggled her sandy toes. It was something that was inconceivable when she was a young woman in her native Jordan standing at the water's edge of the Dead Sea wearing a *hijab*. No swimming, no sand between her toes. *No nakedness....* No fun.

Hunter smiled at her enjoying herself and was mesmerized at her antics. He had little idea what was going through her mind. It was good to see her unwind, relax, uninhibited. Nazy walked back into the crystal clear water and dunked herself, washing the sand from her body. She turned and smiled at Hunter and asked, "I still can't comprehend why you jumped out of your airplane. Duncan darling, that was crazy."

He got up from his vantage point and said, "It's only crazy if it doesn't work." He waded into the water to her and kissed her.

She grabbed the back of his head and kissed him hard. When she released his hair and their lips uncoupled, she pointed a finger at him in mock admonishment and whispered, "Baby, please don't ever do that again. I really don't know what I'd do without you."

"Okay. But it'll cost you another kiss." Duncan stiffened in her embrace, but she wasn't interested in anything extracurricular. Playing in the sand was one thing. Now she wanted a private swim in the lagoon. She backed away from him, teasing him, not taking her eyes off of him, and walked into deeper water. When the water was up to her breasts she submerged, turned, and pushed off with her feet, gliding through the water. Her hair fanned out like a long diaphanous cape.

Hunter scanned the lagoon and followed. Later they explored the island on foot, scaring away tiny pink crabs that lived at the edge of the water. When they found a shaded spot, they laughed and loved as long lost lovers on the brilliant white sand. It was another remarkable thing Nazy couldn't imagine doing anywhere, anytime. But with Duncan, all things were possible.

● ● ● ● ●

The Director of Operations at the National Reconnaissance Office stepped into the Command Control Center. The Deputy Operations Officer stepped to his console and reported, "We've identified and confirmed that we have visual contact on the targets." The NRO DO nodded and guided a computer mouse to the appropriate satellite download. He lifted an eyebrow when the live feed filled his console monitor. *Hair as long as she is tall, and his most distinguishing features were the thick scars on his Achilles, his knee, his hip, his hand. Yep, the CIA Director was correct. Frankenstein's monster had fewer surgeries.* He ordered the controller of the satellite to resume its surveillance of the oceans. He turned to the Deputy and said, "I'll inform Director McGee we have located the specified targets on a remote island near Tahiti. Marlon Brando's old place."

EPILOGUE

December 7
Tetiaroa

Nazy heard it before she saw it. She said, "Duncan, I think we have company." She pointed to the horizon.

"We're not due company until…." Then he saw it. A Zodiac boat at the entrance of the lagoon; he hoped they were friendlies who needed to use the facilities or something. Their resupply aircraft wasn't due for another few hours. Nazy donned her swim suit and covered herself with a silk bathrobe from the bungalow. Hunter stood his ground in his shorts as he slipped on docksiders.

"I hope the Islamic Underground hasn't acquired a submarine and Arab-speaking frogmen. We could be in trouble." *And I do not have a weapon….*

In minutes, the little black boat loaded with armed men pulled up to the beach where Hunter and Nazy stood. Six men in SCUBA gear carried M-4s in waterproof bags. One man pulled out a smaller bag, removed what was in it, and then punched a few buttons on a satellite telephone receiver. He handed it to Hunter. No words were said although plenty of facial expressions were exchanged.

Hunter thought, *You got to be shitting me. Only one person could pull this off.* He recognized the voice at the other end of the satphone and said, "Good afternoon, Mr. President."

Nazy frowned. She pulled a brassy challenge coin from her bag and showed it to the scuba men in black.

The leader of the SEAL Team was astonished to see the red arrowhead. He reached in and removed an identical one from his scuba wetsuit. He walked toward her, and they brought the arrowheads together. When the two arrowheads touched, they lit up, flashing red. The SEAL said incredulously, "You're one of us?"

Nazy smiled and nodded. She said, "Bullfrog said all I had to do was show this, and a U.S. Navy SEAL will take me wherever I need to go, do whatever I need done, and protect me with their lives." She smiled mysteriously, "Is that true?"

All of the Navy SEALs on the black rubber boat smiled and said, "Yes ma'am!" It was hard for them to take their eyes off of the remarkable woman clad in only a tiny knitted swimsuit and a silk bathrobe which flittered open every few seconds from a convenient breeze. At the same time they recognized the overabundance of faint scars on her arms and mile-long legs, a thick scar adjacent to her breast; the obvious handiwork of fanatical bombers and Islamic mutilators. She really had been on the front lines of the undeclared war on terrorists. The SEALs showed a little more respect.

For the first time in years, Nazy didn't think about or feel embarrassed by her scars. She looked at her husband, one hand on one hip, one on the satphone. She determined the outcome of the unscheduled visit. She walked to the bungalow for their things. Two SEALs followed her at a distance ripe for rubbernecking a beauty queen's behind.

The president exchanged pleasantries with Hunter and handed the telephone to the CIA Director. Bill McGee's low rumbling Barry White voice came through the speaker loud and clear. "I need you."

Hunter barked at his friend. "I'm convalescing! I need time to recuperate. I can barely walk! Greg Lynche killed me off, remember? Technically, I'm dead." He remembered having this conversation before. His bullshit excuses hadn't worked then, either.

"Lynche said you get this way when you're cranky—I'm surprised to see this side of you. He told me to remind you that you're still under contract, and that, as the DCI, I'm still buying your jet fuel. Right?"

"Yes, sir." Hunter smiled at the SEAL and then looked away. He knew he wasn't going to win no matter what he said. *They sent guys with guns!*

"And we don't want to have a conversation about what happened to some of the possessions from some former members of the NCS. Wouldn't look pretty."

"Spoils of war, Bullfrog…. Those assholes declared war on me and my family."

"Spoils of war? That's a good one. For the past month while you've been gone missing with my acting Deputy Director of Operations all hell has broken loose. You are nowhere around when an associate justice of the supreme court fell and broke her hip, and the former attorney general apparently slipped and fell, and is no longer with us."

Cosmic justice? Hunter was nonplussed and said nothing. He gazed over to his wife. He had programmed a drone to attack the former attorney general and presidential candidate. Not with explosives or anything lethal, just when she emerged from her mansion the drone would buzz around her head and continually harass her like a frenzied suicidal blackbird from Alfred Hitchcock's *The Birds*.

McGee continued, "If you'd check in now and then, you'd know the President agreed to transfer some of the — what you'd call *spoils of war* — to the hangars in Elmira. I think you know what a Jaguar XKSS is."

Hunter thought, *The Jag Steve McQueen made famous*. He said, "It's got an external muffler like the Yo-Yo." Hunter could hear McGee roll his eyes 10,000 miles away.

McGee shook his head. "Yeah, well…. But none of that's going to happen until your bride is back at work. I need Nazy back here, pronto. No BS. No XKSS. And if you try to give those SEALs some lip, I don't have to tell you they'll execute their orders and leave your stinking ass all alone on that island." Hunter could see McGee grinning at him half-a-globe away. He grinned at being reminded and reprimanded and rewarded.

"Please thank the president on my behalf." He had two more lines. "You really don't expect Nazy and me to leave paradise so soon? We just got here." He waved at her with her bags and sandals in tow and threw her a kiss. She had pulled a delicate white jumpsuit over her swimsuit, which accentuated her long legs and bust even more.

Two SEALs had picked up their bags and placed them in the Zodiac. She carried a subdued flowery Tommy Bahama shirt and brought it to her husband. She walked to the front of the rubberized boat, sat down on the edge, crossed her legs, and combed her hair. Nazy knew they'd be leaving soon, but maybe she had time to get a few snags out of her hair.

McGee said, "Go with the nice men in the Zodiac. You're coming home. The Yo-Yo is enroute. I need Nazy and you…here. Now. Quit your bellyaching, *Maverick*. Look at it this way, you don't have to drive all the way to Washington D.C. like you had me do."

Hunter rolled his eyes. "*I didn't do that to you!*" He couldn't believe what Bill McGee was doing to him. When he heard nothing else, he looked at the satphone and found that the connection was severed. Duncan handed the device to the SEAL and shook his head in defeat.

Nazy sighed, smiled at her husband, and pointed her hairbrush at him as she said, "Baby, you know you can't get away from it. You can't ever get away from it!" She stood up, bundled her hair into one thick large knot and waited for Duncan to help her in the slick rubber boat. She waited, legs akimbo, like bronzed stilettoes stuck into the sand. "Let's get moving. Might be important." *Who sends a nuclear fast attack sub to pick up a couple of wayward beachcombers?*

Before Hunter could say what he was thinking, the lead U.S. Navy SEAL said to the pair, "We'll find something appropriate for you to wear when we get aboard. Beachwear is insufficient for banging around a submarine, sir."

The Zodiac raced across the shallow flat waters of the lagoon before entering the noticeably larger waves of the Pacific Ocean. Within five minutes they pulled along the side of a freshly surfaced black submarine.

Nazy hugged her husband tight and looked into his eyes as they boarded the submarine. She said, "It's never dull when I'm with you." Hunter pulled her in closer and kissed her passionately. He whispered something naughty into her ear.

She gave him one of those looks, between cocky and sensual. She said in her best British Bacall, "Well, then, I'm about to make you the luckiest man on the planet!"

Acronyms/Abbreviations

AC—Attack Cargo, as in AC-130
ACP—Automatic Colt Pistol
AFB-Air Force Base
AG—Attorney General
AGL—Above Ground Level
AI—Artificial Intelligence
AIRRAID—Artificial Intelligence Rapid Retrieval and Analysis
  Interface Device
AK—Automatic Kalashnikov
AMTRAK—National Railroad Passenger Corporation
ANVIS—Aviator Night Vision
APB—All-Points Bulletin
APU—Auxiliary Power Unit
AQ—Al-Qaeda
ASAP—As Soon As Possible
ASL—Above Sea Level
ATLS—Automatic Takeoff and Landing System
AWACS—Airborne Warning and Control System
B—Bomber
BB—An air gun shot pellet 0.175 inch in diameter
BBC—British Broadcasting Corporation
BCC—Blind Carbon Copy
BORTAC—U. S. Border Patrol Tactical Unit
BS—Bullshit
C—Cargo aircraft
CAVU—Ceiling and Visibility Unlimited
CCIP—Constantly-Computing Impact Point
ChiCom—Chinese Communist
CI—Counter Intelligence
CIA—Central Intelligence Agency, Catholics in Africa
CEO—Chief Executive Officer

CFRIS—Concealed Face Recognition Identification System
CMC—Commandant of the Marine Corps
COMMS—Communications
CONEX—Container Express
CT—Counter Terrorism
CTC—Counter Terrorism Center
C-4—Composition C-4; a variety of plastic explosive
DARPA—Defense Advanced Research Projects Agency
D.C.—District of Columbia
DCI—Director of the Central Intelligence Agency
DDO—Deputy Director of Operations
DELTA—1st Special Forces Operational Detachment-Delta
DHS—Department of Homeland Security
DIC—Distinguished Intelligence Cross
DIP—Diplomatic Passport
DME—Distance Measuring Equipment
DNC—Democratic National Committee
DO—Director of Operations
DOD—Department of Defense
DOE—Department of Energy
DOJ—Department of Justice
DOS—Department of State
DV—Distinguished Visitor
E-3AWACS— "Sentry" aircraft designation
EMP—Electro Magnetic Pulse
ETA—Estimated Time of Arrival
F—Fighter aircraft
FBI—Federal Bureau of Investigation
FDR—Franklin Delano Roosevelt
FedEx—Federal Express
FLIR—Forward Looking Infra-Red
FSTC—Full Spectrum Training Center
G—Gravity
G—Gulfstream aircraft
GITMO—Guantanamo Bay Naval Base, Cuba
G-IVSP—Gulfstream Model 4, Special Purpose
G-550—Gulfstream Model 550
GMO—Genetically Modified Organism
GOP—Grand Old Party

GPS—Global Positioning System

GRU—*Glavnoye Razvedyvatel'noye Upravleniye*, the foreign military intelligence agency of the Soviet Army General Staff of the Soviet Union

GS—General Schedule

GTO—Gran Turismo Omologato

H—Helicopter

HIDTA—High Intensity Drug Trafficking Area

HP—Horsepower

HQ—Headquarters

HVT—High-Value Target

I—Interstate

IARPA—Intelligence Advanced Research Projects Agency

IC—Intelligence Community

ID—Identify/Identity/Identification

IED—Improvised Explosive Device

IGA—Independent Grocers Alliance

IO—Intelligence Officer

IPA—India Pale Ale

IT—Information Technology

IRAD—Internal Research and Development

ISR—Intelligence, Surveillance, and Reconnaissance

IU—Islamic Underground

IV—Intravenous, the Latin number four

JCS—Joint Chiefs of Staff

KGB—*Komitet Gosudarstvennoy Bezopasnosti*; the foreign intelligence and domestic security agency of the Soviet Union

LD—Laser Designator

Level 1—Level 1 Yankee White clearance consists of those staff members who work directly for or have direct contact with the president or the vice president

LGB—Laser Guided Bullet, Laser Guided Bomb

LGM—Laser Guided Missile

LIDAR—Light Detection and Ranging

MAC—10Military Armament Corporation Model 10

MD—McDonald Douglas

Mil—Air-Military Airlift

MI—5British Military Intelligence, Section 5

MI—6British Secret Intelligence Service

MM—Millimeter

MPH—Miles per Hour

MSL—Mean Sea Level

M-4—Carbine version of the longer barreled M-16

NASA—National Aeronautics and Space Administration

NATO—North Atlantic Treaty Organization

NBA—National Basketball Association

NCS—National Clandestine Service

NCTC—National Counter Terrorism Center

NDA—Non-Disclosure Agreement

NE—Near East Division

NKVD—*Narodnyi Komissariat Vnutrennikh Del*, the People's Commissariat of Internal Affairs of the Soviet Union

NOB—New Office Building

NOTAR—No Tail Rotor

NRA—National Rifle Association

NRO—National Reconnaissance Office

NSA—National Security Agency

NYPD—New York Police Department

O—Observation aircraft

OD—Olive Drab

ONI—Office of Naval Intelligence

OOB—Old Business Office

OTP—Operational Test Piece

OSS—Office of Strategic Services

PanAm—Pan American World Airways

PDB—President's Daily Brief

PFT—Physical Fitness Test

PLO—Palestine Liberation Organization

PNG—Persona Non Grata

POTUS—President of the United States

P sub-K—Probability of Kill

RFID—Radio Frequency Identification

RNC—Republican National Committee

RPG—Rocket Propelled Grenade

RPM—Revolutions per Minute

ROAD—Retired on Active Duty

RTN—Russia Television Network

SAD—Special Activities Division

SAM—Surface to Air Missile

SAP—Special Access Program

SATCOM—Satellite Communications

SATPHONE—Satellite Telephone

S&T—Science and Technology Directorate

SCI—Sensitive Compartmented Information

SCIF—Sensitive Compartmented Information Facility

SEAL—Sea, Air, Land

SERE—Survival, Evasion, Resistance and Escape

SES—Senior Executive Service

SF—Special Forces

SF-86—Standard Form 86, Questionnaire for Security Clearance

SIS—Senior Intelligence Service

SOC—Special Operations Command

SOF—Special Operations Forces

SOG—Special Operations Group

SOP—Standard Operating Procedure

SPAIC—Special Agent in Charge

SR—Surveillance Reconnaissance aircraft; SR-71

STU-III—Secure Telephone Unit

SUV—Sport Utility Vehicle

SVR—*Sluzhba Vneshney Razvedki Rossiyskoy Federatsii*, Foreign Intelligence Service of the Russian Federation, tasked with intelligence and espionage activities outside the Russian Federation

SWAT—Special Weapons and Tactics

Tally HoA—Very old traditional cry made by huntsman to tell others the quarry has been sighted. Used by aviators to indicate other aircraft or targets have been seen.

10-4—Message Received, from Ten Code

3M—President Maxim Mohammad Mazibuike

TS—Top Secret

TSA—Transportation Security Administration

TS2—Terminator Sniper System

TS/SCI—Top Secret/Sensitive Compartmented Information

TV—Television

TWA—Trans World Airlines

RINO—Republican in Name Only

UAV—Unmanned Aerial Vehicle

UPS—United Parcel Service
U.S. —United States
USB—Universal Serial Bus
USG—United States Government
USMC—United States Marine Corps
U.S.S—.United States Ship
UV—Ultra Violet
WWII—World War Two
Y—Prototype aircraft
Yankee White—Clearances for those staff members who work directly for or have direct contact with the president
YO-3A—Prototype Observation aircraft, model 3, series A
Yo-Yo—Nickname for the YO-3A
Y-12—World War II code name for National Security Complex in Oak Ridge, Tennessee
XKE—Jaguar E-Type; the most beautiful car ever built according to Enzo Ferrari
XKSS—Road-going version of the Jaguar D-Type racing car

Acknowledgements

I owe a special debt of gratitude to Barbara Hewitt, my editor and wife, for her careful reading and editing of my manuscript, and her many excellent suggestions for its improvement. Her continuous good advice and encouragement has been invaluable throughout.

I'm also deeply grateful for U.S. Air Force Colonel George "Curious" Fenimore, Retired, and the brilliant "recovering attorney" Rosemary Harris for their unfailing patience and good humor that helped turn my very rough ramblings and ruminations into something of a set of coherent thoughts and a better story. *Salute!*

A special thanks to Shelby Stricklen, master artist, for permitting me to use his beautiful YO-3A rendering for the cover of Wet Work.

Also a special tip of the old cowboy hat to Dave King, Black Rose Writing Design Director, for turning my manuscript, last minute changes, and cover art into a book that I am proud of. Dave, you're a god.

My publisher, Reagan Rothe at Black Rose Writing, is just a rockstar. *Here we go again, good Sir!*

Any errors found in this novel are my responsibility.

About The Author

Mark A. Hewitt is a retired U.S. Marine Corps officer. The highlight of his career was to fly the aircraft of his childhood dreams, the venerable F-4S Phantom II. He served in senior leadership positions with the Marines, the U.S. Border Patrol, and the U.S. Air Force before leading aviation activities and aircraft operations for international corporations in the Washington D.C. area. Somewhere along the way he became a member of the intelligence community, with a top secret security clearance with SCI and a polygraph. His manuscripts must be approved by the CIA Publication Review Board before they can be published.

Mark's interest in spies and spy planes began when Francis Gary Powers, the U-2 pilot shot down over the Soviet Union, splashed onto the headlines. Immediately afterward, the Director of Central Intelligence declared the CIA would no longer put men in surveillance aircraft over the Soviet Union and China. While Mark's family was stationed in West Germany, he read the Hardy Boys and everything he could sneak into his room, primarily Alistair MacLean, Ian Fleming, and John le Carré. Eight miles from the East German border, MiGs routinely flew over his house.

His Duncan Hunter books reflect many of his life experiences, as well as his love for all things aviation. He has logged time in gliders, jets, Gooney Birds, helicopters and even made a dozen trips to aircraft carriers. Of being shot off the pointy end of an aircraft carrier: "It's the most excitement you can have with your clothes on." It was a natural fit to see his protagonist as a pilot and a spy, flying a little-known spy plane to get deep behind enemy lines and hunt down the world's worst terrorists. More than one CEO has called his novels "a case study for conducting counterterrorism missions with special purpose aircraft."

Mark served as an Assistant Adjunct Professor for Embry-Riddle Aeronautical University. He earned a Master of Arts degree in National Security and Strategic Studies from the Naval War College and holds an MBA in Aviation from Embry-Riddle Aeronautical University.

NOTE FROM THE AUTHOR

Word-of-mouth is crucial for any author to succeed. If you enjoyed the book, please leave a review online — anywhere you are able. Even if it's just a sentence or two. It would make all the difference and would be very much appreciated.

Thanks!
Mark

Thank you so much for reading one of
Mark A. Hewitt's THRILLER novels.
If you enjoyed the experience, please check out our recommended
title for your next great read!

Special Access by Mark A. Hewitt

"Duncan Hunter is a great character... an excellent read."
–*A Good Thriller*

View other Black Rose Writing titles at
www.blackrosewriting.com/books and use promo code
PRINT to receive a **20% discount** when purchasing.